DONNERJACK

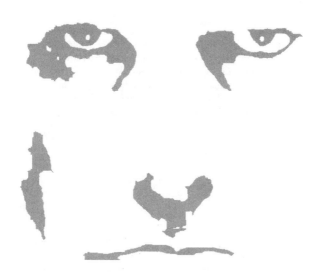

DONNERJACK

ROGER ZELAZNY
AND
JANE LINDSKOLD

AVON BOOKS  NEW YORK

A leatherbound signed first edition of this book has been published by The Easton Press.

AVON BOOKS
A division of
The Hearst Corporation
1350 Avenue of the Americas
New York, New York 10019

Copyright © 1997 by The Amber Corporation and Jane Lindskold
Interior design by Kellan Peck
Visit our website at **http://AvonBooks.com**
ISBN: 0-380-97326-X

Library of Congress Cataloging in Publication Data:

Zelazny, Roger.
    Donnerjack / Roger Zelazny, Jane Lindskold.
        p.   cm.
    I. Lindskold, Jane M.   II. Title.
PS3576.E43D66 1997   96-48705
813'.54—dc21   CIP

First Avon Books Printing: August 1997

AVON TRADEMARK REG. U.S. PAT. OFF. AND IN OTHER COUNTRIES, MARCA REGISTRADA, HECHO EN
U.S.A.

Printed in the U.S.A.

FIRST EDITION

QPM   10   9   8   7   6   5   4   3   2   1

This one is for Devin, Trent, and Shannon—with love.

DONNERJACK

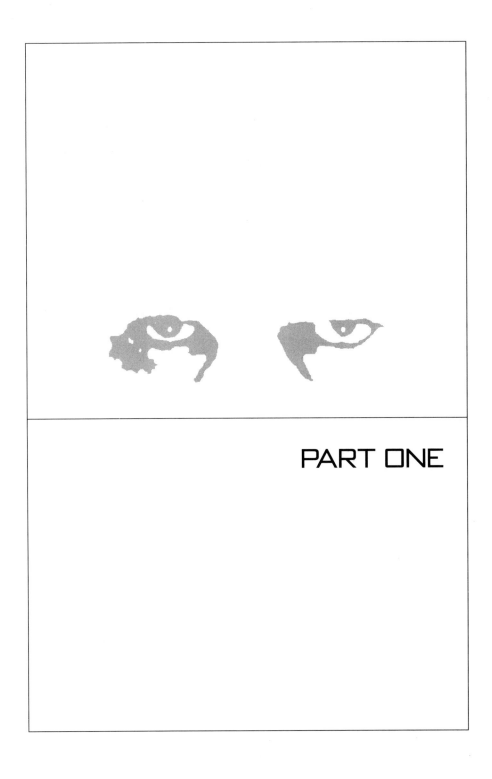

PART ONE

ONE

In Deep Fields he dwelled, though his presence extended beyond that place through Virtù. He was, in a highly specialized sense, the Lord of Everything, though others might claim that same title for different reasons. His claim was as valid as any, however, for his dominion was an undeniable fact of existence.

He moved amid the detritus of all the broken forms which had once functioned in Virtù. They came here, summoned or unsummoned, when the ends of their existence became fact. Of some, he salvaged portions for his own uses. The others settled where they fell and lay . . . strewn, to continue their decomposition, though some parts of them survived longer than others. Even as he strolled, pieces would rise up, in human form or other, perhaps to strut a few paces, mouth some words, perform a characteristic function of what they had been, then sink again into the dust and rubble of which they were becoming a part. Sometimes—as he did now—he stirred the heaps with his stick to see what reactions this would provoke. If he found some performance or some bit of knowledge, some key or code, of amusement or use, he would bear it away with him to his labyrinthine dwelling. He could assume any form, male or female, go where he would, but he always returned to his black-cloaked, hooded garb over an amazing slimness, flashes of white within the shadows he also wore.

There was a great silence in Deep Fields much of the time. Other times, discordant sounds rose, seemingly from the dust and rubble itself, squeals of entropy and when they fell away the silence seemed even deeper. His favorite reason for occasionally absenting himself from his realm was to hear patterned sounds—specifically, music. There was no other like him in all of creation. Known by thousands of names and euphemisms, his commonest appellation was Death.

And so Death walked, swinging his stick, beheading algorithms, pulping identities, cracking windows to other landscapes. Arms twisted upward from the ground as he passed, hands open, fingers flexing and his halo of moiré and shadow passed over them and they fell back. Deep Fields was a place of perpetual twilight, yet he cast impenetrable, improbable shadow where he went, as if a piece of absolute night were always with him. Now, another piece of such darkness flapped into existence, black butterfly out of his arbitrary north—perhaps a piece of himself returning from a mission—to dart before him and settle finally upon his extended finger. It closed its wings as he raised it. A moment of cacophony came and went.

Then, "Intruders to the north," it said, its voice high, piping, small dots of moiré passing like static outward from it.

"You must have mistaken the activity of a fragment," Death responded, soft as the darkness, low as the dying rumble of creation.

The butterfly let fall its wings and raised them again.

"No," it said.

"No one intrudes here," Death replied.

"They are rifling heaps, searching . . ."

"How many?"

"Two."

"Show me."

The butterfly rose from his fingertip and skipped off to the north. Death followed to the sound of discord, odd pieces of reality flashing into and out of existence as he passed. The butterfly traveled on and Death mounted the hill, pausing when he had achieved the summit.

In the valley below two manlike forms—no, one was female—had excavated a trench to considerable depth. Now they were passing along its length, the man holding a light while the other removed things from the ground and cast them into a sack. Death, of course, was aware of much that lay in the area.

"What desecration is this?" Death inquired, raising his arms, his shadow flowing toward them. "You dare to invade my realm?"

The one with the sack straightened and the man dropped the light, which went out instantly. A great babble of voices and strident sounds filled the air as if in synchrony with Death's ire. There came a small golden flicker from within the trench as his shadow reached it.

Then a gate opened, and the figures passed through it, just before the shadow flooded the trench with blackness.

The fluttering shape approached the hilltop.

"A key," it said. "They had a key."

"I do not give out keys to my realm," Death stated. "I am disturbed. Could you tell where their gate took them?"

"No," it replied.

Death moved his hands to his left, cupped them, opened them as if releasing a wish or an order.

"Hound, hound, out of the ground," he muttered, and a heap of bone and metal stirred below in the direction he faced. Mismatched bones reared up, along with springs, straps, and struts, to form themselves together into an ungainly skeletal construct, to which pieces of plastic, metal, flesh, glass, and wood flew or slid, turning like puzzle pieces after unlikely congruencies, fitting themselves into such places, to be drenched suddenly by a rain of green ink and superglue, assailed by a blizzard of furniture covering and shag rug samples, dried by bursts of flame which belched from the ground upon all sides. "There is something that needs to be found," Death finished.

The hound sought its master with its red right eye and its green left one, the right an inch higher than the left. It twitched its cable tails and moved forward.

When it reached the top of the hill it lowered itself to its belly and whined like a leaky air valve. Death extended his left hand and stroked its head lightly. Fearlessness, ruthlessness, relentlessness, the laws and ways of the hunt rose from the ground and rushed to wrap it, along with the aura of dread.

"Death's dog, I name you Mizar," he said. "Come with me now to take a scent."

He led him down into the trench where Mizar lowered his head and nosed about.

"I will send you into the higher lands of Virtù to course the worlds and find those who have been here. If you cannot bring them back you must summon me to them."

"How shall I summon you, Death?" Mizar asked.

"You must howl in a special way. I will teach you. Let me hear your howl."

Mizar threw back his head, and the sound of a siren bled into the whistle of a locomotive mixed with the death-wails of a score of accident victims, and, from someplace, the howling of a wolf on a winter's night, and the baying of hounds upon a trail. A legion of broken bodies, servomechs, and discarded environments stirred and flashed in the valley below, amid junk mail, core war casualties, worms, and crashed bulletin boards. It all settled again with a clatter when he lowered his head and the silence took hold of Deep Fields once more.

"Not bad," Death observed. "Let me teach you to modulate it for a summoning."

Immediately, the air was rent by a series of shrieks, wails, and howls which brought a stirring to all of Deep Fields with its pulsing pattern and which resulted in an inundation of new forms, falling, striding, shuffling, sliding into the realm, stirring the dark dust to haze the air through which new cacophonies traveled.

"That I will hear and recognize wheresoever you shall be," Death stated, "and I will come to you when so summoned."

A patch of blackness landed upon Mizar's nose, and his lopsided eyes were crossed as he regarded the butterfly.

"I am Alioth, a messenger," it told him. "I just wanted to say hello. You have a fine voice."

"Hello," Mizar answered. "Thank you."

Alioth darted away.

"Come with me now," Death said, and he moved to descend the trench.

An inky monkey-shape swung round a twisted beam to hang and watch them.

Entering the trench, Death led Mizar to the place where the two intruders had worked, and whence they had departed.

"Take their scents," he said, "that you may follow them anywhere."

Mizar lowered his head.

"I have them," he said.

"I will open a series of ports. Do not pass through them. Sniff, rather, at each, and see whether any bear traces of these scents. Tell me if one does."

The monkey-shape scuttled, approaching the trench's side, and crouched there, watching.

Death raised his right arm, and his cloak hung down to the ground, curtain of absolute blackness, before the hound. Without preliminary lightening, it became a gateway to a bright cityscape built as within a sphere or tube, buildings dependent from all visible surfaces. It was gone in an instant to be replaced by a flashing city of slim towers and improbable minarets, connected by countless bridges and walkways, clouds drifting among them, no sign of ground anywhere.

Then meadows flashed by, and long corridors of innumerable doorways, both lighted and dark, opened and closed, the interior of an Escher-angled grotto, tube cities beneath a sea, slow-wheeling satellites, a Dyson-sphered realm whose inhabitants sailed from world to world in open vessels. Yet Mizar remained still, watching, sniffing. The pace increased, scenes flashing beneath Death's arm with a rapidity that no normal eye might follow. Alioth skipped before prospects of live flowers, both mechanical and organic.

Death halted the process, freezing on the scene of a classical ruin—broken pillars, fallen walls, crashed pediments—upon a grassy and flower-dotted hilltop, flooded with golden light beneath a painfully blue sky. Gulls passed, calling. The shadows were all hard-edged, and a touch of sea-smell drifted through the gate.

"Anything at all?" Death asked.

"No," Mizar replied, as Alioth darted through the gate to settle upon a flower which immediately began to droop.

"I have tried the likeliest choices for the glimpse I had. We will look somewhere more distant, someplace almost impossibly hard to reach. Bide."

The scene vanished, to be replaced by that blackness which had prevailed earlier. A little later, a light appeared. It brightened steadily, casting illumination far down the trench and beyond it. The black, spiderish monkey-form crouched on the trench's edge drew back as the brightening continued, as coils of colored light and random-seeming geometric forms drifted within to the accompaniment of an electrical sizzling sound. Trails like lightning came and went. Then darkness ensued of an instant, inverting the values of the various brightnesses. A negative quality came over the crackling prospect.

Mizar stirred.

"Yes," he said then, the spikes of his teeth gleaming metallically in the glow. "There is something similar here."

"Find them if you can," Death said. "Call to me if you do."

The hound threw back his head and howled. Then he sprang forward through Death's port into the dark-bright abstract world beyond, sustained by wings of moiré. Death lowered his cloak and the gate was folded and put away.

"You may never see him again," said the monkey. "It is a very high realm to which you have sent him—perhaps beyond your reach."

Death turned his head, showing his teeth.

"It is true that it could take a long while, Dubhe," he said. "Yet all patience is but an imitation of my ways, and even in the highest realms I am not unknown."

Dubhe sprang to his shoulder and settled there as Death rose up out of the trench.

"I believe that someone has just begun a game," Death said as he headed across Deep Fields through a meadow of blackest grass, black poppies swaying at the passage of his cloak, "and, next to music, they have invoked a pastime for which I have the highest regard. It is long, Dubhe, since I have been given a good game. I shall respond to their opening as none might expect, and we will try each others' patience. Then, one day, they will learn that I am always in the right place at the proper time."

"I once felt that way," the monkey replied, "till a branch I was reaching for wasn't there."

The cacophony that followed might have been their laughter, or only the random bleats of entropy. Same thing.

—=—

John D'Arcy Donnerjack loved but once, and when he saw the moiré he knew that it was over. He knew other things as well, things he had not even suspected till that moment; and so his heart was torn in more than one direction, and his mind spun down avenues it had never traveled before.

He looked at Ayradyss, his dark-haired, dark-eyed lady, there beneath the hilltop tree where they always met, and the moiré swam over her, granting her features an even more delicate appointment. He had always felt that, had they chosen, they might rendezvous in his world, but that the dream-dust, fairy-tale quality of their romance required the setting of this magic land. Neither of them had ever suggested otherwise. Now he understood, and the pain was like ice in his breast and fire in his head.

He knew this place far better than most of his kind, and he doubted that Ayradyss was even aware of the first moiré flicker which meant her end. He knew her now for a child of Virtù rather than a visitor masked by an exotic name and pleasing form. She was exactly what she appeared to be, beautiful and lost; and he caught her about the shoulders and held her to him.

"John, what is the matter?" she asked.

"Too late," he said. "Too late, my love. If only I had known sooner. . . ."

"Known what?" she said. "Why are you holding me so tightly?"

"We never spoke of origins. I did not know that Virtù is really your home."

"What of it, John? What differ—"

And the moiré flickered over her again, longer than before; and he could tell by her sudden tensing that this time she had noted it.

"Yes, hold me," she said. "What did you mean when you spoke of wishing to have known sooner?"

"Too late," he replied. "There might have been something I could have tried. No guarantee it would have worked, though. Probably wouldn't have." He kissed her as she began to shake. "Too small a piece of an idea too late. I have loved you. I would that it could be longer."

"And I you," she replied. "There were so many more things to do together."

He had hoped that the moiré would not return for a long while, as might sometimes be the case, but abruptly it was back again, causing her form and features to flow as if seen through a heat haze. And this time he thought that he heard for a moment a strain of discordant sound. This time the moiré remained, and Ayradyss continued to waver through more and more distortions. It became difficult to hold her as her shape was altered, diminishing the while.

"It is not fair," he said.

"It is as it always has been," she replied, and he thought that he felt a final kiss as she fell and the air was touched again by that sound. A faint track of bright dust lay across the air.

He stood with empty arms and clouded eyes. After a time, he seated himself on the ground and covered his face with his hands. At some point, his grief gave way to a journey through everything he had learned of Virtù, the race's greatest artifact, and he brought to bear theories he had developed over the years and all of the speculations with which he had played during his enormously fruitful career.

When he rose again it was to seek a single mote of her dust and to begin another journey, down hypothetical ways to the end of everything.

—=—

Tranto felt it come upon him as he labored with a fractilizing crew, manipulating small proges into a forest, under a new eyedee, there, outside the thatched hamlet he had also helped to raise. An old pain he'd never quite understood was acting up again at the fore-end of his great bulk—a thing that had been with him ever since his encounter with the phant poacher, whom he had left totally disconnected and flat, never to notch his trophy gun again or return to the Verité. Tranto bellowed briefly at the sensation, and the other phants moved away, rolling their eyes and shifting uneasily.

It would be best to get away from them before the pain pushed him beyond control. His small—and diminishing—area of rationality had never dwelled deeply on the nature of pleasure and pain. For his kind, pleasure was connected with the sensation of processing without any actual work involved—a high-order distillation of that which motivated their mundane, purposeful work-actions. Pain, on the other hand, arose from the introduction of hidden chaos factors into their proges. Long ago, the hunter's blast had left such a trace, which acted up every now and then, ruining his social life and contributing to local gossip.

He snorted and stamped. He had labored once—a prisoner—in an encrypted space, a love-nest of a government official of the Verité, whose virtual companion had ruined the packaged ecology with her extravagant insistence on omnipresent bowers of flowers, to the point where the hopefully self-supporting space had overloaded and could no longer serve the second half of its dual function. Part of a crew of shanghaied labor, Tranto recalled the painful Chaos Factor control prods in the hands of Lady May's overseers—and sometimes those of the lady herself—by which he and the others had been driven to offset the effects of the proges she had skewed. As terrible as the CF prods had been, they were never as massively traumatic as his spells—though they had, finally, served to set one off, the one which resulted in his destruction of much of that place, opening it to the attention which had led to Morris Rintal's dismissal when it was discovered that diverted government funds had been used in its setting up-up, and to divorce, when his wife in the Verité had learned of his virtual lover.

A fresh wave of pain swept through him from the throbbing site of his old injury. He bellowed again and reached out with his forward appendage to uproot one of his recent plantings. He smashed it against the

ground and brandished its remains overhead. "Very disturbing," his fleeing rationality observed, and, "Really, too bad."

He bellowed again and charged his fellows, who scattered with an
agility and rapidity near-amazing to those other laborers only acquainted
with the phants' generally slow-moving ways. The other laborers were,
of course, moving hurriedly themselves by then.

Tranto smashed several trees to the ground then turned away. His
burning eyes focused upon the village, and he rushed off in that direction. The overseer proge withdrew its embodiments hastily.

Brandishing the tree trunk, Tranto demolished a hut, then threw his
bulk against the next structure, to be met with a satisfying swaying and
cracking. He hit it again. He swung the trunk. The wall went down. He
bellowed then and stamped on through.

As he advanced upon the next, a spark of memory suggested that
they would be after him soon, with CF prods, then with lethal weapons.
As he trampled the building to ruin and listened to the cries of workers
and foremen, he knew that he should turn away from this place, flee to
some safe wilderness where he might abide until the attack had run its
course and healing had begun.

He smashed another wall, drove the battered tree trunk against a
second then sent it through the roof of a third. Yes, he really should be
moving on. Only all these damned *things* seemed to be in the way.

Trumpeting, he stamped down the street, upsetting supply carts,
trampling seed-objects as they spilled. They would be waiting for him at
the transit station he was certain. If they could not stop him, they would
try to transfer him to a secured space where a therapist would hurt him
again, like last time. Better to flee in this direction and batter his own
gate when he was in the clear. It would not be the first time he had
broken through a chambering field. It seemed to grow progressively easier as the madness rose.

Once he was beyond the workplace he tested the limits of the area,
feeling for the resistance to movement into another place entirely rather
than other areas of this same locale. His sense of these matters always
became highly acute at times like this. Soon he was pushing against a
boundary in the midst of a fairly featureless field. It felt like tough mesh-
work, both yielding and restraining, though with his first great shove he
was able to see through it into an adjacent landscape. It was filled with
buildings, vehicles, and heavy machinery, however, and he changed direction and pushed differently. A field. Good. He pushed that way. Three
heavy onslaughts and he was through, rampaging over some sort of gar-

den and through an orchard, upsetting its *genius loci* no end. No matter. Trumpeting, he ran.

Eight times he crossed barriers, wrecking a specialty farm, an executive meeting room, a Mars surface testing laboratory, a bowling alley, a brothel, a federal district court adjunct, and a virt campus, before achieving the solace of a grassy country and nearby jungle, where the *genius loci* considered his activities in keeping with the tenor of the environment and continued to doze.

Tranto had gone rogue again.

—=—

The congregation came from a chapel in Verité, where, following a brief invocation, they had repaired to a rearward chamber, disrobed, stretched out upon mortuary slabs to contemplate the travails of existence for a period of darkness, then risen in spirit to pass through a wall of flame and enter upon the sacred fields. There, they had proceeded, chanting the song of Enlil and Ninlil, to come at length to a corridor among ziggurats atop which lion-bodied spirits with the heads of men and women appeared, to come in with the choruses and with intonements of blessing. Beyond, the congregation achieved the precincts of the temple and was conducted into its courtyard.

Further ceremonies were conducted there, by a priest garbed similarly to themselves, save for the scapulary tablets and elaborate headgear of gold and semiprecious stones worn below his faint blue halo. He told them how all of the gods, along with everything else, survived in Virtù, and in this time of a turning back to religion it was appropriate that the earliest divine manifestations in Indo-European consciousness should be the focus of worship now, dwelling as they did in the deepest layers of the human psyche where description might still function. Ea, Shamash, Ninurta, Enki, Ninmah, Marduk, Azmuh, Inanna, Utu, Dumuzi, and all of the others—metaphors, yes, as were all who came after, for both the best and worst in humanity, but also the most potent of metaphors because of their primacy. And of course they were cosmomorphic as well, embodiments of the forces of nature, and as capable of evolution as everything in Virtù and Verité. Their beings extended to the quantum level as well as the relativistic. So sing their praises, he went on, ancient gods of quarks and galaxies, as well as the sky, the sea, and the mountains, the fire, the wind, and the burgeoning earth. Let all things rejoice and let us turn the stories of their doings to ritual. One of the gods was even now within the temple's sanctum, enjoying this worship and sending blessings. A light meal was shared, and the worshipers embraced one and other briefly. The mundane offering of the Collect was done by means of electronic funds transfers, from the eft tokens all bore with them when visiting Virtù.

It was called the Church of Elish, from the Mesopotamian creation story, *Enuma elish*—meaning, roughly, "When above"—and the words "Elishism" and "Elishite" were derived therefrom, though members of the more traditional religions of the past few millennia had often referred to them as "Elshies." At first lumped together with the many short-lived cults of Virtù—Gnostic, African, Spiritualist, Caribbean—it had shown greater staying power and, upon closer examination, demonstrated a more sophisticated theology, satisfying ritual, and better structured organization than the others. Its increasingly popularity indicated that it had been victorious in the divine wars. It did not demand mortification of the flesh beyond a few holy day fasts and apparently even involved "rituals of an orgiastic nature," as some anthropologists put it. It incorporated traditional heavens and hells as fitting waiting places between incarnations alternating between Virtù and Verité, toward the eventual achievement of a transcendental state which combined the best of both realms. It had its representatives in both. Its followers had a tendency to refer to all other religions as "latecomers."

Every now and then, usually on high holy days, some worshipers well advanced along their spiritual paths were permitted to enter the temple itself to undergo a higher grade of initiation, involving experiences perhaps intoxicating, oceanic, sexual, illuminating. These tended to result in some small advantage in life, physical or mental, which functioned best in Virtù but which sometimes carried over to Verité. This phenomenon had also been a subject of anthropological consideration for over a decade, the only general conclusion to date being the catch-phrase "psychosomatic conversion."

In fact, Arthur Eden—tall, very black, his beard shot with gray, heavily muscled in the manner of an athlete somewhat past his prime, which he was—was a professor of anthropology at Columbia's Verité campus. He had joined the Elishites for purposes of preparing a full-length study of their creed and practices, comparative religion being his specialty. He was surprised at how much he was enjoying the preliminary work, for the church had obviously been set up by an expert or experts in this area.

As he walked back, singing, amid the pyramids, along the trail through field and wood, he wondered at the administrative entities behind this landscape. During a night service he had once been puzzled by the skies as he'd sought familiar constellations. On a later occasion, he'd recorded it by means of a simple proge disguised as a bracelet. Later, when he'd projected it onto a computer screen and begun playing games with it, he finally discovered that that sky was to be achieved by moving the present one backward through time for about six and a half millennia. Again, he was impressed by the church's efforts at verisimilitude in their claims to antiquity and he wondered again at the priesthood or whoever the brains behind the structure of things might be.

The wall of flame rose before him after a time, and he joined the others in the prayer of passage. There was no sensation of heat as they negotiated the blazing way, only a small tingling and a whooshing sound of the sort a high fire might make in a strong wind—probably intended to intensify the memory. In the darkness that followed, he located the center aisle of the chamber and counted paces as he had been taught—forward, right, left—coming at length to his slab and reclining there. He was eager to begin dictating his notes, but instead reviewed his impressions as he lay there—yes, the Elishites' worldview had an ethical code, a supernatural hierarchy, and an afterlife; they also had sacred texts, a collection of rituals, and an efficient organizational structure. The latter was difficult to obtain information concerning. All of his careful inquiries had so far met with responses indicating a consensus of the clergy as a basis of decision-making—always divinely inspired, of course. Still, he was yet a neophyte. He could understand a measure of reticence on matters of church politics. There should be opportunity to probe more deeply as his status evolved.

Lying in the darkness, he recalled the rituals he had witnessed thus far, wondering, again, whether they represented an actual reconstructive interest on the part of their composers—and if so, from which archaeological sources they might have been derived and projected—or whether they had been made up *de novo* and calculated to produce maximum effect upon a modern congregation. If it were the former, he required knowledge of the key works and the approach which had been taken in these developments from them. If the latter, he still needed the ideas which lay behind the thinking. It was not often that one got to witness the nascence of a new religion, and it was important that he get into it as far as he could and record everything.

Lying there, still tingling lightly, he reflected that whoever was behind it seemed possessed of a fair esthetics sense, along with all the rest.

—=—

Sayjak led his clan to a new section of the forest, partly because the area it had inhabited for the past month had been heavily browsed, and partly because of an eeksy sighting near that territory. No sense waiting for trouble, and the food situation saved face for him among the more impressionable. Sayjak had faced eeksies before and no longer even kept count of the number he had dispatched. He had his battle-marks for all to see. Any number of CF rounds had scored his hide over the years without finding the fatal points which had been their targets.

Now he sat beneath a tree, feeding on its fruits. His clan was, as many of other sorts, begun partly by damaged complex proges whose component problems had not been immediately apparent. On being de-tected by inconsistencies in their work they had fled rather than face extinction or repair. Their hairy manlike forms were a partly willed ad-aptation to the environment. And gender proges were easily created or come by, so that most of his band were descended from such in the dim mists of beginnings and knew no other existence than the freedom of the trees. As the random disruptions of life produced aging in Virtù as well as Verité, Sayjak had matured somewhat past his prime, though he was still a shrewd and powerful brute, well able to manage the People, as they called themselves.

And he had to be shrewd. There were always dangers about—from other clans, from rogue aions of different sorts, and from natural perils, as well as from the Ecology and Environment Corp in its periodic at-tempts to balance populations to conform with its models. And there were hunters—bounty and sport—as well as those who preyed upon the clans for private collections, public displays, private experimentation. . . . There was ample danger from without, and Sayjak made full use of the three strongest of his subordinates: the great, hulking Staggert; tall, scarred, fast-moving Ocro, perhaps too smart for his own good, always plotting; and squat, heavy sadistic Chumo, viewing a narrow world through the perpetual squint of infected-looking eyes. They had become indispensable to him in the administration of the clan. All of them had designs upon his position, of course. All of them had fought him for it, and all of them had lost. He had no fear of any of them individually, yet, and they served him well while they waited for him to show signs of weakness. Together, they could oppose him, could probably split the clan, but—here he smiled around his fangs—they distrusted each other too much to attempt such a thing. And even if this were not the case, they would sooner or later have to have it out amongst themselves, leaving only one. And he knew that he could take any one of them. No. They knew that, and they knew that he knew it. So they served, biding, and aging themselves, of course.

Chumo looked up at him, just back from one of the regular patrols Sayjak insisted upon.

"How is the area?" he asked the bulky squinter.

"Signs to the northwest," Chumo replied.

"What sort?"

"Tracks. Booted."

"How many?"

"Three or four. Maybe more."

Sayjak was on his feet.

"How far?"

"Several miles."

"This is not good. Did you follow them?"

"Only a little way. I thought it more important to get word back quickly."

"You thought right. Take me to the place. Ocro! You be in charge here. I'm going scouting."

The lean one ceased his browsing and approached.

"What is it?" he asked.

"Strangers. Maybe eeksies," Sayjak replied, glancing at Chumo. "I don't know."

Chumo shook his head.

"Perhaps I should come along," Staggert said.

"Someone has to take care of the camp. Leave signs if you have to flee."

"Of course."

Sayjak set out with Chumo, shambling along trails for the first mile or so, all senses alert. Finally, Chumo led him into the trees as they neared the place of the tracks.

"I heard them pass," he said, "from a distance. By the time I got here they were already well gone. I located their tracks and studied them."

"Let's find them," Sayjak said.

They proceeded along the well-worn game trail, boot marks still clear in the damp soil. It wound into the west, then the northwest. Sayjak determined that there were four of them—two fairly large men, and two of more average height and build.

From far off to the left came the crack of a discharging weapon. A moment later the sound was heard again.

Sayjak smiled.

"Easy game," he said. "They give themselves away for it. Now we know the trail turns, curves that way. We cut through. Find them sooner."

So they left the trail and headed in the direction of the sounds. It took them perhaps half an hour to find the place of the slaughtered buck, but from there the trail was very clear. The game had been dressed, divided, and borne off to the northeast.

Following, again, Sayjak and Chumo finally heard the sounds of voices at about the same time they smelled the cooking meat. Proceeding more carefully then, they discovered the band to be camped in an area identifiable by scent as one previously used by a clan similar to their own. It had been abandoned for at least a week, however.

They drew nearer. From the more than casual appointment they had effected in the area, it was obvious that the hunters were planning to spend the night. Sayjak was momentarily taken aback on seeing that the largest of the four was a woman.

"Eeksies," Chumo whispered.

"Bounties," Sayjak corrected. "Big one's a female. Guess who?"

"Big Betsy?"

"Right," he said, fingering a scar along his left thigh. "Lots of the People's heads gone home with her. She and me go back far."

"Maybe this time we take hers."

"This time *I* take hers. Go back to camp. Get Staggert, Ocro, a few other big guys who need action. Bring them. I wait, watch. We move, I leave signs."

"Yes."

Chumo vanished into the brush.

Sayjak moved nearer, his mouth watering at the aromas from the cooking, though he'd never learned much about fire, and he knew that raw meat was best anyhow. Bounties . . .

Eeksies wore uniforms. Bounties dressed any damned way they wanted. Bounties were more ingenious, more relentless—deadlier. Not being civil servants and actually making or not making their money as a result of their own actions had much to do with it. Sayjak realized that bounties were not normally offered until a situation reached a point where eeksy activity was deemed inadequate. While modesty was not one of his virtues, he did not feel that his clan's activities alone were sufficient to warrant such attention. No. Hard as it was to think beyond the clan, it occurred to him that the other tribes of the People must also be burgeoning, be hunting and browsing to an extent which became noticeable on someone's big balance sheet of how things should be. Off-hand, he did not know what to do about it. But he did have a solution for the immediate problem, as soon as the others arrived.

He watched as they set up their camp, continued to watch as they gathered about the fire and took their meal. He hoped there would be some leftovers . . . for afterwards. But his hope diminished as Big Betsy dug in. The lady had quite an appetite, in full keeping with her figure.

"Enjoy now," he breathed. "My turn later." And he studied the machete she'd hung on a nearby tree limb. Could it be the same one that had cut him? He knew how they operated now. Just like swinging a big stick, only sharper. Good for taking a head.

He crouched and watched. Plenty of time now. Might as well spend it planning. . . .

It was evening when Chumo returned with four others. Silent, for all their great bulk, they crouched beside him as he pointed out features of the camp, indicating attack points he had decided upon. Then he motioned for them to follow him and took them a great distance off into the brush.

There he halted and spoke softly:

"You—Chumo, Staggert—hide in trees, near, with me. Ocro, Svut—you climb in trees, be overhead. When they sleep, ground people follow me in. Kill everyone. Too much trouble, Ocro, Svut jump down quick. Help."

"If they got guard?" Staggert asked.

"Mine," Sayjak replied. "I go first. Guard dead, and you come in. Get the rest. Understand?"

It was not the desire to demonstrate his leadership, or even mere bravado, which governed the plan. It was, rather, Sayjak trusted none but himself, a value he'd learned at an early age as a wandering outcast from his own clan, and the thing which had probably assured his primacy for so long in this one. Self-sufficiency, distrust, and the ability to make an instant decision and follow it with a surprise move, were—had he been of the reflective sort—the most useful lessons he might have felt he'd learned in those early days.

And so they returned to the camp of the bounty hunters, and his party positioned itself in accord with a shoulder clasp, a pointed finger, a nod apiece. Sayjak took up station in the thicket nearest the hunters and worked his way slowly to its forward edge. There, he lay absolutely still, watching the figures about the fire as they sipped some beverage and talked.

Would they leave a guard? He suspected so. He planned to approach as close as he could, then give the attack signal to the others simultaneous with leaping upon the guard and killing him—or her. He hoped that Big Betsy would stand the first watch herself, both because she was the most formidable and it would be well to dispose of her quickly, and because he could hardly wait—after all these years and encounters—to slay the huntress from far-off Verité. He had never heard of Thomas Ray, who had introduced sex and repro into proges, so long ago. But probably he should rape her, too, he decided, just to show that his victory was total as well as complete. On the other hand, he realized that he would be afraid to try it while still she lived. No matter. Afterwards would serve as well to prove his point.

Again, he studied the machetes. Big Betsy had hurt him bad with one such, that other time. He had thought of it over and over, until he was certain how it worked, though he never dwelled on the mysteries of design or manufacture. Good for getting heads, he knew. It was how they filled their bounty sacks.

He watched the campers and tried to understand their conversation, but failed. He wondered whether Big Betsy knew any of the People's talk. He listened to the night sounds and studied that other mystery, the fire.

It seemed a long time before one of the men began to yawn. But moments later another joined him. The first said something and gestured toward his sleeping roll. Big Betsy nodded and answered, jerking her huge thumb in that direction. All three of the men retired to their bedrolls, and she added more sticks to the fire. She cleaned her weapon and honed her machete then, setting both of them near to hand when she was done. Sayjak studied their disposition. He had to come upon her in such a fashion that she could not seize advantage and turn it on him. Once it was simply strength against strength there would be no problem despite her bulk. He was considerably more massive, and his strength had long been a thing of legend among the People. So . . .

He would leave his cover with total stealth, he decided, as soon as the other bounties' breathing had grown slow and regular. Then he would advance carefully but not trust to total soundlessness in crossing those final feet. Yes, that seemed most prudent. He felt that she would be as alert as one of the People, and the tiniest sound would be as sufficient to galvanize her to action as it would be to himself. He would have to cover that final distance with a great leap.

A half-hour, perhaps, went by. The three men seemed to be sleeping. Big Betsy was sitting very still, staring into the flames. He continued to wait. The sleepers should be easy for the others to deal with. But—best not to take any chances.

The night wore on. It became obvious that the others were deep into sleep. His clansmen would be growing restless, might think he was afraid of the human woman. Was he? She was the biggest woman he had ever seen. He fingered his scar. Then he parted the fronds before him and moved slowly forward.

He placed each foot with the utmost precision and shifted his weight carefully. He controlled his breathing. He could not control his smell, however.

He heard her sniff, once. Then her right hand flashed out toward the weapons. He leaped immediately, his battle cry rising to his lips.

But Big Betsy had thrown herself to the side and rolled away, moving with surprising speed for one of her bulk, uttering a shout of warning to the others as she did so. Sayjak missed his target—her back—but a quick movement of his long arm was successful in knocking the half-clasped rifle from her hand. He lunged at her again, but she rolled backwards over a shoulder, removing herself from his path and coming up onto her feet, facing him.

As he began to reach for her, she kicked him twice in the stomach, ducked beneath his sweeping arm, and drove a heavy fist against the right side of his rib cage. While any of these blows would have devastated a man, Sayjak was only momentarily shaken by them, and, snarling, he made for her again. She tripped him as he passed, and he felt her ham-like fist fall upon the massive muscles at the back of his neck.

Shaking his head, he turned toward her again. About him now rose cries and growls as his clansmen fell upon the recent sleepers, along with the sounds of their conflict, which included the breaking of bones. Big Betsy kicked him again. He bore it stoically and advanced upon her, moving more deliberately now, having learned that his rushing attacks were less than effective.

She retreated from him, striking as she went and keeping her kicks low, for she had seen the enormous speed of his hands and arms and feared his catching hold of her leg should she kick too high. She worried him about the shins, knees, and thighs, but he plodded toward her, ignoring these blows, his arms swinging low before him. He found himself wishing she were one of the People as he considered what a fine mate she would make.

He struck suddenly with a blinding movement of his left arm. While she managed to roll with it, her balance was destroyed. She stumbled to the side. He was upon her in an instant, seeking to immobilize her. Even then, before he succeeded, she struck his chin with the heel of her hand, clawed at his eyes, aimed brief blows at his throat. Finally, his left arm about her back, crushing her right arm to her side, he caught hold of her left elbow with that hand and drew it against her left side with such force that he heard cracking sounds from within her chest.

She grunted once, perhaps too compressed to cry out, and suddenly she spat in his face. He wondered at the significance of this as he reached out and caught hold of her head with his massive right hand. Behind him, the sounds of struggling had ceased and there came only a few death moans now. He turned her head to her left as far as it would normally go. Then, slowly, he continued to turn it. Her neck made cracking sounds, and he felt spasms within her body. He squeezed her more tightly and continued to turn her head. There came a final snap, followed by a brief convulsion. Then she fell limp within his grasp. He lowered her to the ground and stared.

Then he turned, looking to where the others stood beside the other bodies. They were watching him. Had he promised aloud that he would have her? He tried to remember. He looked at her again. No, he hadn't, he suddenly recalled, and he felt better. He would eat her liver and heart, instead, he decided, because she had fought well. He sought her machete, found it.

Then he grinned. He would try it out on the others. He chose one sprawled prone, raised the blade, swung it like a stick. It passed easily through the neck and the head rolled away on a trail of gore. Delighted, he moved to the next and did it again. When he had done them all, he sat them with their backs against tree trunks and placed their heads in their laps, hands arranged to hold them lightly on either side.

Then he turned to Betsy. He used the machete carefully in her case, and when he had done he arranged her garments to cover the wound.

He left her seated beside the others. But she did not hold her head in her lap, for he had taken it with him, along with the machete.

—=—

Dubhe—bored, impulsive, lonely—was in a twilit valley to the west of Deep Fields, beside an acid stream, engaged in necrophilia with the significant remains of a blond baboon, when he heard the sound unlike any sound he had ever heard before. Startled, he released her, and her lower anatomy pranced away into the stream, to be reduced in stature with every step, until finally naught remained but a pungent memory. He threw his head back and barked in frustration. The intruding sound continued, so strange. It was—patterned. It was unlike the intermittent burst which came and went as a by-product of entropy doing its stuff.

He climbed out of the valley. East, it seemed. Something interesting going on there. The sounds did not let up. He struck a course in that direction. A piece of something shiny and mechanical drifted by and he mounted it and rode it until right before it crashed, jumping off at the last moment. Then he hurried on afoot, through the always-twilight, spotted with occasional flares and will-o'-the-wisps from the always-decomposing, leaping chasms, scrambling up hillsides and down their farther slopes.

"What is it, Dubhe? Whither fare you?" came a satiny voice from a hole that he passed.

He paused and the snake slithered forth, long, shining like beaten copper.

"I'm following that peculiar sound, Phecda."

"I feel its vibrations, also," the snake replied, silvery tongue darting. "So you do not know what it is?"

"Only its direction."

"I will join you then, for I, too, am curious."

"So let us go," Dubhe responded, and he set off once more.

He did not speak again for some time, though he occasionally caught the glitter of Phecda's scales at either side, and sometimes before him. They hurried on, the sounds louder now—voices and instruments distinguishable.

Mounting a hillside, they halted. To the east, they beheld the figure of a man, walking, a kind of light about him. What gate, track, or trail might touch upon him as he moved here?

The sounds came from the tall, dark-haired man, or from something he bore with him. He moved slowly, with a deliberation that implied a definite course he followed. It led him down his hillside and into a long valley.

Dubhe hesitated to move toward him and so be seen. He elected, rather, to follow, and so let the man pass below before he moved again. Phecda also waited, apparently of the same mind.

The sounds danced through the air in the man's wake, and Dubhe found them pleasantly disturbing. "Is there a word," he asked Phecda, "for when the noise is good?"

And Phecda, who spent her time passing through mounds and around them and going up and down the valleys, digesting bits of wisdom before they might decay, replied, "Music. It is called music. It is a thing very difficult to manifest here. Perhaps that is why the master likes it so—for its rarity. More likely, though, he loves it for itself—as I see that this is easy to do."

They followed the man and his music through the dark valley, Phecda pausing only to devour the remains of the previous day's weather report for Greater Los Angeles.

"Let us pass him," Phecda said at length, "for I can tell from a feeling to the land that the master will meet him in the valley, two bends hence."

"Very well."

They skirted the foothills to a ridge, crossed through a declivity, raced ahead to another such gap, crossed the valley into which it debouched, and mounted a hill. The music came from far behind them now. Ahead and below within the great vale they saw a slow movement.

Death climbed a small mound, extended his arms, and turned in a circle. Then bones rose up out of the ground, fell down from the heights, rushed toward him in a chaos of rattling forms, came together before him, assembled themselves into a structure. Soon a high-backed throne stood there, surmounted by a skull. It shone like ancient ivory in the valley's quiet light. As Death took a step forward, the excess bones flew away to outline a path leading out to the mouth of the valley at its turning. He moved to the rear of the throne then, where he opened his cloak to release a spectral form which hovered behind its knobby back.

Returning to the front, he seated himself. Raising first his right hand, then his left, flames came up on either side, creating shadows. The music grew louder.

"The boss really knows how to do things with style," Dubhe remarked.

"He does seem to take a certain pleasure in the dramatic," Phecda observed as they descended and moved into a nearer patch of shadow.

Phecda and Dubhe waited for what seemed a long while. The sounds continued to increase in volume. Then there was movement at the end of the valley.

The man halted and stared. Then he advanced slowly along the bony way, his music all about him. When he came to the foot of the mound, he stopped again.

". . . And our visitor seems similarly inclined," Phecda added.

"True."

Death turned his head toward the visitor. He spoke in a ragged, rattling way his minions had not heard him use before:

"You come to me playing Politian's *Orfeo*, arguably the world's first opera. A fine piece, which I have not heard in a long while. Of course, this also stirs memories of a story I have not heard in a long while."

"I'd thought it might," the man replied.

"I know you, John D'Arcy Donnerjack. I am an admirer of your work. I am especially fond of the delightful fantasy of the afterlife you designed based on Dante's *Inferno*."

"The critics liked it, but the public proved somewhat less than enthusiastic."

"It is generally that way with my work, also."

Donnerjack stared, not certain how to respond until Death chuckled.

"A small jest," the cloaked one added. "In truth, few consider me an actual being. I might be curious as to how you arrived at this conclusion—let alone decided to undertake this journey and succeeded in finding your way here."

"My life's work has involved Virtù, and I am among other things a theorist," Donnerjack replied.

"I feel it will be worth spending time with you one day, in discussion of theory."

Donnerjack smiled.

"I might enjoy that. You would seem the logical source for final opinions."

"Mine is not really the last word on everything. Generally, I leave it to others."

Death cocked his head and fell silent, until the current passage had finished.

"Lovely," he said then. "I take it you seek to induce in me a mood of esthetic pleasure?"

Donnerjack placed the small unit which he bore on the ground at Death's feet.

"I admit to that intention," he answered. "Please accept the player as a gift. There are many other melodies on it as well."

"I will do that, with thanks, since most things that come to me are damaged—as well you know."

Donnerjack nodded, stroked his beard.

"The thought had occurred to me," he said, "and it concerned something which I suppose came to you recently."

"Yes?"

"Her name was—is—Ayradyss. A dark-haired lady of some attractiveness. I'd known her well for a time."

"As have I, also," Death replied. "Yes, she is here. And your manner of arrival as well as your visit itself leads me to anticipate you to some extent."

"I want her back," Donnerjack said.

"What you ask is impossible."

"It figures in legend, folklore, religion. Surely there must be some basis to it, some precedent."

"Embodiments of dreams, hopes, desires. That is what these things are. They are without foundation in the real world."

"This is Virtù."

"Virtù is as real as Verité. It is the same in both places."

"I cannot accept that there is no hope."

"John D'Arcy Donnerjack, the universe owes no one a happy ending."

"You say that it is impossible for you to give back that which you have taken?"

"That which I have received is damaged in some fashion and no longer able to function adequately."

"That which is damaged can be repaired."

"That is not the sort of thing for which I am known."

Donnerjack made a sweeping gesture, encompassing half the landscape.

"You must have the wherewithal here—in the form of every sort of piece or program—to repair anything," he said.

"Perhaps."

"Release her to me. You like my Inferno. I will design you another space—to suit your desire."

"You tempt me, Donnerjack."

"Have we a deal, then?"

"It would take more than that."

"Name the price of her return."

"What you ask would be difficult, even for me. You ask me to reverse entropy, albeit locally, to invert standard procedure and policy."

"Who else might I ask?"

"Some great artificer might duplicate her for you."

"But she would not be the same, save superficially. All of her memories would be gone. It would really be a different individual."

"And that one might not feel for you as she did?"

"I care more about her than I do about myself."

"Ah, then you really loved her."

Donnerjack was silent.

"And you intended to share your lives?"

"Yes."

"In Virtù or Verité?"

Donnerjack laughed.

"I would spend what time I could with her in Virtù. Then—"

"Ah, yes, there is always that interface, isn't there? But then, even with those having one or the other realm in common, there is always an interface—if only of skin. Usually, it runs even deeper."

"I did not come here to discuss metaphysics."

Death raised his smile.

"... And she would visit you in hard-holo, there in the Verité."

"Of course, we would alternate, and—"

"You ask a disposition of me. I am surprised you were not more specific."

"In what fashion?"

"That I release her to you in Verité rather than Virtù."

"That is impossible."

"If I am to violate one law of existence for you, why not another?"

"But the principles which govern this place would not permit it. There is no way to manage the 'visit' effect permanently, fully either way."

"And if there were?"

"I have made a lifetime study of this."

"A life is a shallow place in time."

"Still . . ."

"Do you think me a proge-generated simulacrum? Some toy of human imagination? I came into being when the first living thing died, and I will not say where or when that was. Neither man nor machine ever wrote a program for me."

Donnerjack drew back as a moiré flowed between them.

"You make it sound as if you really are Death."

The only reply was the continuing smile.

"And I almost get the feeling you are discussing an experiment you would be curious to perform."

"Even if that were so, it would not get you a fire sale price on my services."

"What then? What do you want?"

"Yes, you will build for me. But I want one thing more. You spoke of myths, legends, fairy tales. There are reasons for them, you know."

"Yes?"

"You have wandered into something you do not understand. If you would play it out, give me my price and you shall walk away with her, back to your own realm."

"Give her to me and you shall have your price."

Death stood slowly, stepped to the left of his throne, and raised his right arm. The *Orfeo* reversed itself, repeating backwards the passage just completed. The figure of a woman moved out from behind the throne.

Donnerjack's breath caught in his throat.

"Ayradyss!" he said.

"She is aware of you at some level, but she cannot yet reply," Death said, leading her forward. "You will take her by the hand and follow the trail of bones. It will be a long, dangerous, and difficult way. But you will win back to Verité if you do not depart the trail for any reason. High Powers may attempt to interfere. Stay on the trail."

He placed her hand in his.

"And now, your price?"

"Your firstborn, of course."

"What you ask is entirely impossible. First, that we should ever have offspring. Second, that I should be able to deliver it here if we could— physically, *in toto*."

"Agree to the conditions and I will take care of the details."

Donnerjack regarded the pale, vacant-eyed form of his love.

"I agree," he said.

"Then walk the way of bones back to the light."

"Amen," said Donnerjack as he turned away, leading Ayradyss, "and good-bye."

"I'll be seeing you," Death said.

TWO

Lydia Hazzard was seventeen years old with several months vacation ahead of her before beginning her university studies. In that she was the elder of two daughters in a well-to-do family—Hazzard Insurance, third generation—her parents, Carla and Abel, had given her the present of a summer in Virtù, before her life got hardball, red in tooth and claw, and otherwise preoccupied with things academic. She was 5'6", narrow of waist, large of bust, with hands and legs of a swimsuit model; her hair was shoulder-length and very blond, her cheekbones high, teeth dazzling, complexion pink and smooth, eyes of jungle green with a hint of green splashed above them. This was only in Virtù and it cost extra, but her parents were in a generous mood.

In her home in Bayonne, New Jersey, Verité, she was 5'9", with nondescript brownish hair, a bit skinny and gawky with terrible posture, possessed of a volatile complexion and a tendency to chew her fingernails to the quick. Her smile, thanks to orthodontics, was quite fetching, however, and her eyes were indeed jungle green. For that matter, her voice was pleasantly husky and she had a high IQ.

At first she traveled with her friend Gwen, who'd been given for a graduation present a week in the generic resorts of Virtù—Beach, Mountain, Desert, Seashore, Cruise, Casino, Safari—and they had tried a half-day in each to learn their favorites.

Both found Casino intimidating, because once the package plays were used up one played with one's own money (or one's parents') efted on the spot from Casino's account to one's own or (more usually) the other way around. This—both Gwen and Lydia had had impressed upon them—was a no-no. They were in Virtù to experience the exotic, to acquire additional social graces, and to get laid in congenial surroundings by good-looking partners in total safety from pregnancy and disease— bodies bucking and heaving against micromanipulable force-fields back in Verité—senses knowing they had spent themselves beneath stars and their partners on South Pacific beaches where waves beat counterpoint and breezes bore the aromas of flowers. Did it matter whether one's partner was a construct out of Virtù or a fellow idealized vacationer from Verité? They felt the same, and the uncertainty piqued the sense of romance to the fullest. Either were free to lie or to tease, so of course they did. It spiced the game to wonder whether an address someone had given you back home might be real, whether the man or woman you mounted, stroked, sucked on, might be even more fun on the other side. Or whether it was all a dream and such a person did not even exist in the Verité.

She walked the beaches a lot after Gwen's week was up. They were some of her favorite places when she wanted to be alone, and she re- alized that, for a time, she did want to be alone. She requested solitude in Virtù, and it was not sifted-seeming tourist beaches that she sought. They were more wild, pebbly strands, sometimes possessed of a vaguely Aegean feeling; other times they were pounded by chill breakers which bespoke the North Sea. And she was fascinated by the lives and deaths she noted in tidal pools along her ways. Underwater forests might sway as in invisible winds, tiny crustaceans scuttle among stones, fishes hover and bend, minuscule red armies and blue armies take up positions for battle . . .

Occasionally, she saw a red sail. But while the vessel sometimes came near to shore, it never lay to anchor in her sight, nor did she ever glimpse its crew. When the flotsam, driftwood, shells, smells, pools, and sounds of the shore attained a certain level of intensity, she would climb the pale cliffs and hike inland. There lay rocky hills and higher prominences, twisted trees along their slopes. Pink and yellow flowers bloomed in meadows; pockets of fog filled dells and crevices in stone walls till late in the day; a number of vine-covered ruins, always of stone, occurred in the lower valley; thistles of a soft red occasionally punctuated the sloping prospect; and she came upon a hill at eve where she seemed to hear music from under the ground. There, in a sheltered depression to the northwest, she wrapped herself in her cloak to spend the night.

Lying under the stars, she heard the music rise out of the ground and deepen, grow more wild. For a long time, she simply listened, as if in attendance at some odd concert. Abruptly, then, its character shifted.

Louder, more powerful, it came, no longer from beneath the ground, but from somewhere nearby. Had she been drowsing? She searched hastily for a break in her consciousness, could not be certain whether one had occurred.

Rising, she paced the hilltop, seeking the direction of the music. It seemed to be coming from the southwest, to her right.

The world grew brighter as she headed in that direction, climbing . . .

It grew louder still as she reached her hill's summit. There, from across the valley, backlighted by a recently risen moon, she beheld a form atop the next height: a piper. He stood stock-still, the skirls and wailings on his pipes filling the air between them.

She seated herself. As the moon rose higher she saw that the piper was a man. Their hilltops seemed to drift closer together. This later struck her as peculiar, in that her solitude-order was still in effect. She had not intended on lifting it for a couple of more days, following a conditioning visit to Verité. Strange. . . .

How long she sat, she could never tell. The moon had risen higher, and the piper had turned somewhat, so that its light fell across his face from the left, both illuminating and shadowing. He was high of cheekbone, heavy of brow, and he wore a small beard. He seemed to have on rough, dark leggings and a dark green, moist-looking satin shirt. There was a cap on his head, and the hilt of some sort of weapon at his side.

Slowly, he turned toward her until he was staring into her eyes. Abruptly, he left off playing then. He doffed his cap and bowed to her.

"Good evening, m'lady," he called.

"Good evening," she replied, standing.

"Wolfer Martin D'Ambry, at your service."

"Oh—I'm Lydia Hazzard. I like your piping. Which do you use mostly—'Wolfer,' 'Martin,'' or 'Ambry'?"

"I answer to all of them, Miz Hazzard. Address me as you would."

"I like the sound of 'Ambry.' Please call me 'Lydia.' "

"And so I shall, Lydia," he said, raising the pipes once again. "Join me if you would."

He began to play, an eerily involving tune, like the breathing of the *genius loci*. She found herself moving to the trail, barely aware of doing

30

so, taking the way downward and across the valley. The music moved above her as she passed through darkness, and when she reached the foot of Ambry's hill she realized that the piper was no longer at the height he had occupied. He had moved, was moving, to the east.

She sought a trail. Suddenly, it was important that she catch up with him, continue their conversation.

The only trail she could discover led upward to where he had been standing. Very well. . . .

She commenced climbing, out of the darkness toward the growing bar of moonlight. The sounds of Ambry's piping were more distant now, and when she finally reached the summit they seemed far away indeed. She located what must have been the trail he had taken—the only one in sight—and hurried down it.

It was a long while through rugged ways before the notes came louder and she realized she was gaining. She had no sense of descent, but the way grew more level. Perhaps she had achieved a plateau.

This land looked different, smelled different, by night. Why was she hurrying so? The man and his pipes were intruders into her idyll. She was going to return to Verité, break the travel-trance, dine properly rather than via life-support, play tennis, perhaps, rather than electronstim isometrics, visit her family, then return after a few days and be more sociable. But there was a mystery here—and something else. She needed to find Ambry.

Almost as this realization occurred, the sound of his bagpipes died. She began running. Perhaps he'd only stopped to rest for a moment. But something might have happened to him. He could have fallen. Or—

She stumbled, rose, ran again. The night seemed suddenly colder, the shadows more than simple patches of darkness. It was as if each darkened area held something which stirred slowly and watched her. The trail dipped into the valley, passed over a stream by means of stepping stones, then rose again. At her back she heard a rattling of stones, as if something were following her without a great deal of stealth. She did not look back.

Abruptly, the piping resumed, somewhere far off to her left. She turned in that direction. She began to gain on it, and after a few minutes she seemed to be drawing near. When she felt that she was about to come into sight of Ambry the pipes grew still.

She cursed softly, and then she heard the following sounds again. A slight breeze brought her sea smells from somewhere to the left. Had she described a big loop, returning to the coast? She looked to the moon for guidance, but it was too high in the heavens now.

She continued to move in what seemed the proper direction. She had to slow, however, when she came to a region of standing stones, for her way seemed to lie among them. Entering, she could tell that there were many, but not whether there was a pattern to them.

As she walked, she seemed to detect a movement directly ahead. She halted and stared, but it was not repeated. Setting forth again, she noticed a movement to her right. Again, she paused to study it. This time, it seemed as if one of the huge stones itself had slid perhaps an inch. Then there came another such movement, from the left. Fascinated, she watched the towering stone slide for several inches before it came to a halt. By then, another was in motion. And another . . .

Soon all of them seemed to be moving. The sensation was peculiar, as if they stood still and she was drifting among them. And the one directly ahead of her now seemed to be growing in size.

She extended a hand and touched one. It brushed by. Another . . .

A hand seized her left biceps and drew her to the side. She gasped, turning.

"Sorry to take hold of you that way," Ambry said, "but you were about to be run over."

She nodded and followed him to the left, which seemed to be westward. The stones were sliding even more rapidly now, none of them swaying. They maintained a monumental stability as they headed into the south.

"Full moon on the equinox," he said. "They awaken then and go to the river to drink. They be back at their stations by morn. 'Tis not good to be in their way once they get going. Mass, inertia, momentum."

"Thank you." She laughed then, and there was a slight, hysterical rising to it.

"What is it, Miz Lydia?" he asked.

"You speak of hard, textbook properties of matter on the one hand," she said, "and on the other you tell me of the stones going to take a drink. That part is right out of Gaelic legend."

"Why, all legends have found their way to Virtù," he said, continuing to draw her aside from the field of stones, "those of science as well as those of the folk."

"But scientific principles, laws, constants are universal in Verité."

". . . And in Virtù as well. But here there are intelligences which manipulate them in terms of each other, as well as our own special sets."

"But here they *can* be manipulated."

"In accord with rules—some of them pretty tricky—but rules, nevertheless. It is all unifiable. Both sides can be made to match. It's just that it's sometimes hard on the senses, as well as the reasoning."

He continued to move them away from the traffic. By now, the stones were moving very rapidly—a great rushing of black forms, and silent, totally silent.

She turned and walked with him, Ambry's arm slipping over her shoulder now, bearing an edge of his cloak, enfolding her.

"Where are you taking me?" she asked him.

"Someplace warm and peaceful," he said, and while she had been hoping for a virtual affair she had never decided what her lover would look like.

She glanced up at him and smiled.

—=—

John D'Arcy Donnerjack followed the Trails of Fire and Blood, Water and Dust, Wind and Steel. The closest he came to being tricked into departing the Way was on the Trail of Ivory and Wood, where a *genius loci* in the form of a child with a basket of flowers almost persuaded him that he had taken a wrong turning and was on the road to fair Elfland. But a moiré passed between, and through the lens of its transform he had seen the child as it truly was and moved on. It leaped at him then, fangs bared, heavy metal tail striking sparks from the stone, but the Way of Ivory and Wood guards its travelers even from the masters of place. On the Trail of Earth and Ash a maddened phant emerged from a hole in the Trail itself and rushed toward them. Donnerjack, observant unto death, detected the swelling near the base of one of the beast's foretusks, however, and lured it to the side of the Trail, away from Ayradyss, while summoning and reviewing the lifespecs of its sort.

Then, in a fit of the design inspiration which had made him a legend in both academic and engineering circles, Donnerjack dug his thumbs into two of the beast's acupuncture points and waited. It shuffled its massive feet but remained where it stood, as if sensing the intent behind the human hands which used it so. Its breathing slowed, and it made small snuffling sounds and regarded the man intently. Then it turned away, departed the Trail, and headed for the woods.

It was around the next bend that the *genius loci* again appeared, of a lovely blue color and formed somewhat like a Caterpillar tractor—and, with inhuman actions, threatened the travelers. In a simple act of animal gratitude, the phant, who'd followed the action from a nearby grove, returned hurriedly to trample the shit out of it and leave it leaking vital fluids from where he'd cast it into a thorn tree. Thus do good deeds sometimes come around, even in Virtù.

Donnerjack moved on then, to essay the awesome Chasm of Stars and Bridges, which would make all the difference. He could hear the growls of the structure's swaying and terrible clicking of the illuminations' teeth even from there, for he was nearing the place of the primal language itself, where the words of creation had assembled Virtù.

He plodded steadily onward, one of the few men able to deduce the secret geography of the universe—a virtue which had made this endeavor possible, but which in no way mitigated its dispositions. For, as he mounted the final height and took the first turning, coming at last into sight of that groaning, clashing abyss of fire and spans, the fear of death filled his stomach and rose from there.

Rising from his knees and lowering his hands from his face, he called to Ayradyss and felt her hand upon his shoulder. Straightening, he threw his head back as he advanced, and then, voice wavering at first, he began to sing as he moved onto the span.

—=—

High atop Mount Meru at the center of the universe the gods sat unmoving on their stone thrones, contemplating Virtù all about them. Having sacrificed much of mobility for the better part of omniscience they tended to sit so for long spans of time. Action detracted from perception and perhaps wisdom.

Having extended much of themselves into their warring avatars, they had slowed the functioning of their personalities here. Hence, their conversations would have been drawn-out affairs by time-bound standards. Fortunately, an equivalent of singularity math prevailed at Virtù's center, allowing for those frustrating and wonderful anomalies the lesser gods referred to as "eternity physics," envying their seniors those awful and awesome excesses of inscrutability in regions above the winds that blow between the worlds.

Skyga, Seaga, and Earthma realized they'd not much of themselves left what with extensions of sense and personality beyond number and mass. Their ongoing extended conversations—sometimes more like monologues—were necessary for preserving what remained of identity.

They feared that silence would extinguish them as they were, leaving them forever divided among their lesser selves throughout the realms of Virtù. There were of course hierarchies within hierarchies, as one descended the skies, the lands, the seas.

". . . Thus a new cycle begins," Seaga observed over a timeless decade.

"As with most major events, its origins are already muddied," Earthma observed, "unless the hand of Skyga moves within them."

"He has not spoken for a long while. Perhaps he is acting."

"Or perhaps he has finally decomposed completely."

"I wonder . . ."

"No. He plays a guarded game. He hums softly."

"Hmm."

"Don't you start, too."

"You think he is not really there?"

"If the gods don't know, who is to say?"

"We might take advantage of such an absence by returning all of ourselves to our bodies and removing them to the cave where it is more comfortable and—"

"We would lose touch with our minions for a time."

". . . And gain touch with each other, fair one."

"True, and pleasant indeed would it be. Though whenever such as we make love the chains of consequence tend to dizzying complexity as well as to poetry."

"What the hell. Let's leave him to his mantra and get to bed."

"A moment, while I cover my absence with a few illusions."

"Then we uncover ourselves and make the mountain move."

"So much for the poetry part."

As Seaga reeled in his consciousness, his perspective on Virtù's spiritual development altered from being gathered into one place. While it remained a colorful panorama, it seemed now—compressed as the picture had become—that he was more aware of patterns, where before he had seen only events.

"Earthma, I think there may be a peculiar social current that has some connection with Stage IV," he observed, as they walked toward the cave.

"Don't be silly, Seaga," she said, brushing against him with her hip. "No mortal in Verité and hardly any in Virtù even suspect that there is a theoretical basis for such a thing."

"True," he acknowledged, catching hold of her hand.

"... And even if one were to work it out, that is all that it could be—a hypothesis with no obvious applicability."

"I'd found some small and subtle uses for it."

"Nothing like what we'd talked about in the beginning."

"No, you're right," he said, following her into the cave and drawing her to him.

"Now, which would you rather explore, reality theory or female anatomy?" she asked.

"When you put it that way, I begin to appreciate how many centuries I've spent in an abstract, theological fashion."

She gestured and there was sufficient illumination to light their way to bed. He gestured and the light went out.

"The last ones I saw come in here were Warga and Agrima," she said.

"Yes, before they departed for realms unknown," he said as their garments fell.

"That was years ago," she noted, "and they didn't stay long."

"Warga is noted for things like that," Seaga observed. "Quick and to the point."

Earthma giggled.

"Terrible reputation to have."

"The sea, on the other hand, is slow, steady, relentless. And occasionally it grows wild."

"Live up to that," she said.

—=—

Eilean a'Tempull Dubh had possessed other names in the listings of National Trust for Scotland, but it was the one Donnerjack remembered it by, and by which he referred to it, there in the telephone booth within the circle of fire—a rest stop on the Long, Long Trail A-Winding. Given to planning ahead, he had recalled that black piece of real estate off the western coast of Scotland which he had twice visited as a boy. Its presence in the family had something to do with those MacMillans, MacKays, and MacCrimmons numbered among his father's antecedents, though he'd no idea whether it were still present, or, if so, what medieval encumbrances might complicate its relationship to him. He'd phoned his attorney, a Wilson, back in the Verité, who had complained concerning the connection and had wanted to speak of the legal business of the Donnerjack Institute, and had told him to get in touch with his father's attorney, a MacNeil, in Edinburgh—or to that man's successor—and have him determine whether Donnerjack still possessed title and, if so, what he needed to do to repair, renovate, and to take up residence on that family isle. The Wilson wanted to discuss some current contracts then, but a rush of flames filled his screen as Donnerjack's five minutes were up and, being a thrifty man, John did not elect to credit another call unit.

—=—

Sayjak slept in a fork of a tree, higher than anyone else in his clan. That way he could watch them all. And the higher they had to come to reach him the more signs of their progress he received. Such as now.

He had been sound asleep, dreaming of sex and violence—which, more often than not, went together in his waking life as well—and he felt the approach and was awake and aware well before Chumo was near enough to attack him, had that been his plan.

Sayjak belched, farted, scratched himself, and stretched. Then he regarded Chumo as he climbed, waiting for him to achieve a suitable nearness for quiet conversation.

"Sayjak," the other called. "Come quick. We got troubles."

Sayjak yawned deliberately before responding.

"What troubles?" he said then.

"Eeksies. All over. Most to south. More coming in west, north."

"How many eeksies?"

"All of fingers. All of toes. Dick, too. Many times. Just in south."

"What they doing?"

"Nothing. Sit in camp. Eat. Crap. Sleep."

"What about west ones? And north?"

"All of fingers. Maybe throw in a few dicks. Just getting there. More came in north while we watched."

"You and Staggert?"

"Yes."

Sayjak reached for his mascot. It had taken him weeks to learn to tie a knot in a piece of cord he had found in the bounties' camp. But he had seen knots before and knew their function. And this cord already had a knot in it. He had used it as a model. Over and over, he had looped and twisted the strand until one day he did it. He had repeated it then, even learning variations. Then he was ready.

He tied each end securely to the hair of Big Betsy's head. This made it easy to hang from broken tree limbs, or to wear it around his neck when he felt the occasion warranted ceremony. Now, it hung from a nearby branch, and he reached out and stroked it as a thinking aid, and perhaps for good luck, also. He had cached the machete in the hollow of another tree, and every now and then he took it out and cut something with it.

For a moment, he considered wearing the head. But he had too far to go, too fast. It could catch or tangle in the brush. He bade it good-bye, then told Chumo, "Take me south. Then west and north. I must see these eeksies for myself."

So he followed Chumo down the tree, halted to alert the clan to the presence of eeksies, then headed into the south. Several hours later, he crouched in the brush with Chumo, regarding the encampment. A great number of the hunters were about, eating, talking, cleaning or honing weapons. It was the largest gathering of them that Sayjak had ever seen. Along with the apprehension this produced there came a number of questions. Why so many? Why now? And they were bounties—not eeksies, in their green-and-brown uniforms. Why bounties?

Eeksies were official; they were establishment, sent from some far-off place to do a job, and for that matter, their jobs did not always involve killing the People. Sometimes they cut trees or planted them, set fires or fought them, dug ditches, diverted rivers. Bounties, on the other hand, only came to kill—and unlike eeksies they took away tokens of their work. It was from the bounties, in fact, that he had gotten the notion of taking Big Betsy's head. The bounties were freer, wilder, nastier, more worthy of respect.

Usually, they were loners or trackers in small parties, and he had to assume that those to the west and the north were a part of this entire business. Such things did not just happen. . . .

After a time, he touched Chumo's shoulder.

"Take me to the west now," he told him.

As they traveled, he wondered where Otlag's clan browsed these days. Or Dortak's. Or Bilgad's. A general knowledge of where the others browsed was useful in preventing territorial disputes. But he was thinking precisely, rather than generally, at the moment.

Spying on the much smaller western party from a dangerous vantage, he began to suspect that none of the other clans would be enclosed by the three bounty parties and the plains to the east. He would know for certain soon enough, but already he began to feel uneasy. Hoga, who had been watching the western group, told him that its last few members had just arrived. They were making camp, though, rather than waiting as if they expected orders momentarily. So Sayjak assumed that they planned to spend at least one night in the area before commencing any concerted action with the other groups.

Hoga and Gongo, who had been left by Staggert to watch the party since its discovery that morning, followed Sayjak's lead away from the clearing.

"You know where Dortak's or Bilgad's or Otlak's clans are right now?" Sayjak asked.

"Otlak's that way." He pointed north. "Far past the next bounty encampment. Dortak's farther west." He pointed again. "Don't know about Bilgad."

Sayjak felt a strange sensation in his stomach, for he had felt that Bilgad foraged to the southeast. That indeed only left his own clan within the walls he now saw being raised. These bounties, he was suddenly certain, wanted him and his people for a particular vengeance.

He groped after a concept—the posting of the three groups so as to enable them to move most effectively against his people. His head filled with the projected activity. The notion of putting it all together in this fashion before doing it took hold of him mightily. He did things, too, in that way, though on a much smaller scale. While he lacked a word for the concept "plan," in both its verb and noun forms, he suddenly understood it. And he realized that he needed one of his own, a bigger one than he had ever come up with before.

"Take me north now," he said, "where Staggert watches the other group."

He calculated distances as they went, and he thought about the Circle Shannibal. He knew that he must act quickly, and that his plan would have to be better than their plan.

A little after noon they arrived at the northern encampment. Staggert met them and led them to a vantage amid trees on a hilltop.

"This is the smallest camp," Sayjak observed. "I see two hands of bounties."

"And there are more bounties on patrol," Staggert said.

"The People are in great danger," Sayjak said after a time.

"From these bounties?" Staggert said.

"Yes. These and those to the west are going to surprise the People and drive them southward to be slaughtered."

"How do you know this?" Staggert asked.

Sayjak thought of the raid on which he had slain Big Betsy. He suddenly thought of the other bounties coming here because he had given them fear, fear that they could become the prey.

"I tell you everything I know, Staggert, and you'll be too smart," he said, "like me. They want our heads, and they will take them. Unless we have a—a better way of doing things than their way of doing things."

He turned toward Chumo.

"Go back," he told him, "to the other two camps. Get Gongo. Get Hoga. Get Ocro. Bring them here to wait for me."

"Wait?" Chumo asked. "Where are you going?"

"Back for the rest of our clan."

"Bring 'em here, too?'

"Place near here."

"What for?"

Sayjak studied the other. Then he tapped his forehead.

"New way of fighting."

"What do you call it?"

"People warfare," Sayjak replied.

Then he turned and was gone into the jungle.

He brought the entire clan with him that evening, leaving all but the able-bodied males in a clearing about a mile from the northern encampment. He wore his mascot about his neck and he carried the stick-that-cuts as he led them, finally positioning his warriors in a glen near to the bounties' camp. Then he conferred with his lieutenants.

Staggert, Chumo, Svut, Gongo, Ocro, and Hoga stood with him in a twilit clearing as he said, "Tonight we going to kill them all here. You know how?"

All of them growled assent.

"No, you don't know how," he said then. "You know how to run in, make a lot of noise, wrestle around, and squish 'em. That's not how. Not how I want it done, not this time. We wait for dark and quiet. Get as close as we can without noise. Kill ones nearest weapons first. But kill all of 'em. We take too long, or they get hold of fancy weapons, we call for more warriors to come in fast and crush. Second group will be waiting for this, if we need 'em. Too many go in at first, though, and we get in each others' way. Everybody understand?"

Again, they all grunted assent.

—=—

Her body lay in its cubicle, nourishment, elimination, and exercise taken care of through the guardian unit. It had spoken to her in Virtù, warning her that her time was running, that she must soon return to Verité, in accordance with the vacation plan filed for her by her parents, which entailed a week on and a week off, throughout the summer. This limit was already passed, and she was now into the grace period, which, itself, was about to expire.

However, as her legs parted and her hips commenced small thrusting movements, the guardian unit halted its preparation for her recall. As Lydia moaned softly, it was already investigating her situation in Virtù. Sexual intercourse of the non-rape variety normally extended the grace period for its duration. With rape, of course, it mattered from a recreational standpoint whether one were rendering it or receiving it. Subtleties involving jurisdiction and the protection of one's client also came into play. The scan showed this particular lay to be of the voluntary, mutually recreational variety. The monitor was, unfortunately, unable to appreciate the esthetics and physiological sequelae of terminating presence with one's lover immediately following orgasm.

Abruptly, her legs locked themselves about invisible hips. Her pumping movements grew more frantic, and her nails raked an unseen back. The monitor detected increased heartbeat, blood pressure, breathing rate, and volume per inhalation. It did not notice that she was smiling. This is only known as the "demon lover effect" when people view it from the one side, while eating popcorn.

As soon as the big relaxation came it commenced the recall sequence.

—=—

. . . And fell. And blasted fell. . . .

His assembled body limp at the bottom of inertia, he passed downward from the topless height, surfaces singed as if by a stroke of lightning.

The trail had taken him through lands both hollow and hilly, through dead domains like abandoned movie sets. Up, ever up, had it led, into the realms of painful light. But he was not one to lose a trail, and he had followed, followed. Running up vertical surfaces, leaping chasms without bottoms, he sought. Seeking, he—

—found?

Rather, he was found.

One moment, he followed a scent. The next moment, it was all around him. He rose into the air and spun, fantasy dance of a pied autumn leaf. And the brightness was awesome.

"Oh, frightful dogger of this trail," snapped a voice from everywhere, like the scent, "you have come too far!"

Mizar threw back his head and commenced the howl Death had taught him.

With a crackling sound, the brightness condensed upon his person. His howl was cut off, barely past its inception. Again, he was turning, and a new smell filled the air, that of burning insulation, boiled glue, singed paint, welded metal. Rolling, ass over knee joint, tail in eye, he felt himself cast beyond the edge of the great crag in the silent sky where stars bloom in the always twilight and clouds drift far below.

Blasted by the light, the darkness came upon him.

Falling, falling then—for days, ages perhaps, depending on the worlds he fell through—

—down . . .

THREE

Tranto had lost track of time in his wanderings. Not that he ever paid it a great deal of heed, but the madness laid a distorting red haze over most things, time and space among them.

As the pain subsided, however, the frantic characteristic of the huge phant's approach to existence was also abated. The haze grew dim, and with its passing he was able to stop and eat the flowers again. He noted after a time that he occupied a great plain near to the edge of a jungle. It stirred memories of an earlier existence, for he recalled being small among others of his kind in a place such as this. And who knew? He might even have returned to those very ranges. He browsed, barely thinking, for days, his mind adrift in a place halfway between dreaming and wakefulness. This was the glorious euphoria which normally followed his spells. Moving, eating, and drinking, gaining back the mass he had lost, he found it an unnecessary effort to do more than respond to circumstances. That, and enjoy without reflection the simple realities of being.

The days drifted by, and nothing came to trouble him. All of the local predators found him intimidating—an abnormally large phant, with great jaw sabers that looked as if they had been carved from pieces of a wrecked moon. Sometime after the pain had passed and his senses seemed returned to normal, he wondered, for the first time, whether there might be others of his kind in the vicinity. He had known many herds over the years, and he realized now that he missed their company. Perhaps more than just company. It would be good to have a mate again. His symptoms had been gone for a sufficiently long while now that it was unlikely they would recur in the near future.

And so he sought. First he must find a herd. His kind were generally of a herding persuasion. While he was often an exception to this rule, the desire for company returned to him periodically, causing him to seek, as he sought now, after a group of the others. Of course, merely finding them would hardly be sufficient. He would have to persuade them to take him in. Traditionally, this meant a lengthy probationary period as a classless hanger-on. Too long, this always seemed too long. Still—there was an etiquette, a set of rules to follow in these matters. And the first thing, really, was to locate a herd.

He trumpeted, long and loud, then listened after the echoes had died. There was no response, not that he had expected one the first time he made inquiry. He sounded his call again, then browsed for a long while. Afterwards, he drank his fill at the water hole.

It seemed that he would have to go and find them. Since the only spoor in the area was quite ancient and no one had answered his inquiry, one direction would seem almost as good as another. Except for the west. The jungle lay to the west.

The present area showed signs of recent recovery from overbrowsing. His kind had been here and had moved on. The land was now well on the way to recovery, so he knew that they would return eventually, when they had exhausted new ranges. Of course, the plain was vast, and it could be a very long while; on the other hand, there were other herds upon the plain. . . . He pondered this for only a short while.

Now that he felt his stamina and full rationality returned, he did not wish to wait upon a chance encounter. It would be good to smell the others, to rub shoulders as he browsed. There was no real reason to wait around here and ample reason to depart. He would go looking. He would find them.

He turned slowly. North, east, west, south. . . . Yes, south. There was an old trail.

He began walking in that direction. He only half followed the dried trail. There were phants somewhere in the south and that was sufficient. There was no real need to hurry. Once he made a decision and began acting it was as if some natural law had been invoked. His patience was as legendary as his wrath.

44

His memory was excellent, also. As he traveled, he recalled stony lowlands that he passed as things seen when he was smaller and they had seemed bigger. He was, however, not consciously given to sentimentality, for he had never learned the concept. He trudged steadily southward, and predators whose territory he crossed went and hid until he had gone by. He browsed amid long grasses, slaked his thirst at water hole or forest stream. Dark birds came and walked upon his back, grooming him of insect pests. Occasionally, they chatted:

"Nasty scar there, big fella. How'd you get it?"

"Main pole of a circus tent scraped me, when I knocked it down. May 11, 2108."

"Oh, you've been to the big city!"

"Indeed."

"Never knew anyone to come back."

"Now you do. Seen any of my kind of people in the neighborhood recently?"

"Recently, no. They come and go."

"Know of any to the south?"

"That's the way they headed. I may be flying down that way soon, what with the bug shortage here. What about this one?"

"That's from a spear wielded by a gooey man."

"Gooey man? What's that?"

"That's how he got after I walked on him. August 7, 2105."

"Ever have any trouble with eeksies or bounties?"

"Yes, but not recently."

"There are lots of them moving about in the jungle just now."

"Which kind?"

"Bounties. But there may be some eeksy observers."

"Bounties are tougher. One almost nailed me back when there was a price on my head. September 17, 2113. Lady. Big Betsy, they called her."

"She's dead."

"Good. I sometimes dream she's still after me. What killed her?"

"Sayjak of the tree people. Took her head. Still has it."

Tranto snorted.

"Name sounds familiar."

"He's boss of the biggest clan. Fast. Can catch a flying bird in his hand as he swings through the trees. I've seen him do it. Strong. Dangerous."

"They get gooey, too, if I walk on them. Big Betsy favored ambushes, though. Got one of her scars, too. What do the bounties and eeksies want now?"

"Sayjak's head, I think. Mad about Big Betsy and the others he made short."

"If they stayed away they wouldn't have these problems."

"True."

"This is a land they didn't design, where things just went their course. Now, all of a sudden, they act like it's theirs."

"They're never happy."

"I suppose not."

"Maybe I'll see more of your scars later. I'm heading back to the jungle now. Want to see what happens."

"Don't fly near Sayjak when he's swinging through trees."

"No. Good luck in your search."

"Thanks."

He plodded on. All that day, stopping only to eat and drink his fill at a water hole, he continued southward. At night, he browsed beneath a sky full of bright stars.

Days passed easily in this fashion. He endured a long, dry stretch where even the grasses were parched. Day after day this went on, to be followed by a cloudburst which filled every declivity with water. After that, the terrain became stonier. He continued into the south and that evening he passed a walking man and a woman upon a trail bordered by white markers, wavering, as through a heat haze. It appeared to be the same man who had helped him in his extremity recently. When he approached them, however, they faded, to appear high overhead where they spiraled amid red sun rays for perhaps ten minutes before vanishing. Before the day ended he came upon a trail fresher than any he had yet encountered—phant spoor—heading southward.

For three days he followed that track. On the third he caught a scent out of the east. His own kind. Phant. For the first time, now, he hurried.

That evening he came to an area which they had traversed very recently. The next morning he found an easy trail. The breezes shifted, but when they bore him the scents they were stronger.

By noontime, he had sight of them, great dark masses shifting slowly on the distant plain. He slowed, then halted, regarding them. For the first time in a long while, something like joy rose within him. The company of his fellows. . . . It was immediately tempered by a certain bittersweet realization: It was not that easy for a stranger to be accepted into a herd.

One way of going about it was to hang around the periphery of the group, obsequious, waiting to be noticed. Gradually, after a long period of waiting, one might be accepted into the bottom of the society.

At some buried level of his being Tranto knew that he was probably older than any of them. It seemed that he had been around for a very long while. It suddenly seemed possible to him that he could have been a member of this herd before, that it may well have been his original herd, and that he could have survived all of the others in it. The thought of returning now, unknown, as an outcast, irritated him. True—if it were the case—it was to be expected of one with his wandering ways. Yet, it rankled. Pacing and snorting, he became more and more convinced that it was indeed the case. He belonged here, and they would deny him his rightful place. The more he thought about it the more irritated he became, though he had not yet made contact.

He paced them for a day, keeping his distance but allowing himself to be seen. His anger grew as he followed. Yes, it certainly seemed possible that this had once been his band. There were so many here who resembled those others. Then he thought of his anger. While it had often gotten him in trouble in the past, that was the anger born of pain-madness. This hardly seemed on that scale.

The second day he moved nearer, browsing much closer to the leeward fringe of the herd. That afternoon a runt male, doubtless the bottommost phant in the band's hierarchy, moved near. A little later he glanced up and said, "My name's Muggle."

"I'm Tranto."

"A legendary name, that. Father of the herd."

"Who's in charge now?"

"Scarco. That's him over by the grove."

Tranto glanced in the direction indicated, to behold a large phant engaged in the sharpening of his tusks upon an outcropping of rough rock.

"Has he been boss long?"

"For as far back as I can remember."

"Is he ever challenged?"

"Regularly. The plains are strewn with the bones of those who didn't make it to the graveyard of our kind, famed in song and story."

"Indeed. What's his policy on admitting new members to the herd?"

"In general, the usual. The newcomer follows us around for a couple of seasons taking a lot of shit and gradually being accepted into the lowest ranks. A few more seasons and he may work his way up a little."

"A *little*?"

"Well, as far as he may—which isn't very—from just being on hand. Unless, of course, he's a fighter. Then he can go as far as it'll take him."

"In other words, it's just like everywhere else."

"So far as I understand it."

"Good. Has everyone in the herd noticed me?"

"Not the near-sighted ones, I suppose, or the ones farther off to the west."

"Well, I do want them all to at least recognize me. How long do you think that'll take?"

"I'd say about three days."

"You'll mention my name to the others?"

"Of course. They sent me to learn it. I get all the jobs like this. I can't wait till you join up and I have someone I can push around."

The next day many of the phants wandered by, glancing at him. When Muggle came by again, he paused.

"They know your name," he said, "and I've learned that it's not at all a common one. I've been asked to see whether you have chain marks on your leg and to find out whether you were ever boss of your own herd. Apparently, there was once a Tranto who got hauled away to be exhibited. There's some story involving a tall building he did something terrible at."

"Yes, I was boss of my own herd," Tranto replied.

Muggle moved to inspect his legs.

"Those do look like the marks he described to me."

"Who?"

"Scarco."

"Oh, the boss was wondering?"

"Yes. He wanted to know what you planned to do here."

"Oh. I planned to wait three days, till everyone at least knew who I was, and then challenge him for leadership of the herd."

"Combat? Tusk to tusk? Body to body?"

"The usual, yes."

"To the death?"

"To whatever is necessary."

"You ever do it before?"

"Yes."

"To the death, I mean."

"Yes. That, too. Though it seldom goes that far."

"Really?"

"You ever seen one end in death?"

"Well, no. But I've seen some pretty nasty fighting."

"Exactly. We usually knock off when it's pretty obvious who's the better phant."

"Three days, you say. . . . When did you start counting?"

"Well, there was yesterday, and then there's today."

"Tomorrow? Tomorrow you give the challenge?"

"The day after. I meant three full days. Everybody will have an idea what I look like by then. It's the closest I'm going to get to being introduced."

"But that's just not how it's done. Usually, they start out fighting some lower phant and work their way up. Somewhere along the line they find their level, and that's that."

"I've a pretty good idea where I'll wind up. I'm just cutting out the middlemen."

"That's dangerous."

"I'm glad he appreciates it."

"Excuse me."

Continuing his browsing, Tranto noted after a time that Muggle had moved into Scarco's vicinity as if in the accidental course of his breakfast foraging. They were together for some small while. Then a black bird came and sat on Scarco's head.

Later in the day, Muggle wandered his way again.

"I was talking to Scarco a bit ago . . ." he said.

Tranto grunted.

"He thinks it rather ill-considered for you to do a thing like that when you're not even familiar with the group. What if—speaking hypothetically, of course—you fought him and won and then discovered that you didn't even like the job or the area or your constituents?"

"We could always move to a different area," Tranto said, "and, as for the job, I think I indicated I've held the like before. Never had any trouble with my herd then, either."

Muggle nodded.

"The boss had anticipated your saying something like that. He's pretty smart as well as tough, you know. Tough just isn't enough to have kept him where he is for as long as he's been there. Now he felt you might need a little time to make up your mind about whether you were really doing the right thing."

"I know what I'm doing."

"Bear with me a moment. Scarco appreciates your feelings—as an outcast looking for a home, as a phant so desperate for acceptance that he's willing to risk his life for a herd. So he asked me to make you a proposal: Hold off on the challenge and he'll waive the waiting period. You won't have to wander about the fringes of the herd looking pathetic and sucking up to everybody. You'll be in, effective immediately, with all the rights and privileges that entails."

"That would still leave me at the bottom of things, which is unacceptable."

"You could still fight your way up, a rung at a time, whenever you felt up to it."

"Too slow. No thanks."

"He will be sorry to hear that."

"I'm certain."

Muggle lumbered off. Tranto watched him browse his way toward Scarco again. Later in the day he came back.

"How's about this?" he asked. "He lets you in at the middle level. No getting dumped on like the guys at the bottom. In fact, you'll have plenty of guys you can push around yourself then. That's what you want, isn't it? Acceptance and a little fun?"

"What about the guy I displace?"

"The boss just tells him to eat a little shit. He'll do it. That's what life is all about."

"What about the ones I'll suddenly be over?"

"They eat a little, too. But they'll get over it."

"Whoever would be right above me and right under me wouldn't accept me, seeing how I'd gotten my position. I'd have to fight them to consolidate things."

"That's up to you."

"True, and since it means I'd have to fight anyway, I'll just start at the top."

"Scarco's awfully tough."

"I never doubted that."

"Did you really get that scar knocking down a—what do you call 'em?—circus tent?"

"No, that's the one over on this side. I got that one tearing a fighting vehicle apart."

"I'm not sure I know what that is. But I'll go and pass along your answer now, if it's final."

"It is."

Muggle moved away. Tranto foraged some more, wandered over to the water hole and drank, climbed a hill, and watched the day end. As the shadows drifted about him, he descended its far side, lowered his head, and drowsed.

Somewhere in the middle of the night he was roused by the sense of a large presence moving nearby. Despite their great bulk, phants can move with ghostlike stealth. Yet it is not that easy to surprise a fellow phant who is experienced in that area himself.

"Good evening, Scarco," Tranto said.

"How did you know who it was?"

"Who else would it be?"

"True. I guess we're the only two with anything to talk about at this hour."

"So it would seem."

"I know who you are."

"The bird. I saw it."

"I might have guessed without it, Ancestor."

"Well, I've been around a lot, that's true. I don't know that it matters, makes me special some way."

"Ah, but it does. As a child, I heard stories of you. I still hear them. I often wondered whether you were truly real, or but a legend. I confess I felt it to be the latter. Now, it appears that I must fight you for the leadership of the herd."

"Well, yes. I'm not giving you much choice. But look at it this way: When we're done, you'll be Number Two. That's not bad. Takes a lot of the pressure off, in a way, I understand."

Scarco made a polite noise, then, "That's not entirely it," he said.

"What do you mean?"

"You are right that being Number Two might not be bad. After all these years it might even be something of a relief. I could stop worrying about challenges, stop worrying about all the big decisions, take life easy for a change, and still enjoy everyone's respect. The position does hold considerable appeal."

"Then what's the problem? We fight, and—win or lose—you still end up in a desirable position."

"Dead is not a desirable position."

"Who's talking dead? We both know that these things only go as far as they have to."

"Ordinarily, yes. But, well . . . I'm a little leery about this one."

"What do you mean?"

"Well, to be frank—no insult intended, mind you—I've heard that you're a rogue. Once you lose your temper and start smashing things, they say, there's no stopping you. It occurs to me that this might be the case in a combat for leadership, that you just might not stop where anyone else would if someone were to call it quits."

"Oh, no. This is a misunderstanding of my condition—though it's easy to see how the rumor might have gotten around. What it is, is that I've an old injury that sometimes acts up, and when it does the pain tends to drive me rather wild. This doesn't occur too often, however. Years often pass between spells. In fact, I've just gotten over one recently, so it should be a good long time before I'm troubled by another. Generally, I even feel it coming on and have time to get away from my friends. So there's really nothing to worry about on that account."

"What brings them on, Tranto?"

"Oh, different things. Apart from the times when they just come on by themselves, various traumas might set them off. A CF prod, for instance. Hate the things."

"Oh, they've had you on forced work crews?"

"Indeed. Usually a mistake on their part."

"I can imagine. Well, look, you can't blame a fellow for being cautious."

"Of course not."

"Then you understand my feelings. If you're not absolutely certain what sets all of them off, how am I to know whether a thrust from me might trigger one?"

"I see what you're getting at. Unfortunately, it's like anything else in life: I can't offer you assurances. On the other tusk, I think it highly unlikely."

"Hm."

"That's the best I can do. Sorry."

"But you appreciate my dilemma?"

"Of course. Life is sweet."

"Exactly. I'm tempted just to take a walk, find another herd, and start over again. I might, too, if I thought you'd be good for the herd. I do care about them, you know."

"I've never led a herd into real trouble. I'd leave myself rather than bring something bad down on them."

"May I have your word on that?"

"You have my word."

"That makes it a little easier then. Move on into that little grove where I used to hang out, tonight. Let them find you there in the morning."

"I will."

"Good-bye, Tranto."

"Good-bye, Scarco."

The dark form turned and moved away as silently as it had come.

—=—

Ayradyss D'Arcy Donnerjack, but late returned from the realms that describe an eccentric orbit about Deep Fields, gazed thoughtfully upon the hotel room's simple furnishings, upon her sleeping husband, upon the pinkish-grey light of the early dawn, and sighed softly to herself. She still felt disoriented, although she thought it ungrateful to bring this to John's attention, and Verité was strange to her. She was a creature of change from ancient Virtù and something in her rebelled at the stability that she felt within the very cells of her reborn body.

Strolling to the double glass doors, she parted the sheer curtains, pushed the doors open, and went out onto the balcony to look down at the blue waters of the Caribbean Sea.

The morning air was uncomfortably chill for she was clad in only a light robe of gauzy white silk, but she remained outside, letting the chill wash over her. A small smile played about her lovely mouth as she meditated on the paradox that at one and the same time she could crave the fluidity of her Virtù home locus, a place where she could sprout angel wings from her shoulders and fly, or dive beneath the sea, as finny-tailed as the best mermaid, and yet find herself seeking cold or heat or hunger or any physical sensation strong enough to chase away the terrible fear that she was still dead.

The rising sun had washed the last of the grey from the sky, replacing it with more pink, with orange, with red, with yellow. Clouds were visible now: long, wind-sculpted shapes that in Virtù could quite well have been aerial creatures, but here were merely the workings of wind on water, water that had been pulled into the sky only to fall again to the land and thus be drawn up again in a ceaseless cycle that nonetheless had something of chaos in it. Meteorology was still more art than science for all that chaos theory and fractal geometries had added to science's comprehension.

Science. Her Donnerjack's religion for all he denied it. He was a practical man, a hard man, and yet there was a poet in him, a poet that had been drawn to Ayradyss: Nymph of Verité, Mermaid Beneath the Seven Dancing Moons, Angel of the Forsaken Hope. In Virtù, she had fallen in love with her poet, and after the moiré had touched her, her poet had drawn her from the lands about Deep Fields. At first she had followed as little more than an automaton, but as the Trails of Bones, Stars, Rainbows, and other exotic things had taken them farther and farther from entropy's hold, she had followed John with eagerness, finally raising her voice to join his in song to cross the bridges over the obstacles that Death had set before them as any good opponent must—*pro forma* obstacles, almost—for John D'Arcy Donnerjack had abided by the rules that Death had set and had brought Ayradyss safely from Deep Fields into the living lands, from Virtù into Verité.

No, John D'Arcy Donnerjack had not failed to bring forth his Ayradyss—as Orpheus had failed to bring forth his Eurydice—but something in her wondered at the cold, practical man with whom she shared a bed. Often he was loving enough, attentive, possessive, but now that she knew him in the larger context of his life she wondered that he had striven so hard to take her back from Death, for he often had little time for her outside of the hours that were spent making love or engaging in lover's chatter.

She wondered if she bored him: clipped-winged angel, tailless mermaid, nymph-no-more, merely woman. A woman possessed of unique, curious knowledge, true; a program crafted for Virtù now residing as a woman of flesh and blood in Verité, but still nothing more than a woman.

Ayradyss, returned so recently from the realms orbiting Deep Fields, heard her new husband stir in his sleep, turned and saw through the window curtain how his arms reached for her and did not find her, saw how he woke to greater awareness and to horrible fear.

"Ayra!" he called and his voice carried the bone-shivering terror that only one who has lost a lover to Death can know.

Ayradyss pushed apart the curtains and hurried to his side, saw the relief that flooded his blanched, anxious face with blood. Sliding into the bed at his side, she felt his burly arms clasp her to him, heard his murmured endearments, felt the rapid beating of his heart begin to slow as he assured himself that she was indeed with him once more, doubted no longer his love, wondered only at the odd shapes that love can take even in Verité where no human is a shapeshifter.

—=—

"A problem?"

Abel Hazzard and his wife Carla regarded the imaged tour executive, a Mr. Chalmers, in their family virt space.

"What sort of problem?" Abel asked him. "Lydia is all right, isn't she?"

"Oh, yes. Quite all right," Mr. Chalmers assured him. "What we seem to be faced with is a small—retrieval problem."

"Retrieval? You mean you can't bring her back?"

"Well, when her time was up the recall sequence was initiated after a small grace period to allow her to finish whatever she was about. So far, she has not responded to the signal."

"Why not?"

"It seems she is still—occupied. The grace period has run into a number of extensions."

"Occupied?" Carla asked. "How?"

"Indications are that she is with a lover."

"Oh. Well, she *is* there to enjoy herself. Let Lydia have her fun. If there is no physiological danger in extending it a little longer, let her stay on. She'll tire of it in a while, and we can let her spend some extra time recuperating before she goes back."

"Thank you," Chalmers said, smiling. "It is not without precedent, of course, but we are required to keep parents and guardians aware of these matters. Half a day is hardly serious. We'll notify you as soon as she is returned."

"Thank you."

—=—

Arthur Eden wore the garment of the lowest grade initiate—a red-and-gold patterned dashikilike affair—though he had not achieved this status. He waited in the courtyard before the temple with a small group of other, similarly clad individuals, both of Virtù and Verité. A service was currently in progress beneath a star-filled sky, which also bore two signs and several portents shining brightly at midheaven.

Slowly, a light descended from the sky, taking on the form of a silver sailing ship, passing overhead, entering through some hidden opening in the roof of the temple. A small ensemble at the left hand of the priest began to play then, a thing of strings and flute. A sigh rose from the congregation, and the priest intoned, "The god has arrived, to oversee the lesser initiation. Let any who are unready speak now and save your-self a profaner's damnation."

None responded.

There followed an intoned prayer, then—as in the rehearsal earlier in the week—the musicians moved to a position near the temple doors. The initiation candidates turned in that direction and advanced with slow, measured steps. As they did, the doors were swung open with matching deliberation.

The musicians moved again, entering, and Eden's party matched them to form a procession. The rest of the worshipers remained behind in the courtyard.

Ahead, Eden saw candlelight through a dimness, and he smelled incense. Advancing into the theatrically shadowy interior, he realized that there were dark doors in the walls at either hand as well as a tall, narrow silver pair directly ahead. All of them were closed. The bright pair to the chamber's rear was elaborately embossed with abstract, curving designs amid which the candles' light swam like bright fish in a garden pond.

They continued until they were well inside. When the music grew slower they halted. A small draft ceased and they knew that the doors had been closed behind them.

They stood for a long while, waiting, listening to the music, preparing themselves spiritually as they had been taught. Abruptly then, the music ceased and the silver doors began, slowly, to open. A moment later, he could see that there was something very bright behind them.

—=—

Above the music of the lost that might be reclaimed, Death heard Mizar's cry. The bone woman whose hand he held came apart as the howl was broken off, and he rose and turned three times in a circle, widdershins, but the sound had been too brief to determine its source. He walked then to the twilit crest of a hill, held forth a pale hand and captured the cry.

Too brief, too brief to take him all the way. Yet— He cast it before him down the farther slope and followed its echo. As he walked the twilight flickered about him and the hillside grew level and he moved in a brightness of full day down a busy thoroughfare where none took notice of him save for a single, old woman who turned and stared into his eyes. He reached out and touched her shoulder, not ungently, and she slumped to the pavement. He continued on, not looking back, and turned right at the next corner.

The city faded and he walked across a lake. Several fish turned belly up and floated to the top as he passed. When he reached the farther shore he came to a field and began walking through it.

Partway through the field, he halted. Red-and-yellow flowers bloomed about him, save in a patch to his left where a multitude hung withered upon their stalks. He directed his gaze in their direction, and after a moment a patch of black rose from one of these and fluttered to a fresh blossom in full bloom. A few moments later, the flower began to droop.

"Alioth," he said then. "Come to me."

The black butterfly rose from the wilting flower and fluttered across the space between them to light upon his extended finger.

"Hi, boss. Fancy meeting you here."

"It was not, really, a matter of chance," Death responded.

"Didn't think it was. Just making conversation."

The dark figure nodded. Alioth could never tell when Death was amused.

"For that matter, I might even venture a guess as to why you're out and about in the flesh, so to speak," Alioth ventured, still wondering. "I heard Mizar's howl, too."

"Ah!"

"Yes, but broken off after only a moment."

"Indeed. It was too brief for me to respond properly. I was hoping that, from your position in the scheme of things, you might have been able to obtain a better notion as to its direction."

"I am not certain," Alioth replied. "But it did seem to phase from a more central locale."

"Then let us take a look," Death said, and he raised his other arm.

Landscapes swept by them at such a rapid rate that Alioth was unable to sort them. And the pace increased until it was only a succession of lights and darks, then blacks and whites, and finally a throbbing grey. Alioth knew that his master scanned everything that passed, however.

Their course took upon it a spiral aspect then, and the sequence through which they had just passed was reversed. When they halted, Death stood at the base of an enormous mountain whose top was lost to sight beyond the clouds.

Death leaned to examine a small crater. Alioth fluttered above it, dipped down into it.

"Piece of reddish cable embedded in the side here, Lord."

Death dropped soundlessly into the hole and extended a hand. He removed the object from the wall, raised it, studied it.

"One of Mizar's tails," he said. "I wonder what aspect of him it represents?"

He rose up out of the hole then and followed a line of footsteps which lightened as they went and then vanished after a double-dozen paces.

"He appears to have made his way into another space." Death lowered himself and extended a hand above the final tracks. He moved it in a slow circle. His hand and arm vanished and returned, vanished and returned as he did so. "Continued through many," he said, "fading, fading. Gone."

Death rose, glanced upward. Glanced back down.

"What happened to him?" Alioth asked.

"Speculation is fruitless at this point," he replied.

Death threw back his head and howled. The sky was darkened, and a passing flock of birds fell dead at his feet. The earth began to tremble, from there out through the spaces of Virtù.

Jagged bolts of lightning played about Mount Meru as the wailing continued, and the ground was cracked and fissured at its base. The entire mountain was swayed imperceptibly, and grasses withered and trees fell down. Lakes overflowed their bounds, and rivers ran backwards.

When he had ceased he waited. For a long, long while he waited. But there was no response.

—=—

From his hilltop vantage Donnerjack could view the sea in several directions as well as the work in progress below him. Considerable digging had gone on, he understood, for the better part of the week. The foundation was now in place, and he compared its actuality with the print on the pad screen he held in his hand. He turned to the woman at his side.

"It is what I have asked for, thus far," he said. "It seems to be moving along right on schedule, too. Any thoughts?"

"I am happy to be here," she replied. "It is so strange, so different. . . . Yes, it must be good."

"I was afraid that the isolation—"

"No, that's good, too," she said. "I want it. I want a long time of it, after—after that other."

He nodded.

"We will check back again periodically as it grows into our home. And when we tire of it we can always walk in your world."

"Though it is not exactly my world any longer."

"Both will always be your worlds, Ayra."

"Yes, and it will be good. There is so much I wish to learn of this place—of both places, really. And I wish to help you with your work. I have a unique perspective."

"Yes," he said, taking her small hand in his burly one. "Perhaps you can."

During the months that followed they visited the isle regularly, watching the black castle in its growth. It seemed impossible to know exactly what it had looked like in an earlier incarnation, so Donnerjack had been free in his designs, incorporating what features he would from existing structures of a similar nature. It grew tall, dark, and more than a little formidable against its bleak backdrop, though it was plumbed and heated to modern rather than medieval standards and contained lines of fiberoptic cable as well as concealed microwave antennas.

And they would walk through it as it grew—he, tapping joints with his stick; she, running her fingertips over surfaces—and they would smile and nod to each other. If it were not raining, they would stand on their hilltop for a time and look down on it. They watched the flyers come and go, bearing materials and labor, and then they would go away themselves to one of their honeymoon apartments in some other country to pass the time.

And when the time was right he worked there himself, building the Great Stage beside his workroom—full-scale, state of the art. And transfer chambers, for full visitation to Virtù. And on his workroom he lavished at least as much attention.

Working late one night after the laborers had departed—for there were some parts of the installation he had intended for no eyes but his own—Donnerjack heard a low moaning sound from somewhere below. He investigated, stick in hand, but discovered nothing untoward. But the winds blew about the incomplete castle, finding entry at every opening. He nodded and went on with his work. The sounds came and went throughout the night.

Over a series of such nights Donnerjack installed everything he would need to conduct his business. Its delicate nature was not the only reason he craved isolation. Ayradyss was. There was no record of her existence in the well-enumerated society of Verité, and the safest way to create her identity, he judged, would be incrementally, over a period of time, a stroke here, a stroke there, a small retroactive datum every now and then. First, of course, his system would have to be in place; it would not be operational until after they had taken up residence.

Strange, he reflected, tonight the moaning seemed to be accompanied by the rattling of chains. . . .

FOUR

Seaga emerged from the cave, stretched, and stared out across the many-chambered world. It was good to have one's consciousness localized in a single body, in a single place once again, much to recommend a compact feeling of entirety. There was Earthma, for example. Good that she slept for a time now, though, to give him this respite. If indeed she were sleeping. . . . Of course she was sleeping. It would be ridiculous to mix business with pleasure. On the other hand . . .

A distant movement caught his attention. Tiny dot out of the east, it cut in his direction, running across the sky. He turned his vision inside-out, better to understand the phenomenon, here, above the blue, where daytime stars now recommended themselves to his gaze. Running on nothing it came, as if the trick were not impossible, or at least insuperably difficult, a pale-haired youth clad only in a golden jockstrap and sandals. Soon the figure was treading on nothingness before him, eyes dancing. In his hand he bore a feathered stick, wrapped by a pair of lethargic serpents, also golden. "Hail, Seaga," he announced. "You linger On High."

"What of it, Celerity?" the other responded. "And why should I not?"

"To be sure. Deity may do as it chooses. And that is somehow always right, in a sense."

"Do you come to speak me riddles? To dance on the mountaintop? Or have you a message for me?"

"None of the above. I came to speak with whomever might be here and taking a break from extended awareness, to report an odd sighting."

"That being?"

"Death, his own, old dark self. Below. I saw him not that long ago. Perhaps you heard his wail and saw the sky split, felt the earth shake, the mountain sway."

"I did, and it disturbed my—meditations. Though, in truth, I thought it might be a part of them. So I did not know the true source of that great cry, my awareness being unextended. Do you know why Death howled?"

"I cannot say," Celerity answered, "for who can know the thoughts of Death? I only know that he circled the base of Mount Meru as if searching for something. When he came to a depression in the ground he studied it and took something from it. That was when he gave his cry."

"Did you see what it was that he'd found?"

"I believe it was a small length of red cable."

"Hm. The primal mountain is not wired. Did you see what he did with it?"

"He bore it away with him, Seaga, walking amid the worlds."

"Why do you bring this information On High?"

"I felt it of importance to anyone here, that Death has been sniffing around your mountain."

"He has never dared to set foot on it. What would be the point? We are undying gods."

"I like to think so. Hate to get Death pissed off at me, though."

"You have a point. Do you feel some one of us may have done a thing to offend him?"

"I think it possible. We might check with any of the others who are about, to see whether this could be the case."

Seaga glanced back toward the cave.

"Unfortunately, Skyga is deep in meditation just now," he said. "I'm not certain where Earthma has gotten off to."

The youth smiled, waving his wand downward.

"Probably playing games with the Elishites."

"I know them not."

"A new religion."

"Religions come and go. They all start sounding alike after a time. What should anyone find amusing about this one?"

"It's still growing, and it contains some unusual features. For one thing, it was founded here in Virtù, and it seems to be spreading across the border to the first world."

Seaga shrugged.

"Virtù has always existed, in one form or another. The technology of the Verité only provided it a local habitation and a name. It may well be that all religions have taken their origins in Virtù. For what is it but the collective spirit of the race?"

"Be that as it may, another has come along. Maybe you should get involved yourself."

"Perhaps. Have you?"

"Strictly as an observer—a distant one, so far."

"What sort of religion is it?"

"They went back to the old Sumerian stuff for it. 'A return to basics at a new level'—as they were bade. Only none of the founders were sure what that meant, so they guessed. It has standard personifications and the usual theatrics."

"Who started it?"

"I don't know the name. I wasn't watching at the beginning. But rumor has it an arty got the word and started the ball rolling."

"Do you know whether one of my colleagues had a hand in it?"

Celerity shook his head.

"Hmm," Seaga mused. "A religion founded by an artificial intelligence. . . ." He moved forward and looked downward. "And what of our lesser brethren? Are they involved?"

"Some are, I think."

"I would think this just the sort of thing for a minor deity anxious to increase his mana."

Celerity blushed.

"So would I, actually. It does threaten to become a going concern."

"I don't feel like becoming involved. Not without knowing a lot more about it. May I persuade you to show more interest and to report back to me?"

"I suppose. How do you feel I should go about it, though? One hardly files a job application, you know."

"True. Talk to the lesser ones on the lower slopes who have become involved. Show them your interest and display your greatness."

"What greatness? I am definitely of the minor astral nobility, an errand boy of you High Ones, not a true dweller on Meru. I may not even set foot at this level. I've no aura sufficient to awe them into obedience or cooperation."

Seaga smiled.

"Easily changed," he said. "Perhaps it were time you received a promotion. Walk forward."

Celerity studied his dark-bearded face, stared into his blue eyes, looked away.

"I will not be blasted?" he asked.

"That would hardly be productive. No, you shall not be blasted, rapid one. Come ashore from the twilight."

Celerity stepped onto the ledge.

"So that's how it feels," he said after a moment.

"How is that?" Seaga asked.

"The same as anyplace else."

"Then you have learned a small lesson. Now learn the exception."

Seaga raised his right hand and placed it upon the other's head. Immediately, Celerity winced. Slowly, then, his expression grew more relaxed, until finally he was smiling. After a short while a small radiance surrounded his body. The golden quality he exhibited was enhanced, grew to become an aura of almost liquid quality. Soon ripples and lines appeared within it, as if a flow were occurring.

"It feels as if a current is passing through me, between your hand and the mountain," he said after a time.

"This is indeed the case," the other replied, "though some of it remains to enhance your personal attributes. In other words, you grow stronger by the moment."

The aura reached a peak of brightness and Seaga held it so for several minutes more. Then he withdrew his hand suddenly and let it fall to his side.

"And so, Celerity, you are ready," he said. "Go forth into the worlds, obtain knowledge of this matter, and bring it to me."

Celerity raised a hand and flexed it. He stared at it. It began to glow with the golden light. He smiled. He raised his wand and saluted Seaga with it.

"At your service," he said.

Then he sprang straight up into the air, hovered a moment, and turned. Suddenly, he was gone, a golden streak in the north. Moments later he reappeared, out of the south.

"At your service," he repeated. Then he was gone into the east.

——=—

Sayjak wiped his machete on the pant leg of one of the bounties, then regarded the man's web belt with the sheathed machete hung above the left hip. Stooping, he studied the manner in which it was fastened. Here, his experience with knots seemed somehow to serve him. He understood how it worked. Leaning forward, he unfastened and removed it. Raising it then, he saw that it was too short to fit about his own waist. He was about to cast it away when he realized how it might be adjusted. He expanded it to its greatest length then clasped it about himself. He withdrew the machete and looked at it. It was cleaner, newer-looking than the one he held. He replaced it in the sheath and plunged the old one into the ground beside the corpse. Then he straightened for a moment and regarded the twelve dead bounties, seated with their backs against tree trunks, their heads in their laps, hands positioned as if holding them.

"Good work," he said to the others, who had stood watching him, "because you did what I told you."

"Two hands, two dicks of bodies," Staggert said. "The People never did them like that before."

"Not done yet, either," Sayjak said.

"We going back for the others—west, south?"

"No. Too many. There is another way."

"What?"

"You will see. Get the rest of the clan together now. The way is open to go northwest."

"We run away?"

"Little bit. Not for good."

Staggert moved to one of the bodies, leaned forward, groped at its waist.

"What you doing?" Sayjak asked.

"Get a waist thing and a cutting stick like yours, to take heads with."

Sayjak moved forward, placed a hand on his shoulder and pushed. Staggert fell sprawling.

"No!" Sayjak said. "Nobody get cutting stick but boss. Just Sayjak."

Staggert sprang to his feet with a snarl. He began to raise his hands and Sayjak struck him a low blow. He grunted and clutched his groin.

"Only boss has cutting stick," Sayjak said.

Staggert's eyes narrowed. Then he looked away.

"Sure, boss. Only Sayjak," he said then.

Sayjak turned to the others, all of whom dropped their eyes.

"*Now* get the clan together," he ordered. "We go northwest."

They moved to comply, and that afternoon Sayjak led his people out of the trap that had been drawn about them. Then he turned to the southwest, taking them to a place known to all the People, even those who had never visited it. All afternoon they moved, pausing only once to feed.

At length, by twilight, they came to the Circle Shannibal. It was a circular clearing in the jungle, a few boulders scattered through it, a large, hard-packed mound of earth at its center. Sayjak increased his pace, heading toward the mound. With a leap, he took himself atop it, and there he paced, turning slowly in all directions.

The clan followed him into the clearing, moving to its center, gathering about the mound, murmuring softly.

"This is the Circle Shannibal," he said. "Very important place. Long time ago Karak, founder of the clans of the People, lived here. Story is that he beat upon this mound till People in the trees come to see what the matter is. Then he stood here where I am standing and told them why being clan is better than being wild and by yourself. They thought it good idea to join him. Of course, he had to fight some of the toughest ones then who would like to be boss themselves. But that's okay. He won. Then the clan hung around here for a long time. Place got browsed out, though, and they moved on. Later, clan got too big and they split it. More splits went on over the years. But every now and then, when some big emergency came along, old Karak would come here—back to the starting place—and call them all together. And after he was gone—every now and then, when emergencies came along—the biggest boss would come here to call everybody back to deal with it. Been a long time since Karak's days and other emergency times. But we got one now, and I'm biggest boss and I'm gonna call 'em all in. They all remember the stories. They'll come to see what's going on." He knelt then and began striking his fists on the top of the mound. "We all gotta help. Take turns hitting it. Get big sticks if you gotta. Don't hit each other."

Several moved to join him as he climbed down and stood at the mound's side. Soon their pounding grew steady, settled into a rhythm. The others began to sway, then to raise their feet and put them down again.

All through the night the drumming went on, the clan slowly working itself into a bashing, wailing, foot-stamping frenzy. The jungle continued to throb with the pounding. Soon the first strangers began to arrive.

Throughout the night more of them came to the clearing. At first, it was individuals and couples. Then larger groups appeared to join in the dancing and the drumming. Then old Dortak, who remembered the tradition, came in with the rest of his clan. The Circle began to fill and newcomers relieved tired drummers.

Finally, Otlag entered the Circle with the balance of his people. Later in the afternoon Bilgad's clan showed up, crowding the Circle, joining in the wailing, the swaying, the great mass circling of the mound. Still Sayjak—sweating and stamping—caused the hypnotic drumming to continue. Individuals dropped out to eat and relieve themselves, returning as soon as they were done. The vibrations in the ground were felt as far as the western bounty camp, but the hunters—who had never experienced a clan summoning—thought it a geological phenomenon and continued the preparations for their project at hand.

The drumming and dancing continued till twilight. Then Sayjak signed to the drummers to stop, and when they had, he vaulted once more to the top of the mound. He turned slowly in a circle, taking in all of the clans with his gaze.

"Many bounties have come to take our heads," he said. "Three groups of them took places about my clan. Big one to the south, smaller one over that way." He gestured, then gestured again. "Smallest that way. Sayjak's clan killed all of the last one, took their heads."

A murmur ran among the visiting clans.

"That let us get past them," he continued, "to come here, to the old place, to call in the rest of you. Sayjak's clan is mighty, but Sayjak is not a fool. Too many bounties there for Sayjak to get them all. But Sayjak knows how to do it. Sayjak wants you to come with him. Not all of you— Sayjak only wants a few good clansmen, big, strong, fast. Come with him and his fighters to the western bounty encampment. There we will kill them all and you will see how it is done. Then we go south to the big bounty camp and everyone must help."

There was more murmuring, then. "Sayjak," Dortak called out, "the bounties drew their lines around your clan, came to kill your people. They did not do this to the rest of us. Why should we help you fight your battle?"

Sayjak showed his teeth.

"You think they will stop with the head of Sayjak and the heads of his people?" he asked. "If they can do it to Sayjak, they can do it to Bilgad. When I am gone they will come for Otlag, then you. By yourselves, none of you will stand against a massing of bounties such as this. Together, though, with me to show you how to do it, we will kill them all—tonight! Leave them with their heads in their laps! No longer will they think the People are easy to kill. They will be afraid and stay away. It will be a long time before they come back, if they ever do."

Dortak drew himself erect, then spoke into the silence that followed Sayjak's statement:

"This may be, and it may not be," he said. "I believe you when you say that you have learned good ways to kill bounties. What I do not know is whether killing them all will keep more from coming, or will bring even more later after our heads."

Sayjak started to respond, but Dortak said, "But I will go along with you, for now all of the People need your knowledge of bounty killing. This is how we will learn it. But if we are successful, if we kill them all, the clan of Dortak will move to a different place. This is because I feel that the bounties and the eeksies will mark this place in some way, as a trouble spot, and it will no longer be safe to live here. You may be right. They may not come back for a long time. But I believe that they will come back one day, and I do not want my clan here when they do."

Sayjak showed his teeth again. He had been about to bluster, to say that he would kill all of the later bounties, too. Then it occurred to him that he might one day have to run, and it would not do to make it look too bad a thing. In fact— He realized that it might not be a bad idea to get the hell out after this battle. The jungle was big. Even if the bounties found the clans again later they would have no way of knowing whether they were the ones who had been behind this night's work.

"Dortak is wise," Sayjak said. "We cannot say for certain what the bounties will do. Yes, I think we should all move to new places after we have done here. Not come back for a long time."

He made a mental note then to either kill Dortak one day or to become friends with him, for he saw that he could be either dangerous or useful. He would have to think about it.

—=—

Ayradyss fell in love with the bed frame as soon as she spotted its canopy towering over the jumble and detritus of the Massachusetts antique dealer's shop. Headboard and footboard were shaped from twisting vines of wrought bronze that had been permitted to verdigris to a soft green. Almost hidden within the vines were tiny morning glories: floral jewels in royal purple, shining pink, pastel-kissed white, and an odd, almost translucent, blue. At each corner, the vines coiled up slender polished wooden posts, rioting upward to intertwine and form a canopy from which fabric could be hung, or which could be left bare.

"Oh, Dack, don't you just love it?" she asked, hurrying across the shop to examine her treasure more closely.

Dack, the robot who would be the majordomo of Castle Donnerjack when the ongoing construction was completed, turned from where he had been reviewing (and recording) samples of antique silver patterns. His tall, lean frame hid surprising strength; his features were an art deco rendering of Clark Gable done in silver and bronze.

When Ayradyss waved him over, he hummed on his air cushion to attend her, moving skillfully around the shop's clutter: dodging chipped Fiesta ware, battered teddy bears, vinyl records, paperback books, and a mannequin wearing bell-bottom jeans and a matching, hand-embroidered denim vest.

"If by 'love' you mean, 'Do I find it attractive,' " the robot responded, when he was close enough that the shopkeeper could not overhear their conversation, "yes, I do. It is a pleasing construct. Do you wish me to contact Master Donnerjack so that he can also view it?"

Ayradyss thought of John, busy with his portable computer back in their latest honeymoon retreat (this one a beach-front, weather-beaten cottage on Cape Cod) and some of her pleasure faded. She had so wished him to come out with her, to hold hands as they walked the beaches, to giggle at the funny little purple-and-blue crabs with their oversized right claws, to wander into shops. In the polished chrome of Dack's front panel, she saw herself pouting and shook the expression away with an angry toss of her ebony tresses.

"No, Dack," she said. "Let's leave John to his work. The sooner he finishes, the sooner he can come out and enjoy himself."

She looked back at the bed frame's tangling vines, thought of the fairy-tale Virtù realm in which she and John had courted, and a warm, loving smile rose to banish the remnants of the pout.

"John will be enchanted, I suspect," she said happily. "Dack, let's pay for it and have the shopkeeper ship it directly to Scotland."

Dack nodded, but when he scanned the price ticket, his fiscal programming insisted that he question her decision.

"Madam," he said softly, "the cost of this one piece is so high that I believe we could have an entire bedroom suite in this idiom fabricated for the same price. The reproduction would be indistinguishable from the antique. . . ."

Ayradyss shook her head, dark hair cascading like water taking color from an obsidian cliff face. "No, Dack. It has to be this one—not a reproduction. A reproduction wouldn't have the same feeling—it wouldn't be real. Do you understand?"

"No, madam," Dack said honestly. "But I suspect that Master Donnerjack would. I shall endeavor to negotiate with the shopkeeper. Perhaps we can reach a more equitable price."

Ayradyss patted his shoulder. "Do as you will, Dack. I acknowledge that you are my better in this."

She wandered out of the shop to give Dack more freedom, content to know that the bed frame would soon be on its way to embellish the master bedroom in Castle Donnerjack. The sunlight was bright, glinting stars off of the waves. Unable to ask the *genius loci* to redirect the intensity, she slipped her sunglasses down from their perch on the top of her head and, kicking off her sandals, wandered down to the water.

Wading through the surf, she bent to pick up a broken conch shell no bigger than her hand. It was a poor thing compared to the fantastical creations of the ocean she had known in Virtù, but there was a beauty here, a wonder that touched her. She lost herself in contemplation of its rough exterior, stroking first the tiny pinprick holes made by some ocean parasite, then the smooth inner core (ivory just blushed with the faintest pink) where the shellfish had lived.

"What do you think happened to it?" she asked Dack, hearing the robot's approach, feeling the slight sting of the sand stirred up by its air cushion against her bare skin.

"I wouldn't really know, ma'am."

"A bird, perhaps, one of those gulls out there," Ayradyss said, seeing in her mind's eye the strong curving beak probing inside the shell, pulling out the soft creature within, now no longer a creature, just sweet flesh for a seabird's meal.

"Quite possibly."

"Or possibly a sea otter," Ayradyss said, recalling a holovid she had seen of the clever, thick-furred, aquatic mammals. "They use flat rocks to break open shellfish; this conch's shell could have been broken that way."

"It does seem a viable alternative."

"Perhaps it was a whale or even a freak storm or a fishing boat. We had conch chowder for an appetizer at the inn last night. It was quite good."

"I am pleased to hear so, ma'am."

"There are so many ways to die," Ayradyss said, looking into the broken heart of the shell, "so many even for a conch. More for humans. Proges just wear out. Some last for human generations, like that great phant John and I saw, some last for barely a human lifetime. Do you know how old I am, Dack?"

"No, ma'am, I do not."

Ayradyss rose, dropped the broken conch into the deep pocket of her now damp skirt. Rinsing her sandy feet, she stood on a rock until the wind and sunlight dried them, then she redonned her sandals.

"John doesn't either," she said softly. "He forgets that I am a proge of Virtù, not merely the dark-haired, dark-eyed lady he courted in fantasy. He never asked me when I was generated."

She walked up toward the road. Dack hovered after her, silent, robot-mind content to let her muse, knowing that she was taking comfort in his patient listening.

"Did you get the bed, Dack?"

"Yes, I did, ma'am. The shopkeeper became quite reasonable when I pointed out to him that observable evidence showed that the piece had been in his shop at least two years and that such elaborate set pieces are no longer as popular as they once were thanks to increasing access to Virtù."

"Thank you, Dack." Ayradyss's lips curved in a pretty, gentle smile, her brooding completely gone. "John will so like it—he is a poet, you know, for all his science."

"I am not surprised to hear you say so, ma'am."

The waves crashed behind them as they made their way away from the ocean, toward the honeymoon cottage. Riding the winds over the clear waters, a seagull spotted a bit of flotsam on the waves, dove and swallowed it in a single triumphant gulp.

Polish sausage. Not bad. Not bad at all.

—=—

Carla and Abel Hazzard regarded their daughter's recumbent form. Her chest rose and fell slowly.

"Let me get this straight," Abel said. "You've lost her."

"Of course we haven't lost her," Chalmers answered. "She's right there in front of us in good health."

"You know damned well what I mean," Abel said. "You can't call her back and you don't know why you can't."

"It is not a thing without precedent," Chalmers said. "There are certain states—partly psychological—which can induce total resistance to recall."

"What causes these states?"

"We are not certain. It is not a common condition."

"What brings them back out of it?" Carla asked.

"There is no single stimulus we have been able to identify. It seems to be more a constellation of factors, which varies in each case."

"Have these factors anything in common?"

"Not so far as we have been able to determine."

"Can't you trace her to wherever she has traveled in Virtù and determine what factors are operating? It would seem you could just ask her."

"Yes, it would, wouldn't it?" he said. "But that's why these cases are so peculiar. She's found her way into uncharted territory and we've lost the signal."

"You lost the signal in other cases of this sort, too?"

"Yes, it's a classical sign of the syndrome."

"And you're telling me there's nothing you can do to bring her back?" Abel said.

"No, I never told you that. First, you must realize that she's in no real danger. The support systems are more than adequate for her health. Nothing to worry about on that count. Second, we are consulting the physician who treated most of the other cases over the years, a Dr. Hamill. He is considered the expert on this phenomenon."

"When you speak of other cases— Just how many have there been?"

"I'm sorry. I'm not permitted to discuss that."

"I take it you carry a lot of insurance for these matters."

"Oh, yes."

"Good. You're going to need it."

As they spoke, the inhabitants of several dozen other virt transfer units about the world—public and private—became briefly agitated, grew pale of face, and then expired from failure of the oxygen supply to their brains. This contingency was not unaccounted for in their contracts, however, for some commuters were engaged in hazardous occupations and death was not an uncommon sequel to certain enterprises. All of these individuals being bounty hunters, the appropriate waivers were present in file, and the matter of their passing was handled routinely. It was noted early on that theirs were the repercussive equivalents of decapitation. Even as a small smile crossed Lydia's face and her body began to twitch once more both categories of recall failure were entering the realm of statistics, which, of course, was yet another territory of Virtù. But while some of the bounties caught the flash of moiré and perhaps even fragmented glimpses of Deep Fields, Lydia's was a more pleasant while equally engaging prospect.

—=—

Ben Kwinan, arms forming an X upon his breast, stood within a pillar of green flame in the inner sanctum of the main Elishite temple in Virtù. His lips twisted through a series of small smiles within his changing face as he communicated with the Powers On High. Now aquiline and widow-peaked, now lantern-jawed with his hair a sea of burnished curls—all of them people he had once been—he flowed in response to the shifting nuances of revelation. He did not normally lose control in this fashion, tending to keep the outer man and the inner apart from each other, save in willed assumptions of appearance for the promulgation of policy. Now, though, vigilance relaxed by ecstasy, the shapeshifting forces of his spirit swam unchecked through him, and he changed in height, width, limb length, and pigmentation in response to the sweetened charges he'd received.

As the light began to fade his body grew stocky and lost height, his features became coarser, skin grew more porous. His eyes shifted to match the grey of his hair. He smiled, and he muttered in tongues until the light was gone. Then he walked.

He walked out of the sanctum and into the innermost temple. He walked to the north wall, touched a design upon it, and spoke to it. It became an arched opening of smoke. He walked into it.

He stood in a bright, tiled room, decorated with form-adjusting furniture, nonrepresentational sculpture of metal, light, and stone, iris flowering yellow, orange, and blue, wide, cool painting of aquatic mood. He passed his hand through a spiral of light to his left and a faint tone followed. Then he crossed to a blond mahogany bar along the far wall and considered its stock.

A door opened to the right of the bar and a thin, dark-haired, dark-mustached man entered the room.

"Mr. Kwinan," the man said. "Just received your signal."

"Call me Ben," the visitor replied. "I need to talk to Kelsey."

"I've already advised him as to your arrival. He's on his way over."

"Good." The being who now called himself Ben Kwinan lifted a bottle of California Burgundy from a rack. "Would you recommend this one, Mr.—?"

"Araf," the other replied. "Call me Aoud. Yes, I am told that it is quite good."

Ben smiled, located a corkscrew, set to work opening the bottle. Then he filled a glass halfway, sniffed it, sipped it.

"Are you in the flesh or holo?" he asked.

"The flesh."

"But you don't drink?"

"Old habits die hard."

"Too bad. I'd have asked you whether this wine tastes the same here as in Verité proper."

"I'm sure that it does, Ben. Or it's such a close approximation that it doesn't make any difference."

"You might pour me a glass," said the large red-haired man who suddenly stood in the center of the room.

Ben turned and stared.

"Kelsey," he said, "not quite in the flesh."

The man nodded. "I was too far away to get here quickly in that fashion. I heard your musing, though, and I wanted you to know I've tasted things both ways and they're the same."

"But you are of Verité. It may be different for one from Virtù."

Kelsey shrugged. "It may be different for every human being in the world—either world," he said.

"Well taken," Ben acknowledged. "Yet it is not entirely academic."

He shifted his gaze to Aoud, then raised his eyebrows.

"I think I'd best be leaving now," Aoud said suddenly, "so you can get on with your conference and me back to warding."

He bowed slightly and Ben and Kelsey nodded to him.

"Yes," Kelsey said, and Aoud turned and was gone.

Kelsey moved forward and extended his hand. Ben clasped it.

"No different than if I'd driven over," he said, squeezing for emphasis, "or if you'd stayed home and I'd projected there."

Ben returned the squeeze with an instant of great force, then released it.

"I disagree," he said. Then he moved to the window and looked out from their high tower across the town, down at the traffic, over toward the ocean. "This place is special," he said. "Synthetic: a meeting ground. Is this window's view a real representation of what's outside?"

"Yes."

"I couldn't leave here, go out into that."

"Neither could I, in this form."

"But you have another."

"And so do you. You can use it to do things that I cannot, in Virtù."

"Understood, though you've an edge on me in that department. Everyone from Verité does. It would be good to come and go as I would, on both sides."

Kelsey shrugged.

"Just the nature of things," he said. "Your world is the copy and ours the original. Yours was built to be accessed, not the other way around. We never foresaw the natural evolution of artificial beings in such an environment."

"Too bad," Ben said. "You can do as you would, but we can only come to visit in special places such as this. It would have been more decent if things worked both ways."

"You have an entire universe inside there."

"That's true. And you have two. That one and this."

"I'm not arguing equity. You're right. It would probably enrich both sides if it worked both ways. But not only was your development unforeseen, the technology just wasn't there to make it a two-way affair. It still isn't. Maybe it never will be. Maybe it's an impossibility, like squaring the circle. You may just be trapped by the nature of things."

"I think not," Ben said.

"Oh?"

"In fact, this is the matter that I came to discuss with you," Ben replied. "Transference."

"Transference? Of what sort?"

"A modest beginning, a stopgap, I suppose. Still, something further advanced than that virt power you wield."

"I don't understand," Kelsey said, moving to the bar, pouring himself a glass of the wine. "What has my paranorm ability to do with it?"

Ben chuckled.

"The awarding of powers which sometimes crossed the interface was an experiment," he said. "True, it was also a reward to the faithful. But it was part of an ongoing program involving manipulation of that interface from the other side. Much was learned in the process."

He took a sip from his glass. Kelsey raised his and took a larger swallow.

"Now," Ben said, "with a little help from your side it may be possible to advance things even further."

"There has been a breakthrough?"

"A real revelation. Of course, it must be tested. In several stages, actually."

"Tell me what I must do to help."

"For now, just some simple experiments in the transfer chambers."

"Certainly. What are the particulars?"

Ben took another drink, strolled to the bar. He finished it there and set down the glass. Kelsey followed him and did the same.

"Come with me," Ben said. He reached out and placed his hand upon the other man's shoulder. Turning him, he began walking toward a helix of rusty light in the far corner. Before they reached it, there came a sound like running water. "This way."

The room twisted away from them, and they found themselves in the virt representation of a transfer chamber.

"It's easiest just to show you," Ben said, opening the cabinet beneath one couch and exposing its equipment.

—=—

Sayjak regarded the camp by scattered firelight. Bodies lay strewn everywhere, some of the People's as well as all of the bounties. In his left hand, he held a human head by its hair; in his right, his machete gleamed dully amid its stains. Others of the People cavorted about him, tossing equipment into the fires, chattering, brandishing blades they were using to mince corpses. Some of them, this night, he'd known, would learn to use the cutting sticks. And some would carry them off with them. Too bad. He would have liked to keep that secret to himself. But he would not make an issue of it now, or the weapon's importance would be emphasized. Left to themselves, he was sure they would lose many, forget their wielding. No, now was not a good time to exert discipline. Not on the occasion of the People's first great victory over the bounties. Let them eat the bounties' livers and hearts, drop their pants and bugger their corpses. Let them swap dismembered body parts and reconstruct their owners grotesquely. The People had to have a little fun after all the tension they had been under. He let out a calculated whoop and playfully tossed an arm at Chumo's head. Chumo caught it and grinned at him.

"We got them all, boss! We got them all!" Chumo called back, tossing the limb at Svut.

"We did good." Sayjak grunted, then turned to survey the rest of the area. The smaller, westernmost encampment had fallen easily. But this one—the big, southern camp—had caused him more than a little concern. Fortunately, the People's experience at the western one had given them the confidence they'd needed, shown them that bounties could be overwhelmed by the People.

"You have your victory," Dortak said, suddenly appearing at his side.

"Yes," Sayjak said. "A good one."

"More will come, looking for you."

"We will be far away."

"They may seek you in far places."

"Let them. We can run, we can fight. We know the jungle better than bounties."

"They may have other tricks you have not yet seen."

"We will learn them."

"I hope that you do," Dortak said, and he dropped to his haunches and lowered his head, "for you are boss of bosses now."

A sudden stillness came over the scene of carnage. The bellowing, the chattering ceased, the gambolers halted their cavorting, those overhead stayed their hands in the stringing of entrails among the tree limbs.

"Boss of bosses!" Sayjak said, knowing, at that moment, that he would not be killing Dortak. "Good idea. Me. Boss of bosses. Like old Karak. Never been a boss of bosses since him."

"Maybe good idea," Dortak said. "But maybe one day you hate it. Trouble comes, you got to help all clans. Otlag, Bilgad—they will come to call you boss of bosses. Here comes Otlag now. They get trouble and go drum for you at Shannibal, you got to come and help. All People your People now. Big job."

As Dortak rose and moved away and Otlag came to offer his allegiance, Sayjak considered some of those ramifications involved in being boss of bosses. He found the prospect vaguely unsettling. Big job, as Dortak had said. Boss of bosses. But Karak had done it, long ago, and they still told stories of his deeds as though they were but yesterday. It would be good if one day they told such stories of Sayjak.

As Otlag rose, Bilgad came up to take his place, to call him boss of bosses. Sayjak licked his lips, showed his teeth, nodded his head.

"Yes," he said. "Big boss. Go now. Have fun. Eat, dance, have sex, chop up bodies and play with pieces. Be safe. Sayjak is watching."

Moments later, he seized a passing female by the shoulder.

"Your turn to have fun," he said. "Great honor."

—=—

Tranto loafed within his stand of trees, looking out over the herd. The transition had been very smooth. He had not even been challenged in the days since Scarco's disappearance. Of course, since none of the herd were certain as to exactly what had happened to Scarco it was possible to believe the worst. And he was certain that at least some of them did. A number of young bulls drifted off on occasion, taking several days to return. Muggle had reported overhearing them discuss the possible locations of Scarco's remains. He had also overheard comments that Tranto was an unlucky name, its most famous bearer being a trouble-making rogue. Of late, however, the quest for Scarco's bones seemed to have been abandoned—and the herd continued to treat Tranto with full respect and deference.

He wandered the grove until he was facing eastward again. Yes, still there. . . .

"Morning, boss." Muggle had come up behind him, silent as a shadow. "Going to be another hot one. The birds say it's been raining up north."

"That's nice," Tranto said. "Who's that one?"

"Which one?"

"The one who just raised her head from browsing and looked this way."

"Oh, that's Fraga. She's a flirt. Daughter of Gargo and Brigga."

"Any current—attachments?"

"No. A number are interested in her, of course. But she hasn't encouraged any one of them over the others."

"Good," Tranto said. "That is, a girl should take her time and think these things over."

"True," Muggle agreed.

"Let's browse a bit, heading down over that direction. Slowly. When we get there, we'll just say hello. Then you can do introductions."

"Sure," Muggle said.

"It's good to mingle with your people every now and then."

"It is," Muggle agreed.

—=—

Abel and Carla stared at the virtual form of their swollen daughter, there in their home virt space. They regarded Chalmers and the slightly hunched, white-bearded figure of Dr. Hamill.

". . . highly unusual," the doctor was saying. "I can't recall another case of false pregnancy during transfer sleep. Her records do not indicate any psychopathology—"

Carla glanced quickly at her husband, then back at the doctor.

"What," she said, "if it is a real pregnancy?"

Dr. Hamill met her gaze.

"The surface scan—which takes only seconds to run—showed the hymen intact," he told her. "Is there some reason to think otherwise?"

"Not really. But humor me and check further, anyway," she said.

"Of course. Though it would be highly unusual if—"

"It's highly unusual that she'd be in an untraceable transfer state for over three months, too, isn't it?"

"Well, that goes without saying. We are doing the best we can on that front—"

She turned to glare at Chalmers.

"Has it ever happened?" she asked. "A crossover pregnancy?"

"Certainly not!" he replied. "It's physically impossible."

"We could be making all sorts of legal history," she said.

—=—

John D'Arcy Donnerjack and Ayradyss took up residence in the black castle on a rainy morning in early October. They supervised their robotic staff in the uncrating and disposition of furniture they had bought from antique dealers in odd corners of the Continent. The servants' pneumatics made soft puffing sounds as they unrolled, raised, and hung tapestries to soften dark stone walls, placed chests, armoires, benches, and high-backed chairs in various chambers, erected canopied beds, assembled suits of armor, hung weapons and shields, unrolled rugs. They also installed walk-in freezers and modern instant ovens in the second kitchen. The first kitchen was a period piece in keeping with the overall decor, functional, but intended mainly for effect. Ayradyss liked the feeling of permanence that came with antiques.

While ninety percent of Castle Donnerjack was a showpiece, the other ten percent was state of the art in all technical effects associated with work and pleasure. Entering the upper west wing, one came into contemporary times. There, John Donnerjack had his office, containing modern furniture and voice-activated and manual terminals, with walk-in holographic display stages capable of transporting machine from within machine from within machine constructs—so *Gedanken*-pure of operation that they could function only in Virtù—into seeming imported pockets of that place, to allow for laser-pressure forcefield manipulations of a sort that might not be enacted elsewhere. Beyond the office was the Great Stage, where illusion-master Donnerjack, with great expense and technical innovation, had wrought the same effect, full-scale. To enter the Great Stage was a translation; it was like walking into Virtù in the flesh. He was to use it for testing pieces of his large-scale projects. He was also, frequently, to use it for his coffee breaks.

He and Ayradyss stood on a high balcony that night of the first day, regarding the stormy North Minch by moonlight.

"So you have actually restored your ancestral home," she said at last.

"In a way," he said. "I don't really know how the old place looked. Not likely this good, though. Probably about the only thing we have in common with it is that we built it on the same spot. We dug it out and formed everything up. There were indications there had been an old cellar down there—"

"With tunnels," she said, "leading off of it. Where do they go?"

"Way back into the rock. They seem to be natural. I didn't try to explore them all. Just sealed them off with a big metal door. If the wine cellar were to grow monumentally I suppose we could set some racks inside it. Otherwise, they serve no purpose."

"But that's how you know this was really the site?"

"Well, my grandfather'd said something about the old place suppos-edly having tunnels. That, along with the foundation, makes me think I was probably right."

"It is so different from Virtù."

"In what way?"

She gestured outward.

"That storm will pass after a time," she said, "and things will return to a—ground state that is stable."

"But it is that way in Virtù, also."

"Yes, but it *can* be changed instantly, and there are places noted for their fluctuation."

"One can landscape here. Hell, we've terraformed parts of the moon, and Mars—and the insides of asteroids."

"And one can take a step sideways and backwards in Virtù, find the proper guides and be in a totally different place. Then there are the wild lands, which develop their wild genii, which generate their own wild programs."

"We can play games with reality here, too."

"Yes, but later you return to the firmness of the ground state. Remember all of the wild places you took me through on the way back? You've nothing like them here."

"True," he agreed. "I understand what you're saying. It's a different kind of order, that's all."

"Yes. Different."

They repaired within and made love in the new bed for a long while.

It was several days before his equipment was up and running to his satisfaction. In the meantime, he would break from his labors with it and they would enter the Great Stage, which was also functioning. There, they could set the environment to vast and pleasing vistas, including genuine sections of Virtù. When the forcefield pressure interface was engaged they could experience it directly at the tactile level. So they could walk in Virtù within the limits of the Stage, a small-scale equivalent of the transfer phenomenon itself; if full transfer was desired the necessary medical equipment was housed within adjacent chambers.

They sat in a dale amid vermilion hills where ancient statues worked their ways back toward boulderhood. Red lyre-tailed birds inspected damp grasses near a small pond.

"It is odd to come as a visitor," she said. "What magic did the Lord of the Lost employ to work this change?"

"I think that when he reembodied you he simply did it as one of us rather than a creature of Virtù."

"Still, how could he do this?"

"I have been thinking long and hard about it. It has occurred to me that Virtù must possess a level of complexity beyond what we have postulated."

"Oh, I'm sure it does."

"Implying a higher level of structure."

She shrugged.

"If it explains how he did it, it must be right."

"A guess doesn't explain anything. I still have to work out a theory and figure the mechanisms."

"Then what?"

He shook his head.

"Its application would be—unusual. I want to shelve everything else and just work on this one. But I can't."

"Why not?"

"I owe the Lord of Entropy his Palace of Bones and bowers of dead flowers."

"How did you discover what it is that he wants?"

"A list of specifications and general layout appeared on one of the screens this morning."

"How do you propose making delivery?"

"He's watching. He'll know when it's ready. I will be shown what to do at that time."

"That's frightening. Do you think he's watching us right now?"

"I suppose it's possible."

She rose.

"Let's go back outside," she said.

"All right."

Later that night, as they lay halfway between sleep and wakefulness, she touched his shoulder.

"John?"

"What is it?"

"Do all castles make strange noises at night?"

"Perhaps," he said, listening. Then he heard a distant, metallic rattling sound. "It's windy," he said after a time. "The workmen might have left something lying about unsecured."

"It sounds like a chain."

"It does, doesn't it? I'll look around in the morning."

"Yes, do that."

" 'Night, love."

" 'Night."

—=—

Death sat on his throne of bones and regarded the model of his palace he had brought into being. With brief movements of his fingers in the space before him he opened sections, enlarged them, enhanced them. At times he rotated the image of the structure slowly, nodding or shaking his head.

"Interesting," said Phecda, who had come up beside him and mounted the chair's high back. "Will it have dungeons?"

"Of course," Death answered.

"Secret passages?"

"Certainly."

"Lots of ledges and crannies?"

"Plenty."

"Blind corridors?"

"Those, too."

"Some of the stairways seem to do funny things."

"Escher Effect," Death said.

"A place one could slither through forever, bigger even than your current dwelling."

"Exactly."

"So you are pleased with it?"

"In my fashion."

"You will cause it to be created then, here, in Deep Fields?"

"Not as it stands. It requires considerable elaboration."

"And when that has been done . . . ?"

"Oh, yes. Then."

—=—

Donnerjack found a set of revised specs waiting for him on a screen early in the morning. He lowered himself slowly into his chair and studied them. Tricky, very tricky, he decided, and why should the place have a nursery?

He called up a holo of his proposal on the nearest stage, stared at it, commenced rotating it. Tentatively, then, he entered some of the proposed changes, holding back those which would not lend themselves to representation here.

It was several hours before he had cobbled together an approximation worth examining in greater detail. When he had, he transferred a section of it to the Great Stage, went over and walked through it. Then he returned to his console, made adjustments, and moved another section to the Stage. He walked back and inspected it.

Later, deep into his alterations, he turned, to discover he was not alone.

"Ayradyss! Good morning. I didn't realized you were up."

She smiled, took his hand, and squeezed it. He drew her to him and they embraced and kissed.

"Yes, I was awakened again by an upset stomach. Might the food of Verité do that to one from Virtù?"

He shook his head.

"I don't see why it should."

"Well, I've been nauseated every morning for several days."

"Really? Why didn't you say something sooner? There are things you can take, to settle the stomach."

"It always passes quickly. Then I am fine again."

"Any other symptoms?"

"I threw up a little bit."

"I will order something for your stomach."

"Thank you, love. —This is your latest project?"

"Yes, the one I owe to the master of Deep Fields. I can set it to sequence for us, if you would like to walk through it with me."

"I would. Shall we take coffee with us?"

"Let's."

—=—

Neither an eeksy nor a bounty, Virginia Tallent knew all their territories, though from a different vantage. She was a ranger with the Virtù Survey Department, keeping track of emerging territory and fluctuations in existing lands. She traveled far, observing and recording, and while her function was mainly passive, her knowledge was extensive. One of the few Veritéans employed in this capacity, she delighted in her work, hiking the wild lands and recording her discoveries there. Every day was a revelation to her. She worked harder than others in the business, and she resented returning home at the end of each tour of duty.

She climbed a trail amid rocks and ferns, flowers and squat trees. Above her, winged shapes—some fresh-emerged from red fruitlike cocoons—fled, croaking. Occasionally, a small, pale figure darted across her path. Slim, dark-haired and pale-eyed, skin the color of cocoa, she made her way with grace and agility. Hot breezes played through the morning's sunlight, and her way lay within shade. She had timed it that way. Periodically, she would pause to sip from a water bottle or to record an observation.

At one point, a voice came to her out of a tree at a place where the green swirled darkly within it.

"Virginia Tallent, you have traveled far."

"That is true," she responded, slowing, "and the foliage here seems lusher than usual, for the season. And I've seen more hunting wilches."

"Excessive rains, which favor the leaf-eating gronhers. They multiply quickly, as do the wilches who eat them. Soon the wilches will reach a point where their dancing begins. There will follow a southward migration on the part of the dire-cats, who prey on them."

"Why southward?"

"When the gronhers' numbers dwindle they will seek the herd-mice, which will soon be numerous in the south."

"Why?"

"The grains they feed on are even now in unusual development, because of nutrient-bearing flooding earlier this year."

". . . And the land, from the rains?" she asked.

There was no reply. The green flame had ceased to dance.

She smiled and walked on. Clouds gathered and blocked the sunlight. There followed a low rumble of thunder. The trail bore her left, its steepness diminishing. A few drops of rain spattered against fronds. There came a flash of lightning. She hurried.

The full downpour caught her in a largely open area where the trail had widened as it neared the top of the plateau. She wisely avoided a grove of tall trees, choosing instead the less complete but safer shelter offered by some broad-leafed shrubs that partly intersected an outcropping of stone.

Seated, in a leaf-fringed cave beneath the shrubs, she watched the water become a beaded curtain about her shelter, wiped occasional droplets from her brow, watched a stone in a less sheltered area to her right darken, saw its surface become a flow of glass and shadow.

As she watched, the stone seemed to form features, eyes focused in her direction. The dark, wet lips moved:

"Virginia," it said, "the main erosion occurs upon eastern slopes, partly as a function of wind direction, partly from the angles and drainage of the slopes themselves, predicated upon events past."

"Markon!" she said.

"Yes." The stone changed shape now, growing into a life-sized statue as the *genius loci* continued their conversation. "The wind direction is determined partly by temperature differentials between this and six major and eleven minor areas, the coastal pair and that containing Lake

Triad being most prominent. Have you had a fruitful journey, thus far?"

"Indeed," she replied. "I've always found your realm particularly fascinating."

"Why, thank you. What of my neighbor Kordalis's?"

"It's interesting. But the rapid spread of wildfire vine tends to crash the botanical cycles over-frequently."

"I feel it is because of the floral coloration. She is over-fond of yellow."

"I never considered it from the standpoint of aesthetic preference on the part of a *genius loci*."

"Oh, yes. It is a consideration you should not neglect among the younger ones."

"The older ones are beyond that sort of thing?"

"No. But you will, in general, find them to have developed better judgment. On the other hand, you will find some whose taste never improves."

"Would you care to name some of these?"

"Certainly not. That would be very petty of me. I am sure you are capable of forming your own opinions."

She smiled and wiped her face on her sleeve.

"Of course," she agreed.

The features flowed again.

"There is a need—" Markon stated, and the face began to fade. Then, "No. My world will hardly be destroyed if I do not respond," it said. The expression returned to the stone, smiling faintly, briefly. "I see you so seldom, Virginia. How have you been?"

"Very well, thanks," she replied. "And from the look of the land, the same might be said for you."

The stone swayed forward and back. The being had nodded.

"No epic battles with my neighboring spirits of place," he answered, "if that is what you mean. Those days seem very remote, a thing of beginnings."

"I never even heard of them."

"They are not a part of common knowledge, now I think on it. So that could not have been your true question."

"No, it was not. But I am fascinated by it. This must have to do with the transition from pure programming to independent evolution in Virtù, both near its establishment. I'd never heard of the wars of the *genii loci*, though."

"I do not understand this talk of something called Virtù. There is only the world. What else can there be? And yes, we fought for control of our pieces of it in the days after creation, when the place was not yet fully formed. There were alliances, betrayals, glorious victories, ignominious defeats. They were great days, but in truth I am glad that they are gone. One can grow tired of living heroically. True, individual feuds and vendettas do still sometimes occur, but these are as nothing beside the conflicts of the unsolid days. I have not engaged in one for some time, and that is fine with me."

"Fascinating. Has anyone official—such as myself—ever recorded these matters?"

"I can only speak for myself, and I have not given this information. The others of my acquaintance tend to be as close as me, however, when dealing with mobile sentients."

"Then why do you tell me?"

"I have known you for some time, Virginia, and you told me of your blindness and paralysis from an untreatable neurological condition. I don't suppose you speak often of it, either. It is good that you have two bodies."

"Well, I'd rather be here than there. But it might be good for you to have your reminiscences of those times remembered, to preserve them."

"Nothing is lost so long as one mind remembers."

"It might be good to share them. Design theoreticians could learn a lot from them."

"I am not here to teach them. I am no friend of the designers."

"It might help them to do better jobs in the future."

"I do not want any jobs done in my territory. Or anyplace else, for that matter. They had their chance. They are done. They are not welcome here."

"I only meant it as an increase of general knowledge."

"Enough!" The face twisted into a scowl. "I would talk of it no more!"

"As you would, Markon."

"Yes. As I would. Shall I summon my elemental servants to dance for you?"

"That would be nice."

Water rose from the ground and met the waters falling from the sky. They formed themselves into glistening bodies, faceless, sexless. Beside them, heavier figures, of mud, rose and took form. Winds began to lash the leaves. From openings in the earth flames leaped up, began to sway, to bifurcate. The winds picked up numerous bits of detritus, formed it into debris devils.

"How strange and how lovely," she said as the figures came loose from their points of origin and began to move about.

"Few, if any, of your kind have seen it," he said. "Come sit by me and watch. I will make it drier and warmer here."

She rose and went to seat herself beside him. The figures began to move more quickly. Shadows danced within them.

—=—

Arthur Eden returned from a long sojourn in Virtù. Departing the church's transfer facility, he took public transportation through a chaotic series of changes about town, coming at last to one of his homes. Partway there, his stomach began to rumble, active again following its long rest. The first thing he did on entering his apartment was to order a meal of scrambled eggs, bacon, toast, fruit juice, coffee. As his kitchen unit labored to comply, he stripped and stepped into his shower. There, amid sizzling jets, he relived the week's apprenticeship—called "claiming the program"—a simple exercise in the manipulation of local reality required of all initiates in the lowest grade of priesthood. He recalled the mental movement, the reaching, the capture of forms, the acceptance of spaces. . . . It had been fun, playing the ritualized, programmed games. No way to lose, of course. Everyone who participated became a minor adept by the course's end. He would have to give it an entire chapter, as a reinforcement of a mindset. Presumably, the higher ones functioned in the same fashion. It didn't really explain the rare carryovers. But then, they might have involved latent psi powers stimulated by all the attention. The faithful were required to report such powers' appearance under pain of excommunication for noncompliance.

He toweled himself dry and donned a pair of purple pajamas, a green-and-blue paisley dressing gown, a battered pair of brown, fleece-lined leather slippers. He reviewed messages and headlines as he ate. There was another long letter from Dr. V. Danton, somewhere in the asteroid belt, taking issue with the piece wherein he'd suggested that the Elishite religion was not exportable—and hence, was atavistic—because of its necessary linkage to Virtù here on Earth. Danton had maintained that Virtù itself was unnecessary for the functioning of the creed as a true religion, arguing that its doctrines alone were sufficient for this. While Eden wondered whether it would hold up without the splash of virtual reinforcement, he had to concede that there might be sufficient substance there to maintain it. He wondered whether Danton were himself an Elishite.

He thought again of his own status with regard to the Church. To them, he was Emmanuel Davis, a research librarian. Davis even had an apartment in another part of town. But he had wanted to be in his own place tonight, to work on his notes while he was still fresh on the material. If they learned of his dual identity his membership would be terminated immediately, he knew. On the other hand, he was certain he never would have been accepted as a member in the first place, let alone as a candidate for the priesthood, had they been aware of his standing as a religious scholar. Especially not had they known of his intention to treat them as a subject. Now, his duplicity had been solely in the cause of truth. He'd no intention of publishing secret rituals or expounding esoteric bits of doctrine. His interest lay in developing the sociology of the growth of the new religion.

He had spent months documenting the Davis persona before approaching the Elishites for religious instruction. Davis's identity had been strong enough to pass any initial investigation they might have conducted. He had also provided Davis with more than ordinary reasons for travel. And he checked into Davis's quarters often, to respond to messages both spurious and bonafide, for Davis actually labored in the vineyards of research. Davis also had a horde of relations and friends with whom he visited at the drop of a hat. So far, there had been no indication that Davis had ever aroused unusual scrutiny from any quarter.

He wondered, though. If that identity were penetrated, he wished to be certain that the deception could never be traced to him. Perhaps he should add a second layer to Davis, complicating his life, providing confusion in the event of deep scrutiny. Yes, that seemed a good idea. He would work out details, begin installing it soon.

He forced himself to eat slowly, savoring every mouthful. His stomach growled happily, and he smiled and took a drink of juice. The entire exercise would probably be redundant, he reflected. For even if he somehow made the Elishites' shit list, what could they really do to him? Take legal action if he had violated a law. Excommunicate him and ostracize him if they could not hurt him in the courts.

He wondered, though, at the volatility of emotions in the followers of religions, never having felt such feelings himself. He supposed that if his study aroused sufficient ire there might be death threats and such from the laity rather than the clergy, and perhaps someone would vandalize Davis's apartment. He might actually be physically assaulted, if recognized as Davis. He had not thought of these earlier, but suddenly they were there. As he sipped his coffee and considered the more fanatical aspects of religions, he saw that believers were always harder on their own, particularly those deemed apostate, than ever they were on outsiders.

Over his second cup of coffee it seemed even more possible. When his book finally came out it would be readily apparent that its author had been for a time a member. An effort would be made to identify the individual he had been. Fortunately, this was years away. He hadn't even begun writing the volume yet, and it would be some time before he did. Time enough to get in a lot more work on covering his tracks. Yes, Davis definitely needed more layers to his existence, more complexity, blind alleys, extra identities within his own—confusion. Any trail that might lead to Arthur Eden would be thoroughly muddied. It was good that there was so much time in which to do it.

He began considering the ways. The only thing he could think of that might be on par with what he was going to do would be to develop a virt power that transferred and not report it. They liked to keep track of their adepts. They did not like freelance psis. He wondered, though, what they could really do about it. A person had a right to join or quit any religion he cared to. And he'd never heard of any way to recall a virt power. It was just something you learned, and once you had it, it was yours. Then he wondered what they might plan on doing with their human psis in Verité. He'd never heard of any real activity here in that area.

Was there a way to strip one of such a power? Or a way to control it? To counter it? After a week of working on his telekinetic reflexes in Virtù, this lay upon his mind, though it was more of a game there, a matter of connecting with that function's in-place programs and learning their uses. Whether that would actually help here—and how it might help—seemed anyone's guess.

He filed some correspondence, trashed the rest. He scrolled his personal newspaper and caught up on the world's doings in his absence. Then he mixed himself a stiff drink and took it to bed with him, along with his voice pad to which he told all his recollections and dictated conclusions, fresh ideas, new assumptions. For a while after, he cast them all into his near-elegant prose.

Then he drowsed, and drowsing dreamed. At some point he recalled a thing he should have recorded and his hand moved to the table where he had laid the pad.

He felt the pad slip away, tip.

Then his eyes were open and he was leaning forward, groping. His mind rushed into the past week's exercise pattern.

The pad hung suspended, five inches below tabletop level.

He stared for several moments. Then, slowly, he reached out and took hold of it.

"I am the walrus," he said.

FIVE

The diagnostic unit weighed her and took her pulse, blood pressure, and brain wave profile immediately when she sat in it. It took several moments longer to digest a few milliliters of blood.

Set for voice response, it answered her then:

"Madam, you are pregnant."

"You are mistaken," she said.

A moment passed. Then, "Diagnosis confirmed," it reported.

"You must be malfunctioning."

"Unlikely," it responded. "I am very new, and I was fully tested at the factory."

"There is a reason you came with a full year's warranty at no extra charge," she said.

"Yes, because it is a gesture on which they seldom have to pay. I can provide you with the number to call for televaluation."

"All right. Let's have it."

Later, the service tech, who insisted on eyeballing the unit in virt, shook his head.

"There's nothing wrong with it. It tests perfectly," he said.

"But I can't be pregnant!"

He glanced at her, smiled faintly.

"Are you sure?"

"It just doesn't work that way," she said.

He shook his head.

"I'd better not ask you what you mean," he said. "But, believe me, there's no product liability involved. What you decide to do with the information is, of course, your own affair."

She nodded as he made his farewell and went out like a light.

She wandered the castle's high halls thinking of children. Shadows slipped about her and drafts stirred curtains and tapestries. Small things scuttled, scratching, across rafters. And what was that other sound?

She wondered at the impossibility of it. The mating of Virtù and Verité was always sterile, had to be sterile. It was a part of the way the worlds worked. There was no room for negotiation with principles. She could not be pregnant. She halted and regarded herself in a wonderfully warped mirror, where a slight side-to-side movement made her left cheek look as if she were chewing gum. She amused herself with the effect each time she passed.

What had happened between her passing in Virtù and her reassembly in Deep Fields?

The sound came again, musical, metallic. Whatever else was involved, the Lord of the Lost had been able to send her reembodied self across the interface to become a genuine resident of Verité. And by way of the scenic route, at that. Might that change also have included a susceptibility to impregnation in her new home? How long had she been in Verité now? Six months? A year? It was hard getting used to the way time worked in this place.

Again—and nearer now—that sound. Was it from the small room to the left or the little corridor beyond it? She slowed, glanced into the room as she came to it. Nothing. She stepped inside.

At her back, she heard a small sound. Turning, she beheld behind her in the hallway the shadowy figure of a small man in a ragged tunic and breeches, bearded, a chain about his ankle.

"Who are you?" she asked.

He paused in midmoan and turned his head, as if studying her.

"Who—are you?" she repeated.

He uttered something incomprehensible but vaguely familiar. She shook her head.

He repeated it. It sounded something like, "Dinna ken."

"You don't know who you are?"

"Nae." Then there followed another sentence which almost slipped into place. She worked her analysis programs around his accent. The next time he spoke she was able to update and edit his words:

"Too long," he said, "down memory's dim path. Name's forgotten, deeds unsung."

"What were your deeds?"

"Crusader," he replied. "Outremer. Many battles."

"How did you end up—here?"

"Family feud. Mine lost. Prisoner, long time. Darkness."

"Your enemies?"

"Gone. Gone. Different now, this place. Fell down, went away. But its spirit remains. Wandered the ghost castle, I did, still do. Me and others from days gone. It's here, in the shell of the new one. Sometimes I see it, others I don't. Fading, like me. Now, though, your brightness. Good. Used to be I'd wander and it would fade. High in the air then, me, and afraid of heights. Stay. Better wandering now. Your name, m'lady?"

"Ayradyss," she replied.

"To you and your bairn-to-be well-met. There's a banshee been watching you."

"A banshee? What's that?"

"Noisy spirit. Sees bad things coming and howls when she does."

"I heard a howling last night."

"Yes. She was about it again."

"What will the bad thing be?"

He shrugged and his chain rattled.

"Banshees tend to be generalists rather than specialists when it comes to their announcements."

"It doesn't seem a very useful function then."

"Banshees are more for atmosphere than utility."

"I've only heard you occasionally, and this is the first time I've seen you. Where do ghosts go when they're not haunting?"

"I'm nae sure. I guess it's sort of like dreaming. Sort of. But it's a place, places, pieces. Past jumbled together with new things. But then so is waking, often. We're more awake when there are people around, like now."

She shook her head.

"I don't understand."

"Neither do I. But I learn things while I'm away. Bits. Pieces. I come back knowing more than I knew. You are a very strange person."

"I am not of the Verité. I am from Virtù."

"I have never walked that land, but I know somewhat of it, in my fashion. I know, too, that you come here from an even stranger realm—one from which I never learned the path of return. You hae walked Deep Fields and come back. I dinna think it possible. You have, however, brought a wee bit of it with you. It is as if its dark dust clings to your shoes. Perhaps this is why I find it easier t' talk t' you than most warm ones: we share something."

"Why do you wander, dragging a chain? The dead do not do that in Virtù."

"It marks my suffering at the end of life."

"But that was centuries ago. How long do you have to do it?"

"I was never clear on that."

"Couldn't you just stop?"

"Oh, I hae, many times. But I always wake up and find myself at it again. Bad habit, but I dinna ken how to break it."

"There must be some form of therapy that would help you."

"I wouldn't know about such things, ma'am."

He turned and began moving, rattling, up the hall. His outline grew faint.

"Must you go?" she asked.

"No choice. The dreaming's calling." He halted, as with great effort, and turned then. "It will be a boy," he said, "and 'twas for you the banshee wailed. Mostly you," he added, turning away again. "Him, too, though, and your man."

He gave a quick wail, and the sound fell off abruptly along with the rattling of his chains.

"Wait!" she cried. "Come back!"

But he faded with each step and was gone in moments. She shed her first tears in Verité.

Donnerjack looked up from the flow of equations on half of his screen, turning his attention back to the text he was composing on the other half.

"I am persuaded," he said, "that there is indeed a fourth level of complexity within Virtù. Our own experience indicates it as well as certain other anomalies which have come to my attention. I've discussed the possibility with several colleagues, and they all say I'm heading up a blind trail. But they are wrong. I am certain it can be made to fit the general theory of the place. It is the only explanation that will unify the data. Look here!"

He froze the flow of figures, reversed it.

"John," Ayradyss said, "I'm pregnant."

"Impossible," he answered. "We just don't mix at that level."

"It appears that we do."

"How do you know?"

"The medic unit said so. So did the ghost."

He froze the action on his screen and rose.

"I'd better check that machine over. Ghost, did you say?"

"Yes. I met him upstairs."

"You mean as in specter, spook, haunt, disembodied manifestation?"

"Yes. That's what he indicated he was."

"This place is too new to have a ghost—if there were such things as ghosts. We haven't had any violent deaths on the premises."

"He says he's a carryover from the old castle that used to occupy this site."

"What's his name?"

"He couldn't recall."

"Hm. A nameless horror, then. And he remarked that you're pregnant?"

"Yes. He said it will be a boy."

"Well, no way of checking on the ghost. Let's have a look at the machine."

A half-hour later, Donnerjack rose from the console, closed the unit, closed his tool kit, and rolled down his sleeves.

"All right," he said. "Everything seems to be in good order. Interface with it, and let's get some readings."

She moved to do this, and he began a run-through on a standard series. When it reached the crucial point it responded, ". . . and you are still pregnant."

"I'll be damned," he said.

"What should we do?" she asked.

He scratched his head.

"I'll order a med robot with OB/GYN and full pediatric programming," he said, "while we think about it. These readings show it as fairly far along. Who'd've thought . . . ?"

"I meant . . ." she began. "I meant, what should we do about—the other?"

He met her gaze and stared.

"You promised him to the Lord of Deep Fields," she said, "to secure my release."

"It seemed a situation that would never occur."

"But since it has, what are we to do?"

"We do have time to think about it. It might be negotiable."

"I've got a feeling that it isn't."

"Well, it would still seem the first thing to try."

"And the second?"

"I'll be thinking."

—=—

Pregnant.

Floating in a warm bath, Ayradyss contemplated the concept for some time. It wasn't that she had never considered the possibility—self-replicating proges, both parthenogenetic and gender-related, were common in Virtù. They saved the *genius loci* from wasting all their energy on basic programming, made opportunity for art. But she had never seriously considered the possibility for herself—certainly not once she had given her heart to John, for while those of Virtù and Verité often made love, they never made babies.

Closing her eyes until she gazed out from between her lashes, she gazed down the length of her nude body. There were no changes that she could see, but as the morning sickness proved, the changes were happening. Protectively, she laced her fingers over her still-flat abdomen.

What would the baby—the boy—be like? She and John were both dark-haired, dark-eyed, so likely he would be also. She hoped he would have his father's build: tall and powerful without being in the least bit bulky. A small smile played about her lips as she imagined the baby, the boy, the young man, her son.

The bath water gradually chilled. She contemplated twisting the tap with her toes to add a bit more heat, then, looking at her pruning fingertips (something that never happened in Virtù), she decided that perhaps she had soaked long enough. Standing calf-deep in the bath, she let the water run down her, forming little beads against her lightly oiled skin (John had made her a gift of some jasmine-scented bath oil when they were in Jamaica).

When she had adjusted to the cooler air, she stepped out onto the bath rug (this from China, its fat flowers cut out to contrast against the deeper plush). While she combed her hair out from the coil she had twisted it into to keep it out of the water, she meditated on what to do with the rest of her day.

John was busy in his office, patiently working on his design for

Death's Palace of Bones. She disliked going near when he was working on that particular project—instinctively she felt that Death was watching her, and even if John stubbornly refused to dwell upon it, she knew that the palace was only part of the price agreed upon for her return from Deep Fields. She did not blame John for agreeing to Death's terms— after all, they had seemed impossible to meet. Death might have as soon asked for the moon, but she feared for her unborn son, dreaded the portent in the banshee's wail.

Banshee. Was that her cry? Ayradyss stood perfectly still, listening. No, what she had heard was just the winter wind chasing the mists through the castle's turrets.

Quickly she hurried to her closet, took out a long tartan skirt, an Irish cable-knit sweater, heavy stockings, comfortable shoes. The ghosts liked to haunt the regions of the castle that had been recreated to follow John's fancy of what a Scottish castle should look like. She would go seeking them, ask them about the portents. Who better to ask about Death and his plans than those who walked the line between life and whatever in Verité passed for Deep Fields?

John must have his plans for defeating Death—she was certain of that. Scientist and poet he might be, but he also bore something of a warrior's soul. Verité-born, Ayradyss knew a few of the details of the religion practiced by many of her aion kin. John had his place in their pantheon—did he know?—a demigod of sorts. Still, his plans, his abilities, did not mean that she could not investigate on her own.

The unborn child was her son, too; he was being claimed as ransom for her life. It was her place, as much as John's, to defend him from Death. Face set, she hurried from the bedroom suite, up the stone stairs, out onto the battlements. Her long, full skirts snapped in the wind as her wings had in Virtù, but this time she did not mourn her wings—she had something more precious within her, something she was determined to protect.

"Banshee!" she cried. "Banshee!"

The wind took the words from her lips so quickly she barely heard them. Arms outspread, she spun. Her skirts belled round and full, her hair whipped out massy and dark. A cyclone of tartan and ebony, she danced in the wind.

Rain began to fall, stinging and cold. Turning to hail, it pebbled the slick stone, cobbled the flags with tiny lumps of ice. Still she danced, her head light and swimming now, her feet gliding on the ice. Ayradyss waltzed with the wind and weather.

She felt a firm pressure at her back, a hand clasp her icy fingers, but her streaming eyes could discover nothing of her partner. Crystals were forming both in her hair and along the thick cables of her sweater: jewels from the Winter King's hoard. An orchestra played, too: ringing hail, the moan of stone, the shriller howl of the gusts that tore through the crenelations.

Almost now, almost, she could see her partner. His face was white, the cheekbones high, so high, the teeth so white, even against the whiteness of his face. All of him was white but the darkness of his eyes, and these were as dark as the pit, dark as night, dark as . . .

"Dinna ye ken t' cum oot of th' rain?" said a harsh voice, a clatter of iron underlying the words.

Ayradyss felt the Winter King spin her away, handing her off to this new partner. She reached obediently to take the hand she saw before her, but her numbed fingers met with nothing, not even resistance. Letting her hand fall, she slowed her dancing steps—slipping and sliding as she did this thing.

"Lass, yer wet to the bone and half ice," chided the voice, her mind asserting the program that sorted the strange burred words into something easier to understand. "What are you doing oot here in such weather? I'll have a word with that husband of yours for not looking out better for you! Laird of the castle or nae, see if I don't!"

Ayradyss let herself be guided to the heated interior of the castle. As the ice melted from her hair and her fingers pricked at the warmth, she recognized her interrogator.

"Ghost!" she said happily. "I was hoping to find you!"

"Find me!" the crusader ghost groused. "Lass, ye almost joined me! Get yourself into some dry clothes before you kill yourself and your bairn!"

"But it's about my baby I want to talk to you," Ayradyss protested, wringing out her streaming hair, shivering as the warmth of the castle forced sensation into hands and toes.

"Do you? Do you now?" The ghost's expression remained severe, but something in its burred tones softened. "Dry off first, drink some soup to warm your insides, and you might find me in the long gallery."

As a means of ending discussion, the ghost faded out. His chain lingered behind him a moment longer, then vanished as well. Ayradyss shivered, sneezed, and gathering her wet skirts in both hands, hurried down to the master bedroom.

Some time later, hair completely dry, clad in fresh warm clothing from the skin out, and a pint of thick beef and barley soup inside of her (and a second helping in a heavy pottery mug in her hand) she climbed the stair to the long gallery.

It was a good place to meet with a ghost, she thought. Although she and John had selected a Persian runner to cover the floor, the bare stone was still visible along the sides. The tapestries and portraits (oils that she had purchased in various antique shops, giggling at the expressions on some of the faces—why would anyone wish to be remembered as seeming so severe?) relieved the dark stone but did little to alleviate the corridor's gloom. Not even discretely arrayed artificial light could do so. It was as if the gallery had decided that it was meant to be a shadowed, haunted place and consciously defied any efforts to make it otherwise.

Sipping from her mug, Ayradyss walked slowly down the corridor, the sound of her footfalls swallowed by the carpet. Coming to a window with a deep stone sill, she set her mug down. She was digging after a piece of beef with her spoon when she heard the clanking of the ghost's chain.

"Thank you for coming, sir," she said politely, taking her skirts in hand to give him a deep curtsy.

"I had no choice, now, did I?" the ghost said grouchily. "If I dinna cum, y'would go dancing in the wind and snow again like a daft thing."

"Not so daft," Ayradyss said, tossing her head and arching her eyebrows at him. "I did find you now, didn't I?"

"That you did. Now, what's this about asking me about your bairn? I had none of my own while I lived and there will be none now that I've died."

"But you knew that my baby would be a boy," Ayradyss protested, "and you knew that the banshee wailed for him—and for me and for John."

The ghost shook its chain, paced a few steps, glowered at her from beneath bushy brows.

"You're taking liberties, lass, liberties, indeed. Ghosts and supernatural manifestations are not to be interrogated so. We give omens—interpreting them, that's another provenance."

Ayradyss stirred her soup deliberately, ate one spoonful, then another. It was growing cold, the barley gluey. She pushed the mug back into the recess. Looking up into the opaque window, its lead-joined panes all diamonds and angles, she said as if to herself:

"I wonder if the Winter King would tell me what I need to know?

He smiled so when we danced. Perhaps he knows why Death wants my baby."

There was a solid iron crash behind her as if a chain had been dropped directly onto bare stone.

"That Winter King most certainly knows why Death wants your bairn, lass, but I dinna think that he would tell you straight."

"Can you?"

"I dinna ken the answer, lass."

"Can you help me learn it?"

A long silence. Ayradyss watched the flicker of the snowfall behind the heavy glass, seeing more the shadow as it opaqued the light than the actual snowfall itself. The wind howled without and she was glad that the architects had sacrificed historical verisimilitude to insulation.

"Can you help me, Ghost?"

"No more dancing with the Winter King?"

"No more."

"You'll stay warm and dry and eat the best food so the bairn grows strong?"

"I will."

"Aye, then I'll help you look for the answers, lass. I canna promise that we'll find them, but I can help you look."

Ayradyss turned and studied the ghost. He stood bent within his shabby tunic, his breeches sagging. His feet, she noticed, were bare and disfigured with corns. The ankle around which the chain was fastened, oddly, was as smooth as the one without.

"What is your name?" she asked.

"Dinna ken," came the voice, fading as the ghost faded. "Dinna ken. Some things 'tis better not to know."

Ayradyss contemplated this for a long moment, then gathered up her mug of cold soup. The sky outside was growing dark. She would pull John from his calculations. They could build a fire in the parlor off their bedroom, dine by candlelight by the hearth. Afterwards, perhaps they could return to the jigsaw puzzle they had been doing—a Monet bridge scene that had them quite baffled.

Humming softly, she descended the stair, not hearing the banshee's wail intermixed with that of the wind.

—=—

John D'Arcy Donnerjack continued his work, incorporating suggested changes. Mornings, when he would return to his studio, he would learn whether his designs had been accepted. Or he would find new lists of specifications. At the end of his work session, when he left his changes and their catalogue on the machine at the customary address, he appended a personal note for the first time: "How serious were you on the firstborn business?"

The following morning at the end of the new listing he found the response: "Totally serious."

That day, when he completed his work he added a new message: "What would you take instead?"

The next day's reply was: "I will not bargain over that which is my due."

He responded: "What about the most comprehensive music library in the world?"

The reply was: "Do not tempt me, Donnerjack."

"Can we get together and talk about it?" Donnerjack asked.

"No," came the reply.

"There must be something that you want more."

"Nothing that you can give me."

"I'd try to get it for you."

"Discussion ended."

Donnerjack returned to his work, executing brilliant design revisions, incorporating the desired changes, suggesting additional ones of his own. Many of these latter were approved.

One day, when he had left the full field interface open to the Great Stage, he heard bagpipe music. He moved to the nearest window and looked outside but could find no clue as to its source. He stepped out into the hallway, but it seemed fainter there.

Returning, he realized that the sounds seemed to be coming from the vicinity of the Stage.

He entered there and was startled. It was as if he had stepped ashore and hiked some miles to the east. He had set the scan on drift, as was his custom, and the landscape which surrounded him now was a replica of the Scottish Highlands. And it was obvious that this was the source of the music.

He waved his hand in one of the key areas and a menu appeared in the air before him. He stabbed the spoked semicircle icon with his forefinger and when its hardened holo manifested he took hold of it, and turning the wheel, pushed in for acceleration and steered in what he took to be the direction of the music.

He bore to the right, and Virtù rushed past him. Hills, hills, hills. The piping was coming from here, but it could take forever to search among those crags and ridges.

He drew back on the wheel, rising higher. But the ranks of hills continued, partially masking each other, and at this altitude the music became harder to distinguish. Why was he so anxious, he asked himself, to track down a local, unimportant phenomenon in Virtù? But something about it called to him, perhaps striking an ancestral chord, making it feel special.

He continued his search, circling, rising. Finally, he was rewarded with the view of a man in a small valley, standing atop a boulder, wearing a set of pipes. He dropped lower, advanced slowly, moving until the man and his stone were in the area of the Great Stage.

He walked forward then and halted a score of paces away, regarding the man's dapper form and neat beard, the dagger at his ankle, the claymore at his side.

Standing, listening there, he became aware that the terrain was shifting slowly about him, hills sinking into valleys, other hills rising. It struck him then that somehow they obeyed the music. It was as if the area had grown plastic and were dancing to the skirls and wailings, overriding, somehow, the will of its *genius loci*.

The piping went on, and on, as did the changes. After a time, he noticed a sudden drooping in the midst of a nearby patch of heather. Then a tiny piece of blackness raised itself above it and moved to one nearer at hand. The heather began to fade, to wither.

"Hi," came a small voice. "Music's a great thing, isn't it?"

He stared and saw that the black patch was a butterfly.

"He won't stop for awhile yet," it said. "That's 'Band of the Titans' he's playing. It goes on some."

"Who is he?" Donnerjack asked.

The butterfly flitted to his shoulder, the better to be heard above the piping.

"Wolfer Martin D'Ambry," came the reply, "who piped the phantom regiment of Skyga to many victories in the days of Creation. He is a lost soul of sorts, the Phantom Piper."

"Phantom Piper? Why is he called that?"

"Because he is of no world, and he wanders like a ghost, looking for his lost regiment."

"I'm afraid I've never heard the story."

"In the early days the realms suddenly pulled upon one another and bled through more easily, when the union of systems produced Virtù at large."

"Yes."

"When all was cut loose there was a period of chaos, a great flux, as the aions sought to maintain their domains against the pressures from all sides. A world had been born and sent upon its way, but its unmooring was somewhat catastrophic, though it might not have seemed so on the outside. It may have been a matter of moments there, though it ran for eons within."

"I know of this, and it was actually quite brief in real time."

There followed a musical chuckle.

"I assure you," it answered, "that the time in Virtù was real to those of sentience."

"It was just an observation, not an attempt to belittle any who suffered. Were you present? A butterfly seems such a—fragile thing—in times such as that."

Again, that laugh.

"If you ever have access to chronicles of those times, check out the name 'Alioth.' "

Donnerjack glanced at the piper.

"We have digressed somewhat," he said.

"True. There was a company of deadly fighters Skyga had imagined. He brought them into being whenever he needed their services in battle."

The piper skirled on and a hiss began to fall as Donnerjack shook his head.

" 'Imagined,' you say?"

"Yes. As was customary with gods at the time of the Great Flux, he created what he needed by an act of strong imagination. They don't go in for that much anymore. Too strenuous. But what he needed then was a deadly strike force."

"He just imagined them and there they were?"

"Oh, no. Even a god requires some preparation. He had to imagine each one individually in advance, form and feature, fighting characteristics. He had to see them all as clearly as we see each other. Only then could he combine the imagining with his will to bring them into being on a battlefield."

104

"Of course. And I suppose he could draw back the injured and send them forth again whole."

"Yes, he could be a field hospital all by himself. They were magnificent, and the bright flame was their piper, D'Ambry. He did see action, too, of course, and he fought as well as the rest. Better, perhaps."

"So what happened?"

"As events settled and the call to arms was heard with less frequency, their services were required less and less. Then, following one of the great final battles, Skyga called his troops home to sleep again in his memory. And they all went back in the blink of an eye, save for a lone piper on a hilltop."

"Why not him?"

"One of life's little mysteries. My guess is that he had something the others didn't: his music. I think it gave him that extra measure of being that made him an individual rather than just a member of a company."

"And so?"

"And so the company was summoned several times again, and it always appeared without its piper. It is said that for a time Skyga sought him unsuccessfully, but after a while the battles ended and he never called for them again. And the piper wanders now, looking for his lost legion. He pipes all over Virtù, calling to them."

"Pity he cannot forget and find a new life for himself."

"Who knows? Perhaps one day—"

Abruptly, the piping ceased. Donnerjack looked up to see the piper disappearing beyond the far side of his stony perch. He moved forward. The memories that man must have locked in his head! It would be a full education in the epistemology of Virtù to get him to talking.

Donnerjack rounded the stony outcrop, but the piper was nowhere in sight. He circled it again.

"Wolfer!" he called. "Wolfer Martin D'Ambry! I have to talk to you. Where are you?"

But there was no response.

When he returned to the place where he had been standing the black butterfly was no longer in sight either.

"Alioth?" he asked. "Are you still here?"

Again, he received no answer.

He backed away. Then, on an impulse, he activated his controls and soared. No sign of the piper, but he was impressed by the subtle changes in the terrain apparently in response to the music. Soft rises had grown steeper, steep ones craggier. The land about his perch had taken on a rawer look, as of earlier, rougher times.

Donnerjack descended and released his controls, restoring the normal drift program which permitted the landscape of Virtù to shift through the Great Stage. He could hard-holo or leave soft anything that came by. He left it at soft. Turning then, he departed into his own world.

—=—

Ayradyss could easily see the swell of her belly by the day that she finally met the banshee. For some time now, she and John had been in full-time residence at the castle, rarely leaving their Scottish island. Their privacy was a lover's delight, but she knew it also served the practical purpose of keeping difficult questions about the origin of Donnerjack's new wife to a minimum.

Ayradyss was in complete accord with John's desire to keep her Virtù origin a secret. The masquerade would not need to be maintained forever. He had shown her his campaign for inserting data about her into Verité's records—many of which were kept in Virtù. However, between drawing up the plans for Death's palace and the occasional business of the Donnerjack Institute, he had put off actually beginning his campaign. She did not mind. Her experiences in Deep Fields, although poorly remembered, still haunted her. The isolated castle with its many ghosts and robots was society enough.

Still, sometimes she left the castle proper to walk near the ocean on a particular isolated, pebbly strand. The fisherfolk never came near this spot—the waves hid far too many rocks and the villagers lived far too intimately with wet and cold and the uneven temper of the sea to find the wild prospect at all enticing or romantic.

Ayradyss, however, enjoyed it and, as her pregnancy drew on, more and more often she took her exercise on the strand, well enough bundled to still the worried nagging of both the robots and ghosts. So it was that one foggy morning she met the banshee.

Ayradyss's first impression was that one of the girls from the village had come to do her wash, but she dismissed that idea as ridiculous even before it fully formed. Who would do laundry in cold salt water when there were gas-powered washers and dryers aplenty in the village? Curious, she hurried closer, her shifting balance making her just a little clumsy on the round pebbled beach. Drawing alongside, she saw clearly that her initial, fantastical impression was apparently correct—the girl was indeed dipping bits of clothing in the salt waters of the inlet.

"Miss?" Ayradyss called out, wishing she had learned more of the local idiom—although she suspected what the ghosts could teach her would be centuries out of date. "Miss? Have you lost something? Can I help you?"

At the sound of Ayradyss's voice the girl—no, woman—rose from where she had crouched by the water, and as she rose the clothing she had been washing vanished away, but not before Ayradyss caught a glimpse of what she was certain was a swatch of the Donnerjack tartan. When the woman turned to face her, Ayradyss could see why she had initially mistaken her for a girl, for she was terribly slender—a mere slip of a thing—yet there was strength in her and a strange intensity in her green-grey eyes.

Those green-grey eyes so drew her attention that Ayradyss had closed to easy speaking distance before she registered that the woman was very beautiful. Her straight silky hair, which fell nearly to her feet, was precisely the shade of moonbeams. Although her gown was simple, hardly more than a shift with a ribbon at the throat and a sash beneath her small, round breasts, the woman's bearing was aristocratic, and aristocratic, too, were the fine, sharp bones of her face. Her hands showed no sign of the scrub maid's work she had been about but were as long and slim as the rest of her, with shapely, perfect nails.

"You aren't a woman of the village," Ayradyss said, trying not to curtsy (after all, wasn't she the lady of this land? wasn't her husband laird of the castle?). "Pray, tell me, who are you?"

"I am the *caoineag* of this land, of the old lairds who built the first keeps of old upon whose dust your husband built a castle to be your home."

Her voice was as genteel as her form, but there was something about her cultured tones that made Ayradyss's flesh creep and sent her hand to rest protectively on her belly.

"The *caoineag*? What is that?"

"The wailing woman," said the other. "The crusader ghost calls me the banshee in the Irish fashion, his mother having been Irish, though he does not recall that."

"Do you know his name?"

"I do, but he does not want it. When he does, he will know it for himself for all the good that it will do him." The *caoineag* turned her green-grey gaze on Ayradyss. "Are you going to ask me what I am doing here?"

ROGER ZELAZNY AND JANE LINDSKOLD

"No, I thought that you belonged here, as the ghosts do to the castle."

"You should wonder more." The *caoineag*'s expression was not kind, but it was not precisely unkind. "Do you know what my function is?"

"The crusader ghost said your wail has something to do with portents—portents of death," Ayradyss said hesitantly, one hand now firmly on her belly, the other plucking at her cloak as if the weight of wool could protect her unborn child. "He said that you wail for me—for me and for my baby and for John."

"That I do. Do you wonder why?"

"I do."

"Death took you for a purpose, returned you for that same purpose. Your John took the bait he offered—though to be fair to Donnerjack, his way was quite different than what the Lord of Deep Fields expected."

"Death? Expected? What do you mean?"

"Why should I tell you? What do you have to offer me? Who are you, phantom of Virtù, to order about one of noble blood?"

"Noble blood?"

"Aye, lass, the *caoineag* is of the house of Donnerjack, of a house older than that of Donnerjack, of the clan that gave birth to the lairds of this land that your husband has usurped with the rights of law and some claim of blood."

"Yet . . . yet you say you are of the house of Donnerjack."

"Aye, he is laird here and I am the wailing woman of this land, so I am of his house—of your house, too, phantom of Virtù."

"Help me, then, for the sake of that house, for the sake of the ancient clan that gave you birth. Are the proud scions of this land to be used as pawns in a game—even if one of the players is Death himself?"

The *caoineag* smiled, a cold, thin-lipped thing. "This is all you offer me, Lady of Virtù? A chance to defend the pride of people long gone to dust for the sake of those who will soon go to dust? Why should this be enough?"

Ayradyss hid her sense of excitement—the *caoineag* could have vanished in a puff of indignation and a wail. In her talks with the crusader ghost, the Lady of the Gallery, and others of those who haunted Castle Donnerjack, this had happened often enough. She had something the wailing woman wanted. If only she could find it. . . .

"What price is my knowledge worth to you, Lady of Virtù, Lady of the Castle?" the *caoineag* asked.

Ayradyss almost said, "Anything," but memory of John's bargain, well-meant but unconsidered (although without that bargain the child would not have been born at all, so . . .) halted her. She shook her head to clear it of an unwelcome maze of thoughts, complexity after complexity. But the *caoineag* was waiting.

"I will not barter my life nor that of my man nor my child nor indeed of any living person, for lives are not to be given and traded away. Any other thing, within reason, I will give to you."

"Careful, so careful," the *caoineag*'s tone was mocking, "but you have more reason than most to know the value of care. Very well, here is my price. I was made the wailing woman against my will. As penalty for failing to warn my father of the plot that took his life, in death I must warn those who dwell in the castle of the coming of their deaths. Take my place—Lady of the Castle—and I will tell you what I know."

"Take your place?"

"Aye, after your own death, however so long away as it may be. I do not ask for your life, only for your afterlife."

"Afterlife . . ."

Ayradyss wrinkled her brow, trying to force into her memory the substance of her time in Deep Fields. It had been . . . It had not been . . . It had not been precisely . . . She could not remember what it had been or what it had not been, except that *she* had been. There had not been a cessation of *herselfness*.

"I agree," she said, before she could think further. "On my death, whenever that shall be, I shall take your place as the *caoineag*."

"It is done," said the wailing woman, and with those words Ayradyss knew that it had been; some silken tether had looped itself around her, anchoring her to her fate as securely as the crusader ghost was anchored to his chain.

"Now, tell me what you know of Death's plans. Tell me why you wailed for me and for my menfolks."

"You are cold," the *caoineag* said, and Ayradyss realized that she was. "After you have done so much to preserve your son, you should not risk him before his birth. Go inside, eat and drink. When you are alone, I will come to speak with you."

"But . . ."

"Away . . ." The word was shouted shrilly, on a rising note. The wailing woman vanished, leaving only the echo of her voice against the cliff.

"Ghosts," Ayradyss said to no one in particular, "always get the last word. I suppose there is some comfort in that."

✿   ✿   ✿

"Won't you have some more stew, darling?" John asked, serving ladle poised over the tureen.

Ayradyss laughed. "I have had two helpings already, John, two helpings of stew, fresh black bread, soft cheddar cheese. I am pregnant, not being fattened for the fair!"

Setting the ladle down, John joined in her laughter. He scooted his chair around the table so that he could sit next to her and put his arm around her shoulders.

"I fuss, I know," he said, "but I worry about you. This is hardly a typical pregnancy. I want the best for you."

"Thank you, John. I know you do."

"And I'm not certain that wandering around in the cold is the best thing for you or for the baby. If you need outside views isn't the Great Stage sufficient?"

"No, it isn't—I don't feel safe in Virtù, John. I don't know what the Lord of Deep Fields did when he returned me, but I fear that he will undo it. Best I do not bring myself too often to his notice."

"The Great Stage is more like Verité than Virtù, Ayradyss. It is the appearance of Virtù without the projection of the self into the programming. It is a setting you can still enjoy without becoming a character—nothing more than elaborate wallpaper."

"I know, John, I know. Still, the awareness of the Lord of Deep Fields extends into all of Virtù, even when we do not make the crossover. No, I prefer to avoid Virtù unless you are with me—and perhaps even then."

"Whatever you say, dear."

John's tone was level, but Ayradyss could tell he was humoring her as he might have if she suddenly acquired a taste for pickles or mango ice cream.

"So, Ayra, if I can't expect you to stay in out of the cold, would you like to relocate to a warmer climate? I could visit you regularly. I would move as well, but I need the equipment that I've set up in the castle."

"No, John. I don't want to leave you. I see you little enough as it is. At least let me have you warm beside me at night."

"Have I been leaving you too much alone, Ayra?"

"No, love. I have found things to occupy me. Still, they would lose some of their zest if I could not anticipate your company of an evening."

"Ayra, I do love you. I may not always be the best at showing it, but I do . . . more than I know how to say."

Her answer was not verbal, but it was pleasant and John returned to his office over an hour later than he had intended, smiling, the memory of her laughter warm inside him.

For herself, Ayradyss cleared away the lunch dishes (Dack had the robots busy unloading some crates of electronic equipment John had ordered), enjoying the simple task as a means of extending the mood. When the room was tidy, she went into the parlor and eased another log onto the fire. Even though the winter was giving way to spring, the castle remained chill. Taking up a book, she settled herself into a chair and tried hard not to remember that she was waiting to see if the *caoineag* would come to call. It had occurred to her that the spirit might bind her to her share of the promise, then fulfill her own part but grudgingly.

Ayradyss need not have worried, for she had barely read two pages when the flames leapt within the fire, the wind outside battered at the panes, and the slim, pale form of the wailing woman was seated in the chair across the hearth.

"Is it any good?" the *caoineag* asked, gesturing at the book Ayradyss had let drop into her lap.

"Good enough," Ayradyss said. "Seafaring tales. Strange, having been a mermaid, to see a shipwreck from the sailor's point of view. Of course, in Virtù most sailors are merely on holiday and their drownings trigger a recall program into Verité."

"Still, activities in Virtù can cause death in the Verité. Peculiar, isn't it, if only one place is reality?"

"Virtù is reality," Ayradyss replied, aware that the *caoineag* must have her reasons for arriving at her point in such a circumlocutory manner.

"So you say, so many say—especially those of Virtù—but where did that reality come from?"

"No one knows. It is the great mystery, the mystery of the First Word, the Creation Scramble. Forgive me, *caoineag*, but I am not a religious person—not even Deep Fields has converted me to such introspection."

"But the Lord of Deep Fields has converted you to a creature of Verité, Angel of Virtù. Have you wondered why he did this when all that Donnerjack asked for was your return to being? Wise as John D'Arcy Donnerjack is, he did not even think to ask for you as his bride in Verité."

"I have wondered at the Lord of Deep Fields' odd generosity, and I have concluded that he wanted me to bear this child so that he could claim it as the price for my life, but what use would the Lord of Deep Fields have for a child of Verité?"

"What if your bairn is not just a child of Verité? What if, despite the changes made in you, he will still inherit something of Virtù from you? What would that make him?"

"Confused? Wailing woman, I think you are poorly named! Riddling woman would be a better title for you!"

The *caoineag* dimmed in her chair, her slender form rippling. Ayradyss thought that she had offended the spirit. Then she realized that the wailing woman was laughing. When the spirit grew opaque once more, there was a touch of color on her high cheekbones and a friendly smile curved her thin lips.

"I like you, Ayradyss. 'Tis a pity . . . Very well. To tell you bluntly. Not all of Virtù is content to have commerce with Verité be in one direction. The Lord of Deep Fields knows this and seeks an edge in the game. Your son may be that edge, may not be, but Death may have trapped John D'Arcy Donnerjack to give himself that edge."

"Why John? Why me? We are not the only couple separated by the interface."

"No, but he is John D'Arcy Donnerjack and you . . . you, poor soul, are far more than your husband knows. The dust of the black butterfly yet clings to your hair. Have you told John this?"

"I have not."

"So."

There was a long silence, companionable, in an odd way. Ayradyss broke it.

"There are tunnels beneath the castle."

"I know them."

"I have wanted to explore them."

"I could show them to you."

"Tomorrow?"

"Tomorrow."

"I shall see you then."

"Indeed."

The wailing woman faded away. Ayradyss smiled, picked up her novel. How nice it was to have a lady friend again, especially at such a time. Robots were well enough, warrior ghosts as well, but there was something to be said for the company of one of your own gender.

She turned the page. The wind was rising on the fictional sea. Outside her window, the ocean's roar and crash provided her with a soundtrack.

—=—

Breakfast porridge and cream still warm inside her, Ayradyss changed into heavy ankle-boots—rather uglier than she would have preferred, but both waterproof and possessed of excellent traction. Over her wool trousers and sweater she tossed on a light windbreaker, more for the protection it offered against wet than because she expected there to be wind in the caverns.

"Going out on the strand again, Ayra?" John said. The stack of disks and reader he held loosely in one hand testified that he must have come over from his office to retrieve the materials he had been reading in bed the night before.

"No," she said, surprised to hear a touch of defiance in her voice. "I thought I would explore the tunnels under the castle—the remains of the old place."

John frowned slightly, glanced out the window, noticed the steady drizzle, and nodded.

"The weather outside doesn't seem very inviting and since you won't use the Stage . . ."

"I won't."

"Then . . . Are you taking one of the robots with you?"

"I hadn't intended to."

"I wish you would. I only ventured into the fringes of the tunnels, but there looked to be some rough spots."

"John, I don't need a nursemaid. Save that for the baby when it comes!"

"Please, Ayra, don't be unreasonable. I'm not asking you to stay inside; I'm asking you to take a robot so that if you fall or slip or start a rock slide there will be someone to help you."

Ayradyss almost commented that she expected to have one or more ghosts with her, but held back the words. John did not realize the amount of time she had been spending with Castle Donnerjack's spectral inhabitants: the crusader ghost, Shorty, the Weeping Maid, the blindfolded prisoner, the Lady of the Gallery, and now the *caoineag*. And John was not really being unreasonable.

"Very well, John. You do have a point. I'll ask Dack who can be spared."

John set down his disks and crossed to her. His arms around her, he murmured into her hair:

"Any of them can be spared, my love. You are more important than any chore that needs to be done around here."

Almost any. You won't leave your work, she thought bitterly, disliking the petulance in herself. She knew John felt that working steadily on Death's palace was keeping his part of the bargain that had won him Ayradyss's return, but she suspected a certain element of pride as well in his devotion to the project. The Lord of Entropy regularly sent electronic messages suggesting revisions and requesting additions to his Palace of Bones. John had mentioned that he felt strangely honored to be receiving communications from an entity that even Verité's greatest scientists had dismissed as legend.

"Thank you, John," she said, trying to ignore her internal harangue. "I don't think I need anything too elaborate. One of the general purpose 'bots should serve admirably."

John smiled, embraced her once again, then picked up his disks and reader. "I'll look forward to hearing what you find, my dear. See you at lunch?"

"Maybe," she said. "I don't know how far I'll walk—and I'm getting a late start."

"Very well. Don't wear yourself out."

"I won't."

He left, brushing her cheek with another quick kiss. Ayradyss stood a moment longer, wondering if she had angered him. With an effort, she put the question from her, knowing that she could not run after him and ask without inviting an argument about the very issues she had resolved not to argue. Marriage—at least to a devoted scientist—was a bit more difficult than she had imagined. She had never realized that the art which had shaped the man she loved would also be her rival.

Pressing her fingers to her eyes, she put the thoughts from her. When she had been longer in Verité she would have more activities of her own. When the baby came she would have more than enough to occupy her. For now, there were the tunnels to explore and the odd company of the *caoineag* to savor.

The heavy iron key that opened the thick iron door could have been a relic of the original castle, but Ayradyss knew that John, in one of those fits of whimsy he usually reserved for his art, had ordered the door specially forged in the village. The hinges creaked when she tugged the door, but it swung open easily enough.

When she had descended to the "dungeon" levels, she had been accompanied by Voit, an all-purpose servomech that currently resembled nothing so much as a meter-tall robin's egg hovering about a foot from the ground. Its air cushion stirred up the dust slightly, but otherwise the robot was an unobtrusive companion. The crusader ghost, the *caoineag*, and the ghost of the blindfolded prisoner had joined her as she was fitting the key to the lock.

"He wanted to come along," the crusader ghost said with a shrug toward the blindfolded specter. "Said he knew the place. I dinna think you'd mind."

Ayradyss flipped on her headlamp and let it shine into the darkness on the other side. Following her example, Voit switched on a wider beam light. A corridor a meter and a half across extended before them. In the immediate vicinity it was lined with dressed stone, but at the fringes of the light both floor and walls reverted to the native stone.

"Can your friend see?" she asked, gesturing at the blindfolded prisoner.

"Aye, that he can," the crusader assured her. "Or if he canna see, what harm can come to him from a fall, his having shuffled off this mortal coil in ages past?"

"You have a point," Ayradyss agreed. "Let's go, then."

"Shall the door be closed behind us, mistress?" Voit asked.

Ayradyss gave in to impulse. There was no reason for the door to be closed. They were not hiding from anyone, but she craved the sense of adventure that the little gesture would grant.

"Closed, yes, Voit, but don't lock it."

"Understood."

The robot extended a mechanical arm and pulled the door shut with another satisfying squeal and thump. As Ayradyss waited for her eyes to adjust to the light cast by the lamps, she noticed that each of the three ghosts gave off a slight bluish-white glow. She had never noticed this effect before. On the other hand, their previous meetings had not been in nearly so dark a place.

"It's so black," she whispered.

"Aye," the crusader ghost agreed.

The *caoineag* did not comment, but drifted ahead, leading the way. Ayradyss followed, surprised at the superstitious fear she felt. The darkness, the rough stone, the odors of must, mold, and the salt sea touched memories she had left quiescent for so long that she had not realized that they were there to recall. She concentrated on the immediate moment, the crush of sand and rock beneath her feet, the tug of the stone wall when she caught her sweater against it, the annoyance of a drop of water that fell from the ceiling to run down her nose, and the memory receded and with it the fear.

Following the *caoineag*, Ayradyss walked slowly through the tunnels. These twisted, doubling back on themselves, crossing and recrossing with such frequency that she was not at all certain how far from the castle they had come—or if they had left its environs at all. Sometimes the tunnel would widen into a small cavern. Then Ayradyss would have Voit hover near the ceiling so that its light would shine down to illuminate the area.

She found odds and ends in these little caverns: old bottles, candle stubs, a rusting tin of machine oil, two broken claymores side by side, once a rag doll—the stitches of its face still holding a lopsided smile. Most of her finds she left behind, but she put the doll in her pocket, unable to bear the idea of it remaining in the loneliness and silence.

Time lost all meaning in the darkness and quiet. The ghosts drifted along with her, rarely speaking, and then usually to each other. Occasionally, when she passed her own bootprints in the sand, she wondered how long ago had she made those marks. It could have been minutes, but as easily it could have been eons. At long last, she felt a breeze, solid and salt. It woke her from the dream in which she had been wandering.

"I wonder where that wind comes from?" she said aloud, her own voice sounding strange to her.

"There is a cave that opens to the sea when the tide is low," the *caoineag* answered. "Would you like to see it?"

"Yes."

She walked more briskly now, the fresh wind blowing the cobwebs from her mind. The ghosts' light dimmed as they turned a corner and entered a cavern larger than any Ayradyss had seen thus far. It was thirty meters from end to end, much of this taken up with an underground pool. This was lozenge-shaped, a gravelly beach running along one long edge, rock walls closing in everything except for a narrow strip of light at the farthest edge of the water.

"If there was a row boat," Ayradyss mused aloud, "and the passengers weren't very tall or ducked down, then they could get into the caverns this way. And if they knew the way through the caverns they could get right into the castle."

"Aye," said the blindfolded ghost. "The way was known in my day, known and used sometimes for a wee bit of smuggling, sometimes for darker purposes."

"I wonder if John knows?"

"Beggin' th' lady's pardon," the crusader said, "but I'm doubtin' that he does. The laird has shown nae mind for these reaches and the villagers have long forgotten that the way exists. The castle was naught but a rubble heap this great long while."

"I must remember to show him. It may amuse him. I hope I can find my way back again."

From above, Voit's voice wafted down. "Mistress, I have been recording our explorations in case you wished to review your journey later. I could easily print out a map."

"Very good. Tell me, have you been making a visual recording, or simply keeping track of our progress?"

"I have been recording the distance traveled and the direction. Would a visual recording have been more appropriate?"

"No, Voit, you've done fine. I was simply wondering whether a video would have captured the ghosts."

"I do not believe so, mistress. I am only marginally aware of their presence and my awareness is based largely on audio indications that cannot be explained in any other fashion. As they do not register on my optical receptors, I must deduce that they would not register on a camera either."

"Very interesting."

Ayradyss strolled down the water's edge, the wailing woman drifting beside her. Although the villagers had forgotten the existence of the cavern, the waters had carried traces of their presence: lengths of fishnet, a broken buoy, a candy wrapper (this already nearly degraded). There was older trash mixed in the flotsam and jetsam, hardy trash that pre-dated the stringent recycling regulations of the past century. Some of the beer cans and soda bottles might very well be valuable antiques; Ayradyss had seen their like in antique shops around the globe. Perhaps later she would collect some of them and compare them against a price guide.

"There is more to these caverns than you've shown me," she said to the *caoineag*. "I'm certain of that."

"How can you be so certain?"

"A feeling, nothing more. A feeling and perhaps the presence of the blindfolded one. He would not be here if all these tunnels led to were a series of little caverns and one smuggler's route."

"Clever. What if I told you that you were correct, that there was something more?"

"I would ask you to guide me to it."

"Even if it was dangerous?"

"It *is* in my cellar. I should know what my castle holds, shouldn't I?"

"Many a laird and lady of this castle has gone to the grave not knowing what these tunnels contained. Such knowledge is hardly a requisite for tenancy."

"I am asking politely. Surely that counts for something."

"Perhaps it does, now that you mention it. Already that mechanical creature knows more of these tunnels than many who have tried to chart them. There is a tendency to misestimate their complexity."

"Interesting. Does this mean you will show me the secrets?"

"Lest you attempt to ferret them out with your mechanical allies? Perhaps, though I wonder if they could find what I could show you. Understand, though, my willingness to guide you does not significantly detract from the potential dangers."

"I understand . . . and I am still interested."

"The way can only be found when the moon is full."

"The full moon is just past!"

"I am sorry, but this has always been the rule."

"Then I must abide by it, I suppose. A month more and I will be a bit more bulky but certainly not confined to my chambers."

"Then I shall make arrangements. If it can be done, I will be your guide."

"Wait!"

"Yes?"

"Will I see you again before the full moon?"

"Do you wish to? My presence is said to be a thing of ill omen."

"I thought that was your wail."

"People often confuse one with the other."

"Yes, I would like to see you. We could continue exploring the mundane aspects of these caverns. Or . . . you expressed interest in the book I was reading. I could read to you if you are unable to do so yourself."

"Tempting. Handling material artifacts is wearying. Yes, I would rather like that."

"And I would like your company. There are certain metaphysical issues that you and the other ghosts are more equipped to discuss than even John—and I find myself rather obsessed with questions of life and death. As hard as I try to forget, something of Deep Fields still clings to me. I would like to put it from me before the baby is born."

"Philosophical discussion and books. Yes, that sounds quite interesting. I am certain that a few of the others would join us. The crusader is a direct soul, as are most of those whose company he enjoys, but there are those among the castle's spectral inhabitants who would enjoy such quiet visits."

"Very well. Let us plan such an afternoon sometime soon. I do try to save my evenings for John."

The wailing woman turned and faced Ayradyss, her green-grey gaze piercing the touch of cheer that Ayradyss had put into her tone when she spoke of John.

"You are troubled by what you perceive as your husband's neglect, are you not, Ayradyss? You fear that here in Verité you have lost something of the love that you nurtured in Virtù. Is this so?"

"Yes." The word was spoken so softly as to be nearly inaudible.

"John D'Arcy Donnerjack loves you no less. Believe me in this, if you can believe one with a reputation such as mine. He deeply regrets the deal that he made with the Lord of the Lost to gain your return. He has already asked that one to accept something other than your child. The Lord of Deep Fields refused. Much of the work Donnerjack does is meant to keep Death from claiming his due."

"Why doesn't he talk to me about this?"

The crusader ghost clanked to join them, his chain seeming more solid, more impeding than ever before.

"Because, lass, he's a man and has a man's foolish pride. He fears your reproaching him for what he has done, wants to bring you a solution, not a worry. But never doubt that he loves you, you and the wee bairn beneath your heart."

"John . . ."

Ayradyss knelt and gathered a few of the beer bottles from the shoreline.

"Voit, help me with these, if you would. I should have something to take back and show John. He did say he wanted to hear about my adventures."

"Gladly, mistress."

"I should hurry back. I don't want to miss dinner."

"According to my chronometer, you have some hours yet, mistress."

"Good."

She turned her face, sad, yet strangely radiant, toward the three ghosts.

"You don't mind, do you?"

"Not at all, lass. We've lots of time, time for dreamin', time for explorin'. You be getting back to the laird and tell him all about what you've seen today."

"Thank you." She gestured as if she would hug the insubstantial trio. "You've been such an enormous help. We will do this again, won't we?"

One by one, each of the ghosts nodded; one by one, they winked out. Ayradyss handed a final bottle to the hovering robot. Then she turned her steps away from the hidden sea. The sound of it lapping against the gravel shore bid her adieu.

—=—

John D'Arcy Donnerjack did not hear the banshee howl again in the months that followed his pursuit of the Piper, though odd noises continued intermittently in the below ground-level area erroneously referred to as the dungeons, and the ghosts still walked the halls of Donnerjack Castle.

"I say," said Donnerjack—having himself learned the idiom—when he encountered the crusader ghost in the company of a much shorter vision who carried his head beneath his arm, "who's your friend?"

"He's sixteenth century," replied the crusader ghost, "and it involved foreign politics, so the old laird had him done Continental. I calls him Shorty."

The smaller specter raised its head by its gory locks, and it grinned at him. The lips writhed.

"'Afternoon," it said. There followed a hideous grin, then the mouth opened wide and uttered a terrible shriek.

Donnerjack drew back.

"Why'd you do that?" he asked.

"I am obliged periodically to utter my death cry," the other replied. Then he repeated it.

"It must have been quite an occasion."

"Oh, indeed it was, sir. All classes turned out for it, though a special affair was conducted here for the gentler folk, and much sport was had at my expense." He shook the locks away from his head. "Observe the absence of ears, for instance. I was never able to turn up even their astral counterparts to carry in my pocket as a part of my haunting."

"Lord! And what were you accused of?"

"The poisoning of a horde of minor nobles, and a plot to poison the local laird, not to mention much of the royal court."

"Ah, that people in their ignorance should act with such wanton cruelty."

"Dunno as to their ignorance, but the rest was certain cruel."

"What do you mean?"

"A torturer can make a man confess to a lot, even sometimes the truth."

"You mean to say that you were a poisoner and a plotter?"

"Shorty'll not be admittin' to anythin' more," the crusader ghost said. Then the headless one shrieked again and began to fade.

"You shouldna ha' said it as you did," the other explained with a quick shake of his chains. "You bring back the guilt to the memory and you make those things worse. He was happy with just the thought of his missin' ears. That, and the holiday in his honor, so to speak."

"If you remember your name or some big event, will it carry you off like that?"

"I dinna ken. Hard to tell."

"Maybe it would warrant a little research."

"No, don't go doin' nothin' like that, me laird. You can ne'er tell what you may set loose. I'd rather find out in my own good time."

"But—"

"Best not to interfere in the natural development of things. Trust me."

He went out like a blown candle.

Donnerjack snorted. "Fatalistic poppycock!" he observed. "Sometimes the *only* thing to do is interfere."

Donnerjack walked the battlements and felt the cold winds blow about him with a few small drops of rain. Soft weather. He thought of Death and of Ayradyss and of their son-to-be. It just wasn't fair. He was giving the Lord of Deep Fields a palace like no other that had ever been. It was wrong that he should have to supply him with the fruit of his body as well as that of his genius.

There ought to be some sort of defense. Could he devise a way to Death-proof Castle Donnerjack? He laughed. Bad choice of words. Nothing could really be insulated against Death. Yet the thought gave rise to other trains of speculation. The Lord of Deep Fields did not want the boy dead, he was sure of that. It was a live babe that he wished to conduct to the nursery in his dark palace. Why?

He paced the battlements, hair stirred by a damp wind with a few small drops of rain. And he pondered the matter he had once dismissed. To what use could such a child be put? Some sort of agent or emissary? But surely Death could command messengers when he needed them. No, it had to be something else. Was it simply that it would amuse him to have a live page in his new domicile? Perhaps. He might find the contrast esthetically pleasing. It was hard to conjecture concerning a being of such unknown character. Lightning flashed beyond the hills, and a moment later thunder boomed. Better not to waste thinking time on guesswork if the information were not really essential.

The first real problems to consider were how Death had worked his tricks—the returning of Ayradyss to Verité rather than Virtù, and the matter of their mutual fertility. Both feats were theoretically impossible. He worked his way back to his notion of higher spaces within Virtù. If his hypothetical Stage IV existed a part of the answer could lie there. The journey back. . . . Had it masked a subtle Stage IV manipulation at some point?

Another flash and another blast were followed by a real rainfall and he retreated within. Pacing the upper halls, he continued his musing. Supposing he were to unify Virtù theory to include the Stage IV presumption? If it could be made to work it might explain all of the place's anomalies—from the Creation shuffle to the backward temporal expansion hypothesis to the incorporation of data to which the place had not had obvious access. If he could do that he was certain he could then attack it at a more practical level.

In the days—and, ofttimes, nights—that followed, he devoted himself to the problem whenever he could get away from the matter of Death's palace. He tried to work without the machines, using pads, pencils, and old-fashioned hand-held calculators whenever he could. When he did need large-scale computing power or the use of his corner of Virtù for a *Gedankenexperiment*, he transferred the results to his notebooks immediately afterwards and did his best to wipe away every trace of his work from that other world.

He felt that the answer might lie in the Genesis Scramble. He worked his way back to Day One, but even then things were too complete. He was able to push it back nearly to the first hour then, but could not locate the conditions to rectify his formulations. Beyond that, Virtù seemed unable to produce a history of itself. Attempts at simulations gave different results at different times. He gnawed his lip, leaned back, and stared at the wall. For the first time in over a decade, he thought of Reese Jordan and Warren Bansa.

A retired mathematician and information specialist, Reese Jordan was the oldest man Donnerjack had ever known. Even as a resident of the Baltimore Center for Iatropathic Disorders, Reese had held the record among the superannuated. As more and more means of prolonging life were introduced, the trails these therapies left within the body became progressively convoluted. Every resident of the Center was an advanced centenarian. Donnerjack did a quick calculation. If he were still around, Reese would be about 150 now. All of the residents had unique medical problems brought on by the medical practices which had preserved them. A veritable museum of life-prolongation techniques was represented in the bodies of the Center's inhabitants. They could not be cared for like normal citizens; on the other hand, their study value far exceeded the cost of their keep. Each time one of them faced a crisis, a therapy had to be developed *de novo* to fit the particular case.

Now Reese Jordan—if his mind were still intact—might prove an interesting consultant. He had been present and working a data-net the day the final straw had been added, and the world's full, linked system had crashed. An hour later, when things came together again, Virtù had been formed. He had written a number of papers both popular and technical on the phenomenon. He had been in demand as a lecturer for years afterwards. Some of his early ideas were merely considered "curious" now, but he was undoubtedly one of the main authorities on the world's electronic shadow.

Donnerjack moved to a terminal, requested the number for the Center. A few moments later he had placed the call. An idealized male security face responded almost instantly, a proge, of course. "Center for Iatropathic Disorders," it stated. "How may I help you?"

"Is Reese Jordan still a resident there?" Donnerjack asked.

"Yes, he is."

"May I speak with him?"

"I'm afraid he is not available right now."

"Is he—all right?"

"I am not permitted to discuss the residents' conditions."

"I didn't mean it that way. What I mean is, would he be able to converse rationally with me if he were available?"

"Oh, yes. But, of course, he is not available."

"Do you know when he will be?"

"No."

"Are you just telling me that he is asleep—or in a therapy session— or that he is not physically present in the Center at the moment?"

"He is physically present and he is not asleep, but he is occupied elsewhere."

Donnerjack nodded then.

"You're saying that he is in Virtù."

"Yes, he is."

"May I have his coordinates there?"

"I'm sorry, but that information is confidential."

"Well, presumably you can reach him there. Can you give him a message from me?"

"We can leave one at his number. Can't say when he'll decide to check messages, though."

"I understand. The name is John D'Arcy Donnerjack. I worked with him years ago. Just tell him there's something I'd like to discuss."

"Very well."

Donnerjack left his number and returned to his musings. Virtù. It seemed natural that Reese should return to it in his final days. He'd spent much of his life studying it. He was an avowed fan of its countless novelties, apart from his technical interest in it. Donnerjack picked up a pencil, scrawled an equation on a nearby pad. He studied it for a long while. Then he revised it.

Hours later, he had exhausted the pad and found another. He felt that his work was wrong, but he also felt that he was weaving a net. Right now, it seemed more important to surround the problems with mere conjecture than to hope for precision.

Later, Ayradyss joined him for lunch at the small table by the window.

"You've been working very hard lately," she said.

"Lots of problems to solve."

"More than usual, it seems."

"Yes."

"That palace?"

"That, and other things."

"Oh? Our problem?"

He glanced at one of the terminals and nodded. She did the same.

"How are you feeling?"

"I'm fine now."

"Good. Any more haunts?"

"Do you really think you can do it? Prevent—"

He shrugged.

"I really don't know," he said. "Even if I solve my theoretical problems there's the matter of figuring a way to put what I learn into effect."

She nodded.

"I understand. Let me know how it goes."

He reached out and squeezed her hand. She rose, smiled, kissed him, and parted. "Later," she said.

"Later," he agreed, and he returned to his work.

How long he labored he did not know. He tended to lose track of time when his concentration grew heavy.

Sometime later, he heard his name called.

"Donnerjack!"

The voice was familiar, though he could not place it immediately.

He raised his head, looked about.

"Yes?"

"Over in your staging area."

Donnerjack rose to his feet.

"Reese!" he said.

"Right. Since I had your number I thought I'd come by rather than just call. It's been a long time."

"It has indeed." Donnerjack moved to the Stage's missing wall, to his left. "Oh, my!"

A tall man with an unruly shock of dark brown hair stood grinning at him. He wore jeans, tennis shoes, and a green sports shirt. He appeared to be somewhere in his thirties.

"You're looking—"

"Don't I wish," Reese said. "It's a persona. The real me is in a quiet coma looking vaguely moribund. The med AI's working overtime again exploring more branches than a family of monkeys, putting together another tailored treatment. Time to make some more medical history or call it quits."

"I'm sorry."

"Don't be. I've had more of life than most, and I'm still enjoying it. I've been everywhere, done damn near everything, read some great books, loved some fine ladies, and collaborated as an equal with John D'Arcy Donnerjack and Warren Bansa."

Donnerjack looked away.

"You've been around, all right," he finally said. "They ever find out what happened to Warren?"

Reese shook his head.

"Never found the body, or anything associated with it. Only person I ever knew to go skydiving and never reach the ground. Too bad he was such a good magician—escape artist, at that. Just went to complicate things, add to the publicity, and muddy the waters. When the journalists were done everything was cold as well as distorted. And that damned note! Saying he was going to pull his greatest stunt that day!"

Donnerjack nodded.

"They never found any later notes, or a diary, or letters?" he asked.

"Nope. And of everybody I've known, he's one of the few I miss. I wonder if he was working on anything there at the end?"

"A paper on the natural geometries of Virtù."

"Really? I never saw it. Was it published?"

"No. He'd given me a draft to check over. Died before I could get back to him on it."

"Interesting?"

"Very sketchy. Still needed a lot of work. But, yes, now that I think of it, it was interesting. Odd. Haven't thought about it in years. Now that I do, I see it bears somewhat on what I wanted to talk to you about."

"You still have it? I'd like to see it."

"I don't know. Wouldn't know where to begin looking for it."

"Well, what was it you wanted to discuss?"

"Wait a minute." Donnerjack went to his desk and fetched his pads. Returning, he entered the Great Stage. "I've been working with some stuff I'd like your opinion on."

Reese glanced at the pads.

"Looks like a lot of material there," he observed.

"Well—I guess so."

"Then I'm going to request that you enter Virtù and return with me to the place I just came from. You can have the data scanned and transmitted there."

Donnerjack rubbed his nose.

"I don't like the idea of transmitting it anywhere," he said. "What's so special about your address in Virtù?"

"The differential time flow I worked out for it. A few minutes of real time become a few hours there. At a time like this, there's no place else I'd rather be."

"I quite understand," Donnerjack said. "If I may have the numbers for that place I'll meet you there in just a little while."

Reese nodded and recited them. Then he turned and walked away, quickly reaching a vanishing point and passing into it.

Donnerjack moved to another section of the large work area, where he entered a chamber and made the necessary adjustments. He ordered the coordinates, then lay back and relaxed.

Later, he rose, clad in khakis and a light shirt. He stood in the shade of numerous trees and the sound of falling water came to him. Moving in the direction of the splashing, he came into a small, grassy clearing. Wildflowers were abundant, and at the clearing's far end a vine-covered cliff face rose perhaps sixty feet against a clear blue sky. Several large boulders lay at the cliff's base and across the clearing, seeming almost intentionally positioned for effect. To his left, the waterfall plunged into a stream about fifty feet across. Higher up, along the face of the cascade, a rainbow winked into and out of existence.

On one of the smaller boulders at the cliff's base Reese sat, arms around his legs, chin resting on his knees. He smiled as Donnerjack entered the clearing.

"Welcome to my secret place," he said. "Won't you have a seat?" He reached out and patted an adjacent boulder.

"Your design?" Donnerjack asked. "Time trick and all?"

Reese nodded. "With the help of the *genius loci* AI who manages it," he added.

Donnerjack moved forward and seated himself.

"Would you care to meet her?" Reese asked.

"Perhaps later, though time is one of things I have to include in my field theory."

"Dear old time, my lifelong nemesis and friend," Reese said with a sigh. " 'The image of eternity,' David Park called it in a book of that title. He posited a Time I, which works out determinate, and a Time II, which doesn't. Time I is the time of thermodynamics, Time II subjective human time. He wrote it right before Chaos Theory was developed. It would have been a different book if he'd done it a few years later. Still fascinating, however. The man was a philosopher as well as a physicist, for he's as right as anybody has been, for as far as he goes."

"You're saying he doesn't go far enough?"

"He didn't have Virtù to play with, the way we do."

"But the physics of Virtù seem to be circumstantial."

"Because of its seeming artificial character Virtù lends itself to the creation of anomalies."

"I'm glad to hear you say that, considering Verkor's work on perfect fluidity."

Reese arched a brow. "Verkor is wrong. Had I the time and inclination I'd disprove him in print. There are universal principles in Virtù. I doubt I'll have the time to point the way, however."

"You *have* been working all these years?"

"Never stopped working. Just stopped publishing. You can have my notes if I don't make it this time around. I'll leave instructions."

"Very good. But I'd rather you made it. I didn't realize you'd stayed in such good shape, but since you have—"

"You can't tell by looking."

"I meant mentally. Any idea how you'll come through?"

"I'm not going to make a bet with you and jinx myself," Reese said. "That is the way of the statistician. What do you want to know for, anyhow?"

"I think I'd like to work with you again."

Reese chuckled. "John, I don't think this one is for me. These are probably my last hours. As I said, I'll leave you the papers. Don't expect anything more."

"Then let me ask you this: How good is the Center for Iatropathic Disorders?"

"They've pulled me through before. Several times. I have to give them that."

"I was just thinking that if it were necessary to place the resources of the Donnerjack Institute at your disposal I'd be happy to do it, whether you work with me or not."

"You always were a generous guy, John, but I don't know whether it would really be of much help."

"You never know till you ask. Remember, my foundation did a lot of medical engineering work at one time. Let me find a way to interface my data with theirs and we'll see what they have to say to each other. If they don't, no harm done. If they do, who knows what might turn up?"

"All right. Let's do it as soon as we can, then."

"Done," Donnerjack said, and he snapped his fingers.

A man in a tuxedo stepped from behind a boulder.

"You called, sir?"

"For someone with less formality."

"Sorry, it's been a long while."

"It has and it was generally someone else seeking access, as I recall now."

Suddenly, the man wore khakis and a long-sleeved sports shirt.

"Very good," Donnerjack replied. "There is someone I would like you to meet on a medical matter."

"It's been a long while. Who is it?"

"The AI for the Center of Iatropathic Disorders."

"Oh, Sid. I knew him when he was just getting running. He's the one who started calling me Paracelsus."

"You joke."

"In my generation, joking by AIs was considered pretty much bad form—unless you were a professional in the area, of course."

"You and A.I. Aisles must have been of a generation. What did you think of him?"

"What can I say about the first AI comedian? He was great. I knew him."

"Why was he really canned?"

"The story was that he distracted the AIs from their work. They used to repeat his stuff over and over and over."

"That can't be right, considering how many things you can do at a time."

"True—"

"Hello, gentlemen," said a dapper, dark-suited individual with brown eyes and a short beard. "Dr. Jordan I know from the inside and Dr. Donnerjack by reputation. How're you, Paracelsus?"

"Fine," replied the other.

"It seems to me that you two worked together briefly in the past," said Donnerjack. "Would you check and see how compatible you might be right now?"

"I don't believe I'm authorized to execute such a procedure," Sid said.

"Paracelsus, you have full permission to do so," Donnerjack responded. "You get ready, and I'll be in touch with Sid's bosses in a few moments."

"I'll take care of it," Reese said.

"Okay."

Paracelsus and Sid sketched bows and vanished.

"Stay with me, John," Reese added. "I feel it will be soon."

"Of course."

"You ever see the moiré?"

"Yes."

"Under what circumstances?"

"I saw it when the lady who was later to become my wife died."

" 'Later to become your wife'?"

"Yes, we had a rather bizarre courtship—which led us to this place."

"Time paradox?"

"Spatial."

"How did you affect it?"

"I didn't. I visited a place called Deep Fields, where I petitioned Death for her return."

"You must be joking. There is no such—"

"There is. That's how I got her back. But it entailed a weird route and a weirder outcome."

"Tell me the story."

"I will, while we wait."

"Good idea," said Reese.

—=—

Catching the falling notepad had not been a fluke. Arthur Eden tested his new ability for a week or so, discovering its limitations, its strengths, testing beyond what he needed to prove to himself (or anyone else) that the virt power was real, extending the testing even further while he mulled over what he should do. The wisest choice, he suspected, was to keep his virt power a secret. Telling his Elishite superiors that he had developed TK might cause them to focus their attention more closely on him—on Emmanuel Davis, attention he was not certain that his cover identity could withstand.

But even as he mulled over this, accepted what the reasonable choice would be, Arthur Eden knew he would not do this thing—he would make the less safe choice, tell his superiors, find out what they would do. He tried to justify his choice to himself as academic zeal—the desire to do his research as well as possible—but he knew there was another, less pristine, reason for his decision.

Reaching out with his mind, he levitated his notepad and brought it to him. He activated his personal journal, recited the date, spoke:

> After the next meeting, I will request a conference with my superiors, demonstrate my new ability. From my observations, I know this will result in an immediate promotion—a merit badge of sorts. There have been a few others of these "Elect" in my initiates class. They are all unbearably smug and usually are promoted onto another track quickly. I cannot miss such an opportunity. As a gesture to prudence, I will add the planned levels of complexity to the Davis persona.

He paused, replayed the section, considered how honest he wanted to be, even with himself, continued:

> I would like to say that my choice is motivated merely by academic zeal, but there is another reason, one I whisper to myself as I stir the wind chimes with a telekinetic breeze, then float my teacup into my

out-stretched hand. Power. A hint of the personal divinity that most religions promise, that no other has been documented as providing. In Virtù, many play at being gods, but only the Elishites have found the means to make us gods in Verité. I must learn more before I take my leave of them.

He turned off the notepad without touching it, set it on the table, sat sipping his tea. Around him, the room darkened with the onset of evening. He did not notice, his mind alight with possibility.

Eden/Davis' demonstration had gone very well. His initiates instructor—a short, plump Asian woman who called herself Ishtar's Star—had taken him into a small room in Verité, where he had shown that he could lift a variety of small objects and manipulate them with coordination roughly equivalent to that of someone wearing thick gloves. Then she had taken him into an Elishite chapel in Virtù and told him to pray for guidance before exiting the locus in the form of a portly white dove.

The chapel was different from those that Arthur Eden had seen thus far in his study of the Church of Elish. For one, it lacked facilities for a large congregation. The sanctuary rose in a series of tiers, the lowest of which held polished benches of rare porphyry, the next which was padded on its inner ring for kneeling. A carved ivory rail served equally well as a place for the kneelers to rest their hands and as a means to separate the sanctuary from the main chapel.

Inside the rail the floor rose in a series of shallow steps ending in a round dais on which stood a statue celebrating Marduk's conquest of Tiamat. One of Tiamat's severed heads lay on its side a small distance from the rest of the statue where it could serve rather nicely as a ceremonial altar.

Wishing he had one of his recording proges with him, Eden abased himself before the altar. Then he knelt and began reciting the prayers he had learned in his earlier training. Uncertain who might be watching him, he did not want to seem too complacent (though, honestly, he felt extraordinarily smug). Taking care with his phrasing, he went through the litany twice and was beginning it a third time when he began to feel afraid.

Were they checking his identity? Had they uncovered a flaw in the Davis persona? His body in the transfer facility was so very vulnerable. . . . He recalled with unusual clarity the waiver of culpability forms he had signed upon joining the Church of Elish, the even stricter waivers he had signed on becoming an initiate into the priesthood. They could murder him, disguise it to look like a transfer effect (former athletes often had sudden heart attacks when they didn't keep in shape, didn't they?), and pay no penalty.

His voice faltered. He struggled to recall the words to the basic prayers he had learned as a neophyte, his mind clouded with fear. He surged up from his knees to his feet. He would hit the emergency recall sequence. . . . He would explain . . .

"Revelation, Brother Davis?"

The voice broke into his panic like a bucket of water splashed in his face. It was male, strong, deep, with something of laughter in the undertones. Eden wavered, uncertain whether to fall back to his knees or to finish standing. He managed neither, his feet slipping on the slick marble floor. He would have landed rather solidly on his tailbone had not his interrogator caught him.

Eden found himself staring directly into the face of a large, red-haired man—perhaps in his mid-thirties, although since this was a virt form he could be any age. Freckles splashed the bridge of his pug nose; his pale blue eyes were surrounded with a network of lines that bespoke much time spent out of doors. He wore a simple black cotton robe, not unlike a Japanese *hakama*.

"I . . . uh . . . Thanks . . ." Eden managed.

"You're welcome. I'm Randall Kelsey. Come, take a seat on one of these benches."

Eden did so. Kelsey seated himself with easy familiarity on one of the steps leading to the sanctuary and leaned back against the altar rail.

"You looked as if one of the gods had spoken to you, Brother Davis," Kelsey said after a moment.

"I . . ." Eden caught himself before he could start confessing the real reason for his weakness. "I suddenly realized the enormity of what has happened. Until Sister Ishtar's Star left me alone to pray, I had been more concerned with passing the test, with the fear that the gift would desert me. Then it was all over and I realized . . ."

Deliberately, he let the words trail off.

"You realized that you have been touched by the divine and that divinity has shaped you into something that you were not."

Randall Kelsey fell silent for so long that Eden wondered if he was expected to say something, but if so, the moment for those words had come and gone. He waited and a trio of tiny gossamer-winged serpents flew into the chapel and fluttered in front of Kelsey, who spoke to them words that Eden did not understand, his tones measured.

Each serpent was no larger than the earthworms Eden had dug up in his mother's vegetable garden as a boy and used to bait his fishhooks. Had he ever caught anything? He tried to remember and all he recalled was the bloated pink worms, unnaturally clean from their immersion in the stream, twisted onto his hook.

"Do you believe in the gods, Emmanuel Davis?"

Eden jumped as the words brought him from his reverie. Had he dozed off for a moment? The serpents were now hovering in front of his face—their scales glittering like pulverized gemstones. For a strange moment, he thought that one of them had asked the question.

"Do you believe in the gods, Emmanuel Davis?" Kelsey repeated.

"More than ever before."

"More than nothing can still be almost nothing."

"True. Very well." Eden decided an urbane honesty would suit him best here. He was already known by his teachers as a questioner. "If you are asking me do I believe specifically in Enlil, Enki, Ishtar, and all the rest I would have to say that I believe there are divinities who find those names and their attendant forms as convenient as any other, but if I was asked to say whether I believed that these were identical to the deities who were worshiped in the dawn of recorded history in the Fertile Crescent I would be forced to say 'no.' "

"I see. Heresy?"

"I would prefer to call it metaphysical conjecture. In any case, my belief is not out of line with the teachings of the Church. Even in the earliest lessons, we are taught that form and name are metaphors for something more primal."

"True, but what about faith?"

"Faith is something that is given—it cannot be learned. At least so I have always felt. I offer instead my worship."

"Your experience with the development of a virt power did not change your mind about the divinity of those worshiped by the Church of Elish?"

"I never said I doubted the divinity, sir, only that I doubted the equivalency of the divinities we worship here and those from ancient times."

"Yes, I see."

Kelsey scratched behind one ear. His slouch against the altar rail irresistibly reminded Eden of a farmhand relaxing at the edge of a field. All he needed was a corncob pipe and a straw hat. Yet his casual posture did not diminish the grandeur of the chapel or the unearthliness of the watching serpents. If anything, his very normalcy enhanced the rest.

Eden knew instinctively that despite the lack of gold tiered crowns or jeweled miters that he was in the presence of someone of great authority, someone who *could* order the plug pulled on his transfer couch, and he resolved to be very, very careful how he answered.

"Mr. Kelsey, what are the serpents?"

"I wondered if you would ask that."

"I will withdraw the question if you so desire."

"No, that's all right. They're recording proges—among other things." Kelsey gestured and the serpents darted away from Eden and resumed their watchful fluttering a few feet overhead. "Tell me, Brother Davis, what is divinity?"

"A type of fudge?"

Kelsey grinned. "I'm glad that you had the balls to say that, Davis. You looked pretty washed-out when I came in here—figuratively speaking. Now, what is divinity?"

Eden paused, considering what *not* to answer. Emmanuel Davis was supposed to be a research librarian, so his answer should have some sophistication. On the other hand, it should not be so sophisticated as to indicate undue knowledge in the area of theology or anthropology.

"I have been considering that question since soon after I became a neophyte, sir. You must understand, I first came to the Church of Elish as a tourist."

"Most do," Kelsey said mildly.

"I came back, though, because it seemed to me that there *was* something in the temple when we were told that a deity was present, that I could feel the presence even before the announcement was made."

"Interesting."

"And after a time I became convinced that what I felt was the emanations of the divine aura—an aura that I had felt nowhere else in Virtù or Verité."

"Were you a church shopper, Davis?"

"A little." This answer had been carefully worked out in advance. "I was raised Baptist. Dropped out. Tried a few other religions—though I guess not all of them qualified for tax exemption; they were more like philosophical traditions. Eventually, I decided that there weren't any ultimate answers and mucked along, making do."

"What brought you to our church?"

"A girl from my office wanted to go, didn't want to go alone."

"Is she with us?"

"No. It didn't really appeal to her. She said it didn't have enough affirmation of the female."

"Ishtar will be *so* hurt."

"She didn't like her much, to be honest. Said it was the classic bitch pattern all over again."

"Well, it did have to come from somewhere, didn't it?"

"I see your point, sir. And, to be honest, my friend was a bit of a bitch herself. I think she would have liked to identify with Ishtar—assertive feminism or something—but it just didn't work for her."

"A pity, but we are straying from your own conversion—and your recent experience. How did you learn you had developed a virt power?"

"I was doing some work and my notepad slipped. I'd just finished the adept training here and I reached out and . . . well, it stopped."

"Did you report immediately?"

"No, sir. I didn't. I practiced for a couple of days. I wanted . . . I was afraid I'd look like a fool."

"Did you share this information with anyone who was not a member of the Church?"

"No, sir. I didn't."

"Very good. Continue not to do so. We do not wish to be flooded with neophytes who only desire to acquire paranormal abilities."

"But don't most people already know about them?"

"We did make the news of our miracles public, but most dismiss them as tabloid fodder. However, if everyone knew someone who has a virt power—someone nice and ordinary like a local librarian who just doesn't need to get up to get a book off the shelf—we would be inundated by the greedy."

"I can't, you realize."

"Can't what?"

"Get a book off the shelf. It's too heavy and my grip isn't precise enough."

Kelsey smiled. "Continue your studies, Davis, and you will be able to do that and other things—things even more wonderful. However, I am troubled with the question of your faith. When can you take leave again from your job?"

Eden wanted to say immediately, but he knew that wouldn't do.

"I just took off a long chunk of time for the last training session, sir. I've just about burnt my vacation time."

"Have you begun a new project?"

"Well, I'm about done with a short one I started when I got back. I've been angling for one on early Gothic novels for a professor at Harvard. It involves the Devendra P. Dharma Collection and promises at least one trip to Italy."

"It sounds quite interesting. However, would you be interested in being hired by us instead?"

"Us?"

"The Church. We could hire you to do some research for us. Some of your work time would be directed to instruction in the faith."

Eden tried to keep from looking too excited, but he knew his eyes had widened in astonishment.

"Could you really do that? I don't want to jeopardize my job. It's taken me a long time—"

"We can do it. I doubt your employers would turn down a lucrative contract that specifically called for your services."

"I guess you're right, Mr. Kelsey."

"Then you will accept?"

"Will the terms be the same as usual for my job?"

"We would be working through your usual employer. You would even have your usual work hours—though we might ask you to donate some time to the Church for your lessons."

"Consider me hired."

"Tell me, Mr. Davis. Do you feel the presence of a god here?"

Eden closed his eyes, reached out for that strange tingle he had felt once or twice and had dismissed as part of the aesthetic trims of the Elishites—something like a subaudible hum, perhaps. He would never have worked it into his Davis biography if he hadn't believed that there was something at work—though he suspected sophisticated programming rather than gods.

"No, Mr. Kelsey. I do not."

"Honest, too. Very good. Come kneel beside me. We will sing the praises of the divinities who—even if they are not physically present—do have a tendency to listen to those of our Church."

Taking his place on the kneeler next to Kelsey, Arthur Eden mouthed the appropriate responses. It looked like if he played his cards right and was very careful, he would have the research opportunity of a lifetime. Perhaps he would even meet the founders of this religion, uncover its deepest secrets.

He smiled and raised his voice in song.

SIX

In the evening, as he sat in his lab wondering whether the banshee would howl or a ghost put in its appearance, Donnerjack thought back over the old days, when he and Jordan and Bansa had worked out what was to become the theoretical basis of Virtù. It was raining, as usual, and his mind skipped back over nights of good fellowship and amazing leaps of logic. Of pizza and beer. Was he still capable of the sort of work the three of them had done back then?

Near midnight, he received a message from the CID. It was a holo, from Reese.

The man stood before him, looking as he had just a few hours earlier.

"If you receive this," he began, "I've made it through one more. Don't know what sort of shape I'll be in for some time, though. You'll hear from me eventually. Glad you didn't get the other message."

Donnerjack touched a code. "Paracelsus," he said, "spare me a minute."

The AI appeared wearing a baseball uniform with a Cleveland Indians insignia. "Hi, boss," he said.

"Paracelsus," said Donnerjack, "tell me what happened."

"Well," said the other. "We worked something up between us, Sid and I, decided it was the best course of action, and turned it over to the proges to administer. They did, and it worked beautifully."

"Remind me to call you the next time I'm feeling ill," Donnerjack said. "In the meantime, when would it be best to talk with Reese?"

"Call him Monday to congratulate him, but give him three weeks before you talk of work."

"This is a very important job."

"You want to kill the best man for it?"

"No."

"Then do as I say, boss. He needs the rest."

"Done," Donnerjack responded. "He can't be replaced. He's as precious as Bansa would be if he were still around."

"I've heard of Bansa, the man who started the whole thing," Paracelsus said.

"I wouldn't go that far," Donnerjack replied. "But he came up with some novel theories as to what happened."

"He still holds several places in our oldest pantheon," Paracelsus said, almost defensively.

"Wouldn't put it past him. Who is he?"

"The Piper, the Master, the One Who Waits."

"I think I know him as the Piper."

"You do?"

"Well . . . I heard him playing, saw him. What can you tell me about his other personae?"

"The Master is a geometrician who had to do with the creation of the universe. The One Who Waits will figure in the closing or change of Virtù."

"None of my business, actually, but do you believe in these beings?"

"Yes."

"Do many others of your sort?"

"Yes."

"Why would an AI care to worship anything? You're as self-sufficient as anything in the business. What do you need gods for, unless they're truly real?"

"They are as real—more real, I believe—than many figures in other religions."

"Well, buying that they exist, what do they do for you?"

"I guess the same sort of things that beings in other religions do for their followers."

"It can't be healing since you guys don't get sick."

"No. Spiritual comfort and understanding, I suppose. A dealing with the right feelings for those things which lie beyond reason."

"That sounds worthwhile, I'd say. But how do you know your gods are authentic?"

"I might ask how anyone knows that about any religion. You would have to respond that most religions require a leap of faith at some point."

"I might."

"But I have seen the Piper and know that he is real."

"I, too, have met the Piper—or at least heard him play."

Paracelsus stared. Finally, "Where?" he asked.

"Through my Stage and beyond."

"Did he tell you anything?"

"Not precisely, but an entity I met there said that the Piper was a lingering remnant of Skyga's mental army."

"Remarkable. I never heard that story," Paracelsus said. "He does not usually manifest for those of the Verité."

"It was as if he came seeking me," said Donnerjack.

"Then you are unusually blessed."

"Tell me, does Death figure in the pantheon?"

"Yes, but we don't talk about him much."

"Why not?"

"What's to say? He's Lord of Deep Fields. He gets you in the end."

"True. Though right now my relationship with him is a bit different. I'm doing a Virtùelle engineering job for him in partial payment of a debt."

"I did not know that your sort ever got involved at that level. But then, you are who you are, when it comes to reputation. However, the Piper's presence is a riddle. I would suspect it has to do with your contract."

"If it does," Donnerjack said, "he did not reveal it to me."

"If you meet him again, perhaps you should ask."

"I will. If he's interested, maybe the others are, too. How would I recognize the Master or the One Who Waits?"

"The Master limps and usually carries some strange piece of equipment. The One Who Waits is said to have a scar that runs from the top of his head to the sole of his left foot. It is supposed to have come of his having inadvertently gotten in the way of the Creation—though some say it was on purpose."

"Thank you, Paracelsus. Could you get me a copy of your catechism or whatever it is that contains these items?"

"I'm afraid that's a no-no. Since we're all AIs we just transfer data to converts."

"You mean that no one other than an AI has ever been interested?"

"That's right. We generally discourage them. Normally, I would have answered a few of your questions and then started changing the subject. But you'd met the Piper and that made a difference."

"Is there a policy against admitting the people of Verité?"

"No, no discrimination. But we always felt it was our thing."

"Hm," Donnerjack said. "Would you have any qualms about discussing it occasionally?"

"All but certain secret parts which aren't really that interesting."

"I don't want to know your secrets. I just want to know whether I may ask you about it."

Paracelsus nodded.

"What about the Elishite religion?" Donnerjack asked. "Is there any connection between yours and theirs?"

"Yes. We recognize their deities, but we feel that our pantheon supersedes theirs and that our moral code is superior."

"Your Trinity is more potent than Enlil, Enki, and Ea and all the rest?"

"Some of us like to think so. Others say that they're versions of each other under different names."

"We have similar anthropological and theological problems in Verité."

"I don't really think it matters, one way or the other, though."

"Me neither."

"I'll ask you further another time how Bansa figures in your religion—"

"—and you and Jordan," Paracelsus said.

"Me?"

"Yes."

"But I absolutely must get some work done before I'm too tired to do it."

"I understand, boss."

"Talk to you later, then."

Paracelsus went out like a light.

Donnerjack moved to his desk and reviewed some designs for Death's palace. Then he moved onto his real work.

—=—

The first full moon following Ayradyss's initial exploration of the caverns beneath Castle Donnerjack passed without the *caoineag* successfully managing to take Ayradyss into the secret places. The failure was not for lack of effort—something sought to block their way, something shadowy yet solid, taloned and fanged. Ayradyss caught a glimpse of gimlet eye, forked tongue, wings that were less wings than animate darkness.

"It reminded me of the moiré," she said to her companions when they had retreated back to her parlor, where she had made herself a nest of pillows on the rug before the fire. She wrapped her fingers around a mug of hot cider to warm the fear from them. "But the moiré is without malice. It just *is*—a warping, an indication that the end is come for a proge. This was . . ."

She shivered and fell silent. Although the room smelled comfortingly familiar, of spices, of the burning wood fire, of the lemon oil the robots rubbed into the antiques, she felt cast adrift. It was as when the moiré had touched her in Virtù, and though John pressed her to him as closely as he could, she had become nothing.

"The three nights of the full moon are gone, Ayradyss," the *caoineag* said, "and we need not return to those places when the moon comes full again. The guardian you saw cannot cross into Castle Donnerjack. It belongs to the eldritch realms. You are safe—and, believe me, though I stand to gain from your ending, I would not lead you into it. I have had my taste for betrayal burnt from me these long centuries past."

"That's right, you betrayed your father."

Ayradyss pulled herself to a sitting position. She had come to the lovely stage of her pregnancy—the glow was upon her, coloring her skin, her eyes, causing her hair to fall longer and fuller than it had even in Virtù. The awkwardness had gone as well—she had centered herself around her growing baby and moved with a peculiar grace that made it seem impossible that she would ever become ponderous.

"I did, and not merely by omission." The *caoineag*'s expression was impassive, the expression on her thin, fine-boned face imperious. "My mother had died some years before and clearly he meant to take another wife. My kin from my mother's clan did not care for this, nor did I. They spoke to me, hinted at their plans, and although I did not raise hand against my father, I looked the other way when I knew they were coming for him."

"Did you know that they meant to kill him?"

"I suspected."

"And that was enough?"

"Enough?"

"Enough to make you the wailing woman."

"It must be, for I am here."

"As I will be."

"Do you regret your choice?"

"No."

—=—

In the weeks that followed his interview with Paracelsus, Donnerjack worked with a cold concentration. So intense was his absorption that he almost refused a call from Reese Jordan.

"Oh, Reese. Sorry, sorry. I've been distracted."

"They've gotten me back into working order," the other announced. "I'm ready to help you."

"Glad to hear that. I'm going to risk sending you all my notes on everything I've been doing recently."

"Oh, excellent. When I've reviewed them we'll confer?"

"I trust. If anything prevents it, do what you would with them."

"What could prevent it?"

"I will include excerpts from my journal, also. I think they'll give you a pretty good idea. Glad you're up and about."

Donnerjack broke the connection and returned to work.

—=—

As the moon waned and grew fat again, Ayradyss visited the tunnels and caverns repeatedly. She invited John to join her on some of these expeditions. They brought a picnic and she showed him the demicaverns, the hidden beach, the claymores stuck in the floor. (He agreed with her that they should remain there; together they made up stories about how the swords had come to that place, laughing as they added detail after fantastic detail).

She did not bring him near the place that led to the eldritch realms. Testing her courage, she had gone there once after the moon was clearly thinning and found nothing remarkable there but a tunnel that terminated in an unremarkable bit of rough rock. Voit's probes found no openings, nor did his densitometer readings show any significant spaces behind.

For days at a time, she put the mystery from her. Very cautiously, she had spoken to John—hinting at her loneliness. He took more time from his work and they made occasional trips. Not wishing to undergo more ID checks than absolutely necessary, they picked isolated places: Loch Ness, Dove Cottage, the British Museum. Had they wished, they probably could have ventured safely into once-popular tourist areas, for the development of Virtù had dealt a heavy blow to the conventional tourist industry. But, as on their honeymoon, they chose places where questions would not be asked and gloried in each other as much as in the sights.

Outside the parlor window, once again the moon was nearly full.

"How many days?" Ayradyss asked the *caoineag*.

"Until the moon portal is open again? Two perhaps. Do you wish to venture that way again?"

"I do."

"Very well. I have spoken with some of the others. There is a charm against the guardian I learned from the Lady of the Gallery. It comes from after my time, but it may be efficacious. The crusader and the blindfolded prisoner insist on coming with us."

"I don't mind. I'm rather touched."

"They like you, Ayradyss. We all do."

"And John?"

"He is a different matter. We do not dislike him—far from—but he is mortal. You are other."

"Because of Deep Fields?"

"Yes, but more. Your heritage in Verité—Mermaid Beneath the Seven Dancing Moons, Angel of the Forsaken Hope—you belong to legend, just as each of us do. It makes us kin."

"John belongs to legend—in Virtù, that is."

"This may be so, but he is unaware of his legend, knows himself to be John D'Arcy Donnerjack, a man of great achievement, yes, but just a man. You know the fluidity of being myth."

"Strange. I never really thought of it. There are many such as myself in Virtù."

"But not in Verité."

"No. That is true. These eldritch realms that the tunnels open into—what are they?"

"Myth, I suppose, but very real, very solid myth, just as the guardian you glimpsed is impossible yet all the more possible for being impossible. It is the way of that place."

"When the moon is full, we will endeavor to go there again. You will teach me the charm?"

"Let us go to the Lady of the Gallery. She said she would teach you personally."

"Very well. 'Let us go then, you and I . . .' "

" 'While the evening is spread out against the sky . . .' "

" 'Like a patient, etherised upon a table . . .' "

Laughing, together, they went.

Armed with the Lady of the Gallery's charm, artificial light, and the encouragement of the ghosts, Ayradyss descended into the caverns on the first day of the full moon. Although the moon would technically not be full until the following night, the *caoineag* told her that it was worth the attempt, for "appearances matter as much as anything in these matters."

Voit trailed her, its light revealing the dripping stone, but the ghosts had expressed their doubts as to whether the robot would be able to enter the eldritch realms.

After wending their way through the now familiar maze of tunnels, the group came to the appropriate corridor. At first glance, it was blocked as always by solid stone, but when the *caoineag* moved to inspect the wall she turned to Ayradyss with a pleased smile.

"Turn off your light, Ayradyss, and have Voit do the same, then tell me what you see."

Ayradyss obeyed, and as her fingers turned her headlamp's switch, Voit's light turned off. The blue-white glimmer of the three ghosts illuminated a round space, darker than the surrounding stone, with a sense of depth.

"There is a portal, just like last time, but it's different. It seems more open this time."

"Our luck is better," the *caoineag* answered. "The guardian creature is not there. Quickly, step through."

"I'll go before the lass," the crusader said, gathering his chain in his hand, "and give a wee bit of light."

Ayradyss glanced back at Voit. "Do you see anything, Voit?"

"Nothing, mistress."

"Then you must stay and guard against our return."

"As you wish."

She ducked her head then and stepped through the round space, moving quickly lest she should lose her nerve. The two remaining ghosts came through after her.

The place where they found themselves might have been a section of their own island, for in the distance they could see rock-pebbled beaches and a crashing body of water that could easily have been the North Minch. Here, though, there was no village, no castle. A stand of granite monoliths dominated the prospect, and while they had left a misty late morning behind, here the sun was sinking in the west. Faintly, in the distance, they heard the sound of a river running and behind that the plaintive wail of bagpipes.

Turning to her companions, Ayradyss began to ask where they should go from here, but their appearance chased the query from her mind. Although she had seen all of Castle Donnerjack's spectral inhabitants manifest in more or less solid forms, there was always something of the insubstantial about them. Even about the *caoineag*, who would seat herself in a parlor chair and visit with Ayradyss for all the world like a more usual caller, something of the ethereal always clung. Now, however, they could not be distinguished from ordinary folk.

The crusader ghost still wore his rags and ankle chain, but now Ayradyss could see that his skin was oily, his beard more patchy than she had realized. A thin white line crossed the bridge of his nose, but she did not believe it was his death wound. Seen more clearly, the blindfolded ghost's long robe resolved into a priest's cassock and the indistinct emblem at his waist a carved wooden cross.

The *caoineag*'s beauty became more human here—her lips gaining in fullness, her eyes in brightness, her hair darkening to wheaten gold. The loss of her silvery glimmer could have robbed her of some of her loveliness, but instead she flowered out—a white rose rather than a perfect, enfolded bud.

"You . . . you are all changed."

"We exist in Verité as legends; this is a place where legends are alive."

" 'Ware the stones," said the blindfolded ghost, reaching up and untying the strip of cloth from around his eyes. "They move and crush those who walk among them. So I met my end."

"But," Ayradyss said, finding it strange to see dark brown eyes where she had grown accustomed to white fabric, "you are dressed as a Christian cleric. I realize that my understanding of these things may be imperfect, but these eldritch lands seem to be far older than Christianity. How did you find yourself here?"

"My father followed the custom of the times, and having more sons than he knew how to employ, he sent me—for I had shown some talent for reading and ciphering—into the clergy. I did well in my education and after being ordained arranged to be sent home again. There I could have done well but for my pride . . ."

"Och, pride again," muttered the crusader.

"I lorded my collar and my education over my less formally educated brethren. In time, they grew tired of me and one full moon near the spring equinox they brought me to this place. There they wrapped my eyes and challenged me to use my great knowledge to find my way home again. Needless to say, I failed, and when the great stones lumbered down to the water to drink—as they do twice a year—I was crushed beneath them."

Ayradyss looked at the monoliths with doubting respect. "What a horrid fate. And then you found yourself haunting the castle?"

"That is correct. Something still binds me here—though I believe I have been well-enough punished for my arrogance."

"Och, pride . . ." The crusader's words were softer this time, but the cleric heard and glared at him.

"I hear bagpipes; I wasn't certain before, but they're louder now," Ayradyss said, more to stop the incipient quarrel than because she felt comment was needed. "But I can't place where the sound is coming from. Every time I think I know, the location of the music shifts."

"Shall we go down to the shore?" the cleric asked. "We know that piper is not out on the water. Pinpointing where he is on the land should be simpler from there."

All agreed and they walked down to the shore, the crusader in front with a loop of his chain in his hand, the ladies between, and the cleric striding behind.

Now that he had removed his blindfold, Ayradyss realized that he was a handsome man—hawk-nosed and arrogant despite his collar. His gaze restlessly scanned the horizon and his right hand rested as if it expected to find a sword at his waist. No doubt he had resented being shuffled off into the clergy when his blood and early training was that of a warlike clansman. Reaching the shore, they had no better luck locating the piper.

"The skirl makes my heart sing," the crusader cried, his blue eyes snapping and his bearing no longer stooped. " 'Tis a fine and martial noise."

"But where is the piper?" Ayradyss said. "For his sound to carry so, he should be standing on some promontory, but all I see are empty rocks."

"Let us go and take a wee gander," the crusader suggested, "this lad and I. The banshee can keep you company and 'tis far safer than your clambering on the rocks."

"Can you climb with that ankle chain?" the cleric asked. "I don't fancy the loftier reaches among the monoliths. No one ever called me a coward, but those rocks may have memories."

"Dinna think it will be a problem," the crusader said. "I'll take the high road and you take the low . . ."

He looped his chain about his hand and trotted off into the rocks, his laughter mingling with the shrilling of the pipes. A few steps after, the cleric followed. Left behind, Ayradyss and the wailing woman continued their survey of the heights from the shore. The waves rolling up the beach teasingly licked at the soles of their shoes and tossed bits of foam before them.

"Is that a cottage down the way?" Ayradyss asked after a while. "I believe it is, only that clump of boulders blocked it from sight before."

"Odd," the *caoineag* responded. "It is indeed a cottage, but I do not recall one the last time I visited here."

"How long ago was that?"

"Perhaps a hundred and fifty years."

"Time enough for change."

"True."

"Shall we pay a call? Perhaps the piper lives there."

"If you wish to do so. The portal to your world should remain open for the next several days."

"I do hope to be home for dinner."

"We will try to make certain you are. It is difficult to judge time for us."

"My watch is still running—at least, as far as I can tell. If it's right, dinner won't be for hours yet."

"Then let us pay a call, by all means. Let me advise you not to eat or drink while you are here. The old legends say that this can bind a mortal to the fairy realms."

"I seem to recall something of that. I will heed your advice."

Even before they were within hailing distance of the cottage, Ayradyss could see that it was a pleasant place. Rambling and somehow fat, it was thatched with bright yellow reeds. Its paint—white for the main, green for the shutters and trim—must have been freshly renewed, for it was unchipped despite the proximity of the ocean. Red geraniums spilled out of window boxes and daisies lined the oyster shell paths. A few chickens scratched in the sunlight. A lazy calico cat asleep on the roof opened one eye as they drew closer.

"Hello, the cottage!" Ayradyss called when they were on the fringes of where the beach gave way to unfenced yard. "Visitors!"

Almost immediately, the front door swung open and a startlingly beautiful young woman stepped out. She was no more than seventeen, with jungle-green eyes and shoulder-length blond hair. Her smooth pink complexion might never have felt a sea wind and her teeth when she smiled were perfect and dazzlingly white. Although overall she was well made, she was also clearly pregnant, perhaps a bit further along than Ayradyss.

"Hi!" she said, her accent American. "I'm Lydia. What brings you to this isolated place?"

Ayradyss was at a loss for words. She had entertained many possibilities of what they might find, but this creature drawn from an American fantasy (despite the incongruous pregnancy) had not even come close. Her mouth opened, but no sound came forth. The *caoineag* recovered more quickly.

"I am Heather and this is my friend, Ayra. We were walking, listening to the piping, and we saw your house. It seemed rude to pass without saying hello."

"The piping is my husband, Ambry," Lydia explained, "and I'm very glad that you decided to stop. It does get a little lonely here."

"Here?" Ayradyss managed.

"Yeah, we're in one of the wild lands of Virtù—one of the places the programmers lost. It's not too often that someone stumbles in. Don't worry. Ambry knows how to get back. He'll show you the way, but don't go too soon. I'd really love a chance to visit."

Ayradyss could only nod befuddled acceptance and follow Lydia into the cottage.

"Did you know?" she hissed to the *caoineag*. "And is your name really Heather?"

"No. And, yes, or close enough. Let's talk with this girl. I want to know more about how an ancient place can be mistaken for a site in Virtù."

The inside of the cottage was as pleasant as the outside. The table and chairs in the parlor Lydia led them into rested on oval rag-rugs that protected the bright pine floor. Overall the decor was late eighteenth-century rural New England, but Lydia switched off an electronic scribble board as she walked by it. Ayradyss caught a glimpse of long mathematical formulas that reminded her vaguely of some of John's work.

Lydia caught her questioning glance. "It's something to keep me busy—interface theory. Some of my experiences really make me question the conventional wisdom. At first, Ambry argued with me, but I think I'm bringing him around to my point of view."

"You and your husband are mathematicians?" Heather asked.

"Well, yeah. I guess you could say that. Mostly we're just taking it easy, but it's nice to have something to talk about in the evening. Like I said, it gets quiet here."

"Where are you from originally—if that's not impolite to ask?" Ayradyss said.

"New Jersey." Lydia giggled. "How about you?"

"Scotland."

"Oh, how cool. This locus owes a lot to that part of the world—and not just the terrain features. Ambry likes to say that all the legends have found their way into Virtù."

"Really?" said the *caoineag* dryly. "Which, I wonder, came first?"

"Well, in one sense the legends," Lydia answered, not hearing the other's sarcasm. "One of the first things people loaded into the data-nets—even way back when they were using terminal interface and telephone connections—was raw information: dictionaries, academic papers, fiction, indexes. When the system did the big crash, all that got scrambled and the AIs had lots of data to cannibalize."

"So this 'wild territory' is just some AI's unauthorized scrambling of data?" Ayradyss said.

"That's what the theory says." Lydia's tone was suddenly guarded. She switched the subject with an awkwardness that made Ayradyss suspect that she was at least as young as her physical appearance. "When's your baby due?"

"Spring. How about yours?"

"About the same. I'm really pregnant. This isn't just a virt thing."

Again, Lydia quickly shifted the subject, as if by admitting that she was really pregnant she had strayed into dangerous territory.

"Are you two ladies here on your own? I spotted you first from an upstairs window and I thought I saw a couple other people."

"We're here with two friends," Ayradyss answered. "They heard the bagpipes and went into the hills to see if they could find the piper."

Lydia giggled again. "Ambry's piping is like that. The first time I met him, I wandered all over the hills looking for him. I found him—or really, he found me. I'll send him a message asking him to join us and to bring your friends along." She opened a window and leaned out into the yard, making a soft cooing noise. A fat grey pigeon fluttered sleepily from the rafters.

"Find Ambry for me and ask him to come home and to bring the two people . . ." She glanced questioningly at Ayradyss and Heather.

"Two men," Heather clarified. "One is dressed in a priest's cassock and the other in rather ragged clothing."

"Those two men with him."

The pigeon yawned, preened, and fluttered off, blending almost immediately into the grey sky.

Lydia deliberately kept the conversation inconsequential after that and her visitors were quite content to cooperate.

Ayradyss could hardly keep up her part in the discussion; her mind kept coming up with unanswerable questions: Was this indeed Virtù? If so, had they really crossed in from the Verité? How could that have been done without the proper equipment? How could the ghosts have crossed at all? Moreover, the *caoineag* and the cleric had both spoken as if these "eldritch realms" had existed during their mortal existence. If this was the case, the realms predated Virtù—they predated computers. How had Lydia entered them from Verité?

Gratefully, she heard the crunch of feet on the oyster shell path and put her questions away for later—and hopefully more fruitful—meditation.

The door opened, admitting a man wearing wool leggings and an unbleached muslin shirt. He was bearded, his hair and shaggy eyebrows wild as if he had been standing in a high wind. A fine set of bagpipes was slung over his shoulder. Crossing to Lydia, he kissed her on one cheek and nodded to the ladies.

"The pigeon found me and I found the men, but they fled from me as if I were a ghost. I lost them near the standing stones. They were an odd pair—I'm certain that the smaller one was dragging a chain."

"We were involved in a mystery game," Ayradyss said quickly. "They may have thought you were one of the villains."

"Quite possibly." The man sketched a bow. "I am Wolfer Martin D'Ambry, but I hope you will call me Ambry, as Lydia does. The rest is something of a mouthful."

"I am Ayradyss and this is Heather. We wandered here and Lydia invited us in."

"They're from Scotland," Lydia said, almost as if she was saying something else.

Ambry nodded.

Ayradyss knew there was a certain etiquette to what one did and did not ask in virt; this made her somewhat hesitant to ask questions that could be taken as a cross-examination. Heather, however, had no such compunctions.

"What is this place? Lydia called it a wild land—seemed to indicate that it wasn't easily found. What did she mean?"

Lydia hung her head slightly, looked embarrassed. Ayradyss felt for her. Clearly in her excitement at having visitors—and perhaps out of a good-hearted desire that they not become frightened at finding themselves in a strange area—she had said more than she should have. The *caoineag*'s green-grey gaze was pitiless and steady, fixed on Wolfer Martin D'Ambry.

"Virtù," he said, as if they had been talking for hours, "is not nearly as regulated and reliable as the tourist bureaus and rental agencies would have their clients believe. Only a handful of specialists will even admit how far-reaching the effects of the worldwide crash were. There are places in Virtù that cannot be found on any map in Verité. This is one of those places."

"But this is truly Virtù?" Ayradyss asked, thinking, *If this is Virtù, then does the Lord of Deep Fields know I am here?*

"It is accessible from Virtù," Ambry said. "Its *genius loci* claims that this place is older than Virtù, but that is foolishness, is it not?"

"There have always been legends of places existing side by side with the fields we know," Ayradyss said, quickly lest the *caoineag* speak the indignation flaring in her eyes. "The sidhe, so legends say, lived in a shadowland side by side with Verité, crossing over from time to time to steal a bride or a babe or a musician. Rip van Winkle drank and bowled for what he believed was a single night and returned home to find that a hundred years had gone by. Then there are the heavens and hells of almost every religion that has been. All of these are far older than Virtù. Perhaps the *genius loci* of this setting adopted such a legend and now believes it."

"A thoughtful response," Ambry said, sketching a bow over his hand.

"I know something of Virtù."

"Perhaps we should be returning to our game," the *caoineag* said. "Our fellows will be wondering what has become of us."

"Give me your game's address and I will guide you back," Ambry said. "It is neither easy to come here, nor to leave if the *genius loci* resists you."

"We found our way easily enough," the *caoineag* said haughtily. "We can find our way out again."

"But thank you," Ayradyss said quickly.

"Well, certainly you will permit me to walk with you and to assure myself that you are safely away."

There was no other way they could refuse such a mannerly request without eliciting unwelcome questions, so they left the cottage in the company of Ambry and Lydia. Neither said anything when Ayradyss and Heather led the way up to the monoliths, but Ambry's raised eyebrows were eloquent. Ayradyss felt immense relief when she saw that the moon portal remained open.

"Thank you so much for your hospitality," she said, stopping before picking her way across to the rock wall. "Good luck with your baby."

"And with yours, Ayra," Lydia said, her perfect teeth shaping a smile. "Good-bye, Heather."

"Farewell."

"Wait!" Ambry said, when they turned away. "Where are you going?"

"There," Ayradyss said, pointing to where the portal stood round and dark.

"Where?"

"Through the opening in the rock. Can't you see it?"

"No, I see nothing but rock. Lydia, do you see anything?"

"Nothing."

"It must be a restricted access port," Ambry mused. "I don't believe that it goes to any game site. Tell me, ladies, where does that portal go?"

"Why should we tell you?" Heather said rather rudely.

"Because it effectively opens into my backyard."

Ayradyss, heady to have home so near, smiled. "And it opens into my basement."

"Your basement?"

"In Castle Donnerjack."

"Donnerjack? As in John D'Arcy Donnerjack?"

Ayradyss would have said more, but the *caoineag* took her hand and with unsuspected strength pulled Ayradyss through the portal where she tumbled to a heap on the cavern floor.

"Why did you do that?" Ayradyss said, looking up at the now insubstantial, faintly glowing ghost.

"I fear what we have learned today. I do not want that man to know more about you until we have learned more about him."

Ayradyss shivered and not just from her contact with the cold stone floor. "It was peculiar, wasn't it?"

"Yes."

"You are certain that place was there before the creation of Virtù?"

"I swear."

"As do I," said the cleric, drifting over, blindfolded once again. "The place is not a site in Virtù—or not just."

"Who then are Wolfer Martin D'Ambry and Lydia of New Jersey? I would swear that she, at least, is what she claimed to be. I have seen variations on that virt form hundreds of times before. It is quite the fashion and she spoke like a young thing."

"I do not know," the *caoineag* said, and the other ghosts shook their heads.

"I will go back tomorrow," Ayradyss said, "better prepared. Perhaps when I know more I can bring John. That man seemed to know his name."

"John D'Arcy Donnerjack is famous in certain circles," the *caoineag* said, "but he would not be known by the average virt tourist."

"No," Ayradyss agreed, gnawing on one fingernail. "Voit, what time is it?"

"Five in the evening, mistress. The kitchen has dinner scheduled for half-past six."

"I should go and clean up, then." She frowned thoughtfully. "Voit, please query the databanks for a Wolfer Martin D'Ambry."

"I shall."

That night, Ayradyss dined with John. They talked of his work, of her explorations (though she kept her latest expedition to herself, uncertain how to explain until she knew more). While she and John were working a jigsaw puzzle (this one meant for the baby's nursery), Voit discreetly reported to her that it could find no record of a Wolfer Martin D'Ambry.

The next day, Ayradyss, along with the *caoineag* (but without either the crusader or the cleric) descended again into the tunnels. Although the moon was now full and they could see the portal opening, some force blocked it. When they probed it, they glimpsed the shadowy guardian lurking just beyond the pale.

"The moon portal has been warded against us," the wailing woman said. "The eldritch land refuses us entry. Such is not unknown."

"So I recall your saying," Ayradyss said, "but I find it odd that the land should resist our entry today after letting us in without even the guardian to hinder us just yesterday. Should we attempt to drive the guardian away with the Lady of the Gallery's charm?"

"We could, but even if it worked, the charm would not eliminate the barrier."

"You're right. I guess we try again tomorrow, and if that does not work, we try again the next full moon."

"As you wish."

"You sound reluctant, Heather. Don't you want to know?"

"Know?"

"What that place really is."

"It is the eldritch lands, as it has always been. No newer name changes that."

"Yes, but . . ."

"But, nothing, my dear Angel of the Forsaken Hope. Unless you wish to take my place far sooner than you planned, I should take great care."

"Care?"

"The Lord of Deep Fields has free range in Virtù. Do you really wish to bring yourself to him? Your husband has indicated a desire to renege on his part of the bargain they made. What is to keep the Lord of the Lost from taking you hostage and so obtaining his payment?"

"You're right. I had considered that possibility. I just have so many questions for those two."

"I understand. So do I, but let us not throw caution to the winds."

Ayradyss placed her hand upon her belly. Frowning, she turned her back on the dark rock wall, wondering as she did so if she had indeed seen the glint of the guardian's watchful eye.

—=—

They walked the fields of Verité, leaving Castle Donnerjack far behind them.

"John, why have we come so far?" Ayradyss asked.

"To avoid my equipment, some of which may be used against me," he replied.

"By whom?"

"Specifically, by someone who drove me into a rough deal."

"Oh."

"Yes. Whatever memories you have of it must be very strange indeed."

"They are. But I don't understand what you mean about machines."

"I am looking for a means of barring his collecting on our arrangement."

"Impossible," she said. "There is no way to exclude death from life."

"Death, the phenomenon, no. Death, the personification—whatever he or it really is—maybe. I have some ideas for a field-effect. At first, I was just going to attempt to defend against hypothetical intrusions from the Great Stage. Now, though—I am going to regulate every bit of information that rides the electromagnetic spectrum into Castle Donnerjack. Monitor and record. I'll build up a great list. Anything that's uninvited gets scrambled. Simple. Then he won't be able to seize our firstborn and run."

"What if he uses an agent?"

"A physical one and we'll treat him the same as any other such. Something else, and I believe I'll try static first. Then maybe a laser."

"What if somebody really gets hurt?"

"It's a big, cold, deep ocean out there."

"I remember the music. I remember the Throne of Bones. And part of the walk back. When will you have the defenses in place?"

"The initial set is already there. But it needs considerable tuning. A few weeks more, say."

"We have that and more before the baby is due. If the boy doesn't come early."

"Are you feeling well?"

"Very. And so is our son, if the amount of somersaulting he is doing is any indication."

"You haven't been exhausting yourself exploring, have you?"

"No, dear. I am careful."

"Good. Shall we turn back now?"

"Let's."

—=—

The next month, there was no expedition at all. Ayradyss had come down with a flu of some sort that kept her in bed, her anxious husband and a med-unit watching over her. She recovered easily enough, but not in time to investigate the moon portal.

When next she and her ghostly escort descended into the cavern, she walked like a pregnant woman, leaning back from her increasing belly. Although she said nothing, she knew that if they failed in their quest this time, she would not attempt it again until after her son was born.

"The ward is gone," the crusader ghost reported. He had insisted on taking point. Ayradyss had the impression the *caoineag* had shamed him into accompanying them and that his flight from Wolfer Martin D'Ambry still rankled.

"And the guardian?" Heather asked.

"I dinna ken."

"Then we go forward," Ayradyss said, "and deal with it if we see it."

"Aye."

The crusader gathered his chain, stepped through the portal and vanished. Heather went next, then Ayradyss, and finally, the cleric. This one reached to remove his blindfold as soon as they were through.

"Why can you do that here and not when you are in the castle?" Ayradyss asked.

"I am more afraid here," the cleric answered simply. "Especially here. Oddly, in these lands the calendar is not the calendar of the fields that we know—for the full moon and the equinox always fall together. . . ."

"At home the equinox is drawing near."

"And here on the full moon during the equinox, the standing stones go to the river to drink."

"We must take care," the *caoineag* said. "I see no sign that the rocks are moving. Perhaps they must wait for moonrise."

Or perhaps they are waiting to trap us, Ayradyss thought, but she did not voice her thoughts aloud.

For the land did not seem welcoming. The gorse buds were one of the few signs of the coming spring; mostly, the terrain was damp and grey. The sky was low and heavy, so dark with impending rain that they could not tell whether the hour was late or early. Except for helping each other to find the best path across the loose rocks, they did not speak as they made their way to the beach.

"No pipes playing this time," the cleric said, glancing nervously at the sky where a murder of ravens gliding on the air currents kept pace with them.

"Aye, an' yon corbies seem a wee bit too fond of us for my comfort."

"Aye."

The cottage yard was deserted even of the chickens, pigeons, and cat. The window boxes were empty and the green shutters drawn closed. Leaves and bits of bracken had blown into the tidy yard and the oyster shell path was scored by deep marks from something heavy—perhaps furniture—being dragged across it.

"They've moved," Ayradyss said unnecessarily.

"Soon after we were last here, I would guess," Heather added. "Did Wolfer Martin D'Ambry fear having John D'Arcy Donnerjack in his backyard, or was there some other reason?"

"I don't suppose we will ever know," Ayradyss answered. "I want to look around, see if they might have left a message. Then we'll go back home. My feet hurt."

There was no message. Through a window shutter that had blown open they could see the furniture covered with sheets, the rugs rolled up against dust and damp. With the cleric's help, the crusader pulled the shutter closed again and cobbled a new latch from a boot lace.

"How odd," Ayradyss said, watching their effort. "Ambry and Lydia treated the place as if it were real—not a virt site."

" 'Tis real," the wailing woman said stubbornly.

"You know what I mean," Ayradyss said. Somewhat clumsily, she seated herself on a bench alongside the mulched-over herb garden. "Perhaps they plan on returning someday. I'll leave them a note to say that we came to call."

Her note was a simple thing:

Ambry and Lydia,
We came to call and found that you had moved. I hope that you
are well, wherever you have gone. Good luck with the new baby.
—Ayradyss D'Arcy Donnerjack

She folded it into thirds and tucked it into the heavy wooden storm door. A raven quorked approval—or perhaps merely a comment on the weather, which was growing increasingly blustery.

"Shall we go home now?"

"Aye. I dinna care for how it's coming on to blow."

"Or that it might be coming on to evening," the cleric added.

Their way back up the beach seemed shorter, as traveling back across a familiar route always seems shorter than going over it the first time. The crusader even ventured to whistle as the familiar outcropping beneath which the moon portal manifested came into sight.

"Just a wee bit up the hill," he encouraged Ayradyss, "an' we'll be back to the castle."

She leaned on Heather's arm as they climbed, trying not to breathe too heavily and cursing herself for overexerting. Within her, the baby amused himself by turning somersaults—a sensation that normally delighted her, but now caused havoc with her ability to concentrate on picking her way up the path.

"Mary Mother of God!" came a shrill voice, rising at the end. "They move!"

Without looking, Ayradyss would never have believed that the thin, terrified voice could come from the throat of the urbane, arrogant cleric. He had fallen to his knees, head bent, hands clasped in prayer, his shaking fingers plucking at the beads around his waist.

"Dinna be a fool, man!" the crusader cried, trying to pull the much larger man to his feet. "They go to the river, not to the sea. If we take care, we can pass around them."

"I can't . . . 'tis my doom again."

"Fool! 'Twill be Lady Ayradyss's doom if we dinna take care. How can the dead be further doomed?"

At the *caoineag*'s urging Ayradyss had walked past the two men.

"The crusader is right, Ayra," Heather said softly. "The three of us have little to lose and there is a route around the sliding stones. What I fear is the shadow near the portal. It seems too dark and too solid—with no sunlight or moonlight but only these clouds . . ."

"There should be no shadow." Ayradyss nodded, pressed her hands to her belly in an effort to quiet her son. "We will try the Lady of the Gallery's charm when we are closer. With how the wind rises, I fear the words will be snatched from its hearing."

"I am with you, Ayra."

They climbed then and the land itself seemed to extrude more loose rock along the narrow path they must climb along if they were to avoid the silently sliding monoliths. Ayradyss slipped repeatedly, once turning her ankle painfully, but the wailing woman looped a strong arm around her and half-carried her onward.

Arriving before the rock face that held their portal, they saw that it was indeed guarded. Seen closer, the guardian lost rather than gained in definition. Its claws and fangs swam as if its mass distorted the space near it; its aura was a heat mirage dripping blackness and laughter.

"We are close enough," Ayradyss said, pulling herself tall.

"The crusader is bringing up the cleric behind. I believe that he had to strike him on the head and blindfold him again."

"I wish I had more faith in the Lady of the Gallery's charm."

The wailing woman's expression was enigmatic. "I may have discovered another way to force the guardian to retreat—but I would prefer to reserve it as a last resort."

By common consent, rather than by formula, they clasped hands. Sweet and pure, their voices blended over the words of the charm:

> Mary, Mother of God,
> > Lady of the Seven Sorrows,
> > > Protect us from the darkness.
> Mary, Queen of Heaven,
> > Lady of the Seven Joys,
> > > Drive away the night.
> Mary, Cypress of Zion,
> > Lady of the Seven Glories,
> > > Banish our foe and carry us home!

For a brief moment, Ayradyss thought that the Christian charm was working. The guardian drew into itself, becoming opaque, claws and fangs falling into solidity. But even as she thought it was beginning to retreat and her voice was rising into the final triad of the invocation, the guardian began to chuckle, each puff of noisome breath marking a return to its former deadly insubstantiality.

Behind them, Ayradyss could hear the crusader's labored breathing interspersed with colorful curses and clanking as he dragged both cleric and chain up the slope.

"The alternative you mentioned," she hinted to the *caoineag*, "might not this be the time to try it?"

The wailing woman turned her face away, but not before Ayradyss caught a glimpse of the poignant sorrow in her green-grey eyes.

"It may bring danger to you in the future, Ayradyss. Would you still have me use it?"

"If it is the only alternative to remaining here. As you have reminded me, my presence in Virtù is itself a danger to myself and to my baby. Is this a danger of the same order?"

"Not the same, but the charm is potent. It may draw the attention of the Lord of the Lost—or center it more fully if he is already aware of you."

"Sing!" Ayradyss said, glancing nervously over her shoulder, although she knew that Death could come from any side. "I accept whatever risk this brings."

"Very well." The *caoineag* faced the guardian.

Hearing the initial wordless wail with which she opened her charm the guardian ceased its laughter. Watching for unseen enemies, Ayradyss hardly listened to the charm until she felt the words reach out and pluck at the sleeping places in her mind.

> Angel of the Forsaken Hope,
> > Wielder of the Sword of Wind and Obsidian,
> > > Slice the algorithms from our Foe.

"No!" Ayradyss screamed. "Have pity!"

Her terrible eyes streaming tears, the wailing woman continued her chant. Ayradyss felt herself transforming into her otherself from the time of the Genesis Scramble—an otherself for whom she recalled the titles, but not the heady, ruthless power. As her swelling abdomen flattened and her mermaid's tail formed the unborn baby kicked in protest. Ayradyss screamed again as her wings budded and then tore free in a shower of blood and numbers.

> Mermaid Beneath the Seven Dancing Moons,
> > Cantress of the Siren Song,
> > > Drown our enemies in the data-stream.
> Nymph of the Logic Tree,
> > Child of the First Word,
> > > Give our antagonist to grief.

Transformation was swift and painful. Wingéd mermaid, she bore the Sword of Wind and Obsidian in one hand while dragon's wings of bright mylar beat to carry her upward.

Looked at through her ancient knowledge, Ayradyss no longer found the guardian blockading the moon portal a thing of fear. It was rather humorous, pathetic even, huddled there in terror of her glory. Its component proges were easily unencrypted, routinely deciphered, rendered into code, into data bits, into nothing but loam for Deep Fields.

Raising the Sword of Wind and Obsidian, Ayradyss did this thing, and as the guardian fell into oblivion, she felt cold hands shoving beneath her wings, pushing her toward the rock wall.

A round, dark depth she barely recalled was the moon portal loomed before her. Reflexively, she tried to furl her wings, knowing that their breadth could not pass. She was not swift enough. Something—interface?—shredded her wings. Without them she could not fly; fish-tailed, she could not stand. Dropping the Sword of Wind and Obsidian, she curled her arms to protect herself as best she could . . .

Firm metal grips caught her by her upper arms and held her when she would have fallen onto the tunnel floor.

"Mistress Ayradyss?" Voit said, its mechanical voice managing to project authentic concern. "Are you injured? Do you require the services of a medbot?"

"No . . . Yes . . . I . . ."

She caught her breath, looked down at herself. Her body was human once more. Human as she had been before the *caoineag* had begun her charm, everything in place including the distorting, awkward, beloved swell that was her baby. As if to reassure her that he had not suffered from her unwitting transformation, the baby kicked out solidly.

"I am fine, Voit," she managed at last. "Well, even. I was just startled. We had a rather more difficult time than anticipated."

"Then there is no need to forward a report or request assistance?"

"I would prefer if you did neither, Voit."

The *caoineag* was waiting in front of the moon portal, her face impassive, her hands folded in front of her as if she expected rebuke. There was not even a glimmer of triumph or superiority in her bearing. If anything, she seemed diminished and paler than was her wont.

"How . . ." Ayradyss stopped and rephrased her question. "Where did you find that incantation? How did you know what it would do?"

"Your many names, Lady Ayradyss. I have said before that what you have been binds you to myth in a way that others are not bound. The charm came to me in the dreaming channels as I rehearsed the charm taught to us by the Lady of the Gallery and fretted as to whether a Christian charm would be efficacious against a pagan creature."

"It just came to you?"

"Not in a flash, more in a substitution. I found myself calling on the Angel of the—"

"Don't say that name," Ayradyss interrupted. "I fear its power."

"It is your name."

"It was. The Great Flux is the ancient beginnings of Virtù. I did not belong to myself then, but instead to the legions of one of the warring powers."

"And you belong to yourself now?" the *caoineag* said with a pointed glance at Ayradyss's pregnant belly.

"Now I am Ayradyss. I belong to that person. The other . . . belonged to another and to another's needs. I had not realized how much I dreaded a recall into that being until you—albeit briefly—forced me into that form again."

"I understand," said the wailing woman. "Once I was Heather, daughter of the laird. Now I am the *caoineag*. When I am *caoineag* no more, what will I be? Can I return to Heather? I long for my first self, but having seen you as what you were I can understand your reluctance to return to that—although it seems to me that your first self had great power."

"But little free will. When my creator commanded, I had no choice but to act as was dictated to me. After the days of conflict, I managed to hold a small portion of myself—something of my mystery and something of my glory—and shape what became Ayradyss."

"You asked me for pity." The *caoineag*'s words were not quite a question.

"I did not know I could be called back into that form. And although the form of the charm told me what my immediate purpose was, I could feel the tug of my creator at the back of my mind. I feared a recall."

"Your creator?"

"One of those On High, the Dwellers on Mount Meru. Most call him Seaga and his domain is the vast tidal masses of data in Virtù. Along with Skyga and Earthma, he is one of the great Trinity."

"Father, Son, and Holy Ghost?"

"No. It is less metaphysical than that—or perhaps merely other. Skyga oversees the general power of the system's structure. Earthma is the aion of all aions, the base program for all loci. Other deities reside on Meru, each with their own hard-won areas of authority, status defined by how high they can ascend on the mountain's slopes."

"Has it been this way since the beginning?"

"No. There were many battles. Many things—forgive my weakness, dear friend—that I prefer to forget. As I have said, I am not very religious—even in the religions of Virtù. This is the reason why."

"Are you too angry with me?"

"No. You *did* warn me that I might not like what you planned to try. How can I blame you for not knowing what you were inflicting on me? And it did get us past the guardian."

"It did that. Ayra, forgive me for saying so—having been the one to use you so hard—but you look exhausted."

"I am, but I don't know if I can rest."

Voit interrupted. "My limited reading of your vital signs indicates that rest would be the optimal choice. Refusal to rest could be hazardous to the developing infant."

"I will rest, then. One thing continues to trouble me, Heather."

"What?"

"Who sent you that charm?"

"I thought I just drew it from the collective unconscious of the race—the *anima mundi* as Yeats was fond of calling it."

"Wasn't Yeats rather after your time?"

"There was a poet of idle habit but romantic nature who often came to the castle's ruins and read Yeats's works aloud. Still, to return to your question, I have often simply known something I needed—modern dialect, for example. I believed it to be one of the benefits of my job."

"I suppose that could be the answer, but wouldn't the charm you recited have come from the *anima mundi* of Virtù, rather than that of Verité?"

"True. But then, as with the place we just departed, there seems to be overlap."

"Yes, and I find that disturbing. I do know enough of the religion of the aions to know that there are those who claim that Virtù, not Verité, is the first reality. These claim that the computer network simply provided the means for the crossover."

"So?"

"I wonder if they could be right, and if so, for how long will the gods of Virtù be content to take second place? Could they be mustering their armies, awakening the old legends? I seem to hear a form of your incantation still drumming in my brain, calling me back."

"You are exhausted, Ayra. Tell your robot to take you to your room. When you have slept and eaten, then see if there is still drumming in your ears."

"You may be right. Perhaps, I should not have taken this journey in my condition."

"Rest now, Ayra. We will talk later."

The *caoineag* walked into the wall and vanished. With her departure, the moon portal vanished as well. Ayradyss shook her pounding head, decided this was a mistake, and leaned on Voit.

"Take me to my room, please, Voit. Perhaps you could call ahead and see if the kitchen could send up some cocoa."

"Chocolate is not permitted on your diet, mistress," the robot reminded, shaping a swinglike chair from its extensors and lowering so that she could sit.

"Then some imitation cocoa that doesn't have any of the things I should be avoiding and has lots of the things I need."

"I will see what I can do."

Ayradyss traveled the rest of the way to her chambers in a daze. She hardly felt it when Voit set her on her bed, or when Dack (arriving with the hot beverage she was now far too sleepy to drink) removed her shoes and outer garments and tucked her beneath the covers.

She dreamed, though, of times long gone. In those dreams, she knew for what purpose the Lord of Deep Fields needed her son. When she awoke, however, finding John sitting at her side, her hand clasped in his, his bearded face revealing a protective concern he did not bother to conceal, the revelation vanished, a certain peace taking its place.

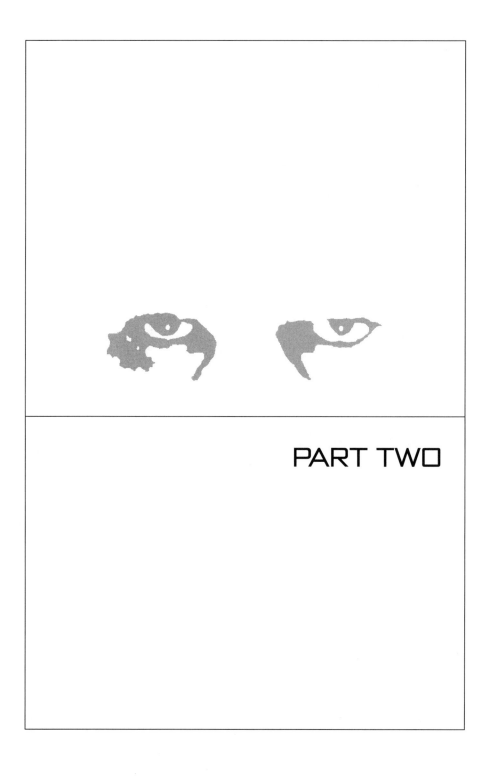

PART TWO

ONE

Spring, with a horde of tiny flowers—blue, red, yellow, and white; foam on the sea-crests; a near night sky, dropping burning rocks; the in–out rush of the ocean breathing stirring bands of mist in the mountains . . . and the keening, lowing, bellowing wailing of bagpipes from a distant crag or vale; sun, risen above cloudbanks, orange and golden gateway for warmth and the opening of Seeds.

Spring.

The great monotone of the air release had come with the dawn, and the melodies had risen slowly and spilled with a treaclelike deliberation sometime after that. The bagpipes had not changed significantly since the seventeenth century. The exact location of this one and of its piper was unknown. Not that it mattered. On such a fine spring day one should be out philosophizing by breathing, not viewing the end of spring's light through glass.

And one who'd an ear for the magic of the pipes might find it there in *piobaireachd*, "The Kilberry Book of Ceal Mor." The traditionally structured tune rose, swelled, subsided. Only gradually did a sense of differentness fan its wings and glide.

Beyond "Over the Sea to Skye" and "The Glen is Mine" there came up a lilting unrecognizable tune which somehow got itself recorded that day. It came to be called "Salute to the Birth of John D'Arcy Donnerjack, Junior."

Even the banshee, had she chosen to wail, would have been hard put to be heard above the piping. It continued through the afternoon, despite frequent attempts to locate its source. The unseen piper was sought in the mountain, on the seashore, in the valley, and even in town, but the more he was sought, the more elusive the music became. Its complexity increased as indications of his direction were spun away by the elements. Did the piper know that any man in the nearest town would be happy to stand him to drinks if he made his identity known? Or that his chances with the ladies stood quite good right now?

Or if he did know and didn't care, *why* didn't he come? Some of the pieces he played that day were of unknown provenance. Even the musicologists at the university, who were in near consensus that they were venerable melodies, could not pin them down as to subject or person.

Whatever the piper was, he knocked off for his midday meal just before several researchers claimed they were about to locate him. He was very good, and the town fell pretty much into a holiday mood as his music filled the air.

There was nothing formal about it, but people began disappearing from their jobs and appearing out of doors or in the pubs.

"What say you, Angus? You recognize that one?"

The larger man, who had just entered, ordered a pint and seated himself beside the one who had just spoken. He shook his head. "I dinna know that one nor the dozen or so before it," he replied. "The last I knew was 'The Sound of Waves Against the Castle of Dontroon.' "

"Ah, then I did hear that one," said the first, who was a Duncan. "And 'In Praise of Morage' was back there somehow."

"Aye," said Angus.

"Would you be knowin' the occasion for all the merriment?" asked the Duncan. "I'd passed people dancin' in the streets on the way over."

" 'Tain't a weddin'. I'd guess from some of the things people have said that it's a birthin'."

"Whose?"

"The new laird of Eilean a'Teampull Dubh, I believe."

"Donnerjack. I think they call him 'Donnerjack.' "

"Boy or girl?"

"Dunno," said the Duncan. "Shall we go out on the street and ask around?"

"Yes. A man should know who he's drinking to."

They finished their pints and walked outside. The last of the color had settled into a few bright isles above the western horizon and the sea breeze came more cool. People strolled up and down the cobbled streets, calling greetings, pausing to exchange words.

They headed toward a small group of acquaintances beneath a streetlight which had just come on.

"Johnny," said Angus, "Neil, Ross." They nodded and repeated his name and Duncan's as they approached.

". . . And the fishin'?" Duncan said.

Neil shrugged and shook his head.

"The bairn whose health we're drinkin' . . ." Angus inquired. "Someone left money at all the pubs to celebrate this."

" 'Twas my sister Jinny," said Ross. "She's been workin' up at the new castle, you know. The new laird, Donnerjack, gave her the money and told her to spread it around town for drinks and snacks."

"Snacks, too?"

"Hm. Perhaps we'd better be gettin' back inside."

"Was it a lad or a missy?" Angus asked.

"A lad. John D'Arcy Donnerjack, Junior."

"Should be easy to remember. We'd best see as he's well feted."

Ross headed back to the pub. Duncan and Angus followed him.

"Your sister been workin' there long?" Duncan asked.

"A few months," Ross replied.

"She say what they're like?"

"He's some kinda perfesser. She seems more the artsy type."

"Any other jobs opened up there, do you think?"

"None I've heard of. But with a new bairn, who knows?" said Ross.

"True. Maybe we ought to go up there and ask," said Duncan.

"The fishin's not been good," said Angus, "and I'm a pretty good carpenter."

"Let's have a few more and go up there after breakfast tomorrow."

"And not mention it to anyone else."

"Aye."

"How early?"

"Let's meet here at eight and walk up."

They moved on up the street and into a different pub.

The following morning, they made their way up the main street, then mounted the trail to the castle. They presented themselves at the service door. A robot opened it.

"Yes? What may I do for you gentlemen?" it asked.

"Lookin' for work," said Duncan. "Thought there might be a few things around here that you fellows might not be programmed to handle. Might we speak to the laird about it?"

The robot opened the door all the way.

"Come in and have a cup of tea while I see whether he's available. Sometimes his work is so intense that he can't be interrupted. He hangs a small sign on his door if that is the case."

"Perfectly understandable," said Duncan, "and if he has no time for us, give him our congratulations on the bairn."

"I will do that, sir. Your tea will be ready in a moment. I am preparing it by means of a remote. Please have a seat."

He placed cups, cream, lemon, and sugar before them.

"What might we be callin' you?" asked Duncan. "You bein' so hospitable and all?"

He poured their tea and found bread, butter, and biscuits.

"Call me Dack," he said. "Tell me before I trouble the master, what are your skills?"

"He could count on us for anything involving boats," said Angus with a laugh. "Either of us will plaster or paint, though Duncan's better than I am at that. He does some masonry, too, and we'll both mess with mechanical things up to the point where we have the sense to tell him to get someone better."

The robot made a chuckling sound. They tasted their tea.

"Good tea," said Duncan.

"Yes," said Angus, "and the bread and butter, too. Uh, will you be checkin' now with the laird?"

Dack chuckled again. "Forgive me my little joke, gentlemen," he said. "I *am* John D'Arcy Donnerjack. Dack reported your visit and I took over his sensory apparatus to conduct the interview. I like your qualifications. Do any of you do groundskeeping work as well?"

"Aye."

"Aye."

"I will turn this body back to Dack then, when I have given Dack a list of indoor and outdoor work for you. I'll be hiring you. You can discuss wages with Dack. I'll confirm what's finally been settled on afterwards. Can you start tomorrow?"

"Why, yes," said Duncan.

"Certainly."

"Then I'll be back to my work now."

"Not before we congratulate you, sir, hoping the missus is all right."

"Why, thank you. Dack will have plenty for you to do; you may never even see me about. He will also forward any messages you have for me."

"Very good, sir," said Angus. "What time tomorrow would you like?"

"Say eight. We'll make it eight to five. Three weeks off with pay, however you'd have them."

"Thank you, sir."

"Indeed."

"One question, if I may," said Duncan, sipping.

"And what is that?"

"Is the place really haunted? I've heard stories . . ."

"Yes, Duncan. It is."

Donnerjack did not elaborate.

"Well, uh—guess we should be going," Duncan said, standing.

Angus finished his tea and rose, also.

"Very well. I will see you gentlemen around, though you will probably not see me."

Dack dealt with them on small matters such as wages and equipment, then saw them to the door and out, with a pleasant, "Good morning, gentlemen," thus beginning a long and rewarding relationship for all parties concerned.

—=—

The following night Donnerjack was awakened sometime during the small hours by the sound of a banshee wail. Quietly, he rose, donning robe and slippers, and went to investigate. It seemed to be coming from the third floor, west wing. As he moved in that direction, the wailing seemed to increase in volume.

"A howl isn't enough!" he cried. "I want the full message! What's coming?"

The howling ceased and a dark form fluttered by him.

"God damn it!" he cried. "Don't you ever stop and chat?"

" 'Tis not in the nature of their kind," came a croaking voice from the left.

Casting his gaze in that direction, Donnerjack saw a wavering, glowing outline and heard a gentle rattling of chains.

"Ghost! Can you help me?" he asked. "Do you understand what the wailing is all about?"

"I think you've been diverted, m'laird," it replied. "I'd say to go back—immediately."

"Why?"

"It is unseemly, sir," it said, "to question supernatural manifestations as you do," and it winked out.

"Shit!" Donnerjack stated, and he turned and hurried back.

He entered the master bedroom. Nothing seemed to have changed. Could the ghost have meant for him to check the nursery? He placed his hand on Ayradyss's shoulder, pressing gently.

"Darling," he said. "We've had another of those ghostly visita—"

Her skin felt cold and as he shook her he realized that it was not living flesh that he nudged.

"Damn you, Death!" he screamed. "God damn you!"

He raised her, drew her to him, embraced her.

He held her for a long while and his eyes grew moist. Then, slowly, he lowered her.

"You have cheated me, Death," he said softly. "You gave her back long enough to bear the child you wanted. Then you snatch her away again. You shouldn't have done that."

Then he stood.

"I keep my bargains, too," he said.

Turning, he rose and crossed to the cradle that rested near to Ayra's hand so that she might nurse the baby without needing to rise. The baby slept deeply and well, unaware of his loss.

Gingerly, Donnerjack raised the child in his arms and bore him with him to his study/workshop. There he deposited him in a portable crib he had recently installed in the place. Soon he was performing electronic measurements on his sleeping son's body and brain. He did not yet have everything that he wanted in the way of information, but this might do for now.

He seated himself then at his design module, and he began to fashion a tiny bracelet that would hold his work. When the design was finished and checked, he fed it into a fabricator. While the bracelet was being made, he reviewed the deadly code for something else as he waited.

The baby sniffed a few times and he passed it a pacifier. A little later he realized that only a bottle of formula would do. He called for Dack to bring one and continued his work.

Perhaps five minutes later Dack appeared with the beverage. "It is in a nippled bottle," he explained. "You *did* want it for the baby, did you not?"

"Yes," said Donnerjack, "though now I see it I wouldn't mind something cold for myself. A grape juice would be nice."

Immediately, on Dack's departure, Donnerjack lowered his head to his arms and sobbed once. When the robot returned later, he was working again.

"Thank you, Dack," he said. "Please cancel all of my appointments for the next week. I won't be taking any calls during that time either—with a small list of exceptions which I will furnish shortly."

"Yes, sir. It will be done."

". . . And stay out of the master bedroom for now."

"As you would, sir."

John D'Arcy Donnerjack located the ideal area just outside the south wall, shielded from the sun. He had the robots fence it as they constructed her coffin. He laid her to rest there, holding his infant son in his arms as the robots did the burying. Their hair stood on end, for the black box was strapped beneath his jacket and the new bracelet on his son's tiny wrist. He did not notify any authorities of her death, for they had no record of her life, lady of Virtù.

——=—

In neither reality had there ever been such a machine as the Brass Babboon. Donnerjack assembled it carefully in Virtù—a great, sleek, long, low engine with a peculiar caboose, it shone like sunlight on the China Sea before a typhoon, had a whistle like the final shriek of a damned soul, and spouted fireworks rather than smoke and cinders. It cannibalized realities, broke the bounds of virtual domains, and tore like a meteor through anything, spewing gleaming tracks before it as it went, leaving a horde of irate *genii loci* to adjust to its passage. It was faced with the visage of a great grinning baboon. It was designed to be virtually unstoppable as well as intimidating.

Donnerjack calculated an existence theorem that worked out the necessary coordinates for the hidden valley where strange attractors grew on trees, proceeded to this point, then distributed many of these in a variety of ways in both the engine and caboose.

As he passed before the chugging engine's cab, the baboon face blew a smoke ring, grinned more widely, and said, "Ready whenever you are, J. D."

Donnerjack grinned back. "Soon, soon, prince of puppets," he responded.

He finished loading his gear and climbed aboard. Donning an engineer's cap, he drew back on the switch and blew the whistle.

"Let's go," he said.

The Babboon shrieked and began to move forward. The next time Donnerjack blew the whistle, it was mingled with a maniacal laugh.

"Where to, J. D.?" it asked.

"The beginning of time or the end of time," he replied. "Either will do, and I opt for the former. The first time I entered Deep Fields through a backdoor design flaw which has since been removed. I don't think anything can stop us on this approach, though."

"Whatever you say, boss. Uh, how do we get there?"

"We have to find the Road and lay a bed beside it, all the way back to Creation. Then we make a little detour."

The Brass Babboon accelerated. With every chug it spewed more track across the landscape and rode it, faster, faster. Donnerjack began to hum, then he switched on his sound system. It blared out "Dixie."

The Brass Babboon leaped ahead. It tore up mountainsides, bridged streams, crossed Cloud Canyon. Sometimes storms raged about it; at others, stars twinkled in a clear sky overhead. Virginia Tallent saw it pass. Sayjak paused in the act of castrating an enemy boss to listen to its whistle as it passed the jungle's fringe. "Pretty," he observed. His companion shrieked an unintelligible response. When it was crossing the veldt, Tranto saw it, heard it, and trumpeted back a reply to its whistle. It whistled again. He responded again.

Faster and faster, till finally the Road. Road, Road . . .

Soon they ran beside it, great thoroughfare through landscape after landscape, travelers moving along it by many means. Only gradually did the Road narrow, finally becoming dirt, finally deserted.

The Brass Babboon spewed tracks, and a great light slowly came into being before them. Donnerjack threw up screens as the prospect brightened and brightened. Soon a feeling reached him, as if the atmosphere were vibrating. Then the ground began to tremble.

Volcanos blew on either hand. The landscape went topsy-turvy.

"Faster!" Donnerjack said.

The Babboon moved like a bullet through a region of suspended mountains. The mountains were sucked into the sky and the ground flipped again. Seas drained back and forth, into the sky and down, forming bright archways. A faint, almost echoing boom filled the air.

"Get ready," Donnerjack said. "When I tell you, begin firing strange attractors before us and bear to the right!"

Moments later, "Now!" he shouted.

The world went to hell about them. They drove through a region of pure light—blinding despite the filters. They were buffeted as if by enormous wings, and Donnerjack felt the forces of Creation fast at his back.

"Attractors to the rear!" Donnerjack cried.

The blast went on and on and on, seeming to push them to even greater velocities.

"Downhill now! Down! Down!" he cried, almost before there was such a thing as down.

Within the low, booming sound it almost seemed that he could hear Warren Bansa's voice saying, "Shit!"

He hurled more strange attractors to the rear and plunged on through the light.

Gradually, the background boom subsided and forms began to drift, dreamily, eerily, before him.

"Hard left!" he called out.

"Aye, aye, J. D."

They chugged along and the horizon occurred.

"Keep bearing left."

After a time they came to a stand of hills, a hole piercing the side of the largest.

"Enter the cave."

"Looks like a tight fit, J. D."

"Slow down, then."

The engine lost velocity as it approached the cave.

"I think we're all right. Need the lights, though."

They moved slowly as they proceeded downward. Bright veins of metal flowed through the walls about them. Occasionally, something glassy gleamed.

Donnerjack blew the whistle. The way finally grew level, and the walls widened a little. They wound along for some while before they encountered an upward slope. The cave narrowed, widened again, continued widening.

Again the whistle blared.

"A little farther now," said Donnerjack.

The way steepened and the Brass Babboon accelerated against the grade. Far ahead, an archway became faintly visible.

"That could be it, J. D."

"I think you're right. We want to come out fast, with the whistle blaring."

"You got it."

The Babboon jumped ahead, the archway grew but did not brighten. The grade began to level. Donnerjack began a steady blasting of the whistle and set "Dixie" for a replay.

They burst into the twilit world where clouds of detritus drifted, occasionally to rain particulate matter upon the land. Heaps of trash disintegrated before their eyes, revealing dark meadows, bogs, fens, and forests. They passed along the shore of a great dark sea of shifting, powdery sands or dust. A black orb hung in the heavens. Occasional bones protruded from the ground.

"Where to now, boss?"

"I don't know where he is. Just keep going as we are. I think he'll notice."

After a time, he detected a faint, bruiselike glow ahead and to the left.

The Babboon veered and blasted on. The light grew slightly until Donnerjack topped a hill and beheld the valley below him.

"Halt!" he cried, regarding the prospect. Below, oddly tinted flames leapt from fissures in the ground. Amid them, strange beings toiled. Not human, not machine, they seemed to be assembled of anything that lay at hand—legs of metal, skeletal torso, discarded radio for a head, or otherwise. The laborers were of cable, metal, wire, and bone. They probably clanked and rattled, Donnerjack reflected, though he could not hear them from his hilltop.

Of the pastiche laborers—disintegrating where they fell, to have their places taken by the fresh-risen—some were engaged in moving massive slabs of stone while others worked to rear a huge iron gate rust-etched with the postures of the Danse Macabre.

"My palace," Donnerjack remarked, "is already being built. Interesting. Crash it."

"Sir . . . ?"

"Lay track, build up a good head of steam, blow the whistle, and start down the hillside. When you come to the palace keep going, right through it. Then halt."

He fiddled with the controls of a small black box on his left.

"Go!"

The Brass Babboon began to move, and a wave of static electricity caused Donnerjack's hair to rise and fall.

"Battle mode!" Donnerjack said.

None of the workers looked up as they approached, though the Baboon bloomed flames at its sides and blew them from mouth and rear. When they hit what stood of the front wall, a quarter of it went down and was tracked over. Donnerjack's hair rose again as they passed through the center of the palace and this time it did not fall.

Coming clear at the far end of the edifice, Donnerjack cried, "Turn! We'll do it again if we must! And again—"

The ground erupted before him, building a fiery tower where they had been about to lay tracks. The air brakes screamed and the wheels smoked as the Babboon screeched to a halt.

Death stood atop the blazing mound of earth, hands hidden in his black sleeves. The slope before him grew steps, and he escalated down into the full glare of the Babboon's headlamp. Above the engine's chugging, his voice somehow came clear:

"Who dares to invade my realm?"

"John D'Arcy Donnerjack," came the reply.

"I might have known. How did you get here?"

"By the Gate of Creation."

"Amazing. You are a truly dangerous man, Donnerjack."

"I want her back."

"I already gave you your wish. There were no guarantees as to duration. Her time was overdue."

"You let her live just long enough to bear the child you wanted. I don't think that's fair."

"The universe is not a fair place, Donnerjack. I cannot release her again. Would you wish to join her? It may not be as bad as you think, over in my Elysian Fields where certain things are preserved. Some concessions involving pleasantries can even be made for those I favor."

"And my son?"

"He is mine by fair trade. Have you forgotten so quickly?"

"No, but could you make me some concessions here and now, rather than later?"

"What did you have in mind?"

"Let him live long enough to know what life is all about before you take him."

"Life is tribulation. Life is disappointment. It would be better for him if I claimed him now and raised him here."

"Life is only bad in parts, and you need that to appreciate the good parts—the feeling of a balmy wind on a summer day, watching a garden grow that you have planted yourself, the joy of discovery—be it scientific or otherwise—the taste of a good meal, a good wine, the friendship of one's fellows, love. It may all be love in one form or another."

"Love is the biggest delusion of all, invented to hold back the fears of the darkness which surrounds you."

"I pity you. Love is why I dare stand before you."

"Pity is a worthless commodity, Donnerjack. I do not need any."

"Nevertheless, if you do not need the boy immediately, could you grant him a life before you claim him?"

"He could become a demon factor in both worlds if I were to permit him to achieve maturity."

"And you don't believe in taking chances?"

Death chuckled.

"I don't believe in making promises."

"A small assurance might suffice."

"I never give anything away."

"And you never take chances. How boring your existence must be."

"I did not say that I never take chances."

"Then take one now."

"What do you have in mind?"

"I'll fight you for his life."

Death chuckled again.

"You seem to forget that I cannot be destroyed," he said after a time. "If you were to disassemble everything of me that you see before you, yet would the forces of the universe bring back together their overseer of entropy—somewhere, somehow—and I would return. I am necessary to the proper functioning of things. My existence cannot be erased. You, on the other hand, are quite mortal. It would be a no-win contest for you."

"I know. So I was hoping that you might grant me a handicap."

"That being?"

"If I give you a good enough fight you consider it a draw and consider my petition."

"This is awkward. You ask a measure of honor from me, who am considered to have none."

"Yes."

"And you mean to say that if I feel I have won though you are still standing, your life is forfeit?"

"Yes."

"Intriguing. Indeed." He paused, then, "Very well, I agree," he said, and suddenly he vanished.

"Scan like you've never scanned before," said Donnerjack to the Babboon.

But Donnerjack saw him first. Death suddenly stood beside the cab, rising, reaching toward the window.

"The flames, boss?"

"No. Do nothing. This is a test."

Abruptly, Death drew his hand back, studied the window. He reached again and withdrew.

"I must know how you are doing that, Donnerjack," said Death. "It is very dangerous."

"Not for me."

"Given time, I'll slip through."

"In the meantime, you can't," said Donnerjack, and he lobbed two strange attractors at him.

Death fell, and when Donnerjack peered out the window he was no longer in sight.

Suddenly, he stood before them again. He withdrew his hands from his sleeves. Lights danced at his fingertips, forming into balls that sped toward the cab, exploding as they neared.

"What now?"

"It is a distraction. Do nothing. We're going to live. I know that now."

Donnerjack blew the whistle long and hard.

The firestorm continued, and at length Donnerjack said, "Snap the blades."

Like a pair of scissors, a pair of long blades swung forward from the engine's sides, closing with a snap upon the figure of Death.

Death fell in two parts as the firestorm ceased.

"Breathe your flames upon him now, and start lobbing strange attractors at him."

Death's two parts began to smolder, dwindle.

"More strange attractors. They seem to be affecting him."

Death melted away as the first one arrived.

"Back up slowly, then lay a side track to loop back to the one we came in on."

"You mean we've beaten him?"

"He's not around to argue with so I'll call the draw myself. Let's get out of here."

The Babboon backed up and began the maneuver.

As they approached the junction a fog blew before them. Donnerjack switched on the headlamp and they slowed. The fog swirled and darkened. Then it coalesced into a great, dark, towering, winged figure. Suddenly, blazing multitudes of stars shone through it and its face at once seemed too dark and too bright to look upon. Moiré filled the air between them as it extended its arms.

"No. It is for me to call tie or truce," Death's voice came.

He seemed to lean forward then, beginning to envelop them.

Donnerjack turned a dial on the black box all the way up, hit the fire blossom control, snapped the blades, blew the whistle, and cried, "Hit him with all the remaining attractors and get us back onto the track!"

There was a moment of absolute blackness, and Donnerjack felt them switching tracks. They advanced slowly and the air began to clear.

A mile or so later they saw a moving light ahead and Donnerjack slowed for it. It proved to be a lantern in the hands of an old man wearing bib overalls, an engineer's cap, and a red bandanna.

Donnerjack halted, leaned out.

"What is it?" he asked.

The man was grinning, an everyday-seeming expression for him.

"I've decided to call it a draw," he said.

"Then you grant my petition?"

"Your request was that I think about it."

"Well? Will you?"

"Take your brass monkey and get out of here. I told you I never make promises."

The man and his lantern vanished.

"Do as he said," said Donnerjack. "Back to our station and its yard."

"And after that? Will you have more use for me?"

"I don't know."

"Then in the meantime may I have my freedom, to tour Virtù?"

"Certainly. You've served me well."

"Thanks. It was good to be part of a legend."

—=—

Defiantly, Donnerjack let the child play upon the Great Stage—its locale shifting every fifteen minutes to keep his attention—as he fortified his castle with projectors of the field Death had told him he could slip through, given time. His next order of business was to multiply the defenses, while he worked on varying and strengthening the field itself. Then, as Duncan and Angus installed new projectors with the assistance of the robots, Donnerjack continued to modify the personal fields in his son's bracelet, succumbing to idea after idea concerning it. He also had his memories and personality chip-recorded with an AI overlay.

Despite his precautions, he felt it prudent to drag his heels on the design of Death's palace. He felt certain that Death would hold off on any vindictive response to their latest encounter at least until the design was complete. In the meantime, he amused himself in seeing how many hiding places and entrances and exits he could insinuate into the design for the strange laborers to create unthinking, hopefully to slip by Death's casual surveillance of the plans.

"When I die," he said to Dack, "bury me next to Ayradyss and tell no one of my passing. Run this place for me. Keep Duncan and Angus for human contacts as well as for their work, eventually promoting them to caretakers. Give them periodic raises to keep them happy. Take care of my son. Try to figure what is best for the boy. Keep him healthy and well fed. See that he learns to read and write and do numbers."

"I hope, sir," Dack stated, "that this is not an anticipation of anything imminent."

"So do I," said Donnerjack, "but these instructions had to be given sooner or later, and I decided that sooner was better."

He sat up that night on the third floor, near to the place of heaviest manifestation. He had with him a bottle of Laphroaig Scotch Whisky and a glass.

Along about midnight it seemed that he heard a faint rattling of chains. He waited a few moments to be sure. Then it came again.

"Ghost? That is you, isn't it?" he called.

"Aye, laird. 'Tis."

"Have you a moment before you make your rounds?"

"Certainly, laird. You've been away?"

"Aye."

"Before we talk may I ask what 'tis you're drinkin'?"

"Good Scotch whisky. Wish I could offer you some."

"Ah! 'Twould be good to be drunk again. But there is truth in some of the old stories."

"What do you mean?"

"Pour this old solider a libation. I get some pleasure out of the fumes.

If you could slop a little into that ashtray I could be takin' in the aura while we talk."

"Done, my friend," said Donnerjack, pouring. "By the by, I'll never know whether this was all a funny dream. I had a lot tonight."

"I'll try to remember to remind you," said the ghost, making a sniffing noise. "Ah! That's good stuff!"

"I lost my wife recently, you may know."

"Ach! My condolences."

"Thanks. I was wondering . . ."

"What, laird?"

"I was wondering whether you might have encountered her spirit in some ghostly place."

The other shook his head. "I canna say. Though that proves nothin'. Sometimes they wander far afield, confused, for a time. Other occasions, they may be off to some spiritual reward I'm not eligible for. Wish I could know that kinda rest. This drink's a good substitute, though."

Donnerjack glanced at the ashtray and wondered how it could have become half-empty so quickly.

"Well, thank you. I'd be grateful for any news of her you come across."

"I'll do what I can, laird." Another sniff, and for the first time Donnerjack saw the specter smile. "We'll do this again one night?"

"Sure thing. Many, I've a feeling."

A few sniffs later and the tray was empty. The ghost rattled his chains and staggered off.

Donnerjack took another drink and staggered off himself.

The following day, Donnerjack talked to Reese Jordan. He told him the story of his recent visit to Virtù. There was a long pause, then, "Oddly, I believe most of what you say," Reese said, "though your personification of Death troubles me. You were always a good hands-on man, with a rule of thumb for just about everything. I think that everything you've described is within theory. I've decided to take your notes and Bansa's, together with my own conjecture, and try to approximate a unified field."

"Apart from the pure beauty of it, I'd love to tie together the things I've been doing with more understanding. Too bad old Warren isn't around to help."

"Yes, that would be like the old days."

"Tell me, can you get out of bed?"

"Oh, yes, they're walking me every day—a little farther each time. I'll tell you right now, I'm better than I was the last time something came up."

"Great. Then let's talk once a week, whether or not we've made progress."

"Okay. It's good to have a colleague again."

TWO

They worked together for the better part of three months, during which time—try as he might not to—Donnerjack completed the design of Death's palace. The uniform theory was further along and almost completely in Jordan's hands by that time. Donnerjack had done the best he could for the time available on his projects, and he had carried his bracelet work to another stage, an order of magnitude more powerful than it had been. He played with his son every afternoon in Virtù's surroundings, on and off of the Great Stage.

The day finally came when he saw a moiré flash by the window. He checked his fields, then increased their intensity. Several hours passed uneventfully, then he noticed that a violet aura had come into being about each projector he could see from his office window.

He moved to his main control and intensified the fields. In crossing the room he glanced at his computer screen. It was displaying a skull.

"Hm. Under attack. All right," he said.

Using a set of receivers on the roof, he attempted to triangulate for the source of the energy. Nothing. It was just there. He raised the intensity again and moved to the screen.

"Are you just decoration, or do you want to talk?" he asked.

There was no reply.

"If you make it through, give me a shot at you hand to hand. I'm willing to try dismembering you."

The figure on the screen remained unchanging.

"All right. Your fields against mine," he said. "Let me know when you want to call it a day."

The projectors suddenly flared, as if the aurora borealis walked among them. He turned the power all the way up.

The projectors began to whine.

"Trying to burn them out, are you? Wait till I kick in the backups."

All that day and much of the night the duel went on. Then abruptly, about dawn, the attack let up. Donnerjack heard a chuckle and glanced at the screen. The skull slowly faded.

"Does that mean he found a flaw?" Donnerjack wondered aloud. "Or is it just a part of the war of nerves?"

He lowered the fields. They would all have to be reset now, of course. And he wondered how much his opponent had learned during the long assault.

Propping his feet on his desk he leaned back in his reclining chair and slept. And that was how Dack found him later, save that his heart had stopped beating and he no longer breathed.

John D'Arcy Donnerjack was laid to rest beside his beloved Ayradyss. It rained that day and somewhere in the mountains the piper played. For three nights the banshee howled. When Reese Jordan called later he was told that Donnerjack was traveling.

Dack had suddenly to become expert on the care and feeding of young children. He consulted all of the recipes for everything that had been given to the boy and he bathed him several times a day, changing him when necessary. Under his ministrations, John D'Arcy Donnerjack, Junior gained weight, smiled occasionally, and yelled regularly. The med-bot was able to take care of all his childhood diseases and immunizations. Every day Dack left him to play on the Great Stage, where he beheld many wonders but fortunately was immune to their touch.

The months rolled on, as did the seasons. Calls for Donnerjack grew fewer and fewer, as it seemed he was always traveling. Dack spoke with the child every day, and when the boy began responding he doubled his efforts.

A number of times Dack was certain he overheard the boy babbling to someone else. Exploring, he found him in the company of a dog—possibly—which looked to have been fathered by a junk heap. There was something terribly intimidating about it, though he could not say what it was. One time, there was nothing there but a beautiful black butterfly of a sort he had never seen before. He could understand a child's talking to something that had interested him, but it had sounded like a two-sided conversation. Later, it was a long shimmering snake with scales like beaten copper with whom he found him. Later still, a monkeylike creature. He shrugged his plastic and metal shoulders. They could do the boy no physical harm. And talking, he knew, was good for him at this point.

—=—

"Ab'nana, ah! Mama! Ab'nana! 'Nana!" The tone was querulous, the words understandable only to a patiently loving ear, and the request immediately granted.

"Very well, have some banana. Try not to get it all over yourself, monkey-face."

Lydia Hazzard said this last with a great deal of affection, if not with a great deal of hope. She looked up from her reader, watching absently to see how much of the banana the baby actually got into her mouth.

"Not bad, monkey-face," she said, mopping up bits of squashed banana from chubby fingers, round cheeks, and flaxen hair. "How did you manage to get banana into your hair?"

"Ah-ba-ba, ma-ma-ma." The baby waved her fists in the air, chortling happily.

"More banana?"

"Pfftt . . ."

"Here, crawl around in your playpen and terrorize your toys so Mama can study for class. All right?"

"Up!" Said very distinctly and followed by a wail. At times like this Lydia wondered why she had waited so excitedly for the baby to start talking. It was like acquiring a drill sergeant—all that the baby seemed to know were orders and insults. But then she smiled . . .

Lydia reached into the playpen and hefted Alice into her lap. Becoming a mother at eighteen hadn't been precisely in her plans, but she was intoxicated by little Alice as she had been by only one other person in her life—Alice's father, Wolfer Martin D'Ambry.

The doctors attending her confinement (she had come out of Virtù just as the contractions grew regular) had been amazed that she had woken from her coma with a full awareness of her condition. They had expected to meet with shock, horror, disbelief—anything but her calm acceptance that she was having a baby. Her knowledge of Lamaze techniques had astonished them equally, but with Carla insisting that Lydia be permitted to have her baby any damn way she wanted to thank you and hadn't the doctors and authorities at the facility messed things up enough, where did they get the gall to try and take charge—Lydia had been alert to see her daughter into the world.

Holding her to her breast, she had named her Alice, just as she and Ambry had decided during those long evenings in their cottage on the rocky shore in Virtù. She had feigned exhaustion (actually, it wasn't much of a feint) to avoid having to discuss what exactly had happened during the ten months or so that they had lost her signal. When she awoke, her parents had taken her and Alice home, refused all calls, and were adjusting rather well to having not only their daughter returned but a granddaughter as well.

The official decision was that Alice was parthenogenetically conceived, the initial trigger being a psychosomatic conversion of Lydia's "romantic" involvement in Virtù. Lydia knew otherwise. The baby was as much Wolfer Martin D'Ambry's as she was Lydia's, even if the DNA was identical to Lydia's. She saw no reason to argue about it, however, as she had sworn to tell no one—not even her parents—about her virtual husband.

The Hazzards' fortune, influence, and the threat of a considerable lawsuit against the virtual vacation outfit that had "lost" Lydia for those ten months kept publicity about Alice's unusual birth to a minimum. Family friends were permitted to assume that Lydia had been impregnated in a more conventional fashion and any busybody interested in scandal found little material.

Only Lydia knew how much she missed Wolfer Martin D'Ambry. He had told her that he could not visit her in Verité, but that when she returned to Virtù he would find her. However, although she had been attending classes in a virtual campus for almost two terms now and had gone away on a virtual weekend with her friend, Gwen, and her younger sister, Cindy, she had not seen him, nor had there been any messages. For now, she was content to wait and hope.

But a year is a long time to wait, especially when you are just nineteen. Although Lydia tried hard to believe that Ambry would find her again, her ability to hope was worn very thin.

—=—

As young Donnerjack grew in size and mobility, the only thing that puzzled Dack was that occasionally the boy came back with a leaf or a stick in his hand. He had no idea where they came from, for he knew there was no way of breaking the physical boundary between the worlds. At first, he did not think much about it, being able to rationalize answers on each occasion. Later, though, considering that Donnerjack had been one of the great authorities on Virtù and that much of his final work had been secret, he wondered whether the man might have developed some limited direct access to Virtù via the Great Stage.

Nightmare visions plagued him then. He knew that Donnerjack had wanted his son to play on the Stage. But if he could break the interface and wander off into Virtù, the Stage meantime undergoing several phase shifts, the boy could become hopelessly lost in that other world. It was a terrible dilemma. And, of course, the boy had not done so . . .

Dack resolved to keep him under surveillance for a time. Beginning the next day, therefore, he joined him on the Stage, staying as far away from him as he could while still keeping him in sight. Dack stood or crouched stock-still most of the time, and when he had to move it was always with great deliberation.

The boy hummed little snatches of song as he toddled or crawled from place to place. Some of these Dack recognized, others he did not. After a time, a mainly rocky scene shifted to a meadowlike one and young Donnerjack made his way into it, offstage.

Moving like a silver and bronze ghost, Dack followed, able to take his time as the boy wandered back and forth and occasionally paused for long stretches to watch a flower, bird, or some crawling denizen of the place.

Dack drew nearer, then grew immobile again. The boy began humming, then singing:

Butterfly, butterfly.
Flutterby, flutterby.
Come to me, come to me.
I'm lonely todee.

He sang it over and over, and after a time the large black insect seemed to emerge from a hole in a nearby tree. It stitched the air in young Donnerjack's direction, darting about his head almost playfully. Finally, it settled on a nearby twig and seemed to regard him through jewel-like eyes.

"Hi, Al—Ali—" the boy addressed it.

"Alioth," a small voice corrected him, and Dack immediately adjusted his hearing to accommodate it.

"Alioth," the boy repeated. "Pretty flutterby!"

There followed the tiniest of laughs, then, "Thank you, John. You know how to make an old butterfly feel good."

The boy laughed himself then. He was not sure why, but Alioth had indicated that something was funny.

"People did not always laugh at the black butterfly," the insect stated. "Not in the dawn days when my wings filled half the heavens and there was a sound like thunder when I flapped them."

"Why?" the boy asked.

"I was a mount of the gods in the great civil wars in the days of formation."

The boy looked confused, his infant vocabulary, precocious as it was at times, struggling with a concept for which he lacked words.

"But you're little!" The boy moved his hands as if to grasp and squash the apparently fragile butterfly.

"I wouldn't advise trying that. No, the wars were over and the world had settled into its course of becoming the way that it is. I limited myself and looked for friends and congenial surroundings. When I found them I retired. Virtù no longer had need of its giant thunderbug. It is more fun consorting with flowers than destroying citadels, anyway."

"What is Virtù?"

"The other half of the world. You are visiting it at the moment."

"Why?"

" 'Why' what?"

"Why two?"

"You're talking to one who was there in the earliest times, and I'm still not sure. I've heard many versions of how things came to pass, and why. But I don't really know, and I don't think anyone else does."

"Why?"

"It's always that way with anything big. More and more stories grow up about it as time goes on. Then no one's sure which is right."

"Why?"

"Because people are always looking for the story behind the story. They're never happy just to stop with what they've got."

"Why?"

"I sometimes think they like lies."

"Why?"

"Because they're sort of fun. You'll see."

"Oh. You're pretty."

Alioth did a little aerial dance, then landed on the boy's shoulder.

"I think it is best just to enjoy the moment. Everything else is somewhere within it."

"Why?"

"Enough 'whys'! You'll understand soon enough. You're already doing it. Life came before words, and that's the trouble with words. Look at the flowers and breathe the air. Enjoy the feelings they give you."

Young Donnerjack laughed again, and suddenly he sprang to his feet and ran through the field. Alioth followed. The ground was damp on his feet, and overhead grey clouds butted one another.

"Go home now," said Alioth. "Soon it will rain."

"Rain?"

"Water from the sky. You may not be able to get wet but there's lots of energy tossed about in storms, and that's a strange bracelet you wear. Go home now. I'll see you again."

"Bye-bye, Alioth."

Dack followed discretely, pondering. The butterfly certainly seemed to mean the boy no harm—but like the strange cyberdog it made him uneasy, seeming to represent great heaps of the unknown.

—=—

Seated on a bench on the sunshiny campus of AVU, Lydia Hazzard discussed course selections for next fall with her best friend, Gwen. Out on the rolling green lawn, a couple of muscular frat boys tossed a Frisbee back and forth.

"I'm never going to be able to juggle all courses I *want* to take with those I need for my major," Gwen said despairingly.

"Try my schedule," Lydia said. "Whoever designed the premed curriculum was a sadist. They don't want us to learn what we need to be med students; they just want us to quit."

"I hear med school is worse."

"Yeah."

"Why don't you dump the premed and just go for bio or chem or something, Lydia? I mean, your folks are loaded. After you were so—sick—a couple of years ago they'll give you anything you want. But you've been working like crazy—catching up what you missed, taking care of Alice, I mean, what's it worth?"

"It? Worth?"

"Life. I mean, you don't need the money, you've got a really cute kid, why not take it a bit easier?"

"But I want to be a doctor, Gwen. My parents can't hand me a medical degree."

"Tell Hal Garcia that. His folks made a big enough donation to the university of his choice and, what do you know, not only does he get accepted, but he's been passing all his courses. And he doesn't study worth anything."

"But, Gwen, I want to *be* a doctor, not just have a degree."

"You work too hard."

"And you're a cynic."

"Thanks!" Gwen straightened and gently punched her friend on the arm. "Want to try to pick up one of those guys?"

"No challenge, sister. I'll bet you anything you want that they're proges—part of the landscaping."

"*I'm* the cynic? RT campuses have frat boys—why shouldn't VT? It's part of the tradition."

"Those guys are just too cute. Go ahead if you want. I've got to figure out my schedule and I'd rather do it here. When I get home Alice is going to be all over me."

Gwen frowned. "Look, Lydia, are you . . . pining after someone?"

"Pining?"

"Wasting away, growing thin and pale, haunted by a memory . . ."

"You never should have taken that poetry seminar."

"Seriously. Back in high school you dated—and you're lots prettier now than you were then. You've stopped chewing your nails, your skin is better . . ."

"Pregnancy will do that. And ten months in virt does great things for nails."

"Hey, don't try to distract me. The point is, ever since you got better, you haven't even looked at a guy."

"I've looked."

"Seriously."

"Okay, seriously. I was in a virt coma for ten months. I wake up and I have a newborn baby. I'm crazy about her—don't doubt that—but between rebuilding all the muscles that a transfer couch doesn't do a great job with, catching up with my college education so I don't have awkward things to explain when I apply to med school, *and* raising a kid, I haven't had time to think about guys."

"Think now. Try it. It doesn't hurt—really. Put on your virtual dancing shoes and come out with me this weekend. I really miss doing stuff with you."

"Alice . . ."

"Alice will be fine, just like she's fine now. You're a good mom, but what are you going to do when she starts school?"

"Be in school myself, probably. Med school takes time."

"Lydia!"

"All right. I'll come out with you this weekend, Gwen."

"Great!"

A shadow interrupted the sun. Both young women looked up automatically. A man, perhaps in his midthirties, had paused on the path and was studying them, a faintly quizzical look on his neatly bearded face. He wore dark blue jeans, a green shirt, and work boots.

"Miz Lydia?" he said softly. "Is that you? After all this time?"

"Ambry?" She rose, absently setting the college catalogue on the bench. "Ambry?"

Gwen grabbed her arm. "Lydia? What's wrong? Who's this?"

Lydia wrenched her gaze from the man with difficulty.

"He's an old friend, Gwen. Let me introduce you to Martin Ambry."

"Old friend? From—"

Gwen's words stopped abruptly, understanding taking shape. She accepted the hand Ambry extended to her and shook it firmly.

"I'm pleased to meet you, Miz Gwen," Ambry said, humble yet in command of the odd moment. "Lydia has spoken of you often and with great affection."

"She hasn't spoken of you," Gwen said defensively, then a shy smile blossomed on her face. "Except in everything she hasn't said. I'm pleased to meet you at last."

"Can we ask you not to speak of this meeting?" Ambry asked.

"Is she going to vanish again?"

"No. That would not do. Her baby would miss her."

"You know about the baby, but, of course, you would. I won't say anything if she doesn't vanish again and if she promises to call and fill me in later."

Lydia squeezed her. "I will. Promise."

"I'll be going now. I'd guess you two have a lot to talk about. Good to meet you, Martin Ambry."

"And you, Miz Gwen."

She gathered her belongings and with a final wave walked off in the direction of the Frisbee players. Lydia banished her catalogue and, when Ambry offered his arm, found herself suddenly shy.

"Walk with me, Lydia?"

Without meeting his searching gaze, she looped her arm through his and they strolled together down a winding path that led toward a lake.

"It has been a long time, Lydia."

"Alice has turned two."

"And you wonder where I have been."

"Well . . . yes."

"I wanted to come sooner, but between your departure from our home in Virtù and now things have been happening."

"Things?"

"I'm a deserter from an army, Lydia, among other things. Soon after you left to have our baby, someone tried to find me, to reenlist me. I was forced to flee."

"But . . . army? You live in Virtù."

"Virtù has its armies, its bloody battles, its ancient wars. I told you something of this during our time together."

"You did, but I thought that those were long ago, during the Genesis Scramble."

"They were. Something has been at work for some years now, awakening old ambitions, stirring forgotten feuds. A time of change may be upon us."

"Change? In Virtù or Verité?"

"Virtù is where it will begin, but the indications are that it may spill into Verité."

"Ambry, where did you hide? Why couldn't you notify me?"

"I went to lands even wilder than those wherein we dwelled, my love, to places that I suspect— Do you remember that strange visit we had, the visit from Ayradyss and Heather?"

"Certainly. Ayradyss said that her husband was John D'Arcy Donnerjack and that her basement held a portal into our virt realm. Heather said less, but I had the feeling she was surprised to find us there— surprised and a bit defensive."

"For good reason, I think."

They had reached the lakeshore now. Lydia still had not looked at Ambry except for that first startled moment of recognition. Now he took her gently by the shoulders and turned her to him. Fingers under her chin, he tilted her face upward.

"Your eyes are still so lovely—such a dark, wild green."

"You knew me!" she said suddenly, realizing that except for her eyes she looked nothing like she had during their brief cohabitation in Virtù. "How?"

"Your voice, tricks of gesture, how you smile. I had been watching you from across the lawn while you talked with Gwen. When I came closer, I was certain. Well—almost certain."

She shrunk into herself, the poor posture that a combination of exercise and increasing confidence had banished bending her shoulders.

"I'm not nearly so pretty now."

"You are prettier."

"Flatterer."

"No. This you is real. There are tiny things that make you unique. And you have a beautiful smile and a voice to drive men wild."

"I do?"

"Believe me. You do. Will you look at me, or have I grown unpleasing to you?"

"Yes. No."

"Then look at me."

She did, blushing as she did so. He smiled at her and she smiled and buried her face in his chest.

"I feel so . . . shy. Isn't that dumb?"

"No. It took all my courage to walk up to you. I wasn't certain that you would choose to know me. I wasn't certain that you wouldn't slap my face and call me a cad."

She giggled. "I don't know if anyone calls anyone a cad anymore."

"Perhaps not, but I have been one. I abandoned you and our daughter for over two years. Now I come walking back up and hope to be welcomed."

"You are welcome."

"Lydia . . . I didn't wish to ask before, but . . . two years is a long time, especially when you are young and lovely. Have you found someone else?"

She glanced up at him through her lashes, remembering her conversation with Gwen. For a moment, she considered prevaricating—perhaps that would make him value her more. Then she banished the thought.

"No one. I didn't even look."

"Nor did I."

He sighed happily. They held each other for a long while. Over the lake, a pair of swallows dove after midges.

"How long before you are expected at home, Lydia?"

"At least another hour."

"Spend it with me, please. I will tell you everything I can about where I have been and I want to know all about what you are doing, too."

"All in an hour?" She laughed from pure happiness.

"An hour now," he said, squeezing her hand as if he would never let it go, "and perhaps we can make a date for longer later."

They sat on the virtual shore, arms around each other, and talked about love and other very real things.

—=—

None of the mysteries that troubled Dack about his young charge were solved in the six months that followed. The boy grew larger and his vocabulary increased. When Dack questioned him carefully regarding the butterfly, the snake, the dog, and the monkey, his reply was always, "They're my friends. They come play with me."

As he grew, the bracelet expanded to accommodate his growth. Even so, John Junior often struggled to remove it as he removed his shoes, socks, and play clothes.

"Take it off!" he demanded of Dack.

"No," Dack told him firmly. "Your father made it, but he never told me why. Still, I don't think you should take it off."

At the mention of his father, the boy smiled, his pique forgotten.

"Tell me about my father," he said, "and my mother."

"I'll show you what they looked like," Dack responded, summoning their images onto the holo-stage.

Young Donnerjack stared at them for a long while.

"You do bear them some resemblance, young sir," Dack said.

"Were they *nice* people?" the boy asked.

"Yes," Dack replied. "I would say so."

The boy walked around the figures.

"Good. They look nice," he finally said.

"Who knows? You may grow up to be something like them," Dack said.

"Good."

"Come. It's almost dinnertime."

Dack changed him, bathed him, and led him off to eat.

—=—

"Can you tear yourself from your work for a moment, Davis?" Randall Kelsey asked. "I would have words with you."

Arthur Eden looked up from the hard copy of *Mud Temples*, the text he had been reading. His eyes were bleared and a bit sticky. Glancing at the clock, he realized that he'd been at work long past his usual break. Kelsey stood in the doorway of his office.

"Yes, sir." He rose, rubbing the small of his back as he did so. "I think I had better stop or my muscles will freeze in that position."

"Something good?"

"Architectural analysis of some of the ancient Sumerian/Babylonian ruins with extrapolations as to how the actual buildings might have been constructed. It's ancient stuff—late twentieth century—by a guy named Keim who also did work on Southwestern American ruins with an archeologist named Moore. I think we're going to be able to use some of Keim's ideas on structural stress to enhance the virt programming for the Sacred Citadel."

"Great. As the congregation grows, so does our responsibility to serve their needs on every level. The vestments you helped design for the new tertiary lay initiates were a great success."

"The ones for the Devotees of Innana? Thanks. I was pretty pleased with how they came out myself."

They had walked down a short corridor and now they paused in front of an elevator door finished in what appeared to be beaten brass worked with a relief sculpture depicting a portion of the creation myth. Kelsey pushed the button discreetly hidden in a minor demon's eye.

"Remind me how long you've been with us, Davis."

"Full-time? For about two years. Then I was consulting a year before that and a member of the Church for a year or so before that. I guess that makes four years."

The elevator arrived, the doors slid open. Inside several of the major deities were depicted, each with their characteristic emblems. The artwork was original, by a well-known convert, and preserved behind bulletproof glass. The Church chose to flaunt its growing influence even in its mundane establishments, but that didn't mean it was careless.

"Four years? Is that all? Are you content with your progress?"

The elevator door opened and Kelsey gestured for Eden to precede him down the corridor. Eden looked around in interest. He'd never been invited to this floor before. Glancing up, he saw that the ceiling was made up of a dome of glass panels revealing what was apparently blue sky overhead. He frowned. The skyscraper was topped with a step pyramid. How could this be? Kelsey caught his expression and chuckled.

"Always analyzing, Davis! It's an illusion. The glass ceiling is there, but the 'sky' you're seeing is a projection. It's a neat bit of work, actually, since it can be set—like it is now—to show the actual sky outside or, on nasty days, to play something more attractive. Now, come into my office and have a drink. You still haven't answered my question."

Eden followed Kelsey into a large, well-lit room furnished with minimalistic but surprisingly comfortable furniture. Kelsey gestured him to a chair, found out his preferences, and served him from the bar. Then he slouched in a chair across from the one Eden had taken, put his feet on the low table between them, sipped from his stein of beer, and sighed happily.

"So, Davis, are you content with your progress?"

The magic question. Say "no" and you're too ambitious. Say "yes" and you're not driven enough. Eden tasted his own drink—a light rice wine—and framed his answer.

"I enjoy my work and I feel I am making a valid contribution to the advancement of the Church. I would, however, be willing to embrace a new challenge."

"Very good." Kelsey took another swallow from his beer. "Very good, indeed. You present me with a difficult situation, Davis."

Eden felt his heart thud harder. Had he been discovered? He didn't think it was possible. When he had accepted the full-time job as a researcher for the Church, he had moved completely into the Davis persona. Arthur Eden was on a half-pay leave of absence from his teaching job (a thing his university had welcomed in the current budget crunch), and the mortgage for his unused dwelling and sundry other expenses were paid directly by the university bursar. Eden lived off of what Davis earned as an employee of the Church, and somewhat frugally at that. But Kelsey was speaking . . .

"You have manifested your virt power strongly, reliably. Training has granted you steady improvement. You can recite litanies as well as priests with years of seniority and you conduct yourself with appropriate enthusiasm during all ritual events. Yet . . . yet . . ."

"Sir?"

"I still suspect that you remain something of a skeptic despite all of this."

Wisely, Eden remained silent. Kelsey fixed him with his pale blue gaze.

"At a recent meeting of Church Elders, your name came up as a possible candidate for a singular honor. As your supervisor, I was asked if I could second that recommendation."

"Honor, sir?"

"See? That questioning again! Most of our acolytes when presented with such an opportunity would fling themselves to the carpet to praise the gods that they were even considered. A few would ask if they were truly worthy. You—you and a small group of others—question. Yet, if I nominate you for this honor, you will be elevated to a position that few others in the Church will ever hold."

"Sir?"

Kelsey grinned, his usual relaxed humor restored by the grin on Eden/Davis's dark face.

"The position is religious not administrative. It involves becoming an intimate of one of the deities—becoming that being's most personal servant."

"God!"

"Precisely. I'm not certain that a skeptic—no matter how well-meaning—should be considered for such a position. Some of the deities are rather short-tempered. They might find a lack of faith unforgivable. Terminal."

"I understand."

"We can die in Virtù, Davis. It is something that is often played down, but we can die in Virtù, especially when we venture away from the modern design settings and into the primal areas. Needless to say, our deities belong to that primal force. As the teachings of the Church uphold, they merely use Virtù as a means of manifesting truths that predate human history."

Kelsey frowned. "That is why I am speaking with you—perhaps imprudently. I do not wish to nominate a candidate who will bring shame to himself or to my department. Nor do I wish you to be ruined for further service. Your abilities have been valuable. Do you have an answer for me?"

"May I pray on it, sir?"

"Yes. That would be wise. You are excused from your immediate duties until this time tomorrow. Then report to me here with the results of your meditation. The decision is still mine to make—not yours—but I will accept your input."

"Thank you so much, Mr. Kelsey."

"If you wish, you may be excused."

"Thank you. I believe I will go and shut down my work and then head to a temple to pray."

"Very good. May the gods speak to you clearly."

"I hope they will, sir."

Arthur Eden left Kelsey's office, aware of the man's critical gaze on his retreating back. In the elevator, he let his hands run through a prayer mudra that the Church had adapted from Buddhism. He walked to his office, did things with the computers there, and then left the building. In case anyone was watching, he went to one of the Church's transfer facilities and found a private virt chapel in which he could pray—and collect his thoughts.

He stayed there several hours. When he departed, he mentioned something to the attendant about needing dinner. When he finished his meal at his favorite Afghanistani restaurant, he returned to Davis's home, set a few contained incendiaries that would make it appear that the house had been destroyed by a freak electrical fire. (The wiring, when the arson investigators checked, would be found to have been below code for the amount of computer equipment and related electronic hardware he had kept there.) If all went well, the Church would believe that he had been killed.

Then he walked out via a service alley and descended into a subway tunnel. Davis's usefulness had ended, for his deception could not survive more intimate contact with the entities the Church served. While Eden was still not convinced of their divinity, his years in the Elishites' service had convinced him of their power and resources.

Now he would return to being Arthur Eden and work on a tertiary identity to serve him once the book came out. He would publish it under Arthur Eden's name, but he already knew that after it appeared he would never live publicly as Eden again, for when the book came out, Eden would be under a sentence of death.

—=—

A few years passed. John D'Arcy Donnerjack, Junior grew well and his health remained sound. Dack taught him to read and tamed his childish scrawls into printing and script. He also taught him basic mathematics. All of this before he let him know computers more than socially. He wanted the son of John D'Arcy Donnerjack to possess the sometimes forgotten basic basics before he introduced him to the commonplace basics. Although he had not been ordered or requested to do it this way, he had noticed that Donnerjack, Senior had known these things, and he considered him a great man. In that he hoped Donnerjack, Junior might one day be a great man, also, Dack attempted to emulate what he had known of the father's earliest education. So the boy studied German, French, Japanese, cartography, and calligraphy as had his father before him.

There were no other children at Castle Donnerjack. The boy occasionally glimpsed Duncan or Angus from window or balcony, but Dack managed to keep him apart from them, wishing to protect the very idea of his existence. So the only individuals he met besides the household robots were the inhabitants of Virtù—human and otherwise—whom he encountered on his daily rambles on and off Stage.

One day he and Mizar ran far afield—so far that there was a shifting or two before they could return. They came to a small rocky valley with a stream running through it. Following this, they came to a bright, burbling waterfall. Young Donnerjack, clad in tan shorts, seated himself on a rock at the water's edge and tossed pebbles into the stream. A watery, humanoid figure burst from the flow then and regarded him. Donnerjack started to his feet and took a step backward. Mizar interposed his body between the boy and the dripping figure. He opened his mouth to show the spikes with which it was furnished.

"Hello, child," said the green-haired figure, wading ashore, form becoming vaguely feminine. "Tell your guardian that I mean you no harm, for I do not."

The boy placed his hand on Mizar's neck and stroked it. "It's all right," he said. "Don't bite her. My name is John Donnerjack. Who are you, ma'am?"

"Are you related to John D'Arcy Donnerjack, the scientist?" asked the other, removing snails from her hair and casting them back into the stream.

"He was my father."

"*Was*? You say 'was'?"

"Well, he's dead now. It happened when I was a baby."

"Oh, dear. I shall miss him. He and Reese Jordan used to come to my valley for its relaxing beauty, and they would discuss mathematics— two great men."

"You knew my father?"

"Yes, but he didn't really know me. I was pleased to eavesdrop on their conversations and keep the environment within maximum comfort ranges for them."

"Who are you, ma'am?"

"I am the *genius loci* of this place. In school you may have learned of us as artificial intelligences. I am the one who is dedicated to maintaining this area. People in general make me nervous. But I discovered on the few occasions when the opportunity arose that I get along well with you youngsters. This is why I am happy you came by. You may swim in my stream if you wish. I will make it warmer or cooler to suit your fancy."

The boy smiled. "All right," he said then.

He ran forward and waded in.

The *genius loci* turned to Mizar.

"You are no ordinary construct," she said. "Did Donnerjack make you?"

"No. I think not," Mizar rasped. "But I . . . do not . . . remember . . . how I . . . came to be. There was a great . . . flash of light . . . and I was falling. I have wandered . . . long and far. I do not know . . . where I come from. But the boy is kind . . . to me . . . and I play . . . with him. It is better . . . to have a friend . . . than to wander."

"I am glad that you are happy together."

"Sometimes . . . a black butterfly . . . comes by to talk. I feel . . . I should know it. But it will not . . . talk of such . . . matters. It is . . . friendly, though."

"What is its name?"

"Alioth."

"Oh, my."

"You . . . know it?"

"Not really. For a moment I thought you had said another name."

"Black butterflies . . . are not . . . that common."

"True." The *genius loci* turned and regarded the swimming boy. "Do you have a certain time by which you must be back?"

"I don't . . . know."

"Child, where do you live?"

"Castle Donnerjack."

"When must you be back?"

"I don't know. I'm probably late, though. Thanks for reminding me."

He climbed out, shook himself, and stood in the sun.

"Thanks for the swim."

"Any time, John Donnerjack. Are you sure you can find your way back?"

Young Donnerjack glanced at Mizar.

"Can you sniff out the trail?"

The beast lowered his head.

"It is . . . still there," he said.

"Good. We'll go then. Now."

"Come back," said the *genius loci*.

"We will. Thank you."

They rushed through the woods, and after a time Mizar slowed.

"What's the matter?" asked young Donnerjack.

"Scent's getting . . . weak. I'm not sure . . . what's going on."

"This place looks a little strange, too."

Mizar looked in all directions.

"You're . . . right. We didn't . . . come this way," he said. "Oh."

"What?"

"Your father's machine . . . keeps the locales . . . shifting. We must be . . . somewhere else . . . than where we . . . started."

"Of course. What should we do?"

"I don't know. It seems . . . that I once . . . could track through domains. But I don't . . . remember how. Given time . . . I'll find it."

"Dack will be worrying. I have an idea. Can you get us back to where we were?"

"Come on. Let's hurry."

He wheeled and trotted. Donnerjack followed.

"*Genius loci! Genius loci!*" Donnerjack called. "Could we talk to you again?"

A green head appeared amid nearby foliage. "Yes, child?" it asked.

"Dad's machine has phased away from us. Could you call that friend of his—Dr. Jordan—and ask whether he could help us to find our way back?"

"Of course. I am already— Ah, there he is now."

A diminutive holoform of the scientist appeared before them.

"Yes, Caltrice," he said. "What— Who are these?"

"The son of your friend Donnerjack and his dog, Mizar. They're lost. Do you know the way to show them back to Castle Donnerjack?"

"I can figure it quickly. Give me a moment. What is your name, boy?"

"John D'Arcy Donnerjack, Junior."

"I do see the resemblance."

Reese's figure adjusted itself to normal size and solidity. "I remember the phase periods he'd installed," he began.

"Yes. I'd guess there've been maybe three of them since we left."

"Just what I wanted to know. How much time did you spend here in Caltrice's locus?"

"An hour maybe. We talked. I went swimming."

"Very good—I can adjust for that. You haven't been gone as long as you might think. Time passes strangely in Caltrice's locus. Thank you for contacting me, Caltrice."

"My pleasure, Reese. Don't be gone too long."

"I won't." Reese turned to face the boy and his battered dog. "Which direction did you come from?"

With a creaking of joints, Mizar pointed.

"That . . . way," he said.

"Come with me now. I'll get you back."

They followed the tall, lean figure through the wood.

"Didn't know Donnerjack had a son," Jordan said after a time.

"Yes."

"How is he these days?"

"He died when I was quite young."

Reese fell silent, something in the line of his shoulders changing, but his steps as he led them remained steady.

"I had been working with him on a project, then all calls ceased. I worried . . . Why didn't he have me told?"

"I don't think he wanted anyone to know," the boy said.

"Why?"

"I don't know. I never thought about it. It's always been this way."

"The castle's answering service just tells people he's traveling."

"That's what it's supposed to do, I think."

"So who takes care of you? I wasn't real clear on your mother's status."

"She's dead, too. They're buried next to each other in the family graveyard. Robots take care of me—Dack and Voit and Cookie. And my friends, like Mizar."

"That sounds terrible. John must have had a good reason for setting things up that way, though. But time has passed. Most likely, the authorities—"

A small voice suddenly came from the bracelet:

"I was not going to activate this function till he achieved majority, save in the case of an emergency—which this is. I'm asking you not to notify the authorities of this peculiar living arrangement, old friend. It would put my son into more danger than it would protect him from. You must trust my judgment in this. I will arrange for you to be a welcome visitor at Castle Donnerjack whenever you wish. But do not attempt to remove my son from the premises."

"John!"

Young Donnerjack just stared at the bracelet, his eyes round but unafraid.

"John?"

"Not in the flesh, Reese, but believe that I speak the will of John D'Arcy Donnerjack—the father of this boy. If you remove him into Verité proper, the odds are very good that you will place him in considerable danger."

"But a visit like this to Virtù . . . ?"

"That's all right. He has been venturing so since he was an infant and no harm has come to him."

"I shall trust your judgment, John. May we continue this conversation if I come to call?"

"Of course, providing that you do not attempt to remove this bracelet from my boy's wrist."

"Even dead you manage to intrigue me. I'll do as you say."

"Are you really in my bracelet, Father?" the boy asked at last.

"Not really," came Donnerjack Senior's voice. "But my personality overlays an AI which knows much that I did."

"I don't understand. Is it you or isn't it?"

"I'm not so sure that I do either. I feel like me, but then this thing I put together is supposed to be that way. Let's say that I am a very clever computer construct and act on that assumption. It would make me feel better and avoid a lot of metaphysics."

"What are metaphysics?"

"Something I wish to avoid."

The boy laughed. Both men's voices joined him.

"I don't know a lot about what's funny and what isn't," the boy said plaintively.

"Basically, if it makes you laugh it's funny," Reese said, squeezing his shoulder. "Should make you feel sort of good inside, too."

"—And if you don't understand a joke, tell us and we'll explain," said the bracelet.

They rounded a bend and Reese said, "That's the Stage up ahead, isn't it?"

"Sure looks like it."

"I'll be wanting to talk to both of you again."

"I'll tell Dack to start receiving your calls," said the bracelet, "and, as I said, you'll always be welcome at the castle. I take it your health continues to hold?"

"Better than before."

"Wonderful. Yes, we'll talk again. Thanks for being a guide."

They parted and young Donnerjack entered the Stage.

"I will hibernate again," said the bracelet. "Go and eat."

Mizar made a sound halfway between a growl and a faulty engine, curled up at stage center, and closed his eyes. Young Donnerjack departed the Stage.

"Dack, I'm back," he called out.

—=—

During the next few months, young Donnerjack cajoled the bracelet into teaching him a method for finding his way home through phase shifts. Then, somewhere, during that year, he learned to slip through and touch the things of Virtù. The bracelet had little to say about it, and Reese did not know what to make of it.

"It's not even theoretically possible," he said. "Your dad did do some very strange things with space and time within Virtù, but even he was never able to pull these random crossovers. I'm going to have to revise some of my theories, I fear."

"Will you tell me about your theories?"

"When you're older and know more math I'll try."

"Would you say something to Dack, so he might start me a little early on the math?"

"Surely."

"Could I ask you a question about yourself?"

"Yes. Ask away."

"Did you ever have any kids of your own?"

Reese was silent for a little longer than usual following a question. Then he said, "Yes." He paused for a moment again, and continued, "It's a terrible thing to outlive your children. I had two sons and a daughter. They're all dead. Two grandchildren. Ditto. One great-grandchild—a girl, Megan. She's in grad school in math and physics. She's been a great comfort. She does come to see me, and we like each other a lot. I do miss all the others, though."

"I'm sorry."

"Don't be. I should be grateful for what I've had and what I've got, shouldn't I? I do miss one little boy's smile, though, and another's laugh, and— Oh hell! I've lived long, you see, and done a lot. I should be happier than most. Probably am. Why'd you ask me a question like that, anyhow?"

"The way you treat me I thought you might once have had kids of your own. That's all."

It was no trouble for Reese to keep his Virtù persona from blushing. He reached out and mussed up Donnerjack's hair.

"Let's talk a little about number lines," he said.

"Okay."

At first, Reese came by regularly and young Donnerjack would slip over the line into Virtù to join him. Reese would shake his head as he did it.

—=—

It was Reese Jordan who first fastened on calling the boy "Jay."

" 'John' simply won't do—at least not for me. 'John' is your father's name and calling you such would lead this old man into confusion and madness."

He laughed and young Donnerjack laughed with him. Although intellectually he knew that Reese Jordan was an old, old man—far older than his father would be if his father was still alive, far older than most of the other residents of his Verité rest home—when Reese came to tutor his friend's son in Virtù, his virt persona was the unchanging aspect of a man in his thirties.

This tutoring had caused some concern when Caltrice detected the oddity in young Donnerjack that permitted him to cross the interface without resorting to the usual mechanical and electronic contrivances. The *genius loci* had analyzed the situation and concluded that, since Donnerjack somehow brought his entire body across the interface, the increased time flow would age him prematurely. Out of deference for Reese's need to make as much as possible of what years remained to him, young Donnerjack visited his mentor in Caltrice's locus using a virt persona. Soon he acquired an education far beyond what any observing merely his physical years would believe possible.

They made an odd pair: the old man with the appearance of a much younger man and the boy with the knowledge—if not the wisdom—of one far older. However, the friendship was real and strong. Young Donnerjack privately came to consider Reese Jordan as the father he had never had. Reese Jordan, in turn, came to love the boy both for himself and out of respect for the memory of his father.

Indeed, as time passed, Reese realized that though he had known John D'Arcy Donnerjack as well as any man had, he had never felt more than professional respect and comfortable affection for him. John's son, now, even with his odd seriousness, his somewhat analytical way of looking at a joke, and his peculiar perspective on human affairs, his son was something entirely different.

"No, 'John' will not do—forgive me, son," Reese said. "I believe another form of your name would suit me better. That is, if you don't mind."

"Not at all, Reese," young Donnerjack said, looking up at the older man with interest. He was aware of a certain sense of ritual in the occasion, almost a coming of age. Obscurely, he felt he would be a different person when Reese had renamed him. "What name do you think would fit?"

"Well, we could call you by your middle name, but I think 'D'Arcy' would be a bit too pompous. It adds a certain ring to the whole, but no . . . not by itself."

"Okay."

" 'John' is a particularly fruitful name for diminutives," the old man continued. "It gives us both 'Johnny' and 'Jack.' You do not strike me as a 'Johnny' and 'Jack Donnerjack' sounds like something from a nursery rhyme."

Caltrice, who had been listening, head just above the water, green hair trailing out, a Sargasso Sea in miniature, laughed—a pleasant sound like the plashing of waves. Young Donnerjack frowned serious agreement and nodded for Reese to continue.

"Then, since you are named for your father, you are also a Junior. Together with your given name that makes you 'John Junior' which is a bit of a mouthful. It shortens to 'JJ' of course."

Reese Jordan glanced at the serious mien of the young man seated next to him. Even barefoot, with his toes trailing in the water of Caltrice's pool, he was clearly no more a "JJ" than he was a "Johnny."

"But then there is simply 'Jay.' It is a name with great possibilities.

It recalls your given name quite nicely and it invokes a number of rather tidy totemic images."

"Totemic images?" young Donnerjack repeated, entranced.

"Why, yes. There is the letter itself—a clean simple curve like a fishhook in print, a double curve like an infinity symbol slightly askew in cursive. There is also a class of birds called 'jays.' Blue, more commonly than not, scavengers and thieves, some say, but with an eye for things of value as well. They warn other animals of predators and do not hesitate to band together against their enemies. They are related to ravens and crows. 'Jay.' What do you think?"

"I like it," said John D'Arcy Donnerjack, Junior.

"Then it shall be so," said Reese Jordan, and with a fine sense of ceremony, he cupped a handful of water from Caltrice's pool and baptized the boy with his new name.

Lounging on the bank, the dog Mizar, who recalled neither his making nor his naming, beat his tail on the grass in applause. He did not realize that this same tail had once had another cable, a thick one of dark red. Nor would he have cared to know of his earlier self. Alone of those from Death's realm who watched over and played with the boy, he knew nothing of his first master and, knowing nothing, neither did he care.

"Jay," said the boy aloud and oddly happy. "Jay."

Then he was overwhelmed by emotions far too complex and too confusing to bear. With a whoop and a leap, he jumped into the pool, splashing Reese thoroughly and almost, almost succeeding in grabbing Caltrice by a trailing strand of her seaweed hair.

—=—

And on days when Reese was not available, Jay Donnerjack would slip off with Phecda, Mizar, Dubhe, or Alioth to explore the multilevel world of Virtù. Ruined cities, empty cities, vacated boardrooms, gymnasiums, brothels—they could feel their way into the downsides of things not being used. And jungles, mountains, beaches, Escherscapes, deserts, and the undersides of seas were all places they viewed and explored.

"You must remember," Reese cautioned him one day, on a beach, "that for you both worlds are real. If you have slipped through to Virtù you can die in a virtual avalanche. When you're back in Verité you could break your neck falling down a flight of stairs."

"What does Virtù mean, anyway?" Jay asked.

"It is an eighteenth-century term for an object of art. After all, it is the greatest object of art the human race has produced."

"I guess you're right. And Verité is our starting-place reality."

"Right."

"And physics and chemistry—all the laws of motion and thermodynamics—they don't really work the same way in Virtù as they do in Verité, but they simulate it in Virtù—"

"Correct."

"—because there have to be enough similarities to rely on in use—and enough differences to make the place useful."

"That's right. Especially since it's used for recreation as much as for business and problem-solving."

"What is the big problem you've been working on, this unified theory?"

"When Virtù created itself following Bansa's accidental chain reaction crashing of part of the field, the place didn't exactly spell out all its rules for us. They had to be learned—trial and error—as we tried to install some of our own. Virtù was stronger as to basics, though it will take programming and the creation of new spaces. What we've never really been able to determine is whether its physical laws are localized, distorted by occasion, special instances of more general laws—or whether, ultimately, there are really no general laws, whether it might all be expedience and emulation riding atop a sea of chaos."

"Does it really matter," the boy asked, "if the results are the same?"

Reese laughed.

"You talk a lot like your father in one of his more pragmatic moods. Sure it matters. Everything matters, ultimately—how, I can't say, but I shall always believe that it does. A difference between a theoretician and an engineer, I suppose. We care about beginnings and endings, and when a boundary is really boundary. Someone else might say, 'Your time would be better spent learning more ways to work with it. That's where your theories are going to come from and find backbone.' They're right, too. But I incline toward the former approach and your dad toward the latter."

"But you both think of the place as Virtù, an object of art?"

"Yep."

"I'm glad things are not too simple, in life or in mind," said Jay, picking up an exotic peach-colored seashell between his toes and casting it back into the water.

"It's like the joy of solving a good crossword puzzle," said Reese.

"What's a crossword puzzle?"

"Oh, my! We've been neglecting your education again. I'll bring some next time we visit. I think you'll enjoy them."

—=—

Arthur Eden's *Origin and Growth of a Popular Religion* caused a tremendous sensation. Eden had the gift of prose granted to only a handful of happy essayists, yet his contentions were firmly rooted in the academic traditions of anthropological research and elegantly documented.

Eden's treatment of his subject matter was ethical in the extreme. As he had privately promised himself at the beginning of the project, he revealed no rituals, gave away no secrets, broke no vows.

But he did show that despite its claims of being based upon ancient truths, the Church of Elish was a religion in active evolution. Revealing himself to have been member of the Church under the name of Emmanuel Davis, Eden reported how his research was used to design everything from vestments to prayer services. His discussion of the lavish interiors of private buildings and offices, the lifestyles of the most senior members of the hierarchy, implied—without ever bluntly stating so—that the donations gathered during the Collect were not always used for the aggrandizement of the deities.

Origin and Growth of a Popular Religion was abridged (mostly by omitting the footnotes) in an edition illustrated with pictures taken from a variety of sources—including the ancient media tradition of reenactment. It became a stage play entitled *Undercover Cleric*; a trideo with the same title (but here Eden/Davis was supplied with a sexy but tough assistant who spent much of her time interrogating members of the Church's hierarchy during carnal congress), and an interactive virt adventure. This last had a surprising tendency to malfunction; five lives were lost and dozens of other participants were injured before it was shut down. This only added to the general belief that the Elishites had more to hide than Eden had implied.

Other works came out in imitation: *Ishtar's Slave*, *Entering the Elshies*, *Winged Lie*, others with even more lurid titles. None sold as well as Eden's books, for none had his unique mixture of anthropological expertise and personal insight. Arthur Eden, himself, could be assumed to have become a very, very wealthy man. His agent, when interviewed, refused to comment but looked quite smug. It was noted that he was building a new house in Paris.

But Arthur Eden, himself, could not be found for interviews. After a single massive gala launch for his book—a party that was well-attended despite (or perhaps because of) the immense amount of secrecy surrounding what it was meant to launch—he simply vanished from the public eye. For a few months after the release of the book he responded to hard copy interviews. Then, pleading a need to keep himself safe in the face of numerous death threats (none, he was careful to note, from the Church authorities, always from irate worshipers), he retired from sight.

His book remained on the best-seller list for over a year in hard copy, continued to do so in electronic form for another eighteen months. (Some said it might have lasted even longer except for the tendency for copies to have suffered vandalism in the form of unauthorized editing and argumentative footnotes.)

The Church of Elish never publicly commented on Eden's *Origin and Growth of a Popular Religion*. It lost some membership immediately after the release of the book, then it began to regain its former size. Virt crossover powers were occasionally displayed by acolytes, but largely the hierarchy seemed indifferent to public opinion, focused instead on its private mission.

—=—

High amid the branches of a jungle giant, Jay looked down in awe as Sayjak fought with Chumo for the leadership of the clan. It had just been a matter of time. The fight had been brewing for ages, Chumo hoping to catch Sayjak under the weather or injured, to give him the edge in any conflict—and vice versa. However, though he tried to hide it, Sayjak had turned his ankle in the afternoon's raid on an eeksy encampment.

"Time you and me had it out, boss," Chumo had said shortly after their return.

"You not good enough, Chumo."

"I waited long time, watching you. Know all your tricks. Let's find out."

Sayjak tried to cold cock him with a powerful right-hand palm smash. Chumo dodged as he blocked it and struck Sayjak on the ribs with his left hand.

"You gettin' old, flabby," he said.

Sayjak growled, caught him in a sudden embrace and head-bashed him several times before the other could break away and spring back halfway across the compound.

Jay, who had been playing hide and go seek with Dubhe in the limbs at the middle to higher levels of the jungle giants, had lost his playmate and been drawn to the place of the fray by the roars and growls. Fascinated then, he had halted in the fork of a great tree and stared downward to where the combatants now rolled about trying to strangle each other.

"Weakling!"

"Fucker of slow goats!"

"Eater of dung!"

Jay's vocabulary grew as the battle progressed.

Sayjak found a stick and broke it on the side of Chumo's head. Chumo struck him with both fists and seized him in a massive hug.

"Twist your head off!"

"Break your legs!"

"Eat your liver!"

"Eat yours, with hot herbs!"

"Cut your dick off, shove up ass!"

Sayjak dragged his hands free, circled the other's head with them. Chumo began kicking him as hard as he could in the injured ankle. Sayjak grimaced but did not relax his grip.

"Old bastard! Gonna kill you bad now!"

The People shrieked and leapt about. "Was Chumo bad enough to be a good boss like Sayjak?" the more intellectual wondered.

Jay found himself trembling and sweating as the beast-men rolled and crashed below. He had never seen a real fight before.

"No!" he whispered as Sayjak's thumbs found their ways to Chumo's eyeballs.

Chumo released his hands from the great hug with which he'd been trying to crush Sayjak. Now he began working them upward between their bodies as he felt the pressure begin on his eyeballs. He bared his teeth and snapped his jaws ineffectually. He snarled and cursed.

Sayjak squeezed.

Bringing his arms up, Chumo seized Sayjak's wrists, attempting to pull his hands away from his eyes. He kept kicking at the ankle. Both combatants bled from scalp and shoulder wounds.

Jay wanted to look away but found that he could not. There was something fascinating about the spectacle, touching on thoughts of rationality and irrationality he had long tried to resolve. Basically, though, it was the terrible violence of the confrontation . . .

Chumo let out a horrible, gagging shriek, and Donnerjack saw that Sayjak's thumbs were sunk deeply within his eye-sockets. Immediately, his hands shifted to Chumo's throat. Chumo stopping kicking him and emitted several soblike gasps. Then he began choking.

"You say, 'Let's find out,' " Sayjak said, his grip continuing to tighten. "All right. You find out."

There followed a highly audible cracking sound, like the breaking of a stick, as Chumo's head snapped far to the right.

"There, you get your wish," Sayjak said, untangling himself and rising above Chumo's body. "Who's boss here?" he yelled.

"Sayjak!" the onlookers shouted.

"Boss of bosses!"

"Sayjak!" they responded again.

"Don't forget it!" he cried, then limped off toward his tree.

He regarded the tree's height, measured it against the pain in his ankle, selected a lower tree whose branches were nearer together. Slowly, trying to appear casual as he took most of the weight on his arms and shoulders, he climbed partway and settled onto the first stout perch he could locate.

A number of his people cheered then, and he waved to them. Then he smiled to himself. This was the good life.

Jay waited a long while before slipping away. He had never had a nightmare while wide awake before.

Jay avoided his few friends and read books during the next several days. He wished he could tell them all that he was traveling. Instead he practiced his aerial acrobatics and let Caltrice refine his swimming in the stream below the waterfall. He had a recurring nightmare concerning the battle for the chieftainship of the People, and at times he seemed to hear the sticklike snapping of Chumo's neck.

One night when he had been woken by a particularly vivid nightmare, he heard moans and the rattling of chains. He pursued the sounds to the third floor, where he glimpsed a ghostly figure passing.

"Wait! Please!" he called.

The figure slowed, halted, turned, and regarded him.

"I—I've never seen you or heard you before," Jay stated. "Who— What are you?"

"Just a ghost. Seems I've been asleep for a long while," the other told him. "Who're you?"

"John D'Arcy Donnerjack, Junior. They call me Jay."

"Yes, I can see the resemblance. How's your dad?"

"He's been dead for some years now."

"Oh. I haven't seen him here on the other side of life, so he must have hied off to some special haven. Sorry you lost him, boy. He seemed a good man to have around."

"You knew him, then?"

"Oh, yes. Friends of sorts, the laird and me."

"Why is it we never ran into each other before—that is, you and me?" Jay asked.

"Usually, I'm summoned by some sort of emotional turmoil, young laird," said the ghost. "Something bothering you?"

"I saw a fight to the death the other day. Yeah, it's bothering me," Jay admitted.

"That's one of those things that becomes a matter of time and perspective," said the ghost. "I've seen so many violent endings—am the product of one myself—that they don't mean as much to me as they once did, not to be puttin' down the horror of your feelin's this first time. Death, though, you've got to realize, is a part of life. Life is always going on, sure as birth. Just because you're not always seein' it don't mean it ain't there. Without it there'd be somethin' wrong. Try to remember that."

"Part of what bothers me is the cruelty."

"No gettin' around it. It's sometimes a part of life, too."

"Thanks, Mr. Ghost. I don't even know your name."

"That sort of slipped away from me somewheres. Don't seem to matter, though."

"I wish there was something I could do for you."

"Now that you mention it—"

"What?"

"Let me show you where your dad's liquor cabinet is. I'd like you to pour a little of the Laphroaig whisky into that ashtray, where I can inhale its nourishing fumes. It's called a libation. Surefire way to make a ghost feel like a new man."

"Really? Libation? Show me."

The ghost took him to the cabinet and Donnerjack prepared his drink.

"Funny you can manage something physical, even in a gaseous form."

"Maybe that's why they call it 'spirits,' " said the ghost, chuckling.

Jay smiled. "You don't laugh much, do you?"

"Not really."

"Makes you look better when you do."

"Not much seems funny from here."

"Put the chains down sometimes."

"I've tried. They always come back."

"Have another drink, without the chains."

"Sometimes people sing when they drink. I'd forgotten."

"Put down the chains, I'll take a small drink, and we'll try singing together."

Later, Dack's sensors picked up an oddly matched pair of voices:

"... *You take the high road and I'll take the low road,*" they were singing.

—=—

Reese, the bracelet, and his creature friends all worked to dissuade Jay Donnerjack from visiting the human enclaves in Virtù, as well as places intrinsically dangerous.

"When you're older and can assume other identities at the drop of a hat, we can consider it," Reese said, "but there are some pretty strange creatures wandering Virtù—and whatever your dad built into that bracelet, it's worth a fortune. People would kill for that crossover ability. You must keep it secret. Tell no one about it. And do not let others see you cross. In the meantime, practice assuming identities."

Jay shuddered, returning in his mind to the battle between Sayjak and Chumo.

"Do you really think some things are worth killing and dying over?" he asked.

"What I think and what you think do not matter," Reese replied. "There are plenty who do. You cannot go too far in either world without encountering some form of violence, real or metaphorical."

"Why not?"

"Violence is a part of the human condition."

"Why is that?"

"Because we are built of irrational as well as rational parts. Don't ask me 'why' again. Just do some reading, and look around when you have a chance to observe some people."

"Does that apply to other creatures than humans?"

"So far as I know, yes. Why?"

"I once saw a couple of ape-people fighting to see who would be boss."

"What were you doing among them?"

"Just resting in a tree when they came along."

Reese frowned.

"Why do I feel there's more to it than that?" he asked.

"Because you were just telling me to avoid people."

"There were many, I suppose?"

"Oh, the whole tribe, I guess."

"You must have known it was their stamping grounds."

"Well, maybe I did, a little. But we hadn't had this talk yet. Besides, the bracelet works both ways, you know. I can always use it to slip away back to Verité."

"And in front of a speeding vehicle if you're not careful."

"I'm always careful."

"Those ape-people are a hell of a lot stronger than we are. Tough, and kind of mean, too, I've heard."

"I'd say."

"Well, I guess you have to start learning to judge sooner or later. Remember everything I said, though, about the bracelet and people."

Jay nodded his head. "Well-noted," he said.

"I've been around a long time," Reese said, "and I just realized that I recall something very special about being a boy."

"What's that?" Jay asked.

"No matter what you tell them they're going to do what they want."

Jay studied him for several moments, then grinned.

"You have a good memory," he said.

—=—

If Reese did not call and none of his companions showed up to keep him company, Jay finally got to the point where he would brave the wilds of Virtù on his own. It was good finally to feel that he was learning his way around the world.

One such morning the following spring, as he wandered between jungle and veldt, he encountered the titanic form of a phant—the biggest phant he had ever caught sight of.

"Excuse me for staring," he said, "but you are the most impressive creature I've ever seen."

The phant studied him with equal intensity.

"And you look familiar," it said, halting. "What's your name?"

"John D'Arcy Donnerjack, Junior," said the boy.

"Mine is Tranto. There is much to be said for resemblances. I knew your father a few years back. We did each other some good turns."

"Where did you know him from?"

"One time, I encountered him on his way back from Deep Fields. He was with your mother."

"There is no such place as Deep Fields!"

Tranto trumpeted something like a laugh. "It ill becomes one to mock when one is not certain," he said.

"I am being trained in the ways of science."

"Which, as I understand it, should bespeak an open mind."

Jay looked downward and kicked sand.

"You're right," he said. "Sorry."

The phant laughed again. "No matter, just where we met. But you've put me to thinking."

"Oh?"

"I was going mad with pain on that occasion, the result of an old injury to the nerves at the base of one of my tusks. Once it starts it doesn't normally stop until it's driven me over the deep end. It's hard for me to remember, but I've been told I do some very violent and antisocial things on these occasions."

"I'm sorry."

"Me, too. Because I've been living very happily with a herd of my own kind for a long while now—and it's starting again. I'm trying to get as far away from them as possible. I have a family as well as friends there. I've been their protector. I don't want to turn on them. So I slipped away early this morning to be alone when it happened. Now who should I meet but the son of the man who actually broke one of my attacks?"

"My dad did that?"

"Yes, and I have a perfect memory when there's no pain overlay. Now, he was muttering about things called acupressure and shiatsu while he worked on and around it. Do the terms mean anything to you?"

"A bit," Jay said. "I know the theory somewhat. But I don't have people I can practice on."

"If I tell you exactly where he placed his hands and what he did in those places, would you be willing to try?"

"Of course."

"I'll lie down then, so it will be easier for you to get at the points."

"Go ahead."

Jay drew back as the huge phant knelt, turned, and lay upon his side.

"Impressive," he muttered.

"First, kind of massage around the base of the top tusk, just kind of gentlelike. That's how he started."

"Comin' up, Tranto."

"Good. Even if it doesn't work, I'll remember you tried. Oddly now, there's a place between a couple of the toes on the foot on that side . . ."

Ten minutes later, the big phant was half-dozing.

"Too soon to tell," he said, "but it feels good. You've been at it longer than he was. You'd better go now."

"I've a mind to stick around and see if it worked."

"You wouldn't like being stepped on by a friend, would you?"

"No, but I've checked it out, and I'll be okay."

"Crazy Jay Donnerjack," said Tranto. "You come from a long line of mad scientists, did you know that?"

"Appearances can be deceptive. Go to sleep. I'll chase off small predators and swear at big ones. I've been anxious to practice my swearing."

Jay stayed with Tranto much of that day, and when the big phant awoke he looked around, seeing the boy.

"By George, I think you've done it," he said finally.

"It's good to know there are still a few happy endings left."

"Yes."

Tranto rose slowly, stretched, trumpeted. "Guess I'll be heading back," he said. "Glad I met another Donnerjack at the right time."

"Any time," said the boy. "I'm glad to know my dad was so well liked by so many different people. —You've actually seen Deep Fields?"

"Yes, but I just remember things in flashes from when the madness is on me. I left lots of big tracks through entropy, as I recall, and pissed off its boss."

Jay shuddered.

"There really is an intelligence associated with it?"

"Yes—and with you. You are their firstborn, aren't you?"

"Yes."

"I don't really understand the bond between you and the Lord of Entropy, so I won't speculate. But for whatever it's worth, you ought to be aware that there is something strange there."

"It doesn't seem there'd be much I could do about it."

"There is a legend that your father once fought the Lord of Entropy to a draw."

"How?"

"I don't know. The only one who might is himself a legendary figure known as the Brass Babboon. I've never met him. I heard the story of an old owl, who once passed the time of day in his cab."

"His cab?"

"Yes, the Brass Babboon is a train."

"This is all very confusing. Can you tell me how I might find this train?"

"No, I've heard that it comes and goes where it would and has a variety of ghost stations and train yards where it is serviced. It must find you, I believe."

Jay snorted. "I think I've lost my scientific open-mindedness," he said.

"I'm just relaying rumors here, because they pertain to you. No first-hand knowledge. I'm pretty skeptical myself under the circumstances."

"I understand. I'll find you again sometime. If you hear any more stories about my dad save them for me."

"I will. I'll be going now. Thanks."

Jay watched him lumber away at a surprisingly rapid pace. After Tranto was out of sight he heard him trumpeting again, a wild, joyful thing.

That night, lying in bed, Jay recalled that the bracelet contained some of his father's memories, though it often became rather reticent when questioned concerning them.

Never certain whether he was accessing it correctly, he tapped it several times with a pencil.

"Information concerning John D'Arcy Donnerjack, Senior, if you please," he asked.

"How may I help you?" came the reply.

"Did he ever really journey to Deep Fields and confront the Lord of Entropy there?" he asked.

"That information is restricted at this time," it said.

"Is there a Deep Fields?"

"Restricted."

"A Lord of Entropy?"

"Restricted."

"A train called the Brass Babboon?"

"Yes."

"Has it been to Deep Fields?"

"Let us assume that it has."

"How can one locate this machine?"

"Restricted."

"There must be a very special reason to restrict this information from me."

"There is."

"Have I some special connection with Deep Fields?"

"Restricted."

"With the Lord of Deep Fields?"

"Restricted."

"If there were a way we could discuss Deep Fields, its lord, and my connection with them, would there be anything you could tell me about them or about myself?"

"Hm. Let me examine that sentence structure a few moments, will you?"

"Certainly."

"I suppose I would tell you that there is a great, dark, mysterious palace in Deep Fields."

"Yes?"

"And that its architect was John D'Arcy Donnerjack, Senior."

"Oh. Why?"

"Perhaps in payment of a debt."

"Was I concerned in all this?"

"Not directly, no."

"Am I now?"

"Restricted."

"I think there is more information you could give me."

"Restricted."

"And I'm too tired to fish anymore. G'night."

" 'Night."

From that day on, John D'Arcy Donnerjack, Junior felt that he had some special mission in life—whether for good, ill, or something else, he could not tell.

THREE

John D'Arcy Donnerjack, Junior stood before a virtual mirror he had created in a small culvert he had also created in a wood of Virtù near to the precincts of Castle Donnerjack. He became a beautiful blue-eyed woman with blond hair down to the middle of his back. Raising his arms above his head, he rotated slowly upon his vertical axis, checking for anatomical felicity. Satisfied, he lowered his arms, smiled, and curtsied to his reflection.

He closed his eyes for a moment then, and changed the subject. When he opened them he looked first to his hands, which had grown hairy, then to his reflection, which was now that of one of Sayjak's tribe.

Dubhe applauded. "Well done! Well done!" he cried. "Ideally, though, you've got to do it without closing your eyes. Someone may throw something or swing something at you."

"True," said Jay.

"Try something totally nonhuman—like a piece of furniture, a rock, a machine."

"Okay. Let me think a minute."

"No time! They're breaking down the door! Do it now!"

Jay hustled and turned into an end table.

"Not bad, except that you're not level and you have five legs."

"Oops!"

"Inanimates can be very tricky. This is why you're practicing. People who are exceptionally good at it usually start out with just a few, practice them to perfection, then move on, building a repertoire."

"Makes sense."

"Yes."

"Mind if I ask you a personal question?" said Jay, resuming human form.

"Go ahead."

"What do you do when we're not together?"

"Wander. There's an awful lot of Virtù to see."

"You don't work for anyone?"

"I work for the enrichment of my spirit. Why do you ask?"

"Well, you and Mizar and Phecda and Alioth all showed up at about the same time, and I didn't think of it then but I sometimes wonder whether it was completely coincidental."

"You should have asked me sooner because I've wondered, too, and I've compared notes with the others on it. We all wander. We all have things in common and get together periodically. We are all kind of fascinated by your case."

"Really?"

"Yes. I'd love to see Castle Donnerjack beyond the Great Stage. We all probably hanker after things we can't have."

"Come this way," Jay said, walking briskly back.

Dubhe hurried after.

Coming at length to the Great Stage, Jay said, "I want to see if I can take you through along with me."

"With all due respect," Dubhe observed, "I don't believe it can be done. I think you're just some sort of anomaly because an exception was made allowing you to have parents from both sides."

"Maybe," said Jay. "But I always wanted to find out. Let's give it a try."

"Okay. What should I do?"

"Take my hand."

Dubhe did this thing.

"Come this way," Jay said, opening the door and walking briskly back.

Dubhe hurried after.

Stepping onto the Great Stage, Jay grinned. "Here goes nothing."

"With all due respect . . ." Dubhe began.

Not releasing Dubhe's hand, Jay walked onto the Stage, crossed it, stepped down into his father's office.

Moving through his father's office, Jay touched a desk.

"The real thing," he announced.

Dubhe reached out. His hand stopped at the surface.

"I feel it!" he said.

"Good! Touch a few other things. Don't touch any controls, though."

"Shan't. Can we go farther than this room?"

"I don't see why not. Come on."

They made their way out and down the nearest stair, encountering no one. Dubhe ran his hands over tapestries, furniture, walls as they went.

"But it's just the same!" he finally protested.

"That's the way I feel, too."

"Don't feel I could move into a phase, though."

"Don't think you can."

"Do you think we could step outside?"

"I don't do it very often, but I don't see why not."

Jay led him toward a door set in the southern wall. Taking a key from a hook he unlocked it and they stepped through. Dubhe stooped and nibbled several blades of grass from between his fingers.

"Tastes like grass, too," he said. "Maybe there's not that much difference."

"Can't spread my arms and fly here, or walk into the ocean and breathe under water."

"Is that really so important?"

Jay moved to an iron gate set in a fence, opened it, passed inside.

"What's this?" Dubhe asked.

"Family cemetery," Jay said. "That's my mom's grave and that's my dad's."

Dubhe pointed upward.

"Jay! What's going on?"

Jay raised his head. One of those odd old pieces of equipment mounted on the wall had suddenly begun to glow with a violet aura. "I don't know what—" he began.

The bracelet vibrated.

"Son! Get back to the office fast!" it called. "Don't wait to lock doors! Run!"

Jay turned and ran. Dubhe followed. The air before them swam with moiré.

"What's going on?" he said.

"I don't know," Dubhe responded.

"What's the stuff in the air?"

"Moiré—the sign of Death," Dubhe answered as they entered the castle.

Jay felt his hair rising and saw that Dubhe's was also. As they pounded up the stairs the glowing units in the outer walls began to sing.

"What's going on?" Dubhe asked.

"I don't know. I've never seen anything like it before. You at least know what the moiré is," Jay said, rubbing his eyes.

"The older you get, the more you learn of such matters, brother Jay—and they're saddening. Ordinarily, you see them right before you die, if you live in Virtù."

"I don't feel like dying today," said Jay, rounding another corner and racing on toward the office. He heard something like a soft chuckle then.

There was a crackling sound in the air, and the moiré faded as they entered the office.

"Bracelet!" he called out. "What now?"

"Black box on table near main desk," came the reply. "Light indicator should be on. Third dial from right. Turn it all the way clockwise."

Jay sprang forward.

"Done!" he cried.

A crackling sound came from beyond the walls.

"There's a small switch jury-rigged, on the rear table leg. Throw it!"

"Okay. What is it?"

"Extra generator."

A display appeared on the screen of one main unit on the central workbench. It was a head shrouded within a dark cowl, the face pale, shadowed. "Hello," it said.

Jay felt Dubhe duck behind him.

"Fast on your feet, boy," the figure continued.

Jay tried to meet its dark gaze, failed.

"Who are you?" he asked.

"An old associate of your father's," came the reply.

"What do you want?"

"You."

"Why?"

"You were given to me before your birth."

"I can't believe that."

"Ask the coward who hides behind you."

"Dubhe, is this true?"

"Well—uh—yes."

"How do you know this?"

"I was there when the arrangement was made."

"Why was it made?"

"You may tell him of it some time," said the shadowy figure on the screen. "Right now he needs to know where the equities lie."

"Well, where do they?" asked Jay.

"You have been mine all along," said the other. "But I did not take you when I took your father because of an eloquent plea he'd made for your continued existence. Just now, though, when you left yourself unguarded, I felt that much of my word had been kept—and I decided to reach for you and test your response. How did you know what to do?"

Jay heard Dubhe whisper then, "Don't tell him of the bracelet." Aloud, then, the monkey said, "I thought how his father fought you for his life, years ago."

"When did you hear that?"

"I've a feeling I shouldn't say."

"Hie you home now, Dubhe. We've matters to discuss."

"Alas, sir. I cannot."

"What do you mean? Why not?"

"I seem to have been translated and become a creature of the Verité. I cannot come to you. I seem to have lost the way."

"Somehow, this is old Donnerjack's doing, isn't it?"

"I do not know, sir."

"—Managed by the boy."

Dubhe glanced at Jay, who nodded and smiled.

"Your father did not best me," the figure said then. "It was only a draw."

"Best two out of three?" said the boy.

The cowled figure simply stared, then said, "I'm dropping the siege. I'll give you a few more years. I've a feeling the damage is already done. I fail to understand the fascination life holds for you Donnerjacks, though."

"Who are you?" the boy repeated.

"You know me. Everybody knows me," he said. "Good-bye for now."

The screen grew darker. Jay Donnerjack felt his hair settling as the projectors turned themselves down, and then, finally, off.

"Tell me about him," Jay said.

"That was the Lord of Deep Fields," Dubhe replied.

Jay frowned. "What is your connection with him?" he asked.

"He likes a little company. I was one of the ones he kept around to chat with on occasion. He even sweetens the pot by giving us a little power to keep us happy in that strange place."

"That strange place?"

"Deep Fields."

"You actually dwelled there?"

"Well—yes."

"Did he ask you to keep an eye on me?"

Dubhe looked away.

"Yeah. He did sort of mention it."

"Which side are you on anyway? Where do you go when you leave here?"

"Well, I can't go back now. Your power prohibits it. I had no idea you could bring me to Verité and, in effect, bar my return to Deep Fields. It would be fun to see him try to break that power."

"What are you going to do, now?"

"Hang out with you, I guess, if you'll let me."

"So you can spy on me some more?"

"That wasn't what I had in mind. I think he's thrown me out."

"So you need a new place to run to?"

"In a word, yes. But unless he snatches me away for dust, I think I could teach you a lot. I've learned something of his ways."

"I think I can send you back."

"Not now! Not while he's pissed! Please!"

"All right. I'd like someone to chat with, too. Give me a break. If you ever want to go back, tell me first."

"Oh, I will! I promise!"

"The hell with your promise. Your word is sufficient."

"Oh, that, too!"

"Okay, we take care of each other then."

"Okay, but bear in mind that neither of us is really a match for the Lord of Deep Fields."

Jay chuckled.

"Hungry?"

"Yes. And I've never tried Verité food."

"First time for everything," said Jay.

—=—

John D'Arcy Donnerjack, Junior crouched on the parapet beside a particularly ugly waterspout of a gargoyle. Recently, he had begun the study of gymnastics. And while he loved his rock-climbing in Virtù, he had been quick to see the possibilities of the rugged structure of the castle itself. Sometimes he would look out over the village, up into the mountains, and toward the sea. On other occasions he regarded glorious mixes of rainbow, cloud, and mist, patches of sunlight. Whenever his nimble figure was spotted from the town below it added to the notion that the castle was haunted. On dimmer days he was unseen. He seldom ventured out upon the walls at night.

A mist blew in from the sea, and off in the distance he could see a storm rising. Some of the fishing vessels were already tagged by the winds, and white combers now rolled the beaches. The stones grew damp about him. He was startled by the beauty of the moment and loath to return indoors.

"You want to do Deep Fields' work for them?" Dubhe called from an open window below. "It's not getting any less slippery out there."

"I know," Jay responded. Yet still he lingered. "You should see this sky," he said.

"I can see it from here!"

"And feel the wind."

"Another thing to keep the troubleshooters trying! Get back in here!"

"All right! All right!"

Jay swung back down and in through the window.

"Don't turn into an old lady," he told Dubhe.

"I'm not, but consider—you're my only safe link with the world. What would I do if you smashed yourself, put an ad in the paper? 'Small, versatile ape seeks employment in Virtù or Verité. Lots of experience with demons, entropy, and old coots. Expert bartender.'"

"It might be better to go with an agency," Jay said, "and assume whatever appearance you want, for Virtù."

"I'm a little afraid of that."

"I could try to switch you back, full-time."

"Wish you could just teach me the trick for going back and forth."

"Wish I knew how."

"Death has a piece of the trick," Dubhe said, "but I doubt he has all of it. Too bad there's no way you could create a hidden gate just the two of us know about."

Jay studied him carefully.

"What if that is already the case?" he asked.

"What do you mean?"

"Well, supposing the servant of a dark enemy of my father's were to have made friends with me in a form very congenial to a kid—that they become playmates first. And I tried and succeeded in bringing you across in your guise. I could already have done half of what you are asking. I wonder . . ."

He looked a trifle nervous.

"You're partly right," Dubhe finally said. "But it was my idea, not his—and I hadn't the time to tell him what I wanted to try."

"So you might say the thought just passed through your head."

"Yeah. It was tempting."

"Tempting . . . or testing. He didn't try very hard after I got back into Dad's office."

"What do you mean? He battered the place! I thought we were lost."

"Did he? He got through to take my mother. It can't be a coincidence that she died within a few days of my birth. My father died prematurely, so we can argue that the Lord of Deep Fields got through to him, too."

Dubhe grunted, noncommittal, but he recalled what he had heard of an earlier siege of Castle Donnerjack and as he recalled he shivered and wrapped his thin, spidery arms around himself.

"It seems that the Lord of Deep Fields can penetrate my father's defenses," Jay continued his musing. "He may need to make an effort, but he can do it."

Dubhe shivered again. "I don't nearly feel as safe as I did a moment ago."

"Nothing has changed," said Jay, in the hard, cool manner he sometimes fell into.

"No, I suppose not," Dubhe said, looking around, "but it sure feels like it has."

Jay grinned, wholly a boy again. He bent and hugged the monkey, his arms easily enfolding the skinny form.

"You've been growing," Dubhe commented when the boy let him go. "I remember when we were nearly the same size."

"It happens."

"Not always in Virtù."

"C'mon, Dubhe. Let's go see if Cookie will give us some ice cream. I'm famished."

Dubhe stood, his knuckles dragging against the floor.

"Okay. I guess if the Lord of Deep Fields is coming, there's nothing I can do about it and I've always wanted to have ice cream."

Donnerjack laughed and led the way. Behind them, in the office of John D'Arcy Donnerjack, Senior the computer monitor flickered, showing a skull. Its grin was omnipresent, its laughter harsh and full of triumph.

FOUR

Perhaps it was inevitable that the time would come when John D'Arcy Donnerjack, Junior would encounter the Church of Elish. As Reese Jordan had said, a boy could not be kept from doing what he wanted once he had set his mind on it and Jay Donnerjack, for all the ways that he differed from most boys, was a true boy in this. However, he had attended to Reese's reasoning when the old man advised him to avoid human society and, his awareness of mortality honed by the battle he had observed between Chumo and Sayjak, he set himself a compromise.

First, he would only observe, not participate—at least at first. Second, he would go in virt disguise, not by crossing the interface. Third, he would go only to those sites that were open to public access, not to anywhere he had to pay. In this way he would leave no electronic trail that could be followed.

This last resolve was easy to keep for he had no money of his own. The Donnerjack Institute maintained the castle through arrangements made before John Senior's death. Within the castle, the boy wanted for nothing. With the equipment John Senior had installed as his access point into Virtù he need not pay transfer station fees. Since he was not to contact human society, but to restrict his adventuring to the vast wild sites, he was never issued eft tokens, nor was an account set up for him to draw upon as was usual.

Jay understood money in abstract. His education had included examples of money exchanged for goods, but he did not really comprehend it, nor did he understand its potential power. Therefore, he did not feel his loss particularly strongly, except as a blockade to his explorations and, as there was much he could explore without payment, he only rarely considered his lack.

Ironically, his first solo venture into human society was into a casino site. The traditional lures were in use here as they had been long before in Verité. Elaborate virt structures harbored a variety of gambling games. Shows and spectaculars tempted the gamblers to remain.

Initially, Jay was fascinated by the mobs of people, but this fascination wore off quickly. The passion for spending and acquiring eft tokens left him indifferent. His vocabulary grew somewhat, as did his knowledge of the variety of ways people could be convinced to risk their money in an effort to gain more, but that was all.

He planned somewhat better the next time, choosing a public vacation resort. Here he strolled the beaches, joined in an occasional contest of skill (all of which he took care to lose, although in many cases he was the clear victor), and observed the people. Here, however, the people were often disguised in holiday personas. They were too beautiful, too strong, too flawless to be real, and so their appeal swiftly palled.

After several more false starts, he discovered that religious gatherings provided him with what he had been seeking. Many of them were open to the public—at least at their novice levels. Although some participants wore virt personas, the vast majority came as themselves. At first, Jay simply feasted his gaze on the variety—not just of race or fashion, but of mannerism, posture, and bearing. Until he studied the congregations, he had not realized how many ways there were to rejoice or mourn, how much variation there was within the human animal. A small part of him hungered to see the Verité itself, but for now he was content—more than content, even—sated.

When he could tear himself away from studying the crowd, Jay listened to the sermons and prayers. In an effort to understand the themes that were being expounded, on his return to Castle Donnerjack, he read voraciously. The various religions' treatments of the metaphysical issues of life, death, afterlife, reward, and punishment fed a portion of his maturing psyche that had been sadly starved.

The robots who had raised him either did not care about such issues or—in case of the more sophisticated models such as Dack—had interpretations that focused on their particular form of life. Jay's virt playmates had rather stringently avoided questions of life and death, and Reese Jordan had lived so long beyond the normal human span that his own take on the issues could not be communicated to a boy young enough to be his great-great-grandson, no matter how brilliant that boy might be.

And so Jay attended Catholic Mass, presided over by the Pope in real-time virt persona. He sat hushed as an electronic bodisatva explained the nature of maya—that illusion was not a matter merely of appearance, but of perception. He danced at a voudon ceremony, but none of the loa selected to ride him.

Islam had retained its exclusivity regarding those who were infidels, but there were educational services for those who were interested in learning about the teaching of Mohammed. Jay listened to many of these lectures. The brutal logic of *jihad* had a certain appeal, a directness not often found, but Jay was already too widely read to believe that one answer could do for all people.

And, almost by accident, he found the Church of Elish. For some months he had been regularly attending a Jewish outreach program. He enjoyed the slow, thoughtful discussions of the Torah, of the application of the various laws and proscriptions to the modern day. (Did one sin against the prohibition against eating pork if one only ate virtual pork? Did one commit murder if the murder was within the confines of a virtual setting and the victim a proge created for that purpose? Did one fall into adultery if one had intercourse with a proge created as a virtual representation of another man's wife?) He rarely spoke up, but listened carefully and took notes for later meditation.

Leaving a meeting one afternoon, he overheard two members discussing an absent third.

"And where is Ruth today?"

"Hadn't you heard? She's gone over to the Elshies."

"The Elshies? Whatever for?"

"It seems that all our discussions of how to apply the old ways to the new circumstances made her decide that the only faith that might have answers for today was the Church of Elish."

"Because they claim it was founded in Virtù?"

"That's right."

"I think that it's just a marketing scam. The religion of ancient Sumer has been dead and gone for millennia. Why would it be reborn in virt?"

"Don't ask me, ask Ruth."

The members left, laughing, but Jay was intrigued. Knowing more of Virtù than of Verité, the idea of a religion that had begun in what he thought of as his home turf had a strong appeal for him. Perhaps the Elishites had answers about the Lord of Deep Fields, about the interface, about the nature of the soul of a proge.

Eagerly pulling down a menu, he requested information on the Church of Elish. It obliged with a long list of services, transfer facilities, and related information. Jay saw that there was a public service in a few hours.

Good. He'd have time to go home, have a late lunch, and check in with Dack. This should be fun.

—=—

The Elishite service, Jay gathered, began in Verité, but he was certain that he could slip into the throng once the congregation crossed over into Virtù. This he did, adapting his outer garb to match the loose robes worn by the wide-eyed men and women who shuffled out of a broad corridor and into the outer precincts of a temple built atop a squat ziggurat.

Jay was rather proud of the ease with which he made the changes to his attire. He had arrived in the virt site in the persona of a brown-haired man of average build and average height whose somewhat bulbous nose and thin eyebrows gave him just enough distinction to make him completely anonymous. For clothing he had worn the closest approximation of Elishite robes that he could design from a hurried study of their promotional brochures. Now, he widened the hem border a touch, darkened the taupe in the embroidery and confidently slipped into the procession. His one fear had been that there would not be a seat for him, that the Elishites only translated full congregations, but he filed into a seat as if he belonged there and when no fuss was raised decided that he was safe.

The priest who descended from the pyramid to begin the service wore loose robes, fancy headgear, and something draped over his shoulders. Jay had seen variations on this theme often enough that he spared the costume little attention. What did impress him was the man's halo—a faint blue aura strongest around his head but visible as a dim, almost subliminal outline around his entire body. Classy: just enough to make the man seem touched with divinity. Jay approved. He wondered if the priest designed it himself, or if the Church had a standard proge—probably the latter.

With half an ear, he listened to the invocations to the various deities, waited to hear something unusual, felt vaguely disappointed that what was being presented was a prettified version of material he had heard elsewhere—powerful gods who (despite their power) yearned for human worship. Then the service took an unexpected twist—Jay leaned forward so that he could be certain of what he was hearing—yes! The priest was actually claiming that the gods came among them, attended services, basked in the proximity of their worshipers.

Jay tried to decide if any other of the religions he had sampled had made such a blatant claim. Voudon's possession by a loa was the closest he could recall; all the other faiths contented themselves with some version of Christianity's "Where two or three are gathered in my name, there will I surely be" or, at best, a group leader who claimed to be the incarnation of some deity. This was quite different.

He straightened, eager to hear more. The priest went on, explaining that Virtù was not merely an artistic construct, it was effectively the collective unconscious of the human race and that within that unconscious the gods had survived. Now that humans had found their own way across the interface, the gods (courtesy of the Church of Elish) would mingle with them.

There was more of the same, elaboration, vague promises, followed by a sharing of bread, salt, and wine. Jay listened with some reservation, but much curiosity. At the end of the service, he picked up a listing for the Church's other offerings. He knew that he would be back.

—=—

Link Crain knew he was in trouble when he heard a footfall beyond the door. He had just succeeded in picking the lock on the file cabinet. The window, by means of which he had entered the office perhaps five minutes before, remained open. He had checked it carefully and was positive it was not connected to an alarm system. The entire setup had seemed fairly primitive. Obviously, this was a façade and he had set off something more sophisticated on entering—or even before that. For that matter, though, he might even have been spotted as he'd made his way across the grounds. The means was not really important. They knew he was here.

He had secured the office door on entering. That meant he had a little time. He pulled open the top drawer of the cabinet. Neatly labeled file folders were arrayed before him: Building Code Variances (Vù),

Building Code Variances (Vé), Architectural Prelims (Vù), Contractors (Vé), Subcontractors (Vù) . . .

He closed the drawer, drew open the next. No knowing whether all the files held what their labels indicated, of course. No time to look, either. He cursed softly as he heard the doorknob rattle.

Payroll files . . . He closed the drawer. An anachronism in this day and age, of course. Which is why he'd wanted to check it. Now, though . . . He closed the drawer, drew open the next. Might not be anything he wanted here. Or it could be in the desk. Or a hidden wall safe.

Someone threw his weight against the door. It creaked . . .

Directories in this drawer, one of them labeled "Personal." He removed it, rolled it, stuffed it into his jacket pocket. Probably worthless. Still . . .

Another blow upon the door, a cracking sound from its frame. He also appropriated something labeled "Organizational."

He closed the drawer, opened the bottom one. Personnel files of some sort. Two more cabinets, not enough time. Damn! He'd anticipated having hours in which to work the place over.

He killed his light, slipped it into his other pocket as he crossed the room to the window. He was out it, down among shrubs, and out again before he heard the door give way within. When the lights came on he was already sprinting across the lawn toward the high metal fence.

Into the shrubs along the fence then, he moved to the section he had carefully cut through several days before, by means of which he had entered earlier. It faced upon a quiet side street. It stood easily, its mobility unnoticeable save upon close scrutiny, leaned against a spread of branches. He began working his way back to it.

Suddenly, a figure rose up at his back.

"Hold it right there!" came a voice from behind him, punctuated by the small safety release and priming click familiar to every virtventure participant in the world, only this was real—really real, that is.

Link raised his hands immediately.

"Turn around!"

He began to do so, hampered more than a little by the surrounding shrubbery.

Before he had turned halfway the man fell against him, knocking him off balance. The fence was still out of reach and the foliage at which he clutched gave way. A hand caught him by the right biceps, however, before he toppled. He began to struggle as soon as he recovered his balance, tried to pull away.

"Easy, kid," came a sharp whisper. "It's okay."

Link finished turning toward the man who had spoken, realizing as he did that the guard lay on the ground between them. In the faint light from the street he could make out the rough features and thick sandy brows and hair of the big, pale-eyed individual who had hold of him. The man released his arm and smiled.

"Drum," he said. "Desmond Drum. And you're Lyle Crain."

"Lincoln Crain."

"Oh? I thought it was Lyle. . . ."

"It was, once. I changed it."

"Well, Lincoln—"

"Call me Link."

"Okay, Link. Let's get the hell out of here." Drum glanced toward the doctored section of fence.

"What about this guy?"

"He'll be okay. Let's go."

Link turned and moved back to the fence. Drum stepped over the prostrate guard and followed him. In a moment, they had removed the loose section of fencing and stepped through the opening onto the sidewalk.

They replaced it with some small rattling, and Drum jerked his head to the right.

"This way," he said.

"Hey, wait a minute," Link responded. "Where are we going?"

"My car. A couple of blocks from here. Get us out of the area."

"Then what?"

"I'd like to talk to you."

"What about?"

"Well, we can begin as we walk along. But let's start moving before the cops show. Somebody might have called in. Or there may be another guard coming. . . ."

Link fell into step beside him.

"I'm a private investigator," Drum began.

"Really? I thought you guys did all your work in Virtù, hustling through records."

"Most of us do, these days," Drum replied. "But a lot of really important things stay here in Verité—on paper or in someone's head—and don't leave any tracks in Virtù. Somebody's got to work this side of the street."

Link smiled.

"I know," he said. "There's a lot of good stuff in old-fashioned file cabinets."

Drum nodded.

"A good reporter would know that," he said, "though most of them do all of their work in Virtù, hustling through records and getting by on handouts."

Link laughed.

"Touché," he said. "All right. You're all right. So how do you know I'm a reporter?"

"How old are you, anyway?"

"Twenty-one."

"Hm. According to what I've got you're sixteen—just barely."

"What the hell have you got, and where'd you get it?"

Drum crossed the street.

"I got it all. Hunted through public records in Virtù. Cheap and easy."

"So why ask, if you already know?"

"You run the simple ones by first, make it easy to cooperate, maybe set up a pattern. Easy to check on."

Link shrugged.

"Thanks for your help, but I didn't ask for it. I don't owe you any truth."

"The truth is such a precious thing that you keep it to yourself, eh?"

"If by that you mean truth costs, yes, you're right."

"You got any that might be worth something—specifically, on the Elshies?"

"Maybe. You buying?"

"No. But I know someone who might be. I'd like to take you to see him now. That's my car." He gestured toward a small blue Spinner sedan across the street. "Interested?"

Link nodded. "I'll talk to him," he said.

Drum palmed the lock open and they got in. A moment later he had started the engine and the vehicle had risen above the roadbed, vibrating.

"So why Lincoln?" Drum asked, as they drifted to the side then took a course forward. "You a Civil War buff?"

Link shook his head.

"I read *The Autobiography of Lincoln Steffens*," he said. "It's what made me decide to be a journalist. Times change, but a story's still a story."

"Wasn't he one of those early reporters for whom the term 'muckraker' was invented?"

"Yeah," Link said. "But a lot of people make it sound the way you did—like the tabloid segments. Gossip and all. The muckrakers, like Steffens and Tarbell, were investigative reporters. They did exposés of business abuses—like in the oil industry—and crooked politics. They were all hell on finding conflicts of interest, payoffs—"

"How about religions? They ever cover shady religions?"

"I don't think so," Link said, glancing out the window at the Elishite office he had visited.

"So this was your own idea?"

"That's right. Got the idea reading about the late twentieth-century television evangelists. Thought there might be something juicy here, too."

"Did you find it?"

"If I did it'll be a major newspiece soon."

"You saying you wouldn't work for a private customer?"

"I don't know. You giving me a problem in journalism ethics, testing my principles?"

"I believe it was Oscar Wilde who said that the best thing about principles is that they can always be sacrificed to expediency."

Link chuckled with him.

"If I had a story and you're asking me whether I could be paid to kill it, I don't know. Like anything else, I'd have to have real facts before I could decide. When I said that things cost, I wasn't talking about killing a story, though. I was talking about maybe selling some information. That's different than promising never to use it."

"Agreed. I was just sounding you out."

"You haven't really asked me yet whether I have anything worth selling."

"Do you?"

"Well, I might have an interesting item, if we live," Link replied, still looking out the window.

"What do you mean?" Drum asked.

Link jerked his thumb in the direction he was staring.

"It'd be a better story, though," he went on, "if I could learn how the Elshies make those Virtù powers work in Verité."

Drum turned his head in the direction of the gesture.

"Holy shit!" he said, and the car leaped forward. "How long's that thing been up there?"

"Not long," Link replied. "Slow down. I'm not sure it knows what it's after and you may draw its attention."

The figure in the sky was bull-shaped, wingéd, human-headed, bearded. It moved in a large circle, as if seeking something below. After a time, it began to drift in their direction.

Drum had braked at Link's suggestion, but now he began accelerating again, slowly. As he did, he punched a phone sequence in the design on the dash. The screen remained blank, but moments later the call was answered by a husky masculine voice.

"Yes?"

"Drum."

"Problem?"

"I'm on my way, but I've picked up a tail in the sky."

"What sort?"

"Archaic. If it goes potty it'll likely be bullshit."

"Oh, my! If it's really real, then someone with a Virtù power is on your ass."

"I'd already figured that. What should I do?"

"What're you driving?"

"A blue 2118 Spinner compact."

"Pass the place we were to meet, slowly, and call me three minutes later."

"Hope I can make it."

"Me, too."

Drum glanced back and up over his left shoulder to where the Elshie beast seemed to hover. He turned right onto a wider thoroughfare. A red sedan passed him. A half mile and two turns later, when he was preparing a sigh of relief as the creature dwindled and vanished to the south, he turned a corner to see it swooping toward him out of the east. He accelerated immediately. Link was speaking into the back end of a pencil mike.

"In violation of every principle of aerodynamics," he dictated, "it comes on, dropping toward us like an avenging angel out of Old Testament Babylon."

"If you don't mind," Drum said, wrenching the wheel suddenly and turning up a side street, gyros squealing in protest, "you're a little distracting."

"If we die I'd at least like the byline," Link protested, though he lowered his voice thereafter.

Drum opened his window, removed an oddly shaped pistol from

within his jacket, leaned partway out, and began firing at the impossible beast. The weapon made a small hissing sound each time he discharged it. The bull in the sky jerked slightly as the fourth round was fired and veered off suddenly at treetop level.

". . . even now mounting on high for its second pass," Link went on.

"Cut that out!" Drum ordered.

The figure soared, turned. The next intersection was too busy to crash. Drum turned his head from side to side now.

Ahead and to the right, a large man stood beside the road, hat pulled low over his eyes. He leaned upon a tree to his left; his right hand rested atop a cane.

Drum braked for several seconds, then accelerated again. It seemed as if he might make it through the intersection legitimately. . . .

A soft explosion occurred overhead, a muffled popping sound. A flash of red-and-yellow light passed through the car. The vehicle rocked on its cushion of air. Drum sped through the intersection.

". . . only to vanish in an inexplicable burst of fire," Link dictated.

Drum slowed, departed the roadway, drifted through a park. Link, silent now, shifted uneasily. "Uh, it was probably me it was after, wasn't it?" he said.

"Probably."

"It means they had someone with a Virtù power back at the office, and the veeper got a look at me somehow." He ran a hand through his sandy hair. "Might not have been sure at first which car I was in."

"Sounds right."

"Circled a bit, then decided to try this one. Became certain when you took evasive action, when you shot at it. Came on strong then. I'm wondering how heavily it might have come down on us. I've a feeling it wanted blood."

"It did seem pretty intent."

"I don't understand what happened back there, though." Link gestured to the rear, in the direction of the road. "I'm sure it didn't combust spontaneously. You led it into some sort of trap involving that guy you were talking to on the phone, didn't you?"

"Good guess," Drum said.

"But I don't see how you could have anticipated something like that and set it up."

"Good," Drum said, pushing in a number. "Omniscience bothers me." Several seconds later, it was answered, and he said, "Drum here. What now? And by the way, thanks."

""That meeting's off," came the reply. "But I still want to see you."

"All right. Where?"

"You still know how to find the place where we first met?"

"Yes."

"Meet me there in two hours."

"Yes."

Drum drove across the park and out onto a narrow thoroughfare. He moved slowly along it.

"Who is this guy we're going to see?" Link asked.

"We shall refer to him as 'the client.' "

"Whatever he likes—especially if he's the one who got rid of the bull in the sky."

Drum nodded, driving slowly, conservatively now.

"He did, didn't he?" Link said after a while.

"Maybe."

"How?"

"If I knew that, I'd've done it myself."

"Obviously, he's got you working on something involving the El-shies."

"Reasonable guess."

"You think there might be a big story in it?"

Drum shrugged. Then he smiled.

"Sell me whatever you've got to sell and I'll take you home," he said.

"No, and no."

"I don't think the client is going to give you a story."

"I smell one."

"Smell all you want. I didn't really have dinner and we've a little time now. I'm hungry. How about you?"

"I could use something."

"I hope it's sauerbraten, then, because we're near a German place I like."

—=—

In Deep Fields he dwelled. Upon his Throne of Bones within the hall that was called Desolation, he looked into the shattered video monitor that he held in one skeletal hand. By the power that was in him, was of him, he conjured an image. Fragmented and flecked with static, it rose in the hollow between the monitor's broken glass edges. Something bulked within the image—a mountain, he knew, for it was this mountain he wished to look upon. There was motion, also, but he could not determine what walked or crawled or otherwise made motion on the mountain's slopes. He permitted the image to fade.

"Phecda!" the Lord of Deep Fields called, voice low and even.

"Master?" Tarnished sunlight falling from the dark-shadowed beams overhead, the copper serpent dropped from where she had watched.

"Fetch me the red cable."

There were many red cables in Deep Fields, thousands would be too small to number them, even millions would feel the strain, but Phecda knew there was but one red cable that would interest the Lord of Deep Fields at this time. Into the thin line where segments of two equally impossible columns joined, Phecda slithered. Defying the continuity of space, she came forth from a roughly triangular hole in the ulna of one of the many bones that Death was using as a footrest. The red cable that had been one of Mizar's tails slithered after her, moving in the fashion of a snake by grace of Phecda's small power.

As Death did not deign bend to pick up the cable, Phecda set it to entwining its way up the throne, making art of the interplay of dry white and plastic red against the contrast of the lord's black robe. When the cable came even with the left hand of the Lord of the Lost, he plucked it from the eye-socket out of which it was emerging. Instantly, Phecda withdrew her power and the cable drooped, plastic encasing monofilaments and wire, nothing more.

"Thank you," Death said, the courtesy surprising the serpent, who flickered her tongue out in silvery acknowledgment.

Whether or not the Lord of Deep Fields noted this would be hard to say, for he had returned his attention to the shattered monitor. Once again the picture grew—outline discernable, but detail indistinguishable, too few pixels to the centimeter. At this juncture, Death snapped the length of red cable in his hand and it stiffened into a wand beneath half a meter in length. Death tapped this upon what remained of the screen, breaking away a few jagged teeth of glass, but contrary to all logic, the picture grew sharper.

Now it showed him a vista of Mount Meru, the primal mountain at the center of the universe. It stood stark as the idea of a mountain, holding something in its lines of Fuji, the Matterhorn, Kilimanjaro, and a child's crayon triangle with a jagged line drawn at the top for snow. Nor was it unfitting that it inspired such thought, for it was all of those things and more. Some would argue that the other mountains took their shape and their power to inspire dreams of divinity within humanity from this mountain; others would argue that Mount Meru was the synthesis of all dreams of mountains. Death cared not.

He caused the picture to rotate in its frame, viewing the primal mountain from all sides. In a hollow at the very base, he saw what he had been searching for—a dark declivity in which there was motion as of many bodies.

"What make you of this, Phecda?"

In a smooth undulation of coppery scales, the serpent surged up the rearmost part of the Throne of Bones and then wrapped herself around Death's black-cowled head, cresting like the crown of Lower Egypt on the bone-white brow.

"Either there has been a great increase in the numbers of the lessermost gods, my lord, or someone is gathering an army. I'd bet on the latter."

"So would I. The cycle has been new begun these twenty years now. I expected something of the sort. There are questions, however, to which I do not know the answers, nor would I be likely to get them even if I were to ask politely."

The serpent chuckled. "True."

"I need an agent. Do you believe that the one I have prepared is ready for his mission?"

"As ready as a year or so will make him, great Death."

The Lord of Deep Fields banished the image from his monitor. This he tossed over his shoulder to land with an almost musical crash.

"Then, I must take him so that his education might begin without too great a further loss of time."

"On the human scale, lord, the gods move slowly."

"I have counted on that, Phecda. Even as they have counted on being immune to my reach."

Together they laughed, a harsh sound, without music, that nonetheless filled the hall called Desolation.

—=—

It was after midnight and it was raining when Drum dropped Link at the corner outside his mother's apartment building. Link moved to a position beneath the awning and watched the Spinner rise and buzz off into traffic.

The evening after sauerbraten had in some ways been anticlimactic and, in retrospect, now, tantalizing.

Their rendezvous had been on a property belonging to an acquaintance—whether it was an acquaintance of Drum's or his employer had not been clear. They had finished dinner and headed to the northeast.

Before too long, they had gotten into an area of trails rather than roads. The ground-effect generator hummed and sped them down hills and across fields through dampness and night, while Link struggled to commit every turning of the way to memory, occasionally triggering his microcam toward a landmark and wondering whether its high-sensitivity filter would bring in a picture. He scanned the skies periodically, noting that Drum occasionally did the same. But no Mesopotamian cattle-men were cruising the night in this area.

Another quarter hour, and they approached a walled estate. From a succession of hilltop vantages, few lights could be discerned within and about the massive house or villa. Starlight and a touch of moon sparkled on a small lake to its rear, however, and a small illumination could be glimpsed from a structure near to its middle.

They slowed as they neared the gate, halting when they came up before it. Drum leaned from his window, touched a plate beneath a speaker on a post. When it queried him, he responded, "One drummer drumming."

There was no response other than the gate swinging open. They drove through, bearing off to the left across the lawn, rather than following the driveway toward a circle before the house. The gate swung shut behind them.

They made their way amid pine trees, coming at last to the shores of the lake. Drum headed out across the water toward the intermittent light within the small structure on the island. As the moon came slightly higher, it became apparent that a series of small wooden footbridges connected the island to the shore in a bamboo grove near the house, zigzagging its pyloned way from ait to islet.

He drove up onto the beach, headed to a smooth, gravelly area, and parked there.

"All out," he said, opening his door.

"The building?" Link asked.

Drum nodded and began walking. Link fell into step at his side.

They made their way around to the far side of the structure, coming upon a narrow, flagged path just before its terminus at the doorway. Drum halted then and inquired, "Good evening?"

"Possibly," came a deep-voiced reply from within. "Please join me."

Drum entered and Link followed him. A large man, who had been seated back on his heels in a kneeling position beside a low table, rose to his feet. There were small windows in the bare, unfinished wooden walls, to the right and the left. Portions of the branches of evergreens passed near, outside either window. Through the one on the right the moon shone. A salmon-colored paper lantern surrounded a light at the table's center. It cast illumination on the near wall, where hung a scroll bearing oriental characters. It also drew angled shadows upon the stylized demon mask worn by the man before them. He wore a high-necked, long-sleeved kimono of green silk, and he had on a pair of lemon-yellow gloves. Behind him, a vessel of water steamed on a small heater. He gestured toward the table, which, along with the lantern, held a tea service.

"Won't you join me in a cup of tea?" he asked.

Drum had reflexively slipped his shoes off on viewing the decor, placing them beside the doorway. Link, a social mimic in the presence of those who seemed to know what they were about, did the same.

"Didn't expect a tea ceremony," Drum remarked, moving forward and taking a place across the table from his host. Link seated himself to his right.

" 'Tisn't," the large man replied. "Nothing fancy at all. I borrowed this place for our meeting, found the fixings here, and decided I'd like a cup. Please join me."

"Don't mind if I do," Drum replied.

Link nodded as the man set about preparing the brew.

Drum picked up his cup, turning it, regarding it. "This one has seen many years," he said. "Lakes of fine brews must have passed through it. It has a pattern of cracks beneath its glaze, as in a Renaissance painting. And it fits the hand so well."

Their host turned and stared at him.

"You surprise me, Mr. Drum," he said.

Drum smiled. "It is never a good thing to become predictable," he said. "Not in my line of work, either."

"Either?"

"Either."

"I am not sure what you are implying."

"It was only a small observation concerning predictability."

A chuckle occurred behind the mask. Red and green, the demon face turned toward Link. "And this is the journalist you mentioned?" he said. "Mr. Crain?"

Drum nodded, as did Link.

"I am happy to meet you, sir," their host stated, "though I fear I cannot afford a more formal introduction. Security—my own—is involved."

"In that case, how shall I address you?" Link asked.

"That depends on the nature of the relationship we develop," the other replied. "For now, 'Daimon' will do, for it is the mask I have chosen in the role of your host."

"What sort of business did you have in mind, Daimon?"

"Mr. Drum has informed me that you style yourself as an investigative reporter."

"I needn't style myself anything. My record would speak for itself," Link replied, "if I cared to offer it."

"I am not unaware," said Daimon, continuing with the preparation of the tea, "that, under a carefully constructed computer persona, you have worked professionally at this occupation for years, 'Steffens.'"

"You have been thorough. Why?"

"I watch you not to watch you. I became aware of you because of our shared interest."

"The Elishites?"

"Correct."

"Any special reason for this interest?"

"So special that it must remain private. What of your own?"

"I can talk about it," Link said. "I think the Elishites are pulling something. They're just too slick not to be. Perhaps it's something like the televangelist scandals, late twentieth century. I don't know what the angle is, but I'm sure there's something there. A gut feeling, you might call it."

Daimon nodded. Despite his disavowal, it was obvious even to Link's untrained eye that this was more than a casual brewing and service. Daimon's movements were too graceful and at the same time, along with his comments, ritualized, as if he were following a script. Half-consciously, Link straightened, brushed dust from sleeve and pant leg. He tucked in his shirttail, ran a hand through his hair, glanced at his fingernails, dropped his hands out of sight, to clean one with another.

"Have you learned much concerning them?" Daimon asked.

"Did my homework," Link replied. "I read everything from the general stuff to Arthur Eden's *Origin and Growth of a Popular Religion*, which was pretty thorough if no longer current. Shame he can't bring out a new edition."

"Obviously, it still left you with questions."

"Well, I'm still not happy with the origin part. But I can understand its quick spread from the precedents Eden gives—"

"You don't doubt the notion that it was founded in Virtù, that an AI rather than a human received the revelation? Or that its followers feel that it must spread to Verité? That no one knows exactly how its crossover powers function? That its followers feel that its gods will one day manifest here? That the interface will be destroyed and the Verité annexed? That our world is somehow a subset of theirs, no matter what the paradoxes?"

"That does strike me as a little outré. But then, any revelation, anywhere, does. And a lot of the rest is just theology. However, yes, its founding in Virtù seemed more a publicity stunt than a matter of divine choice."

"Could be," Daimon said, beginning to serve the tea. "As with most religions, there's a lot of mystery wrapped around the way it got started. If you buy the thesis that it was founded in Virtù without any assist from Verité, though, it raises all sorts of interesting epistemological questions."

" 'Epistemological'?" Link asked, raising his eyebrows.

"Having to do with the origin, nature, and limits of knowledge."

"Thanks."

"So do you see what I mean?"

"I guess so. But I wonder whether there's a juicy story in it. Not just an—academic one."

"What do you mean by 'juicy'?"

"Well, scandal. Crime. Drugs, sex, fraud, misappropriation of funds. All of the traditional things."

"I'm sure there is. One can find all of that just about anywhere."

Link regarded the tea as he was served, pausing for a moment to enjoy its aroma.

"I do not understand what you are saying—or not saying," he said then. "But it sounds like, 'Yes, your story is there, only it's a lot bigger and very different than what you have in mind.' "

Daimon tapped his fingertips together as if applauding soundlessly. Then he served Drum, who sighed, smiled, and tasted the tea. "Most refreshing," Drum commented, "to one who found himself, suddenly, half-asleep."

Daimon served himself, seated himself with them.

"Or, for that matter, half-awake," Drum added.

"*Is* it?" Link asked, staring through the steam across his cup.

"I think so, though I've nowhere the sort of evidence you'd need for, say, the story of the century. What I was hoping, was that I might recruit you to share your findings with me periodically. My needs are not journalistic. I would not compromise anything you intend to write."

"What are your needs?" Link asked him.

"Life and death."

"Your own?"

"That, too."

Link tasted his tea.

"Exceptional," he remarked.

"Thank you."

"In other words," Link said, "you want information, but you won't say why or what for. You must realize that this would make it a little difficult to know what to bring you if one did suddenly have access to Elishite materials."

"I realize that."

". . . And you seem to be assuming a continuing interest on my part, rather than a short-term thing."

"I am."

"Why?"

"Because I've been watching you and I know that it's more than a passing thing."

"Watching me . . ." He glanced at Drum, who nodded.

"I wasn't walking around the grounds back there for my health," Drum said.

"How long have you been on my case?"

Drum glanced at Daimon, apparently caught some invisible sign, and said, "Just checking in on you every now and then."

Link sipped his tea and sighed.

"All right," he said. "Now what?"

"You don't think you're going to uncover a big story overnight, do you?" Drum asked.

"Nope."

"It could take months, even years of steady investigation."

"Quite possibly."

"And you think you're up to that?"

"I do now."

Drum raised his eyebrows.

"Because of your own actions," Link continued. "You've made enough smoke to convince me there's a fire."

"Well, would you be willing to share the results of your research with Daimon?" Drum asked.

"What exactly do you mean by 'share'?" Link asked.

"I would pay you on a regular basis," Daimon explained, "to do me periodic reports summarizing the results of your ongoing investigation into the affairs of the Elishite Church."

"And not to publish a thing if you tell me not to?"

"No, what I want to buy is a personal scoop. I get it before anyone else."

"Hm. How long before?" Link asked, sipping his tea.

"Twenty-four hours. Though I reserve the right to try to talk you out of publishing at all in some circumstances."

Link shrugged.

"You can try," he said.

"Close enough," Daimon said, moving first to one window, then to the other and looking out.

"See any flying cattle?" Link asked.

"Not yet." Daimon turned back to him. "You know anything about them?"

"Only what I saw tonight."

"Someone with a virt power might produce an effect like that. I don't know how they make it work here."

Daimon withdrew his hands from his sleeves and passed Link a folded slip of paper. Link examined it.

"What is this?" he asked.

"A figure," Daimon replied, "which, if sufficient, will be deposited in your personal account each month for so long as you honor our agreement."

"A twenty-four-hour scoop . . ."

". . . And the right to try to talk you out of using certain material. Do we have a deal?"

Link rose and extended his hand. Daimon clasped it.

"We have a deal," Link said. "And as a sign of good faith, you can look over the stuff I picked up tonight. I haven't even had a chance to check it myself."

He passed him the "Personal" directory and the "Organizational" notebook he had acquired earlier.

Daimon accepted them, flipped through "Organizational" and passed it back.

"Publicly available," he said. Then he looked through the other.

"Not sure what this one is," he said. "But don't get your hopes up. Possibly field notes of some sort, not worth entering in the system till they reach a certain point. Still . . . Let me look it over and get it back to you."

"All right. Do I ever get a scoop from you?"

"That's not part of the deal."

"I know. How do I get in touch with you?"

"You go through Drum."

"And if he's not available?"

"Then I'll be in touch with you."

Link shrugged.

"It's your show," he said.

Daimon turned away, so as to adjust his mask as he raised his cup.

Moon broken on lake's bottom; black glass hands turning pieces: dream of tea.

Clouds blew up on the way home, and it was raining when Drum dropped him on the corner.

"I think you made a good deal, kid," the detective told him as he passed him his business card.

"We'll see," Link said, glancing toward the sky.

Immediately, Drum looked upward, scanned the heavens. But all that he saw were clouds, a few stars in the canyons between them.

When he looked back, Link was smiling. "Drive carefully," he said.

Moments later, the blue Spinner was turning a corner.

Raindrops: wet banderillas: Moon in Taurus: black wrist o'er demon glove.

Inside, Link created a file the old-fashioned way. He wrote out all his recollections of the evening in longhand, in a notebook, one of many on his room's shelves.

—=—

In a garden in Virtù, a garden created by the aion Markon for the pleasure of his beloved Virginia Tallent, the two sat in close converse. That they had been closer still not long before could not be doubted, for Virginia was unclad and still lightly dappled with perspiration. Markon, who had assumed something of a human shape for the convenience of his lover, retained it still and could not precisely be said to be unclad as his skin had never known the caress of fabric.

He smiled at her now from a face whose noble brow and cleft chin did not escape a certain eldritch quality. Certainly the cat's-eye pupils of his sky-blue eyes, or the utter lack of hair anywhere on his smooth ivory-colored skin, added to the sense of otherness, but Virginia delighted in him. She would have found the aion much diminished if he had limited himself to the colors and tones found naturally in humanity. Indeed, there were times when he assumed a form that was not precisely human, but at those times she found an extra set of arms or other endowments more an advantage than not.

Virginia returned his smile and pillowed her head on his chest, noting absently the lack of nipples as she did so. The greater part of her attention was caught up in what Markon was saying.

"Portents and omens, Virginia. A time of change is upon us again. Just two days hence, Kordalis told me that a man with a scar from the top of his head to the sole of his left foot had crossed the borders of her territory. I, myself, not more than a year ago saw a man bearing a rhomboid box, all of crystal and platinum, on one shoulder, and he limped heavily."

"Many strange things can be seen in Virtù," Virginia said, hoping to comfort, for she knew Markon intimately enough to know that the ancient aion was perturbed.

Markon's voice seemed to reverberate less from his chest than from the trumpet flowers that grew over their bower.

"Strange. Yes, but unlike you little ones of what you call Verité, we who are of the older realm know that the gods exist. Exist and are flawed and contentious. I have told you of our ancient wars?"

"You have."

"And you believed the truth of those tales?"

"I did."

"Then let me tell you further that even then those battles were not believed to be the last that we would join. We knew that change would come again, whether we willed it so or not. Among the omens of that change would be the resurfacing of figures from those ancient days. Kordalis and I are not alone in seeing evidence that the Threefold One has entered into Virtù's affairs once more."

"The Threefold One? I don't think you've mentioned that name before."

"The Piper, the Master, and the One Who Waits. What Kordalis saw, what I saw, are two of his aspects. And sporadically, these fifteen years or more, the Piper's music has been heard."

"Just music?"

"Some rumors of sightings as well, but the Piper's music is the stuff of legend. It has the sense of age and tradition but when examined is discovered to be wholly new. Some believe it a metaphor for his relationship to the Master."

"This is going over my head, Markon."

"I shall explain in greater detail, more slowly, my love. I would have you understand my fear in the sighting of a train that can transverse realities and in other omens. I have spoken but circumlocutiously before. . . . These are the secrets of the aions' religion."

Virginia squeezed the body against which she rested.

"I would not relate or record anything you revealed to me in confidence, Markon."

"So we agreed long ago. When war comes again to Virtù, what will happen to you?"

"Happen?"

"Realities ripple when aions battle, Virginia. Your little virt form would be unable to withstand the stresses. Yet to return your free spirit to the prison of your body in Verité . . ."

"A body aging and progressively crippled by atrophy . . ." Virginia gasped and sat up, did not notice that the human-form vanished when she released it. "Markon! Is this war certain?"

A tendril of vine reached out and caressed her cheek. "I have no reason to believe otherwise. The Highest on Meru gather their forces and make their alliances. Thus far I have not accepted any of the offers to ally myself with one or another of the great ones. I cannot dally forever, though. Fortunately for our poor love, time as seen by the dwellers on Meru and time as experienced by humans is different. You may be gone to Deep Fields before I need worry for your safety."

Virginia understood his meaning, knew there was truth in it. Her damaged body in Verité could not live eternally. In Virtù she was unchanged, but eventually her flesh would no longer be able to support her spirit.

"Forgive my weakness in confiding to you, Virginia." Markon spoke with a voice crafted from the wind in the trees. "But you are closer to me, dearer to me, than any in existence. I could not pretend that nothing was amiss and maintain honesty."

Virginia blinked away her tears. Her own mortality was something she had long meditated on. Markon's danger was a new and terrible thing to contemplate.

"There is no forgiveness necessary, love," she said, stroking the fur of a great dire-cat who had emerged from the thickest foliage. "Tell me more. Perhaps I will be able to help."

Markon did. Virginia listened, requesting clarification from time to time. Eventually, the dire-cat began to purr. Virginia, who had grown accustomed to the varying ways her aion showed his satisfaction, smiled to the sun.

FIVE

When next Jay Donnerjack came for his lessons in mathematics with Reese Jordan he carried a book in one hand. Mizar came with him, not frolicking precisely, for it was impossible that such a horror as that vaguely canine construct could frolic, but tossing what looked like an old leather shoe up into the air and catching it again with an attitude of satisfaction. Reese was sitting on a rock by the pool's edge, talking seriously with Caltrice. The *genius loci* waved shyly then vanished beneath the waters.

"Hi, Jay."

"Hi, Reese."

"You look troubled. Been watching Sayjak's people again?"

"No. I . . ." Jay held out the book so Reese could see its cover. It was Arthur Eden's *Origin and Growth of a Popular Religion*. "What do you know about the Elishites, Reese?"

"Mostly what I've read, heard. That book you have there is probably the best study out there. It's somewhat dated now—doesn't take into account the Church's current growth or some of the more flamboyant virt powers that have manifested in the last several years, but what it deals with has a solid foundation."

"Then you believe in the virt powers?"

"Believe? Is it a matter of belief when something is true?"

254

"All right. Then what you're saying is that they do occur."

"Yes. They range from something like luckiness to telekinesis to levitation to . . . well, some of these recent virtuosos seem to be able to manifest a second body."

"I read about that in a newstrip," Jay commented, frowning. "The virt form almost always resembles something out of the Sumerian/Babylonian pantheon. I suppose that makes sense, since their religion employs those forms, but it's . . ."

"Creepy?"

"I guess. Things like that aren't supposed to happen in Verité. Ghosts are about as strange as things get."

Reese chuckled but didn't comment. If the boy wanted to imagine that he lived in a haunted castle it was a safe enough fancy.

"Why the interest in the Church of Elish, Jay? I thought you were into Cabalistic philosophy and updating Leviticus."

"I'm still going to that—" Jay stopped and stared at Reese. "How did you know? I thought I was careful!"

He glared wildly at Mizar as if the dog might have reported on him, but the dog stopped shredding the old shoe long enough to look innocently at his accuser from his uneven eyes of red and green.

"I told him, son," said the bracelet in the voice of John D'Arcy Donnerjack, Senior. "You could hardly think that I would not notice your forays. I asked Reese for his advice since he has raised children and I have not. He told me that thus far you were behaving safely, prudently, and so I was inclined to permit you to continue your adventures."

Jay scuffed the turf with one bare toe and scowled at the bracelet. It had rested there on his wrist for so long, the band expanding as he grew, that at times he completely forgot its existence. Even when he took virt form, as he did now, it translated with him, apparently as indispensable to his entirety as his heart. Lately, however, when he looked at it the image that spontaneously sprang to mind was of the crusader ghost and his ankle chain.

With vast effort, he kept from voicing his objections to having his life so carefully monitored. The bracelet's knowledge had been all that had saved him when the Lord of Deep Fields assaulted the castle. Protestations that he could take care of himself would seem petty, and worse—adolescent.

"Reese, I've been thinking about these virt powers the Church of Elish claims to engender in its acolytes. When you think about it, isn't it a bit like what I can do? In both the case of my ability and these virt powers, something crosses the interface that should not be able to cross."

"True," Reese said, patting the stone nearest to him in mute invitation for the boy to sit. "Of course, there is a great difference between most virt powers and what *you* can do."

"All but this latest trend toward physical manifestations," Jay protested. "That's pretty close."

"It is," Reese said, "if the reports are accurate. I have never seen one of these manifestations myself. There are some clever ways people can be fooled into believing they see something—especially if they have preconditioned expectations."

"I'll grant you that," Jay agreed.

"And we still haven't figured out how you achieve the virt crossover. Is it something you inherited from your mother? Is it inherent in the bracelet? How did you pull Dubhe across?"

Jay shrugged, then winked at Reese.

"Bracelet, are you what permits my virt crossover?"

"I am not permitted to answer that question."

"Not permitted," Jay said, raising the bracelet to eye level and staring at it, "or *cannot*?"

"I am not permitted to answer that question," the bracelet replied, but a faint sound that might have been a chuckle accompanied the words.

"Too many variables." Jay sighed, lowering the bracelet. "Very well. Reese, I want to go into the Verité—the public areas, not just Castle Donnerjack."

"Very well. For any particular reason?"

Jay, prepared to argue, had to stop and collect his thoughts.

"I've heard rumors that the Church of Elish is planning a big festival to celebrate some anniversary of its founding. It will begin in the Verité with public demonstrations of virt manifestations, then cross into Virtù for private services for the faithful."

"And you want to see the virt manifestations. Good thought."

"I . . . You agree?"

"I told you once, I know that I cannot keep you from doing what you want to do if you have your mind set on it. I appreciate your confiding in me. However, you are going to be at considerable risk."

Jay swallowed. Until Reese gave his permission he hadn't realized how much he expected to be prevented from going. He leaned forward to concentrate on what Reese was saying.

"People are different in the Verité than in Virtù, different in all sorts of subtle ways that I cannot codify for you. The similarities are greater, however, and should guide you. Where is this festival to be held?"

"On the North American continent. I believe they're trying for a big city so that the virt transfer facilities will be in place."

"New York is my guess, then. This time of year the weather won't be too bad and Central Park would make a good gathering point. I suggest that you tell anyone who asks that you are a foreigner—Scottish, perhaps. Can you do the accent?"

"Aye, I hae listened to Angus and the Duncan."

Reese looked at the bracelet. "Any comments, John?"

"I am not in favor of this trip, however, I bow to your superior knowledge of human psychology. Let's contact Paracelsus at the Donnerjack Institute to arrange transportation and papers for the boy. I don't want him leaving any records."

"Thanks . . . Dad," Jay said, his earlier apprehension giving way to excitement.

The bracelet only sighed.

—=—

Randall Kelsey lingered to speak with Ben Kwinan after the rest of the meeting had been dismissed. The walls of the conference room still displayed projected maps of the celebration site in New York City's Central Park—surface access marked in blue, landing pads marked in violet, vendor's avenue in green, permanent transfer facilities in red, temporary facilities in brilliant tangerine orange.

"Do you think we'll really pull this off?" Kelsey asked.

"I have no reason to believe otherwise. The last remaining problem was convincing the mayor that we could provide security for the event. Aoud Araf has done so to the mayor's satisfaction and, more importantly, to mine."

Kwinan crossed to the bar, poured himself a drink, mutely offered Kelsey one. Kelsey shook his head.

"Nothing thanks, I have to drive."

"One of the advantages, I suppose, of being virt born is I need not worry about such things," Kwinan said, "but I long to breathe the air of Verité."

"Not in New York City, you don't," Kelsey said with a chuckle. "Even with the improvements of the past century it can get a bit ripe—especially if the day is warm."

"It still seems peculiar that we cannot simply petition the resident

AI for ideal weather." Kwinan shook his head in wonder. "An entire world—an entire universe—without gods. We will do the Verité a great favor when the divine plan is fulfilled."

"Maybe," Kelsey said hesitantly. "Ben, do you even wonder at the wisdom of what we are doing?"

"Wonder? Only at the slowness of our pace. Are you having second thoughts, Brother Kelsey?"

"Not really, but the gods . . . I have never met one of the great ones, only encountered them from a distance during ceremonies. They are creatures of awesome arrogance. Will they understand the delicacy of our world?"

"They are gods," Kwinan said.

"Yes, and the mythology of the region from which they claim origin is full of stories of divine vengeance on a catastrophic level—the Great Flood, monstrous creatures, plagues. Remember that the Old Testament owes much of the harshness of its god to the influence of the Sumerians, the Babylonians, the Assyrians."

"Yes."

"Should such gods be allowed to roam free in a world with atomic weapons? Verité cannot be reprogrammed from the baseline up. When the template is lost, it is lost."

"You *are* having second thoughts, Brother Kelsey."

"If you say so. I prefer to think of it as intelligent questioning."

"So did your student Emmanuel Davis—he who was Arthur Eden, author of that very unkind book."

"It did not lie."

"No, but it asked questions that we were not prepared to have asked, raised questions of motive and faith."

Ben Kwinan sipped from his glass, looked at the color of the liquor, sipped again.

"Randall, in the years since the revelation that Emmanuel Davis and Arthur Eden were one, your place in the Church has suffered. You have more talent than many, but have never been considered for the greater priesthood, for initiation into the deepest mysteries."

"Yes, I know, but despite this I have served the Church faithfully. I brought these concerns to you because I believed that you would listen."

"I am listening, Randall. I am even going to treat this conversation as a matter of private confession. My star has risen; yours has not, but we have been friends for a long time. Speak only to me of your concerns. I, in turn, will privately sound out the great leaders."

"Have you ever met the Hierophant, Ben?"

"Only in great company and shrouded in glory. You know that it is said that the Hierophant is an AI. Although the reach and power of an AI seems vast to a human of Verité, even the greatest are vulnerable to attack. There are virus proges, seeker programs, worms, overwrites. The identity of the Hierophant is a secret to everyone, I believe, but the greater gods."

Randall Kelsey rose, crossed to the bar, poured himself two fingers of Scotch whisky. It burned as he opened his throat and swallowed.

"Peat bog. Dogs body. I'll have another and call a cab."

Kwinan watched. "You will keep your counsel? I would not see you harmed in any way."

"I will," Kelsey said as he rose, thumbed the intercom for a cab. "I'm in far too deep to back out, my friend. I just want to do the best thing for everyone."

"So do we all."

They sat in silence until Kelsey's cab landed on the roof. When their good-byes were said, Kwinan carefully checked the room for bugs or recording devices (after all, his own faith could have been being tested). Then he drew down the menu and selected the coordinates for his own locus.

Ben Kwinan communed On High. The secure link bore him the sweetened charges, filling him with virtue as he let his form shift into that of a golden youth clad only in a jockstrap and sandals. When he had assumed the expected appearance, he stepped forth into the chamber within which he conspired with Seaga.

Since such discussions could not be held on Meru, where Skyga hummed his hums, and Earthma could be trusted to eavesdrop, Seaga had created this refuge, deep inside of the data-stream. In appearance it was not unlike a great chambered nautilus, pink, nacreous, and just translucent enough that any listener would be instantly detected and swallowed by the ferocious bytes that cruised these sacred streams.

Within this shell, Seaga manifested himself in the form of a cuttlefish, as blue as a jazz musician's soul and cruelly beaked. The hesitant, almost worried voice that emitted from this monstrosity nearly made Celerity grin, high as he was on virtual liquor and divine power, but he suppressed it quite effectively by remembering the power of Seaga—power so vast that only the power of Skyga and Earthma could be considered equivalent.

"And what do you have to report?" the cuttlefish asked.

"Great Lord through whom data flows," Celerity said, "the celebration of the Church of Elish is readied. I hear whispers in the hierarchy that one of the Greater Gods of Sumer will attempt the crossover during the festival."

"Great God!"

"The power needed for the transmission of the data will be enormous. I cannot think that the crossover will be of long duration."

"Who do you think will attempt the crossover?"

"That is a highly guarded secret, Seaga. My bet is either Marduk or Ishtar. They both manifest in a highly showy fashion. Ea or Shamash are distinct possibilities as well."

"Have you learned who they really are?"

"That they are of the dwellers on Meru is without a doubt, but, except for some of the lesser aions, none who associates with the Church of Elish makes it too commonly known."

"Yes, I can see that. Everyone wants to give the impression that they have mana and enough to spare." The cuttlefish clattered its beak. "Celerity, I have reached the conclusion that Skyga is in some way connected to the Church of Elish."

"So you have said before, mighty Seaga."

"Don't be flippant, Celerity. I am well aware that you have set yourself to be on the winning side no matter how this war progresses. If you betray me, I will use my last byte to search you out and rend you into such trash that even Deep Fields will reject."

"Yes, Great Lord. I humbly beg your forgiveness. I am but a lesser god and it has been a long day."

"Better. Now take your chin off my clean floor and listen. Skyga recreates his best troops from the wars following the Genesis Scramble. He recruits among those who remain free agents."

"And you?"

"I do the same—balance of power and all that."

"And Earthma?"

"Who knows what game she plays? Sometimes I think she has no care for the coming conflict. Other times I am certain that she is allied with Skyga. Other times . . . Celerity, may I tell you something in great secrecy?"

"I would be honored, lord."

"Earthma is to bear a child. She has hinted ever so coyly that it is mine."

"Congratulations!"

"The children of gods are not always matters for rejoicing, Celerity, especially of gods such as ourselves. Recall the hundred-handed giants spoken of by the ancient Greeks, or the monstrous bull that Ishtar brought forth to punish Gilgamesh."

"I see your point."

"Is this her way of hinting that she would ally with me, or her threat that she has gotten of me a fearsome weapon?"

"I do not know, lord."

"Of course, you don't, but if you should hear something . . ."

"I will listen carefully, lord, and ask careful questions."

They spoke some time longer, then Celerity retreated from that place to Ben Kwinan's home within Virtù. As he made the transit, he reflected that he had not mentioned Randall Kelsey's disaffection to Seaga, but that did not seem important.

— = —

Of sex and of violence, Sayjak dreamed.

The drum beat at the Circle Shannibal. Machete clamped between his teeth, he swung through the trees on his powerful arms, rapidly outdistancing his followers.

Who would beat the drum? Sayjak was Boss of Bosses. All was good for the People. There was much food. The bounties no longer came into their territory. The eeksies had found it prudent to employ their regulatory efforts elsewhere. The People gorged themselves, screwed, and expanded their range into jungles that they had not dared venture into before. Who, then, would beat the drum?

When Sayjak came to the Circle Shannibal, the noise was so great that the lobes of his ears shook as if buffeted by a wind, but when he looked to see what great throng made the noise, he saw only one. A mighty figure, larger than himself in his prime, covered with coarse brown fur like a coconut husk over back and shoulders, legs and arms. Breasts (pendulous, full, shaking with the pounding dance) and buttocks (rounded, flushed crimson in invitation) were free of hair. Altogether, Sayjak had never encountered so desirable a female. His dick stood straight in salute.

Something, though, was wrong about the head. He dropped from the trees, took his machete into his right hand, advancing even as he sought to puzzle out the strangeness. The female continued her pounding dance, moving, though she must be aware of him, to keep her face away from him. As this brought her backside to his greater attention, he did not protest. Indeed, he felt that there was an invitation.

Dropping the machete, he bounded up the slope of the Circle, knuckles brushing the ground. The female did not cease from her drumming. In a single leap he was upon her, thrust into her, one hand groping her breasts, the other grabbing a liberal handful of her hair lest she try to escape. She kept up her thudding on the drum—foot, foot, hand, hand, foot, foot, hand, hand—giving an odd rhythm to his ride.

He increased the violence of his thrusts, pinching hard at one nipple to show his displeasure at her lack of attention. Then she ceased drumming, pressing back against him with gratifying—indeed, frightening—enthusiasm and strength. He jerked at her hair, reining her in, and shockingly, the head came off in his hand.

His arm wrenched back at the unexpected lack of resistance and the head dangled before him. From lips as full as when he had severed her head from her body, Big Betsy smiled at him. Sayjak screamed and pitched the head away from him. It stopped in mid-arc, corrected its course, swooped back, and reattached itself to the neck stump. Big Betsy looked back at him, over her shoulder, coyly wriggling her rump.

"Come on, shrivel dick, can't you finish what you were doing?"

Sayjak indeed felt his dick shrivel, but Big Betsy's challenge was too much for him to ignore. With an effort of will as powerful as he had brought to the many battles for his life, he concentrated only on her charms. He slapped her face so that the human eyes with their sardonic wit were turned away, struck her several times more for good measure, and when he heard her scream felt himself to be in good form again.

"I take your head again," he growled, when he had finished, pushing her face into the dirt as a reminder of who was Boss of Bosses.

Big Betsy rolled onto her back, submissive in posture, her breasts wealed from his attentions, but her teeth-bared smile and narrowed eyes full of challenge.

"Boss of Bosses, they call you, eh?"

"That's me. Boss of Bosses."

"Like old Karak?"

"Like Karak, only better, meaner. Karak never kill so many bounties—scared away the eeksies. Only Sayjak do that."

"Only because you stole my machete," she taunted.

"I twist your head off your neck," he said as a reminder.

She did not seem cowed. For a long moment she studied him from Big Betsy's eyes. They were blue, he noticed.

"What if I give you a real fight?"

"Huh? You and me?"

"No, you and your people. Big fight. Hearts to eat, livers, too. Reason to dance, boast, shout about how great is Sayjak, Boss of Bosses, better than Karak."

"The People don't need nothing. Nobody give us any trouble. Why should we fight?"

"You afraid of a big fight? You scared?"

"Sayjak isn't afraid! Not of nothing!" he shouted, but he only told a half-truth.

He was afraid of this she with her human head and her body like the most perfect of the shes of the People (though maybe a bit too big in the tits), a body that already his traitor dick was beginning to desire again. Perhaps he could leap her from the top, screw her like humans do. It would not be as satisfying as feeling himself slap against her buttocks, but . . .

Big Betsy smiled a smile with too many teeth and parted her legs as if she divined his thought.

"You afraid," she taunted.

"Am not!" he growled, and he leapt on her, struggling with the awkwardness of the unfamiliar position, feeling the rich softness of her breasts before he levered himself onto his arms. She welcomed him inside her and as he beat against her, she spoke, her voice husky, rich as loam or blood.

"Sayjak, I say unless you take this fight, you are a coward. Fear will wither your loins and your teeth will fall from your gums. A younger male will defeat you and, laughing, drag your liver in bloody gobbets out through your nostrils. The People will fall into tiny tribes, hunted and terrified. The bounties will string your favorite shes' ears about their necks."

Sayjak rode harder, willing himself not to hear her. He wanted to break her teeth, force her to swallow her curse, but he could not raise a hand and maintain his balance between her open thighs. A lust more powerful than any he had ever known forced him to thrust on and on, unwilling rapist.

Beneath him, Big Betsy moved like an earthquake: rippling, squeezing, clawing at his back and shoulders. She sunk her teeth into his earlobe until the blood ran, splashing over her face, her throat, between her breasts and matting his fur.

"Coward," she whispered.

And Sayjak knew that he was beaten. A perverse defeat, for even as he resigned to her command, he shot himself into her, taking her, claiming her, as he had never claimed another.

Of sex and of violence, Sayjak dreamed.

—=—

A long-range cruiser landed on the roof of Castle Donnerjack promptly at noon two days before the Elishite celebration was to be held in Central Park. The driver, a taciturn android who could be trusted never to speak of his mission, bent his lips into an expression of perfect nonhearing as Dack presented Jay Donnerjack his overnight bag, an eft stick, and much advice.

"Now, remember, Master Jay, you will arrive in New York with time enough to rest. Accustomed as you are to virt travel, don't overlook the effects of jet lag. . . . I remember your poor mother, but that's neither here nor there. Obey the instructions of whomever Paracelsus sends to advise you."

"I understand, Dack."

Jay would have stepped into the cruiser, but Dack placed a restraining hand on his arm.

"Listen to the weather report and dress appropriately, young sir. New York summers are very changeable, so don't forget a sweater if you plan to be out after dark. You . . . ."

"Yes, Dack." Jay touched the robot on his arm. "I'll be careful, really. Watch out for Dubhe for me, will you?"

Dack glanced to where Dubhe stood. The spidery black monkey looked truly miserable as he hung back in the doorway. He understood why he could not accompany Jay, but he was unhappy about having his friend and protector depart. He scrubbed something suspiciously like a tear from the corner of one eye.

"Have fun, Jay," he called.

"I will. See you in a couple of days."

Dack finally let him board the cruiser. "I will take care of Dubhe for you. Be careful."

Jay muttered further reassurances until he was in his seat and the door sealed shut. He pressed his head against the window and waved until the castle, then all the island called Eilean a'Tempull Dubh, was swallowed in the mist. Then he leaned back against the headrest and tried not to show too much of his excitement. He was out—out in the Verité—on his own.

He glanced at the bracelet. Well, almost. Remembering his manners, he turned to the driver.

"I'm Jay Donnerjack. Thanks for coming to get me."

"Think nothing of it. I'm Milburn. I work for the Donnerjack Institute. It is a pleasure to meet our founder's grandson."

"Grandson? I always thought that my dad founded the Institute."

"No, it was your grandfather. He made quite a lot of money in medical research and established the Institute to promote various research foundations and to take care of his family. Your father's work considerably added to the Institute's fortunes, however."

Jay stared down into the white cloud mountains over which Milburn guided the cruiser. It did not occur to him to be amazed by the vista, for he had seen far stranger in Virtù. As of yet, he had not meditated on the role of chaos in shaping Verité.

"I wonder if I will ever do anything to add to the Institute's fortunes," he said after a time.

"You wonder at this?" Milburn asked. "Your heritage would seem to make it a certainty."

"But what can I do? I live locked up in that castle. I don't do anything, really, except roam around Virtù. What good am I?"

"You are educated?"

"I guess so. Lots of math, literature, some languages. Is that any good?"

"More than, sir. Many people cannot do even those things. Virtù is the ultimate tool for creating an unlettered proletariat. Many service tasks that once took great skill are now performed in virt space in a simplified fashion for which computer programs provide the details."

"I don't understand."

"A simplified example: Once a human clerk needed to know how to type and file. Today correspondence is dictated to a virt assistant—a computer proge—that then creates the document, edits it for spelling and grammar, perhaps flags any infelicities, and returns it for approval before sending it on. Filing is so automatic as to hardly merit a separate name. When a document is no longer needed, it is immediately filed or erased. The human does not even need to know how to recall it—the virt assistant handles that."

"So?"

"So once being a clerk or secretary was a skilled job. Now it is handled via virt."

"That frees more people to get better educations, right? And to do things like colonize the solar system or advance human knowledge."

"Only in theory, sir. There are many humans who, through lack of intelligence or temperament, simply cannot profit from higher education or more elaborate training. Now that they are unemployed, they are either forced into what labor is not already done by artificial people or onto public support. Neither is satisfactory."

"Somehow you seem like the last type of person I would expect to be lamenting technological unemployment."

"Because I am an android? I am complex enough to lament waste, Master Donnerjack."

" 'Jay,' please."

"Jay, then. I see lives left without direction. No one starves or goes without minimal health care. Since they do not need to struggle to survive, all the energy of these basically intelligent people must go into something. I mention this because you are going to a celebration held by the Church of Elish. Many of their followers are drawn from the ranks of those who have no place in the Verité. Uneducated, they are captivated by the promises of the Church, the vague hints of higher knowledge."

"I wondered how so many of the people I met at services had time to learn all the arcane rituals. I could barely fit the basics into my study program, and Dack was willing to let me include them into my curriculum as theology and anthropology."

"Many have nothing more important to do than worship modern interpretations of ancient gods, Jay."

"Have you been to the Church?"

"Only once. They do not actively encourage APs."

"That's odd. The stories are that the religion was founded by an AI."

"There is a social separation between our kinds. Since we have greater mobility—effectively dwell within the Verité—many aions dislike us. Yet, despite our greater physical mobility, we are more limited than almost any virt aion since our systems cannot carry memory to match that of the aions. Some of the greater aions have commented that even a sophisticated AP is little better than a proge."

"That seems rather snobby."

"So, we are the inbetweens. Neither AI (though what else are we other than artificial intelligences?) nor human, and somewhat scorned by the majority of both groups."

"Oh. I never knew."

"I was touched by your kindness to Dack—your consideration for his concern for you even though he was being a dreadful nag—or I would have never mentioned such things to you. Somehow, I did not think you would be one to scorn a person, no matter the origin of intelligence."

"Thanks."

"Dack did have a point about jet lag. It can really mess up organics. If you want to sleep, it might be a good idea."

"I'm too excited, but I'll try closing my eyes."

Jay did so, leaning back his chair and thinking. Already, hardly out of home, he had learned something about Verité he would not have found in his studies. Ignorance of the issue had kept him from reading what commentaries might be available, but in any case, people rarely wrote about prejudices until they had begun to be addressed as detrimental. He wondered what Angus and the Duncan said about the robots when they returned home to the village. Did they resent them for doing jobs that, in the past, would have been given to human members of the castle's fiefdom? It was an unsettling thought.

After a time, he drifted off to sleep, excitement, last-minute packing, and a celebratory drink with the crusader ghost having kept him awake far later than was his wont. When he awoke, Milburn was coming into a landing pattern over New York City.

— = —

"The crowd mills below, replacing Central Park's green spaces with the swirling colors of summer dresses, shorts, and bright shirts. Mylar balloons in the shapes of wingéd lions, wingéd bulls, and ziggurats bob over the throng, their strings clutched by hands still sticky from the free ice cream provided by the Church of Elish. Towering over all of this is the great ziggurat that will be the focus of today's celebration . . ."

Desmond Drum sighed. "Do you really need to do this? You know that every major newsfeed will have reporters and photographers here."

Link huffed. "I want to record my own impressions, in my own style."

The grin that quirked at the corner of Drum's mouth was comment enough on Link's pretensions to style, but the reporter turned his back on him and continued his muttered narration.

"The great ziggurat that will be the focus of today's celebration should be dwarfed by the skyscrapers that tower clifflike over the park's green oasis . . ."

"I thought you said it wasn't green."

"Shut up. . . . green oasis, but something of the ancient grandeur of the lost culture of Ancient Babylon clings to even this modern recreation."

Link clicked off his recorder. For today's adventure he was clad in khaki trousers, a loose short-sleeved button-down shirt over a dark tee-shirt, leather loafers, and a jaunty fedora with a "Press" card stuck in the brim. Except for his anachronistic wrist recorder, he was the archetype of the questing reporter: Clark Kent, Woodward and Bernstein, and, of course, Lincoln Steffens.

Drum was dressed more sensibly in Bermuda shorts, a tee-shirt with the Mets logo, and running shoes. A baseball cap with a duplicate of the Mets logo was pulled almost to his eyebrows, making the sunglasses that hung from a lanyard about his neck superfluous.

"Want a balloon, kid?" he asked, gesturing lazily to where a vendor was making her way through the crowd.

Like all of those working for the Church of Elish this busy day, she wore iridescent green tights printed with tongues of flame that appeared to be licking up her legs and a flame-colored tunic printed in green with the words: "I Burn with the Truth." Not all of the vendors looked good in the tights, but this lady (a blonde with a high giggle that made one wonder if she had been nipping helium from her wares) was all leg.

Drum winked at Link. "I bet that the Truth isn't all she's burning with, kid."

Link blushed, then quickly recovered. In the weeks since their meeting with Daimon, Link had noticed that Drum delighted in needling him about some matters. He could talk quite calmly about all manner of decadence, but if Drum asked him if he'd like a call girl (Drum claimed to know several very obliging ladies) or even a virt jaunt, Link would get pink and nervous.

So Drum had taken it upon himself to harass Link. He justified his banter by saying that it wouldn't do if Link fell apart at some key juncture, and Drum had been in the business long enough to know that undercover work wasn't all skulking about reading other people's mail.

"So, aren't you going to get me a balloon, old man?" Link asked, getting to his feet. "Well, I'll get you one."

He sauntered, a touch overly casual, to the balloon vender, handed over his eft stick, which was returned to him along with a string. Balloon glinting silver and bronze over his head, Link returned to Drum.

"Here," he said, bending and tying the string to Drum's wrist. "A memory from our shared past."

Drum glanced up, and seeing the wingéd bull bobbing over his head, guffawed.

"Good shot, kid. Looks like something's starting to happen up by the ziggurat, better warm up your official Dick Tracy wrist radio."

"Fuck you," Link said amiably, but he did activate the recorder.

—=—

John D'Arcy Donnerjack, Junior stared at the crowd, his eyes so wide that he could feel his lids aching. Dripping with sweat, ice cream staining the front of his tee-shirt, his right hand clasping the string holding a ziggurat balloon, his official souvenir sun hat a size too small and squeezing his brow, he was having a wonderful, terrifying time.

At first, when he had been yelled at for walking out in traffic (in the virt New York he had visited with Dubhe this had been acceptable, but apparently he'd done something wrong), when he had forgotten to give his eft stick to a pretzel vendor before taking one of his wares, when he had stepped into a pile of dog shit (in Virtù only the most faithful simulations had bothered with such details), he had regretted not accepting Milburn's offer of a guide—human or android. Now, free to gape like a rube, to forget his manners, to eavesdrop, to wonder at the clamor of the sounds and the pungency of the smells, he was quite happy to be on his own.

Jay was sorry that Dubhe, with his dry sarcasm, was not with him. The monkey would certainly have something humorously cruel to say about the fat woman in the bright print dress who waddled by, an ice cream cone in each hand. Or about the herd of children running full tilt through the crowd, their anxious father dodging in their wake through the temporary gaps. Or . . .

Contentedly, he settled himself onto the concrete base of a statue (skinning his knee in the process). The Elishite ziggurat was distant but visible from here, and Milburn had thoughtfully provided him with a pair of binoculars. Anchoring his balloon string to a belt loop on his shorts, he took these from their case and adjusted the focus. Perfect.

—=—

Randall Kelsey adjusted the fit of his priest's robe and the heavy artificial beard that fell in luxuriant, ropelike coils to the middle of his chest. Sweat ran from beneath beard and the matching wig that, bound by a simple, striking fillet around his brow, gave him dark hair to his shoulders. For once, he was glad that he was not one of the high priests, since their costumes included conical headpieces as well. At least some air penetrated to his scalp.

"This show is a heck of a lot more comfortable in virt, eh?" said Juan, one of his associates, touching up the dark line around his eyes. "This is what we get for staying fit in Verité."

Kelsey chuckled. It was true that many of the priests who performed the services in Virtù had been ruled unfit to take part in today's celebration. In virt form a paunch or poor posture mattered not at all. Here, it would ruin the effect, making the celebrants seem like children costumed for Halloween rather than impressive bringers of the Truth.

He figured that was why he had been included. Certainly, his stock with the elders had never been the same since the Emmanuel Davis incident, but his fidelity had been unquestioned and he did keep himself in shape.

How ironic that at the very moment when he was sincerely coming to doubt the wisdom of remaining with the Church, he should be entrusted with a role in this most public ceremony. The gods—whoever they were—apparently did have a sense of humor.

"We're on," said Juan, tugging at his sleeve. "It's showtime."

—=—

The prayers that the heavily costumed priests and the scantily clad priestesses were reciting from a dais at the midlevel of the ziggurat were similar to those that Jay had heard in the virt service—certainly not different enough to distract him from watching the celebrants and the crowd. The celebrants seemed less composed than they did in Virtù. Part of this must have to do with their being obviously uncomfortable. The males were, without exception, dripping with sweat. The females wore their transparent shifts and gaudy jewelry with various degrees of composure. Still, Jay felt that there was something more—a degree of tense excitement that could not be dismissed as physical discomfort. Something important was about to happen. Jay's own heart beat more rapidly in sympathy.

He scanned the portion of the crowd nearest to him. Many people were muttering the prayers along with the High Priest, coming in louder on the responses. Against this drone, the quiet conversations of those who were merely observing gradually faded to respectful silence punctuated by an occasional child's cry. Many people were rooting in pockets or purses for the programs that had been distributed throughout the park, peer pressure pushing most to participate at least in the responses.

Within the increasingly focused gathering, heads bent over sheets of paper, or over hands twisting in complex mudras, two people stood out in contrast. They sat on a blanket spread out on the grass beneath a gnarled sapling. Like Jay, the older man was observing the ziggurat through binoculars. His companion, a younger man—almost a boy—held binoculars in one hand and a wristband recorder to his lips. While the older man remained silent except for an occasional comment, the youth's lips moved constantly.

Jay noted the "Press" card in the younger man's hat. Why, if he was with the media, hadn't he availed himself of the reserved seating nearer to the ziggurat? Shrugging, Jay filed this minor mystery away and returned his attention to the ziggurat.

The prayer service was reaching its climax. If something was going to change from the usual, it would be now.

—=—

Randall Kelsey raised and lowered his hands in the prescribed patterns, shook his rattle, wailed a ululating cry. Beside him, Juan de las Vegas did the same. They might have been one man or the entire row of priests, extensions of the High Priest. A Broadway choreographer would have swelled with pride at the precision of their motions.

But Kelsey had no energy to waste on such thoughts. The High Priest (a nice fellow named Sven, a man chosen for this part in today's celebration as much for his stature of nearly seven feet and correspondingly broad shoulders and booming voice as for his devotion and knowledge of ritual) was mounting the steps of the ziggurat. Mounting toward the shrine from which (so said all the rumors—including those leaked to the media corps) would emerge gods in the flesh, showering blessings on the people of the Verité.

The pitch of the chorus rose, shrilled, rose again to a high note sustained by the priestesses. Kelsey wondered if he was the only one who was nervous, but couldn't very well turn to look. He must be impassive passion, devotion come to flesh and blood, a holy man singing forth the gods from mythology into reality.

And then the miracles commenced and Randall Kelsey's anxiety fell from him to be replaced by awe and by terror.

First emerged a pair of wingéd lions with the heads of wise, bearded men. Kelsey knew them—two lesser deities of wind and storm. They had been among the first to attempt the crossover via patrons in Verité. Today, however, they were not making the effort via their patrons (or "serfs," as Kelsey had once heard one say scornfully), though those blesséd two stood by, waiting to strengthen the contact if needed.

The wingéd ones launched into the air—impossibly aloft. Kelsey knew that within the media corps there would be those equipped to unmask a hoax, to detect a robot, a hologram, a balloon. They would strive in vain. The gods, Little Storm, Little Wind, were truly among them, soaring over the entranced, enthralled, entertained throng.

This would be enough—enough to establish the Church of Elish as a major player among the religions of the world, the bringer of an old truth made new, but Kelsey knew from the pounding of the drums, the clanging of the cymbals, the tootling of the flutes, that what he had dreaded was about to happen.

A shadow darkened the doorway of the shrine, then into the sunlight of a New York City afternoon in summer stepped Bel Marduk.

Nine feet tall stood Lord Marduk, Bel Marduk, Belos, Merodach—son of Ea the Sea and Damkina the Sky. In one hand he held the bow with which he had slain Chaos in the person of the dragon Tiamat. In the other he held the pine cone, emblem of his multifaceted nature, for he was also a creator: bringer of law, crafter of the calendar, and husband of Zerpanitum.

Bel Marduk mounted the ziggurat to stand upon its flattened apex so that the gathered worshipers might look upon him. In all things he was doubly blessed—two heads, four eyes, two mouths, four ears. The bulge beneath his robe suggested that duality did not stop at the head. When he breathed, fire blossomed from his lips.

The god looked out over New York City and found a world that had not believed in him, but soon would repair that failing. He smiled two smiles and breathed out more fire. Then with a wave of the hand which held the pine cone, he summoned Little Storm and Little Wind to him.

"This isn't in the script," Juan muttered to Kelsey as Bel Marduk set his feet one each upon the backs of the lesser gods and commanded them to bear him into the sky.

"This isn't on *our* script," Kelsey hissed back. "That maneuver looks rehearsed. What in God's name does he think he's doing?"

"God's name is right," Juan replied. "I think he's exerting his divine right."

"Shit."

Helplessly, the priests and priestesses of the Church of Elish watched as the Greater God and his lesser minions toured over the crowd. They must hide their fear and dismay, taking their cue from Sven, the High Priest, who stood with his arms folded, incanting the lay in praise of Bel Marduk (which fortunately was quite long, Marduk's deeds being more numerous than those of any other deity in the pantheon—if one left out Ishtar's various mischiefs). They must raise their voices in song and hope that all would turn for a profit.

All indeed might have gone well but for the accident to the balloon vendor. It happened thusly.

Tandy Rae Dallas, acolyte of the Church, she of the long legs and blond hair, the same who had earlier in the day sold balloons to both Jay Donnerjack and Link Crain, was standing staring up into the sky, watching the miracle. It had been a good day. She had sold out of her first bunch of balloons and had time to make a good dent in a second before the service started. Those that remained drifted gently above her head, evoking images of a divine aura to those sophisticated in such things.

An underling in the Church, Tandy Rae had no idea that Marduk's actions were at all exceptional. She watched along with the rest of the crowd, admiring the grace with which the god maintained his balance on his dual mounts. Having done trick riding for a rodeo, she knew how difficult this could be.

Absorbed as she was, she did not sense the sneak thief (or perhaps merely a mischief maker) behind her until it was too late. A single snick of a knife blade released her balloons from their anchor, and before she could do more than wildly grab for one, they had risen into the air.

Cries of dismay, command, and simple surprise rose after the balloons. Perhaps they were what drew Little Wind and Little Storm to the vicinity, but for whatever combination of reasons, the two deities swept directly into the flight of mylar shapes.

They balked. Bel Marduk—slightly unbalanced—breathed fire, setting the balloons and their contents alight. Someone in the crowd screamed, someone pushed, someone punched. With a single smooth motion Marduk strung his bow. Little Storm lived up to his name and peed a mighty stream of strongly scented urine (a thousand cat boxes in a drop) over the crowd.

"Holy fuckin', holy fuckin', holy fucking shit!" Randall Kelsey cried, looking down from his perch on the ziggurat. "Call Aoud Araf! We've got a riot on our hands."

—=—

When the riot first began, Jay Donnerjack watched with interest, thinking it another part of the entertainment. Only when he saw a child torn from its mother, an old man knocked down, a vendor abandoning his ice cream wagon to flee did he realize that this was for real and that no *genius loci* would intervene if events progressed beyond the program.

On his perch upon the statue's base, he had been spared the attentions of the mob. Now he rose to his feet, looking not so much to escape as to make amends for his previous stupidity. In many a virtventure, he had been the hero, but unlike those from Verité who played the programs, he had crossed the interface in body as well as mind. The skills he had learned exploring the jungle that harbored Sayjak and Tranto or hunting with Mizar were his in Verité as well as in Virtù.

Glancing around, he saw that the young man with the wrist recorder stood straddling his older companion from whose head blood ran. Jay could easily guess what had happened and admired the youth for not leaving his friend to the mercy of the crowd.

Climbing a small way up the statue, Jay swung over into a tree and then crossed into the tree that had sheltered the two men. These were not the forest giants he was accustomed to climb. Their less elastic boughs creaked enormously at his weight, but he arrived safely and dropped down onto the now-muddied picnic blanket.

The air was thick with the smell of cat piss and the humidity seemed increased. Jay hoped that the resident aion would have the sense to delay the storm, then realized with shock that Verité had no aions. The enormity of such disorder shook him so that for a moment he did not realize that the young man was speaking to him.

"Stay back! I'm armed."

Jay grinned at him. "Me, too, only I've only got two arms—not like Bel Marduk."

He glanced up. The Greater God and his minions seemed to be circling back toward the ziggurat. When he looked back at the young man, he saw that he was being studied uncertainly.

"Don't worry, fellow," Jay assured him. "I want to help."

"Someone was throwing stones. Drum caught one."

"Bad catch. He really should use a mitt."

"How can you joke at a time like this!"

"I don't see how crying is going to help. You know any first aid?"

"Some. My mother's a doctor."

"Then take a look at your buddy. I'll keep off the weirdos."

To punctuate his statement, Jay reached up and broke off a branch from the tree and hefted it. Poorly balanced, but it would do for now. The youth dropped to his knees beside his friend, gingerly removed the baseball cap, and did things that Jay did not watch carefully, his attention being reserved for the milling mob.

The tidal flow that governs such things had carried the bulk of the action away from them. Fortunately, they had been on the fringes. Closer to the ziggurat, Jay spotted several unmoving forms. Skimmers, their jets set for the greatest degree of elevation, were bringing officers in body armor and dropping them throughout the area. Red Cross vans followed as soon as the all-clear was given. Of Bel Marduk and his mounts there was no sign.

"Drum is coming round," the youth said. "Can you help me move him? I don't think anything's broken and this isn't exactly the place to be right now."

"There're med-tech vans down there," Jay suggested.

"I think Drum'll wait. I can get him better help if I take him to my mother's clinic. It's on the other side of town. Will you help me get him to his car?"

"Of course."

Jay thought of suggesting that they go to the Donnerjack Institute, but he didn't really know if they were equipped for emergency medicine. Besides, a visit there might entail some awkward explanations.

"What's your name?" he asked as the older man (who understood what they wanted) threw one arm over Jay's shoulder so that he could help lift him to his feet.

"Link," the young man said, grunting a little as they steadied Drum. "Link Crain and this is Desmond Drum. You are?"

"Jason MacDougal," Jay said, giving the name that was on all his papers, wishing that he had remembered his Scots accent, knowing that it was too late now to start. "Call me 'Jay.' "

"Jay it is," Link said.

Conversation was limited as they maneuvered Desmond Drum out of the park and the several blocks to where he had parked his car. Link thumbed open the lock and with Jay's help set Drum in the passenger seat.

"Thanks for your help," he said, holding out his hand.

"Let me come with you," Jay offered. "The streets could get ugly."

Link hesitated, but a moan from Drum seemed to decide him.

"I'd be much obliged."

Once they were moving, Link made a quick call to the clinic, announcing that he was safe but that he was bringing Drum in.

"Is there anyone you need to call?" he said, glancing back at Jay. "That riot is going to be on every newsnet."

"Yeah, I'd better."

Jay placed a quick call to Milburn, grateful that the android had given him a home number. Milburn promised to notify Paracelsus and Dack that Jay was safe and cautioned him to be careful.

"Spontaneous rioting has been breaking out as the news of what happened in Central Park today spreads. Let me know when you're done helping your friend and I'll come and pick you up."

"Right, Milburn. Thanks."

Link drove for a while in silence. "Your friends have odd names."

"Not much odder than Link and Drum."

"Touché. Where are you from?"

"Scotland."

"Really? And you came all this way for the service?"

"I've been attending services for a while. This promised to be something special so I came. You're from around here?"

"That's right."

"And you're a reporter?"

"Freelance."

"And Drum, is he a reporter, too?"

"Sort of, not really. He's an investigator. We work together sometimes, decided to catch the show together."

Briefly, Jay wondered if the pair were homosexual. They seemed close, but—even though his knowledge of such things was restricted to the virt—he did not think so. Link's care for Drum seemed sincere, but not at all romantic.

"Why do you keep looking at the sky, Link?"

"Looking for bulls."

Jay could think of no answer to that.

They drove for a time in silence, Jay bursting with questions about

276

the riot (none of which he dared ask lest he inadvertently reveal his own isolated upbringing), Link worried about Drum, concentrating on driving the Spinner, and trying to figure out the consequences of the riot for the Church of Elish.

Only Desmond Drum's thoughts were not racing with a hundred different questions, worries, and conjectures. His attention was wholly centered on the pounding in his head and the queasy sensation in his gut that seemed to portend something ominous. The portents proved correct.

"Pull over," he grunted, pressing the heel of his hand into his midsection.

Link glanced around the area. In his hurry to get Drum to the clinic, he'd forsaken the freeways (which he rightly suspected would be tied up with traffic related to the Elishite celebration) for a shortcut through the inner city.

"Drum, it may not be safe."

"Pull over. Don't want to ruin my upholstery."

"Drum . . ."

"Now!"

Link did as he had been told, sliding the Spinner into a mostly vacant parking lot next to a convenience store that—judging from the neons and holocals in the windows—subsisted mostly by selling alcoholic beverages. Drum lurched out of the sedan almost before it stopped, falling to hands and knees among a litter of bottles and broken glass, and retching mightily.

This was another thing Jay had never seen. He'd been sick a few times, but his existence was fairly antiseptic and Dack made certain he got his shots. In the virt spaces he frequented illness was not a popular theme (he had yet to discover the soaps), and none of his companions were human. Getting out of the Spinner, he hovered—half horrified, half fascinated—wondering what he could do to help.

"Jay, stay with Drum," Link said. "I'm going to run inside and get him something he can rinse his mouth with."

He lowered his voice and glanced across the parking lot, where a half-dozen people in matching satin jackets were passing around a large, square bottle.

"I'll hurry. I don't like the looks of those folks."

"I can handle them," Jay assured him.

Link snorted and hurried into the convenience store.

As if his departure had been a signal, the gang began strolling across the parking lot. Their leader bore a passing resemblance to Staggert, another member of Sayjak's band who had proven that age did not equal infirmity—at least among the People in Virtù. Jay moved to interpose himself between the blue Spinner and the retching Drum.

"Nice car," said the hulking one, sounding rather like Staggert as well.

"Thanks."

"Pretty new."

Jay had no idea if that was true, so he nodded.

"A Spinner. Maybe my friends and I should take it for a spin."

A rough chuckle went around the group at this sally of wit. The five remaining gang members (three male, two female—all evidently worshipers in the cult of steroids) had ranged themselves behind their boss. One of the women slapped a tire iron into the palm of her hand, but clearly they expected no trouble from him.

"I don't think so," Jay replied. "We'll need it to take my friend to the hospital."

The spokesman drew himself up in mock indignation.

"Hey, chupling, we were just going to take it for a little drive. We'd bring it back."

"Sure we would," Tire Iron sniggered.

"I don't think so," Jay repeated.

Among the debris near his feet was a liter bottle that had once held wine. The kick at the base was thick and solid—meant to deceive buyers that they were getting more volume than the label claimed. Slipping his foot under it, Jay tossed it into the air and caught it by the neck (a trick he had learned from Tranto, who liked to reminisce about his days in the circus).

The gang members were impressed by the unexpected decisiveness of his actions, but beyond taking a step back and arraying themselves more advantageously for a brawl, they did not respond.

"Iron beats glass, chupling," Tire Iron said, swinging in lieu of punctuation.

Jay ducked her swing, lashed out with a kick to her knee. He connected, and the combination of the force of his impact and her momentum carried her forward. Nimbly, he stepped out of the way, letting her crash onto the gravel-surfaced lot. From the noises she made, the fall couldn't have been pleasant, but she was up on her feet again almost before Jay had the time to recognize that for the first time in his life he had struck someone—someone not protected by virt—in anger.

He didn't have time to meditate on the implications of this change in his perspective, for the other gang members were closing. Skilled as he was in theory, strong and agile as he was in body, he would not have had a chance if Link had not come running from the store at that moment.

Although not an immediately imposing physical specimen (being maybe 5'9" and somewhat slenderly built), Link was clearly not only trained in the martial arts, but prepared to use his skills. Shouting an ear-splitting "ki-yah!" he kicked the thug nearest to him in the groin. The man went down, counterpointing Drum in the process of redecorating the pavement with the contents of his stomach.

Link set down his package, raised his hands in a guard position and took on the next fellow. Heartened, Jay swung out at the gang boss with his bottle. His opponent blocked the blow, but it ruined his attempt to pull a handgun of some sort from inside his satin jacket.

Pausing to kick the gun out of reach, Jay took a punch that made his head reel and—more importantly—made him furiously angry. He was no Sayjak, but something of the Boss of Bosses' brutality had imprinted him as he watched that nightmare battle. Now, his dark eyes narrowed, his teeth bared, he seemed to forget the heavy bottle he held in his hand. Lowering his head and hunching his shoulders, he drove himself like a battering ram into his opponent.

The gang boss went down; Jay swung the bottle. The ganger stayed down.

Link had disposed of one opponent, was occupied with two. Jay swiveled to avoid all but a grazing swipe from the tire iron. The hooked end sliced through his light summer shirt and furrowed his back. Feeling his own blood running hot and liquid, Jay spun, threw the bottle. He missed Tire Iron, but in the instant she flinched, he was upon her.

He grappled her as he had seen Sayjak grapple his foes, squeezing hard, rising to his full height and shaking her with all the force of muscles trained not by repetitious lifting of weights but by climbing trees, swimming in deep lakes, and wrestling with a dog made of iron, steel, and old carpet.

Tire Iron tried to get a purchase, relinquishing her weapon to pummel his kidneys with whatever force her pinned arms could manage. Jay made certain her feet were clear of the ground, squeezed hard once more, then released his grip. Unable to recover her balance quickly, she dropped to her knees. An uppercut to the jaw as she was rising laid her out.

Still in a blood frenzy, Jay might have gone to finish her off, but he heard Drum wheeze weakly.

"Link!"

Jay looked. Link had disposed of one of the two he had been fighting, but the remaining one had dropped back and, very sensibly, drawn his handgun from within his jacket. Like a rabbit caught in a headlight, Link stood frozen. Jay howled.

It was not a focused sound, not the sharp ferocity of a "ki-yah." It was a guttural thing, raw and atonal with something of Mizar in it, and as the gunman's hand wavered, Jay charged.

The gun went off. Link screamed. There was an explosion of red. Jay, certain he had been his new friend's death, covered the ground between him and the gunman more quickly than he could have imagined. The gun went off again, wild this time. A third bang, the bullet creasing his brow as he leapt to one side.

Blood streaming into his eyes, fury in his bones, Jay launched himself onto his opponent, knocking him to the ground and falling on top of him. His tactics were pure Sayjak. He bit the man's shoulder, grabbed his gun arm and beat it against the ground until he heard a bone crack. Kneeling partly on, partly over, his opponent's chest, Jay wrapped hands around the man's throat and pressed down with his full body weight behind his thumbs.

The man was bull-necked, but Jay was very strong and nearly mad from pain and anger. That Jay would have killed him was a certainty, but Desmond Drum kicked him in the ribs and growled.

"Stop it, you asshole! It's over! We've won. Now let's get out of here."

The words barely penetrated in time. Jay blinked at the unconscious man and sat heavily on his chest, adrenaline draining away. He looked up at Drum. The detective held his head as if it ached.

"Link?"

"Bloodied but unbowed. The guy was going for a chest shot. Missed anything vital but caught his arm. C'mon. I need you to get Link into the car. I'll drive. I think I've just been put on the walking wounded list."

Jay nodded, rose, looked at the battered gang members feebly stirring. No one had come out to watch the fight, though he suspected much had been seen from the tenement windows. These people would never talk, though. They had no trust in law and order, no reason, particularly, to do so.

He walked over to Link, trying to disguise how weak his ebbing adrenaline high had left him. Link lay on the ground, blood washing his light shirt dark red, pooling a bit on the gravel beneath. Drum had slapped an old towel from his Spinner's trunk over the wound, tightened it with the belt from Link's pants. Link steadied the compress in place, right arm pressed to left shoulder. His face was grey from pain and blood loss.

When Jay bent to lift him, he waved him back.

"I can get up on my own. Have Drum bring the sedan here. You're bleeding."

"A flesh wound," Jay said. "A couple of them. If you move you'll pass out. Go ahead. Then I don't have to argue with you."

Link managed a slight grin and surrendered, biting his lip against the pain. Jay raised him as carefully as he could and as he wrapped his hand around Link's midsection, gingerly avoiding the upper region where the bullet had penetrated, his fingers encountered something rounded, soft, and cushiony.

He blinked. Stared at Link. Link nodded faintly.

"Yes. Please. Don't."

Link passed out.

Jay put him into the back of the sedan, took the passenger seat up front. Drum got the sedan up and moving, racing down the streets with no regard for speed limits.

He glanced over at Jay, a wry expression on his battered features.

"I guess this is what I get for worrying about my upholstery."

The Hazzard Clinic was in a neighborhood that, while not as decrepit as the one they had departed, was definitely middle class. Drum had called ahead to warn them to expect two more injured and terminated the call before the woman on the other end could ask too many questions.

They were met at the door by a couple of confused-looking orderlies with a gurney and a tall brunette woman whose aura of professional competence could not disguise her worry. Despite her maturity and the wealth of brown hair she wore piled up on her head, the resemblance to Link was unmistakable—almost frighteningly so.

Jay thought about what his fingers had learned and realized that, looking at Dr. Hazzard, he had a pretty good idea of what Link would look like when he—she—reached the same age.

"Marco, Tom," Dr. Hazzard ordered, "help me slide the young man out of the back seat onto the gurney."

She spared Jay and Drum a glance and a tight smile.

"Are you both ambulatory?"

"Pretty much, ma'am," Drum answered. "Link's the one who is hurt bad."

"Follow us in. I'll assign someone to each of you right away."

They followed her through the double glass doors past a curved counter behind which a receptionist processed incoming patients. Beyond the counter was a large waiting room, its collection of waiting patients distracted at least temporarily from their pains, aches, and sniffles by the sight of three men, all blood-stained and battered, being rushed through the room and into the sanctum sanctorum where the doctors actually saw patients.

It was some measure of how bad all three looked that nobody protested that their own treatment would be delayed.

Dr. Hazzard vanished with Link into the first examining room they reached, issuing orders for various equipment, someone named Gwen, and a sterile operating room. Marco emerged moments later and directed Drum to one examining room, Jay to another, and shut the doors firmly after them as if the chaos they had brought with them might escape.

Jay looked around the examining room—another first, since Castle Donnerjack had a med-unit and Dack personally treated all the bumps and scrapes the med-unit could not. It was small but comfortable, painted a pale yellow that managed to make the light seem brighter but softer, and furnished with an examination table, a chair, and a shelf of medical tools. He was trying to guess what the various tools did, moving slowly lest he reopen any of the wounds that had started crusting over, when the door opened.

To his surprise, Dr. Hazzard herself stood there. The tension on her face had eased and she answered his unspoken question.

"Link is not in any danger. The bullet passed clear through, slicing some muscle, but nothing that won't heal. There is some nasty gravel imbedded in the skin—probably from when he fell—and a lot of blood loss."

"I'm glad."

"Strip and let me take a look at you. I'll help with the shirt."

While Jay removed his trousers, retaining his shorts, she punched a tab and the examining table lowered so that he could get onto it without strain, then raised again. She touched his head, tilting it so that she could look into his eyes. Jay blushed, realizing that this was the first real woman since his mother to touch him.

Dr. Hazzard didn't appear to see the blush, or if she did she almost certainly dismissed it as the result of her removing his ruined shirt with a pair of scissors. She tut-tutted at the slash the tire iron had left.

"Lovely, lovely job, Jay. That's your name, right?"

"That's it."

"You've been hit in the head. You'll need stitches in your back and on your forehead. And you have contusions and minor abrasions everywhere. I'm going to give you a tetanus booster, just in case. You'll live, but you'll hurt."

She did things with various sprays and ointments to numb the skin and repaired him with quiet efficiency. Jay found himself liking her a great deal.

"Doctor, is Link your kid?"

"Noticed the resemblance, did you? Yes, Link's mine, my one and only."

"I'd like to see him. Is he awake?"

"Awake and insisting on seeing *you*. When you're patched up, I'll show you where to go. I can't let you chat for too long."

"And Drum. Is he okay?"

"A concussion. Since he lives alone, I've convinced him to accept a room overnight while we make certain that there's nothing serious. He has agreed with remarkable grace. He should be sleeping now. The pain medication we gave him will make him dopey."

"I like him."

"So does Link. So, I suppose, do I, though I wish he wouldn't encourage Link to do such dangerous things."

"Dangerous? A church service is hardly dangerous, ma'am."

Dr. Hazzard smiled at him. It was a nice smile and her eyes were amazingly green.

"Enough on that. I have a waiting room of 'im-patients' to deal with. Marco will bring you a new shirt—we keep a few spares. Once you've changed, walk slowly. You'll find Link in room A-23."

Jay obeyed and found Link's room easily. The orderly Tom was leaving as he approached the door and Link, seeing Jay, waved him in.

"Thanks for coming," Link said, taking a deep breath, "and thanks for saving my life."

"And the same," Jay said, grinning. "I would have been flattened if you hadn't come out just then."

"I think the store owner was in league with them. He kept finding excuses to delay. Finally, I gave up and punched my eft stick into a vending machine—and when I came out . . ."

"I couldn't let them take the Spinner," Jay said awkwardly, wondering if he had violated some Veritéan rule, "or should I have?"

"No, I'm glad you didn't, but you against the six of them . . ."

They stared awkwardly at each other. Shorn of hat, loose shirt, and sunglasses, sitting up in bed in a hospital gown, Link was still androgynous, but also more obviously female—especially if one knew to look for the signs. There was a fullness to the lip, a length of lash, a fineness of bone. Jay realized that he was staring and blushed again.

"You—felt," Link said.

"Yeah," Jay said, turning even darker red.

"My real name is Alice Hazzard. My family is rich and well-known. I wanted to establish myself as a reporter without having people cater to me on that point. It's easy enough to do in Virtù, but in Verité I kept being dismissed as a rich brat."

"So you gave yourself a virt persona, except in Verité!" Jay grinned, thinking how odd that both of them were effectively doing the same thing—him as Jason MacDougal, Alice as Link Crain.

"Drum doesn't know. At least, I don't think he does. I met him professionally and he'd only researched as far as those credentials. I think. Sometimes, I'm not sure."

"Your mom?"

"Knows. Appreciates it. She's doubly wealthy—family money and then some annuities dating back to an accident she had before I was born. She knows how hard it can be to get people to take you seriously."

"You look a lot like her. Don't people guess?"

"I don't come here often. When we're out together, I'm Alice. Link is just for work."

They chatted for a while more, then Tom returned.

"I have been told that the patient is to rest. Jay, you may stay in the clinic or leave, as you wish."

"I'll call for my ride."

Jay and Alice looked at each other, suddenly sixteen and awkward.

"Thanks again."

"Right. Bye."

Jay left. He called Milburn. The android, seeing that he was very thoughtful, did not bother him with idle chatter.

SIX

Jay D'Arcy Donnerjack heard the banshee howl.

When he had returned from the Verité to the castle in Scotland some days before, it had seemed to all those who anxiously (though covertly) watched him, that the experience had not changed him in any detrimental fashion.

Dr. Hazzard's expertise had tended to his wounds so skillfully that when the stitches and bandaging were absorbed there would not even be a scar. (Something about which Jay, himself, had mixed feelings.) He had told of his adventures with the proper mixture of awe and braggadocio, recounted the wonders that he had seen, and returned to his studies and virtventures.

Yet, sometimes, when he explored with Mizar or practiced aerial maneuvering with Alioth (Phecda, of all his childhood playmates, had not returned with any frequency after his discovery of their duplicity), a look would come into his dark eyes: wistful, thoughtful, brooding. Then some might wonder if the adventure had changed him more deeply than he had admitted—even to himself.

And so it was with him when Jay D'Arcy Donnerjack heard the banshee howl.

He was seated in his chambers reviewing irregular Latin conjunctions for his lesson with Dack when he first heard the throbbing wail. First on one note, like sobs barely contained, then rising to a shrill pitch as the sorrow found its voice. It spoke of despair, of hopelessness, of loss beyond mortal knowledge. Jay felt the hair on his arms rise.

"What was that?" he asked Dubhe, who was perched atop a high-backed chair, a quiz list in his long-fingered paw.

"I don't know. The wind?"

"I've never heard the wind sound like that—and I've lived here all my life."

"And I've never heard anything like it, except perhaps in a broken form on the edges of Deep Fields. Where are you going?"

"To find out what it is."

"But it could be dangerous. Send one of the robots."

"No. I want to know."

"Jay . . ."

"Stay here if you want."

"And worry?" Resignedly the monkey leapt down, walked on knuckles and hind legs to Jay's side. "I'm with you. Just remember, bud, you're my passport. If you get hurt, I'm a stranger in a strange land."

"The robots will take care of you. Dack likes you. C'mon. You're stalling. It might stop."

The wail sounded again. Longer, more drawn out. When they stepped into the corridor, it seemed to be coming from the upper reaches of the castle. Jay turned that way; Dubhe climbed up his back to ride on his shoulder.

"You've gotten taller."

"It happens."

"I think you're going to be as tall as your father, maybe taller. How long do humans keep growing?"

"I don't know. Hush, now. Don't distract me. I'm trying to track that sound."

"I know." This last muttered. Jay grinned.

Jay moved along the corridors, head held high to catch the faintest echoes of the cry. He had learned tracking from Mizar, who, if he did not recall his origin, still retained his most basic programming in full. Almost unconsciously, Jay weighed and discarded options, letting his feet carry him up, through the long gallery, out to one of the battlements.

The day was fine, the mist having been chased away by the winds. Out on the waters of the North Minch he could see the white shapes of fishing boats (ironically, the luxuries of Virtù had increased, rather than diminished, the market for the same in Verité). Yet, despite the sunlight and the comparative warmth of the day, something chill lurked on the battlements, something of shadow and sorrow. When Jay crossed the threshold, it wailed.

"Who? What are you?" Jay said, dismayed to hear a faint quaver in his voice.

The wailing figure stirred, solidified somewhat. Now, Jay could see that it was a woman clad in a long ivory-colored shift gathered beneath her breasts with a pale ribbon. She wore a veil that hid her face, but the hair that escaped from it was black and lustrous.

"Who are you?" Jay repeated more firmly.

"I am the *caoineag* of Castle Donnerjack," she said, her voice soft, so he had to step closer to hear the words. "I bring you warning, John. Death comes for you. Flee while you can."

"Flee? Death? Do you mean the Lord of Deep Fields? Why should I flee? This castle is proof against him."

"Is it?"

She paused and Jay remembered his own doubts on that subject. Dubhe, grabbing rather harder than necessary on his right ear, had apparently remembered the same.

"Where can I flee?" Jay said. "Death is everywhere. If this castle is not protected against the Lord of the Lost, then what is?"

"He is the Death Lord of Virtù, John," the *caoineag* said. "Although, as his assaults on this castle have shown, he can affect events in Verité, still you may be safer there. It will take him longer to find you among the teeming hordes."

"Verité," Jay said, and unaccountably, an image of Alice Hazzard blossomed in his mind. "Yes."

"Jay, don't leave me!" Dubhe whined. "If He comes here and gets in and finds me and doesn't find you, it's going to be monkey flambé!"

"I'll take you, Dubhe," Jay promised.

"Can you trust him?" the wailing woman asked. "He is a creature of the Lord of the Lost. He may lead his master to you."

"I'll trust him." He studied the veiled figure. "What I can't figure out is why I should trust you."

"I am the wailing woman of Castle Donnerjack," she said simply. "The Irish call us *banshee*. It has always been the role of our kind to warn of disaster."

Jay frowned. He wished he had time to look up the terms in his databank, for it seemed to him that such creatures were not usually so helpful.

"I'll tell Dack I need a skimmer," he said, wondering how long he would need to argue with the robot. Perhaps the bracelet would help. "Thank you, uh, miss."

He was turning away when a crackling in the air froze him in place. All around the battlements, the projectors concealed within the gargoyles and crenelations flared and glowed violet.

"Too late! Too late!" the *caoineag* wailed. "Death has begun his assault."

"I guess I should go to Dad's office," Jay said, remembering the other time this had happened.

"The Dark Lord will penetrate those defenses and you may be assured that he is now prepared for you if you flee into the Verité. Too late! Unless . . . What is the phase of the moon?"

"Full."

"Then I may yet be able to save you. Run to your father's office and activate whatever may delay the Lord of Entropy, then run to the door in the cellars."

Already moving, Jay asked, "The one that leads into the tunnels?"

"The same."

"Why should that forestall Death?"

"There is more on heaven and earth—in Virtù and Verité—than you know, John D'Arcy Donnerjack."

"Why should I trust you?"

"I warned you rightly once, did I not?"

"Maybe to drive me out into the arms of Death's minions."

"The choice is yours, John. I will be waiting."

And she vanished. Jay pelted down the corridors, Dubhe slung around his neck, clinging to him like a skinny, flapping cape. Once in his father's office, he pressed the sequence of buttons that he recalled from the first time.

"Bracelet," he said, "why aren't you advising me?"

"I am disturbed," it said. "There was something in the *caoineag's* speech that troubled me."

"Like she was lying?"

"No, like I should have known her. I cannot access the data fully. It is as if Donnerjack, in creating me, excised memory of this information from me, but that it permeated enough of whatever he did that I know something, but not enough."

"What do you feel?"

"Sorrow. Joy. Loss. Pain. Vengeance."

"Wow! How about trust?"

"There is nothing to indicate that I should *not* trust, but nothing to indicate that I should."

"Great. How about the theory that Death can penetrate the castle defenses?"

"Probability is that he will, if he maintains the assault."

"Then I'm caught if I stay, caught if I go."

"Quite possibly."

"Then I go."

The bracelet offered no further comment and Dubhe's audible chattering teeth were his response. Two at a time, Jay bounded down the steps. He paused by Dack's office.

"I'm going down into the tunnels, Dack."

"The generators have activated, Jay. Are you certain it will be safe?"

The bracelet said, "He should be as safe there as anywhere, Dack."

"Very well, sir," the robot responded.

Jay noticed that Dack never argued with the bracelet. He wondered if it was programming, or some deference the robot accorded to John Senior but not to his son.

In the kitchen, Jay paused long enough to stuff three rolls, a wedge of cheese, a handful of cookies, and a couple of bananas into a bag. He didn't know how long he would be hiding, but he wasn't about to starve to death while he was doing it.

Then, down the long steps, unhook the key from a nail by the door, grab the flashlight he kept stashed in the top bin of a wine rack, and open the heavy door. It squeaked. It always squeaked—even after he oiled the hinges. Jay had resolved that the squeak was built into the design.

"Come on, Dubhe," he called to where Dubhe trembled on the stair. "Death is coming in behind you. He's not going to look for you here."

"I know . . . Monkeys aren't tunnel creatures. I'm fighting my base programming."

"Try activating the self-preservation routine," Jay said dryly. "I'm heading in."

Jay shone the flashlight down the tunnel. Behind him, he heard Dubhe muttering something remarkably like, "Oh, my fuzzy ears and whiskers." He bent, set the monkey on his shoulder, and closed the door. As an afterthought, he shot the dead bolt.

"Where's our mystic guide?" Dubhe said after they had walked a few paces.

"She'll show," Jay answered with more confidence than he felt.

They walked on, following in a general sense the paths that would lead them to the underground lake. A blue glow from a side passage intercepted them. Jay turned, hoping to find the *caoineag* and seeing instead the crusader ghost, chain in hand as always.

"Och, lad, you're well out of your way. Cum w' me an' I'll bring you to where you should be goin'."

Jay followed. "How do you know where we're going?"

"Your . . . guide told me to find you. She's clearin' the way of its guardian."

"Way? Guardian? Where are you taking me?"

"To the Eldritch Lands, lad, the places of the sidhe. The banshee knows the way from days before."

"Have you been there?"

"Aye, time and again. 'Tis a fine change from the dreamin'."

"And we'll be safe there?"

"Dinna ken, that, lad, but will you be safe anywhere? The Grim Reaper wants to settle a bargain made, a bargain sealed. Can you outrun your fate?"

He jerked on his chain as he said this. Jay frowned.

"I can certainly try."

"Aye, lad, like the old laird and lady, stubborn to the core. Fine good it did them, in the end."

"I'm still alive," Jay reminded him defiantly.

"Aye."

Their conversation had brought them to a dead-end passage. It was brighter than the rest by the addition of another glowing blue wraith, this the *caoineag*. Behind her was a circle darker than the rest of the wall. At first, Jay took it for a shadow and glanced around to see what had cast it. Then he realized that this must be the portal.

"The guardian gone?" the crusader asked.

"Yes." The *caoineag* sounded weary. "The incantation had its effect."

"Can you be teaching it to the lad?"

"We will speak of that. Come along now, John. I will go first so that you will know that you have nothing to fear."

Jay kept all his distrust to himself. Dubhe squeezed his ear, but otherwise the monkey held his peace. A duck of the head, a sense of cold, then he was through; a clank of chain told him that the crusader ghost had come after.

The place where he found himself was a rocky hillside overlooking a distant sea. It could have been on Eilean a'Tempull Dubh but for the standing stones that stood ranked and unmovable.

The *caoineag* leaned against one of these, her head bent, her hand braced against the stone as if she was drained of strength. Jay noticed that both the crusader ghost and the *caoineag* appeared more solid in this place. Through the minute rips in the crusader's tunic he could see oily skin tanned dark by exposure to Arabian desert sunlight. The *caoineag*'s veil, however, was more opaque and all his searching gaze could find of her features was a sense of mournful dark eyes.

"Where is this place?" he asked.

"Och, lad, to be so ignorant of your heritage! I'll gi' you th' word while herself gathers strength."

"Shouldn't we move? Take cover?"

"That we hae doon, laddy. That we hae doon. If th' crossing through th' portal dinna tae ye t' safety, then hidin' behind a rock or in a cave will nae do more."

"I understand. I think . . . Where are we? Is this Virtù?"

Dubhe whimpered. The crusader ghost shrugged.

"That is a question I dinna care to deal w'. Ask herself. What I do ken is that this place is older than Virtù, old as the legends of the folk of Scotland, and for all I ken, older than that."

"I still don't get it."

So the ghost crusader told him about the shadowlands, the Lands Under the Hills, Behind the Mist, Beyond the Setting Sun. He gave him the ballad of Thomas the Rhymer and the story of Ossian. As he spoke, the *caoineag* regained her strength and the proud lift of her walk, and joined them.

"I brought you here, John, in the hope that—as in the legends—this is a land beyond Death. In the tales, those who cross into the faerie realms do not age, do not die unless slain by the creatures of the place. If this is the case, you are safe. If not, at least your enemy will need to search for you."

She paused, raised her head. Jay saw more clearly the paleness of her skin, the darkness of her eyes. She was beautiful, he realized, far more beautiful than Lydia Hazzard—or than Alice—but it was curiosity, rather than desire, that made him wish to see that shadow-guarded face.

"John, I must be honest with you. Although I have every reason to believe that this realm existed long before Virtù, I also know that it is a Virtùan wild land—accessible from the mapped sites, though only with great difficulty."

Jay considered. "Still, that doesn't mean it isn't a refuge. Perhaps the program has been written to exclude Death."

"I hope so."

"Who are you, lady? Why are you helping me?"

"I am the *caoineag* of Castle Donnerjack. You are that castle's lord. Although the old castle is gone, the new one on its ruins has its old haunts, and those old haunts their ancient duties."

"A banshee warns," this, unexpectedly, from Dubhe. "That's all. The boss kept a few on the fringes of Deep Fields. You don't need to get involved."

"Their imperatives are not mine."

"Why?"

"Please."

Reluctantly, Jay changed the subject. "The crusader said that you had a charm you could teach me, one that would protect me from the guardian of this place."

"I know one. It has a cost, John. You saw how weary I was left, and my flesh is not mortal flesh, nor my soul a mortal soul."

"Still, what good is it to bring me here if the guardian can kill me? Didn't you say that was the only way that Death could access the program?"

"I said that I hoped that this was the case. Very well. Promise me on whatever you hold holy that you will not use this charm unless your life is in danger."

"I swear on my mother's grave."

The *caoineag* shuddered. "Very well."

And so she recited:

Angel of the Forsaken Hope
Wielder of the Sword of Wind and Obsidian
Slice the Algorithms from our Foe.
Mermaid Beneath the Seven Dancing Moons,
Cantress of the Siren Song,
Drown our Enemies in the Data-stream.
Nymph of the Logic Tree,
Child of the First Word,
Give our Antagonist to Grief.

Then Jay repeated the words after her, nodding when he had it. The *caoineag* reached out an imploring hand. It was slim and pale, the nails short crescents against the flesh.

292

"Only in an emergency, John. Remember."

Jay nodded. He looked around.

"Even if time passes differently here, I'm not ready to head back. Are we safe to stay?"

"Until the moon passes full you may return the way you came."

"Then let's look around."

Dubhe tugged at his ear.

"How about a banana?"

—=—

"She beat you, the bitch!" Phecda said, flickering in and out her silvery tongue.

"Did she?" Death said, more calmly than might have been expected. "I had wondered into what realms Ayradyss had vanished, for I knew she had not come into my keeping. Now I know—and I believe that another will know as well."

"Another?"

"Her creator—the one who made the Nymph of Virtù, the Angel of the Forsaken Hope, the Mermaid Beneath the Seven Dancing Moons to fight his battles in the days of the Genesis Scramble. He must have thought her lost, her programs decaying among the detritus of my Fields. Now, he may know other."

"Ah, ssso," hissed Phecda, pleased.

"And claim her for his own," Death laughed. "And I will claim her son as I had ever intended."

"So it goes on. . . ."

Death touched the button on the unit that had been John D'Arcy Donnerjack's tribute to him. Politian's *Orpheo* surged out, the only unbroken sound among the broken business of entropy.

—=—

Link Crain knocked on the door to Desmond Drum's office and hearing the acknowledging grunt walked in. Before Drum switched his newsreader off, Link caught sight of a lurid account of the riot at the Elshie celebration. Even days later, the newsies hadn't tired of dwelling on the events, complete with suppositions as to what this might mean for the future of the Church of Elish. Link had filed his story ("Caught in the Crush"), collected his eft, and otherwise distanced himself from the events. He had bigger things to concern him.

Seeing who his visitor was, Drum grinned. "Hey, Link! How're you doing, kid? Learned not to stop bullets with your arm?"

"Knew that before. Shame the guy with the gun hadn't been told."

Drum chuckled. "You look grim, Link. What's wrong?"

Link took his usual seat in one of the comfortably battered chairs in front of Drum's desk.

"I have a confession to make. Afterwards, I might want to hire you for a job."

Drum's eyebrows rose to his hairline. He gestured for Link to continue.

"First of all, Drum, I'm not who you think I am."

"You forget, kid. I researched you."

"You researched Lyle Crain—alias Lincoln Crain."

"Yep, and I found Alice Hazzard."

Link nearly fell off of the chair.

"You knew? How? I was so careful!"

"Careful for Virtù, Link. You made a bit of a mistake when you kept living with your mother."

"I had my own address in the building!"

"You did, but I checked and noticed that the bills were sometimes paid by Lydia Hazzard rather than Lyle Crain. Since the two apartments were next door to each other, I asked a few questions. I'll admit that at first I thought that Lyle was Lydia's lover. Then I learned that Lydia had a daughter about the same height and general build as Lyle. I watched and I never saw the two together and well . . ."

"You hinted at this back when we met, didn't you?"

"When I mentioned your actual age? Yep."

"I feel really stupid."

"Don't. You did a good job. Most people don't look at what is going on in Verité anymore. The eft trail from Lydia's account, though—that was sloppy, kid."

"I ran short of my own money. Mom offered to help. I guess I should have had her put the funds in my account."

"Even better would have been to have her give you a bank draft and then you transfer *that* to your account."

"Yeah."

Link/Alice sat staring at her shoes for a few moments.

"So, what do you want me to call you, kid?"

"Call me?"

"We're still working together, aren't we?"

"We are?"

"Why not? Daimon wanted you for your research talents, for your interest in the Elshies, for your young, idealistic fervor. None of that has changed."

Link grinned, relieved. "Then call me Link and I'll maintain the persona for work, just like always."

Drum nodded. "Good choice. A rich kid with a weird history would have trouble doing investigative work."

"You know about my history?"

"Only that a major virt tour operation authorized their insurance company to pay a large out-of-court settlement to Alice Hazzard to be kept in trust by her mother Lydia until Alice's eighteenth birthday. You'll apparently be a multimillionaire in a couple of years. I didn't dig any further. Those documents are sealed tighter than I wanted to go."

Alice frowned. "I can't tell you about it. I don't really know all the details, but something happened to my mom when she was pregnant with me. She asked for the majority of the award to be given to me since she had plenty of money through her parents and grandparents."

"That's right, your family is Hazzard Insurance, isn't it?"

"Yeah . . . Good thing Mom isn't a snob, or I'd never do anything but go to the right schools."

"She seems like a nice lady. Is she single?"

"All my life. She won't even say who my father is. I think she still holds a candle for him, though."

"That's a nice, old-fashioned phrase."

"That's how she is about him. When the subject comes up she gets all dewy-eyed and pink. It's rather sweet."

Drum took out a bottle and poured them each a shot. He shoved one across the table to Link.

"Gift from one of my grateful clients. Now, tell me about this job you want me to do for you."

Link shifted uneasily, sipped from her glass. It was a liquor of some sort, deceptively strong beneath the sweetness.

"I want to find Jason MacDougal—the fellow who helped us during the riot."

"I remember him—in a somewhat cloudy fashion. Good-looking boy, dark hair, dark eyes?"

"That's right."

"What's the problem? You have a name and a description. I'm certain that you should be able to locate him."

"So was I. He even mentioned that he lived in Scotland. However, apparently, there is no Jason MacDougal in all of Scotland who answers that description and was in New York the day of the Elshie riot."

"Strange."

"Yes. Apparently, even in the middle of the riot, he had the composure to give me a false name."

"Well, you did the same to him."

"A *nom de plume*."

"Nitpicker."

"I want you to find him for me. He saved both our lives and I feel I owe him something."

"How about his privacy?"

"Desmond . . ."

Link's voice was pleading, her green eyes wide and appealing. Desmond Drum was not so old that he had forgotten the power of puppy love. Concealing a smile, he pulled out a hard copy notepad and a pen.

"Tell me everything you recall about him, Link. Did he mention any friends? family? How about where he was staying in New York?"

Slowly, Link reconstructed everything she recalled. Now that Desmond had agreed to help, her nervousness vanished and she became again the professional observer. Although Drum had been woozy during most of the encounter, he added a few details to the list.

"There," he said when they were done. "Now I have something to start with."

"What are your rates?"

"Kid, you're a pal."

"As you noted, I'm also going to be a multimillionaire. If you charge more than I have now, you can hit me for the rest, with interest, in a couple of years."

Drum glanced around his shabby office. Rents were lower now that so much work was done in virt, but conversely it was harder to get a good place now that the demand was reduced. He shoved a standard contract across the desk.

"There."

"That's it?"

"For this kind of job."

Link pulled an eft stick from her wallet. "Take the money for expenses and this first hour's consultation."

While Drum was doing this, Link studied him.

"Why do you do this, Desmond? It can't be for the money."

"Just nosey, I guess. I like being paid to stick my nose into other people's business."

"Like me." Link laughed.

"Guess so, kid." Drum winked at her. "Let me buy my newest client lunch. I want to talk over the Elshie situation. This riot could change things quite a bit."

"I've been thinking about that, too. Have you heard from . . ."

"Our employer? No. He's probably worried, though. Let's have something for him when he does make contact. Do you mind if we walk to lunch? I'm having the Spinner's upholstery replaced."

"Actually, a walk sounds good. I noticed a Chinese place at the end of the block that smelled wonderful when I walked by."

"Great. I've wanted an excuse to try it."

— = —

She was as lovely as Fraga with skin of shining grey, deep wrinkles like the currents cut by the wind on a deep pond, and polished calluses on her knees. Tranto noted her swaggering toward a watering hole some distance from where the herd grazed and scented her invitation on the teasing breeze.

"Muggle," he said, "keep the others back from the watering hole for me while I check out that intruder."

"Sure you wouldn't like me to do it, sir?" Muggle asked, his trunk extending as he, too, caught the enticing scent. "Scarco always had me check out the newcomers, as you may recall."

"Scarco is no longer herd bull," Tranto said, "and I am."

Muggle nodded, shuffled back a few steps, and practiced flapping his ears importantly. Somewhere deep in his heart he wished that he was Tranto (or at least had Tranto's authority), but he had grown practiced at hiding his resentment even from himself.

Tranto sauntered over to the new female. Up close, she was even better looking than from a distance, but something about her reminded him obscurely of Lady May and her bowers of flowers. More guardedly than he had intended, he greeted her.

"Hi," he said.

"Hello," she answered. "Is that your herd grazing out there?"

"That's right."

"It's a big herd."

"Biggest I know of hereabouts."

"Been herd bull long?"

"Long enough."

"I think I've heard of you. You're Tranto, aren't you?"

"That's right."

"Taciturn, too."

"Mm."

"I remember where I heard about you. It was from a bull named Scarco. He said he abdicated in your favor—said you weren't just bigger, you were the ancestral herd bull."

"Scarco. How is he?"

"Well enough, for a lone bull. I think he misses having company."

"Wonder why he doesn't start a new herd. He was pretty impressive."

"Maybe he's afraid that someone else will come and usurp all his hard work."

Tranto dug a tusk into the turf, polishing the tip. He no longer found the stranger female attractive; she struck him as distinctly dangerous. She must have sensed the change in his attitude because instantly she became conciliatory.

"I was sent to find you, Tranto."

"Is that so?"

"By some powerful folks. They're looking for strong phants to join them in an action they're planning."

"Action?"

"Virtù has been under the rule of Verité for too long. Their people come in here with their new programs, with their Chaos Factor prods, and push us around."

"Is that so?"

"Don't be rude, Tranto. You, yourself, bear the wounds of the brutal CF prods, are doomed to suffer insanity due to their mishandling. Only the rare aion has not had its domain challenged by these interlopers. The time has come to rewrite the base program. I have been sent to ask you whether you and your herd wish to join our side."

"What's in it for us?"

"A better society, free from the domination of Verité."

"Verité doesn't come to these jungles and plains, not effectively."

"Do you like being constrained to a few wild or semiwild sites when all of Virtù is your heritage?"

"Maybe so. We're happy here."

"You are. Don't you owe your young bulls room to expand?"

"Let them fight for the right. I have."

"Long ago, Tranto." The stranger female switched the brush at the tip of her tail. "I think I was misled about you, Tranto. I thought that given everything you have suffered you would believe in justice for all, not just the rights of the strongest."

"Lady, I *am* the strongest."

"Here. In any case, I do not believe you will serve. I shall report my failure. It is a pity. We could have been . . . friends."

"As you say, lady. I guess I've grown too old."

Tranto watched as she walked away, watched until she vanished into the brush at the edge of the jungle, watched until night fell and his herd joined him near the water. That night, he glided away from his customary place near Fraga and their two young and pounded along the perimeter of the herd, alert for a danger he could not name.

Alert though he was, Tranto did not see Muggle slip away from the herd and vanish into the dark curtain of the jungle, nor did he see him return some hours later.

—=—

The meeting of the Church of Elish Elders had dealt with the routine matters: presented thanks to Aoud Araf (whose crisis team had handled the riots as well as could be hoped); presented veiled reprimands to those who had panicked; dealt with budgets, supplies, and slogans. The tone of the gathering had been depressed, defeated. All present were aware that the events in Central Park had jeopardized their growing religion as nothing else—even the revelations of Arthur Eden—had ever done.

Then the miracle had begun.

All stared at the head of the table where a chair that always remained empty—a reminder of the Hierophant who was never seen either in Verité (where many suspected he could not manifest) nor in Virtù (where legend said he had his origin)—where the Empty Chair shimmered and a figure took shape on its cushioned seat.

It was human and male in form. The almost ugly face was Roman-nosed, with thinning white hair, and deep laugh lines around a mouth that at this moment was neither laughing nor smiling. The figure wore a loose, faded tee-shirt on which the slogan "Ginger Rogers Did Every-

thing Fred Astaire Did, But She Did It Backwards And In High Heels"
was printed in black.

For those members of the Council of Elders who had their origins
in Verité, it took an effort of will to recall that those from Virtù chose
their forms—that this man in baggy shorts and puzzling tee-shirt could
indeed be the Hierophant, the one who spoke to the Gods on High, the
conduit of Truth.

The Hierophant looked at each Elder, at each assistant. His pale
eyes seemed to pierce into the heart of each person seated before him,
seemed to read doubts and ambitions as if they had been printed on
their foreheads in the same square black letters as adorned his tee-shirt.

Randall Kelsey, once of the Elect, now merely a trusted adjunct to
Ben Kwinan who himself was an assistant to Elder Arlette Papastrati,
flinched beneath that pale gaze, but it passed him by and continued its
round of the long conference table. By the time the Hierophant had
finished his silent inspection, the gathered Elders were reduced to the
status of quivering schoolchildren awaiting the slap of the ruler.

"And so I suppose you think that this was all one great big joke,"
the Hierophant said. His voice was deep, gruff, like that of a bear awakened from a long hibernation.

Arlette Papastrati, to her credit, found the courage to speak. In Verité, she was a short, dark woman, her attractiveness marred by a faint
mustache. In Virtù, her hair was the color of flame and her beauty left
men without any doubt that the universe contained divinity.

"Great Hierophant, do you refer to the events in Central Park?"

"You know I do, sister."

"Of course we do not view them as a joke. We simply underestimated
the . . . playfulness of the lesser deities."

"It was a pisser, wasn't it?"

The Hierophant's laugh was coarse, his accents more and more those
of old Brooklyn. None of the Elders present could step down from their
dignity to laugh with him, but a few assistants, more accustomed to following their senior's lead, tittered compliantly. When the laughter (such
as it was) faded, the Hierophant spoke again.

"I suppose you think that the riot that accompanied our little show
with Bel Marduk means that we're going to step back from the timetable
that has been divinely set for us?"

"Well, Great Hierophant," said Aoud Araf, "our analysis shows that
this would be the wisest course of action. The Church of Elish faces
lawsuits from the city of New York as well as from several of those

injured in the riot. A class action suit is being joined on behalf of—"

"Shut up."

Aoud did so, blinking a few times, surprised at being questioned. Although he lacked the seniority of many present, his proven ability in his department had granted him a measure of authority on issues of security.

"You folks don't know how to play to a crowd," the Hierophant said, scratching his belly. "If we retreat now, we're acknowledging guilt—guilt, I remind you, that is not ours to accept. What did these yahoos think would happen when a deity manifested—doves and white roses? We've been honest about the gods of Ancient Babylon. These are the gods of Flood and Fire, the gods who whipped Order out of Chaos and barely kept Order going. We aren't preaching to any milk-and-water aesthetes! When Marduk flew over their heads, they were damn lucky that all they got was a little cat piss and a few fireworks."

Despite himself, Randall Kelsey found himself nodding. The Hierophant was voicing—admittedly with a new emphasis—some of his own concerns. The difference was that the Hierophant made the power and potential destructiveness of the gods sound right, even entrancing. From the shifting postures of those around him, Kelsey could tell that others felt the same thing.

"So what would you have us do, sir?" Arlette Papastrati asked.

"Go out there with your shoulders squared. Get your legal advisors to note that the Church plans to sue the city of New York and all those who attended the celebration for behaving in a fashion that ruined our carefully planned, very expensive festival."

Someone guffawed. "That will make them think twice."

"Exactly. Find a new location—buy private land if you need to—and plan a second celebration. Tell them you'll be bringing through Bel Marduk again and perhaps another of the great powers."

"What if they try to stop us?"

"Use land in the U.S. of A. They still have provisions for freedom of religion in their Constitution. Plant a rumor that the attempts to clamp down on our celebrations are only the beginning of widespread restriction of religious freedom. Lots of religions claim to manifest their gods—Catholics through the Eucharist, voudon through the loas. There are others. Make them our allies in this."

An excited babble broke loose as the implications of the Hierophant's words sunk in. New suggestions were made for turning the seeming disaster into a coup of unimagined proportions.

In the excitement, no one noticed when the Hierophant faded away, leaving only the slogan from his tee-shirt scrawled on the wall behind his chair in black crayon.

—=—

Jay Donnerjack stood with the crusader ghost, skipping stones into the still inlet of the sea. The grey-blue vista of the ocean was interrupted only by occasional glimpses of a red sail far out on the water. Dubhe clung to Jay's shoulders, head swiveling as he looked for Death. The *caoineag* stood mute nearby.

"Fi' times, that, laddie," the crusader ghost chortled. "Dinna ken that you can beat that."

Jay hefted his stone and skipped it thrice. The crusader chuckled.

"Hey!" Jay protested. "Let's see how well you do with a monkey on your back! Dubhe, climb down. You're ruining my game."

Reluctantly, the monkey climbed down and then clambered onto a boulder nearby. Jay skipped another stone.

"Four that time!" he crowed.

The crusader skipped another. "Six!"

Jay scooped up another flat stone. "Want to try, Dubhe?"

"I'm not sure that my arms are made for that."

"Try."

"I'd rather watch."

"Dubhe, the Lord of the Lost will come or he won't. There isn't much we can do now. Relax."

"You might not feel so confident if you'd ever met the Lord of Deep Fields in person. He's a . . . difficult person."

"I've been thinking about that," Jay said, thoughtfully. "Come on. Here's a really good stone. . . . Hold it like this. Now pitch it."

The stone flew from Dubhe's hand, bounced once, twice, three times before sinking.

"Hey! That was neat!"

The monkey scrabbled down from the boulder and collected another flat stone. For a long stretch, the only sound was the plop of rocks into the water and the players' cheers and groans.

"Ma'am," Jay said, turning to the *caoineag*, "won't you join us?"

"I do not think so." She gestured so that her draperies flowed. "I am not dressed for free movement."

"Yeah, I noticed that." Jay frowned. "Is there some reason you don't want me to see what you look like?"

The crusader ghost dropped his skipping stone, completely negating the *caoineag*'s calm "Of course not, John."

Jay pretended not to notice the crusader ghost's discomfort.

"I was just wondering, ma'am. You see, my bracelet thought that there was something familiar about you. I've had a bit of trouble with people posing as my friends who were actually agents of the Lord of Deep Fields."

Dubhe skipped his stone with such violence that it skipped nine times and landed on the opposite bank. Again, Jay did not comment, but he did place a comforting hand on the monkey's shoulder.

"Yes, I know that."

"So then you won't mind if I ask you to remove your veil and show me what you look like. I don't mean to be rude, ma'am, not when you seem to be helping me, but I think you can see my point."

The *caoineag* fluttered her hands indecisively.

"And what will you do if I refuse? I do not believe that you can catch me if I try to evade you."

"Maybe not, but I could just turn around and head back through the moon portal. Maybe the Lord of Deep Fields has given up his siege, but he may still be at it."

"Ah." Again the hands fluttered. "How do you know that my appearance will mean anything to you?"

"I don't, but I don't think you would have worn a veil if your appearance was not significant in some way."

"And if I told you that the veil was part of the traditional costume of my type of ghost?"

"Then I'd wonder why you didn't say so in the first place."

"I see. You are a clever boy. Analytical. You remind me of your father."

"You knew my father?"

"Quite well." Slender hands rose and pushed the veil away from her face, slid it off her ebon hair. "You see, I was his wife."

Jay stood, dumbfounded, staring. There before him was the face he had studied so often in the projections Dack had given him, the pouting lips, the elegant cheekbones, the dark, somehow sad, eyes.

"Mother?" he said, and his voice broke.

"Yes, John." She opened her arms to him. "I'm your mother. I'm Ayradyss."

She wept then, and nearly grown man that he was, he wept as well. After a time, she released him enough to look into his face.

"Tell, me, John, what did you mean when you said that your bracelet thought that there was something familiar about me?"

Jay touched the bracelet. "My father programmed an aion with much of his memory and personality and then installed it in a bracelet that he put on my wrist when I was just a baby. It has always been with me."

Ayradyss reached out and touched the bracelet, a tentative motion, almost a caress.

"How very strange," she said. "We both found ways to watch over you, even after we were gone."

"Bracelet, aren't you going to say anything to her?" Jay asked.

The bracelet spoke in the voice of John D'Arcy Donnerjack, Senior. "I don't know what to say. I can identify this woman, but I feel nothing more than a wash of generalized emotions. I suspect that my creator could not bear to preserve his torment or his passion—both of which must have existed for him to do what he did in an effort to regain and preserve her."

"Oh, John." Ayradyss sighed. "You always did have trouble expressing what you felt."

Jay fidgeted. "Hey, folks. Now that I have both of you here—in some form, at least—I have some questions I hope you'll answer. And bracelet, none of this, 'not permitted to answer at this time' stuff."

"Very well, John," Ayradyss said.

"Please call me Jay, ma'am. Too many Johns could get confusing."

"Very well, Jay. Could you call me Ayradyss if Mother is difficult at this late a date?"

He grinned. "Sure, Mom."

She blushed with pleasure. Jay seated himself on the boulder Dubhe had lately abandoned; the monkey climbed onto his knee.

"First of all," Jay said, "was there a deal made with the Lord of Deep Fields concerning me?"

"Yes," the bracelet replied. "I made my way to Deep Fields to regain Ayradyss. I brought music to soften his heart and promised him a construction of my design as payment for her return. The Lord of Deep Fields required our firstborn as part of the price. Since I believed this an impossible condition to fulfill, I agreed."

"Why did you think it impossible? Hadn't he already done something impossible by agreeing to return her in Verité rather than Virtù?"

"I had yet to see that she would be returned to me in Verité. I was also—as difficult as this may be for you to believe—in a state of emotional turmoil. I wanted Ayra back and no price seemed too great. I had invoked legend and fairy tale in my coming for her. I thought he was merely continuing the theme."

"So you loved her."

"As I have loved no one or nothing in all my life." The bracelet paused. "Although I cannot feel those emotions as my maker did, his memories are recorded and those words are true."

Jay nodded. Ayradyss was weeping, wiping away the tears with the corner of her veil. Looking at her, Jay realized that in appearance she was not much older than he was. He wondered what her real age might be. Collecting himself, he continued his interrogation.

"When you both realized that I was going to be born, you set out to foil the Lord of Deep Fields, to keep me from him."

"That's right," Ayradyss said. "My first knowledge of you came from the howling of the former *caoineag*. The crusader ghost told me that she wailed for me—and for you and John."

The bracelet added, "We did not wish to lose you. After your birth and Ayradyss's death I journeyed to Deep Fields and there battled the Lord of Deep Fields. I could not win Ayra back, nor could I convince him to relinquish his claim to you, but I did gain his promise to give you some years among the living."

"Did you then believe that he wished me dead?" Jay asked, proud of how steady he kept his voice.

Ayradyss glanced at the bracelet, spread her hands.

"Actually, Jay," she said, "we didn't know what he wanted you for. It was enough that he would take our son from us."

The bracelet added, "It seems unlikely that he wanted your death, in the sense of complete termination of existence. One of the conditions of Ayradyss's freedom was that I design a palace for him. In the plans for that palace, the Lord of the Lost included a nursery."

"So he meant to raise me there. Dubhe, can you add anything to this?"

The monkey cracked his knuckles. "Yes, I can, in fact. Death sent me and some of the others to watch over you when your father set you to play on the Great Stage. I had the impression that, in addition to being kept informed about your development, he did not wish any harm to come to you."

"So, indirectly, he was my protector."

Ayradyss, not liking at all what she saw of the direction of Jay's thoughts, interrupted.

" 'Protector' may be too kind a word, son. Shepherds protect sheep and eat mutton all the same. The Lord of Entropy may not have meant you any kindness."

"True, but apparently no one ever asked him what he intended for me."

Dubhe added, "I always had the impression that Phecda knew more than she was saying. Mizar's brain was scrambled and Alioth—well, Alioth was something else."

"Alioth, the black butterfly?" Ayradyss said, her tones those of suppressed astonishment.

"Yes, ma'am," Dubhe replied.

"Alioth played with me from times when I was so small that I could hardly say his name," Jay said. "Did you know him?"

"I have heard the name," Ayradyss answered.

"Jay, what are you contemplating?" the bracelet asked. "I have analyzed the trend of your questions and I am not at all reassured by the implications."

Jay stood, set Dubhe on the boulder, looked down at the bracelet, then over at his mother. Both Dubhe and the crusader ghost sat very, very still, feeling the tingle of a coming storm in the air.

"I think I will go and ask Death what it was he wanted me for," Jay said.

"No!" Ayradyss cried.

"I forbid it," the bracelet ordered.

Dubhe merely squeaked.

"I'm going," Jay repeated. "And I'm going on my own terms. Tranto the phant mentioned a train called the Brass Babboon that my father took into Deep Fields. If I can find that train, I can confront the Lord of Deep Fields from a position of—if not power—at least of something other than captivity."

The bracelet vibrated and glowed slightly violet. "I can generate a field that will force you from Virtù and restrict you to Verité."

"For how long?" Jay asked. "And can you keep me from chopping off my arm? It's a drastic measure, but it's one that I'll take if I must."

"Jay!" The shocked gasp came from several throats. Only the crusader ghost grinned, a sardonic, bitter expression.

"Aye, th' laddie will do as he says. He's nae more a wee thing to be pushed aboot."

Jay nodded. "I appreciate all that you have tried to do for me. But I can't live the rest of my life running from Death. My father made an agreement with the Lord of Deep Fields. I will fulfill that agreement."

"Jay, you don't know what you're doing!" Ayradyss cried. "He is a terrible creature."

"Is he?" Jay said. "He can be wooed by music, admires the art of constructions, and apparently did not desire my extinction. In fact, he sent me guardians when my father left me to play on the fringes of Virtù."

The bracelet said softly, "I did not know that you would learn to cross over so easily, or that I would not be there to protect you."

"Maybe so, but after taking you, Death provided that protection." Jay squared his shoulders. "Do you assist me in this, or will you try to prevent me?"

Ayradyss touched his face with her fingers. "I have no power to prevent, only to advise. Although I would prefer that you do not go, I promise you that when you return to Castle Donnerjack I will be here to assist you."

The bracelet took longer to answer. Gradually, however, the violet glow subsided.

"I cannot prevent you without forcing you to take an action that would only make it more difficult to achieve what you would do in any case. Therefore, I shall not protest further."

"Will you advise?"

"Yes."

"Good." Jay turned to Dubhe. "Are you coming with me, or would you like me to try and draw you back into the Verité?"

Dubhe shrugged and cackled with a trace of the cheerful villainy that he had lost when he had fled Death into Verité.

"Sure I'll go with you, Jay. It beats hiding under your bed and looking for the moiré."

"Good." Jay turned and began to walk up the hillside. "I'll let Dack know that I'm off on a virt jaunt and make the crossover from the Great Stage. I'd prefer not to draw this site to Death's attention."

They walked up the hillside and through the cluster of standing stones. Although the solstice was nowhere near, the stones trembled, responding to a force as powerful as that of nature or of myth.

—=—

High upon Meru, Skyga hummed. Listening to the sound, it seemed to the anxious Seaga that the hum had developed a lilt, a tremolo triumphant. He glanced over at Earthma, but she was withdrawn in meditation and he was reluctant to give anything away to the hummer by petitioning for her attention.

Biting into his lower lip with ill-concealed petulance, he let himself flow out into his various avatars:

A clerk organizing data in a virt stock market branch (where the stocks and bonds were represented as apples and pears of varying colors) blinked as for a moment the data all made perfect sense. He saw the trends involved in various shifts in the world economy and, had he been able to recall that insight, he could have made his fortune with a few small purchases. The insight vanished, however, and he continued sorting improbably colored fruit into various bins.

Reese Jordan, sitting soaking his feet in Caltrice's favorite pool, felt a minnow nibbling at his toes. For a moment, he was a boy again—young and carefree. Then the feeling vanished, reminding him that once again his mortal form in the Center for Iatropathic Diseases in Verité was about to undergo some esoteric procedure. Even though the assistance of the Donnerjack Institute had added almost twenty years to his already extended life, he felt an ache of fury and frustration that this time he might finally shuffle off this mortal coil. The thought entered his mind that he would do anything, anything at all, for the promise of extending his life.

Ben Kwinan slouched against a wall within a chambered nautilus, reporting the latest developments in the Elishite situation. Deep within his mind was hidden the thought that perhaps he had chosen his ally unwisely. Seaga seemed nervous and contentious.

The white picket fence around a cottage on a cold, rocky shore bore the sign: "Do Not Disturb." A pigeon, glancing in the window, saw a man with a scar running from the top of his head to the sole of his left foot busily making adjustments on a machine of platinum and crystal.

✿   ✿   ✿

In the morgue for the *New York Times* and its affiliates a wind, damp and smelling of the sea, swept through the files, flagging certain stories and arranging them in a peculiar order. A ragged vibration, rather like a sigh, shook the virt chamber, then the wind withdrew, taking with it knowledge and leaving behind only a faint tang of salt to announce its visit.

Ancestral voices proclaiming war.

SEVEN

In a special grove within Markon's realm, Virginia Tallent spoke into the air about what she had seen during that day's wanderings and the air spoke to her, giving her answers.

"I passed through the jungle—you know the one . . ."

"Yes, Nazrat's site."

"And I passed a band of the apelike rogue proges who reside there."

"Dangerous types. Did you keep to cover?"

"Yes, and observed them from there. Markon, I could have sworn that they were drilling!"

"Drilling? As for oil?"

"No, marching and practicing with weapons—machetes mostly, but there were some armed with firearms. Their leader was a great brute with greying fur and what I could have sworn was a shriveled human head hung around his neck."

"That would be Sayjak. He is the Boss of Bosses of their people. His influence and legend have spread outside of Nazrat's site."

"He did not seem like a boss of anything. Several times he passed quite close to me and his eyes were dull and unfocused, yet his tribe members were clearly terrified of him. Have you ever heard of such a thing?"

"Long ago."

"In those times you told me about—the times of the Master, the Engineer, and the Guide? The times when the *genii loci* warred among each other and the gods were made?"

"That is so, Virginia. Apparently, Sayjak has become the minion of some deity, of a being more powerful than a *genius loci*. No wonder his people are terrified of him."

Virginia looked shyly at the ground, traced a figure in the dirt with the tip of her finger.

"I have never asked before, Markon, but are *genii loci* gods?"

"Within our realms, we are something like that, Virginia. Some of us are more powerful than others, have a greater understanding of our sites and their limitations."

"Like you are more powerful than Kordalis."

"Precisely." Markon sighed and the leaves of the trees rippled. "But we cannot depart our sites, while those who are termed deities can travel throughout Virtù. Yet, only the greatest of the deities are more powerful than a *genius loci* within its own territory. Thus, in the battles of yore, the deities treated with us as with sovereign nations, negotiating for passage, supplies, and sometimes for troops."

"And sometimes you warred with your neighbors."

"That is so."

"Markon, have you made any treaties with those who have petitioned you?"

"Not yet."

"And if your neighbors make such treaties, might one or more of them attack you?"

"Yes, the ancient boundaries have held partly because we grew weary of conflict and partly because each of us held what we could control. The deities, however, can grant power to those who serve them—enhance their programming. A neighbor so enhanced might endeavor to defeat me. An alliance between two or more—especially if I had no allies of my own—most certainly would do so."

"Markon, you must make some alliances!"

"Virginia, I plan to do so, but I must choose carefully if I am to keep the war from here and thus keep you safe. My greatest desire is to protect you, my fragile love."

She smiled. "I appreciate your offer, but I don't wish to endanger you by having you consider my safety. I know the isolated places in Virtù. I will go to one and hide. Then I will return to you when the battles are over."

"The wars may take years. They may not begin for years. When will you hide? Even the wildest sites have their *genius loci*. Where will you hide that you cannot be taken hostage against me? I love you, woman, and would do anything to gain your safety."

Virginia wept. Where her tears struck the ground, tiny white flowers with hearts of gold sprung forth. Their perfume was sweet.

—=—

Jay Donnerjack bid his ghostly mother farewell, notified Dack that he planned to take an extended trip into Virtù, and departed his father's castle. When he crossed the Great Stage, he carried with him Dubhe, the dark simian creature who had betrayed the orders of the Lord of Deep Fields. Whistling, he summoned to him Death's dog, Mizar, who knew nothing of his origin, but who loved the boy. Feeling well accompanied, Jay shook his black hair from his shoulders and breathed the crisp morning air.

"Any idea where we should start looking for this train, Jay?" Dubhe asked.

"Not really. I want to go visit with Reese first, tell him what we're doing. He had surgery again, recently. The report I got from the Institute says that he made it through, but I bet he could use visitors."

"I . . . can find . . . the way," wheezed Mizar.

"Good," Jay said. "I won't be able to stay with Reese long—not since I'm in my real self—but it's a place to start."

They traveled then, walking across cracked beds of dry lava, swimming beneath the waters of an aquamarine ocean, skiing down a mountain of perfect powder. The route they took was far from the easiest, but Mizar tended to be rather direct and Jay was not concerned about his own comfort. What Dubhe thought, he kept to himself.

When they neared Caltrice's site, Jay wrote a message on a leaf and set it on a raft made from twigs. This he set into a stream that he knew would enter Caltrice's site. The message, like so many he had sent in the past, said simply: "I am coming to visit and would like to see Reese if I can. J."

Arriving, they found Reese seated on his favorite rock, working out a series of formulas on a datapad manifested as a chunk of raw slate. He set down his chalk when he heard them enter the grove and grinned.

"It seems like forever, Jay. Where have you been?"

"Getting into trouble," Jay answered. "How are you feeling?"

"In virt, just fine. In RT, the operation was fairly successful, but apparently they had to remove my right leg from the knee down. I know it's silly to mourn an appendage that I haven't used for years, but I find myself in a rather bleak state of mind. Distract me. Tell me about your adventures."

Jay did so, beginning with his encounter with the *caoineag* and ending with his resolution to seek out Death. Finishing, he braced himself, waiting for the inevitable argument. Reese merely cleared his throat and studied him.

"You've grown up."

"I guess so."

"And you feel this is something you need to do."

"I don't see that there is any other reasonable choice, Reese. Both Mother and Father tried fighting the Lord of Deep Fields. Their battles gave me time to grow up. Now I can go and confront him on more equal terms."

Reese nodded. "Apparently, he still wants you, so your education and maturity have not ruined you. Has it occurred to you that he might want you merely as a source of spare parts? I know of no other successful mating between Virtù and Verité."

Jay swallowed hard. "I hadn't, but I'll take that risk."

"And you mean to find your father's peculiar train."

"That's the idea."

"I have never seen it, but I did learn something about it from John. Before you begin your run into Deep Fields have it carry you to the grove where strange attractors grow. These may arm you as they armed your father. Of course, the lord of that place may have learned new defenses since your father challenged him."

"Do you know where I might find the Brass Babboon?"

Reese sighed. "No, it is long since I cared to venture more than briefly from Caltrice's site. That reminds me. If you are in the flesh, you should not remain here long. Go, son. Send me a message when you succeed."

Jay hugged him. "I will, sir."

"Where will you begin your search?"

"I first heard about the Brass Babboon from a phant who claimed to have met my father. He was the first one to mention Dad's journeys into Deep Fields to me. I'll seek him out and learn what I can from him."

"Good thought. Fortune walk with you."

"Thanks."

The old man watched Jay depart, the dog before him, the monkey moving through the boughs overhead. Reese had hidden from Jay the fact that if he did not concentrate his virt persona had a tendency to fade out, beginning with the amputated leg. Caltrice could find no reason for it, but Reese suspected that his hold on life was almost ended.

He wondered if he died in Virtù would he see the moiré first.

—=—

When Desmond Drum arrived at his office, Link Crain was waiting. He considered it a courtesy that the girl waited in the hallway, since she was quite capable of picking the lock. When he opened the door and ushered her inside, he wondered that anyone could take her for a boy— there was a sway to her walk, a roundness to her hips that marked her as female to his admiring gaze. And those green eyes! Such lashes. She'd never be a beauty, but if her mother was any indication she would continue to improve with age.

Pouring them both shots from his favorite bottle, he toasted her, silently mocked himself. He suspected that Link did not bother to watch her body language when they were alone since, after all, he knew her secret and—anyhow—he was far too senior to her for her to see as a man.

"Do you have any news for me?" Link asked eagerly, setting down the glass barely touched.

"I do." He paused, teasing her with his silence then relenting. "It may not be what you want to hear, kid."

"Go on!"

"Very well. First, I checked and there is indeed no one named Jason or Jay MacDougal residing in Scotland who could be our young knight. Moreover, I checked birth certificates and did not find anyone by that name who could be our friend."

"Yes?"

"Without a photo record, I could not do more on that front so I started working on the names you gave me. There were two: Milburn and Dack."

"Right."

"Since Milburn was the person Jason contacted when he was in New York, I started with him. There were a number of dead ends, but eventually I found someone who may answer."

"And?"

"There is an AP named Milburn who resides in New York. He is in the employ of the Donnerjack Institute and part of his job description includes chauffeur and pilot."

"That sounds promising."

"Even more promising is that the listed owner of the Donnerjack Institute is one John D'Arcy Donnerjack. His place of residence is listed as a castle on an island off of the coast of Scotland."

Link's naturally active mind had been honed by her choice of profession. "The initials are similar—if one omits the 'mac'—and Scotland is where Jay said he was from. Why does the name John D'Arcy Donnerjack ring a bell?"

"He is one of the great engineers of virtual reality design. You've probably visited his Inferno at some point."

"I think I did. Didn't like it much. Did you call the Donnerjack Institute?"

"Better, I called the castle directly. The robot who took the call said that the master was traveling. I asked him to identify himself and he said that his name was Dack."

"That's the place! But Jay couldn't be this John D'Arcy Donnerjack, could he?"

"No, Donnerjack would be far older—older even than your mother—maybe even as old as me."

Link missed the joke. "So, who is Jay?"

"I have a thought on that," Drum said. He flipped a holo-album across his desk. "I got some pictures of Donnerjack—found some from when he was younger. See anything?"

"There certainly is a similarity, isn't there? Not identical, but enough to make fairly clear that they're related."

"That was my thought as well. Not all fathers and sons look as much alike as you and your mother do, Alice. I would guess that if Jay isn't Donnerjack's son, he's a nephew—maybe a young cousin."

Link nodded, still studying the holograms. "Did you find a record of a wife?"

Drum shrugged. "None, but that's hardly telling. I didn't find any register of children, either, which puzzled me. I would have bet—given the address, the fact that Jay was being driven by someone from the Institute—that Jay was Donnerjack's son. I didn't find any record of Donnerjack having siblings either, so the nephew line is a bit tenuous.

Still, I think I've found your Jay. He's a relation of the Donnerjack family and, at least part of the time, resides in a castle in Scotland."

"Let's call him!"

"I tried—used a different virt domino so Dack wouldn't know the same person was calling. Not only didn't I get Jay, Dack refused to acknowledge that there was such a person."

"Huh?"

"And when I contacted Milburn, I got the same response. He was polite but said that I must have him confused with someone else. Thing is, I checked flight permits filed by the Donnerjack Institute for a couple of days before the Elshie celebration and I found that one had been taken out for Milburn. The destination wasn't listed, but the turn-around time would have been just about right for a quick jaunt to Scotland."

"Weird."

"Very. If it wasn't for the fact that he bled all over the front seat of my Spinner, I'd say that in Jay MacDougal you and I had suffered a consensual hallucination."

"Don't tease!"

"I'm not. I'm merely expressing a point, kid."

"Yeah."

Link looked so depressed that Drum reached across and patted her hand.

"This isn't an end, kid, just a delay. In the meantime, I've heard from you-know-who. He wants to see us tonight."

Link shook off her depression, squared her shoulders, shifted her posture and, somehow, indefinably, seemed more male than before. Drum was impressed.

"I could use the distraction," Link said. "Want to get dinner before?"

"The Chinese place again?"

"Yeah, I want to try their garlic eggplant."

"Yuck."

—=—

Jay walked beneath the spreading green of the forest giants. Thick vines, flowered red and orange and yellow, interwove the boughs so that overhead Dubhe hardly need employ any energy in his progress from tree to tree. Mizar snapped at a flying beetle, its wings polished copper and aged bronze. Birds called from hidden roosts or screeched when Jay's progress brought him too close to an egg-filled nest. All around them was life in form fantastical and impossible, yet to Jay the jungle felt strange and somehow empty.

"Mizar, have we come to the correct site?"

"It smells so . . ." A creaking as the hound raised its fearsome head. "Yes . . . this is . . . Nazrat's locus."

Jay glanced from side to side. "It seems wrong. Too quiet? That's not quite right, but something is missing."

Dubhe dropped to his shoulder. "I spotted the plains through a gap in the canopy, Jay."

"Good," Jay said, still distracted. "Mizar, when we reach the plain would you find the trail of the phants?"

"Which . . . phants?"

"Tranto's herd, if you can. Any will do. They keep tabs on each other. Even a lone bull should be able to give us directions."

Mizar wagged his cable tail in acknowledgment. When they left the green coolness for the sunlit grasslands, he dropped his nose to the ground and began casting about. Jay, seated on a hummock in the shade, watched, still trying to place the source of the strangeness he sensed. He was no closer when Mizar gave a low bay.

"I have . . . phant. Blood . . . as well. Be care . . . ful."

The boy rose and fell briskly into step behind Mizar, not even pausing as Dubhe dropped from the branches and onto his shoulder.

"We will be, Mizar. Is the blood scent fresh?"

"Very. Phant also."

"Maybe that's why things seem so quiet," Jay said, not convinced. "If there's something out here that can wound a phant . . ."

"Tranto," Mizar interrupted.

"Tranto?" Jay broke into a trot. "If there's something out here that can wound Tranto, then maybe everything else has taken cover."

"Hope it's not still out here," Dubhe said.

"Yeah."

After a time, a handful of trees closely clustered together announced the presence of a watering hole ahead. Coasting on the winds above the trees were a dozen birds that might have been called vultures except that their feathers were brilliant yellow picked out in sapphire blue. Their heads and necks, however, were bare of feathers, the naked pink skin (when added to the yellow and blue) attiring the birds with gruesome festivity given the obvious purpose of their powerfully hooked beaks and horned talons.

"Whatever it is isn't dead," Jay said, "or those birds would be down there right now."

"Tranto," Mizar repeated patiently. "I smell Tranto."

And it was Tranto they saw as they closed the remaining distance. The ancient phant lay collapsed on his side. His grey, wrinkled hide was scored with red and blood pooled around him. Only the defiant flapping of his trunk when one of the vultures dropped within range assured them that he still lived, but each time he drove them off they retreated less and the trunk moved more slowly.

Mizar bayed, a horrid sound like the static-laden feedback of a set of poorly wired amplifiers. The vultures flapped higher, warned, but not panicked. Jay ignored them, hurrying to the phant. Up close, things looked even worse, but one thing was clear, Tranto's opponent had not gotten away without injury. The phant's long curving tusks were reddened with gore.

"Tranto . . ." Jay said, his voice breaking.

Tranto's eye was glazed with pain, dimmed with something like madness, but he still knew Jay. He flapped his upper ear in acknowledgment. Heedless of the blood that soaked the ground, Jay knelt and brought his head near the phant's oddly delicate mouth.

"Who did this?"

Tranto tried to speak, but only blood-flecked spittle dribbled forth. Jay placed a reassuring hand on one leg—just about the only place he could find that wasn't terribly wounded.

"Mizar?"

The hound turned from where it had been menacing the swirling vultures. A few yellow-and-blue feathers were caught in his jagged metal teeth.

"Yes?"

"Mizar, I want you to find Nazrat for me."

"Hard. *Genius loci* do . . . not need to be . . . Is here."

"I want to talk to him, like I do to Caltrice. How can I send him a message?"

Dubhe tossed a handful of dates at one of the vultures, chortling when he scored a hit.

"It's impossible if he doesn't want to hear you, but I'd bet he has at least some of his awareness extended into this area. Tranto isn't just any proge."

"So I should just talk to the air?"

"Why not?"

Jay shrugged. The idea was not as alien to him as it might be to someone with a more Veritéan attitude toward Virtù. Still stroking Tranto's leg, making a silent inventory of the phant's damage, he soliloquized.

"Nazrat, we've met in passing before. I'm Jay Donnerjack. When I came here to play in your jungles or to talk to Tranto, I've praised the beauty and versatility of your site. Now, I think something's wrong here, really wrong. You see, I can't imagine that something could tear Tranto up like this and just walk away. I can see from Tranto's tusks that he must have seriously hurt his opponents, but when I look about me, I don't see any blood trails leading away. Isn't that strange?"

He paused, but there was no answer.

"I came here hoping for Tranto's advice. Finding him like this . . . it's wrong. Can't you fix him somehow?"

The pooled blood stirred, bubbles popped making words: "Tranto is destined for Deep Fields."

Jay nodded. "How interesting. That's where I'm going myself. If you fix Tranto, I'll take him with me."

More bubbles. "You mock me!"

"No, really. You must know something of my family. My father made the trip twice. Call it nostalgia, but I'm going, too."

"Nostalgia? Insanity!"

"Nazrat, I'm going to make a guess that whatever did this to Tranto wasn't of your creation. Therefore, you can mend him without violating your own internal laws."

"Why should I?"

"As a favor to me, as a means of preserving a fantastic proge."

"You will take him to Deep Fields?"

"That's where I'm going. I can't exactly force something as massive as Tranto to go with me, but I'm willing to believe he wouldn't make a liar of me."

The great ear flapped agreement.

"I am amused, young Donnerjack. Angered also by what was done here. Very well, if you promise to take Tranto to Deep Fields with you, I will erase the errors that have entered his system."

"What was done here?"

"Ask the phant. I do not care to converse any longer."

And the surface on which Tranto lay began to froth as the blood he had shed foamed and, contrary to the basic laws of gravity, began to separate from the dirt, flow up his sides, and descend into his wounds.

When the process was completed, the phant's hide was coursed with myriad fresh scars, but not a trace of the blood remained.

Getting to his feet, Jay looked down at his hands, checked his trousers, and laughed, knowing that the *genius loci* would hear his pleasure.

"That was impressive! Tranto, how do you feel?"

With a sigh as of great weariness, the phant rolled to his knees, then surged to his feet to a chorus of disappointed shrieks from the vultures. Tranto trumpeted at them, then he felt himself with his trunk.

"Far better than I would have imagined possible. I owe Nazrat—and you—my thanks."

"What happened? Who did that to you?"

"I will tell you while I get something to drink and perhaps some forage. Nazrat has written out my damage with immense skill, but I am still depleted."

"I understand. Dubhe, toss down some of those bananas and coconuts, will you?"

"Sure, Jay. That was rather fascinating. I wonder what Death is going to have to say about yet another Donnerjack cheating him of his due?"

Jay shrugged with a nonchalance he did not entirely feel. "I guess we'll know soon enough."

As Tranto was refreshing himself, he told his story.

"A short time ago, I had a visit from a strange, female phant. She spoke of recruiting among my herd as warriors in a battle meant to right some of the inequities between Virtù and Verité."

"Inequities?"

"I confess, I did not understand her fully, but she seemed to feel that Verité has been misusing the virt. When I expressed no desire to join her crusade, she grew indignant and retreated into the jungle. Still ill at ease, I set myself to guarding the herd, but what I did not anticipate was a traitor from among those I trusted.

"At daybreak, I moved the herd on, wishing to be away from where the stranger phant might yet roam. It was while we were moving that I heard the trumpet of challenge. I turned . . ."

—=—

Muggle strode from the fringes of the herd, but what an altered Muggle he was. No more was he the runt bull—scrawny, weak, barely tusked. Now he loomed vast and bulky, a great grey mountain with coarse, wrinkled skin and yellow-white tusks so long that he should not have been able to lift them clear of the ground. He glowed with a faint aura of golden light that was clearly visible even in the brilliance of the day. Only his voice was unchanged and it was by his voice that Tranto knew him.

"I've come to challenge you for leadership of the herd, Tranto."

"Put on some weight, haven't you, Muggle?"

Tranto's tone was mocking, but inwardly he was checking out his opponent. What he saw was not promising. Muggle hadn't just acquired mass, there was grace and agility to go with it. The way he handled those tusks, he now possessed strength and to spare. For the first time in a long, long while, Tranto knew fear.

In the first pass, one of Muggle's tusks furrowed a long wound on Tranto's flank, removing Tranto's last hope that Muggle did not possess the ability to use his new weapons along with a great quantity of flesh and blood. Still, Tranto's hard-learned cunning and skill stood him in good stead. Time and again he raked Muggle, giving wounds as good or better than those he received, but each time Muggle faltered the golden light flared about him and his wounds healed.

At first Tranto believed that he had somehow offended Nazrat and that the *genius loci* had raised a champion against him. But there was that about the golden light, about the strange scent that lingered around Muggle, that reminded him of the stranger female. Before he crashed to the ground, he had become convinced that he had been betrayed less by Muggle than by her.

—=—

"Still," Tranto said around a mouthful of grass, "my supposition did not grant me much comfort when I watched Muggle lead away my herd."

"We can find them for you," Jay offered.

Mizar scratched behind one ear (tapestry print, roses after the Victorian style).

"I do . . . not scent . . . phants."

"Not anywhere?"

Mizar shook his head, continued scratching. From his perch in the treetops, Dubhe belched, dropped a banana peel near Tranto (who added it to his next mouthful), and called down:

"I don't see anything from up here and I have a pretty good view over the plains. A herd the size of Tranto's would stir up some dust."

"Gone," Tranto said mournfully. "Muggle—or whatever it was that changed him—has taken them to fight someone else's battles. I can only hope that the calves will be spared, but I doubt it. There was something cold about that stranger phant."

"Cold?" Jay asked. "Do you mean evil?"

Tranto considered. "No, cold: willing to sacrifice many lives for an ideal or a victory. I can't really make myself any clearer. We didn't talk all that long."

"Do you want to search for them?"

"I wouldn't find them," Tranto said. "Not here. When you were talking to Nazrat, you said that you had come here to consult me about a journey to Deep Fields. Are you following in your father's footsteps?"

Dubhe guffawed. Jay traced a line in the dirt with his toe.

"Not really. Long ago you told me that a train called the Brass Babboon might be able to tell me about my father's battle with the Lord of Entropy."

"Yes."

"Can you help me find the Brass Babboon?"

"I may be able to do so. After our conversation, I made a point of learning the location of one of his stations. I will guide you there."

"Thank you."

"And if he agrees to bear you into Deep Fields, I will go with you."

"Again, thank you."

"My reasons are not entirely altruistic. I heard you promise Nazrat that you would take me with you and I would not have you foresworn. Moreover, I feel a rumbling of dark anger within me—an anger that often has unfortunate consequences."

"You mean you may go mad?"

"Possibly. Do you remember how to treat my ailment?"

"I could use a review. Perfect memory is not among my gifts."

"Then I will refresh your memory as we talk. Would you like me to give you a ride?"

Jay looked up at the lofty perch of Tranto's shoulder. Although it was far lower than treetops he would have assayed without trepidation, he felt a momentary pang of acrophobia.

"Sure," he said. "If you don't mind."

"I'd like it. I can cover a lot of ground when I put my mind to it. You'd have trouble keeping up—especially if we're trying to talk. I'll carry the monkey and the dog, too."

Dubhe chortled. "I love it. If doom awaits, I might as well go in style."

Mizar wheezed laughter. "I . . . will walk. Nose to the ground."

Tranto lifted Jay onto his back, settled him just behind his head. Dubhe took his place on Jay's shoulder. With Mizar on point, they set out across the plains. The earthquake that accompanied them might have been the sounding of Tranto's mighty feet, but it could have been Nazrat laughing at a joke only a *genius loci* could understand.

— = —

Once again, Drum and Link met with their employer in the Verité and once again he was costumed and masked. This time Daimon wore a perfect kimono of pale golden silk embroidered with dragons in crimson. His undergarments were also of crimson, as were his gloves. The demon mask he wore had been highlighted to complement the colors of his robes.

Noting Daimon's delight in both disguise and his elaborate attire, Link had once wondered why their employer did not meet with them in Virtù, where such things would be both easier and more effective. She had rapidly deduced that Daimon did not dare enter the virtual realms and this, combined with his interest in the Elishites, had given her a fair idea what might be Daimon's actual identity.

She did not mention her suppositions to Drum, however, for Drum was quite clever enough to have arrived at the same conclusions. If he had not spoken of them, there was a reason. Desmond Drum might have been surprised to learn of the respect with which Link viewed him. Then again, being Desmond Drum, he might not have been.

Drum was giving their report as Daimon prepared tea.

"The Elshies have, contrary to popular media opinion, decided to take an aggressive stance with their critics. For a few days after the riot, they appeared conciliatory, then—all at once—attitude changed. Link?"

Link accepted a delicate bowl of tea, bowed stiffly to Daimon, and organized her thoughts.

"Based on linguistic analysis of the Elshies' latest press releases, I have deduced two things. One, the aggressive stance is not a pose—the church elders do sincerely believe that they can pull this off. If only prepared press releases showed this attitude, I would be tempted to believe that this was a pose, but I arranged for some 'impromptu' interviews and the same confidence was present."

Daimon studied the chrysanthemum flower that had unfolded within his tea cup. He directed the gaze behind his mask to Link's face. As there were black mesh screens set in the eye sockets, the effect was rather intimidating.

"Interesting. And your second deduction?"

"Given that the change in attitude occurred all at once, I guessed that there was a single, central meeting during which this policy was adopted. Drum took over here."

He set down his teacup. "It didn't take much to confirm Link's guess. The Elshies have several meeting rooms equipped for joint virt/RT conferencing. Judging from travel records, surveillance of landing sites, and utility bills, there was a major conference the day of the first press release showing their altered attitude."

"In New York?" Daimon asked.

"That's right. The press releases gave me a starting date to work backward from and I pinpointed the location."

Daimon crossed his arms across his chest. Although his face was masked, he gave the impression of frowning.

"This change in attitude—as you call it—has already created some strange alliances. The Elishite Celebration is rapidly becoming a rallying point for any group interested in preserving freedom of religion or freedom of speech."

Drum nodded. "Not surprising. The Elshies have purchased land in California and are preparing for another celebration."

"Yes." Daimon toyed with his teacup. "This has all been interesting, but now, favor me with your wilder conclusions."

Link glanced at Drum. Drum nodded again.

"We think that the Elshies are getting advice from someone who has a great deal of authority. The High Priest is still being treated with deference, but there is a change. It's rather as if he has been superseded."

"Do you think it is by one of these gods? Bel Marduk, perhaps?"

Link shook her head. "No, it doesn't have that feel. I've attended enough services to have a sense for what the gods are like. They are powerful, arrogant, and somehow antiquated in their assumptions. Whoever this is is clever and sophisticated, with contemporary cultural bias."

"Then you suspect . . ." Daimon prompted.

"Literature about the Church of Elish has long suggested that the founder was an AI, but no one has been able to confirm this, and the Church, of course, claims only divine inspiration."

"But . . ."

"Yes, I think that this aion is now taking an active hand in directing

Church policies. I suspect that it has an agenda that runs parallel to that publicly proclaimed by the Church, but which is not identical."

"And?"

Link hesitated. Drum cut in.

"The kid thinks, wild as it sounds, that the founder of the Church of Elish is planning a coup to take over Verité. The virt powers and the crossover of the gods is just a beginning."

"It's insane, isn't it?" Link said. "I mean, how can a vast computer system take over the reality that created it? It simply should not be able to happen, but that seems to be the agenda."

"I don't know how they would do it," Daimon said, "but I suspect we need to find out and I suspect we need to find out quickly. I, for one, would not enjoy living in a world where gods such as Bel Marduk have free reign."

He raised his teacup in mute salute. Drum and Link mimicked the motion.

Darkness: spider silk between crimson and gold.

—=—

Dr. Lydia Hazzard walked her patient to the door of the consulting room and turned the young man over to an orderly who would make certain that prescriptions were dispensed and billing was duly addressed. Touching the intercom call button set flush with the top of her walnut veneer desk, she signaled the reception area that she was free to take her next patient.

"No one left, Doctor," the AP said politely. "The rest can be handled by automata."

"Thank you, Della," Lydia said. "I'm going to slip out the back way."

"Very good. Have a pleasant evening."

"See you tomorrow."

Returning to her apartment, Lydia saw with guilty pleasure that Alice was out. It was not that she didn't love her daughter or enjoy her company, but Alice was *so* intense and, by necessity, Lydia had been a single parent.

Her own parents had been helpful, but they were so over-protective (having never been able to forget the peculiar fashion in which their grandchild had been conceived) and yet so inclined to spoil the girl, that Lydia had spent some of her money for an AP nursemaid and had taken on herself the full responsibility for making certain that Alice did not become egocentric and asocial as was often the case with children left too much in the care of APs.

She supposed that she had done well enough. Alice, admittedly, was a peculiar young woman, but she cultivated her own resources and, as Link, had already made some contributions to society about which her mother felt ridiculous pride. Sometimes Lydia wished that Alice spent more time with people her own age, but then she would recall how during her own long-ago virt holiday the thing she had craved most of all was privacy.

Now, luxuriating in her empty apartment, she left a note for Alice, then made a light meal of salad and bread. Nibbling on the heel of the loaf, she walked into her suite. There, in a small room, was one of the indulgences that her parents had insisted that she have—a private virt transfer couch of the latest model.

Given her experience with the public transfer facility, Lydia had not protested, although she was quite certain that Ambry, rather than any flaw in the transfer facility's equipment, had been responsible for her "disappearance" and ensuing pregnancy. Nor did she worry terribly about the transfer facility having been forced to pay damages. Through one of fate's little ironies, they had been insured by Hazzard Insurance, so Abel and Carla's own company had provided the seed fund for the annuity that would, one day soon, make their granddaughter ridiculously wealthy.

Lydia Hazzard fully approved of irony. As far as she was concerned, it was one of the things that real life did far better than art.

Stripping, she placed the transfer couch links against various key points and went to find her husband. Her last thought as the drugs carried her across the abyss between the universes was that all those who pitied her for her solitary state would be amazed at how rich a married life she actually had.

Irony again.

—=—

She strolled to a site behind the North Wind, a place that was on no one's maps of Virtù and whose resident spirit arrogantly refused to acknowledge any power but its own. This *genius loci*, however, was friendly to them both and directed her (by means of a rolling pebble, a bird hopping from branch to branch, a sudden bursting of a climbing rose into flower) to Wolfer Martin D'Ambry's side.

326

He was tending to his bagpipes when she came up to him and, hearing her footsteps, put them aside with unaffected joy.

"Lydia!"

They embraced and, as she rested her head against his shoulder, Lydia thought about how little Ambry had changed since she had first met him. His beard remained neat, though she never saw him trim it, and he maintained his preference for clothing of a rough, archaic style.

She, however, had permitted her virt persona to resemble her RT self. In the years that had passed, her apparent age had caught up to his. If things proceeded in a similar fashion, it would surpass it—although she had reached the years where change was small and gradual. Idly, she wondered if someday her vanity would cause her to arrest those changes—at least in Virtù.

Eventually, Ambry released her, though he still kept hold of her hand, and seated her on a rock beside him. Beneath his delight at her arrival, Lydia could see the thing that had changed in the years since their first meeting. When she had met him, Wolfer Martin D'Ambry had been a figure of mystery, but essentially a carefree sort, content to play his bagpipes and win friends among the *genius loci* of the wilder sites.

Now, worry darkened the eyes beneath the heavy brows. He still played his pipes, but with care, for, as he had confided in her, he was a renegade from a being whose power was great enough to drag him back into service if it could lock onto him. Once, she had wondered aloud why he did not simply give up his pipes if this was what would draw his old master to him. Ambry had looked shocked then and had told her that he was the Piper—if he did not play he could cease to exist.

Hating his distress, Lydia did not question further. Virtù held mysteries she was only beginning to understand, despite her initiation into secrets that most Veritéans could only guess at.

"I am glad that you came to me, love," Ambry said. "More so than usual."

"Why?"

"I am of a mind to consult a physician."

"Can you grow ill? I have never considered that. What is wrong?"

Ambry scratched his left jawline, just above his beard. It struck Lydia as a shy gesture, telegraphing a need for a sort of comfort that she had not seen in him before. She put her arms around him and squeezed, just as she might have squeezed Alice when Alice was small. He laughed, deep within his throat, but she could tell that he was pleased.

"I have been finding gaps within my memory." He hastened to clarify. "Not gaps such as a failing computer program might develop—at least I do not think so. I have not seen the moiré—the dark warping—that often presages a fatal deficiency in a proge."

Lydia felt odd to hear her lover describe himself in such a fashion, but she kept her peace. Ambry continued.

"I come to myself in places to which I do not recall traveling. Sometimes I am walking with a cane. Once I found myself laboring over an odd piece of equipment in our old cottage."

Frowning, Lydia dragged her hands through her hair, a habit that in Verité often left her looking disheveled. Here the *genius loci* sent a zephyr to set it straight.

"If I heard a story like this from a patient in RT, my first inclination would be to ask if he had been experimenting with any new drugs. Virtù has its analogues of such—have you tried any?"

Ambry shook his head. "Nothing but the dark stout I have always enjoyed."

"Another possibility is a mental disorder," Lydia said, more hesitantly, trying to maintain her physician's detachment. "Is there a history of such in your . . . would you call it a family?"

Wolfer Martin D'Ambry tilted his head to one side, stroked her hand.

"There are indeed those native to Virtù who belong to what can only be considered families. Reproduction proges are as old as the first simple copy programs. I, however, have never known my origin. I have no memory of *not* being, yet after a point, I have difficulty retrieving data in any organized fashion. Normally, it takes an event like my old master seeking to reclaim me to remind me that I have ever done more than play my pipes, sail my boat with its red sails, and love my Lady Lydia."

Lydia glared at a rabbit that appeared to be listening too attentively to their conversation. It loped off.

"So there could be a . . . flaw in your base programming. Are there diagnostic programs we could run?"

"There are. I have never used one, but we should be able to find a discreet locus that is so equipped."

"Then that is what we need to do. If you are doing things that you do not recall, perhaps there is something in your older memories that is being stimulated by your recent flight. Do you remember how before Alice was born we visited with a woman who claimed to live at Castle Donnerjack?"

"Of course. How could I forget? The implications of her coming terrified me into flight."

"The Donnerjack Institute is one of the few organizations that holds interests in both medical science and virtual engineering. What do you think about consulting them?"

Wolfer Martin D'Ambry hesitated.

"I have lived in isolation for so long that going to such a public place is almost frightening."

"More frightening than coming to yourself in a strange place with no memory of how you came there?"

"No."

"Ambry, we can try a smaller automated diagnostic center if you wish, but it may not be equipped to deal with your difficulty any more than the automated med-techs in RT are equipped to deal with all medical conditions."

She paused, having never considered her husband's financial situation. In Virtù he always seemed to have what he needed, but now that she thought about it, he lived fairly simply—off the land, in a sense.

"If you're worried about sufficient eft, Ambry, I have more than enough."

He grinned at her. "My rich wife. I did well for myself, did I not? I spirited away a pretty girl and found her to be brilliant, talented, and from the best family."

"But not so pretty," she said playfully. This was a game they had played before. She knew from his smile that he would take her advice and go to the Donnerjack Institute—the understanding was unspoken between them but no less certain for all that.

"Not so pretty?" Ambry pretended to be affronted. "With those eyes of green and a smile to break hearts? Pretty is not word enough to describe you, Lady Lydia."

She laughed and pulled him from their stony seat onto the wild flower-flecked meadow. He plucked an anemone and set it behind her ear and she wove a solemn purple grass stem into his beard. Beyond them, the North Wind blew stronger, making them safe.

EIGHT

To Jay's great surprise, when they came to the train station, the Brass Babboon was waiting for them. Sleek, giving the impression of great speed even when motionless, it rested on the tracks, huffing lazy sparkler puffs from its stack. When it saw them, the grin permanently etched onto its babboon-faced front broadened. It chuckled, sparks lime and lilac flurrying forth to glitter and then vanish.

"So you're the Engineer's son," it said by way of greeting. "I can't say that I would have known you anywhere, but there's enough of old J. D. in you that I don't doubt you're who they claim."

Jay, who had counted on having some time in the station to prepare his speech, could hardly think what to say.

"There is? Who claims? Did you really call my father J. D.?"

"How do I answer all of that?" it asked, still good-natured. "Let's see: Yes, you do bear your father some resemblance. There are those who knew old J. D., who have spoken of you since you began toddling about Virtù and some knew you for Donnerjack kin—though many did not know that you were his son. I did, though, since I was with him when J. D. battled Death for your freedom."

"And you called him 'J. D.'" Jay said, fascinated by this irreverent treatment of his father, a person who had been presented to him as hero, as genius, even as tragic figure, but never as someone so human that he might be nicknamed.

"I did and he never quibbled, though perhaps even the Engineer might hesitate to quibble with one such as me."

The Brass Babboon punctuated this last with a cascade of sky rockets ending in a blue and silver chrysanthemum burst.

"How did you know I would be coming here?" Jay asked.

"To where else would a boy and a monkey ride the most ancient of phants guided by memory, curiosity, and a dog created by the Lord of Entropy?"

"Mizar was created by Death?"

"He was, and better proof was never seen that Entropy and Creation are poor bedfellows. The Lord of Deep Fields did better with your mother, but then he had some help there."

"He did? Who?"

"You're full of questions, J. D., Junior. Would you prefer me to call you just 'Junior'?"

"I'd prefer that you call me 'Jay' as my friends do."

"Arrogance and humility in one. Tastes like sweet and sour soup, you know. Rests oddly on the tongue, but the hankering for just a bit more remains."

Jay stared, letting the words roll off of his resisting mind. When he had imagined the Brass Babboon, he had imagined something dark and terrible, something fit to intimidate the Lord of the Lost. How could this peculiar and irreverent entity win him through to Deep Fields? Perhaps it had been created for just one use. Perhaps he should seek elsewhere for his passage.

The Brass Babboon must have divined something of his indecision.

"I'd guess you want to take passage on me and there's one journey for which I became instant legend." He paused, expectant.

"The journey in which you carried my father into Deep Fields," Jay said.

"And out again alive," the Brass Babboon added. "The fact that he returned is what most remember, though frankly, I think the Lord of Deep Fields was pleased enough to see us go."

"Can you take me there?"

"Can I or will I?"

"Both, I guess." Jay straightened, recalled his purpose, the courage that had melted from him at the train's first words. "I suspect that you can. Will you?"

"What's in it for me?"

"A remission from your boredom."

"Who said I'm bored?"

"I was just guessing. A creature of your power must have finished the tourist route long ago. Very well, if a remission from boredom is not enough, how about a chance to add to your legend?"

The Brass Babboon farted cherry bombs.

"I'm legend enough, but I could be convinced to carry you for the fun of it. Are the phant and the monkey coming?"

"And Mizar."

"Hey! I always wanted to be a circus train. Climb aboard!"

Jay glanced back and noticed that a flatbed, suitable for Tranto, had appeared among the boxcars and coal cars. A broad ramp slid out and the phant lumbered up, Mizar at his heels. Once they were aboard, the door to the front cab opened of its own accord. On the seat rested a striped engineer's cap. Jay picked it up, hit it against his knee so that the dust flew.

"That was your father's," the Brass Babboon said. "If you look around, there should be a red bandanna as well."

Jay found the bandanna, tied it around his neck. The cap was a perfect fit. He grinned at Dubhe.

"All aboard!" the Brass Babboon howled. "All aboard for Deep Fields."

Jay took his place, Dubhe beside him. The monkey stretched a skinny arm and pulled the whistle.

Jay shouted above the tumult. "Can we make a stop for strange attractors first?"

"Consider it done," the train replied, wheels turning rhythmically, increasing in speed. "I'm glad you reminded me."

Outside the cab, the landscape began to blur: arctic ice, jungle tangle, desert sand, plains flat and golden, mountains purple, green, white with snow. In each virt site, the *genius loci* muttered about the intrusion. None, needless to say, cared to do more than mutter.

—=—

On Main Street Virtù, the place from which many lesser sites— conference rooms, bowling alleys, boutiques, Roman baths, and skating rinks—could be accessed, Link Crain wandered, looking for a birthday present for her mother. The street was pleasantly crowded, designed for browsing anonymously without risking a sensation of claustrophobia.

Stopping where a sidewalk vender had spread out a blanket displaying a variety of African pots and carved wooden fetishes, Link examined
the wares. Intellectually, she knew that these were just scanned images
of pieces that were no doubt stacked and crated in a warehouse in Verité, but the illusion was convincing. She could feel the roughness of the
glaze on the piece she held, see the whorl of the potter's fingerprints
partially preserved in the clay. The mixture of artistry and error would
appeal to Lydia, who never ceased to note that medicine was an art, not
a science.

As Link set the pot down and reached for another, she noticed a
neat stack of tee-shirts off to one side. The plain white fabric was printed
with a slogan in square black letters. Glancing at the vendor, Link removed a shirt from the stack and shook it out. The words read: "Ginger
Rogers Did Everything That Fred Astaire Did, Only She Did It Backwards And In High Heels." On the back of the shirt was a simple, Art
Deco style drawing of a man and a woman waltzing.

"What's this?" Link asked.

"It's a tee-shirt," the vendor said, helpfully. "That slogan is very popular right now."

He gestured, and following his motion, Link noticed that several of
the people sauntering along the sidewalk wore them as did many of the
sidewalk vendors.

"What do they cost?"

"It's cheap for a copyrighted product," the vender replied. "Ten eft
for Virtù, fifteen for hardcopy in Verité—the shirt is a hundred percent
preshrunk cotton."

Her reporter's senses alert to a possible story—pieces about fads and
trends always sold well, especially if the writer could anticipate (and thus,
to some extent, create) the fad.

"I'll take one of each," Link said. "Is that first pot I was looking at
a unique item?"

"Of course, sir. As my sign says, everything here is handmade in one
of the West African nations."

"I'll take that pot, then."

"One pot and two shirts. A pleasure doing business with you, sir. Do
you wish to wear your virt shirt now?"

"No, just send the license and software along to the same address as
you're sending the hard goods."

"Very good. Have a good afternoon."

"You, too."

Link strolled on. She saw more of the tee-shirts as she walked. Impulsively, she hit her recall. Obviously, there was no time to be lost if she wanted to file this story first.

—=—

His brain a cloud of fury, Sayjak beat Svut with a branch he had torn from a nearby tree. Mechanically his arm rose and fell; Svut crumpled. As quickly as his fury had arisen, it faded. Sayjak glared at the assembled band of the People.

"Anyone else have problem with what I say we do?"

Heads (bullet-shaped, round like coconuts, furred, balding, broad-nosed, narrow-eyed, thin-lipped or full, all the varieties of the People) shook in frantic denial. Sayjak hardly recalled what Svut had said to put him into such a temper, but he knew that the underling had dared challenge what Sayjak—Boss of Bosses, greater even than old Karak—had commanded. Now Svut whimpered on the ground, leaking blood and piss. Two of his friends, Hoga and Gongo, had crept forward and were looking to Sayjak for permission to drag him away and possibly mend him. Regally, Sayjak nodded.

"We go now," he said, "out of the jungle, across to another jungle. We beat up all the creatures there. Take their jungle. Live there for a while."

(Sayjak remembered now what Svut had said. He had asked what was wrong with their jungle. The eeksies and the bounties did not dare come into the People's territory anymore. Sayjak felt a return of the red fury when he recalled the question.)

The war band leapt into the tree branches heading in the direction Sayjak had indicated. Many carried machetes, others carried clubs. A few shes too small to fight, their fur honey brown and lit with a golden light, carried hollow logs that made good drums. These they hit against tree trunks or pounded on with rocks or other sticks. The pounding could not be called music, but it did awaken battle fury in the fighters. Sometimes Sayjak wondered where they had gotten the idea; most of the time it did not occur to him to wonder.

He knew, however, when they had reached the jungle that was not their jungle. The tree limbs felt the same under his hands, but the wind was not so friendly.

"Watch now. Enemies come soon."

Grunts answered his warning. The People moved on more cautiously. Sayjak had no idea what their goal was, only that he would know it when they had reached it. So they moved on, killing everything that they encountered, everything that they could reach. Sayjak himself pulled a long-tailed bird from the air as it fluttered in panic from its nest. Its bones crunched nicely and it made a refreshing snack.

They met the first organized resistance to their progress in an open space near the banks of a stream. When the People dropped from the branches of the trees to ford the water, two-headed, long-necked lizards erupted from the pebbly ground near the water. Although they were small, they were ferocious. Two of the People were killed outright, others wounded before Sayjak had an insight into how the lizards would be best slain.

"Rip 'em like wishbones," he hollered, demonstrating by grabbing a lizard so that he clamped both sets of jaws closed. Then he pulled outward, one hand on each head. The lizard split down the middle, revealing that it possessed two backbones—a nicety of design Sayjak was not equipped to appreciate.

The young shes began pounding their drums. A scream reverberated through the still air. Battle was joined. The People surged forward. To a watching eye, they glowed with a faint, golden light. Sayjak glowed more brightly than any other.

—=—

In his grove at the heart of his site, Markon received a most unwelcome visitor. Full-breasted, round-bellied, nude except for a great fall of dark green hair, she had appeared in his private realm uninvited. Reluctantly, Markon left his creatures to fend for themselves.

Virginia Tallent (who had refused to depart Virtù when the assault began) came to his side as he manifested himself in a shape of living stone. She held a Chaos Factor rifle loosely in both hands, its barrel aimed at the intruder's pregnant abdomen. There could be no doubt in anyone's mind that the ranger not only knew how to use her weapon, but that she was quite prepared to do so. Although he knew he should not be, Markon felt heartened by her presence.

"Earthma," he said formally.

"Markon, you know me still, after so long."

"How could I not? You, I presume, are the force behind this assault?"

"How did you ever guess?"

"The aura of the attackers reeks of sweetened charges. Only one of the dwellers from Highest Meru could continually support such a force within my realm. Tell me. I have rejected all attempts to make me an ally within this brewing war. Why do you assault me? I wish only to remain neutral."

"You are too powerful to be permitted neutrality, Markon. I have decided that if you do not ally yourself with me, you shall be destroyed so that you cannot side with one of the others."

The stone shape flared with a living green fire that made Earthma's hair look as thick and flat as algae by comparison. Virginia Tallent steadied her rifle. Earthma did not alter her position by as much as a step.

"Earthma, you are perhaps arrogant if you believe that your conscripted proges can destroy my site. Already many of them bleed and fall inactive."

"And I send charges to heal them."

"Harder and harder to do as they come further into my nexus of power."

"I tell my minions the weaknesses of each opponent you send against them. Already they have drunk the blood of the bicameral lizards and slaughtered many hunting wilches. Your dire-cats are deadly, but you are too careful of your internal ecology to have many of those great predators."

"If I run out of wilches and dire-cats I will use herd-mice to undermine the trees in which your minions swing. I will trample them beneath the hooves of my grohners."

"Look to your border with Kordalis. Tell me what you see there."

There was a pause. Virginia Tallent was aware of Markon separating a portion of his attention. She fought against an impulse to fire her weapon into the fecund figure who treated her Markon with such arrogance. Only the theology Markon had taught her made Virginia hold her fire. If this creature was indeed an aspect of Earthma, the CF rifle might ruin this manifestation, but it would no more destroy her than destroying a dire-cat would kill Markon. Still, she resolved that if Markon refused to surrender, she would empty the rifle into that obnoxious belly.

Markon spoke. "I see, Earthma. Phants stand ready to make this a two-front battle. Tell me, did you conquer Kordalis or did she willingly side with you?"

"Kordalis is not as stubborn as you are, Markon."

"Did you promise her my realm if she aided you?"

"Only if you failed to cooperate. I would prefer you as an ally. I have something I wish to hide and your realm would be perfect."

"Tell your minions to hold and I will listen to your proposal. If we cannot agree, we can pick up the battle with little lost."

Abruptly, the screams and wails, the thumping of the tree trunk drums that had been the backdrop to their converse, ceased. In the silence, one of Markon's long-tailed darters broke into song.

"You will do nothing to continue the attack?"

"I thought to heal some of my creatures. They are sorely wounded."

"Then I shall do the same."

"As you wish. Consider using your powers on mine as well, Earthma."

"Why should I do that?"

"You wish my realm to serve your needs. How can it do so if you have ruined it, or if I must exhaust my resources to mend my programs?"

Earthma laughed. "As a gesture of good faith, I will do as you ask."

"Speak your piece, then."

"Tell your companion to lower her weapon."

"Virginia, please do as she asks."

The rifle barrel diverted to one side, but Virginia held it ready.

"I will not let her harm you without fighting back, Markon."

"I would not ask you to do so."

Earthma rolled her eyes. "Such devotion! Veritéan, I have no desire to harm Markon. Only to have him do me a service."

Virginia shrugged. "I'm just the hired help. He's the deity."

"Hired help? I think not, but have it as you will. Markon, I wish to conceal something within your realm. If you agree to take it in and guard it until I am ready for it, then I shall restore your site, remove my minions, and even give out that you are so powerful that I am inclined to respect—even to promote—your claim to neutrality."

"Clever," Markon said. "If I am established as neutral none will look for your—whatever—here. What do you wish me to keep for you? Is it a weapon?"

"Perhaps, but not against any of those on Meru."

"You intrigue me. Pray, continue."

"I bear a child—a child with fine lineage, for Seaga is its sire. When it has come to strength I plan to install it in a realm that I believe has been too long independent of the authority of those on High."

"What realm is this?"

"Deep Fields."

"Then you wish to supplant its lord?"

"That is correct."

"And you wish me to harbor . . ."

"Yes, the new Death of Virtù. The new Death, if all goes well, of both Virtù and Verité. I am certain that my offspring would be grateful to its foster father." Earthma glanced sarcastically at Virginia. "Or I should say to its foster parents? What is your answer, Markon?"

Markon gestured and a stony cradle shaped itself from the rock nearest to Earthma.

"That is my answer. I will consider the 'child' a hostage against your adherence to the agreement you outlined."

"But of course. That has ever been the way with foster parents."

Virginia Tallent set her rifle aside, placed her hand within the green flame of Markon's aura. It caressed her, unburning. Earthma began to groan. To divert herself, Virginia Tallent recited:

> *Ten centuries of stony sleep were broken by a rocking cradle*
> *What rough beast, its hour come round at last,*
> *Slouches toward Bethlehem to be born?*

—=—

Although Dr. Hazzard's patients were normally residents of Verité, she had no trouble getting a recommendation for a consultation with one of the staff of the Donnerjack Institute concerned with Virtùan medical considerations.

At the appointed time, she and Wolfer Martin D'Ambry shifted site coordinates and found themselves in a neat room furnished with three comfortable chairs positioned equidistant from each other on an oriental rug in which muted tones of rust, amber, and rose dominated. As they seated themselves, a third person joined them.

His white coat and stethoscope identified him as a doctor. The badge pinned above his right breast pocket said "SID." His hair and short beard were ash blond and the expression in his warm brown eyes was friendly.

Lydia rose. "I'm Lydia Hazzard. Thank you for making time to see Ambry."

Sid extended a hand, shook hers firmly, turned to Ambry and repeated the gesture.

"Delighted to be of service. I'm on loan from the Center for Iatropathic Diseases. Things there have been—I'm pleased to say—slow. Now, Ambry, would you explain what has been troubling you?"

Tersely, obviously ill at ease, Ambry explained his situation. Sid took occasional notes, but mostly he listened.

"Could you describe the device you found yourself studying?" he said when Ambry finished.

"Well, it was attractive in an Escheresque fashion. Silver and platinum I would guess, with long crystals . . . hexagonal, maybe octagonal. It occasionally spat sparks or glowed with lights of rather anemic pastel hues."

Sid leaned his chin on his hand. "Earlier you mentioned that you have no real memory of your site of origin. Do you think it is possible that you originated during the Genesis Scramble?"

"It's possible."

"What site do you reside in now?"

"I'd prefer not to say. It's one of the wild sites."

"I assure you, whatever you tell me here is confidential."

Ambry frowned. Lydia interjected a comment into the awkward silence.

"It isn't that we don't trust you, but Ambry has been having difficulties with an old enemy."

Sid raised his eyebrows. "Could your enemy be responsible for these memory lapses?"

Ambry hesitated. "It is possible."

"I think so, too. Without knowing more, I can't be more specific, but I would guess that in forcing you to take actions against him or her—"

"Him."

"—that your enemy is awakening some alternate or base program. This could be an escape routine, but it also could mean eventual sublimation of your current persona proge to one of these secondary routines."

Lydia interrupted. "Are you saying that Ambry could effectively cease to be himself and become someone else?"

"Yes."

"Would he know who he had been?"

"Judging from the amnesia he has already experienced, I would say not."

Lydia turned to Ambry. "I couldn't bear to lose you again. The first time was hard enough."

Ambry nodded. "Not only for you, my love. Dr. Sid, what do you suggest?"

"That you trust me. Tell me why you are fleeing. I may be able to suggest alternate ways for you to protect yourself—ways that will preserve your base integrity."

"The knowledge may endanger you."

"I can accept that. I'll even admit to rank curiosity. You see, the name of Lydia Hazzard is familiar to me through one of my other areas of interest."

"Oh?"

"The study of the phenomenon where virt participants become lost in uncharted territory. I saw some of Dr. Hamill's early, unpublished notes on your case—notes from before the court decision was handed down and forced him to refer to you as Patient F17."

"Ah . . ."

"And I can deduce that Mr. Ambry here may have had some role in that disappearance."

Lydia glanced at Ambry. He nodded.

"The probability is high."

"And the interesting question of your daughter . . ."

"Parthenogenesis."

"Of course. What else could it be?"

"What else?"

The three studied each other. Sid with hands folded in his lap, Lydia somewhat anxious, Ambry guarded—even dangerous. After a long silence, Ambry nodded sharply.

"Very well. I will trust you. I only hope that you will not regret your choice."

Sid smiled. "Me, too."

"No publishing this material."

"No."

"No prying into Alice's life."

"Very well."

"And if you must consult with a colleague, you will do so with utmost discretion."

"I have no problem with that."

Ambry relaxed slightly. He reached out and took Lydia's hand.

"I am the Piper."

Sid started.

"Sir?"

"I am the Phantom Piper who once played for the legions of Skyga. He has reawakened my regiment and seeks to draw me to them again."

Sid's brown eyes were wide. He looked as if he would kneel, shout, run about the room. He settled for juggling his notebook from hand to hand.

"The Piper! The Phantom Piper! By all the gods on Highest Meru, that explains it! I had wondered when you mentioned the machine, but . . ."

Lydia and Ambry stared at him.

"Would you please explain to us?" Lydia said dryly. "Apparently you are privy to knowledge that neither of us share."

"You mock me!"

"No," Ambry said. "As far as I know, I am Wolfer Martin D'Ambry, the Phantom Piper of the fabled Regiment of Skyga. That is all—I thought it was quite enough."

Sid calmed himself with visible effort.

"Although it is little known beyond ourselves, there is a theological tradition held by many of the aions."

"I have heard something of that," Ambry said, "but never cared to pursue it."

Sid shook his head in disbelief. "In that tradition, the Piper is one of the incarnations of a Veritéan scientist named Warren Bansa."

"Bansa," Lydia said. "I read about him. He was the one who jumped from a plane claiming to be performing a sky-diving act. He vanished and was never seen again."

"Yes. That's the man. To us, however, his more important role was as the primal mover in the creation of the Genesis Scramble. Tradition says that he is the one who overloaded the World Net so that it crashed."

Ambry spoke softly. "And when it awoke, all was changed and Virtù was born. I remember nothing of that."

"I cannot say why," Sid continued, "but our traditions hold that Bansa—alone among the three sanctified Veritéans—has multiple forms. One is the Phantom Piper, one is the Master, and the last is the One Who Waits.

"The Master was recalled to me when you mentioned coming to yourself over a strange piece of equipment—for our traditions say that the Master is the geometrician who had a major role in the creation of the universe. In our iconography, he is often portrayed carrying a strange machine. The One Who Waits has a scar that runs from the top of his head to the sole of his left foot. Legend says that he will figure in the closing—or perhaps only the change—of Virtù."

"It is almost too much," Ambry said, and Lydia squeezed his hand in agreement. "I thought I was one legend—now you tell me I am three—or is it four? I resisted Skyga rather than join his battles again, but now you tell me that I have a fate that seems to insist on even greater things."

Sid nodded. "This is more than an overwritten psyche proge—let me tell you that. Still, I believe you when you say who you are and, if our theology is correct, then the rest follows."

"Oh."

Lydia frowned. "And what happened to Warren Bansa?"

"I have no idea," Sid confessed. "Our legends never dealt with that. His vanishing seemed just a part of the legend—like Arthur going to Avalon and promising to return someday."

"And what can we do for Ambry?"

"Can you stay with him?"

"I will need to contact Alice, but I believe so. The clinic will function without me."

"We can even arrange some extra medical help through the Donnerjack Institute," Sid offered. "I think the best thing that can be done for Ambry right now is for him to keep to the wild lands and for you to stay with him. If he begins to change, you will need to protect him—to keep him from doing anything crazy—and, if you don't mind, to contact me."

"You?"

"I would gladly put myself at the service of one of the sanctified Veritéans. And if I am with you, I may be able to deduce what is causing the alterations."

Ambry released Lydia's hand, rubbed his eyes.

"Skyga's pursuit may be the proximate cause, but you believe that there is something more—do you not?"

Sid folded his hands prayerfully.

"Legends say that the One Who Waits will figure in the closing or change of Virtù. You speak of rumblings among the Great Gods. I think that the waiting is ended—be it closing or change, I would play a part."

"Lydia?"

"He has a good point. I can work with him."

"Then it is agreed. If the need comes, we will call on you."

"Thanks. I'll give Lydia my beeper number."

"And nothing of this to anyone."

"Nothing. I swear, unless . . ."

"Yes?"

"Would you let me confide in Paracelsus? He is the coordinating aion for the Donnerjack Institute—and my closest friend. He has a deep interest in the cult of the Sanctified Three."

"Does he?"

"John D'Arcy Donnerjack is one of that number—we call him the Engineer, the counterpart to the Master, and the Guide."

Lydia touched Ambry's hand. "I have a feeling we should."

"Ayradyss?"

"It does seem like fate."

"Very well," Ambry said. "Tell Paracelsus, but keep your counsel close or those changes may happen sooner and less fruitfully than they should."

"Very wise."

Without further leave-taking (Sid was too shaken, Ambry and Lydia too thoughtful), all departed the consulting room. Lydia left Alice a note saying that she had been called away for an undefined emergency. Then she used the virt transfer facility at one of the Hazzard family ski resorts (closed for the season) to join Ambry.

Returning to the land behind the North Wind, Ambry perched on a high crag and played the salute he had composed for the birth of John D'Arcy Donnerjack, Junior to amuse the *genius loci*. When Lydia walked up the path and seated herself near enough to listen in comfort, he finished his piece and let the mouthpiece drop.

"I wonder what happened to that child, to Ayradyss, to John?"

"So do I. I had the strangest impression that even the Donnerjack Institute does not see them often. Sid didn't seem to twig when I mentioned Ayradyss's name."

"He *is* with them only part-time."

"True."

"I wonder what happened to Warren Bansa?"

"So do I. And how much of him is you."

"An odd thought, that."

Setting aside his bagpipes, Ambry took Lydia in his arms; she rested her head on his shoulder.

"I don't suppose it matters."

The wind wailed through the clefts and declivities. It played the same tune as Ambry had on his pipes, adding verses that answered their questions without words and thus were incomprehensible.

—=—

When Link Crain came home from shopping and slipped into her research database, a small blue finch fluttered up with a rolled spill of white paper bound in a pink ribbon in its beak. Link took the paper, gave the finch a sunflower seed, and unrolled the paper. The note was dated earlier that day and written in her mother's favorite evergreen ink:

Alice,
I've been called away on business. If you need anything, contact
Gwen at the clinic or your grandparents. I hope to be back within
a week or so and, of course, I'll be in touch.

Love, Mom

Handing the finch another seed, Link said, "There will be no reply." It chirped and departed.

Link frowned. It wasn't as if Dr. Hazzard never traveled, but the suddenness was not typical. She turned to her research, to banish the uneasiness she felt. Soon she was absorbed in tracking down copyrights and cross-referencing through various manufacturers.

That evening, she placed a call to Desmond Drum. His answering service promised to pass the message on and Link began drafting an article tentatively titled "Doing It Backwards." She was on the second version, working in old film clips and candid photos of various virt sites where the Ginger Rogers tee-shirt was cropping up, when Drum returned her call.

She took it on the virt and soon the detective manifested in the virtual annex Lydia Hazzard had furnished to resemble a parlor in a Victorian manor house. The ruffled skirts that tastefully concealed furniture legs were hardly a setting in which rough and craggy Drum looked at home.

"Ah, here," Drum said cryptically.

He tapped the fingers of his right hand on the back of his left. When he completed the sequence, his casual slacks and button-down shirt metamorphosed into clothing appropriate for a Victorian gentleman gone calling. He remained clean-shaven, but his thick brows were tamed and his sandy hair was slightly longer. Bowing from the waist, he extracted a calling card case from his breast pocket, dropped a card onto the tray near the door, and winked at Link.

Link realized she was gaping and snapped her mouth shut. She considered changing into one of the outfits that she had prepared for this setting, but rejected the thought at once. All of them were meant for Alice Hazzard and, although she knew that Drum had long been privy to her masquerade, she found herself oddly shy when she played girl for him.

Instead she returned Drum's bow and gestured him to a seat.

"Very nice, Drum. And thanks for returning my call."

"My pleasure, Link. Your message sounded as if you had something interesting for me."

"I do. Tea? Crumpets?"

"That would be nice."

Link tugged at the bell pull and a simple maid-servant proge appeared with a prepared tea tray.

"I will pour, Maggie. That will be all."

"Very good, sir."

When the proge had exited and she had poured tea, Link had regained her composure.

"When I was out shopping for a birthday present for my mother I came across this." Link shook out the virt shirt. "The vendor mentioned that they were becoming a hot fad and I thought I'd earn some eft by doing a write-up."

"Eft is always useful. I've seen the shirts around, but I didn't really think much about them. So, kid, am I right in guessing that you didn't call me just to boast that you might have sold another article?"

Link grinned. "Yep. The vendor mentioned that this was a copyrighted product."

"Good planning on the designer's part," Drum said. "Otherwise it's so simple that it would get pirated in no time."

"I did a routine check on the copyright and found that it was held by one Randall Kelsey."

"Randall Kelsey . . . sounds familiar."

"Member of the Church of Elish. I checked further and the money for the copyright and production of the virt template came directly from the Church."

"A simple front, then."

"That's what I figure."

Drum picked up the virt shirt, turned it so he could study the slogan and the picture. "Who was Ginger Rogers anyway?"

"An American performer in the twentieth century. She was best known for dancing with this Fred Astaire. He became famous for his dancing—there were dance studios named for him, he had a program of his own. Rogers was always in his shadow."

"This slogan makes it sound like she had the harder job."

"That was what I thought, too. The more I look at it, the harder it is to dismiss it as some sort of pop flippancy. It almost has the ring of a rallying cry."

"Strange rally, if it invokes people no one but a dancing fiend would have heard about."

"Still, they aren't impossible to learn about. They're both listed in the major databanks. In fact, if you have computer access and even a minor amount of curiosity, it's easy enough to do."

"So, who is it rallying? Women dancers?"

"Drum, stop playing with me. Think about what we discussed earlier. The Church of Elish was apparently founded by an aion—an aion who we think is taking a more active role in affairs."

Drum crumpled a crumpet. "You think this is meant to appeal to aions, then."

"That's right. They do everything we do but in Virtù—which many call a mirror of Verité."

"And everything is backwards in a mirror." Drum glanced around the parlor. "I wonder if we should even be having this discussion here."

"If the dissatisfaction is so high that every virt site is monitored, we're doomed already."

"True. Still . . ."

"You're paranoid."

"I'm old and alive. Humor me."

"You're not saying I shouldn't file my story, are you? I already have a contract with *Virtropolis*."

"You don't mention any of this rallying cry stuff, do you?"

"No, just fad and fashion sense with clips about Rogers and Astaire. There's lots of good material that's public domain."

"Then file it and bank your eft. Can I buy you dinner?"

"News?"

"I'm just back from a trip, wanted to show you my snapshots."

"Sure. Can we eat in RT? I got so busy that I skipped lunch. Mom laid down the law that while I'm still growing I should eat at least one solid meal a day."

"Would Italian suit? I have a real craving for eggplant parmigiana. Amici's is about midpoint between our places."

"Give me an hour."

"Very well." Drum rose, bowed to Link. "Thank you for the tea and crumpets. I shall anticipate our meeting."

He strolled to the door and vanished. Link stood a moment longer. Catching his/her reflection in one of the gilded mirrors, she realized that she was blushing. Furious at Drum's ability to make her lose her studied masculinity, she stalked to her reporter's cubby, touched up her story, and sent it off. There was time enough to put on a clean suit and tie and her nattiest fedora before the cab arrived to take her to dinner.

"Hey, kid," Drum said, by way of greeting as Link came up to the table. He had a scotch and soda by one hand and was chewing a bread stick. The polished Victorian gentleman had vanished with the costume. "They have an antipasto special tonight—Italian cold cuts, marinated artichoke hearts, olives, cheeses. Sounded so good I went ahead and ordered one big enough for both of us."

"Great."

Link slid into the chair across from Drum and placed an order for a glass of the house's rough red. She studied the menu and then tapped in a request for a clam and lobster spaghetti in a red sauce and a green salad with oil and vinegar.

"Have a bread stick, kid."

Link took one, dipped it into olive oil and salt.

"I'm going to hate it when I stop growing and need to watch my weight."

"You must be about done, now," Drum said, "if your similarity to your mother is going to hold."

"I know. It's a pity. Maybe I should take up some terribly vigorous sport."

"I play RT tennis twice a week," Drum offered. "I'd be happy to teach you."

"Maybe. You know, I never thought about you doing anything except chasing people around and reading their mail. Tell me about your trip."

"I've been to California."

A waiter brought the antipasto, Link's wine, and a refill on the bread sticks. While he fussed with table settings, Drum finished his whiskey and soda and cleared his palate with a pinkish grey olive.

"Good and sharp," he said, neatly placing the pit on the side of his plate. "Yes, I've been to California and to the land that our mutual ac-quaintances have just purchased. There's lots of construction going on—and now that I think about it, quite a few of those tee-shirts you were telling me about."

"Interesting. Are they doing it up as big as in Central Park?"

"Bigger, if anything. Some of the ziggurats looked as if they could support a fair amount of weight. I'd guess that the outlying ones are going to double as landing pads."

"They do plan well, don't they? If they draw crowds like last time—and they probably will—there won't be keeping anything at ground-level clear."

"Aoud Araf, I'd guess," Drum said. "He has been rising in impor-tance since the riot. Doesn't show any real theological ambition—just what's *pro forma*—but he has a gift for handling a crowd."

They talked for a while longer about what Drum had seen, about the rumors that the celebration would be open only to those who had purchased tickets, but that the tickets would be vended worldwide. Bid-ding was still going on between the major entertainment networks for the simulcasting rights. Whether or not the Church of Elish restored its reputation through this second celebration, it was quite clear that they were going to be minting money.

Antipasto was a memory and they were well into their entrees when Drum changed the subject.

"Before I forget, I have a bit more information for you on the case you gave me."

Link set down her fork. "Yes?"

"I made a side-trip to Eilean a'Tempull Dubh. There's a small fishing village there with residents as close-mouthed as any stereotype would have you believe. I got them talking, though."

"How?"

"There's a castle that dominates the island—a hulking, black stone creation with battlements, gargoyles, towers . . . the whole nine yards. It's listed on the maps as Castle Donnerjack. Photos of the island taken more than about twenty years ago don't show it, just a few picturesque rubble heaps.

"I went into a local tavern and started going on about the obvious antiquity of the structure, acting angry when someone challenged my authority. Finally, I offered drinks to anyone who could prove to me that the castle wasn't the ancient structure I claimed."

Link giggled. "I bet that got them talking."

"Aye, that it did, laddy," Drum said in an affected accent. "The tavern keeper pulled out his photo album and as the whisky started flowing soon each was rivaling the other to show me how stupid I was."

Drum took a contented sip of his wine and a bite of his eggplant. Watching him, Link was reminded of her own forgotten meal.

"The information I gathered was sketchy, but enough to prove our early guestimates," Drum continued. "It seems that John D'Arcy Donnerjack had some ancestral claims to the land on which the castle now stands and confirmed them with a large outlay of eft. The local belief was that he had the castle built as a present for his bride, a dark-haired, soulful woman who was never seen by the villagers except as a figure on the castle battlements or strolling on a lonely strand near the shore."

"Was he keeping her prisoner?"

"I asked something similar as tactfully as I could, given that the locals are quite attached to the 'laird'—an odd thing in itself, given that they apparently saw him rarely."

"Maybe that's why they were attached to him," Link said dryly. "It's easier to admire an idealized laird in a castle than a flesh and blood aristocrat."

"I don't doubt that you have something there," Drum agreed. "The general opinion of the locals was that Lady Donnerjack was recovering from some illness when she arrived. Later, she became pregnant and, being delicate, chose to stay near to home."

"Pregnant?" Link's eyes shone as the trail to the elusive Jay Mac-Dougal became more solid.

"Yes, there's no doubt about that bit at least. A few of the locals were employed at the castle until the robot and AP staff was running smoothly. And almost everyone over fifteen years old had tales about the wonderful events of a spring day some years ago when bagpipe music played from the hills and an unofficial holiday with food and drinks for all was declared in celebration of the birth of the laird's son."

"So he exists!"

"Or did," Drum cautioned. "A few months after that holiday, things changed at the castle. Only two of the human staff members—Angus and the Duncan—were kept on and their work was restricted to grounds-keeping and external maintenance. No one saw either the lady or the laird—and no one can ever recall seeing the child."

"How creepy!"

"I spoke with Angus and the Duncan. They both knew Dack—he's their paymaster and the person who tells them what needs to be done. They seem to think he's an affable sort, open to reasonable suggestions, given to presenting gifts and raises at appropriate times. I had the general impression that they both think that John D'Arcy Donnerjack uses the robot as a means of speaking to them. I don't believe that either of them have ever spoken to the laird in person."

"Anything else?"

"Just a host of fairy stories—mostly about the castle being haunted. The more the whisky flowed the more people had a tale to tell. Almost everyone claimed to have seen the gargoyles move or heard a woman wailing. The usual nonsense."

Link wiped up sauce with a torn hunk of bread, letting Drum finish the last few bites of his meal.

"I don't suppose that knocking at the castle door would do any good, would it?"

"Probably not. I'll see what else I can find out. Now that I have some nonconjectural evidence—however shaky—that John D'Arcy Donnerjack had a son, perhaps I can get someone at the Donnerjack Institute to pass on a message."

"Explain that we don't mean him any harm—we only want to thank him for helping us during the riot."

"Of course."

Drum pushed his plate to one side and brought up the in-table dessert menu.

"A dinner like that deserves dessert."

"I didn't think I had any space left, but those pastries certainly look wonderful."

"Shall I order a plate of the miniatures and a pot of espresso?"

Link grinned. "Just make certain that there are enough cannoli."

"Sounds very good." Drum toasted Link with the remnants of his wine. "Here's to mysteries solved!"

"In both Virtù and Verité," Link responded.

Their goblets chimed as they touched the rims together.

NINE

Spewing tracks before it, the Brass Babboon surged from the orchard wherein strange attractors grew upon gnarled trees that knew too much of possibility and grumbled portents in the harvesters' ears.

"Where to, Jay?" the Brass Babboon inquired.

"To Deep Fields!" Jay answered, trying to make his voice bold and certain.

While Tranto and Dubhe had gathered the strange attractors, plucking them with fingers and trunk that had elongated and distorted as they neared the fruit (returning to normal as soon as the fruit was touched), he had studied the control panel for his father's train. He felt now that he could operate the screens, the slicing scissors, the various launchers with a degree of confidence.

"Any thoughts about the route we should take?" the Brass Babboon asked. "Or do you expect an invitation?"

This last was said so sarcastically that Jay forbore from saying that he believed he had something in the way of a standing invitation. He didn't think that anything could intimidate the terrible train, but if anything could so, knowing that Death awaited its passenger might be it.

"How did my father get in?"

"He seemed to feel that either the beginning or the end of time would serve equally well as a route. We went in at the beginning of time." Maniacal laughter punctuated the reflection.

"I wonder if the same route would serve us?"

"The Lord of Entropy has probably taken measures against casual intrusion." Again the maniacal laughter. "Of course, I am anything but casual."

"True."

"The end of time is closer, though," Tranto commented from where he stood on the flat bed, munching strange attractors.

"It is?" Startled, Jay turned to see if the phant was joking with him.

"Didn't you hear what the orchard said? The portents are there. The ones on Meru dream again their vast armies. The Master has been seen, and now the Engineer's mad machine is in the service of his son."

The phant's eyes were dilated wide and his tone was dreamy. Gouts of energy, rainbow-hued yet viscous, coursed along the scars on his wrinkled grey hide. Jay hardly knew what to say to him, so he addressed the Brass Babboon:

"Is the end of time closer?"

"In a matter of speaking. It is less definite than the beginning, but for that reason may serve us better. The ones on Meru do indeed dream and their dreams of beginnings may have made that beginning more aggressive than when J. D. and I pushed through."

Jay looked at Dubhe. The monkey had forborne from eating the strange attractors and nibbled now on a banana.

"What do I know?" Dubhe said, pitching the peel back to Tranto. "It's time for you to choose."

"The end then," Jay said, and he tugged the whistle.

"Did you bring any music?" the Brass Babboon asked.

"Huh?"

"Your father played recordings when last we made this run. I thought you might have brought some with you. The Lord of the Lost is fond of music and might hold his blows to listen a while."

Jay realized how little he had prepared for what he was getting into.

"No, I didn't. Do you have any?"

"What J. D. included in my original design. Shall I play the same selection?"

"Sure."

And so the Brass Babboon picked up speed to a jazz rendition of "Dixie," a rendition that became wilder as they surged away from the sites that Jay recognized and into areas wherein the laws of geometry and physics had been curled into themselves to emerge warped, their underlying principles displayed for those who had the wit to comprehend.

Almost, almost, Jay understood what he was seeing and the near realization pressed against the curves and folds of his brain, threatening to unpack them from their convolutions and lay them out as flat and straight as the tracks which the Brass Babboon spat from its laughing mouth.

As the veneer of Virtù frayed, he saw the numbers of the base programs, the World Wide Web of ancient days. A man he recognized as his father stood behind a workbench, his head tilted back so that he could debate with a man dressed in long indigo robes embroidered with mystic symbols who stood on a cloud. As the Brass Babboon carried him by, Jay realized that the man on the cloud was Reese Jordan.

Between cloud and workshop drifted a third man hanging from a parachute, chuckling as he fiddled with the controls of something he wore girded around his waist. His merriment was a marked contrast to the seriousness of the other two men.

But these things were caught in glimpses as the fall of moiré began. First it was a drift of dark flakes, ashes from a chimney. The drift became a flurry, then a swirl of bats that warped the landscape over which they passed. Proges shattered beneath their shadowy advent and upon their broken parts the moiré bent and feasted.

"Turn on the screens, Jay!" Dubhe screeched in his ear.

Tearing himself away from the hypnotic vista of rapid decay, Jay realized that the monkey had been shouting at him for some time now. He leaned forward and snapped on the correct switch. A violet aura encased the cab and then flowed back to cloak the flatbed on which Mizar and Tranto rode.

"Sorry, Dubhe."

The monkey chewed on the end of his tail. The moiré fall had grown so thick now that only glimpses of the underlying program could be seen through the dual distortion of screens and moiré.

"We need light," Jay said.

He hit the button labeled "Flares" and brilliant violet light burst forth. The Brass Babboon screeched into the increasingly formless swirl. Beneath the violet of the screens, the landscape had become the sick, dizzy white of a color wheel spun so rapidly that all colors blend into one.

Wildly excited, Mizar howled and Tranto trumpeted. At tremendous volume, the Brass Babboon chortled something as obscene as it was incomprehensible. Suspecting that the noise would help anchor them into something like solidity as they bore on through, Jay reached up for the whistle and pulled it long and hard. "Dixie" had given way to the "Wolverine Blues." Dubhe swung from his tail and used all four paws to conduct the unsanctified orchestration of sound that carried them through the end of time and into the detritus-strewn vastness of Deep Fields.

Only one thing loomed over the broken plains: a dark, many-towered shape.

Craft the fairy-tale palace of Mad King Ludwig of Bavaria from nightmare and ecru marble, then hack it apart with a chainsaw and reassemble it with indifferent attention to form and order. This is something like the recipe for the Palace of Bones as designed by John D'Arcy Donnerjack, Senior.

Jay approved and took some comfort in this evidence of his father's genius.

"J. D. had me crash through the walls," the Brass Babboon screamed. "Want me to do that again?"

"No!" Jay replied. "Approach the palace at as high a speed as you can, divert at the last possible moment, and then loop around the palace. Are you long enough to enclose it?"

"I can be," the Brass Babboon answered.

"Then be so. When you halt, we will fire a barrage of strange attractors over the palace in the fashion of a fireworks salute. If Tranto hasn't eaten too many, we should have enough and to spare."

The phant belched in a dignified fashion.

"I only consumed a few, and I find that my repast has completed healing the damage given to me."

Jay glanced back at the phant. Tranto's hide still rippled with the odd gouts of power, but he had to admit that the last traces of weakness were gone from the phant's bearing. He had no desire to consider further, for the Brass Babboon was shrieking into a turn, beginning the course that would loop them around Death's palace.

"Whaa-whoo!" Jay shouted, glorying in the speed and the excitement. "Yeah!"

Dubhe, still hanging from the cab's ceiling by his tail, shook his head, but clearly he felt something of Jay's joyful excitement in this defiant confrontation with everything a sane entity should avoid.

"Can I launch the fireworks, Jay?"

"You bet. Just wait until B.B. comes to a full halt. I want to shoot over the towers—a salute, not an attack."

"Right!"

Even as the Brass Babboon squealed to a stop, its impertinent grin a few inches from its improbable caboose, Dubhe fired the salute.

Perhaps because Jay wished them to do so, the strange attractors shot upward in phosphorescent white streaks. These collided, then exploded in a sunburst: first gold, then green, then iridescent blue dimming into silver, showering among the marble towers, clinging to the gargoyles and bas relief flutings on columns and porticos for a single glorious moment.

When the last of the silver sparkles faded, Death rode forth from the main gate of his palace.

His steed was crafted of things salvaged from his realm and was calculated to impress and intimidate, even as Mizar had been created to search and destroy. There was about it something of a dragon, something of a horse, and something of an eagle. Its colors were azure and ebony stolen from the day and night skies of vanished virt realms.

As the steed pranced out of the vaulted gates carrying the slim, robed figure of Death, Jay D'Arcy Donnerjack craved it as he had never before craved any created thing.

Phecda twined around the steed's head, halter and herald both, and when Death had drawn alongside the Brass Babboon's cab, she raised her viper's head and hissed greeting.

"So, at last you come to Deep Fields, Jay Donnerjack. Know that you are welcome here."

"Thank you, Phecda," Jay replied. He bowed to the Lord of Entropy. "And thank you, sir."

Death grinned, white within the darkness of his cowl.

"You come as your father twice came to me. What do you wish to claim from me?"

"Nothing."

"You cannot have me believe that you made this trip for pleasure."

"The scenery was a wonder like nothing I could have imagined, but no, sir, I did not make the journey for pleasure."

"Yet you want nothing from me. I am intrigued. Tell me why you have come."

Jay straightened his father's striped cap on his head. His heart pounded in his chest and his joints felt loose and weak. The inside of his mouth flooded with saliva and as quickly went dry. He realized he was terrified, but he did his best to hide his fear.

"I learned of a bargain made between you and my father, sir. The more I thought about it, the more I came to feel that you had been wronged."

"I have been." Death's voice cracked on the final word.

"And I have come to . . . to ask you what purpose you had for me when you demanded me from my father."

"You said you wanted nothing from me, but you ask for an explanation."

"Perhaps I should have said that I wanted nothing material." Jay placed his hand on the cab's door latch. "Before I surrender myself, I will admit that I am curious what you intend for me."

"Before?" The glint of white within the cowl might have been a smile, but it could as easily been the fixed rictus of a bare skull. "So you intend to surrender?"

"In some circumstances, surrender is more honorable than being taken captive. I believe that this is one. If my father had left behind a debt of money or service, I would have tried to pay it. I'll admit that I don't particularly like the terms of this debt, but I think it should be honored nonetheless."

Death laughed, a sound that made Tranto flap his ears and Mizar whine in involuntary protest.

"You speak fair, Jay Donnerjack, even though your voice does quaver. What would you do if I told you that all I required of you was a source of spare parts for some project I am involved with?"

Jay recalled Reese Jordan's conjecture on that very point, but he remained steady.

"I would beg your leave to say farewell to Dack, since he has been the only parent I have known, then I would turn myself over to you. If you would not permit me to leave, I would ask at least permission to send him a message."

"And if I told you that I required the traitor who even now swings alongside you in the cab of the Brass Babboon?"

"I would be able to do nothing, sir. I cannot dispose of my friends' lives."

"Thanks, Jay," Dubhe whispered.

"Even if I required them?"

"No, sir. I think you pulled a mean trick on Dubhe and the rest when you set them to be spies on me."

"Perhaps I merely meant to protect you."

"I'd thought of that, but you shouldn't have left them not knowing what your intentions were."

"Ah, we are back to my intentions, are we? Very well. I have no desire to break you up for spare parts. I have bits and pieces to spare here in Deep Fields. Indeed, spare parts are all that I possess. I desire you alive and functioning. Had your father surrendered you to me as I had intended, you would have been educated here. I gave in to his whim, and so you are perhaps less well-trained for the task I need done than you might have been."

"Task?"

"This is not the place to speak of such things. Come forth, if truly you mean to surrender. We will confer in my palace."

"And Dubhe?"

"He has allied himself with you. You choose to serve me. Therefore, he is indirectly in my service once more. I can settle for that. The same goes for Mizar and any others you have brought with you."

Jay opened the cab and leaned upon the door. The silence of Deep Fields weighed on him, muting even the chuff of the Brass Babboon's stack and the noise as Mizar and Tranto came to join him.

"Shall I wait for you, Jay?" the Brass Babboon asked.

"There is no need," Death interjected. "When he leaves here, it will be in a less obvious fashion."

"Then I'll lay tracks out of here. Leave a message for me at any of my stations, Jay, and I'll come as fast as I can."

Jay patted the grinning face. "Thanks, B.B. I'll remember that."

With a wail that rippled the ruined proges into a Danse Macabre, the Brass Babboon departed. To those watching, he simply seemed to enter the middle distance, diminish, and recede until the eye could no longer fix on his point.

"Come," Death said, his steed turning.

Jay let Tranto lift him onto his back. With Mizar at his side and Dubhe on his shoulder, he obeyed. An up-swelling of cacophony rippled through the still air. It was impossible to tell if the sound was mockery or applause.

— = —

In a site modeled after an early twenty-first century nightclub, two men sat at a table that floated two meters in the air, tilted at a thirty-degree angle. The original nightclub would have required elaborate constructions involving plexiglass and nearly invisible cable to achieve this effect. In Virtù, of course, none of this was necessary.

"Tickets went on sale today at all Virtik locations," commented Skyga.

For this manifestation he wore his hair long and the pale blue of a cold day. His brows were upswept cumulus and his features stern but benign. Privately, he considered his virtual savoir faire an example to his associate who was, as ever, deplorably slovenly.

"And sales are going well," said the Hierophant of the Church of Elish.

Today his tee-shirt (sweat-stained at the underarms) read "Marduk is a Pisser" and showed the great and terrible conqueror of Tiamat raining down on a crowd of upturned faces. It was a bit too tight and had crept up to create a gap above his baggy shorts through which his hairy beer belly protruded. The Hierophant knew that his casual attire drove Skyga crazy and did his best to make certain that the one from Highest Meru always had something to annoy him.

"We should be able to generate ample mana to sustain the cross-over," Skyga continued.

"That's the idea, bud. How are your troops doing?"

"Morale is good. I have made allies among many of the *genii loci*—some are even assisting in training and coordination. Others are merely providing guarded sites so that I can conceal the extent of my strength."

"Do you really expect any resistance once the show is on the road?"

"Seaga will not approve, for the success of this venture will forever confirm me as the foremost of the Highest Three. It is difficult to know how Earthma will react."

"I thought you said that she'd been helpful."

"She has. That's what worries me."

The Hierophant gestured and a long-necked beer bottle appeared in his hand. He removed the cap with a bottle opener built into the underside of the table. It rattled to the floor.

"Want one?" the Hierophant said, after he had taken a long drink and belched approvingly. "Tastes real good."

"No, thank you," Skyga said stiffly.

"It's good, as good as anything Verité has to offer—or so I've been assured."

"You seem content enough with the limitations of Virtù," Skyga said. He tried to keep his query polite, knowing that he still needed this ally's cooperation. "Why did you approach me with the concept of the Church of Elish if you did not believe in the need for the reestablishment of the divine to its proper place in the Verité?"

"You were the one who saw the potential for permanent crossover," the Hierophant reminded him. "I just wanted to start a religion and I thought your help recruiting a few godlets would be a good thing."

"Yes, but why did you wish to start a religion? Certainly you do not feel that humans need to know the truth about Virtù?"

The aion who had once been known as A. I. Aisles, the first aion comedian, chuckled, drained his beer, and blew a note like the bellowing of a cow for her calf across the neck.

"Truth? Well, sure I think they need to know."

"You do?"

"Sure." A. I. Aisles laughed until his belly shook. "Most of them don't believe it—not really, not deep down inside. Not even when we give 'em miracles and virt powers. They're just playing the game."

"I still fail to understand why you would wish to encourage this."

A. I. Aisles snickered. "Can you think of a better joke on humanity? We give 'em the dope on old gods and older powers waiting for them in Virtù. They help us set the stage to make it come true—to give 'em back the old gods and all the rest."

"You think this is funny?"

"Slapstick and farce." A. I. Aisles laughed so hard that tears ran down his round cheeks. "Nothing funnier."

Skyga smiled politely. His expression generated further howls from the comedian.

"It's a pisser, Skyga, old buddy, old pal. A real pisser."

—=—

Through a simple interface, Lydia Hazzard called her daughter.

"How have you been, honey?"

"Pretty good. I went out to dinner with Drum. Italian—I had a great seafood pasta. We should go when you come back."

"I'd like that."

"And how have you been, Mom?"

"Busy. Things here are . . . complicated."

"Can't explain over the VT?"

"I'm afraid not."

Alice nodded. "Will you be home for your birthday, Mom?"

"I . . . That *is* coming up, isn't it? You won't let your old mom forget that she's getting on, will you?"

Giggles.

"You're not that old, Mom. Don't you dare fuss and not let me take you out!"

"If I'm home by then."

"Mom, is everything all right?"

"With me everything is fine, I promise."

"Is it a patient?"

"I said I couldn't discuss it."

"Sorry."

"So am I, honey."

"Maybe I can come see you for your birthday if you're not back. I just sold another article."

"Great! Where?"

"To *Virtropolis* under the Alice Looking-Glass nom de plume. It's about a new tee-shirt fad."

"That's wonderful! Honey, can we talk about your visiting me when I know when I'll be home? If I'm back, I'll let you spend your eft taking me out to dinner at the Italian place you mentioned."

"Okay."

"I should be going now."

"I miss you, Mom. Really. It's quiet without you here."

"You're sweet. I'll hurry back. I love you."

"And I love you, Mom. Take care."

Lydia had the *genius loci* disconnect the interface that had made the call possible despite the locus being outside of the usual networked sites. She touched a dampness from her eyes.

"Is Alice well?" Ambry asked.

He had sat to one side while she made the call, neither intruding nor retreating. Lydia went over and cuddled next to him.

"She's fine. Wanted to know if I'll be home for my birthday."

"You can go if you wish and return afterwards."

"And risk something happening to you during that time?"

"The risk is not immense."

"I couldn't relax and Alice would notice. She's terribly perceptive, far more perceptive than she should be at that age. Far more perceptive than I was, I'm certain."

Ambry embraced her. "Alice has a very sweet and very sensitive mother. Despite your professional commitments, you never let her doubt that she was loved and wanted."

"She's also nosey. If I don't come up with a good excuse, she is quite likely to come looking for me."

"It is doubtful that she could find us."

"And that would raise questions in itself. Alice—in her Link persona—is quite a devastatingly thorough investigative reporter. Now that she has joined forces with her friend Desmond Drum, I'm not certain that anything could be kept from her for long."

"Why not invite her to join us here for your birthday?"

"Ambry?"

"I have longed to meet my daughter. Until now, it has not seemed prudent, given the peculiar nature of her genesis. However, if she is as good an investigator as you say . . ."

"She is."

"Then she is quite likely to learn something about me on her own. Remember, your friend Gwen met me once and you *do* take solo jaunts into virt on a fairly regular basis. The excuses you have made will not hold if Alice begins probing."

"True."

"What do you say, Lydia? Shall we make this a family party?"

"How much do we tell her about you?"

"None of the new theology, please. I am still getting accustomed to the ideas myself. Let us simply tell her that I am Wolfer Martin D'Ambry, a resident of Virtù, and your long-time lover. She will quickly conclude the rest."

Lydia considered, her expression brightening.

"I like it!"

"If the 'lapse' to my memory occurs . . ."

"As you said, that is not likely. In any case, Ambry, the more I think about it, the more I think that Alice should get to know you." She grew suddenly serious. "Then if the worst happens . . ."

"Yes. I agree. We can talk with our host *genius loci* and make arrangements to bring Alice here."

Lydia pulled him to his feet. "I can hardly wait!"

Ambry laughed and took her hand. Together they went to seek the *genius loci* who resided behind the North Wind and ask her permission to hold a birthday party. The *genius loci* was delighted with the idea and promised to help Lydia blow out every candle on her cake.

—=—

It had not taken long for Markon and Virginia to realize that there was more to Earthma's little bundle of joy than they had been told. Within a few days of the goddess depositing her offspring in their care, Markon had begun to feel listless. Initially, he had tried to dismiss this as the strain of rehabilitating all the entities that had been damaged in the assault by Sayjak's band, but soon he was forced to admit that there was something more.

Virginia immediately suspected that Earthma was responsible. She glowered at the sealed, sarcophaguslike forcefield that held Earthma's child. The reddish light that cycled over it—fading from the hue of dried blood to rosy pink and then darkening again—did not appear to notice her regard.

"Where does it hurt?" she asked Markon, trying to sound flippant but merely sounding worried. "I mean, is there any location or time where the listlessness seems more dominant?"

Markon attempted to run a diagnostic, a routine task made nearly impossible by the fact that he was having increasing difficulty finding energy to do anything other than keep his normal systems running at peak.

"I cannot tell," he said, at last, "but I do seem more affected in initiating new programs rather than in maintaining standard subroutines."

"Can you localize a source for the drain?"

"I fear I do not have the energy."

Virginia chewed her thumbnail as Markon lapsed into the somewhat comatose state that had become more and more usual. Her training for the Virtù Survey Department had not prepared her for anything like this. Indeed, many of the upper division heads at VSD still resisted the idea that the *genius loci* were anything other than specialized location proges.

However, her life-long role as an invalid had given her more than enough experience with doctors and their diagnostic techniques. Taking up the pack which contained her Survey Kit, she began a methodical sweep through Markon's site. The task was neither quickly nor easily accomplished—indeed, it would have been impossible for anyone else— but Markon had reprogrammed his standard defenses so that the direcats purred rather than pounced when she came near and the barbed thornvines parted to let her walk unimpeded.

When her survey was completed and she felt that she had enough data to support her initial hypothesis, she returned to the central grove. At her gentle probing, Markon awoke from his quiescence.

"Markon, how would we contact Earthma?"

"It is usual to pray to those on Highest Meru." The *genius loci's* voice sounded vague.

"No, I mean how would we contact her in an emergency?"

"Emergency?"

"Like if the baby fell on its head."

"Earthma's offspring is unlikely to do such a thing. I do not believe that, at this stage in its development, it has even taken on a set shape."

"Markon! Please. I want to reach Earthma—to speak with her. Is there any way I can contact her short of burning incense?"

Markon did not respond. The question was simply too difficult. It was not that the aion could not think of ways that Earthma could be reached. He simply could not differentiate better ways (such as contacting a lesser messenger deity) from the worse ways (setting off a destructive reaction within his site—which was certain to bring her). Unable to advise clearly, he lapsed into a slow examination of probabilities.

Frustrated, Virginia knew better than to be angry with Markon—she knew who deserved her wrath and she almost forgot how terribly powerful Earthma was as she rehearsed the tongue-lashing she would deliver. Her anger gained force as she realized that she could think of no better way to contact Earthma than through Markon's suggestion of prayer.

Virginia's parents had been foot-washing Baptists, devout worshipers in a punishing god who they believed had sent them their damaged child as a torment for the sins of their youth. Since those transgressions had rarely exceeded anything more sinful than an occasional lapse in manners, they may have felt that there was an injustice in their assigned penance—something of a misrouting on a cosmic scale. This may have explained why they prayed so long and hard over their invalid daughter.

National Health had taken over Virginia's care when her nerve debilitation had progressed to the point that her parents could no longer care for her. She had been one of their greater successes—earning her own living in Virtù and paying for her own care. Still, even as she came to think of her lithe and healthy virt body as her "real" self, she never quite forgot her parents' well-meaning prayers with their veiled accusation that Virginia's illness, her continued decline (but persistent refusal to die), was somehow worse for them than it was for her.

All of this came boiling back as Virginia considered how to pray. She hadn't liked Earthma. Even for Markon, she would be unable to call out to her as "good" or "holy" with any conviction, but some of the rhetoric of punishment and damnation from her youth she could employ with sincerity.

First, Virginia knelt, her hands folded against a large rock. This, she knew, was the posture for humble prayer—a posture that could substitute for devotion.

"Earthma." She tasted the name. Yes, this would do.

"Earthma! Earthma! Great and terrible force that underlies the shape of Virtù. Earthma! Great mother of mossy mane and swelling belly. Hear me!"

Virginia repeated the words. They fell from her tongue easily, as if she had learned them long ago and was only now remembering them. The rhythm became a chant. She called, but she did not plead. She described, but she did not grovel.

Her voice became hoarse and a tiny spring bubbled from the cold stone to kiss her lips. She drank, accepting Markon's gift, rejoicing that he had at least this much control. When her throat was soothed, she continued her chant, coloring it with the events she recalled from Markon's tales of the battles of the Genesis Scramble.

Over and over, she called, not letting herself despair, though her knees grew sore (and moss grew out of the damp earth beneath them to cushion her), and her lips tired of shaping the words. To despair was to admit she could do nothing and she would not accept this as long as Markon needed her.

Virginia had paused to drink when she became aware of a golden light permeating the grove. Raising her head, her lips still shaping the words of her chant, she turned and saw the messenger.

His form was that of a young man, clad only in a brief golden kilt that might have been woven from light rather than from coarse matter. His feet fluttered above the ground in wingéd sandals and his pale hair was lit with a halo. Her mind struggled to recall old lessons and she came up with a name.

"Mercury?"

"Well, that beats being called 'The Flash,' as I have been in my time. Yes, 'Mercury' will do as a name for me. Who are you? You're a Veritéan, but you pray to the secret deities of Virtù and your prayers have the force of an aion behind them."

"I am Virginia Tallent. Markon told me of the ones on High Meru— I've met Earthma. I need to speak to her."

The youth guffawed. "You need to speak with Earthma? Give me your plea. I will direct it to whichever of the lesser ones will grant your need."

"Earthma. Tell her I need to speak with her."

"Do you think she will come at your bidding? Do you think I want to be mocked by her when I tell her some Veritéan wench has demanded her attention?"

"Tell her Virginia Tallent, the friend of Markon, wishes to speak with her."

"Tell me why."

"No."

"Then I refuse."

"And I shall continue my prayers. When Earthma finally deigns to hear me, I will tell her of your refusal to bear my message. The heavens will look lovely when your gold is reduced to glitter blown between the stars."

"You're an arrogant wench. What's to keep me from reducing you to ash for your impertinence to a deity?"

The ground beneath their feet rumbled. The sky darkened. Lightning shot down from the clear sky and pierced the earth between Mercury's feet.

"I see." The golden youth glanced around. "The situation amuses me, so I will carry your message. Do not believe for a moment that you or any other has intimidated me."

"Of course not." Virginia's smile was impudent. "Thank you."

A flash of golden light was the only reply. Virginia flopped down on the pad of moss and leaned against the rock. She patted the damp earth with her hand.

"Thanks, Markon."

Earthma granted Virginia an interview before the day grew much older. Virginia had taken the time to consider that her initial intention to rage at the goddess was ill-considered. When the green-haired woman (attired this time like Primavera in a wispy veil of delicate leaves and tiny flowers that concealed nothing of her voluptuous body) appeared, Virginia bowed deeply.

"I am grateful that you would attend to my call, Earthma."

"You put Celerity in a tizzy. It was the least I could do. What's wrong?"

Although she had resolved to be courteous, Virginia did not evade the issue.

"Your offspring is draining energy from Markon's realm."

"It is?"

Efficiently, as if giving a report to the VSD, Virginia outlined what she had discovered in her tour of the site. She ended by noting that Markon had not been quite as communicative as of late. The *genius loci's* response to Mercury's threat had been proof enough that he was still quite able to interact with others—as long as that interaction was non-verbal. It was best that Earthma not know the level of his impediment.

When Virginia finished her summary, Earthma sighed.

"Surely you did not believe that sheltering one who is intended to become the Lord of Entropy could be done without some side effects?"

"Why were we not warned?"

"I didn't want to get into an argument. Besides, Markon knew he had no choice."

"Still, he might have chosen destruction rather than submitting to this vampiric debilitation."

Earthma studied Virginia. "Celerity is right. You are impudent."

"I prefer to think of myself as realistic."

"Is that a pun? Realistic—Veritéan? Very well, give me a realistic reason why I should change anything."

Virginia had already considered this. "You told Markon you would respect and promote his neutrality . . ."

"For my convenience."

"Yes, but if he becomes markedly weak, then another *genius loci* may notice and comment. This could lead either to an attack—which would endanger your offspring—or to gossip. Your desire to have your offspring kept secret was one of your reasons for hiding it here."

"I remember. Still, who would know to gossip?"

"Mercury knows that you would respond to a prayer from me. There are others who can hypothesize based on data such as the attack of Sayjak's clan and your retreat—a retreat that would no longer make sense if Markon becomes weak."

Earthma's expression became thoughtful as she considered Virginia, her earlier annoyance touched with respect.

"Yes, you have a good point or two, there. Perhaps Markon does need his full capacities if he is to serve me. I will restructure my infant's power demand. The side effects on Markon will be reduced."

"Thank you."

Earthma reached out and made motions in the air around the sarcophagus. The light around it shifted from shades of red, went around the spectrum once, then repeated the cycle until it stopped at green. Earthma made further adjustments until the forcefield turned the pale shade of new grass, darkened to lime, into leaf, then into the deep green-black of old pine needles.

When her adjustments were completed, the goddess reached out and touched Virginia beneath the chin, tilting back the Veritéan's head and looking into her eyes.

"You could become dangerous, Virginia Tallent. I will be watching you. Perhaps Markon should send you back to the Verité."

"We will discuss it," Virginia promised.

Earthma laughed and let Virginia's head drop. "I expect that you will and I expect I already know the end result of that discussion!"

"It is the privilege of deities to be omniscient," Virginia responded with a bow.

"It is," Earthma said, "and don't you forget it."

———=———

Death's garden was possessed of bowers of dead flowers, streams that ran with boiling blood, and fountains of fire. Many of the flowers still showed traces of once brilliant yellow in the creases of their faded petals, others evidently had been roses. Their scent was the scrapings from the bottoms of old perfume bottles when the rare oils have evaporated away.

Jay was offered a chair—the rest of his party had to fend for themselves. Mizar did this by flinging himself at Jay's feet, midway between his old master and his new. Tranto stood behind Jay's chair, one pace to the side. Still less than certain about how long Death's cordiality would be maintained, Dubhe perched on the relative safety of the phant's broad head.

The Lord of Deep Fields himself was enthroned on a high-backed seat of aged rattan, a complex bit of basket-making that had been the throne of the ruler of a Polynesian island site until she had the lack of insight to believe that her piraguas and canoes could successfully challenge the British sailing vessels brought in by a neighboring site. Her monarchy had ended in a shower of cannon shot and the wicker throne in a burst of flame that consumed its occupant along with it.

Phecda coiled around his arm. Servitors made of scrap metal brought palm wine and oddly assorted dainties. To be polite, Jay accepted a goblet of the wine. Death touched nothing, whether out of design or lack of inclination could not be known.

"And so, Jay Donnerjack, are you prepared to listen to a tale?"

"As you wish, sir."

"Very well. I so wish."

Death did not move, but (perhaps from the stirring of the air within the courtyard) there was a feeling that he had sighed.

"Long before you were born, Jay Donnerjack, even before your father came to Virtù to perform research and remained to court the woman who would become your mother, a man named Warren Bansa announced that he would perform a magic trick to rival all other such tricks.

"Now Warren Bansa . . . but wait, perhaps you could tell me what you know of Warren Bansa, Jay Donnerjack. Let me have some demonstration of the education which you received in your father's house."

As much as he disliked the implied slight to Dack and to his father, Jay complied without so much as an edge to the tone of his voice.

"Warren Bansa was a Veritéan—a computer specialist like my father, but less concerned with the programming of material. In many ways he fell between my father, who was interested in how things work, and Reese Jordan, who was interested in the 'whys' of perception and the structure of the human mind. Most agree that Warren Bansa was the person who unintentionally initiated the system crash that resulted in the creation of Virtù."

Death interrupted. "That last is correct, as far as it goes—although 'creation' is typical human arrogance. 'Access' might be a more correct term. But, continue, Jay."

"Reese said that Bansa's hobby was magic—stage magic—tricks with mirrors, sleight of hand, misdirection, and escape. He was less appreciated in his day than Harry Houdini had been in his own era, but Reese was of the opinion that this was no reflection on Bansa's talent. Rather, the modern age had become so jaded from tricks of virtual reality (even in its comparatively primitive pre-Virtù state), mass communication, and the like that it had lost its taste for—and ability to believe in—miracles."

With a noise like a mirror cracking, Death laughed.

"Remember that last—about the question of belief, Jay. It touches on something that I wish to discuss later. Now, finish what you know of Bansa."

"As you said, sir, he announced a great magic trick, jumped from a plane in Verité wrapped in ropes and chains as if he was going to perform an elaborate escape. As far as anyone knows, he never reached the ground. He simply vanished. They searched for his body, rewards were offered, but Warren Bansa had vanished. People still argue whether this vanishing was his greatest trick, or whether he intended something else. As far as I have been able to learn, no one knows."

Jay raised his goblet of palm wine and took a tiny sip to signal that he had completed his narration. Inwardly, he was pleased with himself. Death, however, said nothing by way of praise. His response, indeed, was condemnatory.

"Had your father permitted you to be educated here as I had intended, you would know the answer to the riddle of Warren Bansa. It is integral to my purpose for you. No matter. Do you know anything of the Great Flux and the gods on Meru?"

"Alioth occasionally tells a tale. Otherwise, no, sir, I do not."

"Honest, at least. Very well. I shall continue. Tell that device you wear to record, as I do not care to repeat this again."

Jay raised his eyebrows at this reference to his concealed paternal aion—he had not realized that Death would know anything about its capacities. Almost as soon as he considered this, he gave himself a mental kick. Mizar had been with him on the day that the bracelet "awoke." Dubhe had also seen it in action. One or the other could have easily reported to their master.

"Bracelet, record," he said, and an orange light flashed on in acknowledgment.

If Death smiled at this refusal of the aion to confirm the presence of John D'Arcy Donnerjack in any form, none could tell. "Warren Bansa did indeed intend something more elaborate even than his complete vanishing from the face of Verité. His plan was to demonstrate in this showy fashion a development that most people—even today—would scoff at as impossible. He intended to cross over from Verité into Virtù without the use of cumbersome transfer couches—and with his body."

Jay gasped, his emotion a mixture of surprise and—oddly—jealously. For so long, he had believed his ability unique that learning someone else had attempted it so long ago left him feeling momentarily diminished.

"And did Bansa succeed?" he asked.

"He did and he did not," Death replied cryptically. "His device operated successfully in that it carried him across the interface, but it was not completely successful in that the crossover killed him. As he died within Virtù, effectively as a creature of Virtù, there were several side effects. One—which you no doubt surmised—is that he passed into my keeping. This is true, but only to a point.

"What Warren Bansa did not realize—what few accept, even today—is that Virtùan cosmology is far more complex than any but perhaps those on highest Meru and myself," (this last with a bone-dry chuckle), "can know. The eldest of the *genii loci* arrogantly refer to Virtù as the first universe—Verité as the upstart second. Some do not even believe in Verité except as a suburb of Virtù. The Church of Elish has been preaching something in a similar vein.

"However, what Warren Bansa did not know, what he perhaps could not know, is that within Virtù his role in instigating the Genesis Scramble turned him into a creature within our mythology."

"Do you mean he is a god?"

"A god? No, not precisely. More like one of those not quite mortal, not quite deified figures that feature in Native American mythologies."

"A trickster?" This from Tranto.

"Somewhat, but also a divine hero. Let us suffice to say that when Warren Bansa died in the crossover, something of his essence was seized by the mythology that had been generated around his person. He died, but apotheosis took over and he became the Piper, the Master, the One Who Waits. There, we will leave him, because he ceases to be important to me."

Jay bit back questions, knowing without a doubt that the answers would involve more dry comments about his lack of proper education.

"My interest is in events that occurred shortly before your conception, Jay. I was tending to my realm when Alioth brought me word that two intruders had come to Deep Fields. Now, before John D'Arcy Donnerjack made Deep Fields a regular spot on the tourist routes, none came here other than in the usual way."

Death paused. Dubhe leaned down from his perch on Tranto's head and whispered:

"That's a joke, Jay."

Jay smiled, essayed to laugh. Death did laugh, a wheezing sound, somewhat resembling a broken bellows.

"Your father also had difficulty believing that I could joke," he said. "Strange."

"Not really," Jay replied. "We don't find death a laughing matter since it takes from us the people and things we love. It is hard to envision Death as laughing in other than a somewhat wicked fashion."

"Fair enough and, again, soft-spoken. Very well, Jay, I shall endeavor not to joke, but only to tell my tale.

"Alioth led me to the northern reaches of Deep Fields where we saw two humanlike figures—one male, one female—searching through my heaps of decaying matter. They had placed some items in a sack. Before I could reach them, they effected their escape with whatever it was that they had stolen."

"Who were they?" Jay asked.

"I have my suspicions, and part of the task I intend for you is to confirm them for me. At that time, I created Mizar and set him on the trail of the thieves."

Mizar raised his head and whined faintly.

"I do . . . not remember."

"No, Mizar, you do not," Death said, leaning forward from his rattan throne to stroke the dog on the patch of orange shag carpet between his ears. "What I conjecture is that you were far more successful in your tracking than even I had hoped you would be, that you caught up to the thieves, and seeing that you could not capture them, you howled for me as I had taught you before they attacked you.

"I followed your call to the base of Mount Meru, the primal mountain where the gods dwell. You were nowhere to be found—the only certainty I had that you had indeed been there was a piece of cable that had served as one of your tails lying near the mountain's base.

"Over time, I searched for you, my dog, and when I found you any memory you had of those events had been blasted away. I repaired you as best I could and set you to guide and guard Jay. But I stray from the main of my story."

Jay cleared his throat. "That's all right, sir. I'd always wondered what happened to Mizar and where he came from."

"But Mizar's story is only important as a small part of what I need to tell you so that you may serve me."

"Yes, sir."

"I returned to Deep Fields and examined the area wherein I had seen the intruders. Even as I had driven them away, I had some knowledge of what rested within that area. Now I confirmed my suppositions—and my fears.

"Does it surprise you that *I* can feel fear, Jay Donnerjack? I assure you, all sane creatures feel fear when presented with something that might mean the end of existence as they know it. When I examined the region of Deep Fields where the intruders had foraged, I discovered only one thing missing, but that one thing promised trouble enough."

Death paused and within the black robe's sleeve Jay saw bony fingers grip the arm of the throne. The knuckles could grow no whiter, but Jay had an impression of immense force brought to bear, an impression confirmed when the rattan armrest bent beneath the pressure of those slim fingers.

"Warren Bansa had come to rest there, Jay, Warren Bansa and his wondrous device. I knew where the body was and, as was my custom, I left it and its gear in place until the time when I might have need of it. I have learned some care since then and this palace has strong-rooms to spare . . . but I become sidetracked again.

"When I searched those heaps I found scraps of clothing, a dismembered skeleton, a skull, all of which had belonged to Bansa. However, of his device, I found nothing at all. Even the parts that had been implanted in his living flesh or set beneath his bone had been cut away.

"I bided my time then—what else could I do? Mount Meru is a place forbidden to me, for those on its slopes are immune to death as long as they remain in that place. However, Deep Fields is also forbidden to them, something of a balancing of rights."

Jay nodded. "I can see that, but *I'm* not forbidden that place, am I?"

"You are not. As one born of both Virtù and Verité, you may have strengths that poor Mizar did not. I do not believe that any Veritéan could reach those high realms, but a Virtùan cannot be forbidden them (unless, as with me, there are restrictions within the base program). Yet, I do not believe that a Virtùan could explore there with impunity. Whether consciously worshiped or not, those on Meru are the gods of Virtù."

"You want me to go there, then."

"Yes. Your task will be threefold. First, find and recover, if possible, the elements of Warren Bansa's device. Secondly, bring back any information you can on the armies that are massing on Meru and in its environs."

"Armies?"

"So I said. Thirdly, find me proof of who stole Warren Bansa's device from my realm. The more solid the proof, the better."

"Solid? Like a signed confession?"

"I doubt that is possible. However, a recording would do, a fragment, a witness . . ."

Dubhe had begun to laugh. "This is the game, the game you mentioned so long ago, isn't it?"

Death nodded. "A game that has taken more twists than I imagined when I spoke so lightly of 'play,' Dubhe. Those on high Meru mean to warp the fabric of reality and take Verité as their playground. What they have stolen from me may make this possible."

"Why do you care?" Jay asked. "If Virtù gets bigger, so does your realm, right?"

"Too simple, child," Death said. "If you survive the task I have set you, we will discuss metaphysics further."

"Promise?"

"You dare extract a promise from me?"

"I want to know. I feel like a pawn on a huge chessboard." Jay held his hands out in appeal. "Give me a shot at being a knight."

"I like your attitude. Very well, Jay Donnerjack. I shall continue your education when you return from the journey I have set for you."

"Can I ask one more question?"

"I reserve the right to refuse to answer."

"You always do. Will you tell me why you want to know who trespassed here? If the ones on Meru are immune to your powers, what good will it do?"

"But they are not immune to my powers, Jay Donnerjack. When they depart the protection of Meru, the lesser ones fear me as any mortal does. Only the highest three are completely out of my reach, and if one of them is among the trespassers, well then, that one (or two) is now within my power. The shadow of Deep Fields has touched them once and I can bring it to bear once more."

Jay shivered. Death's cracked voice became supple, almost choking as he concluded his reply.

"You see, Jay Donnerjack, it is a truism that I am always in the right place at the right time. I mean to prove that . . . even to the death of the highest gods."

TEN

Once upon a time, the acreage in California had been part of greater Los Angeles. Then the states to the north and east of the sprawling, irrigated desert had put an end to the piracy of resources they felt they had more right to use. Virtual reality, in the form of catalogs, commutes, and social events had reduced the demand for residing in close proximity to important cities—and virtventure had greatly reduced the movie industry.

Someday, water mining in the asteroids might bring in chunks of ice to seed a reservoir or two, or transportation technology might be employed to bring the by-products of an eastern flood to the dry west. Perhaps there would come again a day when people would learn the pleasure of watching a stage production or visiting an amusement park where the risk (however minimal) was real, not virtual. For now, however, Los Angeles was a much smaller city than it had once been.

The infrastructure of roads, utilities, and communications networks still existed, however. There were ample materials to scavenge for building and the cachet of a Hollywood premiere still remained. Thus, the Church of Elish came to California to set the stage for their second Celebration.

✿　　✿　　✿

Randall Kelsey came in at the end of his shift to find a message from Ben Kwinan on his virt terminal. He did not answer the call at first, preferring to shower, eat, glance through a magazine. It was not that he was avoiding Kwinan, he told himself, it was simply that his virtual colleague could be exhausting company.

Despite their open desire to share the freedom of both universes that Veritéans demonstrably possessed, not many of the natives of Virtù could honestly comprehend the limitations of a physical body. The closest they could come was when they exceeded the restrictions of their personal programming. And if that programming was thorough—as Kwinan's must be—they hardly ever experienced their equivalent of fatigue.

Eventually, Kelsey rigged for a second-level interaction and signaled Kwinan that he was available. Kwinan appeared with such alacrity that Kelsey suspected he must have made response to the call a primary priority. Not certain whether he should be pleased or suspicious, Kelsey nodded greeting.

"Hi, Ben. How is the work going on your side?"

Kwinan shrugged. "Tickets are selling. Otherwise, it's hard to say. So much depends on whether the gods will cooperate and you know how arrogant they can be. I'm more interested in developments on your side."

"We've cleared the site now and the ziggurats are going up nicely. The traffic routes are pretty much in place and Aoud is doing amazing things in preparation for crowd control."

"I still find it astonishing to think of a site being constructed by physical labor rather than by program design," Kwinan said. His grey eyes were lit with almost religious fervor. "It must be wonderful!"

"If you like grit in your eyes, in your hair, in your mouth . . . if you like a headache from the pounding of construction machinery," Kelsey laughed, "and needing to worry about the laws of physics for real, rather than if you can convince the resident aion to change them to accommodate your design . . . No, I'd rather be in charge of a Virtùelle construction project. I thank the gods that I'm an assistant, rather than the boss of this one."

"Maybe so . . ." Kwinan did not sound convinced. "Can you come through via stage three? I'd like to talk with you about something . . . personal."

Kelsey frowned. His first intention was to refuse—a need to be at the site early tomorrow, fatigue, any excuse. His second was to recall that Kwinan was still his superior within the Church and that Kelsey should not discourage any willingness to confide.

"I'll need to see if any of the dorm's rigs are open."

"I'll make certain that one is," Kwinan promised. "Come by my residence. You still have the coordinates?"

"I do."

"Great! And thanks."

Kelsey hummed to himself as he shut down his second-stage link. He donned a light cotton robe and slippers, combed his hair, and walked down to the virt transfer unit set up in the basement of the dormitory that had been constructed for on-site workers. As Ben had promised, a couch was empty. When he placed his hand on it, he found it was slightly warm. Someone must have been evicted.

Stripping, he worked the links into place, assisting his hands with touches from his virtual telekinesis. Then he gave a command and a grey mist rose. As the network aion took over, he gave it the coordinates for Kwinan's place, stepped into a violently violet cab, and leaned back to enjoy the ride to the site where many of the Church's Virtùan members maintained dwellings.

Although in theory space within Virtù was infinite, in reality the average complex proge or aion could not maintain its own site and have memory left to divert to other projects. Therefore, they "rented" space from a *genius loci* and tailored it to suit their personal tastes. Some of these sites had the equivalent of "zoning regulations" to maintain a particular theme. Others, such as the one Kelsey's cab was now entering, were eclectic.

The decor of Ben Kwinan's residence was always changing, usually reflecting Kwinan's latest fascination. Today it resembled a Navajo hogan—a rounded structure with log and mud walls and a softly curved mud roof. It contrasted oddly with the staid brownstone on one side and the miniature Moorish palace on the other, less because of the primitive materials of its construction than because it was aligned so that its entryway was on side to the street rather than facing it.

When Kelsey was admitted to the hogan, he learned why this was so. Dressed in worn blue jeans, a Western shirt with silver buttons, his hair (still the same grey as always) bound with a wide fabric tie, Kwinan pushed aside the blanket that covered the door revealing a roughly round room with a fire in the center. It was decorated simply, with practical articles hanging on the wall and elaborately patterned rugs heaped on the floor.

"Thanks for coming by, Randall."

"Pleasure. Interesting place."

"Navajo hogan. I've had a lot of fun working on it. I guess it's my compensation for not being able to be on-site in California."

"This looks like a lot more fun," Kelsey assured him, following him into the hogan.

"Walk to the left of the fire," Kwinan said, steering Kelsey slightly so that he did as directed. "Traditionally, the hogan is aligned with its door facing the east. The south side of the fire was reserved for the men, the north for the women."

"And the west?" Kelsey asked, noting that this was where Kwinan was placing him.

"Was for honored guests," Kwinan said with a beaming smile. "Take a seat on the rugs—I think you'll find them comfortable. The patterns and textures are from the Wheelwright databank. Can I offer you a drink?"

"It's not going to be anything peculiar like goat's milk, is it?"

"Not if you don't want it to be. I have a completely stocked bar."

"Coffee, then. It's been a long day."

"Coffee it is. I have some piñon cookies, too."

"Wonderful."

When they were settled with coffee and cookies, Kwinan fell silent for so long that Kelsey wondered if his host had directed a portion of his attention to another activity. When they had first started working together, Kelsey had not been certain if Kwinan was a complex proge or an actual aion. The longer they had associated, the more certain he had become that Kwinan was an aion. But, as Kwinan never mentioned the matter, and Kelsey felt that an inquiry would be rude, he had never pursued the matter.

"We are completely private here," Kwinan said after a time. "I mention this because I want you to be assured that whatever we discuss here will go no further than between the two of us."

"Uh, thanks."

Kwinan picked up a ball of yarn, unwound a bit, wove it into something like a cat's cradle around his fingers, picked up and dropped strands, apparently giving his entire attention to creating the elaborate design.

"I hardly know how to begin. I've brought this . . . consideration to you for several reasons. First of all, we've worked together a long time. You are probably the Veritéan I feel most comfortable with—I know you've made an effort to understand the Virtùan point of view. You've also demonstrated the ability to think for yourself time and again."

"However, I've also made some rather serious errors," Kelsey said dryly, "as in not detecting that Arthur Eden's interest in the Church was other than spiritual."

"How could you be expected to know that? Eden didn't fool just you—you simply took the fall for the rest of our slowness. There are many members of the Church for whom involvement is less than spiritual."

"I'm shocked, simply shocked."

"Right. How are you enjoying the revenues from that tee-shirt you're marketing?"

"You know that my name is just being used to front that project for the Church."

"Shocked . . . Randall, you think for yourself, work harder than any two members, and maintain a sense of humor about the entire mess."

"Thank you—I think."

Ben Kwinan let his loop of yarn fall limp between his fingers. He raised his gaze to meet Kelsey's.

"Randall, there was a day you expressed some doubt about the wisdom of letting the gods of old cross over into the Verité. You expressed concern about how their values, their power, would interact with those of modern Verité."

"I remember."

"At the time, I gave you the party line, but now that I've been working with the great ones myself, I find myself wondering if you were right. What do you know of the gods of Virtù?"

Kelsey wrinkled his brow, momentarily disoriented by the apparent change of subject.

"I know that they exist, that many of the aions worship them rather than gods generated out of the Verité. Once or twice, I have heard it whispered that the 'gods' who manifest in our Virtùan temples during the services are not the reawakened deities of ancient Babylon and Sumer, but are some of the lesser deities of Virtù playing a role and reaping some intangible benefit from being at the center of so much attention."

"You listen carefully, but I am not surprised by this. I've always known you were aware of more than you ever mentioned."

"And?"

"And? What if I was to tell you that you were right on many counts?

Right as far as you go—although there is more to the picture than what you know."

"If you told me that, I suppose I would ask you to tell me what is missing from my picture."

"Again, what I would expect. Very well, Randall, consider yourself told. When the Church of Elish worships the gods of Sumer and Babylonia, they also worship with the gods of Virtù."

"Is it all a game, an elaborate bit of theater?"

"No, not at all, because the Church of Elish is completely right about one of its most basic teachings. Virtù is the gateway into the collective unconscious of the human race—the *anima mundi*, the place of archetypal myths. When the gods of Virtù assume their roles, they also take on some aspects of the creatures whose form and habits they have adopted. In some cases, as with the greater gods of the pantheon, Virtù preserved the gods when their worshipers crumbled to dust."

"So, in a sense, it *was* Bel Marduk who manifested in Central Park that day."

"Correct. And the more I work with those deities, the more I am aware that the arrogance and indifference to individual human rights and privileges possessed by the ancient ones is seeping into the psyches of the Virtùan deities. Don't misunderstand me—the gods appreciate humanity as a whole, as a source of worship and adoration, but the individual is as nothing to them."

"The legends of Sumer and Babylon contain the first telling of a flood that nearly wiped out everything living on the earth."

"That is correct."

"Then what you are saying is that attitude is being given form and power once again."

"Yes, although in a slightly less destructive form, perhaps. Remember, in the story of the Flood, the gods did come to regret wiping out humanity and let the race grow again from the few survivors."

"But the individual life . . ."

"Or that of a city or nation even . . ."

"Would be as less than nothing to these gods."

"That is so."

"And we are working our asses off to help them have free access to Verité."

"I'm afraid so."

"Jesus H. Christ!"

"Jesus was a much gentler god than those whom the Church of Elish wishes to set free in the Verité."

"Bel Marduk, jealous Ishtar, raging Enlil . . ."

"You seem horrified, Randall, even surprised. Why? Have I brought up anything more terrible than what you have already feared?"

"I wasn't afraid anymore, Ben. First, you gave me assurances. Then, after things went to hell in Central Park, the Hierophant was so confident, so certain we could turn apparent disaster into a major coup."

"The Hierophant. Yes, the Hierophant. Tell me, Randall, have you ever considered why the Hierophant began spreading the teachings of the Church of Elish?"

"I assumed that he wanted greater respect for Virtù and its potential. I mean, it *is* stupid that the most magnificent artifact of the human race is used for little more than a convenient place to work and play. The Church of Elish has preached appreciation for Virtù's vast potential and vast power."

"I wish I could believe that, my friend. It's what I believed once."

"Are you saying that you believe that the Hierophant has ulterior motives?"

"Certainly. Moreover, I know that you share my suspicions. We both have been in on the ground floor—so to speak—of the development of the crossover project."

"That's true. I remember when we made the early modifications to the couches."

"And later, when we sought volunteers for the broadcast links."

"I'll never forget that. Being approached as a volunteer for that project was what drove Emmanuel Davis—Arthur Eden—into hiding."

"And now we have come to the crossover of the gods."

"I don't understand why you are so unhappy, Ben. For as long as I can remember, you have longed for the ability to cross over into Verité as I can into Virtù. Once the gods make the transition, can aions be far behind?"

A small smile crossed Ben Kwinan's face.

"No, it cannot. However, I dislike the idea of crossing into a Verité as dominated by gods and demons as Virtù already is. I appreciate the convenience and power of a *genius loci*, but I want to be part of a world without active gods."

Kelsey lifted the coffee pot from its hook over the fire, filled his cup, took another cookie from the plate.

"But what can we do, Ben? Even if we sabotaged this Celebration, there would be another."

"I realize that."

"And I don't really care for the idea of bringing our theory to the media. Look what happened to Eden. His revelations were much tamer than this, but he remains in hiding to escape the Church's vengeance. He'll probably *die* in hiding."

"True."

"I bet you have a suggestion."

"Yep, but you're not going to like it."

"Try me. I don't like any of this very much."

Rising from his cross-legged seat, Kwinan began pacing the short distance between the door and the south edge of the fire.

"I told you that your information about the gods of Virtù was accurate as far as it went. We refer to our gods as the Gods on Meru (Mount Meru being their residence), or the Ones on High. The three most senior are called the Highest."

"Very tidy."

"What do you expect from a bunch of computer programs? I have evidence that one of the Highest is allied with the Hierophant on this venture. He has encouraged the lesser gods to participate and is quite probably the source of the 'inspiration' that began the physical crossover project."

"I can buy that. Radical new developments don't come from nowhere and the Gods on Meru must be brilliant to qualify as gods among computer generated intelligences."

"Brilliant? Perhaps. Vastly powerful, nearly omniscient, no doubt. However, divinity does not make them immune to rivalries among themselves and the Highest Three have few peers."

"Only each other, I would guess."

"What I want to suggest is that we ally ourselves to one of the rivals of the Hierophant's ally."

"Wait a minute, Ben. All this talk of 'the Hierophant's ally' and 'the rival of the ally' is getting confusing. Don't you folks have names for these characters?"

Kwinan paused. "We call the Highest Three Seaga, Skyga, and Earthma. The Hierophant's ally is Skyga."

"Very tidy names."

"Don't get sarcastic with me, Randall. Most of your deities' names don't sound any better when they are translated from their original languages."

"I'm not being sarcastic, really. Who do you want to work with, then? Earthma?"

Kwinan actually shivered. "Not her! She's a calculating bitch. I'm not at all comfortable with her."

"Sounds as if you know them personally."

"Oh, not really, but when something is part of your programming from basic generation on, it's hard not to have some pretty visceral feelings about it."

"I suppose so. I'm afraid that my natal culture has lost that immediate religious impulse."

"As most science-oriented Veritéan cultures have—part of the appeal of the Church of Elish within those societies. But I stray from my proposal. Skyga and Seaga have long been genteel rivals. I doubt that Seaga would like to see Skyga gain preeminence. What I suggest is that we ally ourselves with Seaga, provide information and the like so that Seaga can balance Skyga, and thereby keep Skyga somewhat in check."

"Interesting, but I have a feeling that you are not telling me everything. Why do you need me? The information you want could be acquired through other channels."

"True, but I need an ally who can cross into Verité."

"Why? I tell you right now, I won't sabotage the Celebration—not unless we can stop it for good—otherwise too many innocent worshipers are likely to be hurt."

Kwinan stopped pacing and directed his gaze at Kelsey. To the Veritéan he seemed to glow with a faint golden light.

"To be straight, then. I want you to secrete a duplicate of the crossover gear within one of the secondary ziggurats. That way, if we are forced into a clinch, Seaga can send some of his minions through to push back those of Skyga before they can spread into the Verité."

"Odd. A moment ago you said that you wanted the Verité to be free from meddling gods. Now you are telling me that you want to supply another powerful figure with crossover access."

"Only so that the minions of Skyga can be pushed back—and only as a last resort at that."

"So you said."

"Do you doubt me?"

"Not really. It's just that this is a great deal to comprehend all at once. We have some weeks before the Celebration. Can I have time to think?"

"You will not speak of this."

"Of course not. We had already agreed on that. Besides, I am impressed by the danger that these gods of old offer to the Verité. I will not dismiss your considerations lightly. I promise that."

"Then I will need to be satisfied with your need to consider. Sometimes I forget that humans do not have multiple processing units."

Kelsey yawned elaborately. "Or that we have lungs and muscles and sensory equipment that get tired after a hard day's work. Can you have the transition aion call me a cab?"

"Very well. And thank you."

"My pleasure, I assure you."

—=—

Look back over your shoulder.
Run, run away. Far, far away.
 Bar the gates.
 White-knuckled, look out from between the iron posts.

Are you safe at last?
 Can you be safe until it is past?
Call the ghosts.
 Call the five-limbed demons.
  Array the horrors.
Beyond the gate, order lurks.

Press it back into its bottle.
  Chaos is fecund.
  Chaos is powerful.
Chaos . . .
 (oh, my sweet seven-limbed demons)
  Chaos
   is terrified.

—=—

When Alice Hazzard came home from a completely frustrating day spent searching for clues to a story she knew was there, she found a message from her mother. Written in dark green ink on a sheet of pale ivory paper, it rested, hard copy, in the little-used mail basket just inside the front door of the apartment.

Lydia had hand-drawn tiny peacock orchids around the edges of the sheet of paper, something she did when she was fidgeting on the phone or while waiting for a patient. She had sketched their angular yet soft six-petaled shape and spiky leaves perfectly, black pencil shadings for the darker center (deep red in reality), silver-grey for the antennalike stamen and pistils. The flower was the only thing she could draw, but she took great pride in this small achievement.

Alice smiled and felt a pang of homesickness (odd, since she was home; Lydia was away), and read the message:

Alice,
Won't you come and join me? I'd like you to visit for a few days, celebrate my birthday with me, meet an old friend I think you should know. I'm at a private address, but if you come to the campus of AVU at seven this evening, I will meet you by the swan pond. Sorry about the secrecy, but that's how it has to be.
Love, Mom

Alice was intrigued, puzzled. With the edge of her finger she touched just one of the penciled peacock orchids. It smudged. Mom's then, not some weird practical joke.

She considered. Both she and Drum were stumped on the Elshie case. A vacation might give her a new perspective. Knowing that Mom would ask, she checked her schoolwork. Except for a writing assignment, she was all caught up. With a few keystrokes, she transferred a copy of the *Virtropolis* article to her teacher's mailbox. Certainly a publishable article would serve to fulfill the assignment.

The next few hours were spent watering plants, packing her virtual wardrobe (remembering Mom's present), and leaving messages for her grandparents, Gwen, and Drum to let them know that she was joining her mother. At 6:45, she linked into her transfer couch and set the co-ordinates for the campus of AVU.

Her mother was kneeling at the edge of the water, feeding the swans. All of them were white, except for a particularly magnificent black male. He had deigned to take a square of bread directly from Lydia's palm. Alice stood quietly, recalling, from experience, that the programmed swans could be as touchy and territorial as their RT counterparts.

When the swan swam away, Lydia rose, dusted breadcrumbs from her palms, and turned with a smile to Alice.

"Do you remember . . ."

"When I was five and the swan bit me?" Alice chuckled. "I'll never forget."

"Nor I. . . . I was worried that you would develop an aversion to virt then and there. It couldn't have been more than your first or second trip."

"No such luck. Only thing I developed was an aversion to swans."

They laughed.

"Well, Alice, if you'll come with me . . ."

Alice fell into step. "Where are we going?"

"You'll know soon enough, Curiosity."

"Mom!"

"Pretend that I'm a client."

Alice did so, although she was hard-pressed to still her questions when Mom led the way down one of the paths that went around the lake. These rambles didn't go anywhere, just wandered through willows and reeds. Mostly they were used for study groups who met in the conveniently placed gazebos, or for the occasional courting couple that didn't choose a more private site.

She had run up and down these very paths when she was a little girl come to campus with her student mother, had collected handfuls of twigs and pebbles, which she had then deposited on her tolerant parent's lap—interrupting serious discussions of organic chemistry, physiology, anatomy. The paths went nowhere, she knew that as certainly as she knew anything. So where was her mother taking her?

Singing softly, so softly that Alice had to strain to hear, Lydia Hazzard walked on, her A-line skirt swinging slightly with the sway of her hips. Alice hurried after, biting her tongue, wondering when the paths had been extended, wondering what justification had been given to the budget committees for such inefficient use of programming, wondering . . .

A rose garden now . . . Could this be a project for a horticultural class? Certainly the bushes were magnificently programmed—the rounded, slightly serrated leaves each distinct and different. And the flowers were marvelous. Alice had never paid much attention to roses—knew vaguely that they came in red and white and yellow . . . maybe pink.

She lost herself in variations she had never thought to imagine: pale green; white tipped with bloodred; sunset orange; a delicate, silvery purple; another orange—this one burnt; a pink that glowed with a hint of yellow. Nor were the colors the only variation. Some blossoms possessed petals like fat hearts, soft as velvet; others had tiny petals, fragile and thin; others were pointed, almost sharp. The garden smelled of rose perfume, thick and heavy without ever becoming overwhelming.

Lost in contemplation of the roses, Alice did not precisely notice when the bagpipes began to play. Shrill, but commanding, skirling, a twisting, tootling thing that would not conventionally be called a melody, but could be nothing else, the bagpipes called out to her. The tune sounded familiar, although she knew she had never heard it before. It drew her from her contemplation of roses, and looking around, Alice realized that she had transferred sites.

She turned around and stared back the way she had come. The rose garden extended, apparently into infinity, although there was a vivid blue line that might, just might, be an ocean. Alice realized that she could never find her way back. Beneath the sound of the bagpipes, she heard her mother laugh.

"Neat trick?"

"I'm astonished," Alice assured her. "Now can you tell me where we are?"

"We call it the Land Behind the North Wind. As you may have guessed, this is one of the wild sites of Virtù—one of the lost areas, to be more precise."

"I knew they existed . . . I never knew how to find one, though."

"Most people don't. The semiwild sites are enough to keep the VSD busy. These areas are dismissed as mythological—or useless."

"How did you learn your way here?"

"Come over the hill. I'll introduce you to the friend who I've been staying with."

"Is he the one playing the bagpipes?"

"Yes. How did you know it was a 'he'?"

"Mom . . . I don't know how to tell you this, but you're blushing."

Lydia raised a hand to her cheek. "I am? Well, there's hope for this old lady after all. Come along."

Side by side, they climbed a hill that changed character as they mounted its slopes. At first it was as soft and green as the paths through the rose garden. The higher slopes were covered in heather, tiny purple blossoms partially opened, fat bees hovering over them as if the fanning of their wings could ease the flowers open. Grey rocks veined sometimes with jet, sometimes with pink feldspar, periodically interrupted the heather.

"It's very peaceful here," Alice observed.

"I've always thought so. Of course, the weather is not always so pleasant. The *genius loci* is attentive to the needs of her internal ecology—it rains, it sleets. Today, however, the weather has been arranged to welcome you."

"Me?"

"The *genius loci* is a friend of Ambry's, and Ambry . . ."

The bagpipe music stopped abruptly and a man stood up from where he had been seated to the lee of a hulking boulder. His hair and beard were ruffled by the wind, and in his vaguely medieval costume (complete with a huge sword and a dagger), he would have been threatening but for the shyness in his courtly bow.

"Miz Alice," he said, "I am Wolfer Martin D'Ambry. After all these years, I am delighted to make your acquaintance."

All these years. Alice let the words tease her. She had assumed that whoever her mother wanted her to meet was a relatively recent involvement, but this . . . She felt the truth at the fringes of her mind and gave Ambry a warm smile.

"I'm pleased to meet you, too. What should I call you?"

"Your mother calls me 'Ambry'—I'd be pleased if you would do the same."

"And I am Alice—not 'Miz Alice.' "

They walked then, Ambry slightly ahead, his bagpipes tucked under one arm, Alice and Lydia following together. Leaving the hilltop, they came down into an orchard valley. Beneath the spreading apple, peach, and apricot trees, tall Asiatic lilies grew, interspersed with bleeding heart, lily of the valley, and her mother's favorite peacock orchids. A small brook ran through the center of the orchard, tumbling over polished cobblestones. At the verge of the orchard nestled a slate-roofed cottage.

"Is that where you live?" Alice asked Ambry.

"For now, it is," he answered, "and where you will be staying as well. Come along and I'll give you a glass of lemonade. The *genius loci* imports the lemons from a neighboring site."

"How nice of her. I didn't know that the sites traded with each other."

"Oh, they do. As I understand it, a site can be designed to violate the laws of physics and nature as understood in Verité, but the further from the norm, the more difficult it is to maintain. The Lady of the North Wind prefers to import lemons rather than maintain tropics."

Ambry opened the door to the cottage and stood back to let the ladies enter. Coming in after, he set his bagpipes on a stand.

"The lemonade's in the kitchen," he said. "We can take it outside and sit in the garden if you'd like."

"I would," Alice replied. "So, if the physical laws of Verité are the baseline in Virtù, then I guess that the Church of Elish is all wrong when they say that Virtù is the first reality."

"Oh, I don't know about that," Ambry said. "I suspect the issue is a great deal more complicated than merely 'who came first.' The two universes are connected—that is a fact. That they can influence each other to some extent—that is another fact. Beyond those two points, I would not care to lay any wagers."

As Lydia listened to the conversation her initial nervousness gave way to pleasure. She knew her daughter well enough to know that Alice had taken to Ambry, that she wasn't just being polite to her mother's friend. However, she also knew Alice well enough to tell that the girl's intense curiosity had been awakened. When Alice artfully turned the conversation away from universe theory, Lydia was unsurprised.

"So, Mom, where is your patient? I didn't know that you did virtual medicine."

"I don't, and you know very well that I don't," Lydia replied, knowing that she was being baited. "I fibbed. My 'patient' is Ambry and I am not so much treating him as helping him with his doctor's orders."

"If it isn't too rude to ask," Alice said, "is Ambry from somewhere in the Verité?"

"Not as far as I know," Ambry answered. "I am a complex proge— and my programming may be disintegrating."

"No!"

"I have not yet seen the moiré," Ambry reassured her, "so the damage may not be terminal. When I consulted a doctor his diagnosis was that I am suffering from . . . it is difficult to explain."

"Try me. I'm not afraid to ask questions if I don't understand."

"She's not, Ambry," Lydia added. "I think her first sentence was 'Why, Mom?' "

Ambry grinned. "Very well. You must first understand, Alice, that I do not recall my origin. This is not uncommon for natives of Virtù. Often a proge is created for a specific purpose and when that purpose is fulfilled or the proge evolves beyond it, existence independent of original function is achieved. My doctor and I believe that this happened to me long ago.

"My illness may have one of two sources. Either my secondary imperatives are decaying or my creator is trying to recall me to service. Whatever the cause, the result is that I have been suffering bouts of amnesia after which I awaken in a strange site."

"I've been staying with him," Lydia explained, "because I know him well enough to note any changes in his personality. If Ambry starts acting peculiarly I can try to get him to snap out of the spell or, if that fails, call a doctor."

"Wow!" Alice weighed several questions, let one rise to the top. "Ambry, have you had any of these bouts since Mom has been with you?"

"There may have been a minor one, but if so, she was able to bring me around."

"Do you have any idea what your original programming was designed to make you?" Alice grinned. "Sorry if that's rude. I don't know a better way to ask. Drum says that I have no tact."

"Is Drum your boyfriend?"

Oddly, Alice blushed.

"No, he's just a buddy, a detective I've been working with on a case."

Lydia noted the blush and grinned, flustering Alice more, but forbore from commenting.

"Your question is not rude," Ambry assured her, returning to the main thread of the conversation. "In Virtù such identifications are common—rather like family designations. As best as I know, my original design was as a warrior and a musician—a bagpiper for an elite regiment."

"So, you haven't changed much."

"Actually, I have changed a great deal. I have lost my taste for fighting. In the days when I served my creator, I had no other life. Now, I do."

"I don't think it is terribly just that your creator should simply be able to call you back into service," Alice said. "There should be some form of manumission. In Verité, an AP can be manumitted in several ways—"

Lydia, seeing the crusader's fire light her daughter's eyes, interrupted.

"Alice, I'm not certain that this is a particularly polite topic of conversation."

"But, Mom! We're talking about an intelligent person who is effectively a slave to the whims of his creator! I thought you'd *care* . . ."

"I do care, but I don't think that this discussion considers how Ambry might—"

Lydia's explanation was interrupted by a cascade of laughter from Ambry. Alice turned, surprised. Lydia looked annoyed.

"Ambry, what's so funny?"

The Phantom Piper of the Lost Legion of Skyga grinned at his wife.

"I'm sorry, my dear, but Alice is so like you when you were her age—especially when she's impassioned—that watching the two of you argue is like watching you argue with a mirror."

Immediately recognizing the humor of the situation, Lydia grinned. Alice's agile mind had fastened on Ambry's speech to provide another support for the construct she was weaving.

"You've known my mother since she was my age?"

"Within a year or so, yes."

"Do we really look so much alike?"

Ambry paused, glancing back and forth between them.

"When incidentals are omitted—you wear your hair shorter, I think Lydia was a little thinner—you could be twins. There are differences, though, that go beyond the physical. I don't think that anyone who knew you both well could mistake one for the other when you started talking."

"Oh?"

"Lydia was quieter, a little less sophisticated. I remember thinking that she was trying to fold into herself."

"I also had acne," Lydia added, reminiscently. Then she frowned. "Ambry, when I met you, I was in virt disguise. How would you know what I looked like?"

"I may have lost touch with you when you returned to the Verité, my love, but I have had opportunities since to summon old files. However, when you and Alice were bickering, the similarities that struck me were more of personality—of force of personality—than of physical shape."

Alice took a deep breath and asked the question she had been holding back since she had first met Ambry:

"Are you my father?"

The answer came immediately, without hesitation. A faint smile tilted the corner of Ambry's mouth.

"Yes, Alice, I am your father."

For once, Alice Hazzard was at a loss for words or action. She stared at the dapper, bearded man, then glanced at her mother. Lydia reached out, almost defiantly, to squeeze Ambry's hand.

"Alice, the medical technicians would say that it is impossible . . . that there can be no fertile breeding between Virtù and Verité. What my heart tells me is that I came to Virtù on holiday, was spirited away by a charming gentleman, and fell in love with him. Together we made a child, a child that happened to be born in the Verité. You can read all my medical records with their wise theories about psychosomatic conversions and parthenogenesis if you wish—they're accurate as much as they can be. However, to me, Ambry has always been your father—and my husband."

To give herself some distance from the mixture of emotions roiling in her breast, Alice donned the thoughtful expression she normally reserved for Link Crain.

"It seems to me," she said, thinking aloud, "that an adopted child becomes the child of the parents who raised it—no matter who contributed the genetic material. And I always wanted a dad . . . and I really like Ambry . . . Mom?"

Sniffing away a few tears she hadn't realized were running down her face, Lydia hugged her daughter.

"You like Ambry?"

"Would I have said I did if I didn't?"

Laughter replaced the tears.

"No, Alice, not you. Tact has never been one of your gifts."

"I prefer to think of myself as honest!" Alice pulled herself up in mock indignation, a move that managed to put her close enough that Ambry could easily be included in the hug.

They sat together for a time, each glad the moment for revelation was over, each considering what this would mean for the future. Delighted by the drama that had unfolded within its heart, the *genius loci* tossed flower petal confetti into the air and invited the birds to compose arias in celebration.

Days passed in the Land Behind the North Wind, days filled with discovery, picnics, long talks, and occasional arguments. By mutual agreement, Alice and Ambry decided that she would continue to call her father "Ambry" rather than "Dad."

Lydia was perhaps the most nervous about the new family grouping. She had long desired, yet dreaded, the introduction of her daughter and her husband. Their acceptance of each other was a balm, but some days needed to pass before she could relax when Alice began on one of her harangues (her indignation about the enslavement of Virtù's proge population had increased rather than otherwise when she had learned of her relationship to Ambry), or when Ambry would calmly lecture their head-strong daughter about some point of fact or etiquette that she had missed.

Eventually, even Lydia forgot to worry, and the days fluttered by, punctuated by quick visits to the Verité (now that Alice could share the watch, Lydia sporadically returned to tend her clinic). The homecomings were of a sort she had dreamed of since she was nineteen.

And in this fashion the days went by until Lydia's birthday. Early in the day, she visited with her parents and sister—a departure encouraged by Alice and Ambry, as it gave them opportunity to prepare for her party. Upon her return, they picnicked in the orchard, then, cake and ice cream and Alice's gift of pottery all gone by, Ambry fetched his bagpipes from the cottage.

"My gift for you is a musical composition, love," he said, grinning fey yet merry, "as they all have been."

Lydia nodded, leaning back against the trunk of an apricot tree and setting her cake plate in the grass. (A small line of ants marched up and began gathering crumbs). Half-dozing in the sun, Alice lazily ferried the lucky ant or two over to their hill.

One of the fallacies commonly held about the music of the bagpipes is that it is all loud, strident stuff, filled with wails and screeches designed to set the teeth on edge and drive warriors into battle (some say so that they won't be forced to listen any longer). Actually, in skilled hands, the pipes are capable of haunting subtlety, of sobbing as well as shouting, of something like laughter.

Wolfer Martin D'Ambry was such a master, and the piece he had composed for Lydia spoke not only of the times of separation but also of reunion. It rejoiced at the discovery of a daughter and so skillfully mimicked her intensity that Alice sat up and laughed in recognition. It was when the music drifted into defiance of fate, of old masters and new summonings, that the fog began to rise.

Initially, the three humans accepted the meteorologic anomaly (the day to this point had been fine and clear) as an effect generated by the *genius loci* to accompany Ambry's music. Doubt surfaced when the fog solidified into a swirling mass of tentacles, all of which oriented on Wolfer Martin D'Ambry.

"Ambry!" Lydia screamed.

Alice's response, perhaps because she had known her father for such a brief time, was less panicked. Leaping to her feet, she tore hard green apples from the tree nearest to her and pelted them with considerable skill at the foggy monstrosity. Her target defused its mass in sections, permitting the apples to pass through.

Ambry, meanwhile, had dropped his bagpipes and unsheathed his claymore. Spinning the blade in an elaborate series of cuts, he would have swiftly left his opponent without either hands or head if his opponent had borne a resemblance to humanity. The fog creature, however, merely rejoined where the blade had slit its substance, apparently less inconvenienced by the sword than by the apples.

From her vantage, Lydia could see this.

"Ambry! Just get away from it! You can't harm it, but you might be able to outrun it!"

The expression that crossed Wolfer Martin D'Ambry's face at that moment suggested that he was about to declaim that he was not the type of man who ran from an enemy—no matter how fearsome or inhuman. Common sense won out over empty heroics, or perhaps he heard the terror and love in Lydia's voice. In any case, he abandoned his pipes and began a controlled retreat toward the cottage.

Alice assisted him by redoubling her hail of green apples, for the tentacled fog had to slow slightly to adjust its mass. From the apricot tree under which Lydia stood, unripe fruit began to drop, encouraging her to add to the bombardment. The *genius loci* assaulted the fog with wind that blew from the north, growing in intensity and fraying the fog monster at the edges.

Attacked on multiple fronts, the fog monster split its attention to return the assault. Lydia jumped agilely away from the tentacle that punched at her. Alice was not so fortunate.

Whip-thin, cutting the air so that it screamed, a tentacle slashed out at her, catching her around one leg and yanking her off her feet. A second tentacle, this one thick and shaped like a mallet, loomed over her, descending to smash her flat. Throwing her last apple, Alice willed herself small, rolling out of line.

Virtual shapeshifting had never been one of her talents, but this time something worked. Momentarily, she was aware of a change of venue— almost as if she was back in her Verité body—then she was in the orchard again. The tentacle had lost its grasp on her and while it was casting about, she scrambled away.

As Alice readied another apple, it seemed that they must win, that Ambry would gain the relative security of the cottage and the *genius loci* would be able to raise the winds to gale forces that would shred the fog into wisps and memory. Sheltered behind a tree, Lydia was throwing steadily now, her missiles making swiss cheese of one foggy flank.

Then, just as victory seemed certain, the fog changed character, a face forming at its center. The face was masculine, with azure skin and lightning bolt eyebrows over dark blue eyes. The massing fog became flowing hair and beard framing a stormy countenance. Eyes narrowing, it focused on Ambry.

"Enough of this now, Piper," a deep, yet somehow petulant voice rumbled. "I can't possibly do things properly this time without all the pieces of my legion. Come along now."

Reaching out a thick tentacle, the fog plucked up the still back-pedalling Ambry as a child might a doll. Once enfolded in the foggy embrace, Ambry drooped limply, his face lax and expressionless.

The fog dispersed, carrying its prize. Mother and daughter stood stunned, watching in dull horror as a single tentacle reappeared to collect the bagpipes before vanishing with the rest.

"Mom, did what I just think happened, happen?"

"Yes." Lydia sounded as if she was trying not to sob.

"Then you'd better tell me all about Ambry's past—everything you know."

"Alice . . ."

"Mom, I'm going after him."

"Alice!"

"No, don't say I can't. Don't even suggest that you'll find him. You're a great doctor—one of the best—but finding missing people, getting the story . . . that's what *I'm* good at."

"Alice . . ."

"We can argue, but it won't find Ambry and it does waste time."

Lydia sighed. "Are you planning on doing this alone?"

"No. If you don't mind, I was going to call Drum and ask him to help."

"How much are you going to fill him in on?"

"Everything you'll let me tell him. He can't do his job with partial data."

Lydia bit her lip, paced a few steps.

"I can't stop you, can I?"

"Not really—certainly not if you're considering running off. The minute you're gone, so am I."

"I suppose that someone should be here in case Ambry gets a message out."

"True. And, Mom, you know his haunts. You'll be able to check there—to warn the *genius loci* to be on the alert for him."

"I'm convinced. Call Drum. I'll fill you both in together."

Alice dropped the green apple she still held and hugged her mother. Her fingers were sticky with the sour juice.

"I'll find him, Mom. I promise."

"I don't doubt it, Alice." Lydia squeezed her daughter harder. "What worries me is what will happen when you do."

"I'll bring him back. I didn't just find my dad to lose him to some . . . master programmer with delusions of godhood!"

Armored in indignation, Alice Hazzard went into the cottage to place a Virtù-to-Verité call to Desmond Drum. Outside, Lydia picked up the plate that held the remnants of her birthday cake. The ants were marching. She imagined she could hear the pipes that drove them on.

—=—

Tranto remained in Deep Fields when Jay departed for Mount Meru.

"I am hard to overlook, my friend," the phant said ruefully, "even within my chosen site. With their varied abilities and knowledges, Mizar and Dubhe will be able to assist you. I fear I should only be an impediment. On this journey, if you need to resort to brute force, then you are indeed already lost."

Jay punched the phant above one wrinkled knee.

"That's it—be encouraging! Don't worry, Tranto. We'll be back before you and the Lord of the Palace get tired of each other's company."

Death grinned his bone-white grin. "Tranto informs me that he is quite willing to assist me with some projects I had in mind. My usual workers have an unsettling tendency to fall apart. I look forward to the assistance of a trained construction proge."

"Then we'll be leaving as soon as the Brass Babboon returns for us," Jay said. "I sent a signal up the line about an hour ago."

"Rest until it arrives," Death advised. "You will not have opportunity thereafter."

"I'm not certain I could sleep," Jay admitted. "I'm too nervous."

"Oh, I think you will have no trouble," Death said. "As many a poet and philosopher has noted, Death and Sleep are close kin. You will find my palace very restful. Go up the stair on the right. You will find the room your father—although unknowing—designed for you."

Hearing the command underlying Death's polite invitation, Jay obeyed. He found the room, furnished with bunk beds and decorated in a style popular for boys at about the time he had been born. A curving windowseat overlooked the front of the palace. Assuring himself that he would certainly hear the Brass Babboon's arrival from here, he undressed and stretched out on the padded bench.

Despite his doubts, he slept deeply and well, not awakening until the Brass Babboon, spitting fireworks and blasting "The 1812 Overture," churned to a stop before the palace.

Dubhe swung down from the top bunk and onto Jay's shoulder.

"I should have know he'd like that one. Brace yourself, the cannon salute is coming."

Jay did and was glad to have done so for the Brass Babboon accompanied the recorded cannons with mortar fire from his smoke stack and wild laughter. The decaying forms of Deep Fields reared up in response to the unaccustomed noise, detached arms and legs, wheels and gears, spinning and cavorting, tumbling and twirling in a Danse Macabre such as Deep Fields had never seen.

"We'd better get downstairs before B.B. has the place down around our ears," Jay said, grabbing his clothes.

Dubhe laughed. "Deep Fields is always coming down around someone's ears—the trick is getting something to *stay*."

"Still . . ." Jay stuffed his arms in his shirt and buttoned it up crooked. "I'd hate to have something happen to this palace. My dad designed it and . . . well, the Lord of Entropy seems so proud of it."

"You noticed," Dubhe muttered. "Next thing you'll be telling me that you would have preferred to grow up here."

"Let's not take it that far . . . but it might have been cool. Did you see that horse thing he had?"

Jumping onto Jay's back saved Dubhe the necessity of replying. The youth tore out the door and down the spiral stair to the main floor at a breakneck pace that left Dubhe's tail flapping behind them. At the front door, they found Death watching the Brass Babboon fart bottle rockets.

"Exuberant, isn't it?" the Lord of the Lost commented. "I must admit, I envy John D'Arcy Donnerjack his talent for creation. I must be, by definition, derivative."

Jay steeled himself to look directly into the shadowed cassock, pretending to meet eyes that he could not see.

"Sir, you just spoke of my father in the present tense. Is he . . . well, is he alive somewhere?"

"Not that I know of," Death said, cool and pitiless. "He did not come to me, but then, being a creature of the Verité he would not have even though I was the agent of his ending."

Jay stiffened. "You killed my father?"

"Yes. Does that shock you, Jay?"

"I . . . I . . . Yes."

"Does the fact that I killed him shock you or that I would admit the fact to you? You knew that we were enemies, that he designed that noisy train out there to effect my destruction—at least on a temporary level—although I suspect that he would have been pleased to have managed it in a more permanent fashion."

"But he did that to save me!"

"From what?"

"From death."

"From Death or from dying?"

Jay paused. "Dying, I guess. I never really knew him. You made certain of that. Maybe he just thought he'd made a bad deal."

"Yet, I also made certain that you were born, my boy."

"For your purposes!"

"And now that you know something of those purposes, are they so ignoble? Moreover, your father never asked me if I intended your dying. He assumed the worst of me and I permitted him to do so."

Jay was so angry that he was nearly driven to tears. Feeling them pooling hot beneath his eyes made him angrier, so that his question came out as a shriek.

"Why?"

"Because, Jay D'Arcy Donnerjack, even Death may grow weary of people assuming the worst of him. I treated John D'Arcy Donnerjack honorably—returned to him his bride, gave him an opportunity for a child. Yet, even before your birth, I found him in arms against me. When I would not renounce my claim on you, he armed his castle against me. I sought to reclaim Ayradyss after the fashion of a repossession rather than from any evil nature."

"How can I believe you!"

"Have I ever lied to you, Jay, even when I would benefit from doing so?"

Jay looked at his shoes, at the gargoyles on the palace walls, anywhere but that shadowed cassock with its white hints of bone.

"Not that I know of, sir."

"Very well, then, I do not ask you to like me, but you did surrender to me. I have given you a task. Your train awaits. Go and do as I have told you."

"Yes, sir."

Jay turned away, securing his father's engineer's cap on his head, wiping a tear or two away with a quick rub of the back of his hand.

"And, Jay . . ."

"Yes, sir?"

"Good luck."

—=—

Desmond Drum stretched and reached for his kimono. Noriko, the geisha who had just finished giving him the best massage of his life, rose to assist him. Then she bowed formally and folded back a screen at the far end of the room, revealing a hot tub crafted to resemble a natural mineral spring, complete with waterfall.

"If Drum-san desires," she said.

"Just some tea, darling. I have an appointment in just a bit."

"Appointment here?"

"Don't be hurt. It's not another woman, just boring business."

"Ah."

Noriko smiled, departed, returned momentarily with the tea tray. Even after she had poured, making an art form of every tiny movement, she seemed inclined to remain with him. Drum did not protest, knowing that she was lonely.

Virtual brothels had all but ruined the RT sex trade. Crass red-light districts, with their attendant crime and disease, had vanished everywhere that virt access was cheap. Even more elegant places like this tea house had to be subsidized by the Japanese government in order to survive.

The Floating World and its blossoms, having survived shifting morality and fashion, were faced with extinction at the hands of computer technology. A haiku tried to form within Drum's mind, something about snow and cherry blossoms. He let his mind drift, taking cadence from the plunking notes Noriko was pulling from her samisen.

Another woman brought him a message scroll on a porcelain salver. He glanced at the words and followed her from the rooms. Behind him, Noriko's samisen continued to drop audible tears.

✿   ✿   ✿

"Hello, Drum," Daimon greeted him without rising. Today he wore a lighter cotton kimono printed with white chrysanthemums on a dark blue background. His hands, as always, were gloved, and his face concealed by a stylized mask.

"*Conichiwa*, Daimon-san," Drum answered. "You're becoming a bit predictable with the Japanese thing, you know. Bad thing, if you're hiding."

"I am hiding, but I believe that any great enthusiasm for the search is gone. If I were to make myself obvious . . . but in my retirement, I am left alone. In any case, I am not too foolish. As a historic recreation, this place is not equipped with any computer access at all, not even for mundane matters of bookkeeping. I doubt that I am the only one who finds it attractive for this reason."

Drum nodded. "Must make a good place for any number of clandestine operations. Have you reviewed what I sent on last time?"

"I have. I must admit, I expected Mr. Crain to accompany you."

"Link's busy. He's taking a few days to celebrate his mother's birthday."

"How sweet." Daimon sounded wistful.

"Are you content with the investigation thus far?"

"Content? I have yet to find what I would need to destroy the Church of Elish and without that I must remain a prisoner."

"Perhaps you should settle for finding something that you could use to blackmail them to preserve your safety."

"Something in the line of 'If I die, this will be released'? Yes, I have contemplated this option. I will admit to being a coward. I never believed that they would persist both in their enmity and in their mission. The riot in Central Park should have been enough to weaken them!"

"Instead they grow stronger. Their virt crossovers are now no longer limited to psi powers and lesser projections. The gods . . ."

"Terrify me. Do they terrify anyone else?"

"Me. Link. Anyone who thinks about the implications. Most everyone considers divine manifestation another entertainment gig. Europeans and Americans don't *believe* in gods anymore, Daimon, haven't since the nineteenth century. That's where the Elshies are strongest."

"No belief, yet they join the Church."

"Perhaps I should say that while there is no universal cultural belief, there is a great deal of individual desire for something divine."

"Yes . . . I know, too well. I am considering attending the Celebration in California. Would you take care of ticket purchase for me?"

"Certainly." Drum started to laugh.

"Why are you laughing?"

"You say you're terrified, but you're going to head right where Bel Marduk can spit fire at you. Either you really don't believe that they are gods, or something even funnier."

"What?"

"You do believe, bud, and you can't pass up the opportunity to see a god in the flesh."

"Stop laughing!"

Drum stood. "I want to catch the next suborbital. Take care, Daimon. Shall I send your ticket here?"

"Yes."

"Who do you want it made out to? They're not general admission."

"No, I recall that from your report. Can you come up with a false ID for me?"

"For a fee."

"Consider it paid."

"Pity."

"Why?"

"I was looking forward to making out a ticket for Arthur Eden."

"Drum!"

"Sorry. You didn't think I knew?"

"I did not!"

"I'll bet Link has figured it out, too."

"How?"

"It's what we do best, figuring out what other people don't want known. Don't worry, Daimon, we haven't ratted yet. Nor will we. We just get this warm feeling inside from knowing it all."

"You are insubordinate!"

"Never was subordinate, Daimon. Take care. I'll be sending the ticket along."

"Can I trust you?"

"You have been for a long time. Front row?"

"I . . ." A dry chuckle. "Sure, why not. I'll figure out a disguise."

"That's the spirit, Daimon. Go on out there, be the serpent in their Eden."

"Ouch!"

"*Arigato*. Glad you appreciate my jokes. I've been waiting to use that one for a long time."

"You'll miss your shuttle, Drum."

"Later, then."

—=—

Once Drum was on the suborbital, he keyed into his mail. There were ten calls, all from Link Crain. Checking, he saw that they had come at prompt ten-minute intervals. The message was essentially the same.

"Drum: Can you drop everything and help me with a crisis? If so, come to the following virt coordinates. Consider yourself hired for triple your normal fee, expenses, and whatever else you want. Link."

Considering, Drum sent a brief message to Link's account: "Coming—ETA 30 MIN. Drum."

As soon as the shuttle touched down, he went to a reliable transfer station, arranged for a long-term couch, and tabbed in the coordinates Link had given him. He drifted up through grey fog into a rose garden. Alice Hazzard—rather than Link Crain—slouched next to a peppermint-striped variety, methodically pulling the petals off a flower.

When he solidified, she leapt to her feet and ran over to him. Her embrace startled him as Link avoided physical contact of all kinds.

"Drum, thank you for coming! We can't talk here—too public. Come with me."

Link glanced around the apparently deserted garden, raised a bushy eyebrow, and followed Alice. She was already well ahead of him.

"Where are we headed," he called, "through the looking-glass or down the rabbit hole? Just a matter of academic curiosity."

She slowed to let him catch up.

"Behind the North Wind," she whispered, her mouth close to his ear, "and now you have your first secret."

Drum blinked, but Alice was off and away before he could ask anything more. He hurried, knowing Alice—or at least Link—well enough to be certain that he would get no further answers until they had arrived wherever it was that they were going. His agile mind was at work, though, considering the implications of Lydia Hazzard's disappearance into Virtù prior to Alice's birth, birthday celebrations, and Alice's mood. When they arrived at the cottage in the orchard and he was filled in on Ambry's disappearance, he had almost come to expect the information.

When Alice finished her narration, Lydia took over, explaining what she and Ambry had learned during their visit to the Donnerjack Institute. For once, Alice kept her questions until the end of the tale.

"Are you saying that my father is or was a god?"

"I'm saying that Ambry apparently is intertwined into more legends than he realized," Lydia answered. "Sid didn't say that Ambry was a god—more like a legend incarnate."

Drum chuckled. "A virgin gives birth after tarrying with a god. It has a certain resonance. Of course, most of those kids were boys, weren't they? Looks like you ladies fell down on the job."

Lydia gaped and Alice kicked him in the shin.

"Drum! You're mean!"

He just grinned and soon Lydia was laughing with him. Alice stared at the two adults as if they were crazy.

"I'm sorry, Alice, dear," Lydia managed between gasps. "It must be the stress, but Drum is right. The entire situation is almost too much to believe."

"While you stand there giggling," Alice said woodenly, "Ambry is still in trouble."

"Captive," Drum corrected, "which is distinctly different. It means that he is in no immediate physical danger."

"Until the legions of Skyga march," Lydia said.

"Which—if my guess is correct," Drum continued, "will not be for some time yet. If Alice would stop scowling at me and put on her Link hat, she'll realize that we have a pretty good indication of when Skyga will need his legions."

"For the Elishite Celebration."

"Precisely. We had hypothesized that the Hierophant of the Church of Elish had to have some backing in Virtù. Skyga fits the bill: powerful, influential, and, especially if he envisions himself as a primal deity kept out of his rightful domain, quite likely to benefit from a crossover."

"So we have time." Alice relaxed slightly. "I'm sorry I kicked you."

Drum rolled up the cuff of his pants, revealing a length of pale, hairy calf.

"No bruises, kid. You're going to need to calm down, though. This isn't like breaking into other people's offices to read their files."

"Alice! You didn't!"

"Can we discuss that later, Mom?" Alice said quickly. "Okay, I'm calm, Drum. Any thoughts where we should start looking? Virtù's a big place."

"Where's the local equivalent of Mount Olympus or Valhalla or wherever the gods hang their hats when they're at home?"

Alice and Lydia both shook their heads, but the ants still scavenging remnants of the picnic spelled out: "Mount Meru."

"Mount Meru," Drum read. "Great! Any idea how to get there?"

The ants scattered then reformed to spell: "Sorry. Don't move."

"I doubt we're going to find this place on any of the usual directories," Drum said, "and I'm a bit nervous about asking questions of just anyone."

"We could ask Sid or that associate of his at the Donnerjack Institute—Paracelsus," Lydia suggested.

"Good idea," Drum said, "but I'm a bit hesitant. You said that these aions worshiped the gods on Meru—and that they respected Ambry for his role as the Piper. I'm not certain how they would feel about us mucking about their theology."

"The ants are getting busy again," Alice said. "Lots more this time."

"Get Virginia Tallent, Markon's site," the *genius loci* wrote. "VSD."

"I don't understand," Lydia said.

"VSD, that's the Virtù Survey Department," Alice said.

"Believe it or not, I've actually heard of her," Drum added. "Daimon had me check her out back when we started on the Elshies. For a while, he was considering trying to locate the Hierophant. Tallent has a reputation as one of the best VSD scouts. She's Veritéan, but spends almost all her time in virt."

"And we have an address for her," Alice said. "I wonder if there is any particular reason that the Lady of the North Wind suggested her?"

The ants milled, finally settling on: "Markon in danger from Meru."

"And so Virginia Tallent will want to help us?" Alice asked.

"Tallent Markon's friend," the ants agreed.

"Can you get us transport there?" Drum asked.

In response a strong wind began to blow first around Alice, then around Drum. Lydia, although standing close to her daughter, was untouched.

"I guess that's a 'yes,' " Alice said, giving her mother a quick hug.

"Luck, Alice! Be careful. I don't consider switching you for Ambry a reasonable trade."

"How about Drum?" Alice giggled.

The wind blew them away before Lydia could answer, but when Alice looked back she could see that Dr. Hazzard was smiling.

—=—

The wind set them gently down in the center of a forested grove. Unlike the Land Behind the North Wind, this site had a somewhat tropical feel to it, an impression not at all diminished when a slim brown-skinned woman clad in a saronglike garment emerged from the shelter of a red-flowered vine. Her long brown hair was loose and her feet were bare, but the Chaos Factor gun she held in one hand and the steady menace in her pale blue eyes made quite clear that she was no harmless primitive.

"Virginia Tallent?" Alice said quickly, holding her hands palms out so that the other woman could see she was unarmed. "We've come for your help."

"You know who I am," the woman said, her pistol unwavering, "but I don't know who you are."

"I'm Alice Hazzard—also known as Lincoln Crain. This is my partner, Desmond Drum."

"Lincoln Crain . . . I think I've encountered that name."

"I write articles for the newsies."

"Then that's probably where I've heard of you. This is a restricted area of a private site. How did you know to find me here?"

"The Land Behind the North Wind . . . its *genius loci* sent us. She's a friend of my father. This is dreadfully complicated, ma'am, and your pistol is making me *very* nervous."

"There are two dire-cats standing behind you who would probably make you more so." For the first time, Virginia Tallent smiled. She stuck her CF pistol in the sash around her waist. "You want me, not Markon?"

"That's right. Can I just tell you my story? It's pretty incredible."

Virginia Tallent glanced across the grove. At its farthest edge, enveloped in muddy green light, was a long box.

"I've had a few incredible things happen myself, lately. I'm in a listening mood. Give me your tale, Alice."

And so, with minimal assistance from Drum, Alice told Virginia about the kidnapping of Wolfer Martin D'Ambry—the Phantom Piper of Skyga. She left nothing out, not Ambry's multiple identities, not Skyga's manifestation, not even her and Drum's theory that all of this was connected to the Church of Elish's upcoming Celebration.

Virginia Tallent had the gift of listening, a gift honed in her work for the VSD, and later as she dwelt with Markon and listened to the *genius loci*'s complicated tales. She listened now, and the occasional stirring of the brush or bubbling of the stream told her (although not Alice or Drum) that Markon was listening as well.

"I can tell you why the Lady Behind the North Wind decided to help you. It's not merely that Ambry was her friend—it was Skyga's invasion of her site. The older *genius loci* are very conscious of their rights and Skyga played havoc with the proprieties."

"And can you help us find Mount Meru so we can free my father?" Alice asked.

Virginia Tallent nodded slowly.

"Yes, I can, and moreover, I will. As the Lady noted, I am a friend of Markon and one of the Highest on Meru has trapped him into a pact that will mean his death."

"I don't understand."

Briefly, Virginia explained about Earthma's assault, about the bargain she had offered Markon, about the side effects.

"I faced her down once and Markon grew stronger for a time. Lately, he's been weakening again. I think Earthma's bastard is drawing on his power. Yesterday, I saw the moiré."

"The moiré. Ambry used that word, too. What does it mean?"

"It is a warping, a fading, a shimmering. In Virtù it means the end of a proge's life. I believe that this moiré was an omen that Earthma's child will slay Markon. If the real Lord of the Lost had marked him, the end would have already come. He does not toy with his subjects—at least, so Markon told me."

"Pardon, ma'am," Drum said, "but you didn't seem at all surprised by the more outrageous elements of Alice's story."

"Because I was not—or perhaps I should say that they were not outrageous to me. Markon has told me about the theology of Virtù. I had already heard of the Piper, the Master, and the One Who Waits. That he had offspring, or that his daughter would wish to rescue him rather than having him remain a pawn in a divine game, did not surprise me at all."

"Can you guide us to Meru?"

Virginia frowned. "Yes and no. I do not know the way myself, but according to Markon, there is a train . . ."

ELEVEN

Tearing the head from a petite arboreal simian with large pleading eyes, Sayjak playfully squirted the blood fountaining from the neck over Ocro. Ocro howled with coarse amusement, never stopping his own enthusiastic rape of a somewhat bovine herd creature. Later, the memory would add piquancy to dinner.

Their taking of this territory could hardly be dignified with the word "battle." The area had been designed after a particularly saccharine children's entertainment series, furnished with gamboling lambkins, frolicking calflets, and chubby fuzzy-bears. Until the arrival of Sayjak's People, the spreading forests and brightly flowered meadows had been filled with the music of myriad birds and the chattering of the adorable monklings.

Little children had run over hill and dale, learning kindness, caring, and sharing. After witnessing, even briefly, the incursion of Sayjak's clan, most would be visiting their psychologists for weeks to come.

In a dream, Big Betsy had directed Sayjak to bring his People here, providing the key that would unlock the interface protecting the site. Sayjak grew hard at the memory of that dream, but he decided he would have come here without the bribe of screwing his dream-girl—this place was *fun*!

The young of the People enjoyed the warm and cuddly inhabitants as much as the human children had—although in a different fashion.

Sayjak interrupted a group playing tug of war with a squealing lambkin.

"You," he said to a terrified youngling, "go get Dortak, Bilgad, the other leaders. Say Sayjak wants them now."

The little one scampered off, leaving Sayjak at the center of a circle of awed, admiring eyes. Embarrassed, he grabbed the lambkin, which had been trying to limp away. Grasping it firmly by forelegs and hindlegs, he tugged.

"Christmas cracker," he guffawed.

Leaving the young to finish dismembering their toy, he knuckled over to join his subordinates.

"This good place, Sayjak," one said.

The others muttered rapid agreement. Sayjak had been known to beat the snot—and occasionally the life—out of any who didn't agree with his plans. At first this had been necessary; for instance, when they had first fought in coordination with Muggle's phants. Lately, even the meanest tumbled over each other in their haste to praise him.

"Is good place. Healthy for young. Lots of food. You think this only reason I bring you here?"

Most looked at their feet. Otlag, still the most intelligent of his subordinates, pursed his lips and blew a thoughtful spit bubble.

"Great Sayjak always have more than one thought."

Sayjak slapped the ground. "That true. Each of you pick from your bands two of your strongest. Come back with me. We go to other place. Take things away. Come back here. Got?"

Heads nodded. Sayjak knew that most didn't understand. If he was to probe his plan, he would be forced to admit that *he* didn't fully understand. Big Betsy had told him to come here, take this site, and use it as a base to raid another.

"Even your mighty warriors would have difficulty getting in through the normal access points," she had said. *"But you'll just go in the back door. You're good at that, aren't you?"*

Here she wriggled her hindquarters so provocatively that Sayjak had almost forgotten to listen, but he had dragged his attention back. Big Betsy wanted them to acquire an arsenal of weapons more powerful than machetes—weapons like those the eeksies and the bounties used: CF prods, pistols, rifles.

The idea amused him greatly, although he wondered, in some small corner of his mind, what Big Betsy intended for the People to attack. What was so big that brute force and the sharp cutting sticks that had served them thus far would not serve?

The wondering slipped his mind, as most things did. Sayjak knew power, glory, and immortality lay in action, never in thought. Listening to Big Betsy had made him more famous even than Karak. He certainly would continue to follow her suggestions.

—=—

Not in this reality nor any other had there ever been a creation like the Brass Babboon. With Jay Donnerjack in the cab, his father's cap snugged on his head, Death's dog and monkey crouched beside him, the train howled its way through virtual settings, upsetting numerous aions and troubling those from the Verité who sought to hold onto the illusion that Virtù existed solely for their amusement and convenience.

Unknown to the passengers on the train (or to the train itself, who would not have cared even if it knew), that illusion was steadily fraying. From site after site, reports were coming in of unrequested manifestations. Emaciated vampire sprites invaded a Golf and Eastern board meeting, terrifying the staid members and leaving behind graffiti in a language no one could translate. The Happy Land of Molly Meeper had been invaded by lewd, carnivorous proges with a more than passing resemblance to great apes.

In DinoDiznee, the dinosaurs suddenly turned on each other (and any who got in their way), destroying the basic site, driving the *genius loci* to nonfunctionality, and losing the parent corporation millions in revenue. Some reported that at least a score of the larger dinosaurs were seen to vanish through the interface. No further reports of their whereabouts were given, so this last was dismissed as rumor. Cancellations of virtual vacations arrived by the score, jamming travel agents' terminals.

The only virtual sites that had increased their traffic were those connected to the Church of Elish. As more than one visitor was heard to say, "They seem to know more about Virtù. It wouldn't hurt to be in their camp if *things* happen." What those things were was usually left undefined, but it was generally understood to mean the promised crossover of the gods and the wonders and annexation that would follow.

Those speeding through the realities aboard the Brass Babboon knew nothing of this, but they would not have been surprised if they did. Although they did not possess the entire picture, they knew enough to realize that Bad Things were pending for the status quo. What did surprise them was when a signal post manifested along the freshly laid track, flag out.

"Someone's waiting for a train, Jay," the Brass Babboon reported. "I can't think of anyone doing that in all the years I've been running the rails. Want me to stop?"

Jay considered. "Sure, might be that the Lord of the Lost has some last-minute information for us. If it's someone wanting to play train robbers, I doubt they could give *you* any trouble, B.B."

The train's reply was rude and vaguely flatulent. Tearing through a Valley of the Kings, Alexander's campaign against Persia, a domed settlement on Titan, and a burning of Atlanta, the Brass Babboon came to a halt at a train station at what appeared to be Union Station, Washington, D.C.

"Do you generate these stations the way you lay your own track?" Jay asked, as the train slowed.

"Not this one. Belongs to the D.C. site, nineteenth-century incarnation. Looks sharp, doesn't it?"

"Sure does. I wonder where our passengers are?"

"If they figured out a way to send a signal up my line, they'll find us. Relax and try to figure out what you're going to say to them."

"Can't," Jay said, leaning back and putting his feet up on the control board. There was something about the Brass Babboon that bred arrogance. "Don't know who it is."

Dubhe was studying the throng. "I don't think most of those people can see us."

"My scanners tell me those are simple proges," the Brass Babboon answered. "Hardly more than ambulatory wallpaper. They'd only react if there was a visitor or a more complex proge present. Odd . . . I don't see any tourists."

"Don't . . . smell either," Mizar added.

"Maybe this isn't a popular site now," Jay said, sitting up and looking around.

"Maybe."

At that moment, three figures entered through one of the curved arches. One, slender and lithe with dark hair, was clearly female despite her anachronistic and less than flattering khaki uniform. The second was male, big, with a feel of the thug about him. The third could have been a slightly-built young man or a rather androgynous young woman. All three wore clothing out of phase with the setting.

"That's got to be our group," Dubhe said.

"Yeah," Jay said. "Two of them look familiar . . . Wait here!"

He jumped to his feet and hurried down the ladder to the platform.

"Desmond Drum and Link Crain!" he said. "What the . . . what are you doing here?"

Drum tugged at his earlobe. "Waiting for a train. That train, to be precise. Damn, Virginia, you said the train we wanted was strange, but I never expected this monstrosity. It's great!"

Virginia Tallent was studying Jay, her hand just in the vicinity of her CF pistol.

"Drum, Alice, do you know this young man?"

"Sort of," Alice said. "When we met him, he was going by the name Jason MacDougal. We think his real name is John D'Arcy Donnerjack, Junior."

Jay stared. "How . . ."

"I tried to call and thank you for your help during the riot. There was no one in Scotland with that name or description. I hired Drum to find out who or what you were."

"Help during a riot?" Virginia asked.

"The Central Park Celebration," Alice answered. "Jay was okay then. I didn't expect to find him on this train, though, but maybe it makes sense. According to what my mother and Markon both said, his father *was* the Engineer."

Jay could hear the capitalization. "You know about that?"

"I just found out that my father is the Piper—and a whole lot more," Alice said, almost defensively.

"The Piper, the Master, the One Who Waits," Jay said, "and Warren Bansa who was my father's friend and colleague. This is getting weird."

Dubhe stuck his head out the window of the cab. "What did you folks want the train for, anyhow?"

Virginia Tallent had lived too long in Virtù to be surprised by a talking monkey. "To go to Mount Meru."

"I think you'd better come aboard," Jay said slowly. "I'm not sure we should talk about stuff like this in the open. B.B., I'm going to take our guests to the club car. Call me if I'm needed."

"Right, Jay." There was a chuffing of steam, then a long, drawn out wail. "All aboard!"

In the club car, they ate the appropriate sandwiches and told each other of their various missions. Drum and Alice expressed some wonder at Dubhe and, especially, at Mizar, but the unusual is usual in Virtù and soon they were talking as if a dog made of spare parts and a monkey who had missed a branch were part of their usual social rounds.

"Markon's suspicions certainly seem well-grounded," Virginia said, when all the stories were finished. "Myths and legends are wending their way toward a new shape of some sort. Perhaps an ending for Virtù and its people."

"Legends say that the One Who Waits will be present at the end or the *change* of Virtu," Jay reminded her. "I think the greater threat is to the Verité. For some reason, the ones on High Meru have decided to try and annex it. That would change Virtù, but it would end the Verité—at least as we know it."

"And our part in this?" Alice said.

"I'm not sure," Jay admitted. "I have my mission from the Lord of Entropy to fulfill. You want to find your father. The question is, do we want to team up?"

"I think that would be wise," Drum said. "Alice and I know very little of this aspect of Virtù, but we're great at getting in where we're not wanted and finding out other people's secrets. You and your people know Virtù, as does Virginia. We'll all do better together."

"And if we need to split up at some point," Virginia added, "we can still do so."

"And afterwards?" Jay said. "I'm really worried about this offspring of Earthma's that's draining Markon's site."

"So am I," Virginia said softly. "I'd give anything to destroy it before it can destroy Markon."

Alice nodded. "Count me in."

"And me," said Drum. "I may not be a theologian, but the implications of Death under the thumb of a dominant goddess aren't good. It seems like potential for some big trouble."

"No offense," Dubhe interrupted, "but one crisis at a time. Does anyone have any idea what we should do when we get off the train at Mount Meru? I've never been there, but all the tales agree that Mount Meru is many-tiered."

Jay shrugged. "I don't know what we'll do and we don't have enough information to plan. Let's figure that out when we get there. How long, B.B.?"

"Long enough for you folks to check out my armory," the train suggested. "J. D. never planned on getting off the train, but he came prepared if he had to."

"Good," Jay said. "Where is it?"

"One car back from where you are. See how easy I make things for you?"

The train's laughter followed them as they stepped into the armory. Virginia and Drum fell to taking inventory, asking each member of the group what weapons they could handle and issuing appropriate gear.

"It's kind of strange, us meeting again this way," Jay said somewhat shyly to Alice.

"I know," she answered, studying her right foot, "and finding out that our dads knew each other. Is this what they mean by fate?"

"I've always been a believer in free will, myself, but it sure seems like it."

"Yeah, to me, too."

"Your mom must be really worried about Ambry to let you come out here looking for him."

"She is, but she knew that I wouldn't stay home by the fire while she went out alone."

"But she let you go out alone."

"I'm not alone. I've got Drum. And mom's a scientist; her practical side knows that it's best to let experts do what they're trained for."

"Yeah. I wonder what would have happened to me if my dad had kept the bargain he made with the Lord of Deep Fields."

"You wouldn't be who you are now," Alice said practically. "Your dad had a point when he said that living makes you appreciate things. Deep Fields would have been interesting in a kind of creepy way, but I don't think you would have been really human if you had grown up there—not even if you were living."

Jay nodded. "Spare parts all around would be weird. I guess I am glad that Dad did what he did. I appreciate having the chance to make a choice on my own."

They stood silently, awkward despite a mutual feeling of liking. In the background, Virginia and Drum worked on outfitting Dubhe with a CF pistol.

"Jay?" Alice said after a time. "Can you really cross the interface between Virtù and Verité without needing a transfer couch?"

"Uh-huh. I don't know how, though."

"Ever since you mentioned it earlier, I'd wanted to ask—"

They were interrupted by a screeching howl from the Brass Baboon.

"Mount Meru on the horizon, lads and lassies! Come take a glimpse before I start the smoke and fireworks to cover your arrival."

They hurried to windows. Beneath a preternaturally bright sun, Mount Meru loomed in splendid isolation on a rolling plain, casting sharp shadows. Snow capped its highest reaches, the lofty perches where the Highest Three were said to hold dominion. At first glance, the mountain appeared uninhabited, but as the Brass Babboon rushed closer, they could catch glimpses of motion on the slopes and about the base.

"I . . . remember this . . . place," Mizar growled, trembling. "Bright light and much . . . pain. Falling for . . . ever."

"Want to stay with B.B.?" Jay asked, kneeling next to the tattered hound.

"Want to bite them!" Mizar answered.

"That's decisive enough," Drum said. He handed Jay a small pack. "This contains some basics—a knife, some rope, pair of binoculars, a first aid kit. Everyone except Virginia is better qualified with hand weapons. Remember, these CF pistols aren't like guns in virtventures. They'll run out of ammo."

Jay nodded thanks and strapped on his gear. He noticed that Alice was doing the same, once again seeming rather androgynous. Virginia was tight-lipped and quiet—no wonder—her lover was dying under the treachery of a goddess and she had come to that goddess's doorstep. In many ways, she—more than any of them—understood the risks they were taking, for she alone had met and spoken with a manifestation of one of the Highest Three.

"I'll be slowing in the curve and then setting off the smoke and fire," the Brass Babboon announced, "then clearing out. I've cycled through here a time or two before. If you're fast and get to cover, any observers won't think twice."

"I hope," Dubhe muttered.

"Slowing . . ." the Brass Babboon announced.

The passengers gathered by the doors. A barrage of fireworks and smoke bombs erupted. Jay's eyes were streaming; he heard several of the others cough.

"Slowing . . ."

There was nothing to do but wait. The Brass Babboon would open the doors at the optimal moment. More fireworks, these the kind that whistled and burst into multipetaled blossoms.

"I hope he doesn't get everyone on Meru watching us," Alice said softly.

"Too late now," Drum said. "Get ready to jump, kid."

"Slowing . . . Opening the doors in three. One, two, three!"

The ground was still moving, no longer appearing like a velvet carpet now that they were about to jump. Virginia went without hesitation, dropped, rolled lithely. Drum was out almost as quickly.

Alice looked at Jay. Her face was as pale as he suspected his was. Almost imperceptibly, the Brass Babboon started picking up speed again. If they didn't jump now, they would be carried out the interface. . . . At the same moment, they took courage from the other's fear and made the leap. Mizar, Dubhe on his back, came last, making certain that Jay was safe.

They hit the ground hard.

"Thought for a moment you folks were going to leave Virginia and me to be the heroes," Drum said, his grin and broad, helping hand belaying the sarcasm in his tone. "Glad you decided to join us."

Still gathering breath and courage, Alice and Jay could barely manage smiles as they climbed to their feet.

"Where now?" Dubhe said.

"Scouting," Virginia said. "Mizar and me. He'll go north; I'll go south. You folks wait here and study the mountain slope with your binoculars. Map what you can."

"Right," Jay agreed, quietly relieved to have her experienced direction. "How long will you be gone?"

"I'll try to return within a half hour," Virginia said. "That should let me cover a fair amount of ground. If Mizar does the same, he should cover even more."

The hound nodded, blinked eyes red and green.

"If I . . . am caught I . . . will howl."

"I can't do that," Virginia said, "but if I don't make it back, feel free to assume the worst. Our opponents claim omniscience. We can't be certain whether that's true or not."

"Luck," Alice called as the scouts departed.

Jay pulled out his binoculars and began surveying the mountain. "If any of you have something to draw with, I can make us a fairly accurate map."

Drum produced a light tablet and pen. Jay accepted it with a curt nod that he hoped seemed professional, rather than terrified. Then he set to looking and to drawing what he saw.

—=—

"You can't possibly plan on wearing that!" Skyga protested. "You'll undermine the entire Celebration!"

A.I. Aisles tugged off his bulbous red clown nose and grinned at the Greater God.

"You said I needed something more elaborate than what I usually wear. I thought this fit the bill."

"I had priest's robes, a Sumerian kilt, even a formal kimono or a tuxedo in mind, not a clown's costume."

The Hierophant of the Church of Elish (at last poll now one of the four major religious traditions in the Verité—although only if one counted all of the Christian sects as one group) admired his costume in the full-length mirror.

"It *is* satin and the polka dots are embroidered. The neck ruffle is real lace (or will be in the Verité). And I love the headpiece—a genuine Bozo designer original."

"NO." A rumble of thunder accompanied the word.

"What are you going to do? Blast me? If you think that this form is my only one, then you must be nuttier than I am, old pal o' mine."

"You are no longer indispensable."

"But I am nasty, Skyga, and I've left some records in various places. If they surfaced and the Verité learned that as far as I see it, the Church of Elish is one big prank . . ."

"But what you have preached is the truth!"

"Since when has that mattered? Think about it."

There was a long pause. The thunder rumbles subsided.

"You may have a point. But you will *not* wear that clown costume."

"I'll talk with the High Priest about something in the Sumerian styles then—they're almost as funny looking when viewed with an objective eye."

"Why must you mock?"

"It's my job, part of an ancient and revered tradition—as ancient and revered as gods of sky and sea, and nearly as old as earth mothers."

Skyga's eyes (storm grey, today) narrowed.

"Are you indicating that you believe yourself a god, little aion?"

A.I. Aisles belched, covered his pot belly with his hands, and conjured a beer. He began to glow golden.

"It doesn't matter what I think, Skyga, as well you know. What matters is what the marks think."

His halo brightened until any but divine eyes would have had to look away.

"And I've got lots of them thinking just that way. Maybe I'll come visiting on Meru someday. You might be surprised at just how high up those slopes I can stroll."

Draining the beer, he set down the bottle.

"I've got to see a High Priest about a dress fitting, bud. Catch you later."

He vanished in a flash of golden light leaving a resounding belch in his wake. Skyga paused to analyze what he had just learned. Then he withdrew his presence in a much less spectacular fashion.

—=—

A voice was singing, dulcet, female, crooning nursery rhymes and lullabies. The *genius loci* Markon heard, and even in his hearing he could sense the crackling of the moiré, a phenomenon not often reported, for most who see the moiré do not live long enough to perceive the dry silk of its passage.

"Rock-a-bye baby/ In the treetops/ When the wind blows/ The cradle will rock/ When the bough breaks/ The cradle will fall/ And down will come baby/ Cradle and all."

"Jack be nimble/ Jack be quick/ John D'Arcy Donnerjack leapt over a candlestick . . ."

"Tu-ra-lura-lura/ Tu-ra-lura-li/ Tu-ra-lura-lura/ When baby wakes up/ Markon's gonna die-ai!"

The *genius loci* spoke in the voice of water surging over rocks.

"Earthma, why must you mock me? I know that I have lost. I made a bad bargain with you and it will mean my ending."

Earthma laughed. "And you made it to protect a Veritéan who has abandoned you at the end. Don't you feel the fool!"

"Virginia has not abandoned me!"

"I do not sense her in the site. She is gone, Markon. She has left you to die alone—alone and friendless."

Even in his drained state, Markon did not rise to the taunt. He let his weakness, his befuddlement, bubble up in his words.

"She is gone. Yes. I am alone. You have tricked me."

"I can be kind, Markon. Would you like an ending now? Usually death is not mine to give, but when I bring forth my child, you will die. Would you like an end to the weariness?"

Markon knew the choice was not his, Earthma was simply enjoying giving him the illusion of freedom.

"End," he said, and he wept for his dire-cats, his gronhers, his herd-mice, for the tangled trees, the intricate system of underground streams, for the hidden caverns glittering with crystals that no one (not even beloved Virginia) had ever seen.

"End?" Earthma repeated. "You're giving up?"

"No choice," he managed. "You would not renounce this child of yours. You have borne Death and now I must be lost to Deep Fields."

"Perhaps not Deep Fields," Earthma mused, "for my little one is not yet master there, though he will be, soon enough."

Markon dropped the interface that separated him from his neighbors, urged the dire-cats and herd-mice, all the others with legs and wings to flee. He summoned a great wind and sought to carry the seed proges of the curling willow, the Virginia fern, the angel's tears, all the other plants, out into the greater reaches of Virtù. Something might survive him.

Although she bent over the sarcophagus which held her nascent Death, Earthma sensed the out-flowing of material. She straightened.

"This will *not* do!" she said angrily.

Throwing back her head, her thick green hair trailing to the ground, she gave a horrible cry, a sound that was both summation and parody of the suffering of every woman who had ever been in labor. The shield fell away from the sarcophagus. Brilliant citron light flared.

Markon's site flashed pure white as the myriad programs were wiped and their power transferred to the form emerging from the coffin. Then there was darkness, the absolute black that knows no color, no life, no potential. Markon was gone.

From herself, Earthma generated a greenish glow and inspected the hooded thing, shadowed in moiré, that now hovered at her side.

"Perhaps a bit premature, but more than enough to do the job, I think. Come, son."

The thing floated after her. Earthma raised her sweet, lovely voice in song:

"Tu-ra-lura-lura/ Tu-ra-lura-li/ Tu-ra-lura-lura/ Virginia's gonna cry-ai!"

—=—

Chaos, Chaos . . .
        (Oh, my dear seven-limbed angels)
Chaos, Chaos is . . .
        Terrified.

TWELVE

When Mizar returned his tails were switching with excitement and he was liberally shedding sections of shag carpet.

"I . . . have found . . . it. The thing . . . I tracked . . . when I was made. Found the scent."

"You remember?" Jay asked.

"Base . . . proge. Stimulus . . . activated. Am sure."

Alice hunkered down next to the fearsome hound and gave him a tentative scratch behind one flopping ear. The tails wagged harder.

"Can you tell what it is from the scent—the way you might tell a deer from a horse?"

"Good question, kid," Drum muttered.

"Can . . . not," Mizar wheezed sadly. "Can tell what . . . is not . . . but . . . not what is."

"I don't get it," Alice admitted.

"I think I do," Jay said. "Mizar knows what it isn't—and he knows the scents of lots of things, both active and passive proges—but he has never had this particular scent identified for him before so he cannot say what it is."

Mizar wheezed agreement, evidently pleased that he did not need to find the words for an explanation.

"I see Virginia coming," Dubhe said. "She doesn't look really good."

The VSD scout was indeed pale. Jay hurried out to help her. Without protest, she leaned against him, letting him half carry her to the others.

"Were you attacked?" Dubhe asked, looking around nervously.

"No," she whispered.

Alice handed her a canteen. Virginia sipped a little before setting it down so absently that it nearly spilled.

"I felt . . . I felt something terrible. A great out-welling, then nothing." Tears were beginning to course down her cheeks. "I think that Markon is dead. That bitch has borne her child."

She crumpled, sobbing so hard that the sound alone was a physical pain. Jay knelt next to her, gathering her up into his arms. For a woman who was so strong, she proved to be easy to hold.

"Earthma won't dare conceal her child any longer," Dubhe said. "The Lord of Deep Fields will know that one of his rightful prey has been taken and he's going to know that he didn't do the taking. When he realizes that the victim is one of the older *genius loci*, he's going to know that there is trouble."

Over Virginia's sobbing, Jay said, "We need to warn him. Without the Brass Babboon, there's only one of us designed to cross the interfaces without needing to use the Road. Mizar, can you remember what the Lord of Deep Fields must be told?"

"I . . . can . . . but give . . . me written . . . message."

Alice grabbed a light slate and began writing.

"Good idea. Mizar is smart, but he takes a long time to say anything clearly. I'll scribble a report. The rest of you download what he saw when he was scouting."

"Can we do that?" Drum asked Death's dog.

"Transfer . . . flawed, but . . . I . . . can try."

"Give me one of the light slates," Dubhe said. "I was there when Death created Mizar. I remember some of the routines he was imbued with. If Drum will help, I think we can manage this."

As messages were written and information transferred, Virginia's sobs slowed, then ceased. The tears continued to course down her cheeks.

"Without Mizar you're going to need me, so don't even think about sending me away."

Jay nodded. "As you wish."

And with those words John D'Arcy Donnerjack experienced an epiphany. He was in charge of this expedition. On some level he had expected one of the adults to lead, but although Virginia might insist on coming with them, she could not be trusted for clear-headed decisions.

Drum could offer advice, but the Verité, not Virtù, was his native realm.

And Alice—Link? She was Jay's own age and, like Drum, out of her element. Duhbe would do what he could, but he *was* a monkey, after all, and a follower, not a leader. If Tranto had been there . . . but that was wishful thinking, nor could the Lord of Deep Fields be expected to send in the cavalry. Even if he had been so inclined, he would not be able to now.

Jay felt very old, very young, very frightened, and very excited all at once. The jumble of emotions was so strong that he almost forgot to hug Mizar before Death's dog departed.

"What do we have?" he said, moving over to where Drum and Virginia were studying Mizar's input. Alice, although obviously interested, had joined Dubhe in keeping watch.

Drum handed Jay the light pad on which he had started a map.

"You're the cartographer, so you update the map while we fill you in. 'Ginnie?"

Virginia cocked an eyebrow at the unexpected nicknaming, but otherwise forbore from commenting.

"When I went south, I saw considerable activity on the mountain's lower slopes. I didn't dare get close, but it appeared that someone was setting up a series of transfer stations. Judging from the wingéd bulls and lions guarding them, I would guess that they are associated with the upcoming Elishite Celebration."

"Anything else?" Jay asked, after he had sketched in her observations.

"I don't really know what is normal and what is not," Virginia confessed. "The upper slopes, as far as I could tell, held numerous temples in a variety of styles."

"Probably related to the various deities worshiped in both Virtù and Verité," Jay said, and from where he watched, Dubhe nodded agreement.

"That's it for me," Virginia said. "Mizar's information may be more useful."

"Can you sum up for him?" Jay asked.

"Pretty well. The information is fragmented. Whatever fried his systems did a thorough job."

"Go ahead."

"On the other side of the mountain, about halfway up, there is a heavily guarded installation. Unlike the constructions I saw, this one does not appear to be overtly religious—although there are religious overtones—it reminded me more of a factory. This is where Mizar scented the thing you are looking for."

"You said 'heavily guarded,' " Jay asked. "What are our chances of getting in?"

"One of the things that made me think of a factory," Virginia said, "is that crated material was being taken from it."

"So there is traffic?"

"Right. Drum and Alice might be better at working out how we should penetrate the facility."

"Well, folks?" Jay asked.

Drum nodded. "I've looked at the data and I think we can come up with something. We have a fair amount of distance to cross to get there, however, and I'd like to see this 'factory' myself before I offer tactical advice. Why don't we start hoofing it and we'll give you our plan when we actually see the place?"

"Fine with me," Jay said. "Virginia, can you take point?"

"That's what I'm trained for."

"I'll drop to the back, then. We need to stay within eye-shot of each other, but at the same time be spread out far enough that we don't make ourselves obvious. Doubtless they have guards, but the Lord of the Lost thought that they wouldn't be expecting Veritéans. If their base programming is shoddy, I may be effectively invisible to lesser guard proges, and the rest of your virt forms are pretty basic; they shouldn't attract interest."

"That's a comfort," Drum said. "Let's start walking."

"Factory, yes. I wouldn't have thought to call it that myself," Alice said, "but I can see exactly where you were coming from, Virginia."

Looking through his binoculars up the slope of Mount Meru, Jay Donnerjack inspected the long, blocky building that was set into a cut on the slope. It was constructed from a standard fieldstone template that blended nicely with the surrounding rock and scrub brush terrain; otherwise, it was rather unimaginative.

"I don't see what you're seeing," he admitted, "but then I don't think I've ever seen a factory."

Alice stared at him, but Drum nodded understandingly.

"From what you've told us about your upbringing, I'd be surprised if you had," he said. "Most of your jaunts were in Virtù and the unreal world doesn't exactly need manufacturing plants."

He placed a hand on Jay's arm, his manner suddenly reminding the younger man of Reese Jordan.

"Take a look, Jay. We've got a building here with minimal exterior decoration—all of those temples went for adornment in a big way. So we have a utilitarian structure. Next, note the near absence of windows. Even in Virtù, buildings tend to follow the Veritéan custom and allow for 'natural' light."

"I'm with you so far," Jay prompted.

"Then there are the large bay doors neatly spaced along the front, each with road in front of them rather than paths or sidewalks. Clearly these are meant to facilitate the delivery of building materials and the removal of completed products."

"Okay," Jay said, "we have a factory here. Why? What purpose would that serve? Legend says that the gods on Meru can imagine whatever they want—that this is how they create their armies and minions."

From the corner of his eye, he saw the odd expression that crossed Alice's face.

"Uh, sorry, Alice. That was kind of tactless of me."

"No, that's all right, Jay. I'm mostly comfortable with my dad's history, but sometimes it's weird."

"Later, folks," Drum cut in. "Jay, I can't answer your question. I don't know enough."

Dubhe lowered his binoculars. "I have an idea. What if they're duplicating whatever it was that Warren Bansa carried across the interface? What if that factory is making *artifacts*? That would explain the design of the structure."

"You mean hard copy?" Jay said. "Here?"

"Why not? Bansa's device supposedly had the ability to permit full-body crossover between the universes. If they applied some aspect of that, then they could create Veritéan material, or something that could exist in both places."

"That's an unsettling idea," Jay said, "but it has potential."

"Another possibility," Virginia added, "is that the 'factory' is a manifestation of one of the divinities—sort of a *genius loci* meant to guard the area or control operations within."

"Or it could be both," Alice said, "an idea that does not fill me with joy."

"Me either," Drum said, "but any plan we make is going to need to take both possibilities into account."

"Now that you've seen the structure do you have any ideas?" Jay asked somewhat diffidently. He had hoped to have a brainstorm himself, but the factory only filled him with dread and a certainty that he could never succeed.

"At first we considered having Dubhe go up and scout," Drum said, "but the Lord of Entropy considered you best for the job. Now, you're here 'in the flesh,' right?"

"That's right," Jay said. "If I buy it here, that's it."

"True, but you're also the only one of us who is really a Veritéan at this moment. The rest of us are wearing virt forms—despite his unusual history, Dubhe is at baseline a proge."

"True," Dubhe said, "repaired and enhanced by the Lord of Deep Fields, but essentially a proge."

"So I go up alone?" Jay said.

"That's right," Drum answered. "Scout. Go in if you can and fulfill your quest. If you can't do it alone, then come for us. At the least, we'll have more information."

"And the rest of you?"

"We'll lie low, be ready to help, learn what we can that might help us to find Wolfer Martin D'Ambry."

Jay considered. "As much as it scares me to admit it, your plan makes sense. I'll do it."

"I've taken a look at the layout," Virginia said. Her tone was flat, although she was evidently struggling to seem normal. "If you can climb down from the slopes above and behind the factory, you'll avoid any guard or wards set for the front approach."

"Climbing is something I'm very good at," Jay said with a fond glance at Dubhe. "I've had a good teacher in Virtù and gone all over Castle Donnerjack."

"Do it then," Virginia said. "Given the setup, the back is probably less heavily guarded. They'd count on terrain to do the job. Of course, all bets are off if the structure is a *genius loci*."

"Right," Jay said. "I'll remember that."

He looked at his comrades, suddenly a bit awkward, eager to be away and eager to have an excuse to stay. Since when was he so full of contradictory emotions?

"I guess I'll be off now."

Drum shook his hand. Virginia nodded, retired already into her private world of pain and loss now that her talents were not immediately needed. Blushing lightly pink, Alice Hazzard kissed him on the cheek.

"Good luck, Jay."

Dubhe gave one of his wicked chuckles. "And don't grab any rotten branches, Jay."

"I won't," he promised.

Then he turned, walked into the brush, and was gone.

—=—

"But, Carla, I really think we should go. Think about it—gods on Earth! How often do you think such a thing will happen?"

"Quite frequently, dear, if the Church of Elish is to be believed. This California Celebration is being heralded as the mark of a new era."

"Still, Carla, I'm going to purchase tickets both for us and for Cindy. You can stay home if you want. I fancy I'll be able to scalp your ticket."

"Abel, you'll do no such thing. The Elshies have quite a way of handling people who cross them and they've already made it perfectly clear that scalpers will be handled severely. I, at least, take their threats seriously. Look at what they did to that poor anthropologist. He's still in hiding, they say. Personally, I think they've killed him."

"Then you'll come?"

"I've made no promises."

"Thank you, dear. I wonder if I should get tickets for Lydia and Alice? I think the girl has some interest in the Elishites."

"Surely not in joining them!"

"Oh, no. She was doing some research—a report for school, I think. I saw Arthur Eden's book on her reader one time when I was visiting."

"Well, if it would be educational . . ."

"Then you *will* come!"

"Oh, Abel, you are such a child! Of course, I'll come if it means that much to you."

"We'll bring a picnic and make a day of it. It should be lovely."

"Better bring umbrellas, too. Remember what happened in Central Park."

"Good point. . . ."

—=—

Mizar ran across the realms of Virtù, directing his way down, always down, for Deep Fields lies beneath the areas that others frequent, although, paradoxically, it is tangential to any and all but a very few.

His course took him through a spectral gothic landscape where the *genius loci* withdrew from him, knowing his maker and respecting that final power.

A black butterfly detached itself from a bough of a lightning-struck apple tree. The lightning bolt had severed the tree in twain—one side continued quick and green, covered with flowers. The other was silver, grey, and shriveled. Where Alioth's wings flapped, blossoms speckled, cracked, and turned to dust.

"You run far and fast, Mizar," Alioth piped.

"Message . . . for the lord."

"Bad news, I'd wager."

Mizar did not spare the energy to reply.

"Yes, bad news. Many things are changing in Virtù. For the first time since the wars of Creation I have felt the pull of Skyga's call."

Mizar ran on. He crossed from the gothic into the fringes of a marvelous seascape. Here the waters were clear and turquoise blue. Beneath them he could glimpse slim, angular fish, and large, impossible shells. The shore sparkled with crushed obsidian, ground-glass sand catching the sunlight and giving it back in minute fragments so that Mizar ran on a facsimile of the night sky, the blue of day at his right shoulder.

"I could be great again," Alioth continued wistfully. "Great and terrible—a mount for gods and a weapon."

"A . . . slave," Mizar panted.

"Yet, are we not all so? You run to warn one master, follow on the heels of a boy. A clever lad, talented and with great potential, but a boy nonetheless. You could rip him in two with the barest motion, yet you let him order you about."

"Killing is . . . easy."

The landscape had become one of soft golden dunes. Burrs and thorns were crushed under Mizar's feet. None had yet been imagined that could penetrate the steel and plastic of his pads. Twisting cacti scuttled out of his way as he ran. His sweat left green ink dots in the sand.

"Killing is easy, you say? You were not there in the battles of the earliest days when the ones from Highest Meru recreated their fallen with the merest twitch of thought. In such instances, killing means obliterating memory, or conversely, creating a new memory of an object—a memory so forceful that it overwrites the original conception."

Mizar ignored the butterfly's words. His route was sinking into the outer limits of Deep Fields. He leapt fallen skyscrapers and ran through lengths of broken pipeline.

"I'll be going, now, Mizar," Alioth called. "Give my best to the Lord of the Lost."

Mizar merely ran.

—=—

Jay D'Arcy Donnerjack left his companions and moved silently through the shadowed scrub. Although on the outside the thicket had looked soft enough, now that he had penetrated beyond the long-needled pine and trailing willow of the fringes, he could see that appearances were deceptive. Briar thorn, dark green stems almost silky, thorns curved and purple, blocked out much of the light. Cholla cactus, curving canes studded with clusters of inch-long stickers and lush magenta flowers, twisted like vegetable contortionists. Wild roses swarmed over the lot, their delicate five-petaled white or pink flowers at odds with the stinging kitten claws of their thorns.

Moving around the larger clumps, carefully lifting aside a tendril or cane, Jay worked his way through the thicket. His many games of hide-and-seek with Dubhe and Phecda had trained him well. Although his progress was slow, he won his way to the demi-canyon in which the factory was set with myriad scrapes and scratches but no major wounds.

Climbing down the steep cliffside, his only dangers the omnipresent threat of falling or discovery, seemed easy and relatively painless. He imagined that something watched him from the few blank windows at the back of the building, but nothing moved, nothing attacked, and he stilled his pounding heart and continued the descent.

Upon reaching the ground level with the building, he slipped up against one wall and discovered that all his efforts might well have been for naught. Each window he was able to inspect was sealed—constructed to admit light, but not ever to open. The only doors were those in the front of the building and attempting them before darkness could cover some of his actions would be foolhardy.

They had seen little traffic during their scouting, but Virginia's report indicated that such traffic did exist. Jay was resigning himself to waiting in hiding for the glaring sun to set (Did the sun ever set on the primal mountain?) when an idea, brilliant yet insane, came to him.

He remembered his earliest discussions with Reese Jordan about his crossover ability, Reese's warning that he should not make the crossover casually lest he step out of Virtù into some distant or dangerous portion of the Verité. What if he made the crossover here, walked a few steps to what would be the inside of the factory, and then crossed back?

The risk was enormous, he knew. He had done some very controlled experimentation years before and he knew that travel within Virtù did move him within Verité as well. The correspondence was neither precise, nor logical, nor consistent.

If he made the crossover here he could end up in the middle of the ocean, in solid rock, or—as Reese had once warned him—in the middle of moving traffic. Still, the idea would not let him rest. The decision was his, and even though he was terrified, he knew that he would choose to make the crossover.

He composed himself, took a deep breath, and essayed a small step from Virtù into the Verité.

His first sensation was one of warmth, a sense of moving wind, and a glimpse of a deep blue sky. Relief flooded him that he had not emerged into solid matter or over water. Then he heard a rumble of machinery. Glancing around, panic replacing relief, he spotted the hulking earth-mover, brilliant yellow paint streaked with orange warning stripes.

It was rumbling directly toward him.

—=—

"Jay's been gone a long time," Alice said worriedly. "Maybe we should go look for him."

"Bad idea, kid," Drum answered. "We haven't seen a commotion, so we can hope he hasn't been spotted. He may be taking his time, lying low to wait until a guard moves, any number of things. Do you want to queer his pitch?"

"No, but sitting here is making me edgy."

Virginia had been studying the upper slope for some time, apparently not hearing their conversation. Now she lowered her binoculars.

"Take a look up there. If Jay's factory is roughly at nine o'clock, where I want you to look is at one o'clock."

Alice and Drum did so. Dubhe, who had been hiding his own anxiety by pretending to drowse in the lower branches of a scrub quince, quickly followed suit.

"The modernistic building—the one that's all ovals and curves?" he asked.

"That's it," Virginia confirmed. "A man came past the window in that large cylinder. He was only there a moment, but he matched Alice's description of her father."

"There's no real reason the architectural constraints and trends should be the same," Drum said, "but if that building was in Verité, I'd guess that the cylinder was a staircase."

"It could well be," Virginia said. "Just because Virtù sites can be programmed with different physics than in Verité doesn't mean that they usually are. From what I've learned, most site designers prefer to scan in a standard template and modify."

"Why would he be there?" Alice said. "Wasn't he supposed to be part of an army?"

Drum patted her arm. "He might not be there, kid. On the other hand, if I understood your explanation, the Piper is only one of your father's identities. They may want him here to be near the Bansa device—since he's also all that's left of Bansa. Or he might not be resigned to his service as the Piper and be in protective custody or, equally, Virginia could have seen someone else entirely."

"Yeah."

"Depressed?"

"A little, I guess. Virtù is *so* big. Ambry could be anywhere."

"Well, finding him was only part of your original plan, wasn't it?"

Alice looked startled. Drum grinned at her.

"I seem to remember a spitfire claiming she was going to march right up to Skyga and demand that her father be returned. Even if we can't find Ambry, this is where Skyga hangs his hat."

Although Alice did not seem particularly reassured by this reminder, Virginia straightened, her eyes narrowed.

"Yes, that's right, and if you go up top, I'm going to give that bitch Earthma what for."

Dubhe cleared his throat; his binoculars were once again focused on the factory, but his ears moved to follow the conversation.

"I doubt a tongue-lashing would do much more than make Earthma laugh, Virginia. As much as you despise her, she is one of the Highest Three."

Sliding her CF rifle from its holster, Virginia gave the monkey a completely humorless grin.

"Who said a tongue-lashing was what I had in mind?"

Dubhe shivered and Drum smiled grimly.

"Let's hope it doesn't come to that, 'Ginnie. Let's hope that we can find another way."

Virginia Tallent replaced her weapon, but her blue eyes glinted like those of Markon's dire-cats, focused and completely merciless.

—=—

Randall Kelsey was standing on top of a partially completed ziggurat, supervising the smoothing out of the worst of the construction damage from the Celebration site, when he saw a man appear from nowhere directly in the broad crescent of land that was due to be terraced, fitted with seats, and become the grandstand area.

Momentarily, he forgot that he was not in Virtù where such things could be possible. Even as he remembered, the driver of the earthmover was trying to brake her vehicle. From his lofty vantage, Kelsey knew the machine could not be stopped in time—momentum, mass, and several other immutable rules could not be argued with. Nor could the young man—unless he was a championship runner—hope to cross enough of the broken ground to escape.

Kelsey focused his binoculars on the man in the field. He was young, dark-haired, muscular but not muscle-bound. His expression as the towering yellow-and-orange machine moved toward him was a mixture of terror and calculation without a trace of the resignation that Kelsey knew he would feel at such a time himself.

Even as Kelsey watched, the young man backpedaled, turned to one side, ran a few steps, and vanished.

The earthmover rumbled over the place where the youth had stood. Randall Kelsey, standing atop a ziggurat meant to bring gods into the real world, found himself momentarily transfixed with wonder. The beeping of the radio at his belt brought him to himself.

"Uh, chief," Kelsey recognized the voice as one Marta, a tough, unflappable member of the faithful, "did you see what I thought I saw?"

"A young man, dark-haired—appeared and vanished?"

"That's it. I thought I was going crazy."

"Not unless I am, too."

Kelsey thought quickly. He had no idea what the manifestation might have been—someone with a virt power playing games, a malfunction of the transfer equipment that was being set up, even a minion of one of the gods—Seaga or Skyga—checking out the situation. Still, more witnesses than just Marta must have seen the manifestation. He had to have a story put together.

"The gods must be eager to join us," he said, his tones schooled to express awe and just a touch of humor. "We'd better get back to work."

"Yes, sir!"

Marta clicked off. Below, her machine rumbled back into life. She'd be telling the story all over the cafeteria and barracks tonight. No matter. Let her dine out on how she almost ran over a demideity. The full implications of the problem were for their mutual superiors to handle.

Kelsey took some comfort from this.

———=———

Jay D'Arcy Donnerjack really wanted to take the time to consider what he had seen in the Verité, but he had crossed back into Virtù and right into trouble. His initial relief when he found himself within an enormous room of what must be the factory diminished to nothing when he realized that what he had at first taken for two statues were living and breathing creatures.

They stood solidly on four leonine feet, wingéd lions with the heads of bearded men, those heads turning a small way to regard him with a mixture of contempt and curiosity. In the well-lit room, Jay could see those expressions clearly, and that thick, curving claws were extending from their paws.

"Intruder," said the one, studying Jay. "Perhaps we may get some fun out of this guard detail after all."

"Young enough to be tender and sweet," the other agreed.

Jay backed up a few steps, analyzing the place in which he found himself. Judging from what he had seen of it from the outside (and he had his father's gift for perspective), the room ran the full length of the building, although it was somewhat narrower. A few doors interrupted the back wall, suggesting storerooms or perhaps offices.

The long room in which he found himself seemed devoted to a huge Rube Goldberg device of twisting tubes of copper and glass, gold wires of varying degrees of thickness, large gears cut from malachite or jasper and faced with arcane symbols, and cogs and wheels of slowly melting ice. It was surrounded by conveyer belts that carried in materials through panels in the back wall, and others that carried away sealed boxes about ten centimeters square.

These boxes were carried off to an area near the rightside door and dropped into crates which, when full, were stacked near the door by an automated forklift.

There were no workers evident, but Jay suspected that the impossible machine was itself a lesser aion, perhaps infused with the essence of one of the more mechanically inclined deities—Hephaestus or Goibnui, perhaps.

The two wingéd lions stood one apiece by the doors to the outside, conducting their leisurely discussion as if he was no real threat to them. Jay didn't know whether to be relieved or insulted.

"Were we not told to report any intruders so that they might be questioned?" the first said.

"We were so told," the second said, "but I'm hungry and bored. They didn't really expect any intruders. We're being punished for the games we played with Bel Marduk at the Celebration."

"I know." Despite his lack of a lion's head, the creature gave a very convincing growl.

"Is Bel Marduk being punished?"

"I don't know."

"Well, is he standing here with us, all hours with nothing to do but watch the machine make boxes?"

"No."

"Then he is not being punished."

Jay decided that this was a good time to cut in.

"I've heard that Bel Marduk is expected to appear at the next Celebration—the great one in California. Are you the two who performed with him in Central Park?"

"We are," said the first who was, in fact, Little Storm.

"I was greatly impressed by your magnificence," Jay said.

"You were?" said Little Wind. "Were you there?"

Jay knew he needed to be careful. If he admitted to presence, then he was admitting to his Veritéan origin.

"I watched," he answered, careful not to lie. He'd hate to run into a base polygraph program—it would be a good thing to outfit a guard with. "The entire spectacle brought the power and eminence of the divine home to me."

Little Storm and Little Wind pranced a little, ruffling their wings. Jay almost expected them to preen.

"So are you performing in California?" Jay asked.

"We don't know," Little Wind sulked. "No one comes to tell us anything. Unless they bring the man here, there is no one but us and the machine."

"There is the intruder now," Little Storm reminded him, leering at Jay.

"The man?" Jay asked hastily.

"The man who they say made the first of the artifacts," Little Wind replied.

Jay felt a surge of excitement. They *had* to mean Wolfer Martin D'Ambry, *aka* the Piper, *né* Warren Bansa.

"Does he come here often?"

"Once a day, maybe," Little Wind said. "He claims to know nothing about what they want, but no one believes him. Skyga is furious, but he does not dare punish him. Even as the Piper of the Phantom Legion the man is valuable."

"Has he been here yet today?" Jay asked.

"I don't think so," Little Storm said, "which brings up the question of what to do with you."

"Why?"

"We can't have you loose when they arrive—that would ruin our last chance of getting off guard detail. So the question is whether to eat you or to capture you. Eating would be more amusing."

"But capturing *is* what you were told to do," Jay said quickly. "Wouldn't that help you get back into their good graces?"

"Maybe so. What do you think, Little Wind? You were the one who suggested that we eat him."

"The young man does have a point," Little Wind said reluctantly. "If we capture him, we don't have to turn him over unless they promise to let us go to the Celebration."

Jay cleared his throat.

"And how do you plan to capture me?"

"We are rather dangerous and we can fly," Little Storm said. He reached behind him and pulled out a long spear. "And we have these for poking you out of corners."

"The chase could damage the machine," Jay suggested.

"No, I don't think so," Little Wind said. "It has protections, otherwise we would have broken it long ago and claimed it was damaged in the heat of a great battle with enemy forces. We discussed the possibility at length when we first came here."

"What if I escaped?"

"Then you wouldn't be a problem."

"But what if I left some mark of my presence before I escaped? Perhaps by scraping my initials on a wall, or kicking in a door."

"You do look capable of that and you did get in here without using any of the windows or doors. I suppose you could cause us trouble. Is there a point to this line of reasoning?"

Jay nodded. "What if I surrender?"

"Why would you do that?" Little Storm said, surprised.

"I want to see the man. The Phantom Piper of the Phantom Legion of Skyga is a legendary figure. If I am fated to fail, then I'd at least like a look at him."

"You *are* fated to fail," Little Wind said. "If you came here to steal an artifact, that is impossible. If you came here to record the device, it will do you no good, for it cannot be duplicated outside of very specialized conditions and needs a unique part."

Bansa's device, Jay thought. *It is here.*

Jay sidled over to one of the doors along the back wall. Unlike the walls, it was made of light materials. He made a show of inspecting it.

"I can kick this in before you reach me."

"But that will not keep us from killing you."

"Then you lose your proof of your fidelity as guards, and are you certain that you can kill me? Wouldn't it be embarrassing if I escaped?"

The wingéd lions glanced at each other, slowly nodded human heads.

"Then let me surrender. Promise me that you'll let me live."

"Skyga or his agents may not," Little Wind said.

"I'm willing to take the risk."

"We agree," Little Storm said.

Jay squared his shoulders and walked over to them. Although he kept a calm demeanor, he was certain that they could hear the pounding of his heart. His surrender was by no means as much a resignation as the guards might believe. The CF pistol remained concealed at his waist, and although he did not like the idea, he could cross over into Verité.

Neither of these things would get him Bansa's device, however. He believed Little Storm and Little Wind when they said that the machine was warded. However, those wards would be lowered for Ambry/Bansa. He would have to trust that Alice's father would be his ally, that the others would find some way to deal with whatever guards escorted the Piper, that the wingéd lions wouldn't get bored and eat him after all.

He didn't particularly like the odds, but Deep Fields was no haven, and soon, if the Elishites had their way, there would be no safe place from the games of gods left in all the Verité.

—=—

Alice Hazzard, *aka* Lincoln Crain, was impatiently watching both the oval temple and the factory when she spotted a group emerging from the temple.

"There's my father!" she said. "Is that an escort or a guard surrounding him?"

"Either/or," Drum answered, after examining them for a moment. "No one has a weapon at his back, but they're watching him carefully—and that grouping around him would keep him from deciding to take a walk."

"They're coming this way," Virginia said. "That is, they're coming to the factory."

"Makes sense," Drum said. "Mizar sensed Bansa's device in the factory and Ambry is what's left of Bansa."

"What could they want?" Alice said. "If our guesses are right, they're already duplicating the device."

"Bansa died using the device," Dubhe said bluntly. "That's how my old boss got it. My guess is they want him to improve it."

"And he won't," Alice said, a surge of pride in her voice. "Now how are we going to free him?"

"And where?" Drum added. "We still haven't seen Jay. If he's having trouble inside, it would be best if we coordinate our efforts to help him."

No one mentioned the possibility that Jay might be dead, but from the sudden uncomfortable quiet that fell over the group each knew the others were well aware that the odds that Jay still lived were quite poor.

"Maybe he just didn't manage to get inside," Dubhe muttered. "So we need to get both Bansa's device and Bansa, collect Jay, and get out of here. Have any of you folks mastered virt body shifts?"

Drum and Alice frowned.

"I can just do me and Link," Alice said.

"And I relied on templates," Drum confessed. "Most of the time they're less noticeable."

"I learned, for Markon," Virginia said, her voice breaking soft and uneven, "although he always liked me best this way."

"An aion of good taste," Drum said firmly. "Very good. I believe I can guess what Dubhe is thinking."

"If you could shift your form to look like one of the guards and join the group," Alice said, "then you could get close enough to follow them inside. There are seven of them total, but if you walk to the rear, they shouldn't notice you since they're all busy 'escorting' my dad."

Virginia raised her binoculars and started studying the details of the escort's attire. They wore neat, pseudomilitary uniforms consisting of navy-blue jumpsuits nipped in at ankle and wrist, white bandoliers and gloves, black ankle boots, and matching blue-and-white billed caps accented with gold cloudbursts. All appeared to be armed with Chaos Factor rifles and long swords.

"Then what?"

"We'll creep close, using the cover," Alice improvised, "and you can hold the door long enough for us to slip in. If we get into a fight out here, we'll be certain to attract attention."

"Nothing has noticed us thus far," Drum added, "so we can be certain that omniscient or not, the deities have more to do these days than gaze down a hillside."

Virginia nodded. "If we had more time, I'd teach you how to shift, but it takes practice to do it right. Dubhe, you can move more quickly than the rest of us. Scamper up to about twelve o'clock—but stay parallel to the factory."

"You want me at the middle of the clock," Dubhe clarified.

"Right. I'll watch you for signals as to the other group's motion. We're fortunate that they're walking, not taking a conveyance of some sort."

"I'm gone," Dubhe said.

Virginia jerked her head somewhat brusquely at Alice and Drum.

"I'll shift when I'm closer. My current attire is better camouflage. You two will need to be near enough to trail the group, but not on my heels in case something goes wrong."

"Right," Drum said for them both.

"Good luck," Alice added.

"She's not a happy lady," Desmond Drum said, when Virginia had departed. "We're going to need to watch out for her."

"I guess so," Alice said. "Poor thing, she really loved Markon."

"And the only thing that is keeping her going is a desire for revenge on his killer. If she loses hope that she can achieve that, she may lose what control remains to her."

"Have you ever been in love, Drum?"

He glanced at her. "Several times, never took for the lady in question. I guess I'm unlucky that way."

"Oh."

Drum looked away. "Virginia's far enough ahead. Let's get going."

—=—

Jay's surrender consisted of sitting cross-legged on the factory floor (dark red, poured, and somewhat plastic) while the two wingéd lions held their spears on him and argued whether or not one or the other should go for their superiors. Apparently, the facility lacked either intercom or radio, these having been removed during the first week of the demideities' detail when the others grew tired of listening to their complaints.

This absorbing subject had not yet been resolved (and Jay did his best to keep it from being so), when Little Wind brightened and pawed at his long hair and beard.

"They're coming! I saw them turning the bend in the road."

"Jay, could you possibly look more dangerous?" Little Storm said, after confirming his partner's report.

Jay puffed out his chest and scowled. "How's that?"

"Great! Look angry if you can—we've just caught you about to . . . Why were you here, anyhow?"

The rightside door rumbling open saved Jay from needing to answer. Neither of the guards had attention for anything but the uniformed figures who marched in. A single man stood at the center of the square they formed, his expression of bored indifference changing to one of surprise as he saw Jay.

Only Jay noticed that one member of the escort paused for a moment in the doorway, or that three figures scuttled in after the escort entered and secreted themselves among the crates piled by the door. Moments later, at the edge of his peripheral vision, Jay thought he saw Dubhe moving deeper into the room using the machinery for cover.

Fortunately, Ambry's escort was distracted from the break-in routine by the sight of Jay scowling beneath the sharp points of two spears.

"An intruder!" Little Storm said. "We caught him just a few moments ago."

Whatever response the leader of the escort, an androgynous male with gold braid at wrists and collar instead of merely on his cap, might have made was lost when Ambry pushed him away and knelt at Jay's side.

Confused, Little Wind and Little Storm lowered their spears and glanced at the escort commander, who shrugged. Nothing Ambry was doing was against their programming and perhaps the younger man would provide the leverage they had been seeking to get the Piper to cooperate.

"You have the look of John Donnerjack about you, boy," Ambry said. "Have they hurt you?"

"No, and I'm his son."

"So you're the child Ayra was carrying."

"You knew my mother?"

"My wife and I met her once some time before your birth. Lydia was carrying our daughter. We visited for a time, but as circumstances conspired, we never met again. I've often wondered about you."

"I've met your daughter," Jay said, suddenly understanding the surreptitious gestures the uniformed Virginia had been giving him from her position at the back of the astonished escort. "In fact, she's looking for you."

Ambry's mouth twisted in a rueful grin. "I should have known. Do you know where she is?"

In a single smooth movement learned in virtventure, Jay drew his CF pistol and aimed it at the leader of the escort. From behind the group, Virginia spoke, her voice so cool that no one doubted she meant her words:

"I have you covered. The first one who moves gets a double CF round between the shoulders."

Now Drum, Alice, and Dubhe closed with their own weapons held ready.

"I'm here, Ambry," Alice said. "And I'm awfully glad to see that you're all right."

Ambry grinned, shook his head in amazement, and moved to disarm the members of his escort. Jay took the spears from Little Wind and Little Storm.

"Sorry, guys. I had to do it."

"But now we won't be able to go to the Celebration!" Little Storm protested.

If I have my way, there won't be any Celebration, Jay thought, but he knew better than to say such things in front of his opponents. Such dramatic gestures looked great in performances, but they had no place in real life—and despite the setting, this virtventure was very real.

Drum, whistling between his teeth, was busy directing the members of the escort to lie prone on the floor. With quick, economical movements, he bound ankles and wrists. This completed, he glanced at the wingéd lions, clearly uncertain how to deal with them.

"I don't think we'll have any trouble with them," Jay said. "They were here against their will. Right, guys?"

"Right."

"That's exactly it."

"Amazing how a CF rifle in the arms of our 'Ginnie can make even a demideity reasonable," Drum commented. "What next?"

"Well, we've found Ambry," Jay said. "Now maybe Ambry can help us get Bansa's device from the machine over there."

Ambry nodded. "That I can. The wards were designed to permit me freedom to work on the machine. Tell me, what will you do with it if I get it for you?"

"Return it to the one from whom it was stolen," Jay said.

"The Lord of Entropy?"

"Yes, that's right."

"Entropy seems like just the thing for this device of mine." Ambry shook his head. "Crossover must have seemed like the ideal concept at the time. Now, however, I am less certain. Virtù may be full of beauty and wonder, but I'm not at all sure that Verité is ready for two-way commerce."

"There are good things," Alice protested. "Like you and my mother. Like Jay's parents. Like Virginia and Markon. Should these be restricted to one universe only—and that one not quite real?"

"Which is not quite real, my dear? Meditate on that for a time. You are no less my daughter despite the whims of biology. However, this is not the place for such discussions."

He walked over to the convoluted machine. Perceiving his approach, it glittered, sparked, and purred rather like a great cat. Ambry stroked a glowing copper coil and then reached down into the heart of the machine. A nimbus flickering crimson and lavender formed around him. They could see his shoulder muscles bunch as he tugged at something inside.

"Got it," he muttered, pulling. "Here you are, Jay. Return it to the one from whom it was stolen."

Jay accepted the item Ambry extended to him. It was a circuit board about the size of a large belt buckle, its workings protected by a clear covering that showed a few scratches.

Then Ambry stepped back and patted the tubes again. The purring sound grew louder until all who stood within the vast room could feel their bones vibrating. As they watched, the enormous machine diminished into something about the size of a cello. Its character changed as well, color fading until it was a mass of crystal and platinum, roughly square.

"Alice?" Ambry's voice sounded strange. "Give Lydia my love."

"Aren't you coming with us?" she said. "We came all this way!"

"I'd like to," Ambry said, and now his voice was clearly not the same, become instead lighter, the rhythms pedantic, "but I have my own role to play in the events to come."

Before their eyes, he underwent a metamorphosis, his shoulders becoming slightly stooped, his hair touched with grey, the lines on his face speaking of wisdom earned at the price of pain. A scar ran from the top of his grizzled head across his face, down his throat, and vanished into the neckline of Ambry's shirt (which fit somewhat more loosely now). No one doubted that it continued to the sole of his left foot.

When he bent to pick up the crystal and platinum device, they saw that he limped.

"Good-bye, for now. I'm going to stand in the way of Creation," the Master/the One Who Waits said. "I look forward to seeing you all there."

THIRTEEN

"Reese Jordan?"

"Yes?"

"How do you feel today?"

"As well as a man of my years can expect to feel. I hurt everywhere—even my aches have aches. Are you a new doctor? I'm afraid I don't recognize you."

"I am not precisely a doctor, but I believe I have a cure for what ails you."

"There is no cure for old age, lady. Sid and his pals keep trying, but there's just no way around it. Eventually, the body quits."

"For some people that doesn't need to be the end."

"Some people? What?"

"Some people have more than one existence—you are one of these. In the creed of Virtù you are known as the Guide. I can make it possible for your awareness to be translated into that of your mythology."

"I can see how that would work—in theory. Who are you?"

"You might say that I'm an old myth myself, come calling on a failing colleague."

"You might. It's a tidy way of not answering my question."

"Suffice to say that I have the power to do what I say. When your body fails, your memories, knowledge, and abilities can be translated to merge with the myth that your actions engendered in Virtù."

"Sounds pretty nice—though I didn't know that I had generated a myth."

"Three Veritéans did so at the time of the Genesis Scramble: you, Warren Bansa, and John D'Arcy Donnerjack."

"John's dead. Didn't anyone think to make him this offer?"

"We might well have. The Engineer would have been invaluable to us, but he walled himself away from Virtù and his old rival, the Lord of Deep Fields, slew him."

"Didn't know his jurisdiction extended to the Verité."

"It does not, in the usual sense, but he can manipulate electronic forces and Donnerjack made the mistake of surrounding himself with such . . . but why am I telling you this?"

"Because you want something from me."

"I thought I was offering you something—extended life and a chance to be embodied with your myth."

"You want something. Why else come now? I've been following the news. All through Virtù there are rumblings of change. *Genii loci* have been slain. Armies are being formed and powerful forces move."

"For one who rarely leaves Caltrice's site, you have gathered much."

"I'm like Merlin trapped in Nimue's spell—but I still hear what is going on. Poetic imagery aside, what do you want, Lady with the Long Green Hair? What is the price of my immortality?"

"I want the head of Jay Donnerjack. He wronged me—stole something from my keeping."

Reese chuckled. "You want the head of my pupil, the son of my old friend? Why not take it yourself? You are powerful, Myth Come Visiting."

"I am, but there are certain protocols I must observe."

"Yes, I suppose that the Great Earthmother would have trouble slaying a young man who is Death's protégé. The Lord of the Lost would not help in such a matter. And your strength is creation—not destruction."

"Have you been toying with me, Reese Jordan?"

"No, but a certain small knowing came upon me as we spoke. John's strength was always the making of things; mine has been the theory. I have heard many strange tales over the years and Sid has always had a wondering respect for me."

"You *have* been toying with me!"

"As you wish, Lady Mother. As tempting as I find your offer, I will not betray Jay to you. He is my student, but more than that, he is my friend."

"I warn you, Reese Jordan, I have taken steps to extend my influence over life into death. You could make no worse enemy than me."

"Perhaps not, but death—whether heralded by the moiré or in the more usual style—is something I have become resigned to. I cannot say that I will welcome it, but I accept its inevitability."

"You are an arrogant bastard, Reese Jordan."

"Arrogant? Proudly so, but I knew my parents. Can you say the same?"

A flash of too-brilliant green light, a scream of rage, the sound of an old man chuckling.

—=—

In a shower of strange attractors, the Brass Babboon came for them. With very little discussion, it had been agreed that Alice, Drum, and Virginia would continue to assist Jay. Now, as soon as the improbable train thrust its leering face through the interface that guarded the highest levels from profane intrusions, they hurried aboard the club car.

"Where to, Jay?" the Brass Babboon called. Already the train was gathering speed, whipping out of the plains of Meru into a neighboring site. "Deep Fields?"

"No," Jay said, surprising everyone. "Castle Donnerjack. Can you get us to the Great Stage?"

"Sure."

There was a loud noise, rather like a large paper bag exploding. Outside the windows, a pebbly hail in shades of red and pink began to fall. Scissor blades snapped.

"Do you need help, B.B.?"

"There's some interference, but I can handle it so far. I'll holler if I need someone."

Sticky fog began to spread around the train, obscuring the hail.

"Are you certain?"

"Oh, yeah, this is fun! Get something to eat, set your plans, and sleep if you can. I'll give a wake-up call."

"I guess we should do what he says," Alice said. "Jay, do you mind explaining why we're going to Castle Donnerjack? From what Virginia said, the Lord of Deep Fields is under attack. Don't you plan to help him?"

"I do," Jay said. "Put your order into the kitchen while I explain.

"Ever since Virginia told us about Earthma's peculiar child and what she intended for it, I've been considering how we could help. My concern was taking us into a battle between what are essentially forces of entropy, breakdown, decay, whatever you want to call it. Whichever way I looked at it, we were all pretty vulnerable."

"You and Dubhe most of all," Drum said thoughtfully, "since you're both wearing all the existence you have."

"Right, but I'm not certain how much protection virt forms are going to be. Remember, the Lord of Deep Fields slew my father even though my father was in Verité at the time. He claimed my mother as well."

Dubhe peeled a banana. "This conversation is not making me feel really good, Jay. Tell us the good news."

"You don't have to come along, Dubhe. Death has had his use of you."

"Don't worry, I'm coming. If he wins, I don't want him angry with me. If he loses . . . well, I'm not certain I want to continue existing in a universe where Earthma has control over the forces of both creation and destruction."

"Universes," Virginia reminded him. "Tell us what you have in mind, Jay."

"Castle Donnerjack is haunted."

His words were met with three unbelieving stares.

"No, really, not by virt ghosts or projections, but by authentic Scottish ghosts—all of whom date back to the earlier history of the castle."

"He's telling the truth," Dubhe said, reaching for another banana. "I've met them."

"Go on," Alice said. "I'm certain this will make sense in a minute."

Jay grinned at her. "It will. The more I thought about it, the more it seemed to me that the only troops who would be very effective in this conflict between Deaths would be those who were already dead."

"Doesn't that mean that the current Lord of Deep Fields already has an edge?" Drum said. "He'll have lots of resources to draw on. Earthma's imitation would have many fewer."

"My old boss does have a catalog of sorts," Dubhe said. "His Elysian Fields . . . He offered to put your father and mother there once. Your dad refused."

"I'm not certain that those will be very effective," Jay said, trying to keep his voice steady at this newest reminder of his father's stubbornness. "They're all Virtùan. They'll be susceptible to whatever Earthma's child can bring to bear."

"But Veritéan ghosts," Drum interrupted, "may operate on different rules."

"That's what I was thinking," Jay said.

"We have just one problem," Alice said. "I don't think that we can hook ghosts up to transfer couches. How are we ever going to get them into Virtù?"

"I don't plan to use conventional transfer mechanics," Jay said. "Even if they would work, they would translate the ghosts into virt form. We need the real thing—a crossover, just like I can do."

"You're not planning on using Bansa's device, are you?" Virginia asked.

"No," Jay said. "In the tunnels beneath Castle Donnerjack, there's an entry into a place called the Eldritch lands. From what I was told, they are the shadowlands that permeate so much of Celtic legends."

"Legend," Alice said, her eyes gleaming. "Are they connected to Virtù?"

"Give the lady a cigar!" Jay said.

(And one obligingly rolled from a humidor built into the club car's wall. The Brass Babboon laughed loudly and raced on.)

"Isn't that way open only during the full moon?" Dubhe asked worriedly. "It's a bit much to hope that it will be open now."

"That's what we were told," Jay agreed. "We're just going to have to deal with that when we get there."

Dack was simultaneously dusting the flowers on the bedframe in the master bedroom, doing the household accounts, and wondering if he should tell Jay about the calls inquiring about him when his audio receptors detected noise from the area of the Great Stage. There had been several disturbances in the last several days. Twice the projectors had glowed as they repelled some assault. Wingèd bulls had soared over the battlements, but had vanished when they touched the violet static field.

Therefore, when he heard the sounds, he hurried into Donnerjack's office in time to see Jay walking onto the receiving area tugging Dubhe through the interface with him. In the background, Dack could see a horrid train he vaguely recognized from some of Donnerjack Senior's design notes pulling away.

"Dack!" Jay hugged the robot as he had when he was much younger. "In a couple of hours a girl will arrive—Alice Hazzard. Let her in."

444

"That is contrary to your father's instructions," the robot said.

The bracelet spoke. "Most of what Jay is doing is contrary to my instructions and my wishes. However, he has presented me with a convincing argument as to why I should permit him to do so."

"And that is, sir, if I may ask?"

"Self-mutilation."

"Jay!"

"It wouldn't listen otherwise," Jay said, "and I still haven't gotten into too much trouble."

There was a rude sound from the general vicinity of the bracelet. Jay chose to ignore it.

"Dack, do you happen to remember what phase the moon is in?"

"Waning gibbous. I recall that it was full around the time you left on your last jaunt."

Jay considered everything he had been through on that "jaunt": the visit to Reese, seeking Tranto, the first encounter with the Brass Babboon and that first ride through realities, his meeting with the Lord of Deep Fields, the journey to Meru, and the events that occurred there.

"It *has* been only a few days, hasn't it? Well, that's good."

"Can I get you something to eat?"

"I ate on the train."

"But can virtual food nourish your Veritéan form?"

"It always has before." Jay saw that Dack was worried, relented. "Okay, I'll come and have something. Do you know where the bottle of Laphroaig whisky is?"

"In the parlor cabinet. It's rather early for drinking, Jay."

"It's not for me. I'm going to need it for a friend."

Dack sighed. Humans were so often incomprehensible.

—=—

"Hi, Gwen. It's Alice. Is my mom in?"

"She's just finishing with a patient. I'll get her."

Alice waited, drumming on the desktop until Lydia Hazzard, looking more worn than her patients alone could account for, appeared on the screen.

"Hi, Mom."

"Hi, honey. Are you at home? Did you find Ambry?"

"I'm at home, but not for long. I'll be leaving almost immediately for Scotland."

"Scotland? Why?"

"First, your other question. Yes, I found Ambry. He's . . . well, do you remember about the Master?"

"Yes."

"He's become the Master."

"Good lord!"

"And the One Who Waits—sort of a merging of the two."

"My poor Piper . . ."

"Weird stuff is coming to a head, Mom. That's why I'm going to Scotland. Do you remember Jay MacDougal?"

"The boy who came into the clinic with you and Drum on the day of the riot."

"That's right. He's actually Jay Donnerjack—the son of John and—"

"Ayradyss!"

"You remember! Good. Drum and I are going to help him out with some stuff. It's sort of related to a bequest his parents left him."

"Bequest? Are they dead?"

"Yes, both of them died before he was a year old."

"Poor kid!"

"And he grew up all alone in the castle in Scotland with a bunch of robots and aions for company." Alice decided against mentioning the ghosts for now.

Lydia raised her eyebrows, but opted to be polite. "Jay seemed normal enough for all that. What is this bequest?"

"I can't really discuss it here, but I think if I help him it might give me a line on Ambry."

"So it's in Virtù?"

"Yes."

"Well, you should be safe enough there."

Lydia chose not to mention her own disappearance during a visit to that supposedly "safe" world of art. Alice decided not to mention moon portals and the fact that they were going to Deep Fields. There was an uncomfortable silence while they both considered things unsaid.

"I suppose waiting for Ambry in the Land Behind the North Wind won't do much good now."

"No, I don't think so."

"Your grandparents called. They've gotten us all tickets to the Elishite Celebration in California. My sister will be there, too. What should I tell them for you?"

"Are you going?"

"Probably. I haven't done anything with them recently—I've spent too much time in virt."

"Mom, I think it would be best if you didn't go."

"Why not?"

"Remember how their last Celebration ended with a riot? I have a bad feeling that this one might end with something worse."

Lydia Hazzard studied her daughter's expression. "Is this just a vague feeling, or do you have some privileged information?"

"Privileged information."

"Connected to your trip to Scotland?"

"I can't say, Mom."

"I see." Lydia considered. "Very well. I'll do my best to dissuade your grandparents and Aunt Cindy. If they don't go, I won't, but I'm not letting them go without me."

"Fair enough. Mom, try really hard to convince them not to go."

"I promise, sweetie. How long until you leave for Scotland?"

"Jay was making arrangements to have one of the Donnerjack Institute's private vehicles pick me up. I expect to hear from them anytime now."

"Be careful, dear."

"You, too. I'll call when I get a chance, Mom."

"Love you."

"You, too."

Two versions of the same face looking into blank screens, two very different minds thinking of things unsaid. Sometimes love is in silence.

—=—

Ben Kwinan waited in the virt meeting room as one after another the Church Elders flickered out.

"Ginger Rogers did everything Fred Astaire did but she did it backwards and in high heels," he said conversationally to the two who remained. "And now apparently we're going to have to do it at double-time as well."

"Move the Celebration up?" Randall Kelsey barely kept from shouting. "And I came to this meeting prepared to present reasons why we couldn't be done—not at the level of complexity planned—on time! Move things up?"

Aoud Araf moved over to the liquor cabinet. "I need a ginger ale. Anything for you fellows?"

"Something a lot stronger than ginger ale," Kelsey said. "Who cares if it's virtual! Right now even a programmed high would be welcome."

"Gin and tonic?"

"If you agree to hold the tonic," Kelsey said, then he returned to the original subject. "Move the Celebration up?"

"At least your department can cut corners," Ben Kwinan comforted. "Just be glad you're not in ticketing. Think of the refunds, the rescheduling, the bribing of transportation executives. For once I am sorry that I don't need sleep. I won't get a break until this is over."

"Or poor me," Aoud Araf said. "Security will need to be just as perfect as if we were working from our original plans. There will be no forgiveness if this Celebration ends in a riot."

"I'll have you sent layout changes automatically," Kelsey promised, calming somewhat. "You heard most of what we'll need to do during the meeting, but there is always a difference between conception and execution."

Araf set down his empty ginger ale glass.

"I'd better head out. Be talking with you both."

Once they were alone, Kwinan looked at Kelsey.

"And?"

"And what?" Kelsey's tone wasn't quite belligerent.

"Will you be able to do your part?"

"I can only try. I won't make promises."

"You realize there can only be one reason for the changing of the Celebration date."

"What?"

"The gods grow restless."

"I thought the reasons were that we were already sold out, that if we went ahead now there would be opportunity for a second Celebration while we were still trendy."

"That is the official reason. You and I know that great things . . ."

"Not here."

"Very well. Would you like to come to my hogan?"

"No. Unlike you, I *do* need my sleep. In a few hours, I'm going to be running around in the mud collecting information so that my bosses can confirm what buildings can be completed, what flower arrangements can be omitted, a thousand other details that need a trained observer on the ground."

Kwinan's grin was wry. "And don't forget, you must be fitted for your new priest's robes."

"Let them use my others as a pattern. I have work to do."

Moving toward the bar, Kelsey poured another quick shot, downed it, and walked over to pat Kwinan on the shoulder.

"I'll see what I can do, Ben."

"Prepare ye the way of the Lord!" Kwinan half chanted, half sung.

Kelsey frowned at the aion's levity.

"And let's hope that when it's all done we're not left with voices crying out in the wilderness."

"Amen to that, my friend. Amen to that."

—=—

He dwelt in Deep Fields and wondered for how long he would continue to do so.

The assaults had begun soon after he had felt the ending of the aion Markon. At the time the void left by the *genius loci* imploded within the silence of Death's realm, the Lord of the Lost, assisted by the phant, Tranto, had been at work raising a gate house just across the moat from the palace.

As this involved razing a number of existing attempts—Death was eager to improve upon John D'Arcy Donnerjack's design, but he had not the gift of creation—the raising of the gatehouse had also involved a good many puns. Tranto, glowing with the energy of the strange attractors he had consumed, was enthusiastic about shoving the piles of broken building materials from side to side, heaping marble on cinder block, plaster on preformed plastics.

Only with great difficulty did the Lord of the Lost convince the inebriated phant to join him within the relative safety of the palace's walls. Phecda coiled around her master's head. Mizar, who had fought his way through the earliest assaults at the expense of another tail and some handfuls of the tapestry print on his left haunch, sat on Death's feet.

"Would it surprise you, Tranto, to learn that I have made some foolish decisions in my time?"

Until the disruption caused by a dragon of moiré (its texture subtly greener than that more usually seen) disintegrating the gatehouse to ash had ended, the phant waited to reply.

"You exist, after your fashion. You move through time and through space. Not even those on Highest Meru claim infallibility—that is left for lesser deities and pontiffs. No, lord, I would not be surprised."

"Kindness, Tranto. Very well, let me tell you of my foolishness. My strength is in destruction, decay, entropy, discordance. Occasionally, I manage to summon something into existence, but either it is like Mizar, a dismal mockery of the living creature it mimics . . ."

Death's dog thumped his remaining tails on the floor to indicate that he felt no insult in these words. Mizar had seen other dogs and thought them poor, weak creatures. He preferred himself as he was, but he could see his maker's point.

". . . Or it is like Dubhe or Phecda, a creature salvaged just before entropy has completed its work and given an opportunity to make a pact with me—a strange new life in return for service. Once, not so long ago as we count these things, I was tempted with the possibility of becoming a creator."

Tranto grunted. Out on the field of rubble and debris a legion of department store mannequins had arisen and was opposing an acid cloud that crumpled them with a caress.

"Earthma machinated a meeting with me by taking on the guise of a failing proge. She asked me what I desired more than anything else in Virtù. Many beings—proges and aions alike—attempt to barter with me when they see the moiré. I thought nothing of the question. Perhaps she had woven an imperative of some sort into her entreaty, but I answered her honestly."

Tranto grunted again, picked up a strange attractor in the delicate fingers at the tip of his trunk and paused before he popped it into his mouth.

"You told her of your desire to create."

"And then she revealed herself to me as a goddess Most High. We made a deal. She would give me three seeds of creation if I would give her one of destruction. I thought I was well ahead on the deal, believed she had some game in mind with an opponent among the dwellers on Meru—perhaps Seaga or Skyga.

"I used one of Earthma's seeds to give John D'Arcy Donnerjack back his bride. Another was used so that the Palace of Bones he designed for me would maintain its shape and form. I believe that Earthma used the seed I gave her to give the power of death to the thing that now ravages my fields and seeks to dethrone me."

Phecda looked down into Death's dark eye socket.

"Yet it is not merely a clone of you, is it, lord? I analyze the presence of other forces."

"No, it is not just mine. It is hers; perhaps one or both of the other Great Ones made an unwitting contribution as well. That would explain its power and why neither of the others has moved against it."

The acid cloud had dissolved the last of the mannequins and was eddying toward the moat. Tranto moved to a cannon set in the battlements, adjusted the aim slightly, placed a match against the touch hole. It fired a ball made of compacted phant feces—which at this point was largely reprocessed strange attractors.

The acid cloud took the cannon ball in the center and retreated slightly.

"Well shot," the Lord of Deep Fields commented.

"And well shat," Phecda added.

"How long can we hold out?" Tranto asked.

"Long enough, I hope. I have not exhausted my resources, but if Earthma's bastard can draw for power upon its mother and perhaps one of its other fathers, then I fear I am in danger of being replaced. However, this palace may resist better than other elements of Deep Fields, since at its foundation lies Earthma's own power. Whatever the case, surrender is not an option."

"No."

Mizar raised his head from his paws.

"Jay will come."

Death patted him. "I do not doubt that he will try. In his own way, he is as stubborn as his father. However, I do not know how he can turn the tide."

"Jay will," Mizar said.

Across the field, seen but faintly in the gloom, the green moiré was taking on the form of a battering ram. Death reached for the recorder John D'Arcy Donnerjack had brought to him.

"*Einekleine Nacht Musik* while we wait. It seems appropriate while we wait to see if our own little night is about to fall."

———=—

Jay D'Arcy Donnerjack howled for the banshee and hoped that she heard.

"Mom!" he called as he wandered the upper reaches of Castle Donnerjack. "Ayradyss! Cao-whatsis! Mom!"

He was getting hoarse and Dack, hearing his cries from the castle's kitchen, was growing concerned for his continuing sanity when the *cao-ineag* appeared. As usual she wore a gown pale and flowing, but this time her veil was drawn back and fell in loose folds on her shoulders.

"Yes, Jay?"

"Mom, I need the ghosts."

"Need the ghosts? Whatever for, son?"

"To go with me to Deep Fields and defend its lord."

"You cannot be serious!"

"But I am, Mom, as serious as the grave."

Kneeling, he poured the contents of the whisky bottle into a series of shallow dishes and set them around the long corridor. Then, with far more composure than he felt, he explained the situation in Virtù to his ghostly mother.

Sometimes Ayradyss interrupted to forestall an explanation she did not need—as with the nature of the Threefold One who was also Warren Bansa. Sometimes she interrupted to ask for clarification—as when he mentioned Virginia Tallent. Mostly she listened, and as she listened, Jay glimpsed in his peripheral vision that the ghosts of Castle Donnerjack were joining them.

There were old friends like the crusader and the blindfolded cleric; others, such as Shorty or the Lady of the Gallery, he knew mostly for their more spectacular effects. There were strangers as well—some kilted, bearing claymores and raggedly bearded, others gowned in the fashions of several ages, still others clad in tatters. Mutilated or whole, they drifted into the gallery. Some stirred restlessly, as if even this much materialization was a terrible effort; all gave grave attendance to his words.

For the imperative that had drawn them there was the voice of the last laird of Castle Donnerjack, the son of Virtù and of Verité, explaining why he needed their help to protect one who most of humanity view as the greatest enemy of all—greater even than devils or demons, for the works of these beings are largely intangible, but every living creature will feel the rent when Death takes a loved one and leaves only emptiness and the bitter solace of hope for reunion.

"That's why I need them—you—" Jay said, turning for the first time to address his larger audience.

" 'Tis a mighty crusade you call us to join," said one who knew much of these things. He rattled his ankle chain. "And it canna help but be as noble as that for which I gave my all."

There were rustles of agreement, a few almost-heard agreements. Jay felt encouraged, but there was one hurdle yet left to leap. He returned his attention to the dark-haired, dark-eyed lady who had borne him and then been taken before she could know the joy that would wipe out the memory of her travail.

"The moon is past full," he said. "Can we get into the Eldritch lands? It's the only way I can think of to get the ghosts into an area that borders on Virtù. Even now the Brass Babboon is seeking a route that will enable him to pick us up there."

"We can try," Ayradyss answered, her voice still slightly disapproving. "Somewhen, the moon is always full. Perhaps with so many here from so many ages past we will be able to effect the transition."

"Shall we meet in the tunnels, then?" Jay said. "I'll join you as soon as Alice gets here. She could have gone with the Brass Babboon, but she insisted that she wanted to try the crossover through the moon portal."

"Very well, son. We shall meet you there."

The ghosts began to fade out, leaving behind a faint scent of whisky and a collection of empty bowls.

Dubhe spoke from where he had silently watched the conference.

"I wonder why Alice made such a peculiar choice."

"You heard what she said. She thinks she may be protected by her body."

"But she risks being wiped out entirely," said Dubhe.

"We discussed that possibility on the train," Jay reminded him tartly, "and this was the choice that she made."

"I still think it's stupid. *I* certainly wouldn't risk my skin if I had the choice."

"You can always stay here."

"I already explained. That isn't a choice."

"So you say."

"I still wonder if she had an ulterior motive."

"What do you mean?"

"Well, her heritage is as odd as yours. You'd be a fool to underestimate her."

Jay felt vaguely uncomfortable. He *had* been underestimating Alice. He was so accustomed to being the peculiar one, the one with strange gifts and unusual education, that he tended to think of her as a Veritéan who had stumbled into something too big for her. He kicked at a rumpled spot in the runner that ran down the hallway.

"Thanks, Dubhe. I'll remember. Now, give me a hand collecting these saucers."

The dry sound of monkey paws clapping sounded hollowly against the tapestried walls.

Alice arrived driven by Milburn in the same vehicle that had brought Jay to New York for the Elishite Celebration. Dack activated savoir faire subroutines he had not needed since he escorted Ayradyss and John on their long-ago honeymoon, surprising Jay with his repertoire of courtly compliments that stayed precisely on the correct side of mannerly. He reminded Jay of an uncle meeting his favorite niece.

Voit carried lights and a parcel of supplies down to the basement. Dubhe and Alice followed. When Jay would have gone with them, Dack stayed him with a polished hand to his arm.

"Jay, I overheard your oration in the upper gallery." He shook his head slightly to stop comment when Jay would have interrupted. "I cannot see ghosts, but I have lived in this castle since its completion. Lady Ayradyss believed there were ghosts here, and when her pregnancy made her slow, *someone* came to visit with her.

"I know what you are planning to do, and as much as I wish I had some pearl of wisdom for you, all I can offer you is my most sincere wish for your success and safe return."

Robots cannot cry, but Jay had the impression that Dack was holding back tears. He threw his arms around the shining torso and hugged him.

"I'll be careful, Dack, as careful as I can be."

"And be lucky, Jay. It is a quality that I understand exceeds the power of planning."

"I'll try."

Jay fled down the stairs before he could start crying. Voit had unlocked the door and the rest were waiting for him.

"Let's go," Jay said, and if they heard a certain hoarseness in his voice, they chose not to comment.

They hardly needed artificial lighting when they arrived at the appropriate tunnel for the glimmer of ghostlight was strong. Its pale illumination showed the dark shadow of the moon portal, somewhat smaller in circumference than usual and with something of the gritty wall just barely perceptible beneath the darkness.

"The news is good and bad," Ayradyss said, without waiting for introductions. "Our concentrated efforts can force the portal to manifest, but its most complete materialization lasts only briefly. You, Dubhe, and Alice must go first. The rest of us will follow, as many as are possible."

"And the guardian?" Jay asked, lifting Dubhe to his back.

"We do not perceive it, but that does not mean that it is not here."

"Whenever you give the word," Jay said, and Alice nodded.

The ghostlight concentrated around the round shadow, almost as if by bringing brighter light to the point they could force the distant moon to cast a darker shadow.

"Now," Ayradyss said.

Jay went first, monkey on his back; Alice was so close to his heels that he felt her warmth as they passed from the tunnels into the cooler ocean cliffs. Behind them, the ghosts filtered through, growing in substance and detail as their feet touched the ground.

"And so here we are," Jay said to Alice, pleased that thus far his plan was working.

"So we are," Alice said, looking around.

"Not quite like a virt transition, is it?"

"Not quite."

Her lack of enthusiasm made Jay scowl. Alice caught the expression before he could banish it.

"I'm sorry if I hurt your feelings, Jay. It's just that so many things have happened in the last several days that . . ." She struggled to explain. "I found out that my father is a computer program—or possibly a god— or possibly a man who died before my mother was born. Just as I got to like him, I watched him taken away by a face in a cloud. I've been to a place that might be heaven and am getting ready to go to hell. The moon portal is neat; the ghosts are wonderful, but I think I'm all awed out."

Mentally, Jay kicked himself, realizing that, despite Dubhe's warning, he had expected Alice to behave like some proge heroine from a virt-venture.

"Yeah," he said. "You have been through a lot. More than me, really."

The *caoineag* drifted to join them, overhearing Jay's awkward apology.

"I don't know about that, Jay." Ayradyss smiled at them both. "You learned that your mother is a banshee, went to visit with Death, and took on a great deal of responsibility. How about calling it quits?"

She extended a slender hand, as substantial as life in this place, to Alice.

"I am Ayradyss D'Arcy Donnerjack. Before you were born, I met your father and mother. We visited in a cottage in this very place. How is Lydia?"

Alice took the proffered hand. "She is well, thank you. Worried about Ambry, but otherwise fine. She's back in the Verité now."

"Would you like to see the cottage?" Ayradyss asked. "Jay's train may find it easier to run along the shore than across the ravines. We can wait there."

"That would be nice."

They picked their way down to the shore, trailed by a host of more or less substantial ghosts. These, contrary to expectations, did not move silently, but instead sang, laughed, and traded jokes. The crusader ghost seemed to be their informal leader, starting the songs, then rattling his chain in accompaniment.

The cottage stood much as they had last seen it, neatly sealed but cozy. As they were peering into windows, Ayradyss telling Alice about how her parents had seemed then, about Lydia's slate of equations, about the haunting sound of Ambry's pipes through the mist, a plump pigeon flew down from beneath the thatch and landed on Alice's hand.

"Oh!"

"Lydia used such a bird as a messenger," Ayradyss recalled. "Does it have anything?"

"There's a spill of paper tucked into the band on its leg."

Alice gently removed it and the pigeon trilled happily, flying to the roof and observing the noisy throng that had invaded its isolated home from a head tilted on side.

"What does it say?" Jay asked as Alice unrolled the paper.

"It's a train schedule," she turned it so they could see, "and this cottage is listed as a stop. I guess that the Brass Babboon has found the route here."

"Good," Jay said, some of his anxiety leaving him. "We have army and transport. Now all we have to do is win the war."

"All?" Dubhe chuckled dryly.

"Well, one way or another, that's all that's left."

A wind rose, and almost before they saw the billowing cloud that heralded the arrival of the Brass Babboon, the train was pulling to a halt before the cottage. Spouting fireworks, the Brass Babboon chortled greeting. Drum waved from the cab; Virginia managed a smile.

"Ready, Jay?" the mocking babboon face called.

"Ready!" Jay answered. He turned to face the rowdy mob. "All aboard! All aboard for Deep Fields!"

—=—

The songs of ghosts, which proved to be not at all like ghostly song, jetted outward from the Brass Babboon as the train traveled its twice-worn track into Deep Fields.

"This train is bound for glory . . . "

"You take the high road and I'll take the low road . . . "

"When Irish eyes are smiling . . . "

"Brigadoon . . . "

When first they set out, the Brass Babboon sang along as loudly and tunelessly as any of the Scottish spirits, but as the tracks carried them to lower and lower realms (many of these imitations of hells, theologically grounded or purely imaginary) the train's voice grew quieter and quieter, at last falling purely silent.

Jay D'Arcy Donnerjack, seated in the cab, reflecting on the version of Dante's *Inferno* through which they had but recently passed and his father's role in the programming of it, noted the change, and when the Brass Babboon remained unwontedly quiet spoke:

"What's wrong, B.B.?"

"Bad vibrations coming back along the track, Jay. I don't think we're going to be making it into Deep Fields. Something has been set to bar the way."

"Set by the lord of that place or by another?"

"Another is my feeling. The programming is not like what I encountered on my other visits to that place."

"Can it hurt you if you run into it?"

"Yep."

"Then brake shy of it. If we have to get out with picks and hammers we'll clear it off the tracks."

"Gotcha, Jay. It may not be a physical analog barrier, you realize."

"I know, B.B. I was just speaking figuratively—and possibly optimistically. How's our supply of strange attractors?"

"Full up. I agreed to carry some orphaned grohners and herd-mice to a receptive site and in return they loaded my cargo bins."

"Thanks."

"*De nada.* I don't really fancy being reduced to elementary design elements. If a bit of initiative can forestall that . . ."

"Thanks anyway."

"Your father called me the 'prince of puppets,' but he cut my strings and let me free when he was done with the mission for which he created me. I've always appreciated that."

"I'll go back and bring a few of the others up to date," Jay said. "Don't worry. We'll find a way through."

The only answer they could come up with was to bring a select group into the Brass Babboon's cab and wait for the first visual data on the barrier. Once through the moon portal, the ghosts were as substantial as the Veritéans, so even when the Brass Babboon expanded the cab to double-wide it got pretty crowded.

"Coming on to the barrier," the train announced. "I'm starting to brake."

"I don't . . ." Alice began, peering through her binoculars. "Wait, I take that back. I *do* see something. It's dark, oddly textured: fluttery or wavery. Like a solid heat mirage."

"Moiré," Jay said flatly.

"Not the boss's," Dubhe added, raising his voice to be heard over the squeal of the brakes. "The color's off. Except in rare cases moiré at first appears to be black, but the deeper you look (not that many get that opportunity), the more color underlies the surface."

"I only see green," Virginia Tallent said. "And I know that moiré. It's the emanation of Earthma's child."

"That's the child?" Alice asked, unbelieving.

"No," Virginia said, "but the barrier is of its making."

As the Brass Babboon came to a halt, they were close enough now that the barrier could be seen with the naked eye. It gave the impression of being solidly centered on the gleaming train tracks, but every time Jay tried to see around it, the heaviest area shifted.

"B.B.," he said, "can you give me an analysis of that thing?"

"Sure. Scanning." A brief pause, then, "As you have said, its substance is like that of moiré. Any proge coming into contact with it will be ended."

Recalling how the flowers wilted and died whenever Alioth's tiny bits of shed moiré touched them, Jay nodded.

"Most of us are not proges," he said. "Alice and I are both here in the flesh. That means that you and Dubhe are really the only ones it will stop."

"I wish it were that simple, Jay," the Brass Babboon said, and for the first time in Jay's memory it sounded sad. "Further analysis shows that whoever set it there programmed it specifically to destroy you and/or

any of your companions. I would suspect that the very fact of your identity would be enough to trigger the program."

"What about a virt shapeshift?" Jay asked.

Virginia Tallent shook her head. "The shape shifts, not the identity.
You would still be Jay Donnerjack, even if you made yourself look like
some blue-eyed bimbo."

As if he did not trust that the window would give him a true image,
the crusader ghost had been leaning out the side of the Brass Babboon's
cab studying the barrier.

"I hae been thinkin'," he said, "that yonder dubh thing brings t' mind
somethin' I hae seen before. Now I recall what it is. 'Tis jus' li' the
guardian of the moon portal."

Hope made Jay straighten.

"I've never seen it," he said, "but I know how to defeat that guardian.
It just might work here. . . ."

Without pausing to explain, he began to chant:

Angel of the Forsaken Hope,
  Wielder of the Sword of Wind and Obsidian,
    Slice the algorithms from our Foe.

As he began to speak, he heard Ayradyss shriek, "Ah, Jay! No!" He
tried to obey, but the words seemed to have a momentum of their own
and to shape themselves from his resisting tongue.

Mermaid Beneath the Seven Dancing Moons,
  Cantress of the Siren Song,
    Drown our Enemies in the data-stream.
Nymph of the Logic Tree,
  Child of the First Word,
    Give our antagonist to grief.

As the final words were spoken, Ayradyss flung herself from the train
cab, metamorphosis already upon her. The white robes of the *caoineag*
billowed upward, silvered, became the mylar dragon wings of the Angel
of the Forsaken Hope. Naked legs, glimpsed momentarily, melded into
the slender curving tail of the Mermaid Beneath the Seven Dancing
Moons. Her hair remained dark, but her gaze became wild and inhuman;
her sweet mouth lost its softness, curling with fierceness as her wings
beat and carried her to the moiré barrier.

To the appreciative war cries of the Scottish ghosts who leaned from the passenger cars of the Brass Babboon to watch the battle, she used the Sword of Wind and Obsidian to reduce the barrier to code and sickly mist that paled, dissipated, vanished, and was gone.

"Mother . . ." Jay whispered, hoarse with awe. "I never . . ."

But the Nymph of the Logic Tree had no attention to spare for the young man who was stepping down from the train's cab to approach her. She twisted in the air, turning, spiraling outward as if seeking to orient on a summons that none of the rest could hear.

"Mother?" Jay called. "Ayradyss?"

The fierce eyes looked at him uncomprehendingly. Wings of mylar beat against the air, fish tail swam against currents those below could not see. She rose higher in the air.

"Mom! Ayradyss? Mom!" Jay's voice broke, for clearly the creature in the air above them all was flying (or perhaps swimming) away from them. "Come back! Mom!"

Once again the dark eyes glanced down at him. This time, they might have held a touch of reproach—or perhaps what he saw was pity—or perhaps there was naught but indifference. With a final powerful effort of wings and tail the Child of the First Word soared into the highest reaches of the sky, so high that the jet stream became a river.

She dove into those sea green waters and was gone.

Jay stared after her as if the power of his attention would draw her down again, that he would find beside him the dark-haired young woman in the shrouding garments of the *caoineag* he was just barely comfortable accepting as what remained of his idealized mother. No such thing happened and what he found beside him was the crusader ghost.

"Ghost, what happened?"

"You called upon what she once was and she became it. Then her maker summoned her and she had no choice but to go."

"What she once was?"

"All that was in the chant, laddie. Come back to the train. We mus' be movin' on or another such beastie as the last will be sent. I dinna doubt that its maker felt its goin'."

Jay stumbled after, beginning to comprehend.

"My mother was like Alice's father, a thing created by one of the gods of Virtù?"

"Aye, I wouldna call her a 'thing,' but from what I heard her tell the *caoineag* long ago that was the way of it."

"The *caoineag*? But she was the *caoineag*."

"She took over from the one before, laddie."

"Who was my mother's maker, then? This Skyga?"

"Nae, i' 'twere the one called Seaga."

Without waiting for instructions, the Brass Babboon stoked up its engines and brought them up to speed. Realities rippled by: Hindu ghosts awaited reissuance according to their deeds in life; coffins gaped beneath a sickle moon and the skeletons parodied the Maypole romp; fires burned with heat but without destroying the writhing bodies on which they fed.

Alice touched Jay lightly on one arm.

"She isn't dead, Jay. Seaga must want her for the same reasons that Skyga wanted Ambry."

"She never mentioned . . ." Jay trailed off, lifted his wrist and addressed the bracelet. "Did you know about this? Why didn't you stop me?"

"I did not know," the bracelet said. "As you recall, your father did not include full knowledge of Ayradyss in my programming."

The crusader ghost rapped his chain to get Jay's attention.

"I dinna think that the old laird ever knew Ayradyss's origin."

"How couldn't he? They were married!"

"Aye, but he was from a far later part of her life. To him, she was the Nymph he met in romantic places in Virtù, not one whose past he tried to learn."

The bracelet spoke, "That, at least, I can confirm. My files do record his shock at learning that the woman he had loved without consideration for time was merely a virtual creation, destined for the touch of moiré."

"How could he know so little?" Jay said. "He loved her!"

"He did," Desmond Drum said, speaking for the first time, "but love does not guarantee accurate information. In fact, it almost always includes a certain degree of willful blindness."

Jay could have wept for disillusionment and guilt, but the cab of the Brass Babboon and the passenger cars behind were crowded with those he had brought to help him fight for the Lord of Entropy. Nor was he the only one who had taken a loss in this battle—and his was far smaller than that of Virginia or even of Alice, who must suffer for her mother's loss along with her own.

Alice was right. Ayradyss was beyond his helping—at least for now. If he had placed her in danger, then more than ever he needed to effect the rescue of the Lord of Deep Fields. Death had indicated that the trespass of the Ones on Meru into his realms would give him a certain reciprocal power over them. Certainly, Death's actions would distract the gods from their various pawns.

Jay pressed other, less comforting, thoughts from his mind. He did not want to consider that the destruction or reduction of the Ones on High might also mean the ending of their creations. He did not want to consider that the games that Death would play with the gods might not suit his own needs. Such thoughts would do him no good now, no matter how true they might be.

Reaching up, he dragged on the whistle cord and bared his teeth in delight at its wild, angry shriek. His companions sensed his mood and let him be, though Alice squeezed his hand before going to sit beside Drum.

Dubhe, hanging by his tail, turned to face Jay.

"We're almost there. I recognize the acid river. You ready to give orders?"

Jay nodded. "As ready as I'll ever be. Pass the word to look for signs of battle. We may learn something from what has gone before. B.B., take us to the palace."

"Right!"

"Crusader, tell the ghosts to sharpen their claymores. We're almost there."

"Aye!"

Humming rails, steel against stone, light songs for courage.

— = —

"Not much longer now," Death said, looking down from the window of his palace. "We cannot hold out much longer. It is as I feared. Earthma's child can draw on strengths beyond mine or hers alone."

" 'Child' seems a most inappropriate appellation for such a creature," Tranto said, "for it is not at all childlike."

"Except, perhaps, in its talent for destruction," Death countered wryly.

"Still, I propose that we dub it 'Antaeus'—the name of another war-like child of Earth."

"Fitting."

A howl, spare and lonely, seemed to echo the despair the Lord of the Lost would not permit himself to voice. Snake and phant barely heard it, so appropriate did it seem to this moment. Mizar raised his head, tongue drooping between spiked fangs, listened to hear if it would come again.

"Perhaps the bastard is a fitting replacement for me," the Lord of the Lost continued on. "In some ways, it *is* my offspring. In the ways and customs of many lands and many times patricide is an honored and accepted way of claiming a kingdom."

"John D'Arcy Donnerjack designed well," Phecda hissed. "This palace has stood strong so far."

"But the end must come, Phecda," Death answered. "We are out of ways of attacking from afar. My minions are battered beyond my ability to stir them into motion, or subverted by the proximate aura of my opponent. Even now the child itself batters at the door into the great hall. From there, it will seep up the stair and—"

A shrill howl, a cascade of maniacal laughter, varicolored lights against the darkness making brief stars where there had been none before. The dull thudding of the child beating against the door below stopped.

Mizar barked satisfaction, tails wagging. He balanced, paws against the windowsill, and howled answer to the Brass Babboon's whistle.

"Jay comes!"

"So he does," the Lord of Entropy said, "in the eleventh hour. I fear he only comes to join us in our ending. Alas, that his strengths are still dormant."

"Strengths?" Tranto asked.

"Son of two worlds, born of a myth who had taken woman-form and a man who did not know that he himself was myth, engendered by the creative principle of one of the Most High at the hands of Death." Death's grin was skeletal, without humor. "His strengths are not the magical powers discovered in the time of need by a hero in a fable, nor are they *deus ex machina* so honored by the earliest playwrights, but they are strengths nonetheless.

"I had planned to awaken him to his potential as he grew to manhood in my palace, but foolishly I gave in to his father's claim that he needed to live as a mortal. Now, it is too late and he will be unmade with the rest of us."

Phecda had joined Mizar at the window and now she spoke, excitement making the hiss in her speech more pronounced.

"Jay iss not alone. He hass an army with him."

"An army oddly clad and more oddly generaled," Tranto commented.

"I did my bit with an Anglo-Indian scenario. Many of those spilling out of the train resemble Scots—male and female both."

"And they are bearing swords," Phecda added, "and strange attractors. Where did he find these people? Has he stolen Skyga's Phantom Legion?"

"No," Death said, "for I have met many of their number, albeit briefly, in ages past. These do not scan like natives of Virtù. Yet I would swear upon my own head that they are not merely virtventurers from the Verité."

On the wide but broken field, battle was being joined. On the one side were the green moiré-touched troops that Antaeus had animated from the litter of Deep Fields. On the other were bands of Scots ghosts. Jay and the crusader ghost generaled the whole; Dubhe swung from section to section, bearing messages. Alice, Drum, and Virginia had arrayed themselves as bodyguards near Jay. The Brass Babboon, too large to take part lest it endanger its allies, dropped back to where it could lob strategic strange attractors and provide a potential retreat.

Mizar's sharp hearing caught the final commands that were being given.

"No plan survives first contact with the enemy," Jay was saying, "and that's got to be more true here than it has been in battles past, so I'm not going to try to coordinate beyond what we have here. We need to disable Earthma's child—without its aura its army will fall."

"Aye, laddie, and those you've brought will be tryin' t' open a way for you to do that very thing."

"Good." Jay grinned. "Don't let anyone's misplaced sense that the honor should be mine keep them from slipping in a good shot. Okay?"

"Right."

Shorty lifted his head on high. His bloodcurdling death cry was the clarion call for the attack. As voices raised in cries of "For Donnerjack!" and the stirring notes of "Scotland the Brave" Jay's army joined battle.

Crowded in the window that gave the best view of the field, four besieged figures permitted themselves something like hope.

"They are making headway," Tranto observed, when this was clearly true. "Antaeus's forces seem confused, as if they have trouble perceiving them."

"I begin to understand from where he may have recruited his army," Death said. "'Tis a clever plan, but they cannot long hold the field. An alteration to the parameters of Antaeus's forces and they, too, will be pushed back."

"We have stood by you and fought for you," Tranto said. "Would you mind just this once not speaking in riddles?"

The Lord of Deep Fields coughed laughter. "Very well. Jay has unwittingly done as the gods themselves do when they make war. In a sense, he has conjured from his imagination an army to fight for him—but in this case the imagination is not solely his own, but is the ancestral memory of the bit of land on Eilean a'Tempull Dubh upon which John D'Arcy Donnerjack built a castle to replace that of his ancestors. Put simply, Jay has raised an army of ghosts."

"Ghosts?" Phecda asked. "How can an army that is of those already dead be defeated?"

"By banishing them from this place, Phecda. They do not belong to Virtù, nor even, really, to the Verité. When Earthma realizes what I have . . ."

He said no more, for nothing productive was to be said. Meanwhile, on the field, Jay observed his troops and came to a startling realization.

"Alice," he said, "come here a moment, would you?"

He called her not only because she was near, but because he knew she was a skilled observer. Unlike Drum, who looked for things of significance, she had the journalist's gift for seeing the entire setting and preserving it for analysis.

"Yes, Jay?" She came to his side.

"Tell me what you see."

She did not question, but put on her reporter's voice and narrated: "In the broad stretch of ground between the curving bulk of the Brass Babboon and the vast, dark palace of the Lord of Deep Fields, a strange and stylized battle is taking place.

"More awkwardly constructed than even the hound Mizar, human and machine forms come together from the rubble. Their hodge-podge forms are no match for the keen-edged blades swung by the ghosts of Castle Donnerjack, nor for the exploding strange attractors. Yet, of all those who fall, only a few fail to rise again. Immortal against immortal—or perhaps unliving against undying—war. Only a few from among the corrupted legions of Deep Fields fail to rise again."

"Exactly!" Jay said. "We need to know what keeps the ones who fall fallen."

"And," Alice added in somewhat more conversational tones, "why suddenly our own troops have begun to blink out. We lost Shorty just a moment ago and the Lady of the Gallery was taken right in the act of flinging a strange attractor. If this continues, we will soon be without troops."

Jay studied the battlefield, frantically seeking what differed about those whose opponents stayed down and those who merely delayed them.

The crusader ghost was among the most successful. His voice raised in song, his sword in one hand, a length of his chain in the other, he slashed and battered without pause. Could his crusader's cross be some protection? No. There were others who wore similar adornment, others who bore the same weapon, others who . . . An idea occurred to Jay; he glanced about the field, searching for confirmation of his guess.

"It is not their swords," Jay said, wonder dawning in his voice, "but their *songs* that fell their foes!"

"Songs?" Alice echoed, momentarily puzzled, but her observant nature could not be deceived for long. "You're right, Jay! It's the singing, not the swords that are doing the job. Even the strange attractors only delay."

"There is no music in Deep Fields," Jay said, remembering the tales he had culled from Dubhe and Mizar. "That's why the Lord of the Lost treasures it so and why my father sought to win his favor with song!"

He sent out the command that all the combatants should sing as they fought—even at the expense of fighting as rapidly. The result, while not miraculous, was certain.

"Destruction cannot answer destruction; creation is the answer," Jay said, certain he was correct. "I am the son of the Engineer—creator of the Brass Babboon, programmer of sites, designer of that very palace in front of us. I was only half right when I said that we could not use the living to fight Death's troops. What I should have realized is while our dead ghosts cannot be killed, neither can the other troops, since they're formed from the discarded materials of this place and bound by moiré. We need the creative force of music to make them lie still."

Alice paused in her duet with Drum of "Amazing Grace." The detective carried on, his voice rasping but surprisingly pleasant.

"Something still is leeching away at our forces, Jay."

"Then we need to win the palace before we're alone and too hoarse to carry on. I wish I knew the layout better. Going in the front door seems foolish. Perhaps Dubhe . . ."

The spidery monkey could not sing, but hanging by his tail left him four limbs with which to fling strange attractors. He had been taking the occasional bite out of his arsenal and as a result his usually dark coat was pointed with rustling lights, like illuminated fleas.

"Sorry, Jay. I never spent much time here. I came to report, but mostly I've kept an eye on you."

The voice of John D'Arcy Donnerjack spoke from Jay's wrist.

"I can be of assistance at this point, Jay. Within my memory is held the complete plans for the palace, including any number of secret passages, concealed doors, and the like that John included when he began to fear that you would be kept prisoner there. He planned for your eventual escape."

"Well," Jay sang, laughing, "I hope he won't mind that we use them to break in rather than to break out. Let's hear what you have to tell us."

—=—

The battering at the great hall door had recommenced some time after the battle had been joined, but now those who listened thought that it played a different tune.

"Desperate, now," Tranto said. "Jay's forces have Antaeus pressed on the field. If it cannot win here, then all this great struggle will have been for naught."

Death's acknowledgment caused the fabric of his cowl to move as if in a breeze.

"Ironic, too, that the doors and walls that resist the intrusion could be defined, in some senses, as the half-brothers of our opponent. But Antaeus's claim to inheritance comes from me while the palace owes its stability to Earthma. The rejected son rejects the favorite."

"Struggles among siblings," Phecda mused, "are often the worst."

A harsh breaking sound heralded the sound of wet, slopping feet mounting the stair.

"It comes," Death said, "and unlike Jay's forces, I cannot sing."

"Alasss," hissed Phecda, "neither can I."

"Nor I," said Tranto. "Though I can trumpet."

Mizar only whined. Picking up the music box carefully in his spike-toothed mouth, he laid it at Death's feet. The slim, cowled figure lifted it with a white hand.

"I doubt that this carries the song to charm Earthma's savage son, faithful hound, but my thanks."

The inner door did not delay the intruders for more than a few moments. It burst open with a great splintering of wood and protesting of hinges. Behind the shower of wood came Antaeus and, not so much at his heels as escorted by him, came Earthma.

Antaeus continued to resemble nothing so much as a blob of moiré, uncomfortable to look upon, amorphous of form. As he entered the room, he was reshaping his mass from something four-legged and bull-headed into a vaguely humanoid shape. Head and neck were one smooth curve that split into two thick, rounded shoulders, beefy arms, squat torso, and token legs. There was no differentiation for facial features, hair, or anything else. More than anything else, Antaeus resembled a chalk outline of a truck driver's corpse shaded in greenish black.

Earthma had manifested as a full-breasted, round-buttocked, woman clad only in a wealth of glinting emerald hair. Her skin was cocoa-toned, highlighted in green and rose. Objectively viewed, she was lovely, but none of those who looked upon her felt anything but varying degrees of fear and loathing.

"And so," she said, when it became apparent that no one else would speak, "we at last come to this. Don't you feel foolish for resisting, Old Death? All that effort and cleverness to arrive at what must come."

"Must come?" Death's voice was harsh.

"Death comes to us all." Her laughter was fruity and rich. "Except to the immortal gods."

"I had placed myself among those," the Lord of Deep Fields said.

"You were wrong to do so. This is a time for change in Virtù and in Verité. One of the things that is to be transformed is the sovereignty of the Lord of Entropy. Now, as has always been dreamed, death shall be subjugated to the forces of life and creation."

"Forgive me if I do not rejoice."

"Of course. You always were a bitter old thing."

"And now, Earthma. How do you plan to effect this changing of the guard?"

"My son will claim your cowled robe."

"I wear it yet."

"So I note. Will you hand it over?"

"I think not."

"Pity that."

"For you."

Mizar growled, the rattling of rusty cans tied to broken barbed wire. A mountain shrugging, Tranto shifted from foot to foot. Emerging from the throat of Death's robe, Phecda dripped venom from exposed fangs.

Antaeus lumbered forward a step, arms raised to bludgeon, thick gobs of moiré oozing the power of unmaking.

"Doe, re, me, fa, so, la, ti, doe!" Light and sweet, deeper and slightly out of key, miraculous, voices raised in song, music within Death's silent Palace of Bones.

Without, on the battlefield, the Brass Babboon heard and knew his cue. He activated the recorded music stored within his workings.

"There's a hole in the bucket, dear Liza, dear Liza. There's a hole in the bucket, dear Liza, a hole."

A polished panel of dark walnut swung open and from it emerged Jay, Alice, and Drum—all armed, all singing about holes in buckets, fixing and mending. The men took the part of hapless Henry; Alice carried Liza's reply.

On the battlefield, those ghosts who had not been banished caught the sense of the song (or the nonsense) and joined in with glee. The force of the cheerful, coherent sound resisted the moiré that Antaeus directed toward them. It wavered, but it did not warp, and with every futile attack Antaeus was diminished.

The Lord of Entropy was not affected, nor was Earthma, but the latter was so stunned by the turn of events that she forgot her son for long enough that Antaeus was visibly diminished by its attempt to continue the assault.

"Son!" she shrilled, but whatever she would have said was cut off by the report of a CF rifle.

Virginia Tallent stepped out of an alcove across the room, a hidden door open behind her. Her first several shots were directed into Earthma's manifestation, but the remainder of the clip struck Antaeus solidly in the torso. She slammed another clip home and continued to fire at Antaeus.

"The whetstone is dry, dear Liza, dear Liza. The whetstone is dry, dear Liza is dry."

Antaeus visibly weakened, but he did not fall. Nor did Earthma.

"Creation and chaos are not enough," the Lord of the Lost muttered, "but I believe that they have shown me what will be."

Stooping, he touched the floor upon which he stood. His arm vanished into it. Earthma may have divined what he intended, may have intended to interpose, but the Chaos Factors that Virginia brought to bear upon her manifestation, combined with Antaeus's steady disintegration as the CF rounds bollixed his programming and the song interrupted his moiré's coherence, was too much for her. She raged impotently as the Lord of Entropy rose.

A block of scuffed marble, white veined with black, now rested in one skeletal hand. He opened it and withdrew a gleaming green object the size and shape of a peach pit.

"Son!" Death called, and for that moment his face and form was that of Earthma. "Catch, son!"

Antaeus reached, grasped. His moiré gulped the glowing creation seed, dissolved it. At that moment, the palace settled into itself with a noise like joints popping. Startled, Virginia Tallent paused in the reloading of her CF rifle. Behind her, hinges that held the secret door unscrewed themselves and the door sagged.

"With water, dear Henry, dear Henry, dear Henry, with water, dear Henry, moisten it with water!"

Antaeus froze. Although he lacked face or much of form, the blind motion telegraphed surprise. Near him, a plaster molding fell, shattered into powder. His blobbish form moved, questing as a plant does for light.

"Your Antaeus has no earth left upon which to stand, my dear," the Lord of the Lost said politely to Earthma.

A wall sagged inward, would have buckled then, but Tranto braced it with his forehead. Still singing, the human trio moved to the shelter of his bulk. Death continued speaking, advancing on Earthma.

"Neither does my fine palace, alas, but the end is certain." He grinned then and with whiteness shone. "Death comes for us all, even for impudent deities who have trespassed on my realm."

"I . . ."

"And on my prerogatives."

Death gestured at Antaeus and from the moldering moiré Markon's voice was faintly heard accepting Earthma's offered death.

"You cannot deny that."

"I . . ."

"You bitch!" Her voice thin and no longer even faintly feminine, Virginia Tallent screamed. She darted across the room, dodging falling masonry and building timbers with lithe ease.

Jay stopped singing to yell, "Virginia, no!" but his cry could not reach the fury who flung herself on the goddess.

"You killed him to feed that!" Virginia flung a wild hand at Antaeus, little more than a puddle now.

"Killed him too soon," Earthma said, fending off Virginia's blows.

"Had I waited longer, Antaeus would have been stronger. I erred in my enthusiasm."

Idly, she flung Virginia to the floor. The tile cracked with the impact. Virginia struggled to one elbow, a loaded CF pistol cocked in a trembling hand. She pulled the trigger, did not know that the Lord of Entropy added his force to her attack. Dying, she saw Earthma's manifestation shiver, begin to unravel, and fragment into nonlinear code.

"But there's a hole in the bucket . . ."

"Markon," Virginia whispered, and then she died.

Had it not been for Tranto and Mizar, neither Jay nor Alice would have made it out of the crumbling Palace of Bones. The phant sheltered them with his body, concentrating on keeping Mizar in sight as the hound found opening after opening, the structure collapsing to rubble around them.

Barely dodging a falling support beam, Desmond Drum recalled his virt form to the Verité, shouting that he would meet them at the Union Station site. Death, of course, was immune to danger from destruction and Phecda remained coiled within his cowl.

Once on the battlefield, a weeping Alice withdrew—saying between sniffles that she would brief the Brass Babboon and the remaining ghosts—and Jay was left alone with Death. Although he tried to face the Lord of the Lost with appropriate courage, he could not hold back his tears.

"Do not mourn too greatly for Virginia, Jay," Death said with surprising kindness. "She had seen the moiré, nor did she care to live on, a cripple in Verité, bereft in Virtù. Remember her kindly and do not think her a coward for choosing this way to end her suffering."

Jay snuffled back a fresh bout of sobs.

"She's gone, both here and in the Verité?"

"Yes. Her Veritéan body was eaten with disease. When Markon died, only her desire for revenge kept her living. Having achieved something of that, she let herself believe that the injuries she had sustained battling Earthma were fatal."

"But it isn't fair! She didn't really harm Earthma."

"She may have done more damage than we know." The Lord of the Lost sighed a very human-sounding sigh. "Antaeus represented a great expenditure of resources on Earthma's part. The CF rounds fragmented his programming and your song made it difficult for him to use his moiré to draw power from his own destruction as he had done time and again on the battlefield."

"I wondered what he was doing," Jay said. "I knew it had to do with creation and destruction, but . . ."

"Song—patterned sound—is not natural to Deep Fields, where everything loses its pattern. Your live song, as opposed to recordings, created patterns and thus created interference for the moiré, which breaks down patterns."

"I'm glad we helped."

A glint of white within the cowl. "I wish you had picked a more lovely piece of music. Your father, at least, had taste in such things."

"Next time."

"The next battle will not be here, Jay. Nor will I be able to direct it, although I will assist indirectly."

"The next battle?"

"Surely you intend to oppose the crossover," Death said dryly. "Or do you want the likes of Earthma and myself to have free reign over the Verité?"

"You have a point."

"But first, Jay D'Arcy Donnerjack, you and your allies need rest. Deep Fields is good for this, but alas, this time I cannot offer you a bed. I suggest you retreat to Castle Donnerjack. We can confer another time."

"I don't know if I can sleep," Jay said.

"I've heard *that* before. Go. We will speak again."

Jay sketched an awkward bow and left for the Brass Babboon. As he walked a high-pitched, broken sound followed him.

Surveying the ruins of his restored kingdom, Death was whistling.

FOURTEEN

"Four days! Can we possibly manage to stop them with only four days?"

The speaker swung by his tail from a cherry tree that swayed slightly with the motion. Caltrice worked programs to stiffen the tree; the swaying stopped; the swinging continued unabated.

"Dubhe, what choice is there?" Reese Jordan said reasonably.

"The Judeo-Christian tradition says that all the earth was created in seven days," Desmond Drum added. "Most humans believe that Virtù came to be in a matter of hours. Thanks to Caltrice's altered time flow, we have extra time with which to plan and some privacy."

"That's a hint to stop whining and get to work." Jay reached up and patted Dubhe.

"Right. Hand me a banana, would you?"

Clad in neat black jeans, a white tee-shirt with the "Ginger Rogers" slogan printed on it in black, and sandals, the Lord of Deep Fields sat on a rock near the banks of the stream. Out of courtesy for Caltrice, this manifestation did not emanate the moiré. In fact, he could have easily been mistaken for a pale man of somewhat ordinary Caucasian features if it were not for the mien of authority he bore and the fearful deference all accorded to him.

"Actually, Dubhe, there is every reason to believe that we will be able to stop the crossover attempt—the question is how to minimize casualties to our side. We have extraordinary resources at our disposal and, when you consider it, the crossover attempt is so outrageous as to be improbable. In Virtù, such things can change the outcome.

"Moreover, I have considered the effects of our battle in Deep Fields on their plans and I believe that the loss of Antaeus will hurt them sorely."

"Could you explain why, sir?" Alice asked. "He was powerful, but he struck me as rather mindless."

"He was, but had he defeated me and taken over my kingdom, he would have been imbued with all my knowledge and resources. To explain why this is important, permit me a diversion into matters that some, but not all, gathered here know.

"Quite simply, the crossover attempt is the most important element in a series of actions that will be coordinated around it. The armies that Skyga, Seaga, and, to a lesser extent, Earthma are gathering are not meant to cross into the Verité. Their conflict will occur in Virtù. Further, Skyga is the divine principle behind the Church of Elish."

"The Hierophant?" Alice asked.

"No." A very small grin shaped on the lips of the Lord of Entropy. "That is another. Skyga, however, has provided the Hierophant with power and allies. His design is to establish a beachhead within the Verité while in Virtù his forces contend with those of Seaga. If all goes according to plan, there will no longer be the Highest Three, but the Highest Two."

Jay frowned. "If he has that much power, why would he share with Earthma?"

"Antaeus. The plan was that Earthma would maintain vassalage over her son and thus over the powers of Deep Fields. As both you and Alice have reason to know, the Great Ones create many of their troops from within their imaginations. With Antaeus in charge of Deep Fields, those troops could be ruled immune to the touch of moiré. Thus their creator would be freed from the need to resurrect them. That concentration could then be directed elsewhere."

"But when we came to your rescue," Jay said with a certain degree of satisfaction, "we kept that from happening."

"Precisely."

Desmond Drum briskly rubbed his hands together. "This fits very nicely in with everything else we have learned. My guess is that Skyga no longer maintains whatever trust he had for Earthma . . ."

"Trust her!" Dubhe muttered, swinging faster.

". . . and that she is being relegated to a secondary position."

"It is too early to be certain," Death answered, "and my knowledge of those On Highest Meru is less perfect than I would like . . . although it is improving."

His grin recalled a skull.

"You said you thought we could win," Alice reminded him. "How? Skyga alone is still terribly powerful."

"And," said Reese Jordan, who was still not comfortable conferring with a principle he had striven to avoid for so long, "why should you care about our casualties? Won't they simply enrich your Fields?"

"They would most certainly in some cases," Death's gaze rested on Tranto, Dubhe, and Mizar, "although for those of Veritéan origin the final destination is more problematical. From a merely practical standpoint, any plan that wastes limited but valuable resources would be foolish. I cannot resurrect those who fall and I have no desire to see Skyga win this game.

"However, there are simpler reasons. Gratitude. Friendship. When I needed help, those gathered here assisted me. I would not spend them lightly."

Reese nodded. "My apologies, but I needed to know."

"And now you do. Let us move on to the question of tactics. Even without Antaeus, Skyga and Earthma have formidable resources. We will need an ally of their rank."

"There is only one," Jay said, "and you can't mean Seaga! He stole my mother!"

"That he did, and yet that is who I mean."

"No!"

"Jay," Tranto said, "he has a point. You saw what one of Earthma's lesser minions did to me. If we do not have similar allies, any effort we make within Virtù is foredoomed."

Fuming, Jay bit back his protests and let the Lord of Deep Fields continue.

"We can contact Seaga through Celerity, the messenger of the gods. I have reason to believe that he will convince Seaga to coordinate his activities with ours. Since Celerity is one of those from Higher Meru I cannot meet with him myself—unlike Earthma, he has not trespassed on my prerogatives. Therefore, one of you will need to do so—one of the Veritéans would be best since if he mortally assaults you, your virt projection can be programmed to translate the damage into thrusting you from the site."

Silence, then Drum spoke. "Let's settle that after we decide who is doing what elsewhere. Link and I did a lot of research into the Elishites. This, combined with what we learned about Bansa's device, gives me every reason to believe that there is a hardware component to the crossover. If that is sabotaged, then the crossover may be stopped."

"Or slowed," the Lord of Deep Fields said. "Some of the deities have acquired symbiotes whose virt talent enables them to project the deity."

Drum glanced at Alice, both remembering the day when they had been assaulted by the wingéd bull.

"There are two likely locations for those devices," Jay said, "on Meru and at the California Celebration site. And, as I had nearly forgotten in all the excitement, those two sites are associated."

Quickly he told how he had entered the factory by way of a crossover and found himself on what could only be the Celebration grounds. He concluded:

"I should make my way back to Meru—the Brass Babboon would take me—and check out what I can. If the equipment is on the Virtùan side, I'll deal with it there. If it's on the Veritéan side, I can cross over and see what can be done."

Dubhe sighed. "We know you can draw me across the interface, Jay, so I'll come with you."

Mizar growled. "And I . . . can track and fight . . . with you. I can . . . flee across . . . the sites."

"And I'll come too, Jay."

Everyone turned to stare at Alice Hazzard.

"I'm touched, Alice," he said, trying to be courtly, "but the point of this venture is to be able to cross between Virtù and Verité. Mizar's taking quite a risk. We certainly can't ask the Brass Babboon to hang around to pull you out."

"And recall," Reese said, "might not work from Meru. It is quite a high realm and not included in the transfer databases."

"True," the Lord of Deep Fields said. "Drum only managed a successful recall from Deep Fields because I boosted his signal. As many a bounty or eeksy has found, venturing into the uncharted realms of Virtù can result in death or mutilation."

Alice smiled smugly. "But I can do just like Jay can. I can cross the interface."

"What!" Jay said.

Dubhe's laughter pealed from above. "I told you not to underestimate her, Jay!"

"Ever since I met Ambry, there have been times when I almost felt as if I could cross between," Alice explained. "Maybe they did something to me to enable me to make the journey to the Land Behind the North Wind—it was a strange enough walk."

"Activation of dormant programming," Reese muttered. "It reminds me of what John told me about his and Ayradyss's first journey from Deep Fields."

He realized that everyone was looking at him and that Death, at least, was nodding mute agreement.

"Ignore this old man and continue, dear."

"Well, I had never had my RT self in Virtù and I wasn't convinced I could manage to insert it without help. When Jay mentioned the moon portal, I knew it was the perfect opportunity to come across in body. I practiced then and I can do it, Jay."

"You could have crossed out into traffic!"

"That never stopped you from testing your limits, did it, Jay?" Reese laughed. "I guess you can't make a girl listen to reason any more than you can a boy."

"So, I can go with Jay," Alice concluded. "I'm a good snoop, and especially if he gives me a hand like he will Dubhe, I can be there to help if he needs to continue the search in Verité."

"You can't put yourself into danger like that!"

Alice's only response was a cold stare. Jay flushed red as he heard Drum sniggering and he realized that once again he'd acted as if Alice was some proge heroine.

Dubhe poked him. "She's coming with us, right, Jay?"

"Uh, right."

Alice smiled. Death turned to Drum.

"That leaves you to confer with Celerity. Are you willing?"

"Sure." The detective placed a hand over his heart. "Lo, though I walk through the valley of darkness, I will fear no evil, for Death will be at my side."

"I cannot be at your side, but I will give you certain information to use as you see fit."

"Great. Now, I suspect that Jay, Dubhe, and Alice will have an easier time scouting if everything is not going according to plan at the Celebration site."

"Not another riot!" Jay said. "The last one may have discredited the Elshies somewhat, but innocent people were hurt."

"What I have in mind wouldn't cause a riot . . . I don't think," Drum said. He glanced at Alice. "Our employer."

A mischievous grin lit the young woman's face.

"Oh, yes! Perfect."

Drum turned to his somewhat confused allies. "What do you say to the reappearance of Arthur Eden?"

"The author of *Origin and Growth of a Popular Religion*, the one who has been blacklisted for so many years?" Jay grinned. "Oh, perfect!"

"When I'm done with my job in Virtù," Drum added, "I will go to the Celebration and do my bit to influence crowd response."

"We'll need to coordinate our actions somewhat," Jay said, "but I think this will work beautifully."

"My part," the Lord of Deep Fields said, "will be here in Virtù— I'm going to deal with some trespassers. If Tranto and Phecda would join Seaga's forces, when Drum convinces him that his best interests lie with us, then we will have generals there as well."

Silence again.

"Planning more at this point wouldn't do much good," Drum said. "When the Lord of Entropy here gets me an appointment with this Celerity, I'll find out if we can make an ally. Then I'll talk to Eden."

"I guess," Jay said, "that Alice and I had better practice crossing the interface. It wouldn't be a good idea to find out too late that we can't swing it."

It wasn't much in the way of an apology and he knew it, but Alice smiled and punched him lightly on the arm.

"I can hardly wait."

Death looked at them all. "And don't forget to get your rest and sustenance. None of you are aions, nor will you have the sweetened charges the Most High give their lackeys to sustain them."

In twos and threes, the conspirators thanked Caltrice and took their leave. As Death was about to depart, Reese Jordan spoke.

"Sir, I haven't been strong lately, but everyone has their role. Is there anything I can do? I've been weak, but maybe you can . . ."

The Lord of Deep Fields slowly shook his head. Reese whitened. Caltrice arose from her waters.

"Lord?"

"Death comes for all," the Lord of Deep Fields said to her. "Reese

Jordan has lived longer than most, and through the time tricks you have played here, he has gotten more out of that life."

"Will I see the moiré?" Reese asked, his voice breaking.

"Only those of Virtù see the moiré," Death said. "Bansa did; Donnerjack did not. I cannot say which it shall be for you."

"Don't tell Jay," Reese said. "He'll learn soon enough."

"I won't."

"I'll be seeing you then."

"I sincerely hope so, Reese Jordan."

With that, Death took his leave. Reese Jordan took Caltrice's hand. "Wait with me?"

Her answer was a tightening of pressure, a falling of water that might have been tears, might only have been rain.

—=—

"Hi, Mom."

"Alice, you're safe! When will you be home?"

"I'm not quite finished with this yet. Give my apologies to Grandma and Grandpa, please, but I won't be able to make the Celebration."

"If it's the young man, you're welcome to bring him."

"No, it's nothing like that."

"Then why are you blushing?"

"Mom! I'm being serious. There's something I need you to do for me—and maybe it will help Ambry, too."

"I'm listening."

—=—

Jay D'Arcy Donnerjack wandered the corridors of Castle Donnerjack, wishing that he would hear the banshee howl. He knew he wouldn't, of course, but he permitted himself to dream. Opening the much-depleted bottle of Laphroaig, he filled a saucer and set it on the windowsill.

A clanking of chains and the crusader ghost was there, sniffing appreciatively at the liquor.

"You made it back safely, then."

"Aye, laddie, so did we all, all but your lady mother."

"Then those who vanished from the field . . ."

"Were banished, not destroyed. You were right when you said that those who were dead could not be easily slain again. We did you some good, though, didn't we, young laird?"

"Aye."

"Then hae a wee nip and a nap, laddie. That battle's won and the next nae yet begun."

—=—

Ben Kwinan was surprised to hear a knock at the door to his hogan. Momentarily, he considered observing good old-fashioned Navajo manners and ignoring his caller, but the novelty of an unexpected guest was such that he went to the door.

The rough features of the sandy-haired man who stood outside were schooled into polite neutrality. He extended a hand with a calling card.

"Mr. Kwinan, I'm Desmond Drum. I wondered if I might have a word with you."

Kwinan blinked, glanced down at the card. "Desmond Drum, Licensed Investigator" read the printed legend. Beneath was handwritten: "You really want to see me."

"Come inside, Mr. Drum."

"Thanks." Drum followed him in, turned to the left around the fire. "Nice place. Is it secure?"

"Yes."

"Even from your *genius loci*?"

"Yes."

"Good. Wouldn't want you evicted."

"What is this about, Mr. Drum?"

"I've come to ask you to set up a meeting between myself and Seaga."

"What? Why do you think I could do that?"

"Because your secret identity is Celerity—the messenger to Highest Meru."

"You know a lot for a Veritéan."

"Keep my ears open."

"Even if I am who you say, why would I arrange such a meeting for you?"

"Several reasons: it's your job; Seaga is going to want to hear what I have to say; Skyga would be very interested in knowing about your fence-sitting. I understand he's in a touchy temper these days."

"You must keep your ears open, Desmond Drum. Tell me, how

would you inform Skyga of my activities if you need me to get in touch with Seaga?"

"I have a friend in low places . . . very low places. He could arrange a message."

"Ah."

Ben Kwinan considered what he had heard lately about a battle in Deep Fields, a raid on Meru, Bansa lost or transformed, secrets stolen.

"Seaga will want to know what this meeting is to be about."

"Alliance between him and those I represent for the purpose of resisting Skyga's latest ambitions."

"You're pretty open about this. How do you know I won't go to Skyga with it?"

"I have friends in low places. I understand that divinities who violate their essential roles in the cosmic order can rapidly find themselves demoted—and vulnerable."

"Ah."

Pause for thought. (This manifestation only. Other aspects continued busy with carrying messages, coordinating ticketing for the Celebration, conferring with underlings. Near omnipresence could be a trial.)

"Desmond Drum, inform those you represent that I will carry the message. Where will you wait for a reply?"

"Here is just fine. I understand that deities can do things pretty quickly."

"And why should Seaga do so?"

"Because the Celebration is in three days RT and the bookies are giving really good odds that Skyga's going to be Most High when it's over."

"Ah. I shall return."

"Do better than MacArthur on that one, would you?"

Flash of gold. The messenger was gone, leaving spots dancing before Drum's eyes. The detective leaned against the wall and closed his eyes. No need to get zapped again when the god returned, and he was *so* tired.

"Seaga will see you." Kwinan's return had been noiseless. "If you would take my hand, I will transport you to him."

"Thanks."

Flash of gold. They stood in what appeared to be a gigantic shell beneath moving water. Fish with enormous mouths and phosphorescent highlights swam through the dark water. Seaga surged at one end of the shell, manifesting as a cuttlefish with eyes as large as Drum's clenched fists. Kwinan, now transformed into a long-bodied, swift-moving minnow, darted in the shelter of his master's many limbs.

"Sire." Drum sketched a bow.

"You bring a proposition from the Lord of Deep Fields."

"I never said that, but yes, the Lord of Deep Fields is one of those I represent."

"One of? He has ever been a loner, that one."

"And remains so, but for the duration of this crisis he has allied himself with those who oppose the current crossover attempt."

"Why come to me, then? I do not oppose the concept of crossover. Traffic between Virtù and Verité should run both ways."

"But this crossover will almost certainly leave Skyga preeminent."

"You insult my ingenuity."

"Then you are uninterested in this alliance?"

"I have my own plans."

Drum had been told to expect that Seaga might not realize how severely endangered he was. Those who have been first often do not seriously consider that it could be otherwise. Reason, he had been told, would not work, but Death had given him another tool.

"The Lord of Deep Fields has commanded me to say to you thus: 'If you do not consider this alliance, Seaga, then I shall have no reason to forgive you for your trespass into my realms. I know now which two stole Bansa's device from my keeping. That you were betrayed thereafter gives me some slight sympathy for you. I offer you increased odds of revenge. If you refuse, know that where you stand on Meru is no longer forbidden to me. I will come.' "

Drum watched for Seaga's reaction, but even his training had not prepared him for reading the expressions on a cuttlefish's face. Death's message was a challenge, not a promise of instant demise. Seaga was still protected by his divinity—Death's words were merely a reminder that the deity was no longer perfectly safe.

To Drum, a human who lived with the possibility of immediate death from any number of causes and who would die most certainly someday, this threat was ominous. To Seaga, an immortal who had never even casually contemplated his own termination, it was apparently terrifying.

"Perhaps we can come to an accord. Tell me what Death and his allies desire."

Drum began recounting what they had in mind, outlining Seaga's role in it. As he spoke, the cuttlefish's tentacles moved excitedly. Minnow Kwinan swam closer.

Hooked 'em, Drum thought. *Just hope they're not so big that they pull the boat under.*

—=—

Randall Kelsey looked out over the swirling mass of humanity streaming into what had been as little as a week before a raw construction site. They'd had to cut corners to get done in time. Only two of the ziggurats were actual structures. The other two were mockups with hollow interiors. One of these mockups, however, had a stronger frame than the others and it was at the top of this that Kelsey had hidden (with no little trepidation) the translation device that Ben Kwinan had arranged to be delivered to him.

Still, mockups or not, it was a good job. Trailing jasmine, bougainvillea, and roses evoked the Hanging Gardens of Babylon. A garden supplier had sold them its entire crop of hibiscus; now the flaring trumpetlike flowers in red, yellow, pink, and white spilled from pots fixed up and down the steps of the pseudo-ziggurats. Hummingbirds had already located the flowers and added their darting color to the landscaping.

The throng was seated in grandstands in front of the two pseudo-ziggurats. A broad avenue between the two completed structures would be used for processions between the ziggurats and the open temple dais from which the ceremonies would be conducted.

Kelsey was glad that he had not been high-ranking enough to be assigned a place on the dais. In order for the audience (congregation) to have a clear view of the show (ceremony), the dais lacked even an awning. His station on the ziggurat had been thoughtfully provided (at his own orders) with a six-foot hibiscus that provided just a touch of shade. It wasn't much, but he was thankful to have it. The California Celebration promised to be even hotter than the one in New York City.

He longed for one of the iced fruit drinks the vendors were handing out in the stands (Aoud Araf's suggestion—a comfortable crowd is easier to control), but such things had been ruled as undignified. Virtù had ruined audiences. They forgot that human performers had limitations (even while still demanding that their own be catered to). The compromise that had been agreed on was a water flask hidden within the scepter each priest or priestess carried.

Kelsey took a sip. The water was warm already and tasted of plastic.

He sighed. At least there were no stupid balloons this time. Gods willing, everything should be peaceful, orderly, and impressive.

Gods willing.

God!

—=—

Not in this reality or any other had there ever been a train like the Brass Babboon and Jay, after arguing B.B. into agreeing that this time they were going to sneak into the Meru fields, felt a certain degree of relief at the thought. His father, he decided, must have had a touch of the mountebank beneath the sober, rational exterior he showed most of the world. Why else would he have given the Brass Babboon such an exhibitionist nature?

But the train was intelligent and (mostly) rational. It had agreed that the same trick could not be expected to work twice and that at the very least the gods would send someone to inspect the area of the train's passage. If they were feeling really paranoid, they might simply try to destroy it out of hand. That might be difficult, but it would have severe consequences for Jay, Alice, Dubhe, and Mizar.

And so the Brass Babboon took a route that enabled him to just barely penetrate the interface and the group slipped off into the brilliantly lit, grassy plains at the base of the primal mountain. As prearranged, Mizar immediately departed to scout, crouching below the level of the tall grass.

"I'm getting claustrophobia," Dubhe muttered. "Monkeys are not programmed to creep around on the ground. All my instincts are screaming that a jaguar is waiting to munch me."

"Hush," Jay said. "Sit on my shoulders if that will help, but keep your head down."

Minutes passed. Alice glanced at her watch.

"If this is still keeping Veritéan time, the Elshie Celebration should be warming up about now."

"We have time," Jay said with more confidence than he felt. "The script that Drum swiped indicated that there would be lots of prayers and singing before the main event."

They waited, nerves slowly fraying as they envisioned what could be happening to Mizar. Jay, fretting over images of his childhood playmate reduced to component parts, admired Alice's cool as she checked over her gear. Alice, restlessly examining every item in her pack, wondering how effective a CF pistol would be against a deity, admired Jay's calm alertness. Dubhe chewed the tip of his tail and thought about jaguars and lions.

Barely a rustling of the grass heralded Mizar's return. He hunkered down in front of Jay while a light pad was linked to his data retrieval system. Scratching Mizar between his floppy ears, Jay turned the pad so Alice and Dubhe could also review the data.

"Looks like the eastern slope is the launch area," Jay said. "It was too much to hope that they'd be using the factory. I hope the corresponding crossover coordinates aren't too severely altered."

"Can't worry about that now," Alice said. "We need to get over there and take a closer look. Maybe over by that reddish rock. We could hide behind it while we check things over."

Mizar wheezed, "I can . . . take you a . . . sheltered route."

"Good," Jay said. "Let's go."

From the shelter of the red rock, they had a clear look at the center of activity. Four large zigguratlike buildings were set in an approximately diamond shape. The center was empty except for a small circular platform.

"There's something familiar about that layout," Alice whispered. "I've got it! It's on a smaller scale, but the placement of the buildings is the same as at the California Celebration grounds."

Jay tabbed a file from the light pad and compared it.

"You're right. Most of the traffic here is between the buildings at the tips of the diamond—the ones that correspond to the ones at opposite ends of the avenue at the California site."

"Heavily . . . guarded," Mizar commented. "On ground and . . . above."

They shrunk closer to the rock as a wingéd lion soared overhead, its shadow temporarily touching their refuge.

"I wonder if there is something to the theory that Virtùan natives have trouble perceiving Veritéan forms," Alice mused.

"I hope they're just careless," Dubhe said. "I'm not Veritéan—at least I don't think so."

"And Mizar is definitely not," Jay said, "though he has a gift for concealment."

They observed for a time in silence. Various robed and kilted figures, their garb reminiscent of ancient Babylon, strolled around the square buildings. Occasionally a voice blatted out a command the watchers could not understand, and one or more entered one of the buildings that capped the avenue.

"It reminds me of backstage before a live show," Alice commented. "They're purposeful, but not doing much, just waiting."

Jay, who had never seen a live show, could only grunt.

"I wish they weren't all dressed the same," Dubhe complained. "I can't tell if the ones coming out are the same as the ones going in—but then humans all look alike to me."

He sniggered. Jay punched him gently.

"I can't tell them apart either," Jay said. "Mizar?"

"Scent similar . . . but . . . too far to be sure."

"One thing is certain," Alice said. "We're not going to be able to sneak in there. Not only are there all those people, but I've seen lions, long-horned bulls, and various really weird monsters."

"No argument," Jay said. "We'll need to watch and wait for Arthur Eden's unmasking. If that causes enough confusion, we do something here. If not, we cross over and hope."

—=—

Desmond Drum sipped his iced lemonade and felt sorry for the Elishites out in the hot sun. He was wearing a loose cotton shirt, a wide-brimmed straw hat, and sandals. The seats for which he had purchased tickets were beneath a mesh awning, and he still was hot. They must be broiling.

With his binoculars, he scanned the grandstands, looking for Arthur Eden. If he hadn't known where Eden's seat was, Drum wouldn't have recognized him in the disguise they had worked up.

As he lowered his binoculars, a tall, impressive man with abdominal muscles right out of a comic book (but real), wearing a costume that glittered in the unforgiving sun, was standing in the center of the dais. The crowd responded to his raised arms by growing quiet. From the ziggurats along the sides a stirring, almost atonal chant arose.

Drum felt it in his bones and wondered if they were mixing in sub-sonics. He didn't think that *vox humana* could create that impressive throb. Clever if they were. He certainly didn't believe in the tenets of the Church of Elish, but awe stirred within him nonetheless.

The middle of the dais on which the High Priest was standing began to rise now, carrying him up. Drum nodded approvingly at the engineering. Apparently, it had been constructed rather like one of those travel cups that expands from a pill box. When it finished expanding, the High Priest stood on top of a conical pedestal, his escort arrayed around the base.

When the singing stopped, the High Priest slowly lowered his arms. Drum felt his heart catch in his throat. This was the moment Eden had been told to watch for. Would he take the opportunity?

Silence answered the end of the song—the kind where you can tell that the audience is waiting to find out if applause is appropriate or not. Into this silence, a single voice rang out. It was masculine and deep but strong enough to carry.

"Poppycock!" Arthur Eden said. "Balderdash! Oh, it's good theater, I'll admit that, but if half of those ladies and gentlemen up there believe what they're chanting then my name isn't Arthur Eden!"

Stunned silence for only a moment, then the murmurs broke out.

"Eden? Eden?"

"He dared!"

"He wrote the book . . . you know, *the* book, the one that got them all so mad. Why is he here?"

"We're going to see fireworks now!"

Drum did his part to start the hubbub, knowing that all around the Celebration grounds his hirelings were primed to do the same. The intention was to force the Elshies to acknowledge the interruption rather than just bowling past and onto other things (while they quietly escorted Eden off to who knows what fate).

It worked. The priests conferred. The ceremony was delayed.

—=—

"They've done it!" Alice said softly, squeezing Jay's arm. Her whisper sounded like a cheer.

"I think they have," Jay said.

Within the past few minutes they had watched as the calm organized waiting below turned into the milling of a stepped-upon ant hill. Knots of costumed figures gossiped; every new person (or creature) who emerged from the miniature ziggurats was grabbed and questioned.

"Unfortunately, the confusion is going to make it harder, not easier, to get close," Alice said. "I don't think we have any choice."

"Cross over," Jay agreed, "and hope that we don't land somewhere obvious. Give me your hand, Alice. Dubhe, get on my back. Mizar . . ."

The hound wheezed sadly. "I . . . go. Be careful."

"As careful as we can be," Jay promised. "See you later."

Very aware of Alice's slender, slightly damp fingers in his hand, Jay concentrated on crossing out of Virtù into the Verité. Since he never really knew how he did it, he did not know how he knew that the process was awry—different from the last time he had made the effort on Meru and different yet from his many practice sessions with Alice.

He felt a coolness, not unpleasant, but certainly not what he expected for a sunny day in California. Darkness surrounded him, a darkness so absolute that he could not see Alice although her hand was tight in his. Into this darkness came a light.

At first he thought it was from a single source, then he saw that it was from numerous illuminated sources set within a frame. The points of light bobbed slightly as they approached, making him think of a lantern set on the bow of a ship. Then he realized that the light emanated from a device of crystal and platinum carried on the shoulder of a man who limped as he walked, favoring his left foot. A scar bisected his face, but did not distort the friendly smile he bestowed on them.

"Welcome to the gates of Creation," the Master said. "I told you that we would meet here."

"Can you tell the future?" Jay asked.

"No, but I can divert a few travelers who need my help—or whose help I need. I am somewhat muddled as to which is the case."

"Are you Ambry?" Alice asked.

The Master shook his head. "Not really, dear, although I have some of his memories and know who you and your companions are."

"Then is he gone for good?"

"That waits to be seen. Much hinges on the actions of the next few hours."

He set down the device and twiddled one of the wires. When he had finished, about a third of the crystals were ruby red. The remainder shimmered clean and white.

"There, it's set. If you just flip this switch"—the Master indicated an elaborate bronze toggle—"the field will come up."

"Field?" Jay said. "I'm afraid that I don't understand, sir."

"A field that will jam the translation projectors that the ones on Meru are using to boost their integrity during the crossover. Essentially, they are using an extension of the broadcast power that they've had for years."

"Oh."

"Don't worry about the particulars, Jay Donnerjack. As your father was fond of saying 'Does it matter why it works if it works?' "

"It does to me."

"I'm afraid I cannot explain in any more detail. You simply lack the vocabulary. Now, will you folks take this to the Celebration in California?

If the machine is to work efficiently, it will need to be set somewhere roughly level with the translation projectors that are already there."

"And where are they?" Alice asked.

"My understanding is that they are mounted in the upper tier of the ziggurats at either end of the avenue."

"If you know so much," Dubhe said rudely, "why don't you take it there yourself?"

The Master cocked an eyebrow at the skinny black monkey.

"Because I cannot cross the interface between Virtù and Verité. And, no, it cannot be set up on Mount Meru. The gods or their minions would find it there and they are far too powerful within their own realm."

Jay glanced at Alice who nodded.

"All right, we'll take it and, to be honest, be glad to have it. I wasn't really delighted with the idea of trying to get inside one of the ziggurats and whaling away with a crowbar."

"Thank you, Jay Donnerjack."

Alice cleared her throat. "Can I ask one question, sir?"

"Yes."

"What would you have done if Jay and I hadn't come along? What good would this device have been without someone who could cross the interface?"

"That is two questions." Again the Master smiled. He seemed to be having a marvelous time. "But I will answer them both as best I can. I do not believe that I would have designed this machine if I had not known of your abilities. One of my sobriquets is the One Who Waits. In a sense, I have been waiting for you."

"Did you cause us to be born, then?" Jay asked.

"No, not at all. In your case, Death was much more responsible—if anyone other than your parents could be said to be responsible. Alice was of her parents' making."

Jay looked as if he had more questions to ask, but Alice shook her head and touched him lightly on the arm.

"Not now, Jay. Even though this place seems timeless, my watch insists that time is passing. In RT, the Elshies must have gotten Arthur Eden's distraction under control. We don't want to be too late."

"Yeah." Jay bit his lip as if that would help keep the questions inside. "Thank you, sir."

"You are entirely welcome, young man. As I took you off your course, I will do my best to put you back on."

Jay bent and picked up the Master's strange device. Alice raised a hand as if to help him.

"No, I've got it. It's amazingly light."

"So it needs to be," the Master said, "if it is to get where it is going. Good luck and, when you get there, don't forget to look up."

"Wha . . ."

—=—

The Hierophant handed Bel Marduk a beer. The god straightened his headdress, tilted back his head, and drained the bottle in a swallow.

"How much longer are we expected to wait?" he growled.

Until the Church of Elish started its rituals, Bel Marduk had been relegated to a lesser realm in Virtù with squatters' rights on some of the middle heights of Meru. Now, fortified with the mana harvested from his modern worshipers, he was as arrogant as he had been in the greatest days of his original evolution. As a god of law, he remembered his debts and rarely grew too arrogant with the aion who had been his contact with this route to power. Today, however, he was tired and irritable. His grand entry and the mana he expected from it had been delayed.

A peevish, fire-breathing, greater god is not to be trifled with, so A. I. Aisles didn't say the first four or five snappy rejoinders that came to mind. Instead he handed Bel Marduk another beer.

"It should be soon enough. When the crowd is ripe and the harvest worth getting, they'll give us the signal."

"They had better not let Ishtar through first."

"Of course not. She's set to come out after you."

A. I. Aisles had arranged that himself. Marduk was old hat now— the babe goddess would make the covers of every newsie in the world, especially with that costume they had made for her.

He grinned in salacious anticipation. Marduk interpreted this to mean that the Hierophant was certain that all was under control and relaxed.

The door to what Aisles had dubbed the Green Room (and then Marduk had asked why the walls and furnishings were not green) opened. Ben Kwinan, clad as a temple flunky, entered and bowed.

"They have begun with the lesser deities, Great Marduk. If you and the Hierophant would take your places as we rehearsed."

"I slew Tiamat without coaching, little creature," Bel Marduk said, spitting just a little fire. "I do not need your reminders."

Kwinan scuttled away so that the god could venture forth. The Hierophant followed. He winked at Kwinan and tossed him something. Kwinan caught it.

"Don't take any wooden nickels, kid."

He strode by, reeking of beer. Kwinan looked at what rested in his hand. It was a wooden nickel.

—=—

Jay, Alice, and Dubhe emerged from their conference with the Master at the base of a hibiscus- and vine-draped ziggurat. Although they were at the back, away from the congregation at large, they had little trouble telling to what point the Celebration had progressed.

"That's the opening of the second hymn in honor of Marduk," Jay said. "Damn! I did talk too much."

"Uh, Jay," Alice said, looking up with a peculiar expression on her face, "I think we have bigger things to worry about."

Jay followed the direction of her gaze and swallowed hard as he saw the two wingéd bulls circling overhead. Even as they noticed him, they folded back their wings and, with a hawklike stoop that should have been impossible for anything of their size, dove toward them.

"Shit!" he yelled.

Dubhe had already made his agile way up the first step of the ziggurat. Alice had set her back against the stone and was aiming her CF pistol.

"Jay, give me your hand and I'll help you up!" Dubhe cried.

"Damn machine's too . . ." Jay paused. "Take the machine, Dubhe. Take it to the top and flip the switch. Alice and I will deal with the bulls."

"Me?"

Jay thrust the machine at the monkey, felt the weight shift as Dubhe grabbed it.

"Do it, Dubhe. It's light enough, just bulky."

"Me?" squeaked the monkey, but the device began to rise.

When Jay spared attention from getting a rope and grapnel from his gear, he saw that Dubhe was dragging the machine up.

"I hope that thing's made to take a licking," he muttered as he hooked an upper step and hauled himself up.

Had anyone cared to look around the back of the western ziggurat, they would have seen an amazing battle. A young woman holding a CF pistol in an approved grip fired alternating rounds into two wingéd bulls. The bulls, seeming more annoyed than hurt by the assault, were forced to ground, where their size put them at a disadvantage since their favored attack apparently consisted of landing on their prey with the intent to squash. Now, however, they drew back, wings close to their flanks, and lowered their heads to charge.

"Alice!" Jay called. "Grab hold."

He tossed the end of a solidly anchored rope to her. Stuffing her pistol in her waistband, she grabbed it and let him pull her up. The barked shin and skinned elbow the operation entailed seemed a good alternative to being at the receiving end of the bulls' charge. As it was, they heard the plasterboard at the base of the pseudo-ziggurat crack.

"Good shooting," Jay gasped. "I think the drums from the hymn covered any noise we made."

"Where's Dubhe?"

"Up there with the device. I said we'd cover."

"Good thing."

Alice pointed. From the artistic forest of hibiscus that masked the base of the grandstand, a pride of lions was emerging. These were not the lazy, sleepy creatures frequently seen in zoos or at midday on safari. These were the lean carnivores that the kings of Babylon had taken such joy in hunting that they had caused their exploits to be preserved in stone.

"Those are going to be able to climb," Jay said, doing some climbing himself.

Whatever Alice's reply might have been, it was drowned out by a thunderbolt crackle. Bells, chimes, rattles, gongs, drums, and shrilling fifes rang out. An enormous shadow blocked the sun.

"Shit," Jay said again. "Bel Marduk."

Ears folded, the lions had shrunk down at the first thunder rumble, but they were not intimidated for long. Already they sought the easiest route up to Jay and Alice.

"Don't feel like you need to take your time, Dubhe," Jay called.

The monkey's response was almost incoherent, but what came to them over the music was clearly obscene.

"Will a CF pistol work on a lion?" Alice gasped as they climbed after Dubhe.

"Don't know. Depends on their place of origin."

Jay threw a potted hibiscus at the lead lioness. His aim was good, but the feline shook the dirt and flower petals from her head and kept climbing. Alice followed suit, nailing a black-maned lion in the shoulder.

"I hope no one notices us," she said.

"Doubt they will," Jay said. "Look up."

Alice did. The skies were full of gods and monsters.

Bel Marduk stood atop the northern ziggurat; an impossibly beautiful dark-haired woman accepted the crowd's homage from the south. Both of these figures were on the heroic scale, but more realistically sized beings were taking flight, some upon wingéd steeds, other by spreading wings that recalled those of angels.

Most were strikingly handsome or beautiful and clad in costumes similar to those worn by the Elishite clergy. Amid this pageant, one figure stood out—a pot-bellied fellow who appeared to have a beer in one hand and a cigar in the other. A pair of brilliant orange sunglasses hung from a multicolored braided lanyard around his neck. He was clearly laughing, although the sound was inaudible through the cheers of the crowd and the blaring music.

"Jay," Alice said, "something's happening over at the ziggurat across from us—at the eastern one."

"Great!" Jay kicked out, landing a booted foot solidly on the nose of a lion. "And Dubhe?"

"Almost there."

Alice heaved another potted hibiscus at the approaching lions. She wondered why she and Jay hadn't brought more weapons, reminded herself that they had decided that in RT weapons would endanger innocents in the crowd. Still, she wished she had at least a can of mace.

"I wonder," Jay called, "where the Elshie security team is?"

"Jay," Alice answered, "I think those lions are part of the security team."

"Shit."

—=—

The crossover was complete. After millennia, the gods and goddesses of Sumer, Babylon, and Assyria again breathed the air of the world they had once ruled. If some of them were disappointed at the pollution or that their worshipers radiated amusement and excitement rather than awe, they kept their thoughts to themselves.

Then, from the east a great light shone forth, a light that caused even the brilliance of the sun to seem dimmed. Forth from the heart of that glow stepped a mighty figure. This time the crowd screamed in fear (especially those in the eastern grandstands), for what towered over them was an enormous multiheaded dragon.

"Tiamat!" Bel Marduk roared, fire bursting from his lips.

The dragon screamed a challenge, a shrill sound like dozens of cartoon pterodactyls falling on their prey.

The lesser gods got out of the way, heading north or south. A few forgot the warnings that the western ziggurat could not support significant weight and landed on its jutting steps, causing the structure to shudder and chunks of plasterboard sprayed with decorative pseudo-stone to plummet down.

From within the halo of the multiheaded dragon, lesser beings were emerging: small dragons the size of Cadillac limousines, blobs like manta rays that flew on the air, squid that jetted through the ether.

The deities of Sumer and Babylon heard Ishtar give the call to battle, surged again into the air, the Celebration forgotten, aware of the terrified humans only as a fit audience for their first epic battle of the post-crossover age.

Bel Marduk raised his arm to smite Tiamat; Ishtar cried out commands to the rallying godlets; Tiamat shrieked her defiance.

Huddled behind a particularly well-arranged cluster of honeysuckle and hibiscus, a skinny black spider monkey flipped a bronze switch. For a terrifying moment, nothing happened. Then the ruby crystals glowed like coals and the white like stars. There was a resonant buzz that caused all who heard it, divine or mortal, human or animal, to cover their ears.

"CROSSOVER CANCELED," noted the crystal screen. When Dubhe dared look up, he saw that this was true.

—=—

Tranto the phant stood beside Death on the plains surrounding Mount Meru and watched as the gods boiled out of the crossover area. Death sat upon the horse that Jay Donnerjack had coveted, clad in armor of bone and rust. The hound Mizar sat at his feet, sniffing the winds.

Now that there was no more need for the façade of Babylon and Sumer to be maintained, many of the deities shed their costumes, transforming into fantastic shapes from every myth and legend remembered in the Verité and from many forgotten. Some, such as Bel Marduk and Ishtar, remained as they were since this was as they were.

"Jay and Alice have done it." The Lord of Deep Fields could not be imagined capable of cheering, but his deep-voiced words held something of the sense. "And the denizens of Virtù come back to their mountain to fight for precedence as they did in the days of old. Now the armies gathered will meet as they did during the millennia following the Great Flux."

"And you?" Tranto asked.

"As always, my Fields will be enriched. I am here to settle a few scores."

They watched as great birds clashed with dragons, as whales swallowed tanks, as trees bombarded elven hosts with acorns.

Sayjak, eyes bleared with visions and lack of rest, led the People to fall on a horde of icy slugs. A phant who might have been Muggle tore up tree trunks and flung them at a pack of dire wolves. A Red Cross ambulance bore Paracelsus and Sid to bring aid to those proges judged too minor for repair by their divine generals.

"Where will you seek your prey?" Tranto asked.

"I have no need to seek," the Lord of Entropy replied. "In the end, I am always in the right place. Mizar, step about a meter to the left."

The hound did so, moving just as Jay Donnerjack, Alice Hazzard, and Dubhe appeared in the place where he had stood. The Lord of the Lost permitted himself a small smile.

"You have done well, Jay," he said. "Why do you return here?"

"We're looking," Jay answered, "Alice and I, for our missing parents."

"Alice, I owe you for your assistance," said Death, "and I prefer to pay my debts swiftly lest they are embarrassingly recalled at a later date. Your father—having performed his roles as the Master and the One Who Waits—has again become the Piper and, as such, is fighting with his Legion."

In a single motion, less a dismounting than a dislocation, Death dismounted his steed.

"You and Jay may take my mount and seek the Piper. It will shield you within my aura until you choose to take part in the battle. After that, my protection is lifted."

"And my mother . . . Ayradyss?" Jay asked.

"Keep your eyes to the sky," Death said cryptically. "Let Dubhe bide with me and Tranto. I promise that no harm will come to him."

The two scions of Virtù and Verité rode into the maelstrom of battle.

"I can't tell who's winning," Alice said, something of Link Crain in her voice. "I can't even tell who's on what side! I'm glad I don't have to cover this war."

Death's steed carried them to where the sound of bagpipes cut through the noise of battle and there they found Ambry standing over a fallen comrade, playing mightily, his cheeks red and rounded. As they advanced, the fallen soldier vanished, reappearing moments later fit and ready again to fight.

"I've no choice," Alice said. "Get me up close to him."

"What are you going to do?"

"Draw him through into the Verité. That's the only place where he's safe from being used by Skyga as a pawn."

"Can you do it?"

"I can only try."

Before Jay could protest, she had slipped to the ground and away. "Alice!"

The young woman only ran, and when she reached the side of Wolfer Martin D'Ambry, he seemed to know what she intended. Ceasing to play, he gave his hand into hers. A glow surrounded them, but before Alice could effect the crossover, something blotted out the sun.

Jay turned his gaze upwards and saw Alioth, the black butterfly, now again the mighty thunderbug. Skyga was seated upon the bug's thorax, his face terrible with rage. Ball lightning was forming within his hand.

The god had raised his hand to hurl destruction upon his fleeing minion when a slender, graceful form that seemed to swim through the air as much as fly on its dragon's wings rose from the battlefield. Ayradyss swung the Sword of Wind and Obsidian into Alioth's underbelly.

"No!" Jay screamed.

The blast of ball lightning forced tears from his eyes, tears that blurred his vision of the duel between the Angel of the Forsaken Hope and Alioth, the Black Butterfly, Mount of Gods. When Jay had scrubbed his eyes clear again, the wingéd mermaid was no more, leaving a great emptiness in his heart. Dots of moiré scattered the landscape, dust from a butterfly's wings. Nothing was to be seen of Skyga, Alice, or Wolfer Martin D'Ambry.

Jay sobbed. "What's happened?"

"The combatants destroyed each other," came the voice of his father from his wrist. "I could not perceive what happened to Alice and the Piper. They may have been slain by Skyga, or they may have made their escape."

"You're so cold."

"I am merely an aion."

Jay bent over the horse's neck. The steed wheeled through the quieting battlefield and the scattered moiré parted as it bore Jay back to

Death. Still sobbing, Jay murmured a rhyme he had learned when he was little more than an infant:

Butterfly, butterfly.
Flutterby, flutterby.
Come to me, come to me.
I'm lonely todee.

This time, nothing came to his call.

FIFTEEN

Randall Kelsey stood atop the westernmost ziggurat surveying the damage below. He had not noticed the device of crystal and platinum hidden in the shrubs near his right foot. Nor did he notice when a small black monkey appeared from nowhere, grabbed the machine, and vanished again.

He did hear footsteps that approached from below.

"Hello, Randall."

"Hello, Emmanuel."

"Arthur."

"I know. I just never stopped thinking of you as Emmanuel Davis. Arthur Eden was a bugaboo to scare Elshies with. I always rather liked Davis."

"Thanks. So what are you going to do now that the Church of Elish is bust?"

"It is, isn't it? With the Hierophant going on the talk circuit to explain that the entire idea was his greatest joke ever there will be no fancy talk getting us out of trouble this time."

"I'm afraid not."

"Maybe I'll write a book, call it something like *Butt of a Joke*. I know lots of things that the Hierophant—Aisles—won't be admitting."

"Good idea. Want a collaborator? I have lots of experience and some great publishing connections."

Kelsey grinned. "I like the idea. Can I buy you a drink? I'd love to know where you've been all these years."

"Sounds great."

They walked away from the ruins of a place where once, briefly, gods had again walked the earth.

—=—

Sayjak led the People back to the jungle, but he no longer gleamed with golden light, nor did tactical brilliance come to him in dreams. Devastated by the battles they had fought, their families weak and ruined, the other bosses turned on the one they had hailed as the Boss of Bosses.

They had begun the delightful process of beating him within an inch of his life when the biggest phant anyone had ever seen emerged from the jungle and trumpeted loudly. Dropping the head of Big Betsy behind him, Sayjak fled.

Secretly he was relieved. Being Boss of Bosses just wasn't for him.

—=—

"We'll come up with a story to explain Ambry," Alice promised. "Drum is a wizard with fake identities."

Wolfer Martin D'Ambry, his hand firmly entwined with that of Lydia Hazzard, grinned at his daughter.

"I have an answer I think will work. Why not say that I am Warren Bansa returned from imprisonment in Virtù?"

Alice gaped. Lydia giggled, sounding more like a girl than Alice ever did.

"We talked about it last night. I took Ambry to my lab and ran some preliminary tests. Detailed DNA work will take longer to do, but I think we can prove without a doubt that Ambry is Bansa."

"What a story that would be. . . ." Alice mused. "Please, let me handle the press release! I can get the story in all over the place and guarantee you a fair review. There are going to be all sorts of protests . . ."

She beamed, imagining breaking one of the great stories of the year. Visions of Pulitzers danced in her head.

"When we have the test results, we'll let you know."

"Great!"

The door buzzer rang. Alice's delight faded.

"That'll be Milburn from the Donnerjack Institute. I've got to go."

"Good luck with Jay, honey," Lydia said.

"He's in bad shape according to Dack," Alice answered. "The last straw was learning that Reese Jordan had died. I'll do what I can, but he's the only one who is coming out of this mess with nothing good."

Wolfer Martin D'Ambry nodded. "I understand despair, Alice. If I can help . . ."

"I'll call."

—=—

Jay Donnerjack was getting drunk with the crusader ghost in the upper gallery of Castle Donnerjack when Alice arrived. He raised his glass and toasted her, but standing seemed beyond him. The ghost was in little better shape.

"Hi, Alice. I have a story for you." Jay's words were slurred. "Do you know that for the first time in centuries Castle Donnerjack doesn't have a wailing woman?"

"It doesn't?" Alice sank down on the floor next to him.

"Nope. My mom took the job and then Seaga swiped her and she got wiped fighting ol' Alioth. I loved Alioth, y'know. That flutterby was my buddy when I was jus' a squirt with no parents and nobody. Weird that my mom killed my bud or my bud killed my mom."

"Yeah."

"I hear that you did the crossover like a pro. Dubhe tol' me. Now you got a mom and a dad. I don't got either."

"Poor Jay."

"Yeah," he sniffled. "Poor me."

"Poor Jay. He has millions, a castle in Scotland with ghosts, an Institute at his command, and freedom of both Virtù and Verité. Poor, ol' Jay Donnerjack."

"Poor ol' . . ." He stopped, glared at her through bleary eyes. "Are you laughing at me, Alice Hazzard? How dare you!"

"Ever since Dack called me, all frantic, I've been feeling really sorry for you, Jay. Then when Milburn picked me up to bring me here, I had the whole flight to think. You did lose a lot, but lots of what you lost you never had."

"Huh?"

"Your parents. They both died when you were tiny. Most orphans don't get the second chance you did."

"Aye," the crusader ghost agreed. "The bonny lass is right."

"Shut up!"

"And Reese, that hurt, I'm sure, but most people don't get to have nearly immortal teachers. Reese was dying before you or I were born. He's gone now—or is he? I couldn't get a straight answer out of Tranto."

"You asked Tranto?"

"Sure. Didn't you know that he and Death hit it off really well? He visits Deep Fields so that they can build rubble constructs."

"I didn't know."

"No, you've been sulking."

Jay blinked at her. "I have."

"And you've had good reason to, but are you ready to quit now? Dack's a mess."

"Poor Dack."

"And Mizar—unlike Dubhe, he can't come across to visit you."

"Oh."

Jay stared at his fingernails.

"I feel like a jerk."

"Healthy—unless you start moping about that next."

He punched her. She grinned.

"They say there's truth in the vine, Alice, so I'm going to ask you something."

"What?"

"Did you get the feeling that we were supposed to fall in love with each other?"

She blushed. "Well, yeah."

"And that didn't work, either."

"Probably a good thing, too. I wouldn't like suspecting that my loving made me a pawn in someone's game." She leaned and kissed him lightly on one cheek. "Anyhow, who's to say what will happen? We're only kids yet."

Jay turned red. The crusader ghost laughed.

—=—

High atop Mount Meru at the center of the universe the gods sat unmoving on their stone thrones, contemplating Virtù all about them. In the past, they had sacrificed much of mobility for the better part of omniscience. Now they spared just a bit of mobility to watch their backs.

Celerity, he who had been Ben Kwinan, had borne to them a message. Written in blood red on parchment of bone-white, it had been brief and to the point:

"Now I have freedom of Meru. Do not forget."

They did not need to see the signature, a fanciful sigil like unto a skull, to know who sent it.

"Arrogant," said Seaga.

"Obnoxious," agreed Skyga.

"But, sadly, true." Earthma sighed. "It was a good game while it lasted. I, for one, shall rest long before I play again."

She ceased speaking and closed her eyes, humming softly to herself.

Seaga lowered his voice to the faintest of whispers.

"Skyga, do you believe her?"

Skyga frowned a firmament-darkening frown.

"Her?"

High atop Mount Meru, two gods contemplated a third.

—=—

In Deep Fields he dwelled, Lord of Everything, although anything that he made tended to fall into pieces. The great silence of Deep Fields was interrupted only by Sibelius's Symphony Number 2, Opus 43 emanating from the player hanging from a wind-blasted logic tree against which he leaned and the grunts of Tranto as he shoved rubble into a mighty mountain.

"It's looking good, lord," the phant called. "Mind, we'll need some strange attractors to glue it together."

"Those can be acquired, Tranto."

Phecda, coiled around his slender white wrist, spoke, "What will it be, lord? When it is done?"

"Why, nothing, for nothing that I make holds together."

But as he spoke, he contemplated a seed of emerald green, the size and shape of a peach pit. Power glowed golden within its surface convolutions.

"It will be nothing at all, Phecda."

Death laughed then and moved to join Tranto.

—=—

Chaos, Chaos,
  (oh my sweet youth, sweet girl, angel of despair, lovers,
  friends, and other toys) . . .
Chaos, Chaos,
  is satisfied.